More praise for
Carey Harrison
and RICHARD'S FEET

"RICHARD'S FEET explores the central trauma of recent European history—the rise and fall of the Third Reich—in rich, unexpected and disturbing new ways. The result is a work of near-demonic beauty, antic imagination and universal resonance."
San Francisco Chronicle

"This first novel by a seasoned British playwright invites comparisons. Indeed, as the auspicious opening of a planned tetralogy, it suggests the completed work may be as thorough an examination of postwar European consciousness as Thomas Mann's *Magic Mountain* was of its era. If the three succeeding novels have the same beguiling power and compulsive readability as Harrison's debut, this will be a series to set beside those of Lawrence Durrell, Olivia Manning, and Anthony Powell."
Library Journal

"Holds the reader spellbound through his insinuating tone of voice, his exultant love of language and sheer storytelling power . . . In its surprise twists and turns, this astonishing, affecting, rich novel mirrors the dislocations of our century."
Publishers Weekly

RICHARD'S FEET

Carey Harrison

IVY BOOKS • NEW YORK

Ivy Books
Published by Ballantine Books
Copyright © 1990 by Carey Harrison

All rights reserved under International and Pan-American Copyright Conventions, including the right to reproduce this book or portions thereof in any form. Published in the United States by Ballantine Books, a division of Random House, Inc., New York.

Library of Congress Catalog Card Number: 90-4367

ISBN 0-8041-0896-X

This edition published by arrangement with Henry Holt and Company, Inc.

Manufactured in the United States of America

First Ballantine Books Edition: April 1992

For Colonel Gesellschaft and his cardboard moon;
for Mark, for keeping the faith;
and for Rosie, my daughter.

"The early loss of a father runs in the family. Richard, my papa, was a solicitor, very respectable, not especially well off, with a compulsion to defend the destitute and a penchant for silly jokes. He taught me, I gather (it's my mother who remembers it), that the moon was not a heavenly body but a piece of cardboard suspended over New Barnet; and died before I was old enough to query this.

"In my case, the disappearing act took place as follows. One fine spring day Father received the news that a paternal uncle had died at his retirement home in Spain, leaving some of his effects to his favourite nephew. The legacy consisted of books and clothes, some war mementoes—the late uncle had liked to be known as 'the Colonel'—and an old jeep. Father flew to Malaga and, three days later, vanished without trace. He had taken the Colonel's jeep out for a spin, which was puzzling in itself, and ominous, since Father had never learnt to drive. Nothing more had been heard, of man or machine. Molly—my mother—went out to Spain at once. She returned without news. Finally, after hellish months, the Malaga police phoned. A goatherd had found the burnt-out jeep and Father's body, in a ravine, hidden from roadside view. Mother travelled to Spain once more, identified the body and made arrangements to have Papa shipped home for burial, amid the appropriate ceremony, in Highgate cemetery; she didn't feel that the crash, and the horror of the ensuing fire, would have done anything to alter Richard's hatred of cremation. It was over. I grew up without a father; and it wasn't till many years later that I learnt some of the odder details surrounding his death.

"Out of delicacy, perhaps, the Spanish police hadn't told Mother the full extent of her husband's burns. It was a shock

vii

when the sheet was pulled back, in the Malaga morgue, to reveal a corpse unrecognizably charred except for two large and oppressively pink feet on the end of it, in front of her. Blistered by the heat but otherwise unharmed, they'd been protected by the Colonel's old army boots. The chief of police raised his eyebrows at Mother; Mother nodded; the feet slid back into refrigeration, and Mother emerged into the spring sunshine, to wander along the Malaga seafront in a daze. The scene in the morgue had left its mark on her. Now, on the beach, there were feet everywhere she looked. She began to study them. They were the same, they were different, some were funny, some were just feet. But would she have recognized her husband's, without hesitation, if they had come padding towards her?

"The relief she'd felt, when the news came that Richard's body had been found, was too precious to abandon and Molly held onto it now, letting it carry her through the funeral arrangements. She didn't tell anyone just how reduced were the remains, in the coffin they buried. It seemed unhelpful for people round a grave to know that they were crying over feet. But feet were all there was, and when the funeral was over and done with they left a nagging doubt in Molly's mind. In the end she hired a man to make his own investigation of the death. Nothing came of it. The only other person missing at the time, from nearby Malaga, was a German tourist, and although neither the local police nor those in the tourist's home town had yet resolved the mystery of Herr Schäfer's disappearance, they didn't seem greatly concerned. He was an underworld figure, a black-marketeer, so the story ran, who had slipped off to Spain with the collective loot, and his 'friends' were confidently believed to have caught up with him. There the trail went cold, to everyone's relief. And Richard—or rather his feet—lay quiet in the grave."

So says Wilf Thurgo, narrator of *Cley*, one of a quartet of novels entitled *To Liskeard*, of which *Richard's Feet* is the first to be published. Each of the four volumes tells a separate story; each has a different narrator, related to the others but separated by circumstance; and each tale brings its narrator a step nearer to a reunion with the others, in the Cornish town of Liskeard. *Cley* follows Wilf's adventures in the summer of 1968, at the end of which he discovers that his father Richard, very much alive, is about to re-enter his life.

What follows is Richard's story.

SOMEBODY IN HAMBURG IS TELLING STORIES ABOUT ME. I could find a man to silence him, easily enough. Hansi would do it. But I'd rather do it myself. I shall be fifty next week, I'm leaving Hamburg for good, and I want to settle the accounts before I go.

Time to put the record straight, to set it down in black on white as the Germans say, *schwarz auf weiss*. (Unlike us—we say "in black *and* white." Or do we? It's so long since I've spoken English that I can't get the ring of it in my head. Interesting—if it's so—that the British see the letters and the page as equals, black and white, and the Germans see them in perspective, black on white, a landscape almost, a snowscape—and for a true German the printed page is certainly more of a landscape than the German countryside, which only comes alive for him when some other German writes a poem about it; till then it's as inert and unconvincing as the papier-mâché décors people build for toy train sets, delightfully elaborate—like the one I remember seeing in Hamley's of Regent Street, over Christmas 1947. Is that still there, by the way? I hope so.)

These stories they're telling: they're saying I'm a Jew, that I killed Martin Bormann, that I betrayed my good friend Wolfgang Zimt, once called the King of Bizonia and later the Al Capone of Hamburg, by naming him to the authorities as the man behind the Walters car-bomb murder; that—worse!—in order to buy up property on the Reeperbahn, The World's Most Sinful Mile, I brought Hamburg's red-light district to its knees. How? By provoking gang warfare, and bringing the *Schmiere* down on us, the police, which led to newspaper headlines and caused a scandal; which brought the politicians running and which played, in time, into the hands of the property developers.

1

(Clean up the milieu! ran the cry. Give it a facelift, get the girls off the streets!) They're saying I betrayed the old days—I of all people!—and that more than any other living person *I'm* the one responsible for the joylessness currently shared by pimps, whores and their customers, by strippers, tourists, street musicians, beggars, vagrants, drunks, by the nostalgic, by bohemians and low-lives of every race and creed, here on Hamburg's redesigned, modernized, mechanized Mile of Sin!

Wrong—wrong on every count.

What offends me so much isn't that people have got it wrong (that some*one* has got it wrong; there's one little bastard at the source of the rumours!) but that anyone in Hamburg should be trying to separate fact from fiction—here of all places! That's the real betrayal.

There was a time in Germany—the best of times, as far as I'm concerned, after the war—when no-one cared who you were. You were whoever you claimed to be. I was Reinhard Sacher, former officer in the Waffen SS, friend and lieutenant of Wolli Zimt, a war hero in his own right. Hansi my right-hand man—yes, take Hansi, for instance: thug, pornographer, and designer of porcelain tea services, one of which, he still maintains, is in use at Buckink-*hem* Palace. An absurd claim? No-one ever challenged it. No-one pointed out that in all likelihood the nearest Hansi had ever got to a porcelain tea service was a two-week spell as a waiter at the Four Seasons Hotel, here in Hamburg. Fantasy was respected in postwar Germany. It was the cornerstone of personality, of nationhood indeed. And why not? Better a pleasant, encouraging fiction than the litany of offenses that might constitute a true history of an individual, or a state. And wouldn't that too, a "true" accounting, contain its share of fiction?

The truth is that I was born plain Richard Thurgo, as was my father before me, in Padstow on the northern coast of Cornwall. Padstow! the holy port that had once seen the arrival of Irish missionaries bearing the glad tidings of Christianity, news of a birth a thousand years before. Like these missionaries of old, my mother came to Cornwall from Ireland, claiming to be a Catholic, but she brought little in the way of gladness to my Cornish beginnings. I was born in circumstances so inauspicious that they've provided me with a lifetime of ready-made excuses. It was the last year of the '14–'18 war, and although my soldier father was delighted to hear of me, my mother was disgusted from the start, referring to me openly, according to my brother Alec, as "that unfortunate child" or as "the spawn of bloody ignorance"—her ignorance having apparently been that she was still, at forty-three, of child-bearing age.

To cap it all my father died of wounds acquired in the final flurries of the war, when the spawn of bloody ignorance was barely three months old. Alec, fourteen years my senior, grieved for him, and grieves still if his visits to Father's Belgian grave are anything to go by. But Alec is more practical than pious, and his trips, I have no doubt, combine business with mournful pleasure. At fourteen Alec was already selling racing tips, in the town, and sending in reports on point-to-points to the sports editor of a local rag, under the pseudonym of St. John O'Malley. Soon he was offered the job of full-time racing correspondent and made the mistake of turning up in person, aged barely fifteen, to accept. Like Mother, he seems to have lacked a sense of the proprieties of age.

For my part, I found no reason to miss the father I had never known. Snapshots of him show an optimistic Cornish face with pale bushy eyebrows and a boulder of a jaw. Clearly not the brightest of men, he failed good-humouredly at several jobs including lobster farming, until the war gave him an all too brief sense of vocation. By Alec's account he was a kindly fellow, attached to children; all the more to be regretted, perhaps, the type of father who would have sought to be a friend. And yet that thought made me regret his absence less. I already had a friend, and a good one: the original St. John O'Malley, whose name Alex borrowed for his premature career.

Old man O'Malley was our sole surviving grandparent, and all of seventy before I got to know him, a tall man with a full head of dyed black hair, a huge and mottled nose which I inherited, and an aristocratic stammer. I doubt if he had ever tried to make friends with his child, my mother. It was a formidable task at the best of times, and in their case they had too much in common rather than too little, one of the common factors being their love of solitude. How either of them married is a mystery to me, at least until I ask myself the same question. I know it took my own father the better part of ten years to win an O'Malley heart. They were both of them, O'Malley father and daughter, made of monastery stuff. But it was not to be; their only faith was in themselves.

It was purely for himself that Grandfather dyed his hair, with one of the more improbable patent devices of the period, ordered in large quantities from Dublin. By the light of day it looked like creosote, but in the twilight of his Galway house, shrouding the tarnished mirrors, it evidently satisfied the old man. He was himself an engineer, and my mother an artist. What they shared was not only the devotional privacy of their work but, in both cases, an extraordinary slowness, and a care reminiscent of the early Celtic gospels. If slowness were beauty then all my mother's efforts would have been masterpieces. She engraved glass, goblets for the most part. Throughout my boyhood, and with a patience that seemed all the more remarkable to my child's sense of time, she fostered minute, uninhabited forests on glass, dotting and stippling with her diamond, little specks and lines so tiny as to be imperceptible until at last a kind of film was breathed onto the glass, an army of little atomies turning to leaves and trees. One punchbowl I think took eighteen months at least; but this was swift compared to Grandfather. His achievements could be counted on the fingers of one hand, and frequently were, by my mother. In all fairness the scale of these enterprises—inventions is a better word for them but one we were never allowed to use—and the problems attendant on a trial run, kept their number in check. Nor was the man, like so many, an inventor for invention's sake. No, his devices shared a common purpose: to raise the wrecks of the Armada, most of which, if Grandfather was to be believed, in full view of his house, to litter the depths of Galway Bay.

Large underwater objects, locally reputed to be stones, he dragged, grappled, and exploded in turn, this last "enterprise"—the use of dynamite—providing the coastal inhabitants with more fish than their fleet caught in a fortnight. But he raised no ships. Grandfather's hopes came to rest on his two most grandiose schemes: the Enormous Magnet and the Submarine Balloon. The balloon, now an increasingly reputable device, was pioneered by old O'Malley, but it depended for its effectiveness, alas, on part-time divers. Deflated, the mass of canvas had to be inserted into the presumed hulk, often at alarming depths. Struggling in the murky water and unable to discern anything resembling a galleon, the local volunteers would dump the awkward canvas beneath a heavy stone, and return to the surface signalling triumphantly. Inflation was a lengthy business—it was the happiest part of the afternoon—but in time a portion of the huge balloon would rise above the waves, draped in seaweed and bobbing like a moody yellow whale, while the divers shook their heads in solemn disappointment. The Enormous Magnet laboured under similar difficulties. It required, in its original version, the cooperation of the very people whose living was undermined by Grandfather's explosion treatment: the Skerries fishing fleet. A graphic illustration in his study showed the scheme at work. Hawsers straining, the gallant vessels churned towards the sea, their cables converging in the waves beside the shore, in what seemed for all the world like an attempt to drag Ireland across the Atlantic to reunite her with so many of her native sons, and save them the trouble of emigration.

A later and smaller edition of the magnet succeeded in drawing an ancient cannon from the depths, in little pieces and at the cost of several rowing boats. If indeed it was a cannon. With a blacksmith's help the thing was reconstructed and mounted on the lawn, the hard black of its modern sections contrasting with the old, encrusted fragments, and reminiscent of Grandfather's hair after an erratic morning with the lacquer. On bright mornings he would take his silver-headed cane and dance a measure, a lavolta he called it, humming and capering on the grass beside his battered trophy. Despite my mother's withering comments, the old man insisted that it was not his own home-made mines that had reduced the cannon to pieces on the sea bed, but the earlier incompetence of Spanish foundrymen—here he baffled us with scholarship—whose artillery usually blew up as soon as it was fired. One merit of this theory, in his eyes, was that it mocked the English victory. Whoever was responsible, broken pieces of pitted black objects were all Grandfather ever brought to light, and they clustered in the study, in the drawing room, and particularly in the room which for years I misheard as the mourning room. Some of these relics were welded into composite form, although this only made their former purpose more obscure. The Skerries fishermen declined to risk their ships and engines prising out bits of volcanic strata, and like Grandfather's dreams of treasure, the Enormous Magnet remained on the drawing board.

He continued, in his eighties, to patrol the shore, hoping that the sea might of its own accord throw up a consolation prize or two. He also talked a good deal to the Galway seals, no doubt about the sunken galleons they knew at first hand. I was thirteen, and visiting Mother in Padstow for the first time since the age of two, when the news came of his death in the waters of the bay. The coroner decided that he slipped and fell, Mother that he was drunk, but I preferred to think that he took, at last, the logical decision: if by hook or crook or magnet the Armada would not come to him, he would go to the Armada.

It was with this Irish disciple of Jules Verne that I spent my boyhood, thanks to a determined mother. Alec left school at fifteen, less because he disliked it than because his thriving mail order concern in racing tips (which bypassed questions of age) left him little time to study. And he'd invested the profits in horse-flesh itself, until he and several shady friends appeared to own a leg in most West Country stables. Being Alec he had bigger things in mind. He traded the mail order business to a fellow schoolboy in return for the fare to London and enough cash to survive three months in lodgings, leaving behind him his pseudonym and a mother glad to be released from duty. At this point she saw before her, like a dream come true, a world of silence in her glassy woods, her Grimm forests where no figures or sign of habitations, not so much as a distant spire or the smoke from a gingerbread cottage, disturbed the landscape. Provided, that was, that she could find someone to take me off her hands.

There were also certain financial considerations. Mother had no intention of marrying again, or of working at anything other than her engraving, from which the income barely fed one hermit let alone two. In this regard Alec had been less than a burden, just as well since our father left little money and fewer relatives to sponge off. (Thurgoes are rather thin on the ground, hardly surprising when you know the etymology: Thorough-good. Alec sneers at this. In time he became something of a warrior, outdoing Father, and now maintains that the origin is "Thor-gar," spear of Thor.) Grandfather had sold a sizeable estate to wrestle with the intractable acres of the bay, and he was rich. He was also tight-fisted, and Mother's pleas for help had always been in vain. Her visits, and her acid comments, only infuriated old O'Malley; now, cunningly, she threatened worse. She would sell the house in Padstow and arrive on his doorstep with the unfortunate child, defying her father to throw us out. Mother was a big woman, built for labours she despised, and removing her would have been a task to daunt the burliest farmhand. A deal was struck. The child would come to Ireland, Mother would stay in Cornwall. And Grandfather, if he farmed me out to some neighbouring family—this was his plan—would be shot of both of us. I was a different proposition from Alec, who had been a loquacious child since infancy, apt to sum people up and tell them his conclusions; I was silent, with a sombre, glazed look (waiting to be engraved, perhaps, rather than spoken to); so silent, in fact, that my mother, convinced that I was an idiot, confided this to Grandfather, and it reassured him that he could dispatch me to the nearest farmyard.

In the event the old man never farmed me out. He found in me what he had never found in my mother or my brother, a willing listener, one who unlike his neighbours didn't interrupt but who was a little more responsive than the seals. Sheltered by his flow of words and his scorn for baby-talk, I refused to speak until I had mastered his own elaborate syntax; and this pleased him.

In the brisk wind of the bay and in the cluttered, gloomy house, staring at the smudges on Grandfather's forehead, I learnt about modern mechanics and ancient history, about bombards and pasamuros, rigging lateen and square, Bilbao shields, breastplates from Biscay, and the glorious brothels of Aragon, always the glorious brothels of Aragon. "*On* the bed, half a reál! *In* the bed, a *reál*!" sang Grandfather, comparing these to modern-day prices. His own visits to Dublin were still, he hinted, for more than the latest block and tackle. There were few pictures of my grandmother, except in the hall, where I once took a hurricane lamp to get a better look at her, giving what seemed to me a rather simple-minded smile, above a shapeless smock. He rarely referred to her, but he would glance up at the distant house now and again while we trawled the bay for the ever-elusive *reál*s, with defiance on his face, commenting once that the saintly bitch, if she could see him now, would hang herself in her rosary beads; it had only been on her death that he had sold the land behind the house to hunt for treasure, and earn the reputation she had dreaded, as a deranged old fool.

Whether out of some unacknowledged piety, or fear that history would repeat itself, O'Malley admitted no more women to his house. With one exception, that is: the Dear Nose, Grandfather's elderly housekeeper and supplier of the rice and tapioca puddings he loved. "The dear"—the dear Lord, I realized in time—"knows," was her answer to all puzzling questions. But whose dear nose? Hers was warty; but dear to her, I decided. Seeing me staring at her, uncomprehending, she would bend down to gaze into my eyes like someone peering through a front door letter-slot. "Anyone at home?" And she'd knock gently at my pate.

"Brutus, thou sleepst! Awake, etcetera!" was Grandfather's way of shattering my dreaminess. Little or no account was taken of my child's understanding, and when I later came across the historical Brutus I was puzzled to find that he wasn't a perpetual sleepyhead, a kind of Roman Rip van Winkle. I was allowed access to old O'Malley's library, but only to the lower shelves at first, the Anglophobe section, where I fed on revolutionary writings intermingled with Shaw. Grandfather's dictionaries were there too and I browsed them from the age of five, coming up with words like acanthine for prickly and algid for cold— alveolar was another of them, though I can't remember what it means—to ambush the old man. "Your soup's getting algid, Grandfather!" Growing taller I graduated to Spanish history and the *conquistadores*. Thence to other Great Explorers, some of whom, unavoidably, were English; those who'd gone native, such as *Igoe in Lhasa*, were preferred. Though strong as an ox I feigned sickness—heaping toys and books at my bedside—to glut myself all day on polar ordeals and Amazonian journeys; tales of African witches who fell into step behind their victim and achieved a hypnotic control over him by mimicking his walk (I tried this unsuccessfully on old O'Malley); and of Himalayan wind-walkers whose trances gave them lightness and enabled them to devour valleys in a stride. Above these wonders Grandfather's shelves threatened me with Latin and Greek. Above these, English literature. I preferred my lead soldiers, explorers in uniform.

Much as Grandfather hated visitors, education had to come, and when I was of school age it was a sequence of young men from Trinity College who came to tutor me. Their holidays were my termtime, and vice versa. They arrived at Grandfather's house, scrubbed and starched in their wing collars, like Baron Frankenstein's guests applying at the castle, and fell in similar fashion under the old man's spell, joining him in his dreams of Spanish gold. One clumsy youth called Meadows, known as Beddows because of the heavy cold he got while all but drowning in his eagerness to help, had to be sent for by his College Tutor before we could be rid of him. Each left more disappointed than the last, without a doubloon to his name. And any payment, even in coin of the realm, was hard to extract from a man afloat in Galway Bay as, come the time, Grandfather made sure he was, deafly erect, addressing a vanishing cable from his rowboat. I had to act as intermediary. Against his better judgement, he loved me, and wanted to be wooed.

"Grandfather! Grandfather, Beddows is leaving!"

"Leaving?" After a pause Grandfather's distant voice, raised in astonishment and sorrow, came across the waves. "Don't leave us, Beddows!"

"He's got to catch the train, Grandfather! He needs money!"

"Money?"

"He says he hasn't been paid!"

"Can't hear!" The figure in the rowboat straightened, revealing a collarless shirt above trousers held up by a gaudy club tie. One spread-fingered, empty hand came up in stiff salute. "Farewell, Beddows!" The other hand paid out cable steadily into the bay. And yet again the Dear Nose would disburse, from the housekeeping jar.

The smell of the sea comes back with that memory and I feel torn, remembering how I loved it then. Sometimes I wonder if I've ever forgiven the sea for claiming Grandfather. I loved its smell as a child and hate it now—the smell of the algid stuff that hates us, that devours breath. And by contrast how I've loved every smell that emanates from this body of ours! Fresh or stale the warmth of innards—offal, entrails, intestinal stench—lingers in it. I should have been a dung-beetle: perhaps if my friend the Bhikku U Thunanda of Rangoon is right and we get another life, I shall have my turn at burrowing.

I loved the sea, and language, to please Grandfather. Most of all it pleased him to hear me recite poetry after supper. I was given a boiled sweet, a jujube as he called them, for a poem well recited, two jujubes if it was a long one. In my efforts to discover whether there was such a thing as a three-jujube poem I learnt great swathes of doggerel and rhyming couplets of the better kind, Macauley ("Lars Porsena of Clusium, by the nine Gods he swore," etc.), Kipling, "Annabel Lee" and "The Raven"—Grandfather loved Poe—or "the boy stood on the burning deck . . . .". When all failed I went for harder, Miltonic stuff, and verses of which I barely understood every other word but can remember all the better for it—Pope's Dunciad for instance—"Thy hand, great Anarch! lets the curtain fall, And universal darkness buries all." Grandfather then nodded approvingly. Two jujubes followed. There *was* no three-jujube poem, I decided.

The first book of my own that Grandfather gave me, bound in dark blue leather with a curiously gritty finish to it, almost pebbly, like coarse sandpaper or whitewash on an outer wall, and inlaid with gilt lettering, was *More New Arabian Nights* by his greatest literary love, Robert Louis Stevenson. Its sub-title, *The Dynamiter*, promised thrills. But at the age of twelve I couldn't penetrate the stories with their mixture of the satirical and the fantastic, like an opium dream of Victorian London with its clubs and cads and hansom cabs rushing princesses through the dark and rainy streets. It was only years later, rereading RLS, that I realized how many of Grandfather's pronouncements—"once you are married there is nothing left for you, not even suicide!"—derived from Stevenson. "What hangs a fellow," Grandfather often said when he caught me infringing one of his rules of behaviour (using the toilet after nine p.m. or before five a.m.; taking fruit from the garden without prior permission), "what hangs a fellow . . . is the unfortunate circumstance of guilt!" Forgiveness was accompanied—just as mystifyingly—by, "It's better to be a fool than dead!" I thought these too bizarre to be anything but his.

Verne, Sterne, and Stevenson. Kipling. Chesterton of course, and Belloc. Poe and Pope. The literary frills escaped me, it was Verne and Stevenson—O the Land of Counterpane!—who peopled my daydreams, just as they intended:

> When I was sick and lay a-bed
> I had two pillows at my head,
> And all my toys beside me lay
> To keep me busy all the day . . .
>
> I was the giant great and still
> That sits upon the pillow-hill
> And sees before him, dale and plain,
> The pleasant land of counterpane.

With Grandfather's death my life changed abruptly, and my new circumstances were so different that I was quite unable, and still am, to connect the earlier memories with myself, Richard Thurgo. They seem to belong to someone else, to the child who hoped to be engraved rather than spoken to, perhaps, or to fable; and I cannot tell them or think of them in any other terms. I appear to have been happy, but at the same time I can tell, reviewing the memories as they come, that I have eliminated all that was drab, the silent evenings with a morose and doubtless drunken guardian, and have retained those stories with which I learnt to amuse my friends at school, and through which I carved myself a place, a popularity, learning early that the past belongs—must belong—to the lies we tell about it.

When I was thirteen it was Alec who recalled me to Padstow, turning up at Mother's door out of the blue, in an Alfa Romeo with a freshly plucked Christmas turkey on the passenger seat,

and demanding a family reunion. In the intervening years he
had abandoned his sporting interests and, like Father, had pursued a variety of trades, only, it seemed, with greater success.
He told me he was in tea. Mother, on the other hand, said he
was a merchant banker and I was equally happy to agree. Whatever it was it paid for my visit from Ireland and a thrilling drive
round Bodmin Moor—"Coming for a spin?"—in the car, the
very car, he assured me, which in the hands of a chum had just
won the Belfast Grand Prix. Still driving he reached into his coat,
brought out a wad of huge white fivers, peeled one off and stuck
it in my breast pocket like a handkerchief. I'd never seen a five
pound note before, and kept a hand over it in case it blew away—
not wishing to offend Alec by tucking the note into a safer place.
After Grandfather's miserliness I couldn't grasp that it was mine
to keep, and when the drive came to an end at last I handed the
fiver back. "Something wrong with it?" Alec frowned, holding
it up to the sun to study the watermark. "Looks all right to me,"
he said as he replaced it in my hand and, seeing my expression,
added "it's not stolen or anything, you know." That was the last
thing on my mind, and I blushed in embarrassment. Or had he
touched a guilty nerve? Perhaps I was already aware, like Mother,
that if Alec's finances were to play a continuing part in my life I
should not be too finicky about their source.

He was twenty-seven, a fine looking fellow with an open face
and golden Thurgo hair, an Englishman with the Irish gift of the
gab that in some of our O'Malley forebears had been compressed, it seemed, into more caustic and telegram-like utterances. He sang us bawdy songs, to the guitar, and told stories
about London actresses over which my mother clucked like a
Dublin matron at bad language on the Abbey stage. I was enthralled. The news of Grandfather's death brought shock to the
household; less at the old man's demise than at the fact that he
had left me all he owned. Not a penny went to Mother (though
she and Grandfather's solicitor shared trusteeship of my legacy),
let alone to Alec. I found myself, all of a sudden, with great
expectations of actresses and racing cars. As it turned out,
Grandfather's cash had run low—I knew where it had gone; into
Galway Bay—but there was enough of it to see me through my
schooling, and the sale of his house would provide me with a
comfortable start in life. When Alec had recovered from the
shock he offered to invest the proceeds of my inheritance on my
behalf. We would all be rich, he promised largely. Mother

quickly rejected his expertise, again on my behalf; and nothing we could say would change her mind.

Despite this setback Alec soon resumed the role he had briefly adopted on Father's death, as head of the family, and since Mother had no great interest in determining my school—which after observing Alec she must have thought of as a choice of betting shops—he made arrangements for me as he thought fit. Most of his friends, he said, had been to Harrow, and so had some of Father's mother's people, the Anstruthers. I had been christened Anstruther, he now announced. Didn't I realize? Richard Anstruther Thurgo; it had been Father's wish. Mother looked blank at this. It would help me get a place at Harrow, Alec said, and was clearly a signal from Father, or at least a portent. With my newfound funds, my studious nature and my tutoring I would, he said, fit in well enough. He was right— though if I did fit in, it owed less to my studies than to my Irish blarney supported by my skill at a curious kind of football played with a leather drum and an elbow in the guts. I was a large and bony boy, with arms hugely developed from hauling pig-iron out of Galway Bay. Lissom Alec took after Father, but I was made of grand O'Malley brawn and took advantage of it. After my solitary childhood, so shielded by Grandfather's misanthropy that I had scarcely met anther child, I found nothing alien in boarding school life. On the contrary I was perfectly equipped for it. I detested other children, and was happiest alone. And compared to old O'Malley the masters were a soft touch: I could woo with the best.

I grew up a fearsome, successful bully. "Pick on someone your own size, Thurgo!" the masters would bellow; all well and good, but there wasn't anyone my own size, apart from "Mr. Carstairs," the stuffed, moth-eaten grizzly bear which dominated the corridors of the science lab. Even though the real Mr. Carstairs, the former science master who had either shot or resembled the bear (according to different traditions) was long since dead, the beast was still known to the school by this name. To entertain my friends I embellished its history with tales stolen shamelessly from Grandfather's shelves; our favourite recalled an American explorer and traveller in the North-west territories, where the Votiaks and the Tlingit believed that bears spoke like humans "when their hide was off" and who himself claimed to have been kidnapped by a female grizzly, "object, matrimony."

In those years I drew my strength not from within the school, but without. My thuggish appearance and coarse, beaky looks,

while they did not make me particularly conspicuous at school—
you can see faces and frames similar to mine in the City of
London every day, raw-boned ex-public schoolboys looking like
yeoman farmers dressed for church—certainly enabled me to
wander unremarked in the teeming North London streets beneath the school. It was there, as soon as I was old enough to
be permitted trips "to the town," supposedly in search of model
aeroplane kits, that I made my real home with the aid of a hold-
all containing appropriate clothes. The school debating society
had organized an outing to the local law courts, and this had
opened my eyes to a world of which I knew nothing. Three
suburban villains were being arraigned for an assortment of
crimes including burglary and "battery," and we were there,
presumably, to remind ourselves of our godgiven place and duty
as much as to learn debating from the eloquence of counsel. I
couldn't take my eyes off the accused. What startled me was the
degree to which they looked like villains and were content to do
so, caricatures of unkempt, shiftless ruffians who would have
defied even the pen that drew our Sexton Blake cartoons. Not
the poorest or most devious Galway peasant had looked so offensive, so unutterably guilty. I took to them at once—drawn by
what? by an odour, by God knows what, but drawn like one of
Grandfather's magnets to the pride of Spain.

Armed with gobbets of the old man's knowledge, I made
history my chosen subject, and the learned references to the
brothels of Aragon and their influence on Imperial fortunes seem
to have tickled my examiners. Meanwhile I explored the clubs
and dives of Wembley and points south until only Piccadilly
would satisfy my curiosity. The whores were not always as delighted with my youth, and what I thought of as my largesse, as
I had hoped, and were a good deal less affectionate than the
good-natured tarts of fiction or O'Malley anecdote. But I relished even their indifference, the key to a world more tightly
guarded still than Grandfather's. I longed to learn a different
silence, that of profound, sophisticated secrecy. The search
proved less romantic than I had thought; when I developed
alarming sores in the inevitable place I felt terror rather than
pride. Our communal baths made my condition a byword, and
it wasn't long before the news found its way to the headmaster,
a man who'd been known to expel boys for lesser evidence of
"lewdness."

"I've only got one question, Thurgo," he boomed. "Was it
love or lust, boy?"

"Love, sir," I said fervently.

He studied me keenly for a moment. "Very well then. You may stay."

Chastened, I turned instead to theft, petty theft, sweets and stationery, sometimes cash—our rooms were never locked—and with this experience "found myself" at last, as Dickens' Magwitch says of thieving turnips down in Kent. It was not a profound self-discovery, there was too little danger for that. But it gave me the idea of a career I might take up, in time. After Oxford. Shavian blarney and an affinity for crime—the boy was born to be a lawyer.

"Bad news I'm afraid, Ratty."

Sometimes a voice is there to give you warning, at other times it's just a voice in the head, alerting you that the landslide's under way and that your life is changing forever in that instant; the moment you touch a loved one's face and realize they're too deeply still for sleep, they're gone.

There's so little left, in memory, of school, that it reminds me what a vacant time it was; my "town" clothes in their holdall felt less like a disguise than did our absurd school uniform. The joke, I always felt, from the back row of class, was on the school, since I was a spy from another country, Spanish, Irish, (I could have passed for either), a fire-raiser learning foreign ways, an infiltrator. *Pay attention, Thurgo! Use your loaf, boy!* This wasn't at all like pulling a book out of Grandfather's shelves and falling to the floor with it, unable to wait, devouring it at once on the sunlit carpet; the bay outside, Atlantic ocean greeting me whenever I looked up, like a guarantee of my boundlessness. I missed it terribly, but it took no premonitions to tell me I'd never go back. I didn't want to; I didn't need to, the bay was in me and accompanied me everywhere.

Alec paid me occasional visits at Harrow, in what I thought was fraternal solicitude till the conversation turned increasingly to the remains of my inheritance and the means whereby, legally or otherwise, I could ferret it out in Mother's ignorance. Then in my last year at school his tune began to change, and one Sunday in early May when I was coming up for eighteen—I was fully six foot six and looked as plausible in my straw boater as a navvy in a baby's bonnet—he took me to the Queen's Head and came to the point. *Bad news, Ratty.* Till my schoolmates seized on it no-one at home had noticed that Richard Anstruther Thurgo made R.A.T., which annoyed me because it didn't fit,

I was a rhino not a scuttling rat; but once I'd made the mistake
of telling him about the nickname, Alec revelled in it. The bad
news for Rat was that Fold Farm, Grandfather's domain of which
only the Georgian pile remained, had burnt to the ground, in-
cinerating the rest of my patrimony and my dreams of Oxford.
The house had been derelict for years now, and it was only
surprising, Alec said, that the fire hadn't happened earlier. Every
attempt to sell it had failed. What's more—"brace yourself, old
son"—Grandfather's cash had run out; Alec himself had been
helping to finance my schooling. All these pieces of information
I believed, and still believe, including Alec's contribution to my
school fees. I believed them then simply because I trusted Alec,
and because despite my dreams of criminality I was utterly and
completely unworldly, as unworldly as Mother in her cut-glass
reverie. I could draw a map of ancient Mesopotamia and spell
my name in cuneiform, I could answer questions on Biblical
heroes from Jehu to Jehoshaphat, but I lacked common sense,
"common" or "nous" as my schoolmates called it ("'Thine is
the genuine head of many a house," I used to declaim at Grandfather, "And much Divinity without a *Nous*"). Alec was counting on this. To cover himself he'd probably concocted some
elaborate explanation as to the whereabouts of the insurance
money—he could simply have said that by an oversight the house
had been uninsured at the time of the fire, and arranged a corroborating story with Grandfather's lawyer—but he didn't need
one for Mother, or for me. It simply never occurred to us to ask.
Later, the fact that he'd never mentioned it led me to presume
that Alec and the lawyer set the fire, re-couped the money, and
split the proceeds. Knowing Alec it seems likely, he was probably in dire need of the cash and it was true that Irish properties
were unsaleable in those days, with or without land. He did the
right thing, even if he hogged the money. And by not asking
him about it, I did the right thing too, for in exchange I got what
I wanted far more than three years at Oxford: a prompt introduction to Alec's world, to clubland, to high-priced tarts and
touts and bookies, to London adventures. When he saw that I
wasn't too disappointed by the turn of events and that all I wanted
was to hold his coat-tails for a while, my brother was only too
happy to oblige; he knew he'd got off lightly.

We sized each other up, that lunchtime, I remember. He saw
a lumbering creature who'd run errands, and ride shotgun if
needs be; useful, if it could be taught some manners; the peasant
would always show through, of course. But he still loved in me,

I think, the big, boisterous dog, the bite. A part of him did. I saw . . . what did I see? I saw his estimate of me; I saw a man who talked less and watched more. The charm was still there but it was no longer involuntary. London had made him taciturn. Or perhaps he'd made the discovery that he was fallible, in business as in love. And since wariness had found no pits or devious pockets to inhabit on the unswerving, ebullient circumference of his nature, it had taken up residence at its core. When Alec was thinking, you could actually see the process going on in his head—a hidden engine bouncing on its cradle as it ticked over—as if it were an unwonted and unnecessary thing for him to do. He'd always reacted quickly, unreflectingly, and whether the course of action was selfish or unselfish he always seemed to know which was appropriate for him at that moment. Now it was like watching someone who'd been taken over by another, watchful self, but one who operated the strings of Alec's familiar personality in such a way that Alec himself could be aware of everything except for the existence of the parasite inside, the London Alec. This was how I saw it, but I saw it with indifference, because although nothing could restore the afternoon on the moor with the red sports car going faster and faster, criss-crossing the open, windy hills, nothing could replace it either, or replace the image of Alec at the wheel that day on Bodmin Moor, grinning, hair streaming; and nothing will.

That day I also mumbled out loud, for the first time, my intention of becoming a lawyer. I didn't see myself at the bar, I said, that was more Alec's style, I was a backroom boy, conferring with the criminals. Alec promised to find me a law firm ready to take on, as clerk and tea-boy, an eager old Harrovian; and he was as good as his word. He promised, too, to retain my services in times to come. It never occurred to me that he had more in mind than wills and deeds of property. Crime to me was street crime, and a crew of ruffians in the dock. Alec went off to the office, several times a week at any rate, and deeds conspired in boardrooms or in armchairs over cocktails lacked the necessary savour to draw my attention. Even the gaming clubs Alec frequented seemed insipid in their elegance. It was the bouncers, rather than the gamblers, that I ogled. Putting on my best bog Galway voice and clothes, I had already applied for the job at several dives, during school holidays, but lacking a patron or a record I was turned down with curt contempt as a probable police mark. In none of this did I feel the thrill of slumming, any more than the fear of being recognized, and ridiculed, "found out." Only this world, and this manner, when I caught sight of myself in dingy shop windows, suited my fierce and ugly face and my solitary disposition. I wasn't down among the dead men but alive among my kind—while Alec, the product of Padstow Grammar School, deployed public school arts and graces, looked the part, and wore my Old Harrovian tie. When I left school that summer, Alec paid for my keep. I curbed my lavishness towards tarts, the last remains of my schoolboy adventuring, and learnt parsimony, except at the racetrack. There I followed Alec, safe in his expert information. There, in his company, I met Peter Lützow, and with this encounter my adult life began.

Count Peter, *Pay*-ter as he bade us pronounce it, was in full *Graf* Peter von Lützow-Brüel, and virtually the sole proprietor of the Schweriner See, twinned lakes in the dark forests of Mecklenburg, and the land for miles around them. He too, he told us when I was introduced to him, was training to be a lawyer, at the advanced age of thirty-five. Somehow I doubted if in his case it involved making tea and learning how to serve writs. He belonged to my brother's respectable acquaintances, to one half of Alec's own double world, though this I was slower to discover. That Alec ignored louts, wore buttonholes as to the manner born, white carnations to match his new Mercedes, and entertained German counts at his Putney home, was what I noted, at eighteen. For all that it was 1936, Germany meant little to me, though I heard Alec and his friends mention aristocrats and business names with respect. You could always do business with the Hun, they said. And they were certainly not alone in speaking rarely, and then with condescension, of "Herr Hitler." "What your Herr Hitler needs," Alec would tell Peter, lifting one arm in a Nazi salute to demonstrate the problem, "is a decent tailor. Fellow's bit short of cloth, round here," and he pulled at the armpit of his own impeccable jacket.

None of this offended Peter, who shared Alec's London tailor. He was an Anglophile of long standing. A Miss Belcher of Bristol had been the family governess, chosen for her plainness by Peter's mother, though this scheme predictably backfired since Miss Belcher, plain as she was, had a tremendous sexual appetite and entertained liberally. Whether or not influenced by Miss Belcher, Peter was himself a democrat (much to the regret, he claimed, of his feudal charges), but he was a true German nonetheless, passionately highbrow, speaking of cathedrals in a lilting voice, of Canterbury and Dur-*hem*, and other places I had no desire to see. He found me, as Alec reported his words, an endearing hound, and promised to show me England. ("It is your country, I know," he said when I protested at this, "that is why I must show it to you, and one day you will show me Germany." That day never came; though for years I have been showing him Germany, in my head, and imagining his response.)

Yes: Peter, Alec, and myself: Peter blond like Alec and a little taller, though nowhere near as tall as I was; beside them I must have looked like a peasant henchman, a bondsman, a body slave, awkward as always in a suit, bouncer by appointment to these Mercedes-borne Teutonic Knights.

Privately, Peter would say to me, "I like your brother very much. He is at ease with everyone, no matter what he thinks of them. This is so English." Then, studying my swarthy and un-English face, "You must tell me about your family—Alec is mysterious about it. You know, I don't mind if it isn't absolutely top-drawer." He gave his little smile of savour for English idiom. "In any case, my lips are sealed."

And Alec, privately, "What do you reckon, Ratty? What's old *Pay*-ter like when he's at home? Does he hobnob with the Hitlerites, d'you think? What's he say to *you*?"

And to each other:

"Wimbledon today, Peter? Perfect weather for it."

"Also for an outing to Hampton Court. You prefer Wimbledon?"

"Toss for it, old chap."

Then came Maggie, and we were four. The first time I saw her she was alone, standing in the foyer of the Coliseum. I was a little confused because for some reason I thought we were going to see a Russian dance troupe (usually I was too much in a dream to take in the details of our evening engagements) but it turned out to be Lupino Lane. The girl in the foyer was evidently foreign, by her looks and touseled hair-do. Or a tart. Either way perhaps available. No-one wore their hair loose then, and it made her look en deshabille, gipsyish, and at the same time oddly like a child, a rather large Victorian child; like Alice. Looking closer, I saw a formidable, almost Oriental hauteur in the face, and backed off, casting her anew as a boyar's mistress. I found Alec at the bar. He passed me a drink through a scrum of dinner jackets and said, "For the girl by the pillar."

I turned to look. It was the boyar's mistress. Alec had forced his way back to the bar, to return with two more drinks. He grinned at me, since I must have been looking impressed. "You don't mind sitting separately, do you? I've bought an extra ticket." And then, taking the girl's drink from me and replacing it with mine, "Come on, I'll introduce you."

Unsmiling, she watched us approach, and took her glass without a word. Before taking a sip she shook her dark hair out of her face and studied me. Then to my surprise she broke into a broad, toothy grin; she'd clearly seen me look her up and down, earlier.

Alec was still gazing proudly at her, as if at an exotic orchid. "Miss Maggie Trimble," he said, making her sound like a transvestite variety act, and nodded at each of us in turn. "My brother Richard."

Miss Trimble was the daughter of a gloomy Hampshire curate and a lady novelist—and as English as a vicarage tea. But to this day what persists is the image of her as a camp follower of the Russian dance troupe I thought we had come to see; walking the streets of Petersburg, say, outstaring married frumps in her ill-gotten furs and finery. Such was the force of first impressions that it took me weeks to reconcile her face to her accent. In tones that anchored her firmly to Hampshire she would pour tender scorn on her background and on both her parents: the one, she said, distributing her fatuous romances among the parishioners, to alleviate the sense of doom brought on them by the other. For Trimble—as I was to discover at first hand—was a great believer in Satan. His direst prophecies were borne out soon enough, but he was hunting for abomination in the wrong quarters, at the time; chiefly female quarters. This was one good reason for Maggie to come to London and escape his ranting. She spoke less harshly of her mother, who had taken refuge farther away, in the eighteenth century. There her bold heroes, we were told, cried "Is there fire beneath your calm, my fair?" in a metaphor all too reminiscent of the curate's dreams. Maggie herself, or rather her long and gorgeous hair, he threatened with the garden shears, perplexed by her dark looks which seemed to derive from the pages of his wife's books, rather than from either of their fair and freckled families. And yet she was in all respects her parents' daughter. Their homely eccentricities brought out the actress in her, but she was English through and through, and the simulated hauteur of the Coliseum foyer was only for presumptuous barflies like me. Beneath it she was vulgar and playful and determined on a good time.

This Alec knew how to provide, and so it began, our quadrille, our lavolta: with Alec on one side of her, and the Count, in melodious form, on the other, singing the praises of the English summer as I rowed them up the Thames from Maidenhead and they plied Maggie with strawberries. Seated in the bows and facing backwards, my rowing position gave me a view of my passengers rather than where we were going, which put me into a happy trance and made their warning cries (Brutus, thou sleepst! Awake, etcetera!) a feature of our boating afternoons.

"Hard left, oarsman, we're running into traffic."

"That's it, Richard."

"Steady now! Good show."

"Yes, *goot* show."

The wiry black hair with its small, obstinate waves swung across Maggie's face as she turned between their cropped blond heads, and her raucous laughter, carrying across the water, drew stares. She posed in answer, a pre-Raphaelite Lady of Shalott. Or lay back and closed her eyes, one hand trailing in the water, where I alone could see it; and where the bangles at her wrist, ebony and bronze, glinted like attendant tiger-fish. It was a glorious summer indeed, *"von gold'nen Träumen schwer,"* freighted with dreams and Peter's beloved Hölderlin. He recited poetry, Alec told limericks, and I pulled on the oars with a flourish, grateful for Grandfather's training. Sometimes I punted them, erect, a solemn bargee, and in imagination, as we moored and I gathered up the picnic basket, watching them escort Maggie ashore, I was a brooding tongueless Turk, pledged to serve her to the death. The harem slave. Gazing at her, I felt no less emasculated. She was twenty-five but seemed younger, while Alec and Peter, though only thirty-two and thirty-five respectively, seemed to my eyes middle-aged.

Or rather ageless, like Jonathan Mansel, the cloak-and-dagger hero invented by my favourite author, Dornford Yates. This was a role for Alec which allowed me to indulge the pride I so often felt in him, in his good looks, in his pose and *brio*, in the very grain and wholesome texture of his skin. And it still allowed me to feel superior in sly, native ways, the wily Pathan bowing to the charming colonial. From the little I'd heard Alec say on the subject, his politics would have suited Yates; in *Blind Corner* the youthful narrator has been sent down from Oxford for "using some avowed communists as many thought they deserved," and receives a mailbag of congratulatory letters from total strangers as well as £300 in cash from a previously tight-fisted uncle in trade. Then he meets Mansel and is swept into a world of sinister intrigue, in a Teutonic castle full of secret chambers, oubliettes, and bottomless wells—Count Peter's home, as I imagined it. The villain of the piece was tailor-made for me, hook-nosed, bulky, with his sidekick the demonic Ellis whose mouth was brutal and whose clothes "argued an elegant taste like that of a blackamoor."

The villain was not, of course, supposed to get the girl, and though Maggie's glances freely included me, the men made sure I stayed the helpful hound. I found that I was ill prepared for this frustration. I was used to pleasure on demand, for cash. *Was it love or lust, boy?* Love, sir! And yet try as I might with fantasies of mute enslavement I couldn't succeed in making myself fall in love with Maggie, much as I desired her. Puzzled, I decided this was because she was too much like me.

With that slow summer and its outings I am inside my memories at last, instead of outside, watching the self that moved beside Grandfather, or in the compartmentalized world of my schooldays, stalking the streets in one guise, the stiff-collared bully in another, muddy sports and furtive homosexual affairs blending the two in violence—rousing encounters, though within only a few years I found I couldn't remember the names of the partners involved, and their faces had begun to blur. My own figure ruled those dark scenes; in the year that followed I came out into the light, and struggled. I found myself reticent with Maggie even when the role of confidant was offered. I almost wanted to see her as someone else's. All my dreams of her were brutal ones, but I suppressed the demonic Ellis during the day. This left me no means of approaching her, though, on well-kept lawns, beneath the august architecture in which Peter instructed us, or at the theatre, in crowded intervals. I couldn't compete for elegance, for savoir-faire or politesse as Peter liked to term it: to him English was amusing and German provincial, and French was the true gentleman's language. I took note, watched and waited.

The contest for Maggie's favours was another source of puzzlement. Why had Alec introduced her to the Count? At first I took it for deliberate insouciance, share and share alike. Alec's girlfriends came and went in quick time and I supposed Maggie his unspoken bequest, ever the perfect host, to Peter. But my cynicism was well in advance of theirs, as I realized from Alec's increasingly anxious eyes and voice. He badly wanted to keep Maggie, and he was losing ground to the walking Baedeker at his side. It never occurred to me in those days, outgunned as I was myself, that Alec too might be insecure in his guise as man about town, or that he might have felt he needed Peter at first, to impress. But only at first—and now it was too late to rid himself of his rival, who was poised to make his own advances. Like us he was entranced. Maggie spoke little, laughed often, and while her dirty chuckle promised volumes, she could be a picture of correctness in polite society, aping her mother, mockingly demure, leaving me to play the country cousin in her stead. She was as bookish as the Count and yet, though we all knew she was brainy, preferred to play the smiling audience. When Peter's learning, or our comic invention, failed, she would read off the Latin mottoes or construe the crests at Audley End and Blenheim. This was a torment to Alec. Yet she met his anecdotes with undisguised delight, while treating Peter to insidious, teasing respect and sometimes leaving him to smile uncomfortably, baffled, when Alec and I laughed at her puns. Poor Alec: more than once I found my brother, who claimed to consider books a waste of time, swotting over titles from the lending library.

Blenheim was the grand finale of our summer, and a cut above our previous excursions, not only in the grandeur of the setting but because we weren't tourists this time, we were guests with printed invitations. And it was here, in the library, that Peter took me aside and recruited my help in winning Maggie. Our presence at the ball was his achievement, but he seemed as ill at ease as Alec did among the landed gentry, and I wondered why. The key lay in Maggie's performance. She swanned, head erect, under approving eyes, stepping proudly through the Vanbrugh décor in a novel of her mother's, all fire, as it were, beneath her calm. She was laughing at it and us and Peter knew it. But despite being a man of delicate ironies about his own rank he was bamboozled by Maggie's mockery, and what he couldn't see was that she loved the part, for all her teasing.

My hired dress suit had given me an unexpected sense of freedom, in its very anonymity, the garb alike of Bulldog Drummond and the Prince of Darkness. Like old O'Malley shuttling between the Dublin whores and his dreams of Granada and al-Andalus, only society's extremes would do, I decided, prince or burnished galley slave. Maggie felt the same way, I was sure of it, and it had brought us together from the start of the evening. Outside Tetworth, on the A40, the nearside tyre had burst, and Alec brought the Mercedes skilfully under control and onto the side of the road, to a halt, waiting with a sigh for dogsbody to leap into action as usual. Jonathan Mansel would have done the same. But Maggie spoke up for me. Was Richard the only one, she demanded to know, who was prepared to get his hands dirty? Grumbling, the suitors set to work, falling into an argument as to the best location for the jack, Alec protesting that it was his car, Peter that it was a German car and he knew best, while we stood smiling by and Maggie poked me in the ribs, delighted.

It was dark before we reached Blenheim, and both rivals were in silent disarray. I found it curious, after so many dreams of desecrating Maggie in a dingy room, that I'd experienced this first rapprochement in the borrowed splendour of a dinner jacket. I soon lost her in the throng, and so did the Count, trapped in conversation with a distant relative. Alec too was nowhere to be seen. In time Peter disengaged himself, and walked over to me. I smiled cautiously at him. No doubt we shared a vision of the other two together on some decorative marble bridge beside the lake, Maggie faintly luminous in her cream-coloured gown, Alec visible only as a shirt-front and a gleaming pair of cuffs. Peter craned his long neck back and considered the ceiling for a while.

"These bold colours are not much to my taste," he said.

Nor bold moves either; the moonlit grounds, as he surely knew, were an eloquent setting for a proposal and one Alec would relish. I watched Peter's raised features, still studying the ceiling. His boyish face seemed too small for his body.

"What do you think?"

I shrugged. "They've been repainted."

"Oh no, this was always a vulgar room."

It was a long way down from the ceiling to the dwarfed figures around us. We contemplated them in silence. I was happy to be with someone who found Blenheim vulgar. "Oh, we have a few acres, and a nice old house," he'd said once, leaving me wondering whether he meant it literally or had learnt this way of speaking from the English and actually owned a nice old house the size of Windsor Castle. "Yes, with servants," he'd said under interrogation. "Mecklenburg is a very backward place. But we are not nobility, Richard, only a small land-owning family with an ancestor who was a counsellor to the Margrave of Prussia. And who had a hand," Peter had added with a smile, as though this was where modesty struggled with genuine pride, "in the commissioning of Bach's Goldberg Variations."

"Richard my friend," he now began, and paused. "I want to marry her."

He sounded firm, and confident. "Have you asked her?" I said.

"The moment has not come."

"You may have missed it."

"You think?" Interested, untroubled.

We watched the other guests once more. Couples strolled in from the dark, but not the pair in question.

"This is not for her, is it," he nodded at the assembly, "these stuffed shirts. You think I should renounce my title? It would not be distressing for me personally, you know, to be plain Peter Lützow."

"I wouldn't."

"You mean, not for Maggie?" He smiled. "She is not worth the candle?"

"I meant that's the last thing I'd do. I'd take her back to Germany, put on a show, light up the castle."

"Yes? You think?" he nodded. "You know her better."

It didn't seem to occur to him that there might be anything awkward, for me, about the conversation, that I might be partisan. The innocent, charming arrogance was always with him, alongside the hesitancy and the skepticism which were just as much a part of his make-up.

"Peter, if you're going to ask me to take your side . . ."

"I *am* asking, precisely I am. Why, you think she should marry Alec?"

It was an oddly loaded question the way he put it, with a measure of incredulity, as though only one answer were possible.

"Why not?" I said. Peter's head was on one side, the expression reserved, though still affectionate. His eyes moved off me, to the door.

"I have asked her to come and visit me, but I did not get a proper answer, you know how she is. It is too cold for her there, I think, where I live."

"I doubt it. You can't have been in many Hampshire vicarages lately."

"Ah hah," he said, and brooded in silence, his small pale face a blank. Whatever he was seeing it was not a Hampshire vicarage.

When Alec reappeared with Maggie, in the doorway, my brother looked pleased and she looked larky. Peter and I tensed together. But there was no momentous announcement in store, only a tale of gatecrashers stripping off for a lakeside dip and

Alec's efforts to restrain Maggie from joining them. I discovered much later that anxious Alec, afraid of bungling a frontal assault—Maggie's grin was so easily triggered—had asked instead about her feelings towards Peter, and been reassured, the fool, by what he heard. Then the bathers had distracted them, or at any rate distracted Maggie.

So did limericks hold the field, for the time being, over Hölderlin? I had no idea at the time, but since neither Alec nor Maggie herself, for all her camaraderie, seemed to require my services, I let my allegiance pass to Peter. I may have believed that when the foursome broke up at last, I'd see more of Maggie in Peter's company than I would in my brother's. It was beyond me to imagine making a rendez-vous of my own with her. In those early, ignorant days, living largely in fantasies, I preferred to project her as the Countess; though whether for her sake or mine I couldn't tell. Autumn drew in and brought with it, for Peter, the pressure of his feudal obligations, back in Mecklenburg; and his impending legal exams. The contest seemed to narrow. I found myself excluded more and more from Maggie's gaze, I was suddenly de trop, and retired to my own law books with their rhapsody of hypothetical crime.

I still saw Peter, separately, at his Pimlico apartment, for councils of war. To be near him I'd taken rooms in Belgrave Road, and rather than have them paid for by Alec I'd persuaded Mother that London life made financial demands beyond her reckoning; Grandfather's library, which had been put in store, thank goodness, long before the fire, was now sent to auction. Peter seemed melancholy, I thought. He had lost the advantage, along with the summer outings and his open-air lectures. Winter meant urban frivolity, and here Alec was the master. My advice was to return to Germany, banking on the charm of absence. He had waited too long for the moment; it was gone. (That I was expert in these matters, at least as regarded English girls, Peter was sure and so was I.) Besides, his stewards required his presence urgently, in the wake of harvest—I imagined him in a tower room, bent over gothic lettering by gaslight, wolfhounds at his knee. Once I asked him, teasingly, if it was so. Oh yes, he said mildly, with regret, but so vaguely that I couldn't decide whether what he regretted was that it was indeed so, or that I—and Maggie perhaps too—would imagine it that way. He made me promise to see Maggie frequently, ready to intercede on his behalf while he was gone. I resolved to do nothing of the sort. A protracted dose of Alec on his own, I thought, would open Maggie's eyes and do my charming, fickle brother more disservice than I could hope to achieve by innuendo.

I was a Spanish spy ready to spike the English guns; my powder was still dry, and if I made a bid for Maggie, if I fired my patent cannon (tempered, with benefit of hindsight, in hotter fires than those of King Philip's fleet), the game would be over. And something else, of course. I might lose Peter.

It was also at this time that the Colonel entered my life. Who and what he was, and even that he really was our uncle, I only have on Alec's say-so. I never met him, but he has played as decisive a part in my life as any of the people I have introduced. He was an Arabist, a personal friend of Ibn Saud, and an active member of the Arab Bureau at a time when that passionate faction succeeded so completely in setting the Foreign Office and the India Office at each other's throats that they finally fought a war to sort it out, using Arab manpower and British guns, Ibn Saud against the Sharif Hussain of Mecca. When Alec first told me this, he omitted to mention that our relative's part in it was to supply both sides with rifles. After the Great War he married a Spanish lady of some means and went to live in Malaga, never, to my knowledge, setting foot in England again. A shipload of English furniture followed him, giving their house an oddly country air, even though from the outside it looked (in the best Moorish manner) as if a child had made it out of icing sugar. Finca Thurgo it was called; I came to know it after the Colonel's demise. His wife was dead then too, but a mistress survived him, and survives him still, now owner of the house. She refers to him only as Tomasito, and perhaps the use of his former rank was kept alive by Alec rather than the man himself. At any rate he seems to have managed to keep a low military profile during the Civil War, when colonels, foreign or not and even in their sixties, might have been expected to take sides; though I am no longer surprised by people's capacity to come unscathed through wars and other nightmares. "We'll get the Colonel onto it!" Alec had said when I asked him if he'd had any thoughts about a law firm I could apply to. What colonel? "Why Colonel Thurgo, man. Tom Thurgo, Father's brother!"

This was in itself a surprise. Mother had mentioned no surviving Thurgo relatives; but then all Thurgoes were to her a shiftless, rather juvenile crew—Father had been ten years her junior—whittling away the wealth of Thurgoes and Anstruthers past, and she was in no hurry to appeal for money to a far-off

Spanish fancy woman. The Colonel, like Alec himself, proved to be a man of many contacts, though he pulled the strings at a greater distance. At Alec's behest he wrote me a recommendation to an ''old friend'' in the City. The Colonel had never seen the object of his confident claims, of course, but this didn't disconcert either one of us; it was how business was done, I took it. The old friend, head of an august law firm, interviewed me with gruff politeness. He had one of those wide-jawed Johnsonian faces, with a short nose, a forehead sloping back to a receding hairline, and the eyes of a fierce old pike. The interview, he assured me, was purely a formality, though when he asked after my uncle's health a guarded look came onto his face, reminiscent of Peter's expression in the library at Blenheim when discussing Alec as an eligible husband. I was beginning to feel uneasy about this expression.

That winter I had few opportunities to probe family secrets. Alec rarely invited me to join him and Maggie for the evening, relishing his tête-à-têtes with her and no doubt suspecting my alliance with the Count. I drew back into familiar ways, my days spent in stiff collars playing the clerk, my nights on the seedy prowl and venting my frustration on dance-hall brawls. In the office mercifully little was required of me, I copied documents, took papers to the courts, and served a writ or two though not, alas, on gangland bosses. My firm did little in the way of criminal law, and consequently even my visits to the courts found nothing more alluring in the dock than stern company secretaries. The nights had to make up for it. I fell in with a large blonde girl called Ellie, who entertained in Leda Buildings, Shaftesbury Avenue, and practiced clairvoyance in Poland Street, under her aunt's tutelage. From time to time I took Ellie to the theatre hoping to meet Alec and Maggie, and provoke them with Ellie's accent. But no such luck. I pored over Roman Law, dreaming of Rex versus the Thurgo gang. Old Bailey Sensation: Rat Acquitted. I dreamed of Maggie. I wrote to Peter, assuring him that I was hard at work behind the scenes. Finally, just before Christmas, the phone call came.

''Richard?'' Maggie, in a gentle take-off of Peter's formality, never shortened my name, scorning Alec's way with nicknames.

''Hello, Maggie.''

''Hello.''

She sounded cheerful but a little muted. There was silence on the other end of the line, as though it was I that had called her up and should now explain why. In time I discovered that this was her particular telephone manner; for my part Mother's periodic phone calls to Fold Farm had trained me not to try and say anything for the first thirty seconds, less because Mother had a lot to say than because of her curious habit of shouting hello, over and over again, very loudly, at the start of a phone conversation, irrespective of whether she could hear the person or not. As a result I tended to begin phone conversations in a passive state. With Maggie this produced stalemate.

"Where are you?" I said eventually.

"Home," she said. "In Hambledon. Can you come down? I want to see you."

I went out to buy my train ticket and a pint of Scotch—a habit acquired at school; now I never went anywhere without this comforter—and returned to pack. When I phoned Mother to excuse myself the family Christmas, she told me Alec had just done the same. But to my relief I didn't find him in Hampshire either.

Trimble, Maggie's father, had arrived in Hambledon with wife and two daughters, and a third on the way. The current vicar was an elderly and solitary man; he offered them the vicarage and moved to a smaller one, in an outlying parish. It was a generous gesture, but he was probably glad to be away from the new curate with his terrible dreams and his burgeoning family. Most of these were crammed into the Riley that met me at the station, its boatlike sides reminding me of our summer journeys up the Thames. Maggie was the eldest of the girls, the rest of whom were blonde and bobbed and, like their mother, noisy. I squeezed between them, with Maggie in the front passenger seat and Mrs. Trimble at the wheel. She had learnt her driving from being chauffeured through India, and sat stately and erect, with no apparent connection to the car, as though it were driving her. Our progress was slow. Mrs. Trimble gazed fixedly ahead, evoking crowds too savage to acknowledge with a wave. Her daughters did plenty of waving at the sparsely occupied pavements, and all talked at once. Maggie watched me with amusement. Local characters, many with gratuitously quaint names, were pointed out as they went about their business. "Look! There's Mungy!" cried the girls. Then came Granny Crabb, Sam Bone, old Curdle, and Captain Lapénotière. I had no idea Hampshire was so exotic; in this context Count von Lützow-Brüel would be quite run of the mill. As it turned out, Maggie hadn't mentioned Peter to her mother or her sisters—I soon found out she'd told her father, just to provoke him—and so I was in the awkward position of being regarded as a suitor by the entire carload of Trimbles except Maggie herself. Her sisters spied on us excitedly; even the curate encouraged me as someone who might with luck take his eldest and wildest daughter off his hands, or at least distract her from the Boche. At eighteen I was an unlikely match for her, but ungainly faces such as mine look older than their years. And besides, Maggie had been telling lies about me.

"You're a lawyer," growled her father as I accompanied him through the garden, hiding my ungainly hands behind my back.

"No, sir. I hope to be."

"What are you, then?"

"I'm studying for prelims." I saw him looking puzzled. He had a tired, kindly face under a balding dome; the eyes were a touch beady, but all the same this wasn't the Witchfinder General I'd been led to expect. "I'm a clerk," I explained.

He looked closer at me, perhaps seeing now that I was barely out of school.

"You're Cornish."

I nodded.

"Believe in ghosts?"

I searched for the appropriate answer, as he stopped again to stare at me.

"Don't look Cornish to me," he said.

"My mother came from Ireland."

"Anglican or Papist?"

"She's a Catholic," I said, adding, to be conciliatory, "I think."

"Not her. You. Or don't you know either?"

"Not really."

"Not religious?"

"I'm afraid not."

"I am," he said, "as you've probably guessed." Then, "Who's this German fella my daughter talks about? D'you know him?" and before I could reply, "Is he a Nazzy?"

"I don't know," I said, truthfully. "I don't think so."

"All I know," he said, "is what my German confrères tell me about the Nazzies and that's pretty grim. I don't want my daughter associating with one, I don't care how good his English is or how many damned Wren churches he's visited with her."

His gaze softened a bit as he studied me.

"So you don't know what you are, eh?" It took me a moment

to grasp his meaning. "Well, I don't blame you. Too many hypocrites. God's lost the fight."

I felt something was demanded of me, in the silence, and I racked my brains. "Perhaps He's only hiding."

Trimble looked keenly at me. "That's right. He'll come out after the fire."

When I got Maggie to myself at last, in the drawing room, I was numb with anticipation. I imagined eavesdroppers at every door, eager for me to make a move. With her first words Maggie confirmed my fears.

"Keep your voice down," she said softly, and sat close. "Peter's written to me. He wants us to come to Germany."

"Us?"

"You and me and Alec."

"He asked for Alec?"

She smiled.

"He asked for you," she said. "I asked for Alec."

There was a gentleness, perhaps more kittenish than gentle, in this vicarage Maggie, a less brittle quality. I liked it.

"I thought you'd already said no to Germany."

"I didn't say no," she said, her voice rising gaily, and then retrieving herself in an admonitory whisper, "I said wait."

"What's all the hush about? Is Germany taboo?"

"It is with Mother, she's terribly romantic about the Jews. Daddy's fears are indiscriminate."

"They seem to think I'm here to woo you."

"Do you mind?"

I hesitated; she took my arm, and I shrugged. In that moment I was glad that I had taken Peter's side in the struggle for Maggie; if I was going to flirt with her myself, I'd feel easier betraying Peter than betraying Alec.

"Where is Alec?" she said.

"Don't *you* know?"

Maggie shook her head and studied me with the curate's canny stare. Her hair was in a mess, giving her pale features a sulky look which roused me to an uncomfortable pitch. Maggie as houri; the subtitle "Secrets of the Harem Revealed" had once drawn me to a cinema in Wembley, and to furious disappointment. Her eyes seemed black, pupils dilated in the dark room.

"Tell me about the Colonel," she whispered.

Did this mean Alec was in Spain? I told her all I knew, which in those days wasn't much, while she watched me with lips pursed. We let the subject hang, in silence.

"You'll come, won't you, to Germany?"

"Of course!" Who's paying? I thought. Maggie saw it at once.

"It's *his* treat." She stood up, stretching her hands to me, pleased. "Good. Then I want you to learn German with me. Alec says he won't—that's why I wanted you to come for Christmas."

Was it the only reason? If I'd believed her it would have been a blow to my vanity, so I decided not to. And as for language lessons . . . surely the audacity of learning German in a chauvinistic Hampshire vicarage, in nineteen thirty-seven, was quite enough without our reciting verbs in tandem? "Nonsense, *Dummkopf*," said Maggie. She brought out a phrasebook and made me solemnly repeat after her, *Danke schön, mein Herr! Bitte, holen Sie mir einen Schnaps!*

In the next few days I discovered that Maggie in the country was indeed a different creature from Maggie in town. At the vicarage she dressed like a slattern, draped in woolen shawls over old clothes—only the bangles remained, to show off her fine wrists—and when her hair became too much of a jungle she shoved most of it under a beret. To me all this only made her more attractive, along with the black hairs that now crept undisguised down her temples towards her jaw. She was well rid of rouge and make-up, I thought, and even in London her dark, mobile mouth always seemed to be busy chewing away any lipstick. To my surprise she outdid the rest of the family in good works, in Christmas visits to the bedridden, to old Nanny, and for all I knew, old Curdle and Captain Lapénotière; she outdid them in goodheartedness too—of all that giggling, posing, charming, sentimental crew of true-blue Trimbles she was the only one who too remembered that old Nanny had hinted at a shortage of firewood, and who took the trouble to set out in the Boxing Day snow like good King Wenceslas, to make sure Nanny was all right. I let Maggie load me up with logs—"Goodness! Can you carry all that?"—and followed in her wake like a good Bohemian churl. It gave her a chance to wade down the High Street in full dishevelment, hair awry and shawl full of holes, looking like the little matchgirl in her final throes. The whole performance was clearly designed to contrast with her sisters, and annoy her mother. Trimble himself rose to it unerringly, referring to Maggie behind her back as the witch of Endor. And it confirmed another side of Maggie, a desperation, an appetite for more than the delights of Maidenhead and Bray, one in which her father refused to see even the slightest resemblance to himself.

I also discovered that I had a gift for languages, or more precisely a gift for mimicry, since it wasn't German that Maggie and I were studying, it was Peter. We vied to imitate his gentle sing-song tones. Inside the house this was too risky, and decency forbade us to be closeted in a bedroom; so to get out of earshot we took to the snow-bound lanes and greeted cyclists with cries of ''Wie geht's, mein Alter?!'' I was glad to be out of the vicarage, where I stumbled like Heathcliff among the antiques. We looked like a couple of tramps in the fields, and skipped and sang accordingly, grammar in hand. The realization that rather than star-crossed lovers we were rivals, rivals for Peter, did not come from within me. It came from Maggie; she never asked about it outright, but her penetrative looks, when we discussed him, uncovered my motives. This bound us together, for despite our rivalry we shared a common greed. I wanted both of them. And Maggie wanted all of us.

Hoping to make her jealous I told Maggie about Ellie and my visits to Leda Buildings. Mischief showed in Maggie's face when I mentioned Ellie's apprenticeship as a Soho clairvoyant, and I withheld the Poland Street address. I could just picture Maggie paying a surprise visit there, and the mocking impersonation she'd come back with. I was learning that, as at school, I had to keep my worlds separate.

There were so many things that at the time we couldn't tell each other. We mimicked Peter's mannerisms and his Junker bearing, safe in our love for him; while Alec, guiltily, we treated with affection, confident that in the end he was the least ruthless of us. We were too quick to guess each other's motives, Maggie and I, and it became a little frightening. There was no escape from one another. I recognized, from school passions, the experience of no longer being able to perceive a face as a whole, the effect of growing intimacy; and when I made the effort to reassemble the picture, felt the wave of nausea that accompanies it. I longed for Maggie's made-up London face, to restore the distance. The German language took its place; our very awkwardness with it protected us and made us strangers again, pulling on Peter's mask in place of our own.

The evenings were devoted to games, and often spoiled by Maggie's early departure, slipping up to her room where the German grammar awaited. I knew she was waiting for me to join her, but out of politeness I stayed downstairs with the family, smiling through recitations and Trimble favourites on the piano. Worse still, I was expected to talk. The homes I'd known were silent, abrupt in speech. Mother said even less than Grandfather. Shaw and Wilde and the Victorian explorers had infected me with words, words on the page and in the head, falling over themselves in their need to get out—and still dressed in the old scented mannerisms, their outdated mauves and pinks and yellows, as unlikely a match for my stormcloud looks as lace frills on a Galway peasant. No doubt that's why I've always censored them, the words, and make such paltry answers when people address me; and why, with Maggie's help and Peter's, I took so readily to formal German, measured and fanciful at once. How can we have so many words inside, and so few to spend aloud? It's not miserliness, in my case. Words don't fit my face, or for that matter my soul, and I've spent a lifetime trying to match up to the one and be an honest servant to the other.

Until that visit to Hambledon I hadn't fully realized how much of a challenge this would be, at least as regards my appearance; or how bizarre I looked in polite company. I'd never spent time in a house with so many mirrors, or so many women, for that matter. Usually I avoided my own image like the plague, but that Christmas it met me everywhere I turned. As always what I saw were the lineaments of violence, but troubled, doubtful of finding an adventure to fulfil them. Where Alec had the serenity of a ship's figurehead, I looked like something hunting for foliage to hide behind. Or a fog to lurk in, a marsh fog like Magwitch my Dickensian model. And later when the film of *Great Expectations* came out I was delighted to find that the actor had a look of me, I mean the one chosen to play the tender-hearted, long-memoried convict (in German we have a blissful compound noun for this, *Langzeitgedächtnis*, long-term-memory): a vulture face with little eyes crowding a prow of a nose, and a big jaw below.

When it became clear that I was no conversationalist, the Trimbles resorted to parlour games. Postman's Knock brought giggling kisses, and Maggie's sisters took full advantage of her evening absences. During the day they were more circumspect. Between snow showers we took to the vicarage garden for Grandmother's Footsteps; there, to the girls' delight, Thurgo footfalls betrayed me instantly, and when it was my turn to play the solitary sentinel it took Trimble laughter to alert me; without it I was as deaf as a snowman to their lightfooted approach. Once I remember a tap on the back within moments of taking up my post, and happy shrieks as I turned to find Maggie behind me. "You're a good sport," she whispered, reaching up to give me a smiling, wet-lipped kiss on the cheek.

My clumsiness became proverbial, yet the more I blundered the more I endeared myself to Maggie's family. Winter is for me the most erotic season, and I might in other circumstances have responded to her sisters' flattering attentions. They certainly reassured me that my face was fit for more than tarts. But I was hypnotized by Maggie's tousled looks as if by a familiar face made ugly in the middle of a row, an angry smudge against the crisp, cold landscape we walked in.

It was hard to tell what her mother thought of me, or of anything. She twittered constantly, but the more Laura Trimble talked the less substantial she became. While her daughters sighed, she interrupted our games to tell me at length about her life, the childhood in a Ceylon she still mourned, and the woes of living with the curate, who was in his study but not to be disturbed, she said, as he was probably busy deciphering the Beast of Revelations. Mrs. Trimble lent me the manuscript of her latest work, entitled *At the Gates of Vienna*, where it turned out that Suleiman The Magnificent was beating loudly. At the beginning the hero, a Spanish mercenary leading the might of Transylvania against the Turk, saved Suleiman's life and received for his pains a peacock feather from the Sultan's turban, plus a book entitled *The Seven Dark Thoughts of Evagrius Ponticus*—I never discovered what these were, though apparently they contained the key to the Resurrection. The Spaniard and the Turk had come to blows over a Maltese lovely, and the Knights of St. John were falling in droves at their feet, when the Reverend Trimble found me pouring over their adventures. It turned out we both identified strongly with the Turk.

"Any good?" he said.

I assured him the book was excellent.

"What's it about? Wait—don't tell me. Is it the Ottoman Wars? Ah yes, the Ottoman Wars," he said, as though he'd survived them himself. "Suppose we'd lost, eh? I'd be up there in the mosque with the muezzin, and you'd be somewhere in the bazaar, I suppose, plying your trade." I wasn't sure what he meant by this. "Pity we won, really," he went on, "those Muslims know a thing or two about how to handle the ladies." It was easy to see why the Bishop's eye had never fallen on him, for promotion. But his fortnightly sermons, alternating with the elderly vicar—they filled and emptied the church in turn, like a bellows—played to standing room only, and caused palpitations for more than just the Trimble family. We were in place early when the day came—too early, as far as I was concerned, and I began to think longingly about the pint of Scotch, still half full, back in my room. But as the church began to fill up excitedly behind us, calming again to an expectant hush, it was possible to understand why Laura Trimble had been so mindful of the Resurrection, in her book; this was like being present at the event, and in the front row. Trimble's arrival sent a collective shiver through the faithful, and he dominated the proceedings that followed, reading both lessons and dictating the tempo of the singing. The first lesson was short but ominous.

" 'How is the gold become dim! How is the most fine gold changed!' " he cried. " 'The stones of the sanctuary are poured out in top of every street. . . .' "

The bare walls of the church gave no hint of this, but Trimble continued, now gazing at the rafters as the verses homed in on their target.

" 'Even the sea monsters draw out the breast, they give suck to their young ones: the daughter of my people is become cruel, like the ostriches in the wilderness. . . .' " I didn't dare glance at Maggie. " 'They that did feed delicately are desolate in the streets: they that were brought up in scarlet embrace dunghills!' " There was a pause. " 'For the punishment of the iniquity of the daughter of my people is greater than the punishment of the sin of Sodom, that was overthrown in a moment, and no hand stayed on her!' " Trimble's hand shut the Bible heavily, and we rose for the second hymn. Early on, Trimble began his slow march to the pulpit, still singing the hymn. He ascended and then stood mute with eyes closed, and with disastrous effect—the last verse was a jumbled effort, deprived of his leadership, the congregation altogether too interested in Trimble to look down at their hymnals, and everyone leaving the words to someone else. Since the pulpit had been built for a smaller race of clergymen, Trimble had to lean forward to avoid the canopy.

"Brethren," he began as soon as the last note had faded, "my text is taken from the Revelation of St. John the Divine, chapter twenty, verses one to three."

Trimble's eyes were still shut and his torso projected alarmingly over our front pew, but at that moment he looked up, and gripped the pulpit.

" 'And I saw an angel come down from heaven, having the key of the bottomless pit and a great chain in his hand. And he

laid hold on the dragon, the old serpent, which is the Devil, and
Satan, and bound him a thousand years, and cast him into the
bottomless pit, and shut him up, and set a seal upon him, that
he should deceive the nations no more, till the thousand years
should be fulfilled: and after that he must be loosed a little
season.' '' The curate paused, and resumed in a meditative tone,
"He must be loosed; he *must*. Why? Why must he be loosed,
if God loves us? Last night before retiring, fellow Christians, I
wrote out this text in full and laid it on my pillow and read it
before going to sleep. As I shut my eyes I asked for guidance.
My sermon was a blank page, my friends. I asked for help."

He gazed round the church, and Maggie nudged me with her
foot. This was the opening she had promised me. On alternate
Saturday nights her father dreamed on behalf of his flock.

"There are dreams," he began, "we don't remember at all,
and dreams we soon forget, and dreams we cannot forget, for
days and even weeks. I shall leave it to you to conclude which
kind this was." Trimble shut his eyes, then opened them again
as though to show there was no need for such introspection, so
powerful was the memory. "I saw faces . . . I saw crowds.
Women and children. And I saw them smiling, separately:
women indifferent to husbands, mothers indifferent to sons,
children indifferent to parents. I tried to shake off the dream, I
knew it was a dream, but I couldn't. I saw women giving birth
in public places; I saw stranger things; I saw a great hall, and in
it files of women smiling and singing in a public register, beside
the name of "Father," one word: Unknown. And I saw men
worshipping these women, on bended knees. Of course, it was
only a dream."

Behind us noses were blown and discreet coughs muffled.
Trimble waited for them to settle.

"It was a dream, but a terrible one. We are the animal that
smiles, we are the animal that worships—but we have a choice,
given to us by God, of when to smile! When to smile, and when
to worship! God gave us this choice because he loves us!"

He spoke the last words heavily, leaving a void in their wake.
Then his voice rose sharply and he looked back up at the rafters,
the words tumbling out.

"Isn't that right? How do we know that God loves us? No
other religion tells us that God loves us, my friends, did you
know that? But we know it's true that God loves us, don't we,
because it says so there, in that book!" He gestured at the lectern
without looking, "John says God sent His only son to die for

us. Well: is that proof? Some people say it's proof, some people say it's *triple* proof! One, he sent his only son; two, he suffered and died; three, he died for us who are unworthy! Is that proof? Is there one of you in this church today stupid enough to believe it's proof?''

Nobody moved, in the silence. Nobody coughed.

"I say: we have proof. Greater proof. He sends us dreams—God sends us warnings, in our dreams, and would He warn us if He didn't love us, my friends? True, he sent his only son—but one death wasn't enough for us, one agony wasn't enough for us. When God looks down on us He cries, I am Unknown! I am the Father and I am Unknown! And we can only answer, help us, Lord, we too look in the faces of our children and are Unknown. Help us! Give us proof that we exist, in their sight and Your own. Give us proof that You exist. Friends, God is not mocked! Out of the pit he sends us whores and smiling children. Instead of wars he sends us worse than wars. For do not be deceived: wars will not save us. A death could not save God. It will not save you and me. Unknown in our homes, we are not yet ready for death. We shall return, the more unknown. 'For in those days shall men seek death, and shall not find it, and shall desire to die, and death shall flee from them.' ''

Trimble bowed his head in anguish, and the minutes passed.

"Help us, Lord," he said at last, "help us to recognize each other without hate and without envy. Help us to know that You exist, and that You love us. For You have sent the proof among us. I say: God loves us. And because He loves us He has loosed the Devil from his prison, for a little season. Let us pray."

As we knelt I stole a look at Maggie, but I drew no response.

Christianity came late to Germany, said Peter as he drove us through the bare Schwerin woods towards his home. Late, and then in martial form; he spoke of the Teutonic Knights who had converted the heathen of Mecklenburg, of the gradual eclipse of the Hansa ports and of the Knights themselves, leaving a territory plundered by successive armies, Swedish from the north, Imperial from the south, until the axis shifted and the French came from the west to take their turn across the land, and back again pursued by eastern armies. Swedes, Danes, Prussians, Hanoverians, Russians, Poles; French and Englishmen too; everyone had been to Mecklenburg, on the way to somewhere else. Gustavus Adolphus, Wallenstein, Napoleon: it was the stamping ground of famous captains, and what remained looked desolate,

and shabbier than I'd expected. It was April and Peter had promised us a reviving landscape. Instead winter clung on, the trees
were dank and still, and the farms squatted beneath low roofs,
sullen, in the muddy valleys. Only the smoke that rose steadily
into a windless gunmetal sky showed that they were inhabited
at all. I saw no faces at the windows as we drove past. Cars and
passers-by were few. Like their animals the inhabitants huddled
indoors, besieged.

Peter had met us at the airport. He too drove a Mercedes, but
it was older than Alec's and less ostentatious, its dull grey blending with the slush that had coated it on the drive to Hamburg. It
was my first trip abroad and I was avid for sights, for pine forests
and towering castles, *Blind Corner* castles full of oubliettes. We
spent an hour or two in Hamburg, which seemed to be full of
familiar faces—this curious sensation, as if London friends were
about to appear before me on the crowded and prosperous
streets, is all I remember of them; I had a different perspective
on the experience in later years, learning how deeply the city
desires to be English (an ideal Englishness, not the real thing)
and apes England in so many of its fashions. But those original
London mirages of mine were also, I think, the reaction to simply being abroad: it was too foreign and it wasn't foreign enough.
As for the streets themselves, their pre-war image has merged
for me with the no less busy city that replaced it in the 'Fifties,
and where not an alleyway remains to stir memories of a port
that once rivalled Amsterdam in its quaint majesty, and now
resembles a face after masterful plastic surgery—a good face,
but you can't imagine anyone growing into it, a face without a
history.

My introduction to the city, that spring, was brief. We lunched
in an expensive restaurant before driving on. There too I was
struck by how little we looked out of place, Alec and I in our
English tweeds (I had bought a new suit, eight pounds ten at
Burtons, and the fly-buttons were still horribly stiff) and Maggie
in a dark travelling suit. It had a greenish tint that shone like
moss when the light caught it, with a distinctly Hampshire fox
draped loosely round one shoulder and biting its tail in an absent-
minded fashion on the other; above it the lurid red of her lips.
The men and women at the neighbouring tables looked no more
Prussian than we did, and there wasn't a monocle in sight, much
less a duelling scar. I was especially disappointed with Peter
himself—no cape, no alpenstock, not even knickerbockers; he
wore one of his English suits and blended in as easily with us,

and with Hamburg, as he had in London. He's doing it all wrong, I thought to myself; but this impression was short-lived. Just as my image of Maggie had been altered by the Christmas spent at Hambledon, so my feelings for Peter, till now no more than a schoolboy crush, sharpened with the choice of setting. I discovered the man, and since it was no longer possible to avoid it I discovered politics.

We had fallen into an odd routine, Maggie, Alec and I, in the preceding months: during the week Maggie would come to London for a day or two to visit Alec, and though she never hid this from me she never got in touch while she was with "the Don" (as Maggie and I had dubbed Alec, in honour of her mother's book; Peter was "the Sultan"). She stayed overnight in Putney, whether chastely or not I couldn't tell. It seemed grossly unlikely given Alec's habits of conquest, but I put nothing, even chastity, beyond Maggie. And for once Alec might be prepared to be patient. I was pretty sure he was in love, and for the first time. Where the German language was concerned Maggie's zeal was undiminished—so whatever her plan of battle was, it clearly hadn't been changed by proximity to my brother. At weekends I went down to Hambledon on my own, and on the station platform at Petersfield we greeted each other with exaggerated cries (a full week of preparation went into them): *Ach! dich endlich zu umarmen, Liebchen! Komm, du süsses, entzückendes Geschöpf!* It was competitive; we matched each other stride for stride. By February Maggie was writing to Peter in fearlessly erratic German and I soon followed suit, growing more excited as our coming visit acquired a date. We were longing to show off. Alec of course ignored all this, though he knew of our weekends and their purpose. He was the man in possession, for the time being, though this wasn't going to be enough and he knew it. His strongest suit, if not his only suit, was his resolute Englishness, and he played it to the hilt. At intervals Alec asked me if I'd heard from Peter and on each occasion he enquired if I thought Peter was involved with the "Hitlerites." As before, I pleaded honest ignorance. As long as the forests and the castles were still waiting for us intact, it was all the same to me.

Schloss Brüel, Peter's ancestral home, lived up to every expectation, even on that first leaden afternoon—though mainly by eluding all classification. Peter had termed the architecture "Dutch-Italianate" which meant nothing to me then and still makes precious little sense. Brickbuilt but rendered a startling white, the Schloss glowed above the fields with their dirty patches of melting snow. What it brought to mind was a wedding cake, and I'm sure I wasn't the only one to think so. Getting closer, other features emerged which explained the cake effect, chiefly the fact that the whole building was ringed at ten-foot intervals by narrow horizontal stripes of a terracotta colour. These turned out to be carved friezes, and were actually made of terracotta. Unglazed, and faded to the colour and cracked consistency of ginger biscuit, they showed a series of profiled heads—Renaissance heroes in the main—each circled by a wreath, and together resembled a huge set of pottery dinner-plates set into the castle walls. Other parts of the friezes showed primitive Christian scenes, transferred with startling effect to a Nordic setting: a boy-Christ on a reindeer; Lucifer with a human body and a snake's head, peering through apple boughs at a blonde, emaciated Eve. "From the workshop of Statius von Düren," Peter informed us as we drew nearer to this extraordinary layered artifact. The building itself was the work of a Dutchman, one Piloot, we were told, with embellishments by someone called J. B. Parr—I never discovered whether this was an Englishman, but Alec was in no doubt and called the place Parr Towers from that moment on. It did have towers, white turrets ending in a conical hat of dove-grey tiles. Low farmyard buildings were attached to the Schloss at right angles, pointing towards us and inviting us into what was part courtyard and part farmyard, giving the place a pleasantly rustic air, turrets and all, like a landowner dressed in muddy Wellingtons beneath his Sunday best.

The Schloss stood alone in the midst of what was, that day, rather melancholy parkland, misty, with only a few isolated trees, and some muddy black-and-white cows making their own cloud of steam in the stillness. We had come through denser woodland, up narrow sandy tracks—a relief after the cobbled roads which made the car reverberate like a swarm of maddened bees—but around the castle and landscape was spacious. To either side of the house, the view gave off that peculiarly drab finality of winter farmland, and the mist gave it the brown and white tones of an early rotogravure. In this setting the Schloss glowed with a theatrical effect as if creating its own light. Neither farm nor fortress, it looked the sort of place where passing generals might be entertained, but certainly not resisted, and the retouching, on the glistening white walls and turrets, was so unblemished that the gothic doorway of pale stone seemed out of place, a relic of an earlier and sterner attitude. Framed in it

as we emerged into an air coarse with fog, was a tall woman
with hair coiled above her head, her broad build emphasized by
the puffed shoulders of her coat. This was Peter's mother *Gräfin*
Agnetha, Swedish-born and widowed, as Alec had informed
me, in the first war, like our own mother. But there the resemblance ended. Looking at her regal face, watching the welcoming smile as Maggie trotted out her well-rehearsed German
greetings, I felt at last the discomposing, pleasurable shock of
being in a foreign country. All the same and without thinking I
hurried to help unpack Maggie and Alec's voluminous luggage
from the rear of the car, where I was politely restrained by
servants, and pointed at the front door.

A firm sense of the house and its personality evaded me for
days to come. Its dual nature, hinted at by the heavy door in its
rococo setting, was pursed inside: above the solemn Rittersaal—
a panelled dining hall of flags and arms and portraits—the bedrooms were bright and homely, with vast swollen eiderdowns,
permanently pregnant, on the beds, and bird or flower studies
on the walls. The climb to the *Gräfin*'s tower sitting room was
dark and cobwebby, the room itself fussily floral. Untidy, it
smelt of dog; but spaniels, rather than wolf-hounds, snuffled on
Agnetha's chintzes.

In her presence we deferred to her poor English and spoke
German, while Alec maintained a gracious armchair silence,
legs crossed and doing his utmost to look like the Prince of
Wales. His cigarette smoke hung uneasily above us; a languid,
punctual gesture, the only movement in the room, took the cigarette to Alec's lips and back to the ashtray.

Haben Sie einen angenehmen Flug gehabt, Fräulein Trimble?
A pleasant flight? A very pleasant flight. Straight out of our
phrasebook.

*Sehr angenehm, Frau Gräfin. Gar nicht ermüdend. Wir dan-
ken Ihnen für Ihre Gastfreundschaft. Mein Deutsch ist leider
schwach, sonst. . . .*

*Sie sprechen aber fliessend, mein Kind. Wo haben Sie das
studiert?*

As I watched Maggie on her best behaviour, acting up to the
setting and Agnetha's dowagerly posture—they both sat as if on
horseback—I had the feeling this couldn't last and that my
brother was gaining more advantage than he knew by keeping
aloof from the small talk. It was still for Maggie to decide
whether or not this was a dry run, as Countess elect; she could
take against the whole thing. We skirted current events at first,

informing ourselves politely on the natural history of the place, its forests still patrolled by elk and wolf and eagle, and discussing the breeding of dairy livestock, which was Agnetha's passion. We listened to family anecdotes; more generals rode past; Tilly, Blücher, Moltke. Taking to the Mercedes once more we reviewed the estates and visited the Schweriner See, twin lakes traversed by a strip of land and a road which had enabled Peter's forebears to claim a toll from passing farmers. These were now rare enough in the bleak weather, and there was little other traffic. In this stunned landscape, seemingly ignored by officialdom, we saw and heard no Nazi, or Nazzy as Maggie's father would have said, and at first it was easy enough to speak none. Devoid of industry, the flat and sparsely wooded countryside seemed to forbid all action, breeding a weary resignation in the landwork and a life of contemplation—judging by Peter—in the landlord. On the North Sea coasts of England, from Essex to Northumberland, you can come across similar scenes on dreary heaths, the same sense of exposure and exhaustion. But nowhere as strongly as here, in Peter's homeland.

I confess that I came here at the harshest time of the year, and tourist guides had led me to expect a land flowing with milk and honey, the German paradise. The beechwoods by the Schwerin lakes promised better things—but at the time the only signs of bounty we saw were on the table. There the flood was endless. *Fünf Mahlzeiten hat der Tag!* Peter announced: five meals hath the day. I counted more like seven. *Morgenbrot,* to which the eponymous morning bread was barely a beginning since it included red cabbage, beans, and beer, with potato soup or else what appeared to be barley grains in buttermilk; *Kleinmittag,* or elevenses; *Mittag,* an unrelenting feast; *Nachmittagskaffee mit Kuchen,* a kind of tea sometimes replaced by the more lavish *Souper*; *Abendbrot,* the evening meal; finally *Nachtkost,* or as Peter put it in his best peasant accent, *'n Bissen vor'm Schlafengeh'n,* a bite before bedtime. By peasant standards this was a skimpy menu, he assured us, since they usually opened the day with not one breakfast but three. At our main meals, chicken, pork, and beef—all of them—arrived in plenty, often with roast goose, and a variety of cabbages, peas, beans, vetches, dumplings, and potatoes in their jackets, along with *schwarzes Roggenbrot,* the hunks of black bread. Dinner brought hams and sausages and fish. I had never been particularly interested in food; now the sheer quantities induced such nervousness that I ate continuously. I remember one Abendbrot in particular: cold roast chicken, a small barrel of lampreys and one of anchovies, with cold roast mutton, veal cutlets, sardines and marinated herring, and four cheeses, one of them a filthy sheep's milk cheese which only the local Branntwein, a sort of eau-de-vie, made palatable.

After four days we pleaded for lighter meals, if only at night, and were indulged. Even Maggie was looking bloated, and I foresaw changes if she were ever to become mistress of the house. Well-fed and comfortable as we were, I couldn't really imagine living at Schloss Brüel, owning it, that is; or rather I couldn't imagine who one would have to be to feel at home in such a curious atmosphere, sumptuous in some respects, pawky in others, part castle and part smallholding. And then there were the antiquities, foreign treasure equally ill at ease among the chintzes as in austere, stone-floored hallways. In addition to soldiering, Peter's father Graf Egon had been an amateur archaeologist, or at least a collector, so that aside from family heirlooms the Schloss sported even more ancient booty. There were Greek and Roman torsoes lurking in alcoves like beheaded servants, and cabinets crammed with Egyptian statuettes whose small submissive figures, arms folded across their chests—they seemed female, but I wasn't sure—had the smug faces of the obedient. It was the torsoes that held my attention, the Greek specimens frail by comparison with the bulkhead strength and metallic sheen of the Roman frame. Some had buttocks attached, some didn't. The corridor to my room was lined with these mutilated shapes; they alternated in the alcoves, Roman, then Greek, then Roman, and the slender Greeks could have fitted inside the Roman ones like flesh under armour. One night, on the way to the drinks cabinet downstairs, where the Branntwein lived, I squeezed into an alcove to inspect the Roman bum-cheeks. They glowered, a pair of bald pates, bony and unappetizing. But at night nothing in the house seemed altogether alien to it; sofas too became mysterious objects, as did drinks cabinets. At night smell took over and a single odour, the faint but persistent smell of cow dung, reconciled what in the day were the warring and confusing features of the house. On my nocturnal expeditions I began to like the place.

The weekend brought our first disturbance. So far we had all been unbearably polite, seeking safety in numbers, and if any of us found ourselves alone with one or other of our company I assume they exchanged the same platitudes with which Maggie and I bade one another goodnight, at out respective bedroom doorways. On Saturday night, as Agnetha rose to leave us, she turned on Maggie one of her most gracious smiles. In the morning the *Fräulein* and her friends would of course accompany them to church, would she not? Maggie glanced at Peter. There were no denominational problems here, it was a Protestant stronghold, and an Anglican clergyman's daughter might well be expected to worship with the family. But we all knew Peter to be no more of a churchgoer than Maggie herself, when away from home. He smiled, and laid his head on one side, nodding encouragingly. "Selbstverständlich, Frau Gräfin," said Maggie, using a word that she and I had often repeated with portentous relish: self-understandable. Naturally she would come. There was a pause after Agnetha left, and I could tell from Alec's expression that he had gathered enough from the exchange to see its possibilities.

"*Kirche,* eh?" he echoed Agnetha, smiling at Maggie. "Home from home."

Maggie's eyes were on Peter. "You're coming?"

"Of course."

"You're as bad as she is, then," said Alec, "kow-towing to the relatives." I'd told him Maggie went to church in Hambledon.

"I am not kow-towing as you put it," said Peter patiently. "You know I am not strictly a believer, but on this occasion I go to show my political colours. A number of our pastors have been arrested in Lübeck."

"Arrested? Why?"

"For preaching against the Nazis. You see, we are not kow-towing—we are a very independent people here."

Maggie was still studying Peter. I knew that face, the expression. It said: are you really just like me or are you actually (as I hope) of a different species altogether?

"And that's all you're going to do? Go to church? I don't call that very independent," said Alec, "especially since you don't believe in any of this religious stuff anyway." He tugged at his nose; a sign of minor nervousness, and it surprised me.

"You have a suggestion?" Peter asked.

Alec studied his cigarette. I saw Maggie, poised at that moment—we were all a bit pent-up, I suppose, none of us had said anything we meant, for almost a week now—and needing to speak. She had to do something with her native truculence, which could hardly side with Peter in his diplomatic vein, but she wasn't yet ready to make trouble for him. She rounded on Alec.

"If they're stubborn, these pastors, that's their own affair—they're probably zealots. Calvinists. Worse than Daddy." She gave Peter a teasing smile. "The kind who suck up to the gentry all the time, that's why they don't like the Nazis."

Peter gave an indulgent smile and said nothing.

"That's something you can't hold against Herr Hitler, Alec," Maggie went on, "that he's having a go at the church."

"Oh, he's quite a good chap really, is he?" said Alec blandly.

This was news to me—or at least confirmation that Alec had an attitude to German politics. Even with regard to English politics his views were a matter of guesswork, right-wing I assumed. Looking back I can remember patronizing references to Baldwin, though around that time the old Alec, the sentimental Royalist who wept for Edward and Mrs. Simpson, and who might even have followed Mosley's flag if the man hadn't been so highbrow and his followers so vulgar, was becoming just what he professed to despise in Baldwin, a cautious investor. In the end Churchill came along and, for Alec, provided the perfect compromise. But German politics? Had he and Maggie been talking German politics? Why hadn't I been in on this?

"He's saved this country from Bolshevism, that's what Agnetha says." Maggie looked uneasy, as if she didn't like the corner she was in. "They'd have turned Communist years ago."

Alec gazed at her. "Really?" he said. "That doesn't say much for them, then, does it?"

The church at Lützow, where we drove on Sunday, was a far cry from the gaunt stone and the rigours of St. Clement's, Hambledon. The dove-grey walls were smooth and featureless, and modern-looking varnished pews shone on the blue carpeting. Here the faithful in their Sunday best also sang lustily; but the effect was more of jolly carols than of hymns. The pastor, squat and merry, seemed untroubled by the fate of his urban colleagues. Locally, at least, it seemed that the clergy had traded in their Lutheran sternness and replaced it with *Gemütlichkeit*, just as they had replaced the altar with a homely table fit for Sunday lunch. I preferred Trimble's crabbed and grimy pulpit, and even his apocalyptic excesses. Lützow itself, some sixty kilometres from the castle, seemed less harsh a place than the hamlets surrounding Schloss Brüel, the towns more prosperous and the citizens fatter the nearer we approached Hamburg. But then, it was Sunday, and no doubt a day for neighbourly display.

After the service there was much saluting and *grüss-Gott*ing outside the church, while *Herr Graf* and his mother introduced us to the dignitaries. Maggie bobbed and smiled obediently, and Alec stood by with a jaundiced air as heels clicked around him. He had decided to come with us, to Maggie's relief, but his silence was beginning to infect us. He spoke up only once, in the car, as we cruised the well-swept streets on our way out of town, to ask if there had been many Nazis, he called them Narzies, present in the church. Quite a few, I should think, came Peter's answer, level. His tone was less than enthusiastic. I stared at the back of Agnetha's erect and motionless head, its piled-up coils of hair thick as a loaf of fancy, braided bread. And I feared for Maggie.

Outside Lützow, on the way home, we visited a property belonging to the family, a huge chalet tiered like a pagoda and dotted with such tiny windows that a race of elves might have felt more at home in it than bony Friesian peasants. This was a retirement home for old or injured family retainers, bowed and stooping as much out of respect for the low ceilings as for the Count's presence. There was a choking smell of drying clothes, and an air, that day, of drama. No sooner were we in the door than several women at once started to pour out a story, in an accent that left me staring at Maggie for help. She too was struggling, but from the words she could make out and from her consequent expression I saw that she sensed an issue at last, an opportunity to throw off her winsome mask as Peter's echo.

She was brooding as we emerged, and it was left to Alec, genuinely puzzled, to set the ball rolling.

"Would somebody mind telling me what that was all about?"

His gaze came to rest on me, and I shrugged. I had no idea. The three of us, Alec, Maggie and I, settled in the back of the car, and he had to lean forward and across her to retain my attention. As we drove off Peter waved back at the house and the crowded doorway, the figures posed before it as for a photograph, though a woodcut was more what they brought to mind. A rough track led us back to the road and we bounced, like effigies ourselves, in silence.

"The woman's son has disappeared, it seems," said Peter finally.

"Which woman?" said Alec. "There were rather a lot of them."

"Yes, there are rather a lot of them, as you say, but the house has ten bedrooms, it was once a small hotel, a Pension. So they are all comfortable, the people who live there.''

''Yes I'm sure they are,'' said Alec, baffled by Peter's touchiness.

''The woman was mostly sitting and said less than the others. An old woman, perhaps you didn't notice her. Her son is fifty now, at least. He is a dock worker in Kiel, a trades unionist. It seems he had brought himself to the attention of the Nazis and into their disfavour.''

''And they've killed him?''

''Unlikely. Killed him? No. I should think he is in a prison, or a camp.''

''A camp?''

''Yes, a prison camp, Alec.''

We reached the tarmac, Peter turned the wheel, and we accelerated smoothly away. Agnetha sat, in silence, beside her son.

''On what charge?'' There was no answer, and Alec turned to stare at Maggie, his face expressionless. As he moved on to me, I avoided his eyes. ''Well, I'll be damned,'' he said mildly, leaning back once more. ''And I suppose they're waiting for you to get him out of trouble, are they? Seeing he's one of your people?''

''He is not one of my people, Alex, we are not in the Middle Ages now. This is the son of a woman who worked for my father, he knows where he is and what he is doing.''

Peter spoke sharply, but said nothing in the ensuing silence to soften its effect. Alec gazed at Agnetha for a time and then away; I took it that her motionless face yielded as little from his angle as it did from mine. Outside the windows the woods gave way to ragged pasture and distant, lowering farms. Maggie leant forwards, as if to disown us.

''Why does she live here, Peter? Her son must earn enough to be able to look after her himself.''

''You think she would prefer that? To live in a back street in Kiel?'' There was a pause. ''He has a mistress, the son, and they do not hit it off, she and this woman.''

''You knew about it, I suppose, about her son being arrested. You took us there deliberately.''

''You object to going there? No, it was not for your sake that we went. I wanted to hear the story for myself. Do you object, Maggie?''

''Of course not.'' I saw blood suffuse her already dark face.

"I just want to be told what's going on in Germany, not to be set some sort of moral obstacle course like a little foreign fool who needs to have her eyes opened." Then, after a moment, "Are you going to help this man or aren't you?"

"No, I am not going to help him."

"Why not?" But Peter remained silent. He'd spoken about showing his political colours; was his mother's presence restraining him? He'd also mentioned that he was waiting to hear the results of his law examinations, and I wondered whether there was a connection. It didn't seem the moment to ask. Maggie was being quite provocative enough, and I could see that Agnetha's observant, appraising eyes had finally ignited her. My fear for Maggie—and my own motive for caution—was not that she might find herself living here in the midst of tyranny, which to me then was merely dark and interesting and no more than Jonathan Mansel would expect in foreign parts, but that she might turn on Peter the full force of her own vexation, something I'd glimpsed now and again. And I felt that Alec and I had much to lose by this; that our place in her life, and in Peter's, stood or fell as witnesses of her performance here.

Dinner was oppressive under the eyes of Peter's martial ancestors, including a Crown Prince of Sweden. I distracted myself by construing Peter's facial heritage from the portraits, and found him increasingly Scandinavian, with his pale eyes and mouth. But the head was smaller and tighter and too round for the long neck which, like Agnetha's, seemed to demand a narrower skull, a taller forehead. It gave his face a curious effect of floating some distance above his lanky frame, and made Alec seem stocky by comparison. Peter ate slowly and as fastidiously as a cat, seeming utterly withdrawn. Agnetha watched me studying the paintings, smiling at me as if I held the key to our uncomfortable silence. During the rest of the drive home we had watched the view, far and clear that day beneath an unbroken grey sky, and reflected in the chilly lakes. It seemed colder than the day we had arrived.

"Mein Mann," said Agnetha as my glance lighted on a smaller frame. The features were strong and unfamiliar. It seemed that as with me, though more happily, Peter's looks came from his mother. "He was killed on the Russian front," she continued in a German decelerated for my benefit, and I nodded gravely. "We defeated the Russians utterly and completely, they were at our mercy—one reason why so many people in this country have resented the conditions imposed on Germany after the war.''

"I see," I said, though I thought it had been the Allies and not the Russians alone who had imposed conditions. I held my tongue. Maggie had asked for political instruction, and at this point I felt it was really she whom Agnetha was addressing, through me.

"The Russians have their revenge. We were no longer strong enough to fight them. You understand?''

I nodded. Maggie and Alec were eating quietly, and Peter gazing down the table in a dream of his own.

"We have been made weak, and the Russians know it. But now we have an army again.''

"Will you fight them, then?'' I said.

I glanced at Peter but could not draw his attention.

"We will frighten them," said Agnetha in measured tones. "They will think twice when dealing with Hitler.''

"What's that?'' Alec had looked up at a word he recognized.

Maggie murmured, "He's going to frighten off the Russians.''

"Ah," Alec smiled at Agnetha.

"He will first destroy the Communists in this country.''

"Was he—this man today," I said, "the dock worker . . .''

As I fumbled, Peter came to life. "Breitenbuch," he said. "Haro Breitenbuch. He is a man of the left," he began eating again, carefully, "not a Communist precisely; I would not say so. He is a follower of Leber.'' A glance at Maggie. "There are many shades of opinion.''

"He's against Hitler, that's all I understand," said Maggie impatiently, "and he's not afraid to show it—''

"I am for Hitler," Agnetha interrupted her. "I voted for him, and I shall vote for him again. You are not German, Miss Trimble; neither am I, I am from Sweden. And because of this I can see certain things more clearly than many Germans of my class. First of all, Germany made peace. As a result her children were made to starve—and we have seen them starve, here in Mecklenburg. That is the first consideration.''

"I was going to say," said Peter, "that Leber is in prison also, in Sachsenhausen.''

Maggie was gazing at his mother. "Surely what matters," she said, "is someone's right to their opinions, no matter who they vote for.''

"We have had many opinions, my dear, many opinions and many political parties, and no work."

Maggie set her knife and fork down on her plate. "Well, given the choice between starving and prison camp I know which I'd—which I'd . . ."—the German phrase escaped her.

Lieber leide, Peter supplied. Maggie held Agnetha's gaze. Now nobody was eating except Alec, safe in his incomprehension. He caught my eye, impassive, as he reached for a plate of pickles; I grinned down at my plate—he knew exactly what was going on. When I glanced at the other end of the table I saw that Agnetha's gaze had softened forgivingly, though Maggie had turned aside, openly furious at the patronage. Peter began to pick at his food once more and we followed suit.

"Have you seen the film 'Metropolis'?" he said.

"Film?" said Alec keenly. "Is it on?"

Peter turned with a patient smile and spoke in English for him. "I do not know if it is on, Alec. It is a famous film of Fritz Lang. In it, and this is why I was thinking of it, the people are swallowed up by a huge machine, a power station, a terrifying place, but in the end the people destroy the power station with its metal and its lights, and they dance in the ruins hand in hand." He let a pause fall. "A very hopeful ending, don't you think so? How they later obtain their fuel, these happy people, we are not told, I think. But it is an important film. You see, we distract ourselves with politics, in order to ignore what is happening to man, in the jungle of the city. Karl Marx and Adolf Hitler are not dancing in the ruins of the power station, they are talking politics, but their power is nothing compared to the power of the metal and the lights, and the power to be free of these things. Do you understand what Lang is saying?"

There was a moment in which he seemed to have turned the conversation, but he had underestimated Maggie.

"And what are you going to do about it? Take a walk in the woods?"

Peter held her gaze until she looked away, and he went on watching her clouded face.

"Yes," he said, "with our children perhaps."

We sat for a time, motionless. I didn't dare look at Alec, knowing he must have been as flabbergasted as I was that Peter should choose this moment and this way to declare himself in public. Hearing Agnetha murmur, I glanced up at her.

Schnee. . . . She was gazing at the window.

"Lord above," said Alec, turning. "Now it's snowing."

"I hate the woods," said Maggie, quietly but with venom.

As the thick snowflakes fell, dappling the light, we sat in silence and a manservant removed our plates.

After the meal Agnetha made some polite excuse to go up to her room, leaving us to wait distractedly for coffee, in the drawing room. Maggie slouched among the antiques, and Alec followed her at a distance, as though in inadvertent parody, striking elegant poses, in a chirpy mood. Peter had once more withdrawn into himself and would not answer my questioning looks.

"What I can't figure out, Peter," said Alec airily, "is why of all people your mother's such a Hitler buff."

"A *buff*?"

Something in Peter's bemused tolerance of Alec, his wariness of slipping into contempt, nagged at my mind. There was something more to it than innate politeness or the circumspection of rivals.

"Call it what you like. I mean, imagine the fellow in here."

Alec turned to Maggie to relish the picture, but she had slumped into an armchair, eyes averted. Peter smiled.

"For many years we have had splendid fellows, in office, field marshals with moustaches . . . and do you know something? This is the first man who has not made money for himself. He had no private fortune, he lives simply, eats simple food. . . ."

"Well, it's what he's used to, I should think. He looks the bangers and mash type."

"More mash than bangers. The Führer is a vegetarian, Alec."

More *mesh* than *bengers*: I grinned at Maggie—it was one for our repertoire, but she was staring coldly at Peter now, unamused by his accent.

"And that's enough," she said, "to make people admire him?"

"I was trying to explain to Alec something of my mother's feelings. She is herself a frugal person."

"What you mean is, she's afraid the Communists might take away the family silver," Maggie sneered. "The way things are going it seems to me you might as well have Bolshevism anyway."

"Yes," said Peter. His voice was light, amused. "I think so too. Why not have Bolshevism?"

Alec gave Maggie and me a loaded look, eyebrows raised at such blithe indifference. We turned as the door opened and a small, stern-looking girl with cropped red hair, wearing a plain black dress, brought in the coffee. Outside, the snow shower had stopped and just as suddenly the sun was out, throwing light off the melting snow into the high ceiling of the drawing room, making its mouldings seem to lift up and away from us, flooded with the soft light, as we moved a little closer to the trolley.

Hard as I tried, in the days that followed, to talk to Maggie alone, she made it impossible, increasingly allowing Alec to draw her away from the Schloss on little expeditions of their own. They borrowed Peter's Mercedes and drove to Rostock for the day; or took rides on horseback through the woods, returning joyous and spattered with mud. The sun had broken through, and a crazy alternation followed, snow and sun in turn, the warmth melting the snow again so fast that the seasons seemed to change three or four times in one day, leaving a glistening morass in their wake. I doubt if I even knew what I would say to Maggie; it was Alec I needed to warn, and try to explain to him that she would drop him like a hot coal as soon as we got back to England, out of shame at the way she'd behaved here; but he wouldn't have listened. And it was, I suppose, unkind of me not to give Maggie credit for her beliefs, some genuine idealism affronted by Peter's spinelessness. At the time I felt nothing but approval for his attitude to politics—while Maggie's posture seemed to me just as willful and spuriously noble as my brother's. Perhaps it was Peter I should have spoken to, urging him to plead his case or at least to see through Maggie's challenge. But I was tongue-tied in his presence, and bound, in the minefield of the public issues, by his wordless, affectionate protection.

In any case, when I was left to amuse myself my thoughts were less with the fate of Germany than whether or not the drawing room was empty and the Branntwein unattended. The best time was of course late at night, when I crept past the Greek and Roman statuary to the stairs, happy in my work, at least until the night when I came face to face with the major-domo— we called him the butler—a middle-aged man called Ludolf, and a dignified fellow even in the dressing-gown he was wearing. That night Ludolf's silver hair, less groomed than by day, caught the light from the candle in his hand as he studied me. He was at the door, I was at the drinks cabinet, and I gazed back, bottle in hand and horribly embarrassed. He said something in German which I couldn't understand. It sounded both polite and disapproving.

"Nightcap!" I said. To make the point I raised the bottle, smiling. Ludolf looked blank, and I realized I still had the initiative. *"Nacht-mütze,"* I offered firmly, though to judge from his expression it wasn't a term which translated directly into German. He waited for me to put the bottle away and then slowly withdrew.

There were no repercussions in the morning. But that night I found the drinks cabinet locked, and between meals—when Ludolf had become rather slow, I noted, to refill my glass—I resumed the life of a sober English guest. Maggie's restiveness had put a strain on any communal activities; indeed, our visit seemed at an end, waiting only an excuse to leave. Once more Alec borrowed the Mercedes for a trip with Maggie, and invited me along this time. He had business friends in Rostock, he said, who would give us an English meal and show us the sights. I cried off, pleading my studies, though I hadn't opened a law book since we'd left England and I didn't intend to.

From my tower room I saw them leave, speeding in Alec's jaunty fashion down the drive. The sun shone from a clear sky, and a greyish, reluctant green had spread across the empty fields like a ground mist. Water sparkled in the footprints of Agnetha's cattle. In the distance the first trim fences of the estate gave way to sad lines of assorted, sagging posts, askew among the leafless trees and jutting from the mud like relics of trench warfare. I felt no kinship with this landscape, it rendered me gaunt and exposed, dangling my heavy hands and plodding across boggy spaces without a football. But on fresh, bright days like these, my very opposition to the emptiness, a heroic isolation, made it tempting. I saw myself, a monstrous silhouette against the wind; appropriate, even in such a setting; a young troll. Beneath my window Peter appeared, strolling out with long, lithe strides, and the view took on a different mood. It was he who was at home in it, picking his way unerringly, head raised, eyes on the horizon. He covered the ground with a wind-walker's ease, his limbs light. The grey tones like a gauze, the sheen of coming grass, became him—I no longer saw it as a rugged place, no, it was even-tempered and remote, as mournful as its chilly lakes behind their screen of reeds. Peter was carrying a sack-like object, white, it seemed a shirt, the bundle weighed down by a sodden shape. In his long brown jerkin—too wide for his shoulders, the leather torn and the slashes showing orange in the sun—he looked like a poacher with his booty. A hare perhaps, by its size. Then I lost him from sight as he turned towards the distant, unseen barns.

When I reached the front door and came down the steps Peter

was nowhere to be seen, and I ran, first to be free of the house and then for running's sake alone, excited, kicking an imaginary leather drum across a muddy football pitch. At the first thicket I slowed to a trot and made my way through brambles to the huge barn. Opening the door I peered into the rustling darkness, and called, but there was no answer. The cows paused; I left them and edged my way along the barn, skirting the puddles. As I rounded it I saw Peter standing beside a rotting workbench. An oblong metal case stood on it, open. Before turning to me, Peter shut the lid.

He moved away from the bench, inspecting my muddy shoes and trousers. Something glittered in his hand, and I saw that it was a small, delicate pair of sugar tongs with a scallop-shaped paw on the end of either arm. Peter shook his head at me, smiling.

"We have boots here too, you know, just like in England, to prevent you ruining your shoes."

I shrugged. His hair had blown, like a cap, to one side, a dark wing—no nation has such forelocks as the Germans, you could almost tug them yourself—blonde only at the edges. He looked even more boyish than usual, and slight under the broad jerkin. I saw a shaving scratch beside the pallid, almost lipless mouth. At that moment it was I who felt protective. Still recovering my breath, I searched for something to say, under his gaze.

"Your studies are quick," he said, advancing.

"I don't really expect to pass first time—unlike some people," I said, and hesitated. "I haven't been working. I didn't want to go with them to Rostock, that's all." His unchanging expression told me he knew that. "Anyway I'll never make a lawyer."

Behind us, over towards the house, a dog began to yap insistently. Peter was very close.

"I think you will," he said. "I have considerable faith in you, Richard."

He put an arm around me, comradely, and squeezed. I stared ahead. The white collarless shirt—the shirt he'd used to bundle up the hare, or rather not the hare, the metal object on the workbench—sprawled on the ground a few yards in front of us.

"What's that?" I asked, nodding at the object on the bench.

"That?" Peter eyed it for a long time. It looked like a shoebox. I felt him give another squeeze as though reluctant to let go, and then drop his arm from my shoulders.

"That is a bomb," he said carefully.

* * *

So many small surfaces glistened in the wet field that it was hard to be sure whether it was the metal case I was watching with such attention or a patch of ice in the area, some hundred and fifty yards away, and well removed from the barns, where we had placed the device. Peter raised his watch and we both looked at it. Incredibly only a quarter of an hour had passed. Peter looked back at the peaceful meadow.

"The fuse is set, I understand, for room temperature. Shall we give it five minutes more?"

And he twirled the silver tongs, on his forefinger.

Time is a dimension about which we have grown sceptical; sequential time that is. But to me it is all-powerful and inexorable. Growing older we get flashes of emotions long since lost to us, often a sense of excitement grown increasingly guarded with age (the way you see an old man make a gesture that could only have been adopted in his youth, and largely discarded since then), and by such instants measure what we think of as a loss of innocence. But it's only time we lack; the gaping void of time ahead, now no longer there, which once permitted us a sense of possibilities; it's future time, not innocent emotion, that we've lost. With the same fashionable disrespect for time in its strict sequence, we speculate about the childhood moment when death becomes real, when we grasp that our life is finite—a moment that must surely mark a change, a humanizing in the darkest sense. There is no such moment. As children come to grasp the concept of finality they accept it with ease at first, for the most part, simply because it is still so unimaginably far ahead, as they know time. All our ideas of aging and its emotional cost are no more than this: reflections of the loss of time. True, each of us lives in a different world of time, and lives with repeated illusions of the elasticity of time which vulgar explanations of Einstein's theorem have encouraged people to think of as relativity (it's nothing of the sort; merely temporary inattention). But for each of us, with our separate clock, time is strict, and as true as the turning heavens.

For me personally space exists as time is often held to do, in fits and starts. Places are only there infrequently, around me, so I approach space taxonomically, like a diligent naturalist, learning the names of trees and flowers in order to label them present. This is of little avail: places come and go and vary at the whim of the personalities lodged, quite vividly, in the foreground. In this connection I have a theory about old O'Malley, my grandfather and surrogate parent, I feel, in spirit as well as in deed. I believe that, contrary to what he may have thought, it was not the submerged wrecks of the Armada that fascinated him, it was the sea (which was what he mostly came up with, from the depths), the sea itself, unyielding to him, featureless, and like my own spirit of place, subject to mood. So when I feel, as the phrase is, at sea, myself, on terra firma among the trees and flowers, I turn the phrase around to find its true meaning, since the sea is never null. Its moods can be intense or subtle but they are above all single, as landscapes so often are to me, unanimous, every feature in unison, making it as idle to name them as it would be to name the waves.

At Schloss Brüel that morning, I had my first glimpse of this inversion of the conventional properties of time and space. Racing across the muddy field towards the barn and kicking that imaginary ball, the sense of brutal exaltation came back in a rush. And the shock of it stayed with me as I covered the distance to the thicket—I wanted to hold onto it, to the sense of time restored, irrespective of the place. How could so intense an emotion, something that had been so much a part of me, have become foreign in so short a time (to be recaptured in a place that really was foreign)? It wasn't for lack of brutal encounters, even now, in London dives and dance-halls; but the exaltation had been missing without my knowing it, not only missing but entirely forgotten. I stood, puzzled, in the trees and brambles of the thicket, as if peering from a husk; as if I'd been dead for a time. Such tripwires, then, awaited one in adult life. It took many more before I was able to rationalize them—at first it seemed that time had been dissolved, that I'd tumbled off my curve of the spiral and landed on the curve below; as these moments recurred I realized it was simply time's way of reminding me of its power, allowing me to measure the distance I had covered along that winding, rhyming spiral, which never quite repeats. At that moment, at eighteen, it seemed more like a recovery of time than a warning, an alarm going off.

The sensation felt quite independent of its setting, yet it was far from arbitrary, it merely owed less to the landscape than the figures in it. Peter was at the heart of it. I knew this as soon as I saw him beside the metal case, cupping the absurdly genteel tongs with its thin arms and its paws like scallops. But the revelation that the case contained a bomb postponed the consequences. I forgot Peter's arm, around my shoulders a moment ago. I was staring at the workbench, and at him, in disbelief, and repeated the word: a bomb?

"It is inactive," Peter smiled.

"What are you doing with a bomb?"

"I am going to test it, Richard."

He was still smiling at me. I grinned in relief.

"You're joking—that's not a bomb at all, is it."

"See for yourself."

Peter saw me hesitate, and fetched it, deliberately casual. He put it in my hands. At a touch the lid came up: revealing wires, nodes, a metal rod, a glass capsule, and beneath them, packed into one end of the crude tin box, two grey clay-like lumps. It was a bomb. Amazed, I looked back at Peter's taut-shaven face.

"What's it for?"

He glanced briefly aside and pushed his mouth.

"As a matter of fact I don't know. I am going to test it, that is all."

"What do you mean, you don't know?"

"What I say, Richard. I am only the delivery boy. They go to some friends for military purposes."

He looked away, leaving me free to believe him or not as I wished.

"They? There are more of them?"

"Two more."

He made it sound so perfunctory they might have been egg-beaters.

"What's it got to do with you? You sell bombs?"

"I? No."

Watching me closely, he chuckled and took the metal object from my hands.

"But I have access to them, let us say. You see, this is a special kind of bomb." He raised the tongs and poked inside the casing. "It has a chemical fuse, so-called; strictly speaking, chemical-mechanical. Of course I am no expert, but it is unusual. You can see for yourself. You break the capsule, and the acid eats away the retaining wire—the time this takes depends on the temperature, of course—which releases this, the firing pin." He pointed with the tongs. "The pin strikes the detonator, and the plastic, here, explodes. Sometimes there is instead a powder charge, but the important factor is the fuse." He paused, proudly, as if the invention were his. "It is silent. In Germany we have no such fuses. Shall we test this silence?"

He brought the tongs down on the capsule and cracked it. I

must have gasped in terror, because he turned to me at once, grinning broadly.

"We have lots of time. Don't be afraid. You shouldn't be afraid because, you see . . . this, old boy, is a British bomb."

He walked with it, cautiously now, away from the barn. I followed at a distance, anxious not to distract him but also still thoroughly nervous of the thing. Even so I couldn't wait for an explanation.

"You bought them here?" I called.

I saw him shake his head.

"Where then?" A pause; I gaped. "You mean you brought them from London?"

Peter shook his head again. There was a silence, and Peter glanced round, just as it began to dawn on me. Alec. Alec and his litter of hand-tooled luggage; Alec and his business trip to Rostock, Alec and his secrecy. I ran after Peter.

"You and Alec? You're supplying the German Army with these things?" It was preposterous. Limericks, Hölderlin, and bombs?

"Not exactly."

I caught him up. "That's what you said."

"I said it is for friends, and they are in the Army, yes."

He stopped and placed the bomb carefully at his feet. We stood over it, Peter gazing at me calmly, relishing the suspense.

"I have told you the truth," he said. "I don't know what the bombs are for," he stood there conscious of my gaze, "they are bombs, that's all."

But they weren't at all. They were special bombs, bombs with a silent fuse. My mind was whirling. To what use would Mansel have put a silent fuse? Only one thing came to mind. Assassination. No, that was absurd, they were just regulation bombs (did regulation bombs look so home-made?), for sale or export. In which case what was this poetry-mad Count doing as the "delivery boy?" And would the German Army buy British bombs? Alec and Peter, rivals but comrades in arms . . . the melodrama took me by the throat. It had to be assassination. And there was only one worthy victim. Tyrannicide then! With Alec, my brother, no longer a charming ass, but a romantic hero—it was all too much, and it must have shown in my face; Peter was watching me as if my eyes were a cartoon.

"Does Alec know what they're for?"

Peter laughed. "Richard, I'm afraid not—he thinks they are

for the 'Narzies.' But then . . . I do not know what they are for either.''

And he chortled as we made our way back across the meadow to a safe distance, giving me time to think, to rethink. Alec's persistent questioning, trying to tie in Peter with the Nazi "high-ups" . . . but no hero himself, if Peter was telling the truth, no, just an Alec peddling wares. Alec's in tea; in teabags with a silent fuse. And Peter cultivating him, smiling at Alec's nouveau riche pretensions. Peter's lilting words, *He thinks they are for the Narzies.* . . .

"And they aren't?'' I insisted. But all I got from Peter was an ambiguous grunt.

"I have no Nazi friends, Richard,'' he said at last. "And so far no Nazi enemies either.''

Once more I jogged to keep up with him. He covered ground so much faster than I did, with his dancing stride. As I reached him he turned, still walking, and his look made it clear that this was all he was going to say on the subject.

The minutes passed, as we waited at the edge of the field for the explosion, and then five more minutes, and we were still waiting. I didn't know whether it was a puff of smoke we were expecting, or a great cataract of earth, shaking the peaceful morning, or some sort of merry firework.

"Perhaps it's a dud,'' I said, "given who sold it to you.''

"Alec knows his business,'' said Peter lightly.

That did rock me: it was true, then. It was his business. I felt humiliated, not even knowing; certainly not humiliated on Alec's behalf—if anything my first response was to envy him his line of work. But all my insights into adult behaviour were collapsing, they were jejune, to say the least. And then the real shock hit me: was it this, was it purely business to which we owed our presence at the Schloss? The whole lovers' intrigue—(including Maggie? She had said "he"—Peter—"asked for you; I asked for Alec"; and surely Alec was the lynch-pin of the visit from Peter's point of view?)—was it simply a front? After all my machinations! Pique must have been plainly written on my face, because Peter continued:

"Also Alec is a pleasant companion, and brings even more pleasant companions with him.''

I found this rather patronizing, even a little sinister, in its tone. He paused, eyeing me keenly.

"You understand, I hope, that Maggie is in ignorance of this. And she is to remain in ignorance.''

I nodded, and once more he put his arm around my shoulders; but now I felt uneasy and no longer, as before, the covert aggressor. Now I had no idea where we fitted into Peter's schemes. I'd spent so much time with Maggie fitting him into ours; I'd been so certain about our motives, Maggie's and mine, and Alec's; but who and what did Peter want?

The bomb went off. I broke free of Peter in sheer fright, I hadn't expected flames, yet it was fire that burst from the centre of the empty field, with a roar that seemed to come, not from it, but to rush screaming towards it like air into a vacuum, as though the sky itself were crying out to smother the explosion. Clods flew, along with streaks of muddy water. Specks appeared on Peter's face. A hot wind struck us in their wake and I put up my hands, fighting to keep my eyes open, watching fascinated as the flames subsided and a cloud of smoke floated up, ochre colours rolling out from underneath the white. The stench came, but by then the ground was still, as if at peace again after its monumental fart. Air shimmered over a dip of dry earth where the bomb had been.

Peter was crouched beside me, rocking from side to side. I saw he was laughing, but I could only hear a hissing in my ears. He rolled onto his back, mouth wide, and I realized the hissing, gasping noises came from him, helpless with glee. Unnerved by his loss of control, faced with a new Peter, I thought for a moment that the blast had overwhelmed him, winded him; then I saw it was me he was staring at.

I raised my hands, pawed at my face, and came away with smears of mud. I saw my shirt and trousers, pockmarked with the stuff, and began to laugh too, out of relief. We'd been standing too close.

"You could have killed us," I said. "Didn't Alec say how powerful it was?"

Peter sat up, composing himself. But when he looked at me he started to laugh again.

I said, "What do your friends want to do with the things, blow up a battleship?"

He gave a military nod. "I will pass on the suggestion." He began to cough, his eyes watering, and pulled himself to his feet. The clod-spattered vista seemed to gratify him, as if it were a welcome gesture of self-mutilation, however futile. Ignoring me, he walked towards the dip. This time his customary sure-footedness failed him and I saw him stagger several times and stop to shake the mud from his boots. Watching him resume, arms swinging, surrounded by the flat, resigned planes of the pasture, I had a glimpse of the Sunday face of war; however many bombs there were, however many uniforms and corpses, guns, grenades, and packs to carry, the ground you struggled over would resume its tractable stare between explosions and offer the banal prospect of a stroll. Peter's tread was leaden as he returned, his expression once more remote. I asked if there was anything left, in the dip, and he shook his head, gazing at his boots, which were hugely plastered with earth. We retreated to the barn, picked up the shirt, and headed back towards the Schloss to wash and change. I tried in vain to get more information out of Peter, saying I'd thought he was a bit of a pacifist, until now.

"Yes," he said, unsmiling. "But I am not a pacifist."

"Don't you think you're perhaps . . . misrepresenting yourself to Maggie, then?"

"No," said Peter.

Don't you care whether you lose her to Alec? I wanted to cry. You can see the line she's taking! I just couldn't fathom Peter; we were in the thicket where I had clung half an hour before to my brief, baffling exaltation; now I was lost again, playing the wise counsellor. Peter stopped, looking down.

"You did not tell me in your letters that she and Alec have become so close. You should perhaps have told me, Richard. Don't you think?"

I wanted to tell him I knew it hadn't mattered, not really, far from it in fact, that it didn't matter now, not even if they'd slept together, and that Maggie would always favour the person she was about to ditch—ah, but I couldn't take Peter's feelings for granted any more, on any subject. I couldn't speak. The ribald atmosphere of our Pimlico afternoons seemed to have vanished for ever.

"Perhaps I have lost her already."

The lightness in his voice made me quite furious.

"Don't you care at all? Or is it only the bombs that matter to you?"

Had I said that aloud? I had. He looked at me for a short time, his eyes cold and unfriendly.

"It is my concern, I think." He paused. "Better if she does not like me the way I am, Richard, that she should learn it now."

Everything was reversed. It was no longer Maggie who was throwing out the challenge (this was how I understood her; the only way I could understand her), take me or leave me, warts and all, no make-up and black looks, sudden tendernesses, toothy grins, sullen silences. Now it was Peter who was refusing to play for sympathy; and I too was to be excluded. We walked back to the gleaming Schloss without a word. Agnetha waved to us from a distance, surrounded by her gods, serene, as if explosions and erupting pasture were all part of a day's work at Schloss Brüel. This too was incomprehensible—or perhaps they *were* an everyday occurrence. She must have heard the noise, and if she knew and approved then the bombs could hardly have the heroic destination I'd first supposed. For nothing Agnetha had said, since her first outburst on the subject, suggested she had less sympathy with Hitler's cause than she claimed. Indeed one story in particular, received by Maggie in stony indifference, had reinforced the impression. It was the night before Maggie and Alec's sudden trip to Rostock, and the experiment with the bomb.

Apparently out of the blue, but with her eyes on Maggie, Agnetha had recited some events of twenty years earlier, in the November of 1917, when a rabble—*Pöbel* was her word for them—invaded the house, demanding quarters in the name of revolution. By their accent mostly Berliners, she said with distaste. And for these louts her husband had died, fighting the very men in whose name they now demanded the run of her home: the Bolsheviks. She had locked herself in her room, listening to their gleeful rampage, eating nothing for ten days rather than serve them; and emerged to an empty house, the servants fled, the mob vanished, leaving behind them dirty plates, a pall of tobacco, the smell of urine in the corners of the rooms. Revenge was swift. In the ensuing election not so much as a social democrat was returned, so fast had Mecklenburg's rural conservatism returned to its senses. The whole of the region, Peter had told us, belonged to some five hundred landowners, and evidently few serfs stepped out of line. Peter listened heavy-lidded to this familiar tale. He had been at school, at *Ritterschule*, he said drily, and missed the fun. Agnetha smiled.

It was this frivolity in Peter that seemed to gall Maggie now, where in England she had found it charming. I couldn't help; I was sworn to secrecy, and in any case after the morning with the bomb I knew less than ever about the man. Maggie had a sombre air after the visit to Rostock, and paid no attention to me.

"Troops," reported Alec, "passed nothing but troops, on exercises."

"Yes, one shell landed here," I said, and Alec's face, under my pointed gaze, took on something of the shifty tipster's look I knew from childhood.

There was much to think about; and I was in no hurry to leave Schloss Brüel. As I lay in bed that night, swathed in down and surrounded by drawings of garish orange cockatoos and other Amerindian species crowing on the walls of my bedroom— "Cock Of The Rocks," one of them proclaimed, in English; had Miss Belcher of Bristol brought these?—I made plans to disassociate myself from Maggie and my brother. I'd find some way of ingratiating myself with our hostess and prolong my stay (as a secret agent of the *Pöbel*). There was a soft knock on the door and it opened to reveal Peter standing very erect, chin up in a curiously regimental manner.

"Je peux?" he said stiffly.

"Natürlich." He came in, shutting the door, and stood smiling but still hesitant.

"I think I owe you an apology."

"Do you?" It was all very Germanic, suddenly. "Can't you do it sitting down?"

He nodded, and although there was a chair, chose the end of my bed. My feet stuck out beyond the quilt. I tucked them in. I was all too obviously an agent of the *Pöbel*, in this aristocratic bed—it was too short, for a start, I could only come to rest under the covers with my bony knees folded up against my chest like some skeleton in the ancient burial mound formed by the eiderdown, which though heavy was oddly buoyant and liable to bobble off onto the floor like a gigantic marshmallow. Oh for English sheets and blankets! I was now training myself to sleep hanging onto the inflated quilt with arms and legs, as to an overturned rubber dinghy in a mild swell.

"I spoke severely this morning," Peter said, "about your letters to me. That was wrong. I did not show my appreciation and also I did not mean to suggest that you were disloyal, since on the contrary it was I who was demanding a disloyalty."

"But you know where my loyalties lie, Peter."

"Thank you. However, I was rude."

"You were rather secretive, that's all, about the other business."

"I had no intention of involving you." He had put his head on one side, like one of the orange birds; I was beginning to wonder if this mannerism showed when he was telling a lie.

"You knew I was here, and I'd have heard it. As a matter of

fact I'm surprised we didn't find all the windows blown out."
This drew a grin. "Your mother must have heard it, surely. What does she think is going on?"

"She knows better than to ask." The tone was firm, the Herr Graf speaking. "I told you, Richard, we have military friends, and they have sometimes performed manoeuvres on our land. I have not come to talk about that, but rather to clear up a misunderstanding, from this morning. I want you to know that whatever happens with the others, you are very dear to me."

The old, tender look had returned, but with a curious pleading note to it which I didn't like. I felt absurd beneath the patterned quilt and with the lace borders of the pillowcases sticking out around my beaky face; I could see their frilly edges framing my vision. Little red riding wolf. I smiled back at Peter.

His gaze went to my hands on the eiderdown, with their broad spatulate nails; I'd always been ashamed of my hands, slablike things the colour of lard, where his were slimmer and ruddy. Leaning forwards he grasped my fingers in his; I returned the pressure gladly.

As his face approached mine I could see again the daily battering it took from the razor, tight as if braced for the next assault. His eyes seemed to be searching for a blessing more than a kiss; but he looked far from innocent, and I hesitated. I couldn't place his motives yet. Being so close to him evoked watching presences as if none of us could kiss without the others' greedy participation, but even this was a more charming thought than Peter's expression brought to mind. When Maggie and I had summoned his voice and manner, at the vicarage, it was to intervene, to raise and spread our power, by the magic of our own restraint. What was happening now was different. I wasn't prepared to be Maggie's stand-in.

"If I'm so dear to you," I said, "I'd like to be let into your confidence."

He released my hands.

"I see," he said, and studied me in silence. If the moment had passed, as Peter seemed to think, it wasn't out of coyness on my part—indeed the murkiness of the act was what appealed, as long as I could be in charge, and enjoy the figures in the wings.

"It is like this," said Peter slowly, with a sigh. "We Mecklenburgers are far from being natural revolutionaries, we are a lazy people. This is the first thing you must understand. We do as little as possible and we think as little as possible. Truly. We have no artists here, not to speak of, in fact we have no history at all. You think this could be the home of Goethe or Schiller or Kant? They would never have been born in Mecklenburg. If Beethoven had come to live here he would have composed sausages. Here men of spirit leave home, they go to Berlin, to America, and are never heard of again. Or like Schliemann they go to Greece. You have heard of Schliemann, the archaeologist? My father met him as a young man. You have also, I take it, heard of Bismarck?''

I nodded.

"He said that when the end of the world came he would move to Mecklenburg, because everything there arrives twenty years late.''

Peter grinned, looking away; perhaps like me he was remembering the bomb and its utterly indifferent, placid aftermath.

"Naturally we are conservative, so after 1848 people believed we would become a police state. This was nonsense, we are much too lazy: we had no police. The landowners were like kings here, they needed no policemen, they even helped men to escape from prison, though this was to cheat the Prussians, not because we believed in revolution. You understand? You must not expect too much from us.'' He was in his old stride, expansive and relaxed again. "When we fight we do it with humour. And a great deal of wine.''

Belatedly I realized he had been drinking, and it helped to explain his earlier formality. I felt a surge of tenderness for the schoolboy Peter, and he saw it in my face.

"Also we have learnt to be a secretive people,'' he said, "with or without wine.''

Someone knocked at the door. We both turned, uneasily expectant, and spoke together:

"Herein.''

It was Alec, in his woollen dressing-gown; he stood expressionless for a moment, taking in the picture, Peter sitting up stiffly once more, beside me on the bed, I with my head on the pillows like a child waiting to be tucked in.

"So sorry,'' Alec said, as if it was the wrong door, and went out shutting it discreetly behind him.

"Come in, Alec!'' called Peter.

There was silence.

"Alec!'' But Alec had gone. "What is the matter with him?'' said Peter petulantly. "He is so cold towards me.''

"Come on, Peter,'' I said. "Stop playing games.''

He turned his pale eyes on me, genuinely hurt, as if the contest for Maggie were irrelevant to good form—and of course he was right in his own terms, win or lose Peter would never behave coldly, it wasn't cricket. Besides, not one word of the Mecklenburg character, as he'd described it, applied to him; except the deviousness perhaps. He stood up and steadied himself.

"So," he said distantly. "I will leave you to your slumbers. I was going to tell you the story of an ancestor of mine, Baron Adolf von Lützow, but it will wait until another time. I only came to say good-night."

He gave a mock bow and went quickly to the door, concentrating on sober-seeming movement.

"Goodnight then," I called as he disappeared.

He peered guiltily round the door.

"Goodnight, my dear fellow," he said.

"Peter . . . you haven't told me *anything*."

He paused, heavily, then glanced down the corridor, and turned back.

"I was asked to find a certain kind of bomb," he said slowly, "In England, and to buy it from the kind of man who sells such things. His name was Alec Thurgo. Now you know everything that I know."

I didn't believe him for a moment. In the morning I received some odd, enquiring looks from Maggie, which gave me a good deal of pleasure; no doubt Alec had mentioned finding Peter in my bedroom the night before. She had been avoiding my gaze, and now I could stare her out. Though she remained aloof from more than routine conversation, the relentless meals brought us together, and with them her suspicious glances. At the same time I was beginning to detect Peter's strategy, even if she wasn't, and though it pushed me into a corner, pursued by our host for a further course in Mecklenburger history, I basked in Maggie's attention and smiled back at her reproachful eyes.

I don't know if I've said that Maggie was beautiful, which she wasn't, to my mind; but she was striking, and her looks had something of the muted aggression you often see in the faces of Eastern European girls, its violence strangely accentuated, not diminished, by the small features and the weak chin. The slippery mouth was her most dangerous feature, slack and seemingly forgotten in repose; then transforming the face in a blinding smile all teeth and dimples. In the morning Maggie was a wonder to me. She slewed her features into grimaces of distasteful flesh, delighting in her ugliness, chewing her lips and ignoring my gaze. These breakfast faces were more intimate than any smile, and evoked a harsh desire. I can see her, flattening her nose with a rubbing hand, and frowning at the bone china before her. At such moments she seemed a mute. And happily so since her voice was always variable, straying from a weak, dull monotone to her mother's silvery timbre. But then what did she know of voices? Her mother's had, for Laura herself, the curious effect of making her personality evaporate, and Maggie only used it for impersonations. Trimble's pulpit growl, breathing anathema, was somewhere inside her but she suppressed it. Sometimes Maggie would start a sentence twice, in different cadences, searching for the key; and when I recall her it is without sound, a watchful, mobile face.

The day after the explosion the rain came, as if to soften all traces in the meadow. We were stuck with one another, indoors, making Peter's demonstrativeness towards me only more noticeable to the others. Sensing Maggie's mood, Alec hinted at the need for his presence in London, and I thought the die was cast. But Peter was on his guard; he chose that evening to take the stage in the guise of storyteller, and to tell Maggie—under cover of the story he had promised me—who and what he was. Dinner was in slow decline through soups and *kalte Platten* to the cheeses, when Peter switched to English.

"The time has come, the Walrus said." He left it unfinished, as Maggie looked up. "Better that we should be less polite, on certain subjects. Don't you think? I come straight to the point. I should not like you to leave with a poor opinion of our German courage, in defence of liberty—or, since we are in such distinguished company," his eyes briefly crossed the portraits above us, "to think that this room shows an unbroken line of petty tyrants and servants of tyrants. You must not think so."

His glance came to rest, not on a portrait but an ancient breastplate, set at chest height atop a thin column of wood, like a phantom warrior, and shining as brightly as ever it had on the morning of battle.

"Verzeihung, Mama," he added, and Agnetha smiled, "kennst doch die Geschichte. . . ."; she knew what was coming. Peter's gaze stayed on the burnished metal for a moment.

"Permit me to tell you a story of eighteen hundred and eight, to which this piece, the Lützener Brustpanzer, bears witness. It concerns a man who is much in my thoughts, and a period which is in some respects more real to me, I think, than our own century. I hope you are not weary of historical episodes."

I glanced at Maggie, knowing her feelings about people—her mother for one—who took refuge in history; the breastplate was all too reminiscent of tale of the Sultan and the Don. She caught my eye before turning to Peter.

"As long as it isn't about two heroes battling over a lovely lady."

"It is not," said Peter, and waited for us to settle.

"The Lützen Breastplate," he said, "plays a small part but a rather curious one, in my story. It is Swedish, and landed in Mecklenburg during the Thirty Years' War. It came ashore," Peter glanced easily at Alec, "perhaps at Rostock." Yes—now I knew what the Rostock "business" trip had been for; Peter was once more in full flow. "Its owner certainly rode with the Protestant armies of the north, who went looting the Catholic south of the country while the Catholic armies of the south did the same to the Protestant north, a good arrangement for both armies. Finally they had to meet or they could not get home, and when they did meet at the battle of Lützen the Swedish king was killed. Also our knight of the breastplate—we have no idea who he was. But at this battle a strange thing happened. Instead of the Protestants losing heart at the news that their king and leader was dead, they fought twice as hard and won. That is in a sense the meaning of pro*test*ant," Peter grinned, "life is something to protest about, not to celebrate—or at least your protest is your celebration; and bad luck is not only what you jolly well deserve, it is what makes you work twice as hard. Isn't it so? Or we could simply say that the Protestant armies were less superstitious than their Catholic enemies. I personally am superstitious, and the second wearer of the Lützen breastplate, which came into our family by marriage, as an heirloom, was superstitious also, I think. He chose the breastplate to die in.

"Before I begin—an apology. The other night in a mood of vanity, perhaps even of vainglory, I promised Richard here the story of Adolf, Freiherr von Lützow." Peter smiled, adding, "Lütz-*ow*," one finger raised, to ensure we noted the difference, "not Lützen. Also in order to think for once about a different Adolf—since this one is an undisputed hero; an ancestor too, although some proof is missing, and my mother, who likes to count our heroes, hesitates over Adolf von Lützow. Worse luck, the chap was born a Berliner. But a hero he was, and he has a line in every German history book as the founder of a Freikorps, the first private army drawn from all over Germany, and licensed by the Kaiser to fight against Napoleon. On the field of battle the Lützowsche troop was not so very successful, but they had opened their ranks to young idealists and to poets whose songs made the troop famous—even the colours, black, red, and gold, became Germany's own. It is a story with many little skirmishes and marching songs and young men who make their wills in rhyme before going out to die at the hands of the enemy. Lützow himself, *hélas!* loses most of the troop, becomes a Prussian general and dies where Prussian generals die, in bed; and for such pantomimes I have no time tonight. Rather I am going to tell you about a man who served under Lützow, though only for a few days. His name was Kuno von Brüel, and he is more certainly an ancestor than our Prussian general, in fact he lived here in this house—and for me personally he is a hero.

"Kuno was during his short life a kind of literary man, a pamphleteer, the author of at least one play, and a disciple of Jean-Paul Richter, who is a writer little read today, and justly so, the author of simple-minded rural idylls, a man so little interested in civilisation that it is no wonder he welcomed Napoleon with open arms. Of course he was not alone here in this attitude. Princes and professors, peasants too, men from every station of life hailed this second Alexander, this Julius Caesar, this Augustus Caesar, this genius of the age!"

Peter allowed us a moment for reflection. He did not look at his mother, who was sitting silent and serene, on horseback in some quite other landscape, at the opposite end of the long table.

"This . . . artist! Such a man needs only to memorize a few poems and all the intellectuals adore him. Goethe too—even a true genius can be a child of vanity—was seduced by the Légion d'Honneur and a well-rehearsed speech about the *Werther*. Later, when the catastrophe of his Russian campaign revealed to such people the demented egotism of the man, Germany awoke one morning to be told by the princes and professors that far from having betrayed their country to a madman, they had been nothing less than secret patriots! Yes, under the bushel of collaboration had these wise virgins hidden their light, they now claimed, the light of nationalism, or radicalism, or conservatism—or world citizenship or anything of course except their own ambition. At least the second Alexander made no bones about his ambition, let us grant him that, but his former German friends made it known, like all survivors, that they had only been biding their time, waiting to serve the cause of liberation.

"Kuno was no survivor, by which I do not mean that he was

a weakling. On the retreat from Moscow when Napoleon himself had abandoned his armies, Kuno ate the flesh of his dead companions, volunteers from Mecklenburg also, in order to survive the Russian winter. This he did, and reached home. But for him the sense of betrayal went too deep to simply turn around and start again, with only a change of enemies, a change of banners. He had been betrayed, he had himself betrayed his own ideals—so he felt—or you might say he had grown up. But I anticipate.

"We do not have the history of his life, though I should like some day to try and write it. There are letters full of his ideas about art and nature, grand designs that in another epoch he might have lived to bring to fruition. . . ." Peter broke off, smiling. "Of course we Germans often make this excuse—didn't you know that our Shakespeare was killed in the Thirty Years' War before he was able to write a single play? So . . . we have Kuno's letters, with here and there portraits of his friends, amongst whom he counted Henri Beyle who became later known to the world as Stendhal. From these *tableaux vivants* I have reconstructed a kind of history, beginning in the autumn of 1808 when Kuno was twenty-one and travelled to Erfurt in Thüringen to see the great Bonaparte arrive in state.

"He was not disappointed. Napoleon came to Erfurt partly to make a treaty with the Russian Czar in order to protect his eastern boundaries, those eastern boundaries he was shortly to violate, although during this autumn the war in Spain occupied his interest—and England waited, England whom he feared most of all." Once more Peter paused to make sure that the modern parallels were not lost on us. "This was, as I say, partly his purpose. He came also to Germany to show off and to impress his hosts. For this reason he brought with him soldiers and statesmen and even the Comédie-Française, who played every night in Erfurt to a crowded theatre. The city put itself at Napoleon's feet with lights and flags and home-made verses in the windows singing his praises . . . for their conqueror a defeated nation made carnival, and fought to offer their wives and daughters, we are told, to French hussars. They stood day and night in the streets only in the hope of a glimpse of Napoleon—*mein Kaiser*, Goethe called him. With hindsight one can speak slightingly of this, but there were of course good reasons, excellent reasons, to acclaim the man. For a hundred years Germany had produced the greatest thinkers in Europe but politically we were still in the Middle Ages, with our tiny principalities, and the peasants living like slaves, unable to send their children to school because they must first go to work on the estate, without payment. The schools and the universities taught Latin and Greek and obedience. Under Napoleon we would enter a modern, united Europe, this was what people thought then. And it is true that the *Erbuntertänigkeiten*, the hereditary servitudes, were abolished, in theory at least, because you cannot end such things in a night. But in place of one kind of censorship the universities and booksellers received instead another just as strict, forbidding ideas contrary to the wishes of the state. Some people were still full of hope, as some people always are, believing that this temporary repression would pass. Others were in such despair that they prayed—this is perfectly true—for England to come and make Germany a part of the British Empire instead.

"And some, like Kuno, simply believed that might was right and watched the Emperor with fascination, in the theatre: his Emperor—ah, what a word, what a sound; what a thought— sitting on a little raised platform beside the Czar but ignoring the Russian and gazing attentively at the drama through his opera glasses made of gold. A strong, squat figure dipping from time to time into a golden snuff-box. So it is described, that Napoleon watched the play and the audience watched Napoleon. An audience of crowned heads, warriors, and celebrities—Kuno was only there by mistake, as you will learn. Talleyrand was there, and Monsieur Goethe, of course. Here in Erfurt Kuno was introduced to Henri Beyle, by no means a celebrity at the time but merely a civil servant, a colonial official posted to Germany, who was in Erfurt for the reasons always most pressing to him, reasons of the heart. A mistress had left him, and she was in the city. Her name was Mélanie Guilbert, formerly of the Comédie-Française, and she was breaking her journey to stay in Erfurt with friends in the troupe, on her way to Moscow and a glittering marriage to a Russian general. Beyle came to Erfurt in vain, since she no longer loved him. Perhaps he did not love her either until she left him, since Kuno's words are, I like to think, exact: he was a small, vain, insecure and ugly man, a splendid talker known to posterity for his worldly-wise sophistication, but in those days noticeable for two things only, his contempt for all things French, and his worship of Napoleon. No contradiction, believe me; ah, if only there were." Peter paused for effect. "But he is not the last man, nor the French the last nation, to choose a foreigner, a native of their country by adoption only, through whom to persecute themselves. Or, if you like, through whom to realize their worst fears about themselves. In other words, to choose a scapegoat for a leader. As in love, so in politics, you see: to save ourselves from betraying a loved one—as we fear we shall—we choose as the loved one someone who will betray us first.'' Peter paused again, gazing down and picking his words. ''Only to find our own face reflected in their no less armour-plated breast.'' Now he looked up. ''This was Beyle's story, and Kuno's too in time. The difference was that Kuno's breastplate came from Sweden,'' Peter smiled, ''and Beyle's from the Comédie-Française. So—true to his character—when Napoleon failed him Beyle replaced the real hero with those of fiction, and took his pen-name Stendhal from the name of a town in Saxony. He was not without irony, this Monsieur Beyle: the town of Stendhal had once been the centre of colonial communications. But what do you do if irony is not for you a sufficient protest against the degradation of all human values, against the corruption of the times? What do you do if you cannot or will not resort to fiction? I shall tell you—for Kuno did not resort to fiction.

''Unlike his friend he failed as a *littérateur*, but he was a successful man of action and in Erfurt he discovered this. He came to the city a poet, and left it a soldier. And this is how it happened. I should first explain that resentment against Napoleon was not confined to a minority among the subjugated peoples but was also felt in his own country, and this before his reversals on the battlefield. It took the form of a secret society calling themselves *les Philadelphes*, the lovers of brotherhood, who had infiltrated the Emperor's entourage and hatched an assassination plot—but without reckoning on the interfering presence, the accidental presence of a young German idealist.'' Peter sat back, gazing round; I was now all ears. ''Kuno was of course no part of the plot, and knew nothing of such matters, his was not even a political idealism, it was a romantic natural philosophy which drew him to the man of humble birth who had risen to eminence by individual qualities, by innate qualities if you will. Here in Napoleon was a specimen of the natural leader, and politics must bow before his sense of destiny, his will, and his unspoilt imagination. A young man on a private income could afford such ideas.

''The plotters were themselves a little confused, some wanted to restore the Republic, others a Bourbon monarchy, and they were held together only by a common hatred of the upstart tyrant. Those who were later arrested were for the most part Army officers, one of whom had succeeded in recruiting sympathizers into the Emperor's personal guard, and if more senior figures were involved—as they must have been to safeguard a *coup d'état*—their names have not been revealed although they may be guessed at. It seems that the initial plan was to surround Napoleon with hand-picked guards, on the evening of October the tenth, and to cut down the tyrant in the narrow streets of Erfurt, on his way to a performance of Racine's *Mithridate*— the play had been specially chosen by the Emperor himself. But it was Napoleon's third visit to the theatre on successive nights, and the Philadelphes should have struck earlier, since by now the people of Erfurt had learnt the route, and anticipated the great man's schedule. They thronged his coach in such numbers that on the Lange Brücke across the river Gera they separated Napoleon from his bodyguard and escorted his coach to the theatre themselves—while the would-be assassins watched, frustrated . . . perhaps, who knows, a little relieved too. That night this ancient city of woad, the same woad your Druids painted on their faces, was celebrating greasepaint of another kind, and Bonaparte reached the theatre unharmed. However one of the plotters, an officer with the English-sounding name of Patrick Granville, from Touraine, was determined that it should be the fatal night. Only one problem: he now had to get into the auditorium where the Emperor, on his raised dais beside Czar Alexander, offered an excellent target. To reach the milling corridor behind the *loges* was easy, but a place inside them was beyond the means or influence of a mere *sous-officier* like Granville.

"Now on the night of the tenth Kuno had just such a place, by the good fortune of his new friendship. Henri Beyle was an intimate of the great Talma, the Mithridates of that evening's performance, for whom all doors opened, even those into the Emperor's presence. How close Kuno's seat was, to Napoleon himself, he does not tell us, but in his box overlooking both stage and audience—it is in any case a tiny theatre; and still exists today; I have been there—he was certainly close enough to attract Granville's interest. And now picture the scene: Granville standing in the corridor behind the boxes, unquestioned there in the uniform of the Emperor's Praetorian guard, watching the guests as they enter their *loge* . . . to the assassin this shy, soberly-dressed young man, so out of place among the dignitaries, must have seemed like a gift from heaven. Using his authority as Imperial bodyguard Granville informs an usher that he has Kuno under surveillance, and is suspicious of his presence in the theatre. Perhaps some money changes hands; in any case, with the polite pretence of a message awaiting him below, Kuno is persuaded by the usher to leave his seat and then marched less politely to the foyer. Meanwhile Granville slips into Kuno's seat. The ruse must have needed little more, only sufficient time for Granville to survey the scene at his leisure, to wait till his entrance no longer provoked attention from those in the box beside him, then unobtrusively to settle, and as the rising curtain drew all eyes, to raise his pistol, aim, and fire.

"It was *le moment propice* in more than one respect—that is, propitious in view of the play itself. Napoleon had not chosen *Mithridate* lightly, for the Erfurt audience. Nor, I believe, had the plotters chosen that evening by chance. Talleyrand tells us that when the Greek warrior king reminds his sons, in a famous speech, of his implacable hatred of Rome, the audience were expected to recognize in that mercantile empire Napoleon's greatest foe, the shopkeeper English. The play, however, opens on a very different note. As Granville took his place in the box above the Emperor, the actor behind the curtain—perhaps just as tense—was preparing to declaim, *'Rome en effet triomphe,'* Rome has indeed triumphed, *'et Mithridate est mort!'* . . . and Mithridates is dead! For the piece begins, as Aristotle prescribes, with a reported action. It is a false report, but Granville intended to make it true by cutting short both the play and the life of the modern Mithridates in the audience.

"And there is one more perspective, stranger still, to be mentioned before the Erfurt curtain rises on that scene of deceiving grief. It is Napoleon's perspective I mean, and his curious choice of entertainment." Peter drew himself up, Napoleonic. "In Paris I imagine him interviewing the Director of the Comédie-Française: *'Athalie* is not to be played, Dazincourt.' 'Non, sire.' 'Too revolutionary—and nothing by Voltaire.' 'Non, sire.' 'Corneille's *Cinna* perhaps . . . and *Mithridate.'* Yes, but why? Its hero's premature death is of course only a rumour—more, it is a ruse inspired by Mithridates himself to flush out the designs of his impatient heirs . . . and then the warrior king returns, striking fear into all disloyal hearts. This is fitting enough for Erfurt, a warning to over-eager German nationalists. But in the last act—here we have the mystery—the hero dies indeed at Roman hands, and with his last words contradicts his earlier defiance. He urges a tactical retreat: *'Allez, réservez-vous.'* Hardly a battlecry! Hardly a suitable attitude, you might think, with which to inspire a loyal audience against the enemy. And in fact it is not a play about conquest at all, it is about renunciation, about a futile struggle against an enemy more invincible than Rome, or England. I have revenged the universe, says the dying king, as fully as I could—death alone disturbed my plans. *J'ai vengé l'univers!* What does he mean? What is it that has happened to affront the universe and make the king its champion? And what were the good citizens of Erfurt to make of his defeat?

"What has happened—in the play—is a stab in the back; simply that. Mithridates is a man betrayed, by his wives, by his sons, one after another until no friend remained, and without his ever understanding that he himself has inspired each betrayal in its turn. Such, indeed, became Bonaparte's cross in later years—for him too the great adversary who outrages the universe was called betrayal. It seems he was fascinated by the play, since he had it performed over and over again, but you have to conclude that he learnt nothing from it. It is not written in self-pity. Racine knew better than most how the victim too pursues his destiny, and *Mithridate* is a tale of self-inflicted wounds; but this it seems that Bonaparte could not see. I should add, since Maggie says that I am not permitted to tell a story of two heroes battling over a lovely lady, that the play concerns not two but three heroes battling over the lady! Mithridate himself, Pharnace the corrupted son secretly allied to Rome, and Xipharès the noble son who nonetheless betrays his father by falling in love—since the lady in question is Mithridate's betrothed. Shall I stop here?"

He surveyed us with an open grin; none of us took him up on it. "Dying, Mithridate grants her to noble Xipharès. The chain of betrayal may be broken at last. But the boy will not adopt his father's military strategy and retreat. He will fight Rome to the last breath, nobly perhaps, or perhaps foolishly. His reason is that his mother has once offered to betray Mithridate to Rome, hoping to win Rome's mercy towards her infant son. Guilt chains the grown-up Xipharès—and the cycle begins again. . . .

"But in Erfurt, in the theatre, a man awaits who can rewrite the evening's drama. Picture him, dizzy with anticipation: *'Rome en effet triomphe,'* and he draws his gun. What a death knell, what a call to arms! He cocks the gun, *'et Mithridate est mort!'* Sublime prompting for an assassin! But Aristotle would have warned him that history and drama are not always good bedfellows. That night the curtain is delayed—an actor has mislaid a prop perhaps, perhaps some Grand Duke loiters in the foyer, self-important, to be sure that he is the last to enter the auditorium. Napoleon's life is saved, his destiny, as in the play itself, deferred, though only to follow more closely that of Mithridates. Outside the playhouse a young Mecklenburger who has travelled far for a glimpse of his hero—adventure enough, he must be thinking, to tell his grandchildren one day—will not be denied his chance because of some stupid misunderstanding. One usher will not restrain him. The other officials are busy holding back the crowd, who also want to see Napoleon. The line breaks, and as the sons and daughters of Erfurt pour into the foyer to hammer on the auditorium doors, multiplying the three blows that announce the stage performance, Kuno is carried back into the theatre before them and runs unhindered up the stairs, back to his *loge*. Inside, all eyes are turned to the doors at the back of the theatre, where the clamour is fading and order being gradually restored. All eyes except those of the man in Kuno's seat—and Kuno's, fixed on him in shock as Granville draws the pistol, impatient, death knell be damned, and aims it unaware of being watched.

"Thus far," Peter sipped at the fresh cup of coffee Ludolf had supplied, "I have drawn mainly on Kuno's own account, but also on the letters of Caroline Sartorius to her husband, those of Major von Knebel to the philosopher Hegel, and the memoirs of *le grand Talma*. The account of Granville's movements we owe to Talleyrand himself, who investigated the conspiracy. Kuno, writing to his sister Adelheid, describes the *dénouement* with typical brevity. Entering the box, he says, I found a French officer with a pistol aimed at the Emperor and I fell on him, seizing his weapon. That is all, except that like a modest chap he goes on to say that he was sadly obliged to miss the performance in order to help the investigations, but that he heard that Talma was excellent. And he curses this luck.

"So there was no shot, no more than a brief commotion as the man was disarmed and led from the box. Of course I prefer to picture the events less swiftly. For Kuno a moment of trance: the gilded auditorium with a cast of crowned heads to match anything in Racine . . . a man with a pistol raised, in his own place, his own seat . . . were they not all on stage and was he not, alone, the audience for whom this play was made? But Kuno mentions no such hesitation and I am sure there was none. He had found his calling and it was not as he had thought, that of a dreamer.

"By other accounts of the commotion, more flattering perhaps to the participants, there was more of a struggle than Kuno suggests. Several German princelings present in the box claimed, and received from the Emperor's hand, medals for their bravery in overpowering the traitor. It was in Napoleon's interest to decorate his new allies, so the rewards were lavish. Granville himself was shot with less ceremony the following day. As for Kuno it seems that against all the evidence, some stain of suspicion may have clouded the honours available to him, since Granville kept to his story that he had seen the young man in the company of other malcontents, and that he himself had only drawn his weapon to anticipate an attack. When the Philadelphes were rounded up this pretence was useless. But by the time Kuno had been cleared of any revolutionary association, the furore had died down. A medal, the cross of St. Joseph, and a commission, were offered to him. It was in fact a substantial commission, a captaincy in the one of the volunteer brigades of the Rheinbund, the confederacy of German states under Napoleon's protection, which included Mecklenburg.

"Was this a double-edged reward, perhaps? If you are indeed loyal, Monsieur von Brüel, and a hero . . . then show us, in the front lines. At first, to judge by his own words, I think Kuno would have exchanged his commission for the lost opportunity to see the great Talma as Mithridates. He wrote this perhaps in jest, but he did not yet see himself as a soldier. Nonetheless some instinct was stirring in him; he accepted the captaincy and became, in time, more of a soldier than he would have believed possible. Kuno also came to see *Mithridate* and Talma in the role, though four long and eventful years had passed before he did so, and the setting was as different from the gay city of Erfurt with its welcoming banners and its bunting as it was possible to be. It was in the ruins of Moscow, still smouldering from the self-destructive deeds of its own departing citizens, in a Moscow empty of people and increasingly without food, that the Comédie-Française once more performed the play, with Kuno in its sombre audience.

" 'How beautiful it is,' wrote Kuno as the Grande Armée set out for Russia, 'to be a wave, anonymous, *une vague anonyme*,' turning to French for the pun which also translates as 'a vague anonymity,' 'in the most irresistible tide in European history!' Not since Xerxes, he might have continued . . . and then remembered Salamis. But they hardly seemed to think that when their three weeks' supply of food ran out, the Russian people would not greet them with the bread and circuses of Erfurt.

After Borodino the enemy fell back, leaving Napoleon to reach Moscow across a sea of corpses, acres, we are told, glittering with gold braid. To live through such a battle was to lose a part of oneself to the cannon and the cries of the dying—on entering the deserted city Kuno felt himself to be a ghost in a borrowed uniform. The French themselves, knowing less of Slav obduracy than did their Prussian allies, rejoiced. And autumn held on that year, deceptively mild. Talma arrived in Moscow with his troupe, to play *Cinna* once more, and *Mithridate*. All around them mansions burned, and splendid furniture, and no food came; no word of surrender from the Czar; instead, the first flurries of snow, the first horses secretly killed and eaten.

"Kuno wrote to Adelheid, a little news and a long discourse on the French imagination. He had seen *Mithridate* at last. This time it was Napoleon who did not grace them with his presence. *'Rome en effet triomphe, et Mithridate est mort!'* Ominous words now; how they must have rung, in that theatre! 'He is in the Kremlin,' wrote Kuno, 'so we are told, and know as much from infrequent appearances on a balcony. Some say this is not the Emperor and that he has already left for Paris . . .' Even Beyle who arrived in Moscow with a letter from the Empress Joséphine, a suitable duty, received no audience and could not contradict the rumours. Napoleon was there of course, nursing his pride in secret, but to heal the wounds he needed more than loving messages. Not so Beyle—his most urgent need was for news of Mélanie Guilbert, newly married in Moscow and most cherished when, like Racine's Monime for her three suitors, she was least accessible. Leaving Malmaison with Joséphine's letter, Beyle would have had little news of the eastern front other than the fall of Moscow itself, and eagerly accepted the mission in the hope of finding Mélanie there, a prisoner along with her Russian husband, the general. Ah, and then to play the magnanimous victor; modestly to obtain their joint release . . . or only hers, perhaps. . . . In the event Beyle searched Moscow's prisons in vain, and then its streets, and even its deserted houses. Mélanie had fled to Petersburg, alone and pregnant—a dreadful journey through a landscape devastated by her countrymen."

Did something premonitory stir in me as Peter drew this scene? Frantic, ugly Beyle ransacking roofless, snow-filled houses for an actress who wasn't there; it was probably just the word "Petersburg" that made me glance at Maggie, restoring her looks that first night at the theatre, in London.

"Beyle's despair left him blind to the fate of the military campaign," Peter continued, "and when he left Moscow on the fifteenth of October, four days before the city was evacuated, his love for Napoleon was like his love for Mélanie, untarnished. He took with him another letter, this time a more anxious one, from Kuno to Adelheid. She opened and read it in one of these rooms, perhaps here at this table. Beyle too had a beloved sister, so he knew how much such letters meant to both parties—he had often promised his own sister that they would share everything, always. Alas when in later life the destitute sister came to live with him, he found her a bore and threw her out. But in Moscow Beyle did Kuno a better turn than simply to carry away a letter. His indifference to the disaster of the invasion opened Kuno's eyes. It explained to him the true meaning of their enterprise and just as importantly, since the man of letters was still alive in Kuno, the logic of *Mithridate*.

"You must understand: Kuno was now blooded in war, but he was still the disciple of Jean-Paul, and a man of abstractions. It was not the carnage of Borodino, nor starvation, nor even the horrors of the homeward march after barely a few weeks of hollow possession, that marked the turning point in Kuno's allegiance. Such things were too vivid to be entirely real. Kuno needed explanations, and he found them in Racine's grim Jansenist creed—frustration as a noble fate. Behold this Beyle, this brother intellectual, this soldier-poet like himself, oblivious to the great forces at play and hunting instead for a former actress through the uninhabitable shells of great houses. So too, while Mediterranean fleets waited impatiently in the bay—ah the false sunshine on that Moscow stage!—and royal chariots stood poised to leave, horses chafing in their gilded traces, Racine's heroes shrank the world and its business to a single imploring gaze, a jealous and impossible love. Was it not grotesque to come so far, for this? Wounds and privations were to be endured; a soldier-poet did not march under Napoleon for comfort or even for victory, but the thing of which poems and monuments alike were made—for History. Not for a hopeless love, not for a private war against the universe!

"As such, Beyle's unrequited passion was understandable to Kuno, and he reports it tenderly. His friend's vision of crowning failure, even when conferred on Napoleon and ascribing to him the role of tragic hero—this too could be borne. Failure itself could certainly be borne. But to Kuno, who believed in the united and enlightened Europe that Napoleon alone could bring about, the idea of a quest for failure, a longing for failure, was repulsive. Beyle, he says, described the Russian campaign—which Beyle had not experienced till now—as a 'challenge thrown down to Nature,' *un superbe défi!* And by Nature Beyle did not mean the unforgiving Russian countryside but a godless universe with its crushing indifference to such adventures. For him, as for Kuno, the Emperor was not the small pale man they had observed taking too much snuff at the theatre, but the model man, in his uniqueness, the model of man's ambitious will. Where he and Beyle differed, as Kuno found to his dismay, was that the Frenchman saw this will as doomed from the start and admired in it the empty insult, the fist waved at a vacant sky. Beyle's Prometheus was born in chains. It was a play, and they themselves were the last act: snow gathering on their abandoned billet, chairs being smashed to feed the fire, Beyle drinking, since there was no shortage of wine in Moscow's cellars. Beyle short and fat, stiff collar puffing out his jowls, gesticulating in a room without furniture and whose great windows give onto more fresh snow and empty, printless, Moscow streets. Beyle talking . . . they were besieged, but by no army, rather by its very absence, and there was no-one to fight—for who needs an enemy in the last act of his tragedy? *J'ai vengé l'univers*, a universe which is only the struggle of the void to be reborn. Kuno could comfort himself with the knowledge that his comrades-in-arms were not giving the scene such a poetic gloss. They were merely starving. Yet if the will of poets failed, if nihilism could be embraced by men of vigorous and worldly intellect, what hope was there of a new enlightenment?

'' *'Réservez-vous!'* Napoleon gave the order to retreat, and burn what was left of the city, in their wake. But whether the snow or his soldiers' indifference won the day, even this final gesture was denied him. Of the Grande Armée one man in five remained to pick his way back across the field of Borodino, slush now and dulled metal and rotting bodies. As History recalls with relish, few survived the journey home. But this relish—Beyle would be glad to know it—is tinged with admiration: the retreat from Moscow, man against the elements, Napoleon walking with his troops to share their suffering . . . and it is true that for short periods Napoleon walked, because stiff-limbed on his horse all day he would have frozen to death. From Kuno we have a less heroic account of the retreat. Those who took part knew that their enemy was neither the cold nor the Cossacks but incompetent leadership, and the German troops were the first to recognize it openly. When the mad French Emperor left off his tantrums, took a sled and abandoned them to their officers, they left the column and begged for refuge in the countryside rather than be led by other Frenchmen to their death.

"Kuno watched his countrymen run into the woods, called after them, but could not follow. He was lame, one leg unfeeling, frozen. It saved his life. Those who escaped to nearby farms were welcomed in, fed *schchi*, the peasant broth, then lulled to sleep and butchered in their beds. The column continued, smaller and smaller, and each night Kuno went to bed expecting to wake up with his good leg frozen, and be released to die. One by one those who did not survive the night's bivouac were thawed and eaten by the others. Now tell me . . . do such things change a man, such acts, such experiences? Of course they do, we say, for the rest of his life. But the events themselves—they pass like a lurid dream, isn't it so? Too vivid to be entirely real. They change us, then, only because we remember them—because we choose to remember them; because we are trained to remember the things we call real. Dreams themselves we let go, no matter how horrible they are, we do not let them change us. But do you insist that if you or I did such a thing as Kuno did—a fearful act—we must be haunted by it? Wake up screaming; stare at our face in the mirror? We may not come to eat a man, you or I, in our lifetime, but let us say we kill a man, out of necessity. When it is done, shall we live it again and again, as in Shakespeare? Perhaps not to justify ourselves, if the necessity was truly there to begin with, but to find again the scab, the moral itch, when in fact it is not morality that compels us to remember, not at all. It is our need for a past, our need to be bound, to be bounded by something: our longing for a past of real events, a history like a photograph album. And a man does not need to have eaten human flesh to be tormented by memory. Moments of social embarrassment may trouble him as much, may pursue him everywhere, different photographs but the same need to review them. So when I ask myself whether Kuno returned home a changed man I want to know if he was free of his past, not if he had new chains.

"In this house here, Kuno recuperated. He walked here from Moscow, most of the way with a kind of crutch, a piece of wood torn from a Russian fence. The frostbite made him lame until his death. But Kuno overcame his injury, and more importantly perhaps, his memories. I do not say that he was free of them—I am sure he was not—but that he was free of many earlier illusions, and that this was the true change in the man. In his short life there were changes yet to come, but these were possible only because he was not fettered by his own story, he could jump, as we say, *über seinen Schatten springen*, over his own shadow. Other German soldiers who survived the retreat became, in the main, professional cripples. They had little choice—the private armies such as Lützow's troop, that were springing up to fight Napoleon under the banner of a new Germany, regarded such former mercenaries as potential spies. If you were not an invalid already, it was better to lie low. Of course the fact that these new liberators, these Freikorps nationalists, were also turncoats, turning now on the hero when he was down, and had merely lacked the courage of their earlier convictions—this was no comfort for the despised cripples.

"Napoleon himself was in Germany again in April, with a new army, another reason for disenchanted followers to stay out of sight. Yet was this not the moment to admire the man? It was surely the most remarkable achievement of Napoleon's life: six months before, he had led half a million Frenchmen to their deaths and now nearly as many again, men and boys, were willing to follow him once more! How like a god Bonapart must have seemed to them! Was it not once more, as Beyle said, *un superbe défi,* a challenge thrown out to Nature? Once more Napoleon came to Erfurt, where he could be sure of quarters. It was a subdued and shuttered city now. No more carnivals outside the playhouse. To the Erfurters the man was no longer even a hero. And to Kuno? Ah, to Kuno, limping through this house—musing at this table . . . I must imagine him so, because we have only one more letter from him to Adelheid, and that was written on the twenty-ninth of April from Erfurt itself. It is a letter unlike all the others, a personal narrative of his shame and terror, and a warning to all those who follow a flag: as a child already I committed it to memory.

"When Kuno heard that the Emperor was quartering there, he put on his Rheinbund uniform and rode to Erfurt. His regiment was disbanded and his commission void, but veterans such as Kuno were in short supply—if he had been French he would have been a general by now. The cross he wore, the Croix St. Joseph, this was his passport. And wasn't he after all the man who had saved Napoleon's life, five years earlier? But this time Kuno's reason for going to Erfurt—so I believe, though he never says as much to Adelheid—was to kill him.

"With whom did Kuno stay in Erfurt? With Henri Beyle. Beyle was there too, after adventures of his own, amorous ones, for Mélanie had regained Paris in the meantime, and Beyle had regained Mélanie. Now he was again in Napoleon's retinue: you can read the account he has left us of the battle of Bautzen, or rather the sights and sounds of Bautzen from a distance. We know from Kuno's letter that Beyle was sick, of a mysterious ailment which Kuno does not identify. He tells how he arrived at Beyle's cheerless lodgings to find his friend unconscious with fever, and how he ran through the streets to find a doctor, but none would answer his cries, only a certain Doktor Wuth, an untidy man making speeches and sighing more like a doctor of philosophy than medicine, who finally agreed to come within the hour.

"For Kuno there followed a terrifying experience. That night, he says, I found myself in the streets alone, facing the little theatre in Turmstrasse. The place was dark and still but there was no bolt on the doors and I felt, or rather I knew, that they were unlocked. Then I was trying them and found that it was so. I entered the foyer in darkness. Before me another pair of doors led to the auditorium, and a faint light showed beneath them. . . .

"Picture Kuno now, a tall man, fair-haired like me, erect. Younger than I am, but older by five years of hell. Somewhere in this gloomy foyer are the stairs he once galloped up like a schoolboy, with the crowd that carried him inside. He had two good legs then, and it is dark now, too dark to stumble up the stairs and disturb Granville's ghost, in the box that now belongs to him alone. The auditorium doors are ahead of him. He pushes them open and goes in. One light above, whose muddy surface moves as though it holds a restless liquid, reveals the seats, and more dimly the empty stage. Kuno is alone in the silence. He inhales the musty air that vacant threatres retain like vaults, the tomb of so much sweat and spurious excitement. It would seem a tawdry place now, without expectancy—but for Kuno's memories. He forces his eyes up to the box beside the stage with as much anxiety as if he were himself the target of an avenging Granville, but there is no-one between the heavy curtains.

"The stage beneath them is bare of décor, and recedes into darkness. Only a fringe of paper leaves, the remains of a rustic scene, hangs at the front of the proscenium and catches the light. Then, says Kuno, a man walked quietly onto the stage, so softly that he might have been walking on real earth, real turf, with a slow contemplative tread, and I saw that it was the Emperor.

"In that doll's playhouse of a theatre they are no more than twelve paces apart, though Kuno still stands with his back pressed against the doors, in shadow. Napoleon stops and gazes attentively, it seems, at Kuno, then slowly raises his eyes to the dish of light in the ceiling, with its moving yellow coils. His gaze now sweeps the stalls as though preparing them for speech. But none comes. He seems not to see Kuno, he looks up at the balcony, motionlessly recreating some lost performance, without gesture, with looks alone, as the lights grow dimmer and then brighter again. Kuno has the pistol, he knows that he can kill him. Now, praying that the tyrant will not start to speak, for when the play begins Kuno knows he is lost—he takes the weapon from his coat. Raises it. And Napoleon turns to him at once. As they stare, Kuno lives the instant that ends the assassin's dream. This meeting of eyes, this tableau, is the climax, for with the shot the enemy vanishes, and with him the meaning of the deed. Under his gaze Kuno can feel the Russian snows claiming his body without pain, but with the same remoteness, the siren song of death. The numbness rises to his arm. His mind clouds, he sees again a soldier in the snow with his weapon trained on his horse, the soldier swaying like a drunk. In the horse's head the eyes roll up, the mouth is flecked with foam. Kuno tries to shout. The words are on his lips, a whisper. When he tries again he hears himself cry them aloud: 'Sic pereunt . . .'

"The lights are out, he lunges forward, in darkness, staring. Kuno is staring in the dark of Henri Beyle's foul-smelling room, sitting, and shaking, awake. Then moonlight comes, and before it fades he has a glimpse of Beyle's head, by the window, staring back at him from the bed. When the clouds pass he sees Beyle clearly. The eyes are bulging, the expression fixed, the face a pale and ghastly deathmask on the pillow. Yes, for a time Kuno believes it is his friend's death he has lived in his nightmare— since it was a nightmare, nothing more. The untidy Doktor Wuth has been and gone, Kuno is in bed, he has not been to the theatre in Turmstrasse. When at last he goes to Beyle he finds that the man is breathing, and his fears abate. I knew their cause, he says: I had woken beside too many dead men.

"He returns to bed and this time forces himself to stay awake. But it only serves to keep the dreaded images before him. Doors opening on a ghostly theatre, the sullen, fleshly figure beneath the paper leaves, drawing life like a succubus from the cowering soldier in the audience. Now he tries to sleep, to drive away a greater fear, the fear that it has actually taken place. *Sic pereunt* . . . but no, only his shout was real. Later that night his roommate begins himself to cry out in his delirium, and Kuno must abandon all thoughts of sleep. I lay there, he says, an imaginary assassin—a failed assassin, even in dreams—listening to Beyle in our stinking room, poor dying Beyle crying out for Mélanie, for love, for human comfort, crying out for the love he has destroyed and will always destroy. . . .'

Peter paused. To my surprise he was smiling, and caught my eye.

''Actually it was venereal disease that made Beyle cry out, not a despairing love. And he didn't die, except in name—as Stendhal he rose again to try his hand at novels and was reborn. But for Kuno . . . for Kuno there remained only the final gesture. What follows in his letter is written, I think, purely for Adelheid's sake, since in it he returns to the fiction that he came to Erfurt to re-enlist. He says that now there is nothing left for him in Erfurt—now that his feelings with regard to the Emperor have been made plain to him by his dream. Rather, I think that this so-called dream was his way of telling Adelheid the truth, that he went there to finish Granville's work and that his courage failed him. The Emperor has not betrayed us, he insists, the Emperor is true to himself, it is we who have betrayed ourselves, in dreams. But does he mean, betrayed our hatred of him, confessed it, or does he mean betrayed ourselves in foolish dreams of glory? Somewhere in his words I hear a different voice, saying more simply: we have betrayed the Emperor. Of the followers of a new Germany he speaks with the same contempt, as though they too were traitors. The old rhetoric comes back: Prometheus was a liar, he says, and man seeks fire not to serve but to destroy the earth. To enable the void to be reborn—this has a ring of Beyle to it, indeed of *Mithridate*. But as always with Kuno, his actions speak more clearly, even when they contradict his words. When he left Erfurt it was to find Baron von Lützow and on the basis of their family connections to beg a place among his volunteers. Then he came home to say his farewells. Here, to this house once more. Here he insisted on taking the armour of his ancestor—sadly I'm afraid only the breastplate was later rescued, but there were more pieces in Kuno's time—and on the field at Lützen he rode to battle partly dressed in this absurd, outdated costume. There was, you see, in our history a second battle of Lützen, and that day it was Napoleon himself who led the victorious charge against the Germans and their allies, Kuno a gleaming target among them—among the 'traitors.'

''When and where exactly Kuno died I do not know, but it

was on this field and so within a mile or two at most of where his knightly ancestor had fallen, at the first battle of Lützen. A deliberate, ridiculous death—I do not think it should be seen as a romantic gesture, but as a mocking one. At the end of the Erfurt letter he says that an honourable part in war is now inconceivable, but that to stand aside and watch the chaos is more dishonourable still. In short, that we must take part, even though where there is no choice there is no honour, least of all in death. Europe was now scattered with corpses, hundreds of thousands of men, and families starving so that the tyrant and his followers could eat. Hundreds of thousands dead, hundreds of thousands more advancing over them, insatiable for death. No wonder if it seemed to Kuno that destruction was now mankind's deepest desire. His own part had been to save the tyrant's life—and finally to turn his hand against himself, since at Lützen Kuno was doomed. Once off his horse he was helpless as a mediaeval knight. The will to live had failed him, just as the will to kill had failed him in the dream. It is just this that interests me so much.

"Why—why did it fail him? Kuno was not a coward. Why then? If it was because he saw the angel of destruction in us all, as much in himself as in others, is it so terrible, this discovery? He was after all a soldier. Or was it that our Kuno, despite everything he had endured, was still in love with Napoleon? Was this his last dream, that with his shining armour he would draw on himself an avenging army to pierce his traitor's breast and rid him of his own despairing love?

"For me it is the only explanation. The lover betrayed . . . who courts this, so that he himself will not be the first to betray. This ritual is observed by each of the characters in the story, each in his manner. Each in his armour, each a hero, each betrayed. You could say this was the stuff of comedy—that only a Frenchman could take it seriously—and I agree. So let the breastplate stay where it is: I do not wish to put it on. I am not a soldier like Kuno, much less an idealist. You see, I would not die for Hitler. I would not even jump forward to save Hitler's life, in a box at the theatre. I do not love him in the least, and I have no desire to follow such a man, as Kuno had. But I understand Kuno's dilemma. In Mecklenburg we are still the knights of old, the *grands seigneurs* watching the masses trample over each other towards the precipice. I share his attitude towards this madness. As he says, where is the honourable part to play in this?''

Peter cocked his head, and sighed.

"But suppose a part is thrust upon you, unchosen. Suppose the tyrant is placed in your hands, not in a dream, not in a theatre, but in reality. At your mercy. What then, if the play has already begun? Kuno was right of course, there are times when it is dishonourable to act—but more dishonourable not to do so. Don't you think?"

What does a man do on his fiftieth birthday? In my case I shall wake up early, I suspect, and lie in bed smoking a cigarette, gazing at the rich grey plaster of the walls with their synthetic rubber look, built to resist a hammer blow. Gaze at my bags packed for a journey, in this Hamburg flat as bright and antiseptic as the décor in the porno films that flicker in the Vegas-Girls, a short walk from my front door. I say the Vegas-Girls, but there are other, similar, cellars in St. Pauli, of course, many others. The Vegas comes to mind because it's mine, I own it. Who is this I, naked in bed, smoking a cigarette? Not Richard Thurgo. Richard Thurgo is a name no-one remembers. No-one has been addressed by that name for twenty years, except in memory.

Lie in bed smoking, gaze at the walls. Get up and brush my teeth, pack my toilet bag, put on a suit and go out to a rendezvous to kill a stranger, on my fiftieth birthday.

Getting up will be the difficult part. I think I shall wait until I hear the doorbell ring, then I shall go and open the door, naked, to Hansi, who will disapprove, and make him wait while I brush my teeth and pack the toiletries and get dressed. Hansi is what you might call my trusted lieutenant, in the language of children's books and childhood gangs. And as a matter of fact, I do trust him. If you want a trusted lieutenant, get a German, even a beady, thin-lipped, thirty-year-old German queer like Hansi. Hansi will avert his eyes from my body and say nothing, although this is not the way *der Chef* should answer the door, especially today. He disapproves of my bright, antiseptic little flat, it isn't the way *der Chef* should live. (I had a lot of trouble getting him to stop referring to me as *der Boss*, which I think sounds even more stupid.) Most of all he disapproves of the fact that *der Chef* is going to kill a man today, because it is he who should do such work, not I. But he will say nothing, because I am *der Chef*.

Besides, I fought in the war, unlike Hansi who was seven years old when it ended, and for Hansi this places me beyond reproach. I don't know how England treats its war heroes these days, shabbily I suspect, if my memories of the postwar years are anything to go by. No, shabbily isn't the right word. Simply indifferently, as though the ending, and the winning, of the war had relegated it at once to history. This was already true, you could sense it in any public bar, within a matter of months; and I watched the laurels fade from Alec's brow (as they would have faded from Father's, I suppose, had he returned in 1918) as victory turned him by degrees from a demobbed hero into an unemployed civilian. In German I learnt that it takes victory to bring this about, and not just peace. Here we—I almost wrote they—still treat veterans, even now, as though they were contemporary gladiators, yes, we make way for them, buy them drinks. Old soldiers rarely talk about the war but it isn't shame that prevents them, it's modesty. They don't need to talk about it, they're still heroes. Perhaps the losing side always behaves this way. After all, they have no future to address with that brusque pride that conquerors affect. The past is an uneasy topic, but the present lives forever on its memories, waiting for handouts. Of course I should have mentioned, à propos Hansi's respect for my status, that he like others understands me to be a German war hero. From time to time I have considered telling him the truth—and on the whole I think his regard for me would be all the greater if he knew Reinhard *der Chef* was an Englishman. No, the problem is quite different. You see, I doubt if *anything* I could say would convince him that what I was saying was entirely true; or rather, since we both inhabit a world where to challenge anyone's account of their past is the unpardonable sin, almost unthinkable (and I treat Hansi's tale of having studied porcelain in Vienna under Rosenthal himself with the same bland nod I would adopt if he claimed to be a fully qualified brain surgeon), nothing I could say about my own past would strike him as true or false. Any more than a carnival mask is true or false. Perhaps Hansi is an expert on porcelain, it's not impossible, and an artist, as well as being a pimp and a thug and a murderer. It really doesn't matter. Hansi is his real name (for once I happen to *know* this), but everyone calls him Oxfart, which has nothing to do with his digestion, it refers to the striped scarf he wears nine months of the year, a green-and-purple striped college scarf which the Hamburg shop assistant assured him was an "Oxford University" scarf; and for fifteen years I haven't wanted to put Hansi right about his "Oxfart." Once more: does it matter? Not a bit. That's why I get on so well with him, and with everyone in our well-regulated little world. Today I am the man Oxfart will accompany to a killing. He is my solemn, anxious second, ready to die for me if fortune turns against us. Is there in all this some painful loss of that probity, that heart's ease, that integrity of those whose past is either true or false and whose present is true and shocking even in its triviality? I will tell you the answer: not a bit.

Not for us the delicate agonies of conscience that Peter revealed—under the eyes of his ancestors, a true and inescapable past—in the guise of a noble, charming resignation that evening in Schloss Brüel, talking of honour and betrayal, and assassination. It was 1937 and you might say the world was comparatively innocent then, for all Peter's talk of Napoleonic slaughter, inscribed in blood in the family annals. He himself was an innocent, a lifelong innocent. And I was eighteen years old.

As I recall it, Peter's tale—or allegory, perhaps even confession—had differing effects on us, his listeners. I seemed to be the only one who understood his final question about honourable deeds as more than a rhetorical question. I was on the edge of my seat. Alec, bored out of his wits by ancestral stories, it seemed, was half asleep over his coffee, and Maggie too answered with a thin, barely polite smile. Long-windedness, she seemed to be saying, was not the way to win her round. She was with Alec still, she was English, and impatient.

But she was no fool; she collared me the next day as we trooped obediently to the stables in Agnetha's wake, to inspect a newborn calf. Peter had hurried on ahead to help the stockmen, while just in front of us Alec ambled beside our hostess, praising British livestock in pidgin German, and I hung back to avoid this.

"What was all that yesterday," Maggie murmured, "you know, about the tyrant being placed in his hands?"

We slowed our pace, letting the others draw ahead. I recalled Peter's words: Maggie is to remain in ignorance. True to myself, I told her at once. "He's got a couple of bombs."

Maggie stared, and I decided to suppress Alec's contribution for the moment. It might come in useful later, depending on Maggie's response.

"Bombs? How do you know?"

"I've seen them. You're not supposed to know about it."

"He's got bombs *here*?"

It was like Hambledon again, we were secret agents, chums. "Then what did he mean last night?" Maggie studied me, still amazed. "Come on . . ." I gave a shrug, and Maggie halted. "Is Hitler coming to dinner or something? What's going on?"

I smiled again as though I knew, and walked on. Shouts came from the stable block, Peter's voice raised among them. As we approached, Alec turned to us from the doorway.

"Spot of trouble," he frowned, not altogether displeased. "Hopelessly inbred, these Holsteins, I'm afraid."

We could hear the cow threshing; the men beside her grunting with effort. Maggie made a face and stopped once more, while Alec turned back to watch the proceedings.

"You can stay here if you want," said Maggie quietly. "I'm going home."

I stared her out. But it was no surprise, after the way she and Alec had been carrying on, talking more and more about England and English ways, in our hosts' presence.

"Tell me one thing," she said, "truthfully—is he a bit . . ." she tapped her right temple with a forefinger, "you know, _non compos_? D'you think? I mean, he seemed normal enough in England."

I shrugged, straight-faced. "Yes, but hopelessly inbred, I'm afraid."

In the stall a huge wet bullcalf only minutes old lay staring stupidly at us, head up and faintly nodding as if someone had told him an unpalatable truth. He was as slick as a conker fresh from its sheath. Behind him a group of kneeling men, up to their arms in blood and straw, were trying to stuff back a mass of brownish-purple membrane into the stunned and silent cow, under Peter's direction. "Prolapse," said Alec in answer to my look. "Womb's popped out." I heard footsteps as Maggie approached the stall. The extruded womb was immense, with the sloppy, ill-designed look of innards never meant for the light. As it slid through the stockmen's fingers and over their hands and arms, gelatinous, I longed to join in, to feel its secret, clammy weight. "God," Maggie muttered after a moment, and walked away stiff-legged. I waited for Alec to respond and when he didn't I glanced back at the steaming, deflated bubble-substance in the stall, hesitated, and went after Maggie.

I carried with me the luxurious image of the cow's insides, and realized I didn't merely want to touch their apocryphal slim-iness. I wanted to eat it. (Apocryphal, yes! Designed for God alone to see and know.) Looking back I sometimes think it was this instant that released in me the flood-tide of delight in spicy, viscous substances, sperm, saliva, the inside-out of flesh (breath-spice congealed!), that I was able to indulge in time. An illustration in Grandfather's copy of *The Conquest of New Spain* showed an Aztec priest holding aloft a heart torn from the living chest of his sacrificial victim, and my own heart had begun to pound in sympathetic terror whenever I studied the picture; which was often. I should have been a surgeon, I suppose. Except that I'd never have wanted to sew up a wound.

Maggie stood pressed against an empty loose-box, shoulders hunched over the stable door, inhaling a faded stench preferable to pure and steely German air, it seemed. Perhaps the smell restored her to the vicarage pony shed, though nothing else recalled Hampshire. The scale and elegance of the Schloss Brüel stables dwarfed us, we were dressed like a couple attending a concert rather than a rustic scene, a bloody mess in the straw. When she drew back it was to look at me resentfully as if I were gloating over her distress. I could see she was fighting not to vomit, unable even to speak to tell me to go away, and I looked away, up at the steeply tiled roofs. They were frosty, with lichen turning to gold as the tiles thawed.

What had Maggie been saying before we were distracted by the commotion in the stall? That she was going home; defiantly, she'd said it, as if she feared she were letting me down. "*I'm* not going to stay, then," I said. "I mean, I really don't know what I'm doing here, I should be studying."

"I don't know what you're doing here either," she growled, "you've been no help to me. I came here to marry Peter—or didn't you realize that? I came here to marry him and I'm scared rotten."

The words seemed to free her from nausea. Her face glowed with sweat.

Don't marry him, then; it was quite simple. I couldn't say it, though. "But . . . you've been carrying on with Alec," and I couldn't find less clumsy words; we both sounded like bickering children. At last I managed to stumble out what I meant. "Do you love him? Do you love Peter?"

She nodded, all too faintly.

How easy it would have been to misinterpret that diffident nod—as the shyness of the bride-to-be, or as delicacy towards me even though I had no claim on her affections and had made none; or as doubt. Even as deceit. But I was sure I knew what her silence meant. She was too tempted by the role Peter was offering her to be able to gauge her feelings towards him. So I thought; and for the time being her withdrawn expression prevented any further questions. Besides, we were children of our genteel and sentimental class, and in Maggie's case, of a romantic novelist. Once spoken, the word love admitted no prevarications. Only someone we would have called a cynic—we played at cynicism, which a true cynic never bothers to do—could have spoken for her then and said that love too was a role you had to play, not because it was false but because it was real and uncertain, because it was something willed as well as willing, something you had to rehearse. Which was just what I told myself whenever I replayed the moment in my head. In this fantasy I remained as silent as I was at the time, in the sumptuous stables. I didn't say I loved her, I didn't say a thing. And not because I was afraid of a rebuff—if anything a warm response would have been more bewildering, a whirlpool of unreliable words, more stultifying. No, it was that I felt too close to her, now as in Hambledon, for love, or what I thought of as love, a possessive passion. I had decided I possessed her too completely to feel passion. Though if that makes any sense I certainly couldn't have expressed it to Maggie; what she saw in my face must have been something like anxiety, the expression of an eager, fretful friend.

"I just hope *you* find what you want, one day," she said, in a bleak attempt at motherliness. The sweat was drying on her face, she still looked ill. You're as fickle as I am, her glance said, you just need to grow up.

Blueish veins were still visible in her face. I was watching her like a hawk and consequently missed the obvious: she was still blinded by what she'd seen in the nearby stall, the prolapsed womb. Soon to be breeding stock herself, in a pedigree herd—but no, that was the least of it; and it wasn't the pain either; it was the body, grotesquely manifest as bowel-work, that revolted her as much as it excited me. Peter should have appeared between us at the moment, hands and forearms freshly scrubbed—or better (for my benefit) with some flecks of blood still drying on his upper arms—and come to clasp Maggie to his breast, but he didn't, either too busy with the cow or too polite to steal a march on Alec. Besides, he wasn't in the clasping vein; he was master here, and he was waiting Maggie out.

The cow died. It was a long-drawn-out affair, punctuated by visits to her stall, but although the cowmen had succeeded in cramming the fleshly parachute back into her, the animal couldn't incorporate the shock and gave up soundlessly the following afternoon. Agnetha mourned her loss as if she were a favourite child; it was impossible for Maggie and Alec to announce their departure while her grief was at its height—and they would have left, I feel sure of it, had the circumstances been less awkward. Maggie would have declined the proffered role, she'd have ducked it, and although this might have been her salvation and mine, I prefer to think that it would have destroyed her. She would never have become the bohemian her looks and hair proclaimed her, but merely an eccentric manquée; she would have married—whom? someone in the wine trade, some harassed and forgiving man, and turned into a Kentish virago, terrorizing the servants. Dreadful thought; today I would be visiting her, occasionally, for tea and asperities; I would be her solicitor. I have that dying Holstein, Waltraut by name, to thank—at least in part—for sparing me this. As for Waltraut herself, she took no interest in her own tragedy, never so much as glanced at the cowmen in her labours, but turned her face towards the partition wall as though the drama was no part of her and only the pain was real.

So far during our stay we seemed to have been quarantined on the estate, and except for Sunday bowing and saluting outside the church, met no Germans other than the Lützows and their retainers. This could have been out of politeness, in order to give Maggie time to settle in, or because they were hesitating to exhibit her. But such pretexts were scarcely needed since the Lützow household was so self-absorbed, a world all its own. We were not in Germany, we were—in my mind—travellers held in one of those fairy-tale castles where riddles are spun by a mysterious host. Meanwhile we were jockeying for position, waiting for the ogre (myself, temporarily disguised as one of the travellers) to appear. In time I learnt that this isolation really was habitual and had nothing to do with our visit. Since widowhood Agnetha had withdrawn to the society of animals, leaving seigneurial duties to Peter, and these were made tedious for him by the lack of kindred, cosmopolitan souls; both took a lofty view of their allotted role—even Peter's contempt for his own aristocratic status was rather lofty—and both had despaired of Germany, enabling them in their separate ways to accept, like the followers of Napoleon in Peter's story, that Hitler was its destiny.

Periodic visits from old and cherished friends only underlined the Lützows' solitude. The visitors brought news of German affairs like Roman expeditionaries to some outpost of empire, where they were wined and dined accordingly. No doubt Mecklenburg had always been like this, a distant province, a Northumbria, though our castle was no stern Alnwick and you must imagine it (free of my fantasies) as it really was, a turreted confectionery set in woods and fields and orchards. Soon after Waltraut's death we saw the house being scrubbed, the breastplate and other armour polished, heard the weekend menu, always a subject of eager discussion, being drafted and re-drafted, but it was left to me to ask in whose honour these preparations were being made.

Ludwig Beck, said Peter, looking round to measure the impact of the name. It had none. He then explained that Beck, his godfather, had been a mentor since his father's death, that the man was a distinguished soldier and former comrade-in-arms of Count Egon; a German, Peter assured us, who represented the best of the Fatherland—noble, generous, scholarly, firm, a military strategist who was as much at ease in the realms of Greek philosophy or botany as in discussing Clausewitz or the campaigns of Moltke. Indeed Beck had been called a Moltke *redivivus*, the highest imaginable compliment for a military man. He was so admired and beloved of his troops and junior officers that his nickname was God: *der liebe Gott*. What Peter did not mention was that General Beck had never actually led an army in the field; neither did he tell us that Beck was the focus of resistance to Hitler, within the army, and the only man in Germany whom Hitler was said to fear. At the time Peter stressed that *der liebe Gott* was his mother's most trusted confidant, which led my suspicions in another direction. Conveniently enough Agnetha's mourning lasted till the eve of Beck's arrival, and it was clear from that alone that this visit from Peter's surrogate father was no coincidence. Well than, this was a test, a public outing for Maggie. In effect an audition.

Why hadn't the Lützows, mother and son, long since given up on this sulky girl? True, Peter loved her, but even I who was no less devoted had begun to feel ashamed of her. On home territory Maggie was proud and larky, but Peter surely knew that coaxing brought out the obstinate and the perverse in her; he must have been waiting for her to show what underlay her sullen disguise: that she had spirit. And still she hid it, taking refuge behind Alec's tweedy airs and his manner of unruffled superiority. Together they had developed a habit of imitating Ludolf the butler; they'd decided he was Peter's illegitimate elder brother, who had been very well-trained in matters of etiquette but was so stupid that the family hadn't dared acknowledge him in public—and who was now reduced to serving upstart foreigners in his own home. Ludolf did have a pained expression on his face most of the time, and his erect carriage would have done credit to the House of Lords. So whenever Alec and Maggie met in the castle corridors or in the park, or at mealtimes, they struck stage poses, exchanged Ludolf's slow, sombre bow, eyes closed, and made to pass each other like grieving, disinherited princes, before collapsing into giggles. To my relief Agnetha missed most of this childishness. She took meals in her room, emerging only for short, solitary walks round the estate before returning to the tower which formed her apartments. I couldn't believe she was up there mourning for a cow, but Peter said she was probably poring over pedigrees, bringing her livestock files up to date in tribute to Waltraut and the newly christened Willibald, her bullcalf son.

Peter and I were once more thrown into each other's company, yet hard as I tried to resume my role as confidant, Peter only smiled, making me feel eighteen and presumptuous, and when I asked him why he didn't try to wrest Maggie from Alec or at least call them to book for their insidious mockery, he gave me a fishy stare of silent amusement. One day as we were walking by the little lake at Tempzin and I began to try and explain Maggie to him, Peter reached into his pocket, brought out a gold-rimmed monocle—his father's, it turned out—and stuck it in one eye, to peer at me. My days as a sexual counsellor were over. Bombs too were a closed subject, and Peter had developed a new technique to keep me at bay. We spoke German. It made my questions clumsy, giving him the upper hand in a relationship which was becoming increasingly flirtatious. Yet if he chose my company not for its own sake but to provoke Maggie, well, I was flattered rather than insulted, flattered to be supposed an object of Maggie's jealousy. And as for who really had the upper hand, I never doubted that it was I.

Na, Junge? Peter would say, finding me loitering in the entrance hall, both of us behaving as though it were a chance encounter: well, boy? And then, as one might address the family dog, *Spazierengehen, oder?* Literally: to walk go, or? Ludicrous to listen to, German was delicious to speak, and I soon found I was talking to myself aloud in it. What I loved was its unremitting sensuality, all those compound nouns greedily locked in daisy chains of buggery; it was like sodomizing language, with decorum. *Selbstverständlich, Herr Graf,* but of course my dear Count. I had found my native tongue.

We went by car to Tempzin where the church, a triple-tiered barn with a tiny wooden bell-tower like a pimple on the highest tier, was ringed with low hedges of box. Their sweet-urine aroma, so humanly familiar, gave me a dog's sense of territory: a precinct lovingly staked out by smell. Once or twice we drove to the Schwerinsee and walked along the sandy margin of the lake, stepping over the thickly corded roots of the surrounding trees, and into the woods where the pine trees came down to meet their reflection, at once placid and menacing. We had a favourite place where a spit of land jutted from an elbow in the lake, clear water, mossy rocks beneath the surface, and all around us a Scandinavian solitude of firs. To melt Peter's monocle-frost I told him Thurgo stories. It was a subject on which Alec had been reticent, so I told Peter of old O'Malley; of Mother and her glass. And once, eyeing me, Peter remarked, "You know what there is beneath that mask of the cynic?" I glanced at him. *Tzü-niker:* it sounded like tourniquet, and I had to ask its meaning. "Yes," he nodded, "behind that defiant look of the young rebel. You know what I think? I think, a boy who was never his mother's favourite." I laughed; it was such an understatement. I thought of Mother with her broad wash-erwoman's face, as blandly alien to me as I was to her. (Mother on her knees scrubbing the consistory floors while the Celtic saints murmur their prayers in some tiny, adjoining church; Mother, climbing wearily to her feet, tiptoes into Brother Ignatius' cell where the gorgeous, decorated manuscript lies, work in progress, on the oaken desk; Mother gazes, and sighs.) How could someone like Peter ever hope to understand? I said: "I used to think I was a foundling. I mean, I used to imagine it. A daydream." Peter nodded solemnly. "So have many great men," he remarked. For a moment I thought he was referring to himself; then I saw he wasn't, and hesitated, grinning. "You think I'm going to be a great man?" Lord Thurgo of Galway; Grandfather's researches into our ancient Gaelic kin, I recalled, had once led him to style himself a Baron of the Holy Roman Empire until laughed to shame by his neighbours. My grin faded before Peter's earnestness. It seemed as though he was going to say something important, something momentous. Instead he said, in the same serious tone, "Do you know, for instance, why you are so timid with Maggie?" "I'm not timid with her," I said, but before I could add, "*you* are," he went on, "It is for the same reason you choose girls not of your class." "How do you mean?" "Your friend in London there." Who had told him about Ellie? Maggie no doubt. "So," said Peter. "Do you know why you are so timid?" I shook my head. "Because," he smiled politely now, "you are afraid of your mother's refusal." I wanted to say . . . I wanted to say, you've got it all wrong, Peter, my mother's not like your mother, she really isn't! But I was shy of him, afraid of being rude, where in England I'd teased and mocked him without thinking. I was a little in awe of Peter now, and it made him all the more attractive; far more so. The small neat blond head, a dusty grey-blond, unshowy, the long expressive limbs—there remained something charmingly girlish about him, not so much in his features, a boy's features, but in his animation, in his gawky, scarecrow gestures. These weren't effeminate, they were fantastical, they made you want not so much to caress as to be clasped by them, to be caught up in the whirling and master it.

Instead, as he warmed to me again, I listened to his discourses on the English character (pragmatic yet romantic), the Prussian character (the same, without a sense of humour), on German history, the rise of the German nation, and the glories of its literature. In a hushed caressing tone he recited Hölderlin, Brentano, Novalis; he also told me something of their lives, but all his respect was for their work; for their person they were thieves and lackeys visited by Poetry, and if fortunate (like Bach) commissioned by lordly von Lützows. An edge, a trace of mockery in the caressing tone kept them, and me, at a distance—thank goodness, since a German speaking his language reverently always sounded to me like a man reading a street sign as if it were Shakespeare. Above all Peter recited Goethe, brief poems which to my relief I found I could follow. The words were short and simple, and the language seemed to me lyrical by default, as though its agglutinating energies were in abeyance, sieved away, or neutered, a kind of pre-German. The books of philosophy Peter gave me I simply couldn't understand at all, even with a dictionary by my side. At the Bösendorfer in the castle drawing room he played Bach exercises, his face expressionless with piety; then with a lofty smile, broke into Händel (and how often I think of that today, that alternation). It was Peter I enjoyed in all this, rather than the objects of his reverence, so it was always a relief when Hölderlin gave way to doggerel—a brisk walk usually brought this on—and Peter mocked his own exalted delivery. Our favourite was a piece known to all German schoolboys, Peter said, as "The Shirt," a kind of Scots ballad in German, made more comical by references to Stirling Castle and King James as Schloss Stirling and König Jakob, and concerning the fate of Graf Archibald Douglas, a greybeard whose family had made war on König Jakob and who now begged his liege lord's forgiveness.

I soon knew it by heart, and heathland and pine woods resounded to the Douglas, or rather the *Doo-glass* cry: "Ich hab es getragen sieben Jahr, und ich kann es nicht tragen mehr!": I've borne it for seven long years, and I'll bear it—or "wear" it—no more . . . hence the schoolboy sub-title, although the "it" refers not to a shirt but the ignominy of carrying the Dooglass name. For all our mockery my heart went out to the hero as he knelt before his king, a pilgrim's homespun robe over his rusty *Harnisch*—armour, but harness seemed more appropriate to the gaunt old warhorse—and recalled the days when he had held the infant king in his arms, and later taught the boy to ride. It was highflown sentimental rubbish, *Edelkitsch*, but there were tears in my eyes as the king forgave him at last: "To horse! We ride to Linlithgow! You shall ride at my side once more, and there shall we gambol, and fish, and hunt, as we did in the days of yore . . ."

All of which may have contributed to my disappointment when the evening came of General Beck's much-awaited visit, and the warrior stepped from his chauffeured car. In place of the Dooglass in his rusty harness I saw, through the castle windows, a little man with slim shoulders and a small, sad, scholarly face. Peter and Agnetha were waiting for him on the steps. Mother and son embraced the stiff, unsmiling figure. Beside me in the drawing room Alec fidgeted, hastily finishing a cigarette.

"Bloody girl. Where is she?"

I glanced at him, surprised. Whatever the occasion Maggie was always the last to arrive. Alec studied me as though I were to blame.

"If she's up there sulking. . . ." He broke off. "She'd better bloody well put in an appearance. Or we'll all be frog-marched to the border, in the morning."

I watched him stub out his cigarette in a majolica dish, and couldn't fathom his anxiety. It was surely in his romantic interest for Maggie to fail the feast, as conspicuously as possible. No such luck. As we came into the hall and stood in readiness under the faded regimental flags, she made her entrance down the stairs. Alec and I turned, and stared, so startled by the figure she cut that we quite failed to acknowledge the appearance of General Beck and our hosts at the door. I doubt if they noticed; all eyes were on Maggie.

Her mother would have been proud of her expression, and her carriage. As at Blenheim she was a Laura Trimble heroine made flesh. A plain black dress; no jewellery; yet apart from Beck—unless he had been warned about her slovenliness—we were all taken aback. She had put her hair up. In a sense it only made her look like everybody else, and it didn't entirely work because her hair was so obstinately frizzy and continued to frizz at her temples. But it came as a surprise that she had ears, and a really rather good neck, an eloquent neck. She stepped towards us as though she and not Agnetha were the hostess here. Beck took her outstretched hand and bent low over it without kissing it. Then he straightened, put his other hand over hers, clasping it between both palms, and smiled into her eyes. It was a smile to melt the gods, though it took place only in the corner of a mouth which was normally turned quite sharply down, a mouth all skin and no lip, like a line drawn firmly across his face with a butterknife. For an instant it recalled the way Peter's faint but tender mouth vanished in his smile, and I felt a shudder at the similarity. They looked so like a family standing there in line, Agnetha, Beck, and Peter. Then Peter spoke, introductions began, Beck bowed again, Alec and I bowed, and Beck, still holding Maggie's hand in both of his, turned his priest's smile on her once more, confiding, shy, and wise, before releasing her. It had taken—how long? Less than a minute. But by the time Beck let go of Maggie's hand and glanced at us again, Alec and I were no longer suitors, we were escorts in the Queen of Sheba's retinue, delivery boys at the court of King Solomon. I saw it confirmed in Maggie's face as we trooped from the hall.

Or so I thought. Perhaps it didn't happen that way at all, perhaps there are no decisive moments except in retrospect; yet it seems to me that Beck was the magnet we had been waiting for, and we fell into line like metal filings under the spell of his fatherly presence. After all, that was just what was missing, from all our lives, and Beck behaved as though he knew it.

The weekend that followed was hectic, with further visitors and the ball the following night which finally gave me a free run at the drinks again. As a result I lost sight of the General. Everyone seemed to have a prior claim. But I had plenty of time to observe him that first evening, in the drawing room and over dinner in the Rittersaal, smiling at the portraits and the heir-

looms, in turn. As commander of the occupying forces I shall
defend these with my life, was how I read the look. Despite
being a regular guest and an intimate friend of the family, his
manner was benign rather than familiar. He greeted the servants
with austere politeness, as though they and he had never met
before. And Peter, though he said he'd known him since childhood, addressed him as Herr General.

Over dinner we spoke English, in deference to Alec, but in
the drawing room beforehand Beck had been seated near enough
to Maggie to open a conversation in German without slighting
her guard of honour. The questions were polite and predictable
enough, and her answers, well-rehearsed, created such an illusion of breeding that when Ludolf appeared and Peter rose to
offer her his arm and lead us into Abendbrot, Maggie took it as
her due without a glance. Until that evening we had shambled
off to dinner like strangers at a buffet. Ludolf's expression now
conveyed a lofty blessing. Beck followed with Agnetha on his
arm, and I avoided Alec's eyes as we formed up behind them.

The Herr General had some difficulty eating; his expression
of patient suffering, as I later discovered, was due to perpetual
toothache rather than what I took to be a warrior's memories.
But his gaze, when it addressed you, was as candid as a child's.
Peter was right: the man breathed nobility of spirit. There is no
more winning combination than evidence of culture in a man of
action, and Beck seemed to me the epitome of this, the complete
man, as he led the conversation from zoology through mediaeval
commerce to music and a tale of Bach at Brüel, breaking a
youthful journey to Hamburg by playing the organ at a little
country church. A passing farmer, hearing the thunderous notes,
was supposed to have declared, "if it's not the devil, then it
must be that fellow Bach!" Peter was wearing what I took to be
a sceptical face. A further anecdote described how Bach had
once auditioned for a post with an aristocrat of the period, who
commented favourably on Bach's playing but urged him to give
up composition. We chuckled dutifully.

"Did you know that in Leipzig they have pulled down Mendelssohn's statue?" Peter addressed no-one in particular. For a
moment, in the ensuing silence, I had an image of the statue,
not of Mendelssohn but of Beck, rigid with dignity, being lowered from the pedestal; how tempting to dethrone such an all-
knowing, all-forgiving butterknife smile.

Why? Maggie was asking. And with the old flippancy, "Well,
he's a rotten composer."

"He's a Jewish composer." Peter held her gaze. "You understand?"

Agnetha was quick to intervene: her guests wished to know about more amusing things than statues. Conversation promptly died, and we addressed our plates.

"What we really want to know, General," said Alec smiling his clubman's, come-on-old-chap smile, "is whether there's going to be another war or not. What's your opinion?" In answer Beck gave a bleaker smile and hesitated. Alec didn't wait for him. "You see, you all say you don't want a war, and *we* don't want a war, I promise you. I think we've made that pretty plain, too. Surely your Führer knows that? I mean, you've got your army back, you've got the Rhineland—is it?—and as far as your colonies are concerned . . . everyone seems to be agreed on *some* sort of restitution. I dare say we should have done it in the first place."

He sipped his drink. To my knowledge it was the longest political speech Alec had ever made. Maggie sat very still.

"If there is a war, Mr. Thurgo," Beck's toothache became acute, "it will not be of my making."

"That's just what I'm getting at. You've given your oath to the Führer, haven't you? So you're in his hands now." Alec fought back another smile. "At his beck and call, if you'll pardon the expression."

No-one cared to look at him except Agnetha, a puzzled watchdog who had missed the pun. Beck wiped his mouth with care.

"I think I can say, as a soldier, that my highest allegiance is to my country. As yours is, no doubt."

"Yes, I suppose it is. Is it?" Alec twiddled his glass. "I'm not at all sure it is. Take my father—he took the shilling, and as a loyal Tommy he went to France, got shot and killed." Glancing at Peter, "By your father, for all we know."

"No, not by him, Alec."

"You never know—it was what they called the last big push, in 1918, you probably remember that, General . . . the last big push," he repeated roundly, turning back to Peter, "whatever that was. Was your father there?"

"Alec, my father fought and died in Galicia, against the Russians."

"Did he?"

I had been longing to make a contribution, anything to stem the flow of Alec's performance; with the silliness born of impatience I opened my mouth to suggest that *I* had been the last big push of 1918. But Alec had fastened onto Peter.

"At least I take it from everything you've said recently that *you're* not going to follow in the family tradition."

"On the contrary. He is."

Beck's words seemed to surprise Peter as much as they did Alec, who found his voice first.

"Really? You mean he'd fight us? What do you think, Maggie?" Maggie avoided Alec's eyes. Instead Alec became aware of the basilisk at the other end of the table and suffered her stare for a moment, before weakening. "Of course, if it's to save us from Bolshevism, then we'll *all* join up . . . I think the *Frau Gräfin* and I see eye to eye on that."

"There is more than one sort of Bolshevism," said Peter.

"I don't quite follow."

"I think the Herr General understands what I mean."

We turned to Beck.

"Yes," said Beck, holding the pause. "I understand perfectly. But you are mistaken, Mr. Thurgo, if you think that your host is ashamed of this family tradition." And, glancing at the portraits above, "I am sure he will be loyal to it."

Peter studied his food. The silence held; Alec had shot his bolt, thank God; but it was clear that Beck now wanted a response. His gaze, after reviewing the ancestors and finding them in order, had descended on his godson. Peter looked up at him, a long look in which I imagined much to be at stake, altogether too much, and I saw my opportunity.

" 'Der ist in tiefster Seele treu . . .' "

It came out of me as a sort of nervous growl. But it earned me Beck's smile; he seemed to notice me for the first time, and his nod acknowledged the words from "The Shirt": "loyal at heart and ever true . . ."

It worked better than I could have hoped. Beck turned to Peter and continued, with me, " '. . . der die Heimat so liebt wie du!' ", "who loves his native land as you!" Agnetha joined in, and Peter eyed us, amused, as we finished the poem in chorus, Beck and Agnetha and I: " 'Zu Ross!' To horse! We ride to Linlithgow! You shall ride at my side once more, and there shall we gambol and fish and hunt . . ." As we did in the days of yore.

I was inspected with new interest. Ludolf even refilled my glass. And though we didn't exactly gambol, then or later, the mood had changed. We passed into a wordless after-dinner trance, a truce, as Peter doggedly played the piano for the General and the General appraised Maggie with fatherly glances. I felt a part of it at last. For a few hours in the drawing-room they were my family, I had won my spurs and now I could enjoy the setting to the full (playing over and over in memory my dinner-table coup). A soirée at Schloss Brüel, straight backs and Bach-faces. Beck and Agnetha, Maggie, Alec wreathed in cigarette smoke, and Peter at the piano, playing fugues.

We woke to fog. Throughout the morning figures loomed out of it while others, invisible, patrolled the gravel of the drive. This activity was partly explained by the preparations for the ball; but the day had already begun in mystery. Not a soul in sight when I came down for Morgenbrot, except for Ludolf, and he wouldn't be drawn. Where were the others? They had already breakfasted, *mein Herr*. And gone off somewhere, leaving me behind? Perhaps forgotten me altogether? So much for winning my spurs. But some part of me was pleased. The room was full of odd smells I could enjoy at my leisure, last night's food and last night's perfume were still in the air along with echoes of last night's conversation. This could be recalled now, free of illusions that I had saved the day.

Like Maggie's German answers it had all sounded well-rehearsed—at least until the General announced that Peter would be following in the family footsteps. (To become what? Soldier? Assassin? Or both, a second Kuno von Brüel? It was so hard to imagine Peter's windmilling arms on parade.) Or had Peter's surprise been part of a charade?

The bombs—the bombs were the key to it. If it was Beck to whom Alec and Peter were delivering them, then last night's behaviour, their show of falling out, would certainly have been an act. But for whose benefit? Ludolf, placing before me a bowl of warm, fatty stuff with pears and beans floating in it, looked as though he knew the answer to everything; perhaps he did. Ludolf. Ludolf the spy? Now we were getting somewhere. Ludolf watching at dinner, listening too: could it have been to fool him that Alec had made crusty English speeches and the General had pledged Peter's loyalty to the Fatherland? I studied Ludolf's creased, impassive face. Country house charades, for the butler's benefit? No, no, it was ridiculous, it was as silly as Maggie and Alec's own Ludolf-fantasies.

Maggie appeared at the door, dressed and groomed as if the intervening night had never happened, the same ensemble except for the return of the familiar bangles at her wrist. I realized I was a bit unkempt. "The dragon wants to see you." As she spoke she raised her eyes towards Agnetha's tower rooms, but there was nothing confiding in her manner. "When you've finished eating," she added graciously, and left.

Again I felt excluded and yet found a way to savour it. The stage was set, my entrance had been called; I longed to work out what was going on but I didn't want to sacrifice my vantage point, or any of the roles I could invent for us. A multitude of roles, as many as I wished. How did Kuno put it? Napoleon, brooding alone there in that little German theatre . . . Napoleon must not begin to speak, for when the play begins Kuno is lost. This I was sure I understood, this sense of a minefield still intact, of a truth that lay in things infolded and not in events too vivid—Peter's phrase—to be entirely real; of possibilities unfolding. We had a Mithridates now, in Beck; an imperious Monime (was Monime imperious? She was now, with her hair up); and in love with her, various sons, princes noble or corrupt, loyal to the Fatherland or secretly allied to Rome. As yet no-one knew (which was to say I didn't know) which son was which. The bombs had yet to go off.

Dressed as I was, no tie, I knocked at Agnetha's door. I had to stoop when she opened it, all smiles, and led me by the hand towards a brightly-coloured sofa. "Sit by me." I did; the sofa was harder than it looked, and taut as a trampoline. Her smile never wavered as I steadied my bouncing, one hand on the upholstery. "This morning I want you to tell me a little more about yourself," she said as though it were a special treat, indeed as though it were a renewed invitation, thought I couldn't remember telling her anything about myself. Perhaps Peter had. "Begin with the beginning, we have plenty of time." When it moved, her face divided into woodcut sections as though it had been put together like a speaking doll's, in blocks: the smooth cheeks, brow, and chin became separate continents drawn to and fro by tendons. I was mesmerized by the inflexibility of each solid, smiling part.

Gradually, as I stumbled through my story—every avenue was met with eager nods—I realized that her questions were being angled towards my acquaintance with Maggie, and I understood why I was there. When had I first met Maggie? Ah, so recently! Had I visited her home? Had I formed an impression of her parents? Indeed I had. This was much easier. I made mad Trimble sound like a distinguished clergyman, "well known," I said, "in the south of England"—that much was almost certainly true—and stressed Laura Trimble's childhood association with Maharajahs. Agnetha's impenetrable smile threatened to snap its strings. But the disappointment in her eyes . . . no, it wasn't disappointment, it was dullness, a kind of disappointment with herself rather than with me or Maggie, misled me at first. She was now seriously considering the girl as a daughter-in-law, for the first time it seemed. She was going through the motions. I saw her glance down, tired of smiling, and pretend to disentangle an eyelash. That was it: yes, that was what disappointed her, that the motions were so hollow. No matter who or what Maggie was, no matter how encouraging my answers, the effort she was making had brought home to Agnetha what she'd been putting off, I imagined, for as long as she'd dared: that she couldn't bring herself to look ahead. And suddenly I warmed to her. Her face, with its mechanical formations, allowed no half-truths, it smiled, or frowned, or stared. The pale blue eyes were deadly clear, it was only their colour that to a casual glance looked overcast, and I read there something her features would not express—being moulded from infancy into permanent Scandinavian shock; something they could not express, a sense of irony.

Released, I wandered through the empty downstairs rooms, listening enviously to the distant bustle in the kitchens. I couldn't find a soul. I went to the piano and played "Chopsticks" in protest, hoping to raise someone. I played "Chopsticks" for half an hour, then with my brain wadded with echoes I went back into the hall, where I found Alec pulling on his greatcoat. He looked flustered.

"Morning!" I watched him pat his brilliantined head.

Turning, he studied me for a moment, as if I might be drunk; I did feel a little groggy from the clanging chords.

"Flies," he said, lifting his chin to fasten the collar of his coat.

By the time I realized what he meant, Alec was out of the door and gone, but he was right all the same—white shirt was visible between my flies and I hastily reached for the top button, wondering how long it had been undone. Perhaps there was a simpler explanation for Agnetha's Scandinavian shock; she'd never previously interviewed a young man with his flies open. Slightly open; really only an inch or so. I put it out of my mind and fetched my coat, pretending it had never happened. What did it matter anyway? I wasn't a suitor here, I was nothing to do with this absurd German household!

As I emerged into the freezing mist I could see Alec disappearing at a trot towards the gatehouse. Then I could only hear him, and I was alone, no longer enjoying it. I felt cheesed off and wanted to go home to Ellie; perhaps it would accelerate things, I decided, if I disgraced myself at the ball that evening. I could count on unlimited Branntwein. And a change of food at last—during the afternoon I watched trays of curious sweets enter the house, which normally wouldn't have caught my attention; but they were little marzipan animals, delicately coloured and with a faint sickly smell that drew me like a wasp to marmalade, or more exactly, given their smell, like maggots to a corpse. It was the smell of them I liked, more than the taste, but since I couldn't very well loiter round the crowded food table sniffing the sweets, I spent the evening eating to inhale the rancid perfume that came off the little things and clung to my hands. Peter and Maggie danced, and I ignored them; they weren't getting me onto the dance floor. As guest of honour, Beck was only intermittently visible behind taller men, lanky Friesian officer-types; when I caught sight of him, the swallow-tailed collar of Beck's dress uniform seemed to be drooping towards his medals, like his mouth, with the same finicky sorrow. Across the room, brother Alec had been penned into a corner by a large Mecklenburger matron in yellow organdie—I was sure she smelt just like my marzipan animals, but I didn't care to confirm this—whom I heard saying loudly, "But what can you do, when a King is in love?" Alec nodded gravely. All was well. I took up a position behind the food table where the waiters stood idly by, like me watching the dancing, and hoped that I might be mistaken for one of them and left to guzzle my marzipan animals in peace.

The thrill of spying and speculation had gone utterly flat, despite a last flicker of excitement in the park that morning. Too peeved to run after Alec, I'd lost him, though I did peer in at the windows of the gatehouse, which loomed out of the greyness like a ship at anchor. Then, returning down the drive, I caught a glimpse of someone running by the fence beneath the trees. It was Alec. Beyond him were the paddocks; beyond them, the barns. By now I was cold, I wanted to run, and set off in pursuit across the grass, crouching, noiseless on the turf. Heading for some rendez-vous, Alec held one arm bent stiffly across his belly as he ran, as though to lend some dignity to his haste. I thought he looked rather German, and ridiculous. At that moment a voice pulled me up short. *"Wer reitet so spät durch*

Nacht und Nebel?!'' Peter was standing watching me from the drive, his voice carrying as clearly to me as if across water. "Come," he said, "I have something for you." I had no choice, as he started firmly towards the house.

The something proved to be his father's splendid old *Frack*, my get-up for the evening, a little tight around the shoulders but to my surprise—the portrait in the Rittersaal had Peter's short trunk—long enough in the leg, as I measured the trousers against my own. Peter stepped back to study me, amused. "This will be strange for my mother, to see the *Frack* live again, on a young Englishman."

His words were more prophetic than he knew, since it was all over Count Egon's ancient dress suit that I threw up that night, outside the front door.

At this point all was no longer well; but at least no-one could see me there, crouching in the shadows at the foot of the balustraded steps, and it was far too cold for any couple to seek privacy outdoors. I bent over to take better aim, and heard my name being called. I couldn't answer. My heaving stomach spoke for me.

"Richard?" I heard Maggie's shoes on the flagstones above me, descending the steps. "Oh, look at you." And then rather surprisingly, "Poor you. Ludolf said you were looking green." I could feel the wet trousers beginning to freeze. One more heave and I'd feel better. "He's really a dear after all," Maggie was saying, "he came to tell me you'd gone outside." She held my shoulders as I bent over again. She was being much kinder to me, now that the tables were turned, than I'd been to her when she went green in the stables after Waltraut's prolapse.

But why not, she was always at her best when tending the wounded, as now, taking my handkerchief from me and mopping my chin.

"Ludwig's dancing with Agnetha, do come and see. Everyone's made space for them, they've got the dance floor to themselves."

Ludwig? Impossible to think of General Beck as Ludwig. And now Maggie was chattering on about how nice everyone was, so friendly, not standoffishness at all. The icy air was bringing such relief I didn't care that I was shivering or that she was talking twaddle. Eyes shining, she took my hands. "You go back," I said. "Go on." She didn't move. *Reizendes Geschöpf,* Beck had murmured, watching her as we went in to lunch: enchanting creature. Was she? I still thought she had the look of someone on the cusp (as she had that evening in the foyer of the Coliseum, at first sight) between, as it might be, aspiring ballet dancer and fallen woman; a look that took me back five times to see "Waterloo Bridge" in Amersham. Fog, and the bridge at night, and a voice, "Chilly tonight, care for a stroll, miss?" Vivien Leigh glancing up at the invisible customer.

"If he asks me tonight, I'm going to say yes."

"Who? Ludwig, or Peter?" I knew the malice was uncalled for.

"Do come in and change. Look at the state of you."

"In a moment."

"Richard, *please*."

I shook my head, withdrew my hands and shoved them in my pockets. The misty house loomed like an iceberg. Now she was turning to climb back up the steps.

"Maggie, have you got the faintest idea what you might be letting yourself in for?"

"Yes." Her glance read: I know more than you do. "I'm marrying a lawyer."

I'm a lawyer, I wanted to say. But I didn't feel like one, at that moment.

It was time to follow her in. I did, slowly, praying there would be no-one in the hall to see me making a dash for the stairs in my bedraggled state. But my luck had run out. A silver-haired figure stood sternly waiting, just inside the front door.

"Nachtmütze," it said, and beckoned.

Nachtmütze . . . I followed Ludolf submissively towards the kitchen quarters; a nightcap was the last thing I wanted, but this turned out to be the butler's idea of a joke, since what he brought me were bitters, "*Magenbitter,* good for you." He sat me down, pointed at me to remove my trousers, and I was suddenly too tired to argue or do anything except sit and sip my bitters by the fire, in my underwear, while the guests danced on upstairs. I could hear them, picture them, revolving marzipan animals in organdie and lace. I think Ludolf knew how much happier I was there in the kitchen, even with my trousers off and servants coming to and fro pretending not to notice me. One girl with a tussock of thick blonde hair and eyes set wide in a bullcalf head, she couldn't have been more than fifteen, stood and stared at me till Ludolf moved her on. It was warm, lovely and warm, Ludolf had taken care of my soiled *Frack*, there was bustle and talk and sounds of crockery. And the bullcalf was staring at me again.

I woke to a dark, gleaming armoury, the firelight low, the silverware all put away now. Ludolf lay in a blackened leather armchair, opposite me, asleep. Between us my dress suit was steaming. I took it off the clothes-horse, pulled my trousers on, and tiptoed out.

Up, past the paintings and the statues, the ghostly marble torsoes in their alcoves, hiding their Mussolini-pated buttocks, Roman, then slender Greek, then Roman, inviting mischief—slip the dinner jacket round the armless shoulders, belt the trousers to a Roman waist. Or a slimmer Greek one, leaving the flies open around the little shrunken genitals? No, tiptoe on. Softly opening my bedroom door, switching the light on, and staring: a jacket lying neatly folded on a chair, and shoes beneath it. I had shoes and jacket in my hand. I was in the wrong room.

I was in the right room. Peter lifted his head and hauled himself upright on my bed, in shirt and trousers. "Na, Junge," he tried to say, swinging his feet to the floor, without looking at me; the words came out indistinctly. I watched him struggling to clear his head, rubbing his face. The duelling scar I'd looked for in vain in German faces had appeared at last at one temple, though it was only a pillow-crease, a mockery scar. "Where have you been all this time? We thought you had gone to bed."

"I'm going to bed now, I think." I wasn't in the mood for German chats. Walking over to him I dropped the warm, heavy jacket on the quilt, beside the pillow. "Thank you very much for the clothes, though."

"Richard, I have a bone to pick with you."

"Can't it wait?"

"I am very angry with you." But he didn't sound it, he was trying to remember how it felt. "You told Maggie about the bombs," and, staring up at me now, "it was our secret, I understood." He saw me hesitate, and added sharply, "No, boy, Alec did not tell her. And I asked you not to tell her, it was our secret. I should really give you a good thrashing."

"Look," I said, "Why don't we all just go home and leave you to your ruddy bombs?"

Peter considered this sleepily; he seemed to notice that I was standing there in vest and trousers.

"Is there something the matter with your clothes?"

"No."

"Where did you disappear to in the middle of the evening?"

"I had a drink with Ludolf."

Perhaps I was imagining it, but he seemed more alert.

"*Why* did you tell Maggie, please?"

"Don't you think she ought to know what's going on?"

"Yes, damn you, but from me and in my good time." *Dem* you. Peter turned away and stared around the room, one arm propped stiffly on his knee. Then he stood up, as if making up his mind. "She has done me the honour of consenting to be my wife."

"Congratulations," I said. "Heil Hitler."

Things were deteriorating fast, they were on a drunken sleepy slide, and for a moment I thought he was going to swing at me; hoped he would. But he controlled himself and went on as if I hadn't spoken.

"However, my friend, she thinks it proper to make certain conditions."

"Oh?"

Peter nodded solemnly. "You see, she has talked to God about the bombs."

"She's done what?"

"Talked to Beck. *Der liebe Gott.*" There was a caustic tone I had not heard him use about the General. "They are to be destroyed, the bombs, these . . . ruddy bombs as you call them." He gave a laugh.

"Why?" I was wide awake now. "I mean, I imagined he knew all about them. Or did he?" Still no answer, only Peter's reproachful gaze. Silence. "Can't you at least tell me what they were for?"

"Don't play the child. I have explained, they were requested by friends in the Abwehr, our intelligence service."

"Then why must they be destroyed?"

"Let it go, Richard."

He walked past me to the chair, made to pick up his jacket and then seemed to change his mind.

"I hope you are just a little bit ashamed."

"I don't see why. Just because Maggie's in the know . . . why must you do whatever she says?" I could feel contempt rising in me.

"It is not because she says it, Richard. Now that Beck knows, there is nothing to be done. You understand?"

I shook my head. "You're not one of his men, you don't have to take orders from him." But Peter just looked at me pityingly. "Not yet, anyway. Are you really going to join up because he tells you to?"

Peter nodded.

"Does Maggie know that too? She thinks she's marrying a lawyer."

"She is. In fact it is the only way she can marry a lawyer. You see, I will explain to you: I have made my examinations but I cannot pass until the authorities are satisfied with my political qualifications. It is the same for all of us, we do not have to join the Nazi party, but all the same colleagues are questioned, has so-and-so been heard to make provocative remarks, is so-and-so reliable? As you can imagine, I have made provocative remarks. And I will not join the party to prove that I am reliable. But . . ." he was smiling now, lopsidedly, "there is a law, passed under the Weimar government, that no member of the armed forces may join a political party. That law is still good. You see? So I shall join up," Peter said smiling, lipless, "then they cannot say, why is this one not a member of the party . . . and when they have passed me through my examinations I shall resign my commission and practise law. It is Beck's idea."

Something about his face nagged at my mind.

"Have you understood what I am saying?"

The smiling mouth—it brought back a picture: Beck's smile, beneath the regimental flags in the hallway; Beck, Agnetha, Peter, in the entrance hall.

"Is he your father?"

"What?"

We gazed at each other; Peter looked genuinely astounded.

"My *father*? Beck? That's my father, there," he pointed at the crumpled *Frack*, where I'd dropped it on the bed.

"Are you sure?"

Laughing, "Quite sure, dear boy. My mother did not even meet Ludwig Beck until after I was already in the world. Beck came here for the first time when I was four years old."

"You said he and your father were comrades in arms."

"They were. That's why he came here, to meet my father's family." And, grinning at me, "I think you are really a funny boy, you are obsessed with this business, because you want a great man for your father. Remember what you told me."

"It's got nothing to do with that. It was just . . . seeing the three of you together."

"You insult my mother," he was still smiling, "never mind *den lieben Gott*."

"Do I? He's human, surely."

"No, Beck is not human."

The smile had gone.

"However . . ." Peter continued at last, "he has his honour and I have mine. I hoped I would never have to choose between them. But now I must choose." He was staring at me accusingly again; we were back with the bombs. "Do you understand that, at least? I must sacrifice *my* honour, if I want Maggie."

For some reason this maddened me, it was highflown nonsense, I didn't believe him, it was stupid; it made me despise him.

I said: "I think you wanted me to tell her."

"No, I took you for my friend." He paused. "But instead you are a big clever donkey who will kick when anyone comes near."

"I'll tell you what I think, Peter. I think you wanted me to know, I think you wanted me to tell Maggie about the bombs. I think you wanted an excuse to ditch them, because you're a coward."

This time he did strike out at me. It was meant to be a cuff more than a slap, the way a German count might cuff a cheeky valet, but as I turned my head it caught me behind the ear, against the bone, and it was Peter who grunted with pain. Enraged, I pulled him by the shirtfront, trying to throw him towards the door, out of my room.

He caught my shoulders, pushed and wrestled, pinching, it was like fighting a child, his face was growing pink and tearful. It was twisted; snarling mouth showing little teeth. As I shoved him back he aimed another blow, and when I lunged for his arm he punched me in the belly with all his might. For a moment other fights, other moments of being winded came back so clearly I didn't know whom I was grappling with. I reached for his face without looking, my hand found it, and I grabbed and gouged and pulled him down towards the bed where I could catch my breath. I held his face against the eiderdown, against his father's steaming, faintly stinking jacket, on top of the quilt, and used my weight to pinion him, while I struggled to breathe. Then I could hear a noise above the panting, and felt Peter go limp as he began to cry. Either that or he was suffocating. The side of his head was flushed and red, I didn't want to see his face. But lying on top of him I could feel how excited I was, and how vengeful. He made no move to stop me as I reached under him for his trouser buttons, pulled his trousers and pants down to his thighs, wrenched open my own flies—at last!—with both hands, and fell on his slim body like Roman upon Greek.

* * *

We flew home two days later, Alec and I. Business was Alec's excuse, and I was more than ready to leave.

It was a tongue-tied journey. Sheer noise, in the aeroplane, prevented lengthy conversation and Alec was in no mood for small talk. He sat stiffly behind a copy of the *Times* he'd bought at Amsterdam airport—his expression on finding it indicated that we were back in civilisation. In point of fact we could have flown direct from Hamburg to Croydon with Lufthansa, but Alec insisted that we fly British even though this took us on a tour of the Low Countries. Ah *ha*, I thought, scenting a vengeful hatred of all things German; but no, it was just that the German airline didn't allow smoking.

He had lost fair and square, he was Jonathan Mansel, and above such pettiness. Wasn't he? I stole guilty glances at him. I had urged Peter to bring Maggie to Brüel, I had sided with the Hun, and the Hun had won. Though I wasn't sure whether Alec knew I'd sided with the Hun.

And *had* the Hun won? There had been no mention of a wedding date, before we'd left; no announcement of their engagement—either it was Maggie and Peter's secret, or Maggie had imposed some further conditions Peter hadn't told me about. Maggie was staying on: that was the official line, as Alec and I received it.

As for what had happened between Peter and myself that night, I still hadn't worked out the consequences of it, if there were any, the internal, emotional consequences, that is—since there were no external consequences at all. It was quite bizarre. I had fallen asleep, fairly drunk and thoroughly sleepy, against Peter's body; which was gone when I woke, as were his father's clothes, proof at least that I hadn't dreamed the whole incident. We *had* both been drunk, and the way Peter behaved in the morning implied, without actually saying as much, that whatever rowdiness had occurred was now lost in the fumes of Branntwein past and would not be mentioned.

This suited me. It had been an odd sort of encounter, gratification I was going to call it, and gratification was what it was, full-bloodedly so, harking back to schooldays and, strangely, to Ellie, as though there was something here—I knew it really, but was forming an idea of it for the first time—that was neither hetero- nor homosexual but simply sexual, at least until a romantic attachment called for one or other prefix. Odd to realize that heterosexual and homosexual were romantic categories, not natural ones; and that it was surprisingly easy (perhaps all it needed was Branntwein) to locate that wellspring of attraction where another body's physical polarity mattered less than the metaphysical qualities which, as always, drew one to it; where that body could be enjoyed as a matter of circumstance, man, boy, girl, or goat.

And yet all kinds of strange resonances complicated and shrouded the event. I couldn't escape the feeling that I had anticipated Peter's wedding night in some distasteful way (distasteful for him, not me); or at least the stag party preceding it, but with some defloration involved . . . no, I wanted none of the responsibility for that, nor to be the spirit of his humiliation by the combined forces of Ludwig Beck and Maggie and his mother, in the matter of the bombs. If he had chosen to be buggered by his destiny in the shape of Richard Thurgo, let that be his cross, it wasn't mine.

Years later, having read and reflected on the German resistance to Hitler both before and during the war, and knowing that at least forty assassination attempts were mounted by a variety of groups, and individuals acting alone—to speak only of the cases that have come to light and were serious enough to term a plot—I saw Peter's abortive conspiracy in a different light. He never admitted to me that the bombs were intended for the Führer, but in view of Peter's later involvement in the plot led by Count von Stauffenberg, I have no doubt about it. I'm also pretty sure the bombs were to be delivered to a group of Luftwaffe officers around Cäsar von Hofacker, a relative of Peter's and a man who proved his own bravery in that July of 1944. As did Peter: he was no coward, despite my foolish words. But Göring's Luftwaffe, though an admirable cover for a plot—it was thoroughly loyal, unlike the Army's General Staff headed by Beck—was an unlikely base for a coup d'état. In 1937 and '38 there was no shortage of German revolutionaries. Their problem was that in most cases they were acting independently and even within the better organized factions there were cells completely at odds with each other. Beck himself was part of one of these muddled pre-war conspiracies, though at the time when Alec and I met him he was still fighting desperately to avoid a confrontation. "Mutiny and revolution," he had stated, "are words not to be found in a German officer's dictionary." Ludwig Beck was one of those intriguing men, a soldier whose devotion to peace is no mere slogan; he loathed war, and it was Hitler's implacable desire for war (one which Beck was sure Germany would lose and from which Europe would never recover), which led Beck, in the end, to commit himself to mutiny. It was not the *Führerprinzip*, the principle of an all-powerful leader, that provoked his disloyalty, any more than it did for Claus von Stauffenberg, and there were many National Socialist tenets which both men found excellent, concepts that had roused a nation to selfless labour and resurrected its pride. Here Peter was, I like to think, in a minority. It was the *Führerprinzip* that he hated above all things. And his detestation of tyranny, admirable in itself—and intense as it can only be in someone who, like his ancestor Kuno in Peter's own rendering of the story, is deeply drawn to power, half in love with the Napoleonic dream; I can still see Peter's helpless, childish glee when the bomb exploded in his pasture—had become a hostility to leadership of any kind. In Peter I imagine it turning by degrees, as all anarchist impulses must, into a fear of action, until the banked and thwarted energy of life lashes out like a cornered animal, and anarchy becomes the thing it hates, violence pitted against violence. If so I was surely right to think Peter was relieved that I had betrayed his secret and, via Maggie and Beck, defused the plot and his role in it. Perhaps I was even right to think he intended it that way, or hoped for that result. I simply didn't know how brave a man he was, for all that; not then, not till many years later.

On the morning of my departure he took me to our favourite spot, the spit of land by the Schweriner See. There he flung the first of the two remaining bombs far out into the lake, his long arm lending the metallic object a great discus loop into far, deep water. It was then, as he turned to me for the second bomb, which I was holding, that the idea came to me of burying it instead; really I just hated to see it wasted, drowned, I think. What other reason? Premonition is what Auntie—Ellie's mentor—would say, if she's alive and practising in Poland Street: everyone's psychic, dear.

We dug a pit in dry, compacted, sandy soil between pine roots pointing out along the sandbank to a reciprocating spit of land on the other side of the lake, and planted the bomb with a care that had less to do with what was inside it than the impulse that— yes, surely—had made me suggest it, and the echo in Peter that had made him agree. It was our own bond that we were burying like a deadly treasure chest on this sandy beach, rather than sink it like a corpse at sea, or drown it like a rat. Now it could rise again, another day. As we dug out the sand together, on our knees, I looked at Peter's small, peaky face, slightly puffy this morning, eyes reddened, and I understood one part of the night before that had been hidden from me. That sense of anticipating Peter's wedding night—of course! Absurdly, given Maggie's absence; except that she wasn't absent. It was her, not Peter, that I was deflowering. I realized this for one reason only. He had lost all attractiveness for me, and at the same moment, as it were, regained all the respect he had lost in my eyes. I could begin to see the man's dilemma. He'd consented to involve himself in a tainted drama whose noblest gestures, in his view, were hollow; and through my casual act of betrayal that decision, costly enough already in terms of his own principles, had been revalued to include his love in its price. He had decided not to pay that price, or at least not to pay it now; and I honoured him for it. I saw that my part in this had been contemptible. There was no way round it, I had buggered my host metaphorically before I did so literally. But I knew quite well that my career as a tunnel rat was barely beginning. It was too early for regrets, and I didn't want to abort an intriguing future digging pits and planting bombs.

It was spring, balmy, sunny, in London, positively tropical compared to the mists of Mecklenburg; strange to fly south to England, yet we did, south to London in its yellow and purple crocus glory. Even Alec smiled at the sight, and he turned in the taxi to include me in his smile, as if to reassure me that his remoteness during the journey hadn't been meant as a punishment. I didn't really think it had; and it would have been wasted on me. I took him so much for granted, as if he was less a brother than an uncle to be adored and mocked and still hero-worshipped, an icon or perhaps a totem pole. Yes, a totem pole, or a bowsprit figurehead—it was both his posture and his skin that suggested this. Sometimes it brought to mind the lifesized statue of a pipe-smoking Red Indian I'd seen in one of the Mayfair tobacconists Alec frequented, and where I'd been in his company. I didn't smoke, it seemed in those days to be "putting on airs," an affectation of gentlemanliness which was the opposite of the role I was cultivating. Seeing Alec standing at the glass counter sniffing cigars, right next to the shiny red mahogany Chief who looked, as Alec sometimes did, positively cured in tobacco smoke like an exotic ham, I had felt a pang of love for him—he'd no idea how funny he looked next to the Indian—and for the very woodenness of his personality. Wooden not (you have to understand this) in the sense that he seemed inflexible or dull, no, he was sly and charming, but it was the surface of Alec, his skin, that struck you about him. It was so healthy and so firm, like teak sometimes, you wanted to stretch out and touch it as if it was polished wainscoting; it wouldn't give. He was fully-formed and finished, all his mannerisms bedded in, he was a member of the adult race and he was mine, my brother Alec. How I cherished him, just as he was! And, in fact, though time and events have closed the gap between us (those fourteen years which separated our childhoods by far more than the Irish Sea had done), I suppose I still think of him as a very large mechanical toy, a kind of guardian robot.

"Toodle-oo," said Alec as he dropped me off at Victoria, where my rooms overlooked the station. Oh but there was so much I needed to ask him, to know from him, about his role in the bomb business, about why Maggie was staying in Germany, about what he felt, what he was going to do. He'd only have put me off with vague platitudes as he had so often before. Wait and see, old cock, never you mind, there's a good chap, there's a good Rat. I clambered reluctantly out of the cab. Something of my frustration must have showed in my face as I glanced back in at Alec's perfectly composed figure, not a hair, not a thread out of place. "Pecker up," he said kindly, "she'll be back in a week, you'll see." But he was wrong.

Salmon on Tort, Chitty on Equity, Stable on Bankruptcy, Underwood on . . . what was Underwood on? I didn't think I'd ever forget those names. The White Book on Court Procedure; there's another. Visits to Gibson and Weldon, just off Chancery Lane. I can remember the smell of it, pure sweat and cleaning fluid. They were a firm—still are, for all I know—of law tutors. "Today we're going to take the three 'B's," I can remember the bearded one saying, "Buggery, Burglary, and Bankruptcy." I listened with particular interest. You could still be executed for buggery in those days.

And the wretched Garnham—the pike-headed man who'd interviewed me when I got taken on as a clerk, he was the senior partner and clearly felt he ought to keep on eye on me on the Colonel's behalf—would walk me to the courts jawing about intestacy, and Chancery procedure, and the Settled ruddy Land Act of 1926. I learnt several of Marshall Hall's summings-up word for word, though this did me little good. Occasionally I went with Pike-jaw to a conference with some barrister in Chambers—this was meant to be an honour and a privilege but the cases were mostly so dull I had to bite my lip to stay awake.

When the cases came to trial they were just as dull, and I got myself a bad reputation for wandering off to listen to criminal proceedings in neighbouring courts. It wasn't so much that I wanted to be enthralled by the law, I just wanted to forget about Schloss Brüel, the "Slosh" as Ellie called it. She was always asking for stories of the Slosh, and unwittingly bringing Maggie back into my mind. Where before I'd never thought about Germany, now every hoarding, every conversation overheard in public seemed to be about the "Nazzies." A shop in Holborn which stocked German newspapers drew my attention like a magnet every time I passed. In the end I succumbed and bought a daily copy, hoping to cause a small stir at the Old Bailey— Crown Retained Nazi Solicitor, Claims Accused—by reading it in open court, behind learned counsel's back. Then Ellie took on a Jewish refugee, a bespectacled child called Minna, as her maid. Together, to Ellie's patient amusement, we sang "You Are My Heart's Delight" in the original German, and I had a daily excuse to speak the language I loved.

And yes: I'd better say something about dear beloved Ellie. I'm so used to keeping her a secret from everyone else in my life, that it's hard to break the habit. And I still feel an odd need to protect her (absurd thought; as well buy an extra padlock for the Tower of London), after thirty years. She was 24 when I met her, my iron butterfly, and blonde—though her hair was rather stiff and wiry and not the stuff grown by the blondes of imagination. She was blonde then, I should say, but around this time she became an auburn colour, tending to magenta on days when in her short-sightedness (like Grandfather's, and with similar effects) she overdid the dye. She had big features, a big nose in particular, big breasts, and emitted a great deal of nasty perfume which I could never get her to change for the more expensive stuff I gave her. She never felt she could splash on the posh stuff—she knew it at a sniff, it was no good my pretending it was cheap—with the same abandon. I found her pretty, intensely pretty, though she could look startlingly ugly, and knew it. Ellie had dropped kissing from her repertoire because, she said, her nose got in the way. Her repertoire wasn't especially extensive but it survived without kissing.

She entertained at number 5, Leda Buildings, a pleasantly horrid block of flats a few steps from Cambridge Circus, in upper Shaftesbury Avenue, and also lived there, with her cat François. This was a female cat, and although I always addressed the animal as Françoise, Ellie obstinately clung to her original habit—in this as in everything. She loved me, she was fascinated by my life, my ways, my habits, my dreams, my talk, but she would never change one iota of her life to make it seem more appropriate to what she loved of mine. In Leda Buildings she also employed the "maid" who came during working hours and was paid a shilling, a little more if trade was brisk—half a crown perhaps, which for girls like Minna made the difference, as Minna told me herself, between one meal a day and two. You might not think a maid was a prerequisite for a 24-year-old dancing instructress, as Ellie termed herself (I believe she had actually taught various dances, though the dance hall where I first met her offered follow-up courses in more than foxtrot or jitterbug), but Minna was useful if Ellie was entertaining when a further guest arrived. Besides, it raised the tone.

One of her earlier guests had presented her with a samovar, and from this hideous urn we drank "Russian", which was Ellie's way of describing tea without milk in it. Milk was too expensive, she said, so we drank "Russian" instead. A lot of her regulars were, to my discomfiture, young gentlemen from the universities. Term-time or not, they seemed to find their way to Leda Buildings like ravenous swans direct from Ox or Cam, and I resented their casual ardour—I imagined them tremendously potent but barely pausing to discard their blazers—far more than any samovar-toting seaman.

Tea was my hour. I often took Ellie out in the evenings, but I was always there at tea. Auntie was often there too, Ellie's elderly lady-friend and tutor in clairvoyance, who wore a head-scarf with what looked suspiciously like curtain rings sewn into its fringe. But she like Minna knew when to make herself scarce, as the samovar emptied. I never did discover what Auntie's relationship to Ellie was, it could indeed have been auntie, or no relation at all; or, as I suspected, that of a former foster mother. One, perhaps, of many, since although I could never prise childhood memories out of Ellie, there was something about her that cried orphan. It was less a pleading quality (I couldn't imagine Ellie pleading) than a battery of defensive walls which made me think . . . well, which made me think of Auntie again. To explain: Auntie sported an accent so dense and exotic—it was only raw Geordie, but quite foreign to me—that it lent something to her professional manner, if not authenticity then at least an air of mystery and incomprehensibility. She had been born and bred in Alnwick, "under Percy walls" as she liked to say with relish, and it was only when I saw her fortune-telling booth in Poland

Street, which was full of postcards showing Alnwick Castle, the Percy walls themselves, that I grasped that her past had nothing to do with a Mr. Percy Walls.

Ellie's protective armour was no less formidable than Alnwick's Percy walls, but she was no battle-axe, she was rather shy, nervous even, long after we knew each other too well to maintain disguises. When we'd been together for a year or so she gave up trying to hide her short-sightedness and wore her glasses when we were alone, clumsy things which matched her big nose and, as she knew, destroyed every vestige of her prettiness. But—even alone with me—she couldn't settle to her own appearance, and her anxiety made the encounter between Ellie's glasses and her perpetual feather boa into a duel to the death between inanimate objects. This would begin with Ellie nervously winding the boa strands round and round one arm of the spectacles she'd taken off out of vanity or to peer at something near, and always ended the same way, with Ellie putting her glasses back on her nose, only to find the boa now rising with the glasses to drape her face for a moment before dragging the glasses back off her nose again into her lap. Clumsy as I was myself, disentangling Ellie's boa and spectacle frames was my job: she couldn't see to do it. Ellie in dark glasses was even more of a disaster. She had discovered that film stars used them to hide hangovers and would emerge after a hard night wearing large and lurid ones. The air of dignified suffering they lent her was worth more to Ellie than breakfast, just as well since she had to lean so close to her teacup, to see it at all, that the steam immediately misted the lenses and left her sitting there blind as a bat, unable to eat or drink.

I was fascinated by her attitude to sex, to our hours in bed where it seemed to me that—of all things—her nervousness persisted. Perhaps what seemed to me to be an awkward reserve, but one which never ceased to excite me, was simply professional indifference. Yet it was no longer a cash transaction between us, and I paid in other ways, in nights out, and treats and clothes and visits to the seaside. It was on one of these, at Worthing, that we saw a Punch and Judy show in progress. Ellie clapped her hand to her mouth and began to rock with East End laughter. For there in front of us in the little booth were our facsimiles: Mr. Punch with his monstrous nose, who really did look just like me (and traditionally owned a monstrous organ, as I liked to think I did, to match his nose), and Mrs. Punch who in this case had a nose to match her husband's and Ellie's own. It was the two puppets doing a mock kiss, swaying around each other like muscle-bound boxers looking for an opening, which had caught Ellie's eye and reminded her all too perfectly of our own attempts. I was "Punch" from then on. But we never fought like our originals. You couldn't fight with Ellie, she was simply too remote under the good-time gaiety, and she sulked if there was something that displeased her. She wouldn't fight. It was undignified. What I wanted to know was where she went when she sulked, where she went when we fucked (pointless to say made love, although I often can't help feeling that Ellie is the lasting love of my life), where she was when we did it. Was she secretly there enjoying it, amused by it, puzzled by it? Or was she doing the shopping, pricing the biscuits and the tea? Whatever it hid—perhaps nothing at all, a dreamy nullity—this elusiveness never lost its fascination for me, it gave me an Ellie-mood to conjure up, more powerful than an Ellie face or an Ellie posture, as I sat in my own poky rooms over baked beans on toast and Salmon on Tort. With a little *Nachtmütze* to help them down.

And there was the Slosh back again in my head, Schloss Brüel on its flat pasture ringed with woods, a white and ginger layer-cake smelling faintly of dung; a huge, odoriferous, hoar-frosted turd. Acrid outdoor smell like metal filings in the air, sweet-urine smell of box hedge at the church in Tempzin, stench of stables, winter smells. The lights of the funny little ship-like gatehouse, in the fog. Maggie on the steps outside the front door; and the taste of regurgitated marzipan. Another sip of Branntwein—I'd finally found some in a vintner's in Old Compton Street, not quite the same taste but close enough. The same landscape, in liquid form. The foggy morning of the ball, the misty trees, and Alec running through the fog with one arm bent stiffly across his British Warm. Bent so carefully: for the first time I saw it clearly: holding something under his coat. But what?

I was dreaming again. Forget the Prisoner of Zenda; back to Underwood on whatever Underwood was on. Leave Alec to his secrets. Since our return we had hardly spoken, he and I. No doubt it had to do with what had happened in Germany—I certainly thought so then, but looking back it all seems part of a perfectly natural progression. I'd been a useful fixture in the days of our foursome not only to fetch and carry but to help dissipate triangular tensions. Now all that was over, and besides, I was growing up, I was busy.

A mad froth of cow parsley along the Hampshire lanes made Mecklenburg seem as distant and implausible as Oz from where I sat among the freckled effervescent girls—a spray of Trimbles—as Laura drove me once more from Petersfield station to the Hambledon vicarage. Alec had his secrets; but there was one thing I had kept secret from Alec. In our last conversation before I left, Maggie had made me promise to visit her parents' and "explain." She'd write to them of course, she said. And of course she hadn't, thought I could imagine her drafting and crumpling incoherent pages, her mouth crooked and pursed in frustration. Maggie's writing style was suited to quick intimate notes, no punctuation and no capital letters, not to considered declarations. So here *I* was to "explain." But explain what? They'd surely guessed by now, and presumably the authoress of *The Enchanted Flagon of Ostend* wouldn't find it hard to understand that her daughter had opted to become a countess and chatelaine of Nordic forests, fields, and lakes. I could paint a charming verbal picture—this was plan A—of how Maggie would occupy her days there, giving balls, raising cattle, distributing Christmas largesse to old Mecklenburger Nannies in place of Hambledon ones . . . although this wasn't at all what Maggie had depicted as her future with Peter. They would leave the castle in Agnetha's capable hands, she'd said, in order to move into a modest apartment in Rostock. There Peter was going to practise law, defend the destitute and challenge the forces of evil, nearer, as it were, to the enemy trenches. I was already converting it into language the Reverend Mr. Trimble could understand. Wouldn't this seem to him a crusade fit to redeem his daughter? Plan B was to tell this version, the truth, which might distress Maggie's mother but would pacify the curate.

In the event Trimble dispatched both my plans in one breath.

"I've been in touch with a pastor out there, in Hanover," he said, fixing me with a demented stare, "and he informs he that the whole damn countryside is seething with bodies—woodland orgies all over the place. And it's not just the *hoi polloi* who are at it, from what I gather the aristos are the worst of the lot, they have their own clubs where they do nothing but flog and sodomize each other from morning till night. I knew she'd end up with a bad egg," his gaze made me feel I'd been on the short list, "but I didn't expect her to sink this low."

We were standing under the dismal conifers at the back of the house, watching from afar as the girls saddled the pony for an

afternoon waddle. The poor animal looked as if someone had
taken the heavy roller to its back and then used the creature as
a trampoline. It was only now, in mid-afternoon, that I was able
to dispense news of Maggie; on my arrival Laura had made it
clear by a volley of bright questions about my own life that the
subject wasn't to be raised in front of her remaining daughters.
I understood why when one of these, the middle one of the three
who were left, took me aside before lunch to tell me she was
boning up on her German, using Maggie's discarded books. If
I came across a spare count could I send her his address? She
understood there were more than enough to go round.

I did try, that afternoon at the vicarage, to impress on the
Trimbles not only Peter's sober virtues but Alec's view that
Maggie wouldn't actually tie the knot, that the matter was far
from settled. Laura only shrugged as though slightly deaf.

"She's awfully obstinate, don't you think? Or am I being
unfair to her? It's so hard to know, with one's own children.
What do you think? She was *such* an enchanting child. I used
to read her Walter Scott when she was little, she was the only
one who really took to it, was that a terrible mistake d'you
think? I suppose it was. My father used to read us Scott, and he
did read it so beautifully. I just wish you'd seen her when she
was a little girl. Of course later she couldn't wait to get away,
and there was simply nothing I could do about it, was there—
d'you think? What *do* you think? How well do you know her?"

Laura Trimble had a way of softening you up with perfectly
meaningless enquiries, stalking you under cover of this fluting,
fluttering, innocuous noise before finally delivering a small tap
which blew you off your feet. Thinking about it on the way home
I decided I didn't really know Maggie at all well. I'd idolized
her, and desired her, but I didn't know her Trimble world and I
didn't feel at home in it, a world of sulphurous revenges disguised as family games and Walter Scott and girlish laughter,
like sprigs of hemlock in the frothing hedgerows. The day after
my visit (I only learnt this five years later) all of Maggie's things
were taken from her room, clothes, books—the middle sister
had done well to pinch her German library when she did—
knick-knacks, even Maggie's childhood toys. Then they were
taken by wheelbarrow to the coalshed and unceremoniously burnt.

I felt at home in Leda Buildings, I was even at home looking
down at Victoria from the window of my strange-smelling
kitchen, watching the antheap of commuters. Ants, real ants,
were a problem in my kitchen itself, that summer. Only kero-

sene seemed to deter them permanently, and it's a smell that takes me straight back to those rooms, to that kitchen, to the hissing of trains, to pleasant solitude and Underwood on Branntwein and nights with Ellie in a world I knew.

"Hello?! Hello?! Hello?!'' began my mother, summoning me to Padstow for Christmas. (I have a feeling she learnt this telephone manner as a child, watching her father's arduous long-distance calls from furthest Galway, in search of engineering equipment; perhaps she thought he was warming up the ether with these cries and preparing it for more sophisticated transmission.) An hour later the phone went again. "Coming for a spin?'' It was Alec, and I duly set out for Cornwall with him in the Alvis, his splendid new Alvis which had replaced the Mercedes shortly after our return from Germany. The upsurge in Alec's jingoism had taken place after all. He'd even joined the Territorials and been busy on manoeuvres during the summer, the very idea of which filled me with apathy, not because it was warlike but because it wasn't. It sounded more boring than Salmon on Tort, all map-reading and foot-slogging and no women. I had already decided that if it came to it I would be a fighter pilot, combining solitude, danger, and plenty of interludes with women; colossal ignorance kept this dream alive (duels with aging ace Peter, above trenches of cheering Alecs) since at six and a half feet tall I could no more have squeezed into a cockpit than into one of Mother's cutglass bowls.

The drive down to Padstow was glorious, the A30 winding like a forgotten Indian trail through snowbound countryside glowing in the sunshine, with Alec at the wheel, where I think he was happier than anywhere in the world; shades once more of our "spin" on Bodmin Moor. That one ride in the Alfa Romeo had inspired me with a schoolboy vision of myself as Alec's mechanic on the Grand Prix circuit, and during my schooldays I'd tried tinkering with engines; I loved the stink, the oil soaked gaskets, but it was all too fiddly for those clumsy weapons, my hands. Now I vowed for the umpteenth time to start saving up for a car, or at least for driving lessons. And I did, this time, I cut out the luxury of Branntwein over a period of six months, substituting cheaper fare. For some reason, though, fate has decreed that I should never own a car, or drive one—legally at any rate; the only time I've ever got behind the wheel it ended one life and changed half a dozen others including my own. But that was in the mercifully unforeseeable future, that Christmas, hidden in what Auntie liked to call (darkly, and perhaps with tribal memories of Dunsinane) "the fatal womb of time."

I hadn't seen Alec since he'd invited me over for a birthday tea—his birthday rather than mine, which was long gone, a golden July day spent with Ellie down at Worthing. I bought him a natty handkerchief-and-tie set. Unasked, Ellie had brought me a box of Turkish Delight to give to Alec "from his brother's friend," so I took her along to meet him. November fog was drawing in around dimly lit Putney villas—recalling Stevenson's Arabian Nights in London form—as we arrived. My brother greeted us in a silk dressing-gown over his Savile Row trousers and expensive shirt. I'd never seen him in this get-out before, and my startled reaction may have had something to do with the fact that I never saw it again. It was hard to gauge what Ellie thought of it, or of Alec, since she wore a furiously stern expression suggestive of Auntie at a Northumbrian prayer meeting, and spoke in clipped sentences. For his part Alec oozed unnecessary charm, as though I was a distant acquaintance, the son of a friend.

"Tell me about the law, young feller. Any hot cases at the Old Bailey these days? And what do you do, young lady?"

I hoped Ellie would say she was an apprentice clairvoyante; failing this, that she wouldn't stumble over her answer. She didn't. "I teach."

"That's good," said Alec, and we sipped our tea reflectively. At least he had the tact not to ask her what it was she taught.

There was another reason to relish this Christmas drive with Alec. I'd got him alone, and more importantly I had him bang to rights at last. I struck early, just beyond Richmond, once we were out of the traffic and before he could go into a brown study and become as incomunicado as Grandfather.

"Good picture of you in the newspapers last week."

"What's that, old bird?"

"I said, it was a jolly good picture. Didn't you see the *Illustrated London News*?"

Pike-Face took this relic of Victorian vanity, and while he was out of the office for lunch I sometimes borrowed it. There, sandwiched between "The Transylvanian Plateau—A Region Of Many Charms" and a report on the fighting in Waziristan, I had come upon a repulsive photograph of a plague of ermine-moth in North-East Essex, which held my attention for a while. Next to it was a picture of a crowded gangplank at Southampton docks. "Glad to be home," the caption read, "is Lord Edward Tremaine, seen here descending from the liner Jutland at South-ampton. Thinking twice about adventures in foreign uniform, the second son of Earl Tremaine of Launceston returns after a happy escape from execution at the hands of Nationalist troops.'' We were told that thanks to what was vaguely termed ''a dip-lomatic intervention,'' misguided idealist Lord Edward had been spared by General Franco himself, to gladden the hearts of his aged and guiltless parents. In the photograph the young lord looked cheerful enough about all this, and right behind him on the gangplank, paler but just as cheerful, stood my brother Alec.

For a mile or so Alec parried my thrusts—Jonathan Mansel would have done the same—and insisted on a chance resem-blance, but I wasn't having any of that. How many wars was he involved in? I demanded. I'd told everyone my brother was a Merchant of Death and I didn't want to disappoint them. Whom had I told? Oh, just friends. It was all bluff, but Alec fell silent. He was visibly thinking; I knew I'd won.

In my imagination Alec-as-Mansel turned to me now, with an endearing, lopsided grin. ''Alright, old scout, I think you've got the high ground. Where do you want me to start?''

Instead we drove through four counties in silence.

His profile never wavered. Since he'd joined the Territorials a further change in Alec's personality was on the way. It was to be the final one, and although he had gone a long way round, via racecourse spiv to businessman and social butterfly, it was only, in the end, to come home to our father's one successful guise: the military man. This had been coming in his posture for a while. Gone were the evenings when he bent to strum a banjo or danced for me as he imitated his favourite vaudeville artists. These days his head was held a little higher, chin up, a piece of advice he took literally; the double-breasted suits were less roomy; there was less handkerchief on show. Two hours had passed, and we were entering Ilminster. Quite without warning, but in the measured tones of an officer of the line, Alec began to speak.

''You know . . . it's a pity you never knew Father, he was a very decent sort of chap. You may not realize it now, but Mother loved him a hell of a lot, she never talks about it but I think he . . . how shall I put it? Kept her in touch with things—you know? Women have a way of turning in on themselves, you'll find that out yourself if you haven't already. They're probably better equipped than we are in the old survival game. They live longer, too. Can't do without them though, can we?''

He smiled uncomfortably at me, then fell silent again and drove more slowly. After a while he gave it another shot.

"Seems to me, perhaps I'm wrong, and no offence, but a chap like you could turn in on himself, become a bit of a dreamer. You see, if Father had lived, you'd never have been bundled off to Ireland. No way for a child to grow up, I know you were fond of the old bugger but he really *was* a bit cracked, with all his schemes, and none of them working. Went round in a dream, that's what I'm saying. You've got to leave all that behind? D'you follow me? The world's a rather boring place, it's got its rules, the written ones and the unwritten ones, you learn them both if you've got any sense, and you know when to speak and when to keep your trap shut instead of talking a lot of drip." Now I could see the anger watering his eyes. "I'm not a—whatever you called it, a merchant of death, any more than I'm the blinking Admiral of the Spanish Armada. And if I've been a bit hush-hush about things, it doesn't mean I've got anything to hide, it just means that some things *are* a bit hush-hush, and that a person with a mite of sense could rumble that without having to be warned. So what I'm going to tell you now isn't for publication, it isn't for your saloon bar friends or your girls or your legal eagles at the Temple for that matter. Yes? Good. If you don't mind my saying so you should get yourself a decent suit, that pinstripe's disgusting. And keep off the bottle, I don't know where you picked up that habit, it's the Irish in you, is it? I don't know," he mused, "you can be quite a sensible chap, now and then, when you stop talking like the Fifth Form at St. Dominic's. Now, this Spanish business . . . I've got a private arrangement, that's all it is, d'you see, with some of Tom Thurgo's friends—the Colonel's friends, are you with me? He knew Freddie Launceston at Oxford, and there's a few more like Freddie with sons who've gone overboard, communists some of them, found their way to Spain but we still keep an eye on them. Sort of bush telegraph if you like. If they've gone missing or done a bunk or got captured, Tom pulls a few strings—doesn't always work but it's a sweet racket if it does, and I pop down to Spain, give them a quick boot up the stern and bring 'em home. It's a sweet racket all right," grinned Alec, forgetting the dignity of this "private arrangement." "The old folks are pretty grateful, I can tell you."

But how on earth did the Colonel manage to pull those kinds of strings? Was he fighting for the Nationalists? I asked.

"Good God no, but he's a pal of Franco's, that's all it is. He and a few others,'' added Alec more vaguely, ''didn't you know that? Oh, he's a resourceful chap, Tom Thurgo—you'll have to meet him, the old boy's had quite a life. He didn't hang around in Cornwall, taught himself Arabic at Oxford and got out while our papa was still cleaning out lobster pots. Says he had four wives, one in Jedda and three in Damascus, when he was working for the Arab Bureau in 'Fourteen.'' I could see Alec's anger draining away, the glitter going out of the eyes, as he talked about our uncle; and I encouraged him. ''It all went sour on him, I think, after the war, the French were getting back in everywhere and we'd sold the Arabs down the river, sold them to the Jews is what he says, so he ended up doing a little business out of Malaga. He prefers the climate there, says the desert's a young man's game. But he keeps his hand in, goes over to North Africa a good bit. He gets on with the Bedouin, you see, and they know they can trust him, and that's how Franco's men caught old Tom, one day, hiding down a well with a hundred and fifty Lee Enfields. This was a year or two back, when Franco was just another colonial warlord trying to keep the tribesmen down, so he wasn't too pleased with our relative for flogging them damn good rifles. But the way it turned out, Tom charmed the pants off Franco and his friends. Instead of shooting him they signed a contract with Vickers Armstrong for twelve hundred machine guns. What do you say to that?''

''He just happened to have a Vickers contract in his pocket, did he?''

Alec shot a glance at my sceptical face. ''Tom Thurgo works for Vickers, didn't you know that? Worked for them for years. Lord yes. Yes, he had General Franco eating out of his hand, the way Tom tells it. They'd caught him red-handed supplying the enemy and by sundown he had Franco signing on the dotted line. That's salesmanship, eh?''

''And Franco gave him a peacock feather from his turban. . . .''

Alec only stared; he evidently wasn't a Laura Trimble fan. ''What?''

''I didn't know we had an adventurer in the family.''

''Adventurer?'' said Alec scornfully. ''He's not bloody Lawrence of Arabia if that's what you mean. He *works* for *Vickers*, you twerp. It's business: we had boatyards out there in Spain, till a few years ago we used to build their bloody gunboats for them—for the Spanish Navy.''

''We?''

"Didn't you know I worked for Vickers too?" He laughed at my expression, taking his eyes off the road. "Not on the engineering side, you ass. More a part of the sales force, if you like." He softened. "Look, I work for several companies, old bird, on a retainer basis. It's really a two-man concern, a little family concern. If you ever came back to earth we might find you a place in it. I'm in business with the Colonel. D'you follow me? I don't sell arms, Ratty. I make introductions. There's a world of difference."

"You sold arms to Peter," I said, and he was silent for a while, watching the road.

"That was something else," he said at last. "I didn't know Peter had told you where he got the things. No, that was . . . official, you might say, it wasn't Thurgo business. Oh, you'd better know," he groaned, "your imagination'll only run away with you and you'll be shooting your mouth off all over the place."

I swore never to breathe a word.

"Tell your tart," said Alec evenly, and with a handful of syllables altered our relationship for ever, "and you might not see her again."

There was an instant before I took it in, then I felt slightly sick. And bewildered. Alec had told me to put behind me Grandfather's world of make-believe; now it was Alec who was speaking the language of Dornford Yates villains—only the demonic Ellis made those kinds of threats, surely. Alec was watching me with a strange half-smile on his face. For a moment I was sure he was going to grin and say, "Just pulling your leg, old bird . . .".

When he didn't, my nausea returned and I looked away for a moment, to stare at the cosy Somerset cottages going past outside the window, at chimney smoke rising into the cold, still air. I waited desperately for all my Mansel-fantasies to answer back— damn it, *I* was the demonic Ellis! But no, I was nineteen and I was stuck in a car with a man I clearly didn't know at all.

"Don't take it too hard, boy," came Alec's voice. "I can't trust you, can I, if you don't get a grip on yourself and at least *try* and understand what's at stake. Ratty? Are you listening?"

I nodded.

"You see, in my line of business you meet the best and the worst—one day I'm having a drink with Carlos Blanco's Mexican crew at the Ritz, the next day I'm having lunch at the Admiralty. As it happens, your friend Peter was passed on to me through, well, let's say semi-official channels, as a chap who needed some under-the-counter stuff. Bona fide chap, I was told, treat him nicely. The thing is, he wanted me to believe it was for use by the Abwehr, who he claimed were going to put a bomb under Stalin's backside. You'd have to be pretty innocent to try and sell that story—they might have wanted him dead once but now they need the blighter worse than we do. So I got in touch with a few people, I'm talking about government level now, d'you understand? We've been trying to get a line on what Beck and company are up to, whether they're any use or not when it comes to pushing Hitler over on their own. D'you follow me? I'd discovered that Peter had a lead to Beck before I clinched the deal with him. I knew certain parties would be interested. And between ourselves, Mr. Churchill gave me some messages to deliver.''

He had my full attention again. ''But . . . so you did supply the bombs?''

''Oh yes, but that was always a hopeless little hole-and-corner show. I was told to scupper it myself by letting Beck in on the story, and that put paid to it, of course. He'd never want a Johnny-come-lately like Peter going off at half-cock and spoiling his own chances.''

I took this in, a little dazed; Alec's earlier threat was still ringing in my head and I just couldn't think straight. But memories were falling into place now. Alec running to a rendezvous, the theatrical air of Alec's dinner-table confrontation with Beck—staged for Peter, evidently. Peter's voice, releasing all his blind contempt for Alec, for the effete Englishman, ''He thinks they are for the Nazis. . . .''

Alec's own words kept coming back, the words he'd said a few moments ago. Did Alec really have the power to dispose of people? That had been the inference—or was merely phrased to scare me into thinking so? This was easier to accept. And it was only now that, reassured by this solution, I began to think about Maggie's part in the ''hopeless little hole-and-corner show.'' I could feel my temper rising.

''Then you weren't really running after Maggie? You didn't care about her at all—right from the beginning—''

''Steady,'' said Alec. ''I wouldn't go so far as to say that. But she was a jolly useful way of keeping tabs on the Count. And getting to Beck, you see.''

Now he grinned, studying my face for an instant before turning back to the road.

"She knew all about the bombs, didn't you twig? I told her on the way to Rostock." Alec chortled for a while. "When Peter told *you*, and you went and let on to her, you did us all a good turn. It meant that she could warn Beck on her account, you see, and so far as old Pay-ter was concerned, you and Maggie had spilled the beans. Otherwise, when Beck told him to chuck it, he'd have guessed that I'd told Beck, and began to smell a rat. Then I don't think his Abwehr friends would have let me out of the country without a few questions, do you? Of course Maggie still wanted to marry the blighter, God knows why, and he's besotted with her, so it was better all round for her to take the blame. What does she see in *him*? Do *you* know?"

For a moment it was like being quizzed by Laura again; I didn't think Alec wanted an answer any more than she had.

"I don't know what Maggie said to you," Alec went on, "but she told me if there was a war she and Peter would come to England. I told her we'd lock them both up."

He turned another grin on me, pleased with himself, or perhaps pleased with my cowed expression. I was feeling cowed, more so than I could remember; too much so to hide it. No wonder Alec couldn't trust me, I'd been a convenient blabbermouth, but I was a dupe and a blabbermouth nonetheless.

"Don't you want to know how we smuggled the bombs in?" he was gleaming at me. "What's the matter now? Ratty? Fellow's a broken reed," he said in mock grief, when I didn't respond. "Have a guess."

"In your luggage?"

"No—not in the luggage. It wasn't my pigeon at all in fact . . . no, the Admiralty dropped the damn things off by submarine. What do you think of that? Picked up by a chap from our consulate in Rostock, that's where I collected them. We came across a few nosy policemen, but my papers were in order—and that's the thing about the Germans, I'd remember this if I was you, might come in handy since you've already got the lingo: they're perfect innocents, they're innocent as little lambs, they may have evil in their little hearts, but they think *you're* a frightfully good chap unless proved otherwise. Like poor old Pay-ter. If you say, look here, I'm the Kaiser, they won't say don't be so damned silly, they'll say let's see your papers then. If your papers say you're the Kaiser, then you are. That's worth bearing in mind."

I remember that I was the one who sat in silence now, on that long, snowy drive through the West Country. Before we got to Mother's I had to know one thing, though.

"Come on," said Alec at last. "Spit it out."

"It's just . . . what you said earlier, about not telling Ellie. That was just to scare me, wasn't it."

He snorted, amused at my circumspect tone. "I'm glad it had that effect, old bird," he said.

The invitation came the day I discovered that I'd passed my intermediate finals—three more years to go, an eternity, before finals themselves and, with any luck, admission to the Rolls of the Solicitors of the Supreme Court, there was my name in black and white on the notice-boards of the Law Society, R.A. Thurgo, and I was giddy with excitement. It was June, London was in shirtsleeves again, the three years would pass, I saw myself certificated by the Lord Chancellor in person, and in this ill-founded euphoria I came home to Belgrave Road and a large envelope on the mat. It contained a card so decorated that even the Lord Chancellor's Certificate of my dreams would have paled before it, so incomprehensible in fact that I looked again at the envelope to be sure it was really addressed to me. Then it sank in. It was the formal announcement, in antique script, of Peter and Maggie's wedding in Mecklenburg.

The year before, on our first visit, Peter had sent an aeroplane ticket. There was none enclosed this time. Did they think that would put me off? Ensure that I wouldn't come? On the kitchen mantlepiece I had twenty pounds' worth of "Branntwein money" in a cocoa tin. My car could wait.

"Oh can't I come?" Ellie moaned when I translated the invitation for her, that evening.

"If you've got twenty quid to spare." I was confident she didn't, knowing what her rent was, and knowing that she couldn't find that sort of ready money even if both Boat Race crews repaired to Leda Buildings to celebrate. I'd have loved to take her to Germany, but aside from the sheer cost I wasn't going to do anything with Ellie that might arouse Alec's suspicions. I still had visions of Carlos Blanco's Mexican crew, whoever they were, pouring Ellie's "Russian" on the carpet as they sharpened their machetes on the samovar. Taking the ornate invitation out of her hands, I replaced it against the cocoa tin, where it gazed back at us with an almost cabbalistic air.

"Tell you what, we'll go to Southend instead, seeing as I can't afford it either.'' Ellie didn't know it wasn't Bourneville's in the cocoa tin.

But she was still gazing at the invitation, her long-nosed face growing more mournful and more mouse-like by the minute.

''Don't *want* to go to bleeding Southend.''

I lifted her up (this took more doing than it had when I first met her), and bounced her in stages towards the bedroom.

The Gothic lettering on Maggie and Peter's wedding announcement brought to mind a story Alec had told that Christmas in Padstow. To my surprise he had opened up about Germany, and treated us to inside knowledge, so-called, ''not to be bandied about,'' as if Mother was likely to tell anyone, or even remember. And his other listener was well and truly chastened. Perhaps Alec was feeling guilty about having been heavy-handed with me in the car; more likely it was just that neither Mother nor I were talkers and so every year we left him no choice but to entertain us. He told us that Hitler's secret police had been trying to discredit various Generals, but were so inept that they had mistakenly charged a Field-Marshal with homosexuality when it was a man with a similar name that they were supposed to be blackmailing on the same grounds. The Generals' response had been to challenge Himmler to a duel, and even this pathetic move had misfired. Beck himself, said Alec, had written out the ancient, formal challenge—I saw parchment, a quill pen, mediaeval flourishes; it was this I now pictured in terms of the embossed message on my kitchen mantelpiece—and had given it to a fellow General to deliver. Instead of doing so he'd wandered round for weeks with the thing in his pocket, and it never reached Himmler. In Alec's eyes the moral was plain: no-one was going to stand up to Hitler unless we did. ''You do realize there's going to be a war, Mother?'' said Alec, bending lower and lower in his chair as though trying to see under her heavy eyebrows.

She had watched us as though not hearing a word we said, so great was her annual wonderment at having brought into the world two large suits with whisky-drinking adults inside them, laughing and joking and clearing their throats and clambering noisily up the stairs of her cottage. She herself had shrunk, it seemed to me, not in height but in width. The fat had begun to recede; it had never been fat as one imagines it, yielding, as Ellie's was, but some hard compacted lardy substance, and beneath it—visible now—lay a frontierswoman frame wasted by years of cheeseparing. Gazing at her I felt awed, and touched, and saddened. Her eyes strayed to me occasionally, she seemed to recognize me beneath the "disgusting" pinstripe, and was satisfied. Whereas something about Alec troubled her. It wasn't his talk of war, war left her cold, it had already done its worst in taking Father from her. Was it that Alec had changed, that he was now impersonating Father and she didn't like it?

One more thing I should mention about that Christmas, because although thank God I didn't know it, it marked a beginning. The night before we drove back to London I had an odd and frightening dream which for the first time in years, perhaps the first time ever, took me back to Fold Farm along the winding, weedy drive to where the old house and its faded yellow brick frontage came into view; and I saw its sour colours now with dread. A curiously pedantic reflection came into my mind in the dream, fully formed: the way a Georgian building goes to seed—the dream formula ran—makes you understand why so many of them have been pulled down. As if to bear this out, Grandfather's house looked like a tired old prison or a boarding school waiting to be sacked by its inmates. The dream obeyed my thoughts. A moment later I was inside it, and I knew it was going to burn down. Then I heard the fire. I never saw flames but the sound was frightening enough, and I knew as you know things in dreams that it was fire and that it would devour the house and me and the dream with it, and that I would never wake up unless I found a door out of the house. This was such paralysing knowledge that I couldn't search, I couldn't move, I could only see a small, shrinking circle of light at my feet which was the shrinking, dying dream itself, and yet suddenly as my anxiety reached an intolerable pitch I was on the front lawn where the old cannon, to my surprise, no longer stood. In its place an old horse was drawing a mowing machine, led by a man in braces and a collarless shirt with thin, reddened cheeks, unmistakably Irish, mowing the lawn steadily and patiently. And yet I didn't know him, I'd never seen him before, and when I rushed up to him gasping and calling about the fire—the house behind me was still strangely intact—he replied quite distinctly, just before the dream at last evaporated, "I can't hear a word you're saying—I only speak German." This absurd sentence (inspired in some odd way by Mother, I decided later) troubled me less than the terror of the fire which was still with me as I woke, and stayed with me all day, through our return to London, where I couldn't go into the kitchen in my flat because the smell of kerosene put me in an irrational panic.

Against Ellie's advice I'd recounted my dream to Auntie. Perhaps because she dabbled in it herself Ellie had an indulgent, sceptical smile for anything "magical." "Must you spend money on it, Punch?" No doubt Ellie knew the tricks of the trade and was right to be sceptical. "She'll read your palm for free, you know that." Palms cost only a few pence per scrutiny, then there was the "little crystal" which cost a tanner to have Auntie gaze into it, and the big one which cost half a crown. I usually paid for the big crystal, feeling—as Auntie intended— that she would try harder if I paid more.

My dream confirmed all the vague forecasts Auntie had ever deduced from "the big one": a life full of travel and conquests, she always assured me. "All doors will open for you, and you'll fall on your feet." It was in my stars too, she said, sun in Leo, Sagittarius rising: I was born to conquer.

Though now she phrased it a little less auspiciously. "You're going to make a few fresh starts in your time, I can tell you," she said, fixing on me the clairvoyant's professional stare. Sewer smells from the corridor seeped in under the door as we sat there.

"Is that what the fire means?" She didn't answer. "Auntie?"

"That's what it means, bonny lad."

I'd assumed that Maggie and Peter were long since married and had turned their backs on the Thurgoes, as I'd been trying to do to them, so that the arrival of the wedding invitation that summer raised more questions than it answered. Why had they waited till now, more than a year later, to marry? Alec couldn't tell me, he knew nothing, he insisted, and he hadn't even been invited to the wedding. This was said with a quizzical, pitying look, one of Alec's favourites. He pursed his steeply-planed, saurian lips, tongue literally in cheek, mocking, amused, daring you to stand up to him. He gave me a letter to take to Maggie, however, "wishing her all the best and so forth," as he said blandly. This rang a bit hollow. I'd half convinced myself that Alec had merely been using the romance as a cover for a business transaction. But when he gave me the letter for Maggie, claiming not to have heard from her apart from a Christmas card, "not much point in writing back, they open all letters from England, you know," a touch of the old Alec transparency showed through, telltale as a throbbing vein, and told me that some part of this was a lie.

I carried Alec's letter back to my rooms and sat it on the

kitchen mantlepiece, behind the invitation. I held off for two whole days before steaming it open.

Darling Mags, it read—this beginning alone exceeded my expectations; but I'd have done better (oh how much better) to stop there, *I'm sending this via the Abominable Slowman, and by putting it in his horny hand hope to get word to you at last.* This nickname was news to me; but I was familiar with the reference, from the Great Explorers shelf at Fold Farm, and during my childhood Grandfather had cut out a series of newspapers articles about this purported Himalayan beast—curiously enough, Abominable Snowman wasn't a reporter's coining but a literal translation from the Tibetan. I was almost inclined to take the sobriquet as a compliment. *My darling,* Alec continued, *I've sent so many letters to you that don't seem to have got through, judging from yours! I wrote three times this month, is it possible you still haven't got any of them? If you've finally received any of my letters at all you'll know that the answer is yes, of course yes, always yes, a thousand times yes! I love you now as much as ever, as much as I'll always love you, my darling one. Come at once—damn it, get on the first train, I'll meet you anywhere you say. I've been absolutely desperate, I've written to you over and over to tell you to come. If you don't give the Slowman an answer I'll know it's too late—for you perhaps, but not for me, my darling. Couldn't you trust me? Didn't you know how I felt? You know I adore you and would lay down my life for you, I knew it from the first moment and I thought you knew it too—* and half a page more in this vein, "sloppy" stuff as Ellie would have called it, I couldn't bring myself to read it closely. Then I came across another reference to me, in the last paragraph. *Young Lochinvar has managed to track down the ugliest whore in London and is madly in love at last so don't let him give you any guff about his devotion to you. The only broken Thurgo heart round here belongs to your very own, Acting 2nd Lieut. (Non-Comm.), Thurgo, A.*

But for those final comments, perhaps I'd have been touched by the situation and the truth about Alec's feelings towards Maggie, and . . . though maybe not; no, I'd still have envied their intimacy too much, even in the tortured circumstances revealed in the letter, and despite its half-baked endearments. However, his reference to Ellie and me blinded me to anything else. Coming on top of his threatening words in the car it unleashed a resentment I barely knew was there. For the first time in my life I started to make a mental list of my grudges against Alec, going

back to the vanished insurance money on Fold Farm—my God—
I found myself repeating this under my breath—my God, the
man burnt down my childhood for his personal gain! I was furious. No, I wasn't furious—in fact I still couldn't get angry, for
some reason, about the missing money or the burnt-out house.
It was just . . . how dare he describe me to Maggie as being
madly in love, "at last," with the ugliest whore in London!

And was it all wounded vanity or was it pique, too, that I'd
been left out of the drama of Maggie's appeals for rescue? To
judge by Alec's words, she was panicking. Typical Maggie, I
thought. But why hadn't she written to me? Because I was the
contemptible, abominable Slowman, obviously. I'd written several times to Maggie and all I'd received was a Christmas card
identical to Alec's with a photograph of her (he'd got one too)
in a perfectly hideous hiking outfit, long German socks and long
shorts full of pleats and seams and zips. Even so I kept it in my
wallet, which was more, I was prepared to bet, than Alec did
with his.

I decided to destroy Alec's letter then and there, and with it
Maggie's escape route and their dreams of a reunion. Then I
relented, put the letter back in the envelope and glued the flap
down. I packed it, in my German phrasebook; I could always
destroy it later. Or keep it as a memento. No, that was a horrible
idea. I didn't know what to do with it.

To my surprise the trip cost less than the twenty pounds I'd
put aside, just fifteen guineas for a flight to Hamburg and back,
so I decided to take myself there a day early without alerting
Maggie and Peter, and do some exploring. I set out with confidence in my linguistic powers, money in my pocket, a new hat,
and a delicious sense of freedom, every inch the seasoned traveller. Everything on that second Hamburg journey conspired to
make me feel both strange and comfortable. Even our rattling
de Havilland with its homemade look had been replaced with a
glistening Lockheed Electra, its nosed pointed dramatically at
the sky as if it could fly to the moon if it chose but would
condescend to drop us off at Hamburg. At Fuhlsbüttel airport I
told my taxi-driver to take me to the best hotel; as I signed the
register I noted with pleasure that English business-types were
few and that I drew more attention amid the Teutonic heads and
the uniforms. In the streets the swastika was much more in
evidence than it had been the year before, as though Hitler had
conquered the city in the meantime, and brought goose-stepping

into fashion. I saw nothing distressing in this behaviour, it was exotic, rather like the thigh-slapping dances performed for us by Ellie's maid Minna, who hailed originally from Munich, and which we made our own attempts to imitate until we all collapsed in giggles.

I sat in Adolf-Hitler-Platz blissfully drinking real Branntwein again until night fell and I set off carefully around the lake and back to the hotel, in a stupor. Like most people and certainly most Londoners, I was perfectly convinced that war was coming, a war that would destroy us all in a matter of weeks, days, or even hours. We were all raised on H.G. Wells and fed with newspaper tales of the fiery hell that would descend on us from the skies—and we were also perfectly unable to think about war for more than thirty seconds at a stretch. We lived with the vague terror and the indifference produced by graphic descriptions of doom in those prewar years, and then it never materialized for us; at least not in its most lurid and Wellsian form. Which is why, as I tell Germans today, Englishmen who lived through that Armageddon atmosphere are sceptical about doom whether it's plagues of locusts or atomic bombs. And on another level there was something about the theatricality of the Nazi régime— by now we'd seen plenty of news-reels—that above all else made them seem peculiarly un-English, unlike the Kaiser and the officer caste of the previous generation. For that very reason it was harder, not easier, to imagine ourselves at war with them. You have to remember that the Great War had not been fought against a comic-opera dictatorship but against our own kind, in appearance as well as in fact. Now that this familiar enemy, our shadow selves, had been replaced by a pantomime cast almost Latin in their squawking, hysterical behaviour, it had the effect of reassuring us that the Continent was back in the hands of posturing foreigners, where it deserved to be. I was delighted to feel foreign in Hamburg, it was just what I'd searched for in vain on my previous visit. I even returned a few *Heil Hitler*s on my walk home round the lake.

Of course the newsreels had showed us less humorous sights, crowds stretching to the horizon before Hitler, and these crowds were shown to us from Hitler's point of view, as it were: we looked out from the dais at men as far as the eye could see. Clearly anyone confronted by this saluting horde would want to overrun the world, and would be absolutely right to do so. You felt that yourself, just watching the film. But it looked like a film, a fiction, none of it resembled the people or the nations you knew, whether at peace or at war. We watched with a puz-zlement that can no longer be imagined now that the images have become so much a part of our real history and acquired an unreality of a different sort, the opposite of what we felt then: not a discomfiting but a reassuring sense of disbelief.

Peter and Maggie collected me from the Vierjahreszeiten at lunchtime the next day, and they both seemed to think my pres-ence in what they said was one of Europe's smartest hotels was tremendously funny. Which I suppose it was if I was the Abom-inable Slowman; I'd decided this sounded like a Maggie gibe, born of my struggles through the Hambledon snow—''hither, churl!''—with Nanny's firewood; whereas ''young Lochinvar,'' etcetera—oh I hadn't forgotten a word of it—had a ring of Alec to it.

I was hungover, my hosts on the other hand were cheerfully drunk. Peter arrived tie-less; Maggie in an expensive, loosely belted coat thrown over her country clothes like a towelling robe. I couldn't fathom this reckless, disshevelled look, this refusal to dress for town. But it warned me that much had changed in the year since I'd seen them. Like Alec, Peter had sold his Mercedes, and bought a large improbable Packard which stood out—it was a pale cream colour—from the rest of the traffic and set the tone for our journey. They talked all the way, loudly and laughingly, without a single question about London life or my news or Alec's. They told each other anecdotes—as though for a third party, except that the third party had no means of enjoying them—about local Mecklenburger figures, with pro-longed impersonations much applauded by each other in turn. They told jokes, presumably for my benefit, about the Nazi lead-ership, in which Goebbels turned out to be a Jew, Göring im-potent and a drug addict, and Hitler a demented epileptic with only a matter of weeks to live. ''Hitler orders a carpet for the Reichschancellery,'' Maggie yelped. '' 'Do you want it wrapped, mein Führer, or will you eat it on the way home?' ''

The Packard swayed majestically through a Saxony of sculpted fields, toy farms and villages, where the frequent lines of ar-moured cars were greeted by Peter with obscenities, a wave of one gangling arm, and more jokes. On the eve of their wedding, on the edge of war, they were entitled to this dismaying cabaret, but for a time I wished I hadn't come. It wasn't the jokes that were dismaying, it was the way their eyes wouldn't settle on me and kept returning to each other as to an invisible lifeline, as if to lose sight of the other might cause them to disappear, like lovers in some nightmare fairy-tale; or was it a two-man tug of war, each combatant daring the other to let go and dump the opposition on its backside? I can see now that a presence more formidable, more directly threatening than mine was to them might have drawn their depression to the surface. My arrival was only an irritant, a nagging splinter, and it drew the hysteria instead. They were each other's audience and mercifully this allowed me to look out of the window, where now and then a soft ochre-gold shape, bent over seedlings, raised its head and unfolded into a young deer, alerting me to a larger discovery. The first slivers of water had begun to wink through the thickening beechwoods, I knew we were in Mecklenburg and I began to realize how utterly wrong I had been about its landscape.

The cold and mournful place which had served as background to so many fantasies, the place I remembered so clearly, had gone and instead I experienced a rolling, pitching ride through different vistas, up through gaudy, restless beeches on their coppery hills of leaf mould, swooping down again into the cathedral stillness of the pines, motes floating thick as incense in the greyish-purple columns of light, and emerging again to a broad rustic comedy of farms and orchards, where heavy-set housewives pedalled fat-arsed and billow-skirted down the cobbled, tree-lined roads: horse-chestnut and lime, squat hawthorn and hazel, here and there sentinels of elm and willow trying to keep a straight face, wild plum and apple trees fruiting fit to burst; then back into the glorious beechwoods.

Being in Germany (I thought it was simply being abroad) made the images so vivid, and as before the mood was dictated by the people in the immediate foreground. The great rustling cloak of leaves around a beech was now like a gigantic mussed-up Maggie hairdo, waves of leaf shaking like a mocking, teasing head, now like a shimmering, faceted costume on a gangling scarecrow king—though it only dawned on me later that this plasticity was born of the German landscape itself and explained my own responsiveness to it. Above all it was a landscape full of holes I saw that day, holes filled with light: the Mecklenburg lakes glimpsed through the trees and glowing with reflected sky, when above us in the woods the waves of leaf overlapped and met to shut out the daylight. And there was the quicksilver again, glinting beyond the pines, between the hills of soaring beeches, between birch and ash and oak, the lake-light making them all weightless, surrounding the coppery-leafed slopes with cloudscapes and lifting them up, like a stage woodland suspended in the air for gods and goddesses to sit in, like the land Jack reaches by climbing up the panto beanstalk, a terra firma in the sky. With a castle in it of course.

Before we'd even got in the front door Maggie seized hold of me, as Peter galloped up the steps with my overnight bag. When he was out of sight she turned, barely able to control her face. Her voice struggled to find the pitch. Was there any news from Alec? Had I spoken to him? Had he got her letters?

In a strange way this was a return to sanity after the forced gaiety of the journey, but it released some of the feelings that hadn't found an echo in the landscape, some of the anger. I might have pitied her, despite her treachery to Peter; I might have, but I didn't. She was staring confusedly at me, waiting for an answer. I could see Agnetha moving towards us from the hall.

"Yes, he's fine," I said. "He told me to wish you all the best and so forth."

Maggie gazed at me for a moment or two longer, then looked away and with a jerking nod resumed her nonchalance.

Inside the Schloss a palace revolution had evidently taken place. It was Maggie who orchestrated the evening's events, moved us in to *Abendbrot*, indicated with a glance when plates were to be removed, instructed Ludolf on tomorrow's menu; and Agnetha seemed content, withdrawn, silently devising bovine pedigrees, or so I took it. I was shown to my old room, where I grappled once more with the eiderdown, under the crowing orange birds, and tried to keep the memories at bay. There was no way to pick up the threads. Peter had been subdued all evening, as if to tell me I was there at Maggie's bidding, not at his. And perhaps only in the hope—did he know this?—of last-minute news from Alec. I slept fitfully, wondering while I lay awake whether the drinks cabinet was locked, under the new régime. I didn't have the nerve to go and look; the house was foreign again.

"Would you like to come with me in the car, Richard? Just to Tempzin, a short journey."

Peter made it sound as if we'd never been on such journeys before, and the breakfast-time formality continued for a time, as we drove down the sandy paths beneath the beeches and out onto the main roads. Then he began to speak, quite freely—in a different tone, as if it didn't matter any more—about the opposition to Hitler, about bungled plots and fresh conspiracies, addressing the windscreen, never looking at me. I learnt that

Beck had decided to resign from the General Staff, that he was going to lead a group of disaffected officers and politicians in some secret coalition. But Peter didn't mention whether he was to play a part in this himself. I asked if he and Maggie had found a place in Rostock. Was he practising law, "defending the destitute" as Maggie had put it?

Peter shook his head, still fixedly watching the road. "My friend, it has been a most difficult year. My association with Beck and with other more openly critical people seems to have deprived me of my living." Now he glanced at me. "Yes . . . the way things stand I have made all my examinations but without the Nazi's party's approval I have no permission to practise. Sadly it did not succeed, this plan to escape attention by putting on uniform, I am afraid they were not fooled. They cannot prove anything against me, but they don't have to, you see, since some years now we have the *Gesinnungsstrafrecht*, this is a law that punishes you for your thoughts, your *Gesinnung*, if these thoughts offend the Nazi party. And they are quite right, they have guessed my thoughts." The heavy car lurched onto the track leading to the church. "I sometimes think that without Maggie I would have little left to live for. My mother, as you can see, has become a statue." He paused and cocked his head with the old humour. "We should put her in the *Brustpanzer* in an alcove."

"So you never joined the Luftwaffe?"

"On the contrary, my dear chap, you see before you one of Göring's élite!" We clambered out of the Packard, and he gazed fondly at it. "Sometimes when they see this coming they think it *is* Göring. *Zu Befehl, Herr Reichsmarschall!* He raised an arm, clicking his heels and unsettling the Tempzin crows. "Oh yes, they drive to the side of the road when I come. Yes," he smiled, "you will see me in my uniform tomorrow—it will be a military wedding. And the next day I shall get into an aeroplane and fly with Maggie to London for our honeymoon." I glanced at him in alarm. "What do you think? Shall I take a Messerschmitt?" He studied me for the first time, put a hand on my shoulder, squeezed. "No, you can't imagine what it's like, poor boy. But I am not a footsoldier, you see, I will not die in the mud and freeze in the snow like poor Kuno. Cheer up! I don't think I'm a German really—do you? I'm too light for this place. Some days I feel I could fly away—on your back—shall we? You can be my horse." We both remembered the same moment and the words he'd used. "My donkey," he amended, grinning.

"With his feet on the ground. Firmly on the ground, I think, and too heavy to fly, unless I take you with me. I have thought of it that way sometimes. You are earth and I am air. Don't you think? Maggie is water, Alec fire. Don't you think that's good? She can slip through your fingers," he flexed them in demonstration, "unless . . ." then cupped his hands, carefully. I was about to tell him that according to Auntie it was I who was born under fire, sun in Leo with Sagittarius rising, but Peter seemed to mistake my expression and raised a hand. "Don't be deceived about Maggie. We're all frightened, it's natural. But I love her," and, lightly, cupping his hands once more while keeping his eyes on me, "and I have learnt how to hold her."

The intensity of Peter's gaze brought it home to me: was it he who had been intercepting Alec's letters? I couldn't take the risk of asking, in case it wasn't. The pastor stood waiting at the church door, dwarfed by the building with its drab brick face, and as Peter joined him to discuss the coming ceremony, I took a stroll instead around the churchyard plots, perfectly tended with their little low box hedges enclosing a rectangle of well-kempt ground, miniature Germanies. It was dull weather, typical weather, bright enough but sunless, I can see it now, I think I always carried it around with me, that flat sky that falls vertical and grey behind the handiwork of fields and forests, like the wall at the back of the model railway landscape in a toyshop.

There was music coming from the church, a music that fitted the well-ordered graves, I took it to be Bach because to my ill-educated ears it sounded constipated; Bach was constipated toil. I needed to see Peter playing it, and went inside to watch him at the organ, seated well back from it; Peter with his little concentrated face. I only knew Bach and Händel, from his playing, and Händel seemed to me the joyous one, a fairground barker crying come buy! It was Händel I took to then, a plump all-consuming Händel, it was inconceivable to me that this devious monkish stuff Peter was playing was the music of a joy beyond joy and a tenderness beyond grief, that it was love itself, when all I heard was an unworldly resignation, a tidy refuge for Peter's aborted hopes.

Of all the inhabitants of the Schloss that summer, it was Ludolf who gave me what I felt was the most genuine welcome. No doubt he saw me as the drunken, probably decadent Englishman, or less harshly as the wayward younger son. It seemed to have inspired a look of tolerant understanding; even of affectionate memory. Though we had nothing in particular to talk about, and all we had in common so far was my German word for "nightcap," I sought him out in the kitchens, when Peter brought me back from Tempzin. I loved those kitchens, with their armoury of knives. But Ludolf wasn't there. The huge rooms were deserted in the sleepy afternoon. I could hear chopping, somewhere, the resentful sound of someone butchering a turnip or some such with an old-fashioned root cutter, and I followed the sound. It led me to a pantry full of pickles, and there stood the blonde, tussock-headed creature who'd stared so boldly at me on the night of the ball, while Ludolf dried my stained *Frack* and I'd sat before the kitchen fire in my underclothes. The bullcalf as I thought of her; Herta was her name, or Gerda, it was hard to tell. Her voice was gruff and her vocabulary centered around one grudging, ominous word of agreement, *"bestummt."* The word is *bestimmt*, meaning "for certain," but Herta's accent introduced *"stumm"* into the word, aptly for her silent and silenced nature. She gave me an unsmiling stare and went back to savaging the hunk of root—it was a massive sugar beet. I suppose she was fifteen; she could have been an overgrown twelve. And she ignored me.

I sat at the table, took a knife and a slice of the beet—it was broader than my own broad hand—and carved it slowly and meticulously, removing sections as I went, into a swastika. Since Herta kept her eyes averted, maintaining her sullen indifference while I worked on the hard white substance, the effect was all the greater when I leaned back from my efforts and she consented to look. She glanced at me uncertainly, then started to wheeze with laughter, like an old man, as I solemnly ate the thing. It was a costly joke since it sat on my stomach all night and I could still taste its bittersweet cabbageyness (I belched cow's breath for days) all through the wedding the following morning. But it won me the bullcalf's heart. I offered her the last arm of the swastika and she ate it with what seemed like genuine enjoyment. We smiled at each other, glowing with a wordless understanding, though whether the ritual had made us both honorary cattle, Nazis, or Nazi-haters, I never discovered.

As the wedding guests began to roll up in their finery, next day, I took to the kitchens again, but it was a mistake and I was simply in the way. Ludolf has his team working flat out in the heat and steam and clanging of giant pans, and I was reduced to watching them with an idiotic smile of encouragement, like a first-class passenger loafing in the engine room. But Herta hadn't forgotten me; as we exchanged our third or fourth grin

Ludolf caught my eye. "Meine Enkelin," he said with a grave smile. Granddaughter. "Tochter," he added, pointing at one of the women pummeling dough, a plump blonde powerhouse in whom I could see my Herta twenty years on. Beside her, greying but with the same squat build, stood the sixty-year old model. "Frau," Ludolf nodded, and went back down the line via daughter to granddaughter Herta. I nodded too, taken back, since like Maggie and Alec I had fallen for Ludolf's aristocratic bearing and couldn't place him; and also embarrassed because my presence was now clearly open to a new interpretation, fitting the role of wayward younger son: messing with the serving girls.

I made my way upstairs, past the bowing, clanking uniforms in the hall. No *Frack* for me today, clearly one disastrous outing was all I was going to get. But I was no better off here; in my pinstripes I now felt less like a loafing guest than a bookie trapped in the royal box at Ascot. I knew where Maggie's bedroom was, and though I was pretty sure this was a total breach of etiquette, I squeezed down corridors and past maids, knocked, and entered.

"Can I come in? It's the Abominable Slowman," I said, as I was barely through the door. The words were out before I knew what I was saying. Afterwards I did wonder if it was purely accidental; Alec's letter to Maggie was in pocket; but I was far from ready, consciously at any rate, to own up to my knowledge of their correspondence, and I added hastily, "That's my nickname, isn't it? Alec told me."

Maggie was at a dressing-table being primped by the girl with the short red hair, whom I only knew from her coffee duties. She stopped in mid-gesture and held the pose until Maggie glanced in the mirror and nodded to her, turning back to study her hairdo while the girl left.

I should like to be able to record that Maggie looked beautiful on her wedding day. In truth I thought she looked bizarre. The outfit was imposing, with yards of tulle, and lace at her shoulders—I wouldn't have been surprised to see the red-haired girl deposit a tiara on Maggie's head—but her face looked as if a photographer had isolated the dish of central features and coyly enclosed them in a cut-out of flowers: her frizzy hair had been curled into ringlets round her face, God knows how long it had taken, making her features appear more unformed than usual, and a little stiff and stunned like those of a child on a winter walk. Her mother's words came back to mock. She was *such* an enchanting child. Right now she looked bewildered, as though the infant-Maggie that stared back at her from the mirror had robbed her memory of the expressions she'd formed in the intervening years. I watched her make a few faces at herself as if testing her make-up, but the startled look, like someone surprised by a flashbulb, kept returning. She gave up and gazed at herself in patient disbelief. It was only then that my words returned to her.

"Yes, hello," she said abruptly. "What else did Alec tell you?" She talked carefully, still trying out her features. "I knew you were lying, yesterday." Maggie studied me for a time, in the mirror. "Damn you, what did Alec say? He must have given you a message. I knew you were lying right away." To break our gaze, she reached for a brush, then seemed to remember the ringlets, and put it down. "Oh, for goodness sake. . . ."

She turned to me laboriously, shifting the heavy dress.

"Are you trying to protect me? Is that why you're doing it? You can tell me, it doesn't matter." But I couldn't tell her. Released from the mirror, life began to find its way back into her face. "It really doesn't matter. Don't you see, I could have just walked out, any time. Couldn't I? If I'd wanted to."

I didn't know what to say to her—that in that case she shouldn't have played with Alec's feelings; that she shouldn't be playing with Peter's? They were mechanical responses I didn't feel. And the odd thing was that from the very beginning, this was what I'd wanted, not just what I wanted for her, but for myself: Maggie and Peter, married.

"All right," I said slowly, "I did have a talk with Alec."

"I've told you, it doesn't matter."

"Yes of course it does. I gather he told you all about his government connections. And his secret missions for the Admiralty. Well, I'm afraid that's only one side of the story," I said. "D'you know how he really earns his living?"

And I told her about the Colonel, and about the family firm, and about "making introductions." She didn't flinch. "He doesn't like to be called a Merchant Of Death, because he doesn't actually sell arms, he just makes introductions, between people who want to kill and people who can get the killing done."

"Richard, stop it. I don't believe you."

"Thurgo and Nephew, introductions guaranteed. They'll do business with anyone who can pay, it doesn't matter which side they're on, for or against Hitler, or Franco or Stalin or anyone you like. Some of the deals they do would probably make your hair curl. If you hadn't made such a mess of it already.''

For a moment I thought she wasn't going to react. The sceptical expression looked stuck on. Then I saw her mouth crumple into a grin.

"Is it that bad? My hair, I mean.''

I wanted to hug her, tulle and all.

"It's awful,'' I said. "It makes you look like Ophelia dredged up and stuffed.''

She covered her face with one hand, as if trying to keep everything in position.

"And worse,'' I said.

"Go on.''

"You look like the little piggy who went to market.''

"Yes,'' she nodded; I could see tears, tears of laughter, forming behind her fingers.

"It's Pigling Bland's wedding . . . you look like a pig in a pram, in all that lace.''

"Yes,'' crying and laughing. "Oh come here,'' she said.

I shook my head. "Your make-up's starting to run.''

"Please,'' she said.

But I didn't move. I didn't want a chaste, tearful embrace, babes-in-the-wood. She took her hand away from her face, and looked at me, and there was enough of Maggie in that look to be going on with, both an offer and a threat in one slack stare, all the expression in the eyes, with anger gradually winning through.

"All that nonsense about Alec . . .''

I shrugged. "You don't have to believe it. But that's the message he told me to give you. I was to tell you the truth.''

After a time she turned back to the mirror and began the reconstruction work in silence.

The sight of Maggie walking down the aisle, in the church at Tempzin, explained why the wedding had been long in coming. You could see a new personality emerging, it seemed to me, by force of habit, and almost reluctantly, from the conflicts of the old. And out of this I could imagine its gestation period, I could picture Maggie fretting and delaying, balancing in her head—I saw her face working, alone—love and pity and tenderness for Peter, and romance too, and the imminence of tragedy, balancing these against the frivolities of old England, the familiar camouflage; while getting slowly sucked into the habits of the Slosh, the pleasures of command, and its peculiar atmosphere of sombre gluttony. The church was poorly lit by windows, and as we waited in the half-light the candles achieved an almost Catholic splendour. Astonished, I remembered the Mass: visits with Grandfather I'd completely buried. Then the music rang out and I turned to look for Maggie's entrance. To my surprise she had not only regained the composure I'd disrupted earlier, but worked herself free from the bridal cocoon, the numbed self-consciousness that seems to come with the occasion. It wasn't the Blenheim performance, or the stairway descent that had charmed Beck when they met: this time she led the ceremony, greeting us with smiles as she advanced on Beck's arm, welcoming us, telling Peter's friends they belonged here, and she belonged to them. She'd thickened, yes, the wedding dress revealed that in a way that her dark outfits didn't; the face was still a little beady Trimble face, enabling me to conjure up all her equivocations, and the long delay; but it was too late, as she'd said, she'd already become the Countess; that's what she'd been trying to tell me.

I felt a little less ashamed, thinking of Alec's letter in my pocket. And the candles all around us now brought something else to mind. I'd find somewhere to burn the letter.

Looking at Maggie as she passed me, I noted that her waist was definitely plumper than I'd seen it before. It was curious: everyone I knew had thickened, even Ellie who didn't have much room for it, but people seemed to put on weight in those last days before the war, as though storing up fat, or perhaps it was simply a surrender to despair, what the Germans call *Kummerspeck*, sorrow-greed. And that day I had Herta on my mind, Herta whose broad bottom and sausage-tight skin reminded me (perhaps Peter was right after all) of Mother's; Herta who seized me by the hand as soon as I was able to escape from the wedding reception into the coolness of the kitchens. The staff were in attendance on the lawn, all in their liveried best, bowing and curtseying to Generals and their wives. I glimpsed Beck, holding modest court among the dress uniforms, and in recognition—ah, hello, the English boy who knows "The Shirt"—he gave me one of his sad, enlightened smiles. But it was Herta I was looking for. I think she knew I'd seek her out, and from the kitchens she led me without explanation through the scullery and the backyards, across the vegetable gardens and past the chicken run, out to the freedom of the orchards, and beyond, into the Friedrichswald.

* * *

The Frederick who gave the forest its name was The Great, of Prussia, who ran a post road through it, giving rise in its turn to a village called Weisser Krug, White Jug. I'd noticed the name on my first visit, and Peter and I had discussed whether it would have been the pallor of the beer available there or the foaming head that determined the name; though it could have been the jug or pottery stein itself, a grail for incoming riders. I'd quenched my own thirst, liberally and fast, at the reception, and I was ready for anything; or so I thought. I wasn't sure how much I was going to enjoy fooling around with Herta—or being fooled around with, since she was at least as heavy as I was and probably stronger. But she had a feral quality, as distinct from her bullcalf exterior, which was strictly bucolic; and in my tipsy state I decided this was promising. I'd had my fill of erotic elusiveness. And I'd just attended a wedding where I'd had the groom and desired the bride, so who was I to be choosy? As we made our way through the woods I couldn't shrug off the sense of awkwardness and humiliation I'd felt among the uniformed guests, since the day began. The revenge I wanted was more than a roll in the leaves with Herta, it was a duel in the skies, machine-gunning their Messerschmitts. It wouldn't be long, I told myself, before I had the opportunity.

We'd stopped, and Herta looked upwards, glancing at me. Following her gaze I saw the treehouse for the first time. I wasn't expecting it, and I wasn't greatly impressed, from the outside. It clashed with its surroundings. Too many different materials had gone into its construction, wood and tin and wire netting, and some compressed fibre torn from a outhouse and stained with chicken droppings. The whole thing was patched with flaking magazines and metal advertisements. It had no window that I could see. What was it? A hunter's hide? It was so garish; perhaps the animals had got used to it, or never looked up, but to human eyes it seemed painfully out of place.

The setting, though—that was perfection. At the time I tried to imprint it on my groggy brain, because it seemed so complete; it was the woodland scene, as beautiful as you could hope to see it. I memorized it, but I never felt a part of it as I stood there. Messerschmitts and machine-guns were gone, certainly, I was there with Herta in a fairy-tale glade, with dappled light and trees in their summer glory rising high over a bed of twigs and leaves, acorns and beech mast, and with a stream curving through it, in and out of the sunlight, a stream with water so

clear it was only by the fine brown sand and the twitch of minnows that you followed its course; and then too, looking closer,
by the dance of insects out over the middle of the stream, keeping their distance from the banks where basking, heavy-lidded
frogs watched them like sated potentates. Lazily watching the
dance. But they weren't watching in the sense that we were
watching them. The frogs were pulsing, and digesting, they were
accumulating frog-strength till the hour came to strike, intricate,
fallible mechanisms among the springs of the great forest clock
that brought the hours back again, century after century. And
we were the watching-creatures in this world, the witnesses,
reading the clock, filling our senses and imagination, turning
frogs into potentates, and accumulating—what? Delight, and
memories. And transformations. With a kiss the toad became a
prince. O happy toad (I saw Maggie plant the kiss, on my brow).
But these frogs were untouched by the kiss of my imagination.
Here in the woods around White Jug, were we completely spurious, or indispensable, God's spies or dreaming, interfering
spectres at the feast? It felt as if we had no place here—yet it
had place in us. I knew exactly where I was. These were the
woods of childhood, so intensely seen and heard, alive with bees
and small sounds magnified in the stillness and protected from
the wind by bright enclosing foliage, hazel and elder playing
hide and seek with shafts of light under the beeches and the
oaks, and birdsong echoing and overlapping, close and far and
all around, continuous. Observed; preserved. Transformed, in
a kind of dream. I stood there, passive, drowsy, trying to understand, till Herta tugged at me and broke the spell.

A route, part ladder, part convenient branch, led up the trunk,
with a rope hanging beside it to hold onto as we climbed; a rope
attached to the floor of the treehouse, fully thirty foot above the
ground. There was a door, with a metal catch. Inside the windowless hut it was pitch dark and it smelt of entrails, not the
spicy smell of a slaughterhouse, where the odour of fresh blood
predominates, but a pungent, decaying stink. Herta reached up
to a shelf, pulled something down, matches, and lit two candles
on an up-ended crate. Candles: perhaps this was the place to
burn my Alec-letter. Above them hung a deer's head, un-
mounted but presumably stuffed, I wasn't sure; it was hanging
nailed through one ear, in profile, as if newly decapitated. I
looked round. There were more animal heads, and skins, small
skeletons and skulls and antlers, and things in bottles, frogs and
eels and other things that looked sickeningly like embryos, and

further along the shelf a row of glass jars with a blackish liquid in them. Around the walls and between these grisly trophies, newspapers were nailed, and photographs, though I couldn't make out a common theme or read them in the dim light. Only the black and red of the old print stood out, Nazi colours, but the Führer was nowhere to be seen. A pair of fatuous wooden manikins, one smoking an implausibly large meerschaum, were the only cheerful touch, but they were crude and mass-produced. I felt something heavy on my shoulders, Herta was placing fur around them: rabbit skins, dozens of them sewn into a kind of cloak. She took my hand—I could picture hers snapping the rabbit necks—and pressed something scaly into it. Looking down I saw lizard and snake and perhaps frog skin too, sewn together to form what seemed to be a little shapeless sack. I couldn't make out what it was until she gestured, showing me how to put it on, and then nodded approvingly as I followed her actions. It was a kind of mask, leaving my cheeks and eyes free. Herta leered at me, and I knew where she'd taken her inspiration—from the Schloss itself and the pottery figures where the snake-headed Lucifer grinned at Eve out of the apple boughs. The skin was rough against my face, the cloak was heavy, and the air stank; but I watched her, fascinated, as she now fetched down one of the jars of liquid and placed it, ceremonially, between the candles. Then she dipped a finger in it, brought it out, eyed me, and licked it. She handed me the jar. The liquid was a dark reddish brown and sticky; and it tasted salty on the tongue. Herta reached out and touched my cheeks in turn with one bloodstained finger, poking up under the snakeskin eye-mask to smear my cheekbones. And she laughed her wheezing, unaffected laugh, a naughty child. I felt relieved, it was all childish after all, and comical, standing there in a tatty costume, in a treehouse full of stuffed animals, and licking bloody fingers. I gestured at the cloak. Her work? I asked. "Bestummt." Her work, for certain, all of it, her face told me proudly. And the stuffed creatures too? *Bestummt* they were. Herta raised a finger to her lips, a fat finger. I waited, watching her expression change. Her blubber lips were pressed into a kiss against the finger. She turned back to the makeshift altar and poured some more liquid into one hand, rubbed it into the other hand, and raised her palms towards me as if offering to play pat-a-cake. I brought my hands up too. She moved her hands to mine, and slowly smeared the blood from her palms onto mine. They stuck together. We stood for a time in that windowless hutch, facing each other, palm to palm. Then she bent and blew out the candles.

RAISING AND LOWERING A BALLOON WASN'T EXACTLY WHAT I had in mind when I joined the Royal Air Force. I had to remind myself that Balloon Command was a vital part of our heroic defences and that Queen Mary, our barrage balloon, was as noble a fighting machine as any Spitfire. But we spent more time oiling the flying cables, laying out our kit and bedding, and doing gas drill, than we did winching her up and down. Once up, we had to keep our enormous kite—she looked like a toy sub out of water—head to wind, as the saying was, on her bed. This, and such suggestive terms as bedwires, slips, screw pickets, and tail guy snatch blocks, kept our imaginations busy. But it was tedious work. She required constant "tickling" as the wind changed, and we all developed semi-permanent neck-ache from craning back and staring up till we felt dizzy from watching her; I became so sick of moorings and guy ropes that the sight of a marquee or even a small tent still makes me queasy.

I still dreamed of dog-fights with Messerschmitts. Short of bagging one of our own planes by mistake I could see no conceivable way of making the kill I'd so often pictured. And yet I did, the day a lone German fighter tried to weave through our lines and strafe the airfield. In time the Luftwaffe learned not to try this, but the early sorties usually contained a few daredevils eager to make mock of Balloon Command. This time, as I told it later, Jerry had chosen the wrong balloon. He had, but my terrified unit and I were flat on our faces in a ploughed field when it happened, and we did damn all to bring down the intruder. He miscalculated his approach, the Queen Mum's moorings ripped through one wing like cheesewire, and down he went.

I was the first one on the scene, galloping across the muddy furrows. It was a Messerschmitt: this was fated—it must be Peter.

Instead it was a heavy-set young man blinded with blood, and with terrible gashes in his face and head from the splintered windscreen. The plane itself seemed small and tattered, as if someone had stamped on it; so defenceless in its grounded state that I couldn't imagine it as the terrifying metal hornet that had sent us running for our lives and diving head first into the mud. It was almost easier to believe the German had flown off on one wing and dropped this crumpled counterfeit to fool us. But the boy in the cockpit was real enough. I picked some of the glass from his face. There were shards at his temple and in his head that I didn't dare touch. Before he passed out I was able to ask him where he came from, and he told me; told me his name and rank too—Feldwebel Butzinger, Hans. I even asked him if he knew Peter, which of course he didn't. He couldn't see, all he knew was someone holding his hand and talking to him in his own language. I don't think he knew where he was.

It hadn't occurred to me that my fondness for the German language would do anything but get me into trouble—the very sound of it had become like the smell of sulphur to us all, it was the Devil's calling card—and far from revealing what I'd been told by Feldwebel Butzinger, I kept it all to myself. Name, squadron number, airfield of origin . . . the very details that exercised a whole corps of interrogators, as I discovered. It was only when I mentioned it to a member of the unit who knew something of my past contact with Germany and Germans, that at his prompting I went along and told the duty officer. I set out grudgingly, wishing I'd kept my mouth shut.

During my two years raising and lowering the Queen Mum (not the balloon's official name, but we saw a resemblance to the old heffalump, loyal as she was, and huge, and shapeless) I'd had plenty of time to gnash my teeth over Alec's war. From the Territorials he'd joined the Duke of Cornwall's Light Infantry, or London Infantry as he called it—to his disappointment most of the men had been recruited not from Cornwall but the East End, with a promise of three square meals a day and training by the seaside. "Freddie" Launceston, father of errant Lord Edward, was Honorary Colonel of the regiment (which Alec had chosen for this very reason) and through the Earl's good offices Alec got himself posted to Chelsea Barracks. Cushy number, I thought. But the first winter of the war found him in France, and I got brief, scathing letters from Lille and the unpronounceable Oignies. In my envy I thought of it as the sound of a German pig with cold steel up his arse. Alec was a lot less blithe. Bloody Canadian rifles, he complained with a connoisseur's contempt, all right for match shooting, no bloody good for warfare, give me some Lee Enfields—and no doubt he could have found them, given a free hand. He complained about his superior officers too. Windy, he said; didn't like the sound of cannon; had enough in 1918. This wasn't bluster, either. Alec knew and liked the sound of cannon. I discovered later that he'd distinguished himself so promptly in the field that the ''London Infantry'' were loath to let him go, after Dunkirk. But let him go they did. He was back in England with the remains of his battalion when I met him in Putney. He looked chipper, altogether too chipper. It wouldn't do.

So: what had happened at Dunkirk? I mocked.

''Reasons for withdrawal of British contingent,'' he said curtly, ''one: ran out of tea. Two: lack of cover.'' He was a little more forthcoming about his own adventures. ''Against my better judgement I got on a boat, decided it was up to God to look after A.T., and went to sleep. While I was sleeping the crew mutinied and said they'd chuck us overboard unless they got more money. Somebody woke me and we got that sorted out.'' He was proud of me, he said, keeping my end up at Balloon Command. ''Hope you're keeping your cable oiled,'' he grinned—I'd introduced him to Balloon smut—''What happened to your little friend? Is she around somewhere?''

The gleam in his eye took me completely aback. It was clearly for himself that he was asking about Ellie. My ''little friend'': she didn't fit the description, but I knew whom Alec meant, from his face. The hypocrite! After the way he'd described her in his letter to Maggie—and now he wanted to move in, did he? I'd told him that Ellie and I had fallen out, which was true, the reason being not her littleness but her largeness. Unsuspecting, foolish Rat; no wonder she was so heavy to lift, that day at the flat when I'd bounced her into the bedroom. Eventually she'd had to admit why she was thickening, and that it wasn't grief or gluttony, or laying in supplies for war.

At the news that she was pregnant I'd felt . . . what had I felt? If it was more than annoyance, and I'm sure it was, quite sure it was, I never managed to acknowledge it. Her absurd insistence that the child was mine made little difference. Why pick on me? If she was going to dun someone, I said, surely among her customers there was an Oxford youth with more money than sense, who would be moved (to cash if nothing else) by the sight of Ellie bulging on the river bank as he punted past. I offered to write to the fellow's Tutor—once we'd identified a suitable mark—on Ellie's behalf. *Dear sir, I am only a poor girl who teaches dancing lessons*. . . . Ellie wasn't at all amused. "Sod you, Punch," she said, "you miserable bastard." But I wasn't having a little Punch, or Punchy-poo as Ellie referred to the thing kicking in her belly, on my hands. I told Auntie she was going to have to deal with it, get rid of it. But no, too late for that, bonny lad. By Dunkirk all I knew of Ellie was that she'd had the baby, it was a boy, and of course she'd called the poor bugger Punch. Through Auntie I kept in touch, I even passed on some of my salary, but I never visited Ellie and Punch. It wasn't lack of curiosity, or fear that I'd get enmeshed in a family I didn't want. It wasn't high moral tone either, God knows. I was more than happy at the idea of siring a son by a "dancing instructress," though I'd have liked some proof. No, the reason was meaner than all of those. I was afraid that Ellie might want me to make love to her, now or in the foreseeable future, and I was repelled by the thought. Irrationally, and as it turned out, temporarily. But that was reason enough at the time, a short-sighted reason and a cruel one too, since I knew from Auntie (I knew it myself really, but Auntie confirmed it) that Ellie cared for me. All the more reason, it seemed then, to keep away.

Nonetheless I wasn't having Alec going anywhere near my son (as I thought of Punch junior when it suited me), mauling Ellie and spoiling the boy's milk. The old lecher! I thought, and that was my one comfort at this time, that Alec was old, he was pushing thirty-six, far too old to carry out and steal my dreams of heroism. The abortive "show" in France would be his last glimpse of the fighting. It was a desk job for A.T. now, and God would doubtless look after him there, but without arousing my envy.

"The Germans are getting a bit beany," said Alec that afternoon in Putney. I didn't know what "beany" meant but it sounded threatening. "We've decided they need a bloody nose, so we're rounding up a little corps d'élite. The C.O. got a circular about it, didn't like it much and sat on it till it was almost out of date. Finally posted it in the mess, twenty-four hours before the deadline. 'Wanted, men of utmost intrepidity,' " Alec gazed blandly at me, " 'who can swim and navigate.' " I knew Alec couldn't do either, and hated boats. " 'No age limit,' " Alec continued, beginning to gleam again, " 'Apply Rumsey, in person.' Somewhere in Sussex. Well, we were in Bideford. But I thought: I'll put in. Borrowed a motorcycle, I'd never been on one before but I rode it round the C.O.'s tennis court a few times to get the hang of it, and off I went. The kick-start fell off at Yeovil, then I got stuck behind a charabanc most of the way and I'd forgotten how to change gears. I was filthy black by the time I got to Rumsey, but the chap there didn't seem to mind: I went in, threw one up''—saluted—''smartish . . . and, d'you see now, Father told me one thing I'll never forget, he said 'Lecky: d'you know how Scott picked his men for the Antarctic? He picked the ones who looked him in the eye,' so when the chap said, 'Are you on for this sort of thing?'—those were his exact words—I looked him in the eye and said by God I was. 'Any good with small boats, Thurgo?' 'I'm a Cornishman, sir.' And I saw him scribble something in a huge book. I'm going to find out what it was, one day.'' (He did; it was two words, ''right sort.'') ''Anyway I had a heck of a fight with the C.O., told him it would be a poor show if the Duke of Cornwall's couldn't find a volunteer with the necessary spirit. He grumbled but I think I'm in.''

And that was how Alec joined the Commandos. Their training weeded out the duds in short order, those of whom ''right sort'' should have read ''brazen fraud,'' so perhaps the selection process wasn't so ludicrous after all. Alec, brazen or not, was never one to fall by the wayside. He was no fraud either, and he became one of the hardiest of them, the only survivor of a full hand of Commando missions, Guernsey, Norway (twice), Dieppe, Sicily, Italy, and finally Burma. Major ''Lecky'' (it became ''Lucky'' behind his back) Thurgo, M.C. and other bits and bobs. And hero.

Meanwhile the tide of my life was sweeping me towards Cockfosters. Or more precisely Oakwood, a little-sung district of North London which more than earns its obscurity. When I recited what I'd learnt from the dying German pilot, the duty officer told the intelligence officer, the intelligence officer told the station's commanding officer, who liked to take an interest in such things, and he phoned Ryder Street in Whitehall, where I was summoned to display my German to a man who spoke it poorly. In no time at all I was walking down the long beech-and-oak-lined avenue (dear, beloved avenue!) from Oakwood Station to Trent Park, carrying my gas-mask, that idiotic metal nosebag, in its Easter Egg box. I had a fresh stripe on my shoulder: Flight Lieutenant Thurgo, R., code-name . . . would I never be free of those damned initials?—Rat. As code-names go it was a pretty thin disguise, and luckily the nation's security didn't depend on it. All it meant was that if someone needed to speak to me while I was at work, they'd send a WAAF with the message, " 'Pitmarsh' wants to speak to you, sir," (this was Tom Vaughn-Fisher, a colleague who hailed from the West Country village of Pitmarsh), or " 'Face' wants to see you, p.d.q.," (this was Group Captain Towle, my immediate superior). The idea was to keep our German interviewees confused. I had been transferred to "Sisdick," to give it its least obscene title. Properly speaking, the Combined Services Detailed Interrogation Centre. My job was grilling captured aircrew.

"Name?"

"Deutsche Offizier sagt nichts!"

This was pidgin German (to make it easier for the stupid English) for "I'm a German officer and I have nothing to say."

"Rank?"

"Deutsche Offizier sagt nichts!"

"Squadron? *Geschwader?*"

"Deutsche Offizier sagt nichts!"

"Airfield?"

"Deutsche Offizier sagt nichts!"

"Cigarette?"

"Danke schön."

And every one, as they came through the door for the first time, was going to be Peter.

I had roomy digs in Oakwood, and a batman in Trent Park who polished my kit; I had WAAFs who saluted me and typed my reports, and German officers who sulked under my questioning; I had a gun, a heavy Smith and Wesson—issued to each of us in case, we were solemnly told, of a German parachute drop to liberate our prisoners. I was taken out into the woods to be shown how the pistol worked. A pheasant got up in front of us and, to my instructor's amazement and my own, I shot it dead. I was in heaven. There were friendly, cynical colleagues, and there was "Face."

Group Captain Towle, only a year or two older than I was, and in charge of my interrogation unit, had been transferred in ignominy from Fighter Command. He was a deeply melancholy man, newly recovered from a nervous breakdown, and he was quite the most beautiful-looking individual I've ever come across, a man of medium height, though his build and bearing lent him stature, with broad shoulders, a long noble face, and hair the colour of faded gilt. His code-name was apt, even though it was facetiously coined for "Face-Towle," because his face caused everyone to stare at it despite themselves. The strong, classical features were delicate and powerful at once, a slim long nose, a slim wide mouth, and eyes of an extraordinary dark blue. Denis Towle had been a dashing and successful fighter pilot—everything I'd dreamt of being—in the opening skirmishes of the war in the air, before succumbing to the illness known with cruel fastidiousness as Lack of Moral Fibre, or blue funk. With some exceptions it was genuine heroes who were laid low by L.M.F., since most of us, having no moral fibre to begin with, could hardly draw attention to our loss of it. From everything I heard Denis was one of those genuine heroes, until one morning when he was simply unable to get out of bed, for no physical reason. His subsequent melancholy didn't derive from his disgrace—in fact far from it, the only thing that cheered him up was talking about his "crack-up," which I think was to him the only real occurrence of his life, and probably the only inglorious one (there was a connection here; though which was the cause of the other, God alone knows); no, his melancholy was due to his beauty which, according to Denis, had always encouraged people to expect too much of him. As a result he carried it around with him like a scar, entering rooms with the apparent diffidence, and the barely concealed defiance, of those poor fellows who'd been trapped in a cockpit fire and whose faces had been redrawn into a leprous mask. Denis Towle was a man who couldn't help being beautiful. Even his walk was beautiful, as were his gestures and the very way he stood, though he held himself apologetically as if to say that the habit of elegance had been formed too early to discard, had come with the box, as it were, in the original set of instructions.

He treated everyone with a pained politeness, but his eyes would give a flare of involuntary pleasure when it was me they saw (this fleeting sign of gladness was rescinded as soon as Towle GHQ received notice of its presence, but it lasted as long as it took for the countermanding order to get back to his face); it was a memory trace of the many evenings we spent getting drunk together, in the course of which I had allowed him to relive, to pore over and analyse yet again, the day when he could not bring himself to report for duty. As he described it, his body had simply refused to obey. Denis recited these humiliating and—for anyone else—bewildering hours as though they were God's grace itself. (Indeed he often spoke of the squadron chaplain, who had helped him through the days that followed. This "wonderful man," as Denis called him, had prescribed a stiff dose of prayer, like a powerful emetic.) But there was nothing masochistic in Denis' account. It was not at all as I imagine victims of stigmata, rejoicing in the suffering they perhaps feel they deserve; or feel they deserve to share with others, in Christ; nor was he experiencing a relief and release from the strains of combat—which would have been only too understandable. No, these were the hours in which for the first time in his life he'd felt at home in himself. I say the hours; but time had stopped for him. There was one simple thing that prevented him getting out of bed: he didn't know who he was. Another man might have failed to get out of bed because he did, at last, know who he was, a coward, or if you prefer a rational being whose nervous system said no to another suicide mission in the skies. Denis had no idea what his name was, how he moved or how he spoke, and so neither was possible. But underneath all this, and because of all this, he was at peace. Denis experienced . . . I wouldn't call it freedom, since it was so dependent on inertia, but certainly a kind of liberation. There are schools of Indian philosophy, according to my source of spiritual wisdom here in Hamburg, one Wolfgang Zimt, in which the self is described in a most unusual way. This thing the self, the entity we think of as ourselves, is not, according to Wolli, anything to do with us at all. By this theory the self is a person watching us—we each have one, as I understand it—who gradually comes to identify with the person he is watching. Or *not*, I sometimes want to suggest . . . and here was a case in point. As he lay in the upstairs bedroom of his modest digs on the outskirts of Alfriston, within sight of the airfield, the person watching Denis Towle (happy person, to be appointed to so watchable a specimen of humanity)—and who, perhaps, had been so overcome by Denis' beauty that he simply *couldn't* identify with him—took pity at last. He saw Denis weeping and without dignity, his face distorted, limbs useless, and released his power of identification, granting the benighted Group Captain the gift of gifts: the sense that he possessed a soul, although his mind and body were in chaos. In short a complete nervous breakdown was the salvation of Denis Towle, and when, a few years after the war, I heard that Denis had committed suicide, I felt—immediately and involuntarily, straight from GHQ as it were—a wave of happiness for him, only an echo of the joy I think Denis must have felt in the moments that preceded his serene, drugged death, as deep a joy—it is the only joy—as any of us will ever know, no matter how long or how furiously we live. When we find it for an instant, this selfhood, it's anything but our own tawdry personality, much less a one-ness with the universe, that idle boast: I say it's time fulfilled in us, incorporate in us, time from its first breath utterly accumulated here, in this, its latest instant. Most of us, luckier than Denis or simply more optimistic, hope to find that sense of self at a cheaper price than physical self-annihilation. If I am right about Denis, he had little choice. I like to think (and to hell with Wolfgang Zimt and his theories) that Denis was so beautiful that he was, in effect, hollowed out by it, robbed of autonomy and robbed of time; like madness, death is time perfected, and it was his only way home.

In those days home for me was No.3, Maidment Road, where Mrs Sampson kept house like a tigress, but perfumed her soft beds with lavender-smelling linen. The mattress yielded as if it wanted to enfold me, the blankets settled heavily, the sheets closed round me like a bud, and I dreamt of Ellie in the old days, before she'd thickened. Nights in Mrs Sampson's linen— and the days at Trent Park, grilling Germans . . . oh, for a time I took my revenge on the dress uniforms at Schloss Brüel, but it palled. They were young, the German fliers, like ours; and as for Peter I learnt later that he never flew a Messerschmitt or any other plane.

The interrogations began to take over my dreams: Name? Rank? Squadron? Airfield? Then on into the technical questions about air-speed and engine capacity. "Messerschmitt! Die Höchstgeschwindigkeit?!" You had to be careful, I'd soon discovered, to speak clumsy German with a heavy accent, in case they thought you were a compatriot who'd been turned, and then clammed up completely. After a few months Denis told me they'd been monitoring my progress by hidden microphone— bugging me, in fact, as they did all novices. I was the first recruit they'd had who didn't have to overcome native politeness: "Look, would you terribly mind telling me . . . ?" No, not Rat. Name? Rank? Squadron? Airfield? Sit up straight, *Mensch*! More often than not we knew the answers to our own questions. We'd bugged the prisoners' quarters too, and it was all in the *Scheisse*, the "shit," our name for the transcript of their conversations. Every so often we'd tell them the answers, just to rattle them. And read about it in the *Scheisse* the next day: "*Mann, ist er scharf!* He knows all about us!" It was a game, transparently so, but our prisoners couldn't bring themselves to

recognize the fact. Where an Englishman might have sat on his
bunk (I liked to think) in silence, the Germans simply had to
talk. Some did nothing but cry, in their cells. I knew this—I'd
listened to them crying, on the tape—but I didn't care. Next!
Stand up straight! And salute properly, you're in the presence
of an officer of the Royal Air Force! That's better. Sit down.
Name! Rank! Squadron! Airfield! Answer, or I'll have you
transferred to the Polish barracks! D'you think you'd like that?
Cigarette?

The war was passing me by, it was headlines and news broad-
casts and bombers overhead, it was bevvies at six in the mess
to hear the latest, getting drunk in the blackout and listening as
the bombs fell on somebody else. We were on an enchanted
island. The Luftwaffe wouldn't bomb us, intentionally at any
rate, while we housed German prisoners. Even during raids
Denis and I would walk through the grounds, drinking from our
hip-flasks, chatting, watching a sky raked with searchlights,
hung with barrage balloons and bombers and sometimes tiny
sticks of falling bombs caught by a beam, drifting down in for-
mation into the fire-flecked city beneath them.

Then one night as I was walking back home down the long,
narrow drive to Oakwood, I flashed my torch, without thinking
really, on a couple pressed against one of the trees. It happened
where the little hilly path—no more than that, a tarmac path,
unlike the grand main entrance from the Cockfosters end of the
park—changed its character, the frantic, spastic oaks I loved
giving way to a dense soldiery of beeches. A man and a girl,
perfectly commonplace, were caught now in my torchlight beam
like the battle in the sky earlier that night. But the girl, three-
quarters hidden, had such a look of Maggie that I stopped dead.
"Oi," growled the man. I was slow to react, I was drunk—
feeling no pain, as we used to say—and too transfixed to switch
off the torch or swerve the beam away from them. The girl
turned, giggling: only the hair and the way she held herself,
with a wilful sloppiness, belonged to Maggie, the Maggie of
old. And the Hambledon Christmas. I hurried on, but my heart
was pounding absurdly. Maggie hadn't been in my thoughts at
all; the bizarre episode with Herta had darkened my memories
of the Slosh, and I'd even used it, when sympathy threatened,
in my interrogations. But now, full of alcohol and the strange,
pent-up aftermath of playing spectator to the Blitz—a kind of
madness, I think Denis felt it too, as we strolled philosophizing
through well-tended gardens, lit by a burning city—yes, now

the missing memories returned. They were precisely moments of inhibition, unable or refusing, I still didn't understand why, to act, when that was all Maggie seemed to ask. It took an almost painful effort, like tearing something out of myself, to formulate at last the idea that I loved her.

I stopped again, not wanting to reach Oakwood. Knowing the Ellie-soft bed was waiting for me.

Above, ahead of me, row upon row of Queen Mums floated in the sky above New Barnet on their bedwires; and among the balloons, mocked by their evident roundness, their Ellie-pregnant bellies, hung a silly, flat, and cardboard moon.

"Aircraftwoman Trimble reporting for duty, sir!" The curious thing about the way I met my wife, apart from the fact that she was wearing a shirt and tie at the time, was that the moment I saw her or rather the moment she turned, I knew beyond the shadow of a doubt that I was going to marry her. Perhaps it would be truer to say that I knew I could marry her if I wanted to. I'd seen her before, of course: she was a Trimble sister, the one who'd rescued Maggie's books to bone up on her German—it had come in handy at last; we were recruiting WAAFs to type the growing *Scheisse*—and had asked me to find her a spare Count. But she'd settle for a spare Thurgo, it was written on her face. I could claim it was a marriage cobbled together out of seconds, she was getting a substitute Peter and I a substitute Maggie, but that would be a convenient lie. It merely brought us together (though we didn't admit it). I was nothing like Peter, whom she only knew of by hearsay, and she, God knows, was nothing like Maggie. If I'd wanted another Maggie, the last person I'd have picked was Hermione Trimble, mercifully known as Molly.

She was small and round (she'd been small and thin once) and still freckled, and chirpy, and she had the dirtiest mind I've ever met in man or woman. I speak as someone who not only frequents the Reeperbahn, the World's Most Sinful Mile, but who once owned several hundred yards of it, and spent years of his life auditioning artistes for the Grand Théâtre Érotique. Molly's penchant was for the Comique-Érotique. This showed itself early on, we'd only known each other a week or so, and we'd bought some ice-cream, in Oakwood, from a Walls tricycle. They were everywhere in those days, Stop Me And Buy One was their slogan. The uses to which Molly could put ice cream would have surprised the manufacturers, but I only discovered this after she'd thrown herself onto the bed in my digs, naked and exposing a choice of orifices with the cry, "Buy me and stop one!" She was irresistible.

We made that afternoon last. It was our only frolic in a Sampson bed, since our headquarters was soon moved out of London and for the next two years we had to be content with so-called "friendly houses" in Amersham, plus whatever corners of the Buckinghamshire landscape caught Molly's imagination. She preferred haystacks to beds, and abandoned piggeries never failed to get her going. Fine for her—she only had to drop her Churchills, the ghastly regulation bloomers. Not so easy for the chap who had to generate an erection amid the dried manure. But Rat wasn't consulted when the powers-that-were decided to transfer Sisdick—along, as Molly put it, with his dick—to larger, country premises; to a fine old red-brick pile called Latimer House, on the edge of the Chilterns.

Cavendo Tutus, "in caution (or wariness, perhaps), safety," warns the Cavendish family motto at the entrance gates. According to Denis Towle the same motto can be seen from the top of a London bus, on the coat of arms over the Burlington Arcade; at Latimer House it was variously translated as "beware of girls in tutus," "always wear a Johnny," and by those with Latin, "watch yer arse." There were no girls in tutus at the home of the Barons Chesham. It had a dignified setting on a bluff overlooking the river Chess, and our officers' mess was in the baronial drawing room, with a view to match. There were WAAFs and WACs and Wrens galore, though, quartered well away from the main building to reduce hanky-panky. As a result an evening walk through the woods to the pub in Chenies or the cinema in Amersham brought Graeco-Roman mythology to life. The Chilterns were suddenly stiff with nyads and dryads, imprisoned souls—every tree seemed to have a couple glued to it. The woodland, as Molly's father would have put it, was seething with bodies. The fields too, in daytime; and when I think of Latimer it's the smell of the grass and the farmyards and the cawing of irritated crows that I remember. And of course Molly's body.

Perhaps I have the Rev. Mr Trimble to thank, in a perverse way, for these wartime delights. He certainly made his family aware of carnal sin. But the curious thing about Molly's sexuality was that although her powers of invention were astonishing, the act itself was quite without mystery or darkness. Her love-making was fizzy, quenching, and faintly medicinal, like Lucozade—

in, as it were, a variety of colours. Whatever the choice of site or position, copulation was always jolly. It dealt deliciously and reliably with the foreground of my lust, leaving the hinterlands in the privacy both they and I desired; or so I decided. This was oddly restful. We both enjoyed ourselves vastly, but for Molly sex was an activity expressing only itself, it was no more a glimpse of the sacred or an exploration of personality than a drink or a shit, merely a great deal more elaborate. And yet she expressed herself completely in it. How was that possible? She fascinated me. Had she divorced eroticism from whatever murky Trimble recesses she contained? It seemed not; she was all of a piece, and in that sense utterly inaccessible. This tubby, cheerful creature had accepted loneliness—or solitude, rather, since I never knew her to be lonely—in her soul. She was gregarious, she never needed to be alone to seek herself out, since there was no danger of this item disappearing, unlike poor Denis with his ungrateful self (the one who kept forgetting to watch him). Hers was always there; and because she never needed to consult her reflection in the mirror of other people, she moved among them without anxiety. When she was with me I had her complete attention. In between I had to be patient, and sue for her time. I thought at first that it was insecurity that drew her into the giggling groups of her colleagues. In time I realized it was the other way about: she didn't need to be with anyone in particular.

Our visits to Amersham, and our jaunts in Baldwin's Wood and Flaunden Bottom were kept strictly separate from our working relationship, a small wave and a smile in the canteen, a chance encounter in the corridor. "Good morning, sir," and she'd salute me smartly. Then saunter off to the typing pool. The uniform suited her and she knew it; she joined the WAAF because the colour matched her grey-blue eyes, she told me. Much as she loved to take it off, she loved the uniform, and the company, and the wartime irreverence. For her as for most people, the war was a welcome escape from home, where she'd lived in the shadow of Maggie's misdeeds. She, Molly, was the true eccentric of the family, she insisted, denied her rightful place by this pouting, self-dramatizing creature. In Amersham teashops she would go into an imitation of her elder sister at table, "Milk, somebody . . . who made this tea? It's *foul*. God, I feel awful. Oh do shut up, all of you. Beastly brood. God it was boring at the theatre last night . . ." and she'd reproduce Maggie's morning performance, complete with hand rubbing her face like a bad-tempered cat. The other two sisters were goody-goodies, Molly said, and she herself had been pretending to be one of them for years. This was her forte: like Maggie she lacked a voice, or rather a steady timbre, but she had adapted differently—she was a natural mimic, and the war, with all its posturing, provided a field day for her talents.

And as with Alec, it was where she finally came to rest. I was reminded of a schoolfriend called Brigham, Brigham Farquhar—he claimed to be descended from the Restoration dramatist—with his stammer, F-f-f-Farquhar as he was inevitably known; though it was only when I visited his parents' home, in his company, that I discovered that his was a borrowed stammer. An elder brother was the family stammerer, from early childhood, and Brigham's mocking imitation had finally stuck, remaining long after his brother had mastered the tic. It was exactly what we were threatened with at school when adults heard us mocking Brigham. In his case it stuck for good, because while his brother was fighting to control the mannerism, confining its influence, Brigham's second-hand version spread from mockery into a convenient disguise, it infiltrated new areas and became a social strategy. Stammering was an excuse for laziness, a kind of challenge to authority—teachers rarely asked him questions in class, knowing the delay and amusement his answer would cause—and from there it turned into a comic tool. Girls found it endearing. Finally it was indispensable. Something similar was happening to Molly, though it didn't take effect until a year or two later when tragedy came into her life for the first time, and the brusque military manner she'd adopted for a favourite impersonation became useful as protective colouring. Then, like Brigham's stammer, it assumed the character of a familiar house guest, paid its rent, and never went away. At first Molly's brusqueness was borrowed from Matty, Squadron Leader Matthews, the senior WAAF whose bull-dyke tones were familiar to everyone who worked in Latimer House. In WAAF parlance, she was the Queen Bee. Molly made a friend of Matty, and cultivated her out of affection, I think, certainly not out of ambition, though it made her an unofficial liaison for the station gossip that might not otherwise have reached the centre of the bee-hive quite so fast.

I was the next to hear this gossip, or to hear Molly's version of her meetings with Matty.

" 'Morning, Trimble!'

" 'Morning, marm.'

" 'Wonderful morning, Trimble. Seen the headlines?'

" 'Yes, marm. Eighth Army Missing.'

" 'Don't be a fool, Trimble, Eighth Army Massing. Are you blind?'

" 'Yes, marm.'

" 'Good show. Give us a kiss, then.'

" 'Oh, marm. . . .' "

" 'Buck up, child. What's the matter?'

" 'It's Cartwright, marm. She's in the club.'

" 'At ten in the morning? I'll have her stripes for this!'

" 'No no, she's joined the pudding club, marm.'

" 'Joined the pudding club? That's all right, every gel should learn to cook, Trimble.'

" 'She's been knocked up, she's got one up the spout, she's pregnant, Matty!'

" 'Pregnant? She can't be! Damn it, Trimble, you know I've got a Johnny fitted to my dildo.'

" 'Oh marm, you're so thoughtful.' "

Several WAAFs, including Molly, claimed to have been fondled in the Queen Bee's office. In the end somebody familiar with Molly's obscene monologues—it could have been Molly herself, but I doubt it, she was too fond of the old bat—got their revenge, leaving their C.O. a Christmas present in the mess, "from your ever-faithful hive." Matty opened it in public, bringing out a nine-inch length of rubber hosepipe encased in a contraceptive and with two ping-pong balls strapped to its base. Shortly afterwards Matty went home to her mother, never to return, and we got a new Queen Bee.

Leading Aircraftwoman Cartwright also went home to her mother, discharged, though not "dishonourably": the WAAF was merciful. But the fallout rate was alarming, and we were having difficulty finding enough girls to type the voluminous *Scheisse* issuing from the German barracks. For this situation, and for most of the pregnancies, "Pitmarsh" was largely held to be responsible, and became known as Hitler's Secret Weapon. Bridge, Tom Vaughn-Fisher's other passion, acquired new connotations, and when Tom strolled in late, announcing, "terrific hand last night, you chaps," we knew it meant another WAAF was up the spout. But as time went on I found my own work getting easier: there was more *Scheisse* not only because there were more Germans but because they were more loquacious, both in barracks and interrogation room, where the pride that had once endangered my sympathies was now more quickly broken. And we had larger dossiers to work from.

"*Kampfkörper 4, Stafel 3*, isn't it, Oberleutnant Maier?"

"Deutsche Offizier sagt nichts!"

"Oh really? And how are your twins, by the way? Isn't it their birthday?"

Maier would boggle—but it was child's play, given all the documents, the newspapers and letters and station gossip sheets we'd gleaned from German aircraft. Poor startled Maier was impressed, and touched, in his loneliness, and ready to talk. There was no more need to threaten him with the Poles up the road, which had been my invention anyway; there were no Polish barracks close to hand. It had become a popular threat among the other interrogators, since it didn't break the Geneva Convention and it rattled Maier, who knew, however dimly, what his compatriots had been up to in Poland. "Trust a bloody Irishman to think of that one," said Denis. I'd told him about Grandfather, and like Alec he now attributed my drinking habits to Irish blood. Irrelevantly, since he drank as much as I did. We all drank, it was a feature of life of Latimer House, along with boredom, gossip, sex, and nervous breakdowns. Never in the field of human conflict had so many gone off their heads for so little, we decided (out of Denis' earshot) as someone else went home to mother, often for the second time; one breakdown wasn't really trying. It was as if the nation had been waiting for permission to be crazy, and the vicarious excitement tipped them over the edge. In Latimer we never heard a gun fired in anger, my pheasant was the nearest I got to combat, and the only V-1 that fell on Buckinghamshire killed a cow in a field at Brill. Meanwhile we ate well and caroused till all hours, and traded second-hand heroics. It took Alec, who knew the genuine article, to bring the war a little closer home.

Being Alec he also knew the owner of Latimer House, Lord Cavendish, though I don't think he'd rescued a Cavendish from Franco, so when he came to visit me one weekend he arrived in style with a letter from his Lordship, granting him overnight access to the private apartments. On Sunday he drove Molly and me to Maidenhead, and silenced us with anecdotes.

"The fourth grenade rolled to about ten foot away from me, just about where that waiter's standing, too damn close to try to get away, not worth bothering, and too far to reach it and lob the damn thing back. Well, I just stared at it. Of course if it had gone off I'm afraid A.T. wouldn't be here. Thank God for the Norwegian climate, I say. The jelly stuff they pack the little beggars in froze solid, and every so often you got lucky—no bang. Another Pimms, anyone? Rat'll have one, what about you, Airwoman?''

He insisted on calling her this, which Molly took as a slighting reference to her waistline, while I, more charitably—easy when someone else takes the offensive—understood it as embarrassment at being faced with another Trimble and the name he was trying to forget. Maggie herself was never mentioned, though Alec did ask politely after Molly's parents, with an avuncular glance at us both. He was Captain Thurgo now, a leader of men. Apparently this was thanks to the impatience of Three Commandos's senior officer, who got cheesed off, Alec said, waiting to see some action, and threatened to return to his regiment. "Look here, if you don't want to run this show, I will," ran Alec's version. "Oh do," said the cheesed-off major, and put in for a transfer.

My reaction to all this took me by surprise. It was Molly's presence that did it, I suppose. I was bursting with pride. We were a military family (forget the Irish lunatics), the Thurgoes! I was sure Molly was impressed, once she'd got used to the way he addressed her. In fact the weekend was a success in so many ways, restoring my love for Alec, and my admiration, and marking a milestone in my relationship with Molly, that I wanted to find a way of thanking him for what he'd done, whether he'd meant it or not. I prepared the words, and the moment came as Alec dropped us off back at Latimer, in the driveway; Molly was distracted for a moment by a gaggle of passing friends who whistled at the Alvis. Instead Alec beat me to the draw, rolling a small, unfrozen grenade under my feet. "I saw your boy, by the way," he murmured, and before I could recover, "little Punchy-poo. He's got your hooter." Molly was turning back. Too late to ask Alec why and how, or to berate him. "Mum's the word, eh?" said Alec with a coarse wink.

The visit was a milestone all right. It was after Alec's visit that Molly and I began drifting apart. I'd completely misread her reaction, not for the last time in our lives, though after this I became a little warier of her capacity to blend into a social context—as she had as a Hambledon goody-goody—while secretly despising it. She didn't blend in to please people; she was stalking them. And it was only through mimicry that she expressed her true feelings. She'd never have come out openly and told me she found Alec ludicrous, a Laura Trimble war hero. Or that she found him patronizing, to both of us. That was quite clear enough from the way she began addressing me in Alec's tones, "old bean," "old bird," "me old cock-sparrer," till it got on my nerves. It was hypocrisy on my part this time, but I wanted her to say she thought Alec had style and charm, that he was amusing, brave, and modest. Instead she went, "Ratty old chap old bean, did I tell you about the *fifth* grenade? Damn thing landed in my lap, froze solid to my pecker, thank God for the Norwegian climate I say. Bless'd inconvenient, though, couldn't bugger the chaps without blowing myself up!"

I'd have been tickled to hear this sort of thing from her sister; why did it irritate me so, coming from Molly? Finally I couldn't stick it any longer and told her sharply to stop taking the mickey. She gave me a long look, with something of Maggie's blank inexpressiveness in it. But I read it differently: I've got your measure. And for the first time since we'd met we both began making the occasional excuse to be unavailable when the other was free; I can't remember who started it. I didn't admit to myself that the affair was cooling. I filed my own withdrawal under tactics, treat 'em mean and keep 'em keen, a Pitmarsh maxim. It was only when I saw Pitmarsh himself taking an interest in Molly's free time that I woke up to my foolishness. Christmas was coming. Did she have any plans, I asked?

It was that Hambledon Christmas '43, that broke us up. It began with the business of the dog. Some months before, Molly had taken on a puppy, a Scottish terrier called "Matty" after the Queen Bee, who was still with us then; Christmas '43 was the Queen Bee's dildo Christmas, a turning point for her too. The dog Matty was a male, but his namesake took no offence. Molly was enough of a favourite to be allowed to drag the animal into the typing pool, and for walks in the grounds. This was another source of friction between us, spoiling our "cosy get-togethers" as Molly termed the acrobatic fucking I had come to depend on. Now we had the blasted dog yapping at us as we heaved and squidged and squelched. I found this less amusing than Molly did (and a lot less amusing than the dog), quite apart from the way he drew attention to us with his noise and his habit of taking issue with the crows over their use of airspace. "Can't you put him in kennels, just for a week, just over Christmas?" "He'll pine," said Molly sternly. "Well, he'll never sit still in the train, it'll be hell for him, never mind us." "If you'd only learnt to drive, like a normal person, we wouldn't have to *go* by train."

It was true; there was something more than just chance that had intervened between myself and cars. I longed to sample

Alec's way with speed, and at the same time some instinct baulked, dug its heels in like a horse halting in fog, sensing danger.

We went by train, with Matty wriggling and whining in Molly's arms, and pissing on the floor when set free. This cleared the compartment on the London train. On the Petersham train the dog had calmed, but Molly emptied the compartment herself with a monologue about dog fleas and how to tell them from nits. She'd learnt all about nits at WAAF training camp.

"Your father doesn't really approve of me, does he?" I queried when we were alone. "You can tell me. That's the impression he's always given."

"Nonsense," said Molly. "He's a perfect sweetie. It's Mummy you have to watch out for."

"He is mad, though, isn't he? I mean *bona fide* mad, off his chump, not just Latimer House mad."

"No, I don't think so, is he? Why d'you say that?"

"Well . . ."

"You've been listening to Maggie. If you mean all that stuff about sex . . . I mean, I don't agree with him, of course. But he certainly knows what he's talking about."

I hesitated. "Does he? D'you mean . . . he was a gay dog in his youth?"

"Oh God no. Look, I'll smuggle you into his study one night. He's got the best pornographic library in the South of England."

"He's got *what*?"

"That's what they say."

I thought about this. "That's what *who* say?"

"Oh, the Know-Thine-Enemy brigade, that's what Daddy calls them. It's virtually a lending library. Clergy drop in from all over the diocese."

This information, though I did my best to hide the fact, came as a relief. I had assumed that Molly had known a lover of hideous sophistication, and since she hadn't volunteered his name (*her* name? A series of them? Captain Lapénotière? Old Curdle? Granny Crabb?) I had resolved not to ask. The last thing I wanted to carry around with me, haunting me during our cosy get-togethers, was an image of Molly with this hoary old roué. Now I could attribute her repertoire to books; it didn't matter it was true or not, what counted was that I had an alternative, at last, to the imaginary seducer, to the captain Lapénotière who'd already acquired a face and perfumed lodgings. No: little Molly creeping into the curate's study at dead of night—alone, please

God—for basic small-arms training with Frank Harris, matriculation in Oriental pillow-books, advanced theory from de Sade.

All this time Molly was watching me, studying my reaction, smiling. I looked out of the train compartment window, pretending not to notice. Molly began to hum.

" 'You are my sunshine,
My only sunshine,
You make me happy
When I feel blue. . . .' "

I glanced at her. She pursed her lips, sent a kiss, and sang:

" 'You are my sunshine,
My double Woodbine.
My box of matches,
My Craven A.' "

She pursed her lips again, and blew me another kiss. Then she started singing the obscene version.

A pyramid-shaped turd sat steaming on the vicarage drawing-room carpet, right in the middle of the room, in the afternoon sunlight; and we'd barely been there five minutes. The dog knew what was going on, though, before I did. The atmosphere reeked of cordite. Molly didn't or wouldn't recognize it, she spanked the dog and cleaned the carpet and told jolly stories about Matty chewing the Queen Bee's nylons, eating everyone's lunch, and for dessert consuming yards of our precious *Scheisse*. Matty watched his own *Scheisse* disappear with a puzzled, mournful expression. I began to like Matty.

There were only the four of us there in the vicarage, five with the dog, that Christmas. Laura cooked, and the result was dismal. One sister—"the gifted one," Molly sang viciously in her mother's treble, and in Laura's presence—was a war artist, shivering on a destroyer somewhere on the Iceland run; and the remaining Trimble sister, the eldest after Maggie and a former gymkhana champion, had been seen "escorting a high-up" in Whitehall. Molly gave a private sneer. Out of Laura's earshot, she said "Elizabeth's got awfully good hands." This was all entertaining, but what Molly refused to notice was the quiet antagonism the Trimbles were displaying towards us, and especially towards me. Gone were Laura's frothing questions. "I simply don't know how you can bear to talk to Germans every day," was all she said. "Oh but Mummy they're much nicer than we are," Molly beamed. Perhaps this was what she wanted, to be provocative, to be herself at last and show me off as a symbol of her newfound freedom. But for her parents I was a Maggie leftover. It was the past I conjured up. "Show me the library and let's clear out," I begged. "Are you *terribly* bored?" said Molly, playing Trimble sister. "Am I keeping you? Goodness, I'd rather you did go if you're going to sit around like Patience on a monument. You might at least ask Daddy about his work." "What work?" "Ask him, silly, he'll tell you."

"Oh, it's just something I've been doodling with for years," said the curate airily, drawing me with a grip of iron into the study. I scanned the bookshelves quickly for lubricious titles, but in vain. "I try it out on my parishioners, you know, on Sundays," he was saying, "theology of evil, that sort of thing—mediaeval witchcraft—rather fascinating—I gather you're interested in the literature."

"Oh certainly." Then it sank in. "You mean . . . ."

"My daughter says you want to see my private collection."

"Ah!" I said, now distinctly embarrassed.

"What do you make of her?"

"Molly? I'm very fond of her."

Trimble moved towards his desk, paused, and gave me a sharp, kindly look. "She's a bolter, you know."

"A bolter?" A Boulter? What was Laura's maiden name?

"She's always been a bolter. The other one was a witch. This one's a bolter."

"In what respect, sir?"

"Used to run away from school. Ran away from here a couple of times. Never the slightest reason—always perfectly amenable. Suddenly, one morning, gone." He put both hands on the desk, and leaned forwards towards me in his pulpit manner. "Got a secret life. Impenetrable—funny child—can't tell what's going on in there."

Trimble's conversation, I began to realize, was like notes for one of his sermons. Still, he was introducing me to a new Molly.

"You a lawyer yet?"

"No, sir, I've only done my intermediate exams."

"Read the fine print, when you marry her."

Marry her? I thought. Good God, what had Molly been saying?

"She's got a mind of her own." The curate added, fumbling in a drawer, "if you can find it." He brought out a key, held it up and waggled it jovially at me, then set out towards a locked, blind-fronted cabinet. He turned, before unlocking the books. "You're probably damned already, aren't you?"

"Oh yes," I said. "I think so. Look, sir, I don't know what Molly's told you," but I'd lost him.

"Who can touch pitch. . . ." he pulled the wooden wings wide to reveal shelves of books. Trimble turned and studied me. "I keep the Devil under lock and key."

"And loose him for a little season. . . ." I said, quoting his sermon back at him. "So I understand."

Trimble scowled at me, a theatrical scowl. "Yes," he said, "you'll make it a lawyer."

Like an idiot I confronted Molly with her father's words; the mention of marriage, that is. It was a fatal mistake. Molly clammed up angrily, as if this were a ploy of mine to introduce her to the idea, which infuriated me. I became more and more silent and resentful. I hadn't enjoyed looking at the curate's library under his heavy-eyebrowed gaze; and Molly wasn't offering any consolations. Sympathetically, the dog Matty shat in her bedroom, in the hall, and finally in the drawing room again. Molly, fed up with us both, began telling stories of Latimer House which seemed to feature me in an unflattering light, variously drunk, cynical, ingratiating, and out of place. And I had thought I fitted in so well. Looking back, I always felt my wartime attitudes were formed by others, they weren't Thurgo attitudes at all; for the only time in my life I marched in step, and after the vicarage, oh I was so happy to get back to Sisdick and the dear old *Scheisse*.

Where Molly was concerned I now took the initiative, and courted a WAAF, "the one with the teeth" as Molly called her, who carried her own packet of contraceptives with her everywhere and seemed grateful for takers. So much the better. This time I was done with treacherous bloody Trimblitude for good.

There was no getting away from Molly, though. Matty ran to me whenever he saw me, baffled by the turn of events; Molly sat and chirped calmly with her girlfriends, ignoring me. Every day I expected Pitmarsh to come in with "jolly good hand last night," but the months went by and it never happened.

Instead I received a letter addressed to *R Thurgo Interogting Ofice*, one spring morning when the Chess was beginning to unfreeze, Baldwin's wood was in bud, and the headlines were fretting over Tobruk.

Dear Punch, gues what your brother Alec came to see me and I got your adress off him isnt that a scream Bet your pleased. He said young Ronnie Purdy one of my boys joined his regimint and my name come up in the mess he said. I hate think what

*was said dont you. Spiffing chap Ronnie is thats the way he talks
your brother isnt he a scream we didnt do nothing just taked.
Honest Punch or I wouldnt be telling you about, punch I've got
to see you just this once its important I'm still at the old place.
Come soon when you got leave its important. You was fixed up
Alec says are you happy? I hope so you know that but one time
I out of sorts I got Auntie to put a jipshun on you dont worry I
did that before and it never worked you know how useles she is
Punch I don't believe in it no more the stars and that its bolocks
heaven keep you safe my dear I always think of you the old cow
sends her love Auntie I mean bye for now, your Ellie.*

With foreboding—though not over the "jipshun," one of
Auntie's "Egyptian" spells—I took the London train, and a taxi
brought me through thick, freezing fog to Cambridge Circus,
here and there skirting roped-off rubble and holes in the street.
London was an underwater city in the fog, headlamps looming
up like deepsea fish, inquisitive but uncertain, and wary of ob-
stacles; the irregular outlines of bombed houses, lightless,
shrouded in fog, resembled undersea boulders as much as buildings. It was unnerving, as if I'd missed the war entirely until
now. Against all reason I felt my taxi was a clearly visible target
for the bombers—a special flight containing the friends and colleagues of the German airmen I'd tormented, who knew (thanks
to the Thurgo dossier, and a network of Sisdick spies) that it
was me in the cab.

There was something nightmarish about our pub that evening,
people swaying and singing in the smoky light, shouting across
the bar. I'd got used to the Red Lion at Chenies, with its sleepy
customers, and after the gentrified atmosphere of Latimer House
it was like entering Valhalla. I was home. I would be, when the
eerie cab-ride cleared from my head.

"Hello, Punch." I turned, but it was another girl, one of the
regulars, and I stared at her, at her clothes and lipstick, trying
to summon up her name.

Snatches of conversation came and went across the singing.
" 'Im and 'is bloody pisspot," came a raucous voice from a
nearby table. "All the way to Peckham!"

"Cat got your tongue?" The girl was smiling at me. "She's
over there, your friend."

Ellie was sitting in the snug, where I'd so often imagined her,
under the light. But seeing her there, just where she was supposed to be, was like a reproach; as if I was merely late. And
something else was nagging at me, the thought had formed be-

fore I could call it back. She looked like a tart. Of course she did, she'd been a tart for ten years; more—and that too made my mind swim; had I known Ellie ten years?

"All the way to Peckham," the voice kept repeating, as though it was droll enough in itself. " 'E walked all the way to Peckham with a ruddy metal pisspot on 'is 'ead."

"Ellie! Look who's here!"

"I don't feel safe without my helmet, he says. And when 'e gets to Egypt what's 'e do? Steps on a bleedin' land-mine."

The singing rose to drown the voices. Behind the cut-glass partition that separated us from the saloon bar I could see figures dancing, men on leave with their gaudy girls. Dancing; a tankful of tropical fish mocking the grey waters outside. I tried to remember: was Valhalla supposed to be below the waves, or above, or beyond? I felt Ellie's arms around me, she was kissing me, and crying, and pulling me into the snug, sitting me down, smearing her tears and make-up on my cheeks, Punch and Judy puppet kisses. I couldn't catch her words.

At last the singing stopped. *Trust an Irishman*, I heard someone say, quite distinctly, and saw Pitmarsh leering at me from the bar, although he wasn't there; heard Denis Towle's precise, pained tones. *Is it the Irish in you, or what?* Ellie's head was on my shoulder, her voice at my ear.

"You're not angry, are you, about your brother? He didn't mean no harm. I could have thought up any old excuse, how I knew where to write to you, but he was so nice, I knew you must have made it up, the two of you. You have, haven't you?"

I turned to look at her. Ten years come Christmas; I was sixteen when I met her.

"D'you know, he even gave me money for little Punch—" Her eyes flooded, she couldn't go on, and I knew what she was going to tell me. I knew it from her voice, her face. "I swear I looked after him, the doctor said so, he said I done what I could but they got no proper defences when they're little. It was disptheria, come from the bombs. The ones with germs."

What bombs? When?

And when 'e gets to Egypt, what's 'e do? Put a jipshun on you.

When, Ellie?

"He's been dead four weeks."

I didn't understand. *What* bombs, for God's sake?

Hadn't I heard? Hitler was bombing us with germs, everyone knew that. Everyone except the clever-dicks in country houses.

I nodded, but she could see I didn't believe it.

"It's everywhere, the disptheria. Fat lot you know."

I saw it leaking, in Ellie's dreams, from bombed sites. Dripping from the sky.

"Diphtheria, not disptheria."

Ellie nodded sad agreement. "That's what the doctor said, disptheria."

After a while I rose to fetch some drinks. She held me back, angry. "You wouldn't've come if I'd told you in the letter, would you?"

"I guessed," I said, but I felt nothing; nothing but relief, and pity.

"I'll never believe in them bloody stars again so help me God, as long as I live. Auntie said he was going to keep me in my old age." The tears were rolling down both sides of her nose.

I fought my way through the linked arms and the bawling, to the bar; stood, and nodded, hearing the girl's reedy voice: the usual? But when I looked up I knew she hadn't spoken; she wasn't there; in her place there was a stranger leaning back against the bottles, singing, a raddled man in a woman's wig. Face like a peeling tenement, a black wig framing it, lank as black-out drapes. He/She lurched forward to peer at my uniform.

"Sing up, Flight. It might never happen."

Ten days later I proposed to Molly Trimble, and was accepted. It seems I was the only person at Latimer House, apart from the new Queen Bee, who didn't know that Molly already had a bun in the oven. I was stunned.

"You're pregnant? But they'll send you home to mother!"

"Not if you're going to marry me. I'll be discharged, that's all. We'll find a house. Somewhere close. I think Sarratt might be rather nice."

"What would you have done if . . . if I hadn't asked you to marry me?"

She shrugged. She'd have managed.

"Are you sure you want to marry me? It's not just to give the baby a father? I mean, I am the father?"

"You're the father, Richard. And of course I want to marry you."

"Why didn't you say so at Christmas, then?"

"You didn't ask. You wanted to know if I told Daddy you were going to marry me."

"Did you. Tell him, I mean?"

"He's awfully indiscreet, isn't he. At least you finally got hold of the idea." She saw me looking doleful. "Oh come on, you know I want to marry you. Why d'you think I joined this stupid outfit?"

"Because of me? I thought it was the colour of the uniform." She smiled patiently.

"But how did you know I was with Sisdick?"

"Tom told me."

"You knew Pitmarsh?!"

"Of course I knew him. His father's the Bishop of Exeter—terribly interested in witchcraft. I've known Tom Vaughn-Fisher since I was a little girl."

"Why . . . why didn't he tell me? In *witchcraft*, did you say?—wait a minute—did *he* teach you all those tricks?"

"What tricks? You mean sex? Of course not."

"I'm going to have a word with Pitmarsh."

She grinned. I saw it all. I was the victim of a pincer movement. Bloody "Pitmarsh"; bloody Vaughn-Fisher. Bloody ecclesiastical plots. Eighth Army Massing had nothing on it.

And anyway: did I want to marry her? If so, why? Why had I proposed to her? I'd told myself it was because I couldn't bear to think of her with someone else. Which was true, but Pitmarsh had craftily fanned those flames. And because she made me laugh more than anyone else I'd ever met; certainly more than anyone I'd be likely to meet with her additional qualifications, her expert knowledge of what the curate was pleased to call the theology of evil. But at the same time I had to tell myself I was doing it despite the fact, not because of it, that she was a Trimble. And I pretended it had absolutely nothing to do with the evening I'd spent with Ellie in the underwater city. No, Molly had her own, unique charms. Where would I find her like again?

Marry her, then.

"Never laid a finger on her. Word of honour," said Tom Vaughn-Fisher. "Played bridge with the mother. Took out the elder sister. God's truth."

"Which elder sister?" I said. "Maggie?"

"Oh God no. Appalling creature. No. The horsey one. Elizabeth."

"Ah," I smiled. "*Awfully* good hands." And to my amazement, Pitmarsh blushed.

Marry her. Give the child a father.

"Would you mind very much if we called the baby after Father?" said Molly.

"I think *she*'d mind very much, if she's a girl."

"Oh, nobody has girls in wartime."

"If it's a girl I won't have it called Laura."

"It isn't going to be a girl. Now will you answer my question?"

"Your father's Christian name is Wilfred."

She saw my expression. "He'd be so pleased. Really."

"He won't be pleased at all. You're not supposed to go to the altar pregnant."

"That's the whole point. It's to make it up to him."

I couldn't follow her logic. But I knew a bargaining point when I saw one.

"I'm not having Pitmarsh as best man."

"Then you're not having Alec as best man."

"Face?"

"Alright, Face." I saw her hesitate. "Well, ask him, anyway."

Marry her. Go through with it.

Denis closed his eyes in quiet grief. "As your friend, you can reasonably expect me to turn a blind eye to the fact that you're taking to wife a pregnant colleague, but as your superior officer you can hardly expect me to sanction it in public, much less give away the roly-poly bundle *and* be your best man."

"What do you mean, give her away? That's her father's job."

"I understand her father isn't coming, for all too obvious reasons. Don't you know *anything*, Richard? She's asked me to give her away."

"Well can't you do both?"

Denis groaned.

"Look," I said, once more glimpsing some leverage, "I didn't want to mention it before asking you, but I'd really like to name the boy after you."

"What boy?"

"Well, Molly says it's a boy. And she wants to call it Wilfred."

"That's a pretty awful name."

"Exactly."

"But so's Denis. I mean, I'm desperately flattered."

He looked to be in pain.

"Well," I said, "I don't know. Have you got any other names?"

"Names I like, you mean?"

"No no, of *yours*. Other than Denis."

"Yes," he said, brightening. "I've got several other names."

"What are they?"

"Well, I'm Denis Arthur Bonaventure Towle."

"Ah," I said. "Bully for you."

Too late not to marry her, now that everyone's expecting it.

One encounter I would have paid to witness was that between Molly and our new Queen Bee, a kindly, trusting woman who had been persuaded to believe that Matty was the official Sisdick mascot, and that *Scheisse* was the German for coffee (down the corridors of Latimer House "Where's my damn *Scheisse*?" was admittedly the most popular cry, after "Where's my bloody tea?") which may well have caused the lady some post-war embarrassment. After so many Queen Bee interviews in which Molly had been the bearer of sad tidings about other prematurely pregnant WAAFs, how was Molly going to handle it now that she had, as it were, to rat on herself?

"Shan't say a dicky-bird," said Molly. "She'll never notice."

And she didn't, even as we stood blinking in the sunshine outside St. Mary Magdalen ("an admirable choice of saint," breathed Pitmarsh), the little chapel attached to Latimer House. It was a preposterous building, with a vaguely Byzantine boil on it instead of a bell-tower; but we were a preposterous-looking couple.

"A little ill-assorted, don't you think?" was all the Queen Bee said. It was an understatement. No-one at Sisdick was prepared to take responsibility for the wedding photographs, which was a mercy. Beside my lanky frame of six foot six, with my hands sticking out of my ill-fitting uniform jacket like spades, Molly was a well-rounded five foot one and looked more like a mascot than Matty did.

The family graves of the Barons Chesham were gaily interspersed with primrose, violets, and speedwell; it was a glorious May morning. Denis made a lugubrious speech, Pitmarsh kissed the bride without permission, and our various relatives, praise God, were either absent shocked, absent on active duty—in the case of Alec and the Trimble sister on the Iceland run—or, in my mother's case, absent utterly indifferent to human affairs.

"Cup of tea, anyone? Anyone want a cup of tea?" were the first words I heard after the bomb hit Alec's house. The voice belonged to an air warden. Unlike Alec at Dunkirk, it seemed we weren't going to run out of tea; but we were distinctly short of cover.

On his return from the "Sicilian show" where, in his own phrase, Alec "picked up" the M.C.—tripped over it, as it might be, in a passing trattoria—Alec was keen to lay on a do for the newlyweds. So were the Luftwaffe. We heard the whoosh of the missile, Alec yelled "Down!" and pulled Molly from the table as I dived off my chair, and there was nothing to be heard for long panic-stricken instants except the faint whine of the descending bomb; then the explosion, deafening but releasing us, breaking the tension with something more familiar than the unearthly whine: noise, intolerable but reassuring. It meant we were still alive. The thing had landed in the garden, and the effects of the blast took the roof off the house, sent glass slashing through the rooms and destroyed the back wall from top to bottom. "No use boarding this one up," said the air raid warden with a laconic smile. "Clear out and count yourselves lucky." Inside the house, after our eardrums had recovered from the shock, a small pattering noise came, the hissing of mortar as it settled in the sagging walls. I remember turning from Molly's stunned face, her hair and features whitened by the falling plaster, to the dinner table where we'd been sitting when the bomb fell, and searching in vain for a clean glass, to bring her some water. The celebration meal, so appetizing only a few moments before, and prepared with such care, had turned into Miss Havisham's macabre wedding feast in *Great Expectations*, dishes, cutlery, and glassware all mummified by a lifetime's dust. The warden's tea more than compensated for his sardonic manner. Molly looked like Miss Havisham herself, and grotesque as the effect was, as chalky as a crude stage make-up, it gave a startling indication of what she would look like as an old woman. Alec and I, seeing each other unharmed but equally transformed by the plaster dust, aged by forty years, began to laugh helplessly at each other.

When we turned back to Molly, there was blood beginning to seep through the whiteness on her forehead.

The shock in her eyes couldn't have been greater if she'd glimpsed herself in a mirror. But she was seeing nothing, looking inwards at death. Then she stirred, moved a hand to her belly, and I knew it wasn't her own death she was seeing. She closed her eyes.

"Ratty? Ratty?" I felt Alec's hands under my armpits as I sat in the hospital waiting room, and for all my size he pulled me up onto my feet like a child, and hugged me. "You'll have another one, old chap, lots of 'em. She's perfectly all right, old bird. Ratty? Molly's all right."

I nodded but I couldn't stop crying.

"Give her another one, eh? Eh? Come on now. Shape up, Flight."

I didn't tell Alec about little Punch; I didn't tell Molly—how could I?—that I knew there was a curse on me, a jipshun. I would never have a living child, a child who lived. It had to be the jipshun; it was the jipshun because I hadn't believed in it.

At the hospital I kept coming back to the same thought: there was only one person who could help me now, and that was Auntie, in her stinking Poland Street flat, under Percy walls. But I kept the thought at bay. I wanted a normal child, not a spirit exorcized by Auntie's foul-smelling herbs and mumbo-jumbo. I didn't believe in all that "bolocks" any more than Ellie did. And yet—that was just it: Ellie didn't, now that it suited her not to do so. We could all be sceptical when we were beyond help or harm; but even the greatest sceptics stretched a point when their own lives were at stake. Or their children's lives. And weren't the sceptics, by common consent, those who wanted most profoundly, most uncompromisingly, to believe?

I wanted to believe. From the way Molly grieved over the miscarriage, month after barren month bringing a disappointment harder to bear than the one before, I knew that unless I did something my marriage would be blighted as completely as the dinner Alec had given in our honour. But by then our life had changed; and with the changes my vision of Auntie's beneficient spells turned back, for a time, into a pipe-dream.

We'd rented a cottage some eight miles from Latimer, in a district of Sarratt quaintly called Under The Heavens. Not even the most ancient locals could tell us the origin of the name, and being sunk in a wooded valley it was rather less evidently under the heavens than the other parts of Sarratt; but there was no part of that countryside left unblessed that summer, burgeoning with fruit and flowers and green things as if to tell Molly that she was the only infertile clay under our portion of the heavens. She had begun to knit the regulation woollens, long before the anticipated arrival of little Wilfred. On my insistence she'd knitted them in both pink and blue, matching piles which I was at pains to hide before Molly's emergence from hospital. She tracked them down, though, brought them out, and began adding relentlessly to them. Not all the feckless WAAFs, WACs, and

Wrens of Sisdick put together in their hour of need could have exhausted Molly's reserves of baby-uniforms.

Before the bomb our married "get-togethers" had been more playful than ever; I woke one morning in the cottage to find Molly's ration book open on my naked stomach at the page where, as she'd read to me more than once, mothers-to-be were sternly told "Mother! Eat this piece of meat entirely by yourself! Do not share it with your family!" and Molly was suiting her actions to the words. But now we rutted with a desperation that we both knew could only provoke the gods to mirth, not pity. Worse, Molly would scarcely leave the house, as though it were a nest she had to keep warm at all hours; as though leaving it had brought down the bomb in the first place. This was normal, people assured me. It would come to an end. I was patient, but what I feared most was a reaction to extremes. Her father's words often came to mind, and I became obsessed with the idea that I would come home one evening to find she'd bolted. Every day as I left the cottage I saw her in my mind's eye, packing. *Suddenly, one morning, gone.* Old, pleasant habits came to an abrupt end. Gone for me were the Latimer House evenings playing billiards or table tennis, I left "Face" to drink alone in his quarters—a step which had its own repercussions—and cycled the eight hilly miles to Sarratt in frantic haste, muttering half-remembered prayers. It all came to an ignominious climax on the hill leading out of Latimer, where I gave myself a hernia.

This was a blessing in disguise, not least because it made Molly chortle. I'd despaired of finding an excuse to get myself to London, and to Poland Street, though if Molly had been in a calmer frame of mind this would have been easy enough. As it was she tolerated my absences at work no better than I did, and if I was five minutes later in the evenings she was convinced that I was the victim either of a V-1 or the WAAF with the teeth. Had it been both at once it might have appeased her sense of divine injustice. But her suspicions that I was betraying her—I, exhausted by her demands—with every female at Latimer House were more than a match for my own fears that she would bolt. Little short of a national emergency and a persona, signed summons from Churchill would have reassured Molly that I was going to London on innocent business.

And was it innocent? There were days when it was Ellie I pictured in Auntie's chair, Ellie for whom the old, obstinate desire had put up fresh shoots in my head. The simplest thing would have been to explain to Molly about Auntie, though not about the origin of the jipshun; merely say I knew a fortune teller with unique powers over fertility. I could hear Molly echoing me: unique powers over fertility, eh? The worst excuse she'd ever heard for a night on the town. She'd already decided that Tom Vaughn-Fisher and I were scouring Amersham for similar powers. Melancholy Denis was the only one allowed to come to dinner, because he made absolutely no attempt to cheer her up, and she loved him for it.

"You've got a choice, Flight Lieutenant," recited the M.O. pleasantly, "you can queue up for the Surgeon Admiral, he's cheap and he'll slit you from shoulder to crotch, or you can see Mr Gambol in Harley Street who'll charge you a bloody fortune for a neat incision."

"I'll have the neat incision, please."

I had my excuse to go to London. Even Molly could see the necessity, if I was to father her child, of an expert hernia operation.

Auntie and I parried each other's enquiries for ten minutes or so like tennis opponents warming up, without giving anything away. Yes, Ellie was well, and sent her love. Yes, I knew lots of interesting war secrets. She knew something must have happened in my life, to bring me to Poland Street, something unhappy—clients, as Auntie liked to point out, never bring clairvoyants their good news. But what? I chose the big crystal. She nodded solemnly, fetched it from under its russet cloth, blew on it, polished it briefly, and settled.

"I'm afraid your mother's not been very well, has she."

"Really? In what way, Auntie?"

Auntie considered. She knew I didn't see Mother very often, so it was a safe opening gambit.

"Could be gall bladder. Does she get stones?"

"Not to my knowledge."

"I can see migraine here."

"It's her back that gives her trouble."

"Yes, it's the sciatica. I've had it myself. And the plumbago."

"Lumbago, Auntie. Plumbago's a plant."

"Is it? I've got some herbs would do wonders for your mother's back."

"Another time, perhaps."

"Some people won't do nothing for their mothers."

Finally she moved onto more exposed ground.

"You've got a young lady, haven't you, bonny lad."

"Yes."

No doubt Ellie had told her Alec's news, that I was "fixed up."

"Yes. I thought so. I can see it in the crystal. One of the girls there, where you work."

"That's right."

"I hope you haven't told her any secrets."

"No, Auntie."

"She likes you, my dear."

"I hope so."

"Oh I can tell you she likes you. But she's upped and left you, hasn't she."

Panic shot through me. Molly, packed, gone.

"Yes, she's got fed up waiting. And she's an independent lass. Am I right?"

I nodded, numb.

"She wants you to marry her, doesn't she, and that's the trouble. You don't want to."

"What?" I breathed again. "No, Auntie, I *have* married her. I'm married." In my relief I couldn't resist it: "D'you mean you couldn't see that?"

Auntie abandoned the crystal and gazed at me instead.

"I can see it now from looking at you, Punch. I don't know why I use these bloody things, I do better without them. You're married, are you. Well, it's not going right or you wouldn't be here."

"It's not my marriage that's the problem, Auntie."

"Isn't it?"

There was a pause.

"You ill or something?"

"Doesn't it tell you in the crystal?"

"You're a devil, *you* are." She turned back to the opaque ball, with a sigh, and mused for a time. "Nothing wrong with your health, bonny lad. Got to watch out for boils, though."

"Boils?"

"And water's no good for you."

"You mean I shouldn't wash?"

Auntie gave me a hard stare. "I mean you shouldn't bloody drown. There's deep water here."

"Anything else? Migraines?"

She said nothing.

"Auntie, I've just had a ruddy operation, this morning, for a hernia. Couldn't you tell?"

"Well I said you were in perfect health, didn't I? You are, now."

I shook my head, stalemated. There was no point in prolonging this.

"You did an Egyptian for Ellie, didn't you?"

After a moment she shrugged a yes.

"What was it? What sort of spell?"

"Just herbs, bonny lad, that's all."

"Auntie, what *was* it? What did Ellie want?"

"She wanted you, Punch. But she can't have you. If I've told her once I've told her a hundred times."

"She wanted me? That was the spell?" Auntie nodded. "And if she couldn't have me?"

The old girl studied me.

"If you're born under Saturn you have to be patient in this life."

"Auntie . . ."

"I don't do those sort of spells, Punch. Just good luck, that's all."

"What was the spell, Auntie?"

"It was to bring you back to her." She picked up the cloth and covered the crystal. "What's happened, Punch dear?"

I told her about the miscarriage, and Molly's desperation. The old girl listened with her professional, beyond-good-and-evil face.

"Auntie, I've seen you cooking up those herbs for other customers. Don't tell me they weren't hurtful spells."

She caught hold of my hands and held them tight. "Just good luck, Punch. Believe me. That's all I'd ever wish you."

I wouldn't leave until she swore to me the jipshun was no part of what had happened. Then, as I stood up to go, she said abruptly, "Don't drive with the petrol in the back."

"What?"

She repeated it.

"What do you mean, Auntie? I don't drive, you know that."

"Well, that's good."

"But why did you say it?"

She shrugged. "You see lots of mugs driving round with petrol cans. Daft way to get yourself killed. Be careful who you travel with, eh? Some of them are a bit dicey."

"Some of whom?"

"You should know."

"I like dicey companions, Auntie."

She smiled. "Haven't you got a kiss for me?"

I kissed her carbolic-smelling old face. "I'm sorry I wasn't better for you this time," she said. "I've got a migraine meself today, no wonder that's all I see in the bloody crystal. Heaven keep you safe, my dear."

I steeled myself.

"Will I have another child, Auntie?"

Why did I even bother to ask? Why didn't I just leave?

"She'll be pregnant within the year, Punch. Sure as I'm sitting here."

"Will you do a spell for me to make sure?"

"No need, dear; trust me. And I'll tell you the truth, the smell of the herbs is murder for a migraine."

"You're sure it'll be all right? The baby?"

"He'll be all right, Punch. Don't fret over him. The Lord looks after his own."

And that was all she would say. I went to the door, feeling relieved, almost weightless. As always, it was like leaving the dentist. Auntie smiled at my delighted face, and sighed.

"Just don't call him Punch, will you. Call him something else, it's bad luck."

"I'll call him Percy," I said, nodding at the old postcards behind her. "Percy Walls Thurgo." After all, Walls ice cream had brought Molly and me together, in a manner of speaking.

But on my return to Sarratt things began to worsen. The days of Buy Me And Stop One were gone, and the nights were becoming joyless, a means of an ever-receding end. What heartening signs there were on Molly's side were undermined by greater anxiety on mine. I was allowed to take Matty for walks again; apparently the woods of Under The Heavens were no longer stocked, in Molly's imagination, with WAAFs on carefully timed assignations. This was just as well, because since Molly wouldn't leave the house to give him some exercise, Matty had started to deposit *Scheisse* in the cottage, in protest. Unfaithfulness receded; infertility remained. And I was the fretful one now. Molly only had to bring out the sedatives her doctor had given her, or complain of a bad night, and I would ring up Latimer House with some excuse for staying at home. By the autumn my colleagues were fed up with filling in for me. I'd phoned in sick so often that even the telephonists were making sly remarks. "Isn't the honeymoon over yet, Flight? Where can I get one like you?" Finally I was summoned before our Commanding Officer, a shy, remote man called Potts, who preferred to communicate by memo. This time I was certain I was for the high jump. I'd been "sick" both previous days. A reprimand, perhaps a demotion. Loss of pay; that was all I needed.

"This way, Flight."

I couldn't tell anything from the faces of the WAAFs in the C.O.'s outer office.

"The Wing Commander will see you now, Flight."

I had my excuses ready in mental note-form, taking a leaf out of my father-in-law's book. Wife under sedation—miscarriage—tragic circumstances—compassionate leave. I wasn't very hopeful. I'd already made one appeal for sympathy, to the M.O., whom I'd visited about my hernia. "Broody, is she?" "No, I really think it's more than that, sir." "Nonsense. It'll pass," he said. "Don't pay her so much attention, man. Treat her normally."

"Sit down, Flight," said Potts without preamble. He was short and stout, with no visible neck and a head wider than it was long, as if his desire to fit inside a cockpit had only been achieved with the help of an enormous winepress. "I see you've been with us nearly four years . . . so you should have learnt the value of secrecy by now."

The first part of his sentence had convinced me I was for it; the second part baffled me utterly. I nodded.

"Thurgo . . . what I'm going to tell you is in ah, the strictest confidence."

Potts turned a pencil over in the fingers of one hand, bouncing it on the desk. Whatever the problem was, he was clearly wishing he could deal with it by memo.

"It *is* your brother, isn't it? Had a hand at Dieppe? Cavendish speaks well of him." He put down the pencil, interlaced his fingers and with a flick of the wrist turned the palms outwards, the finger joints snapping like a shuffled deck of cards. This species of manual fart seemed to bring him release at last. "I've got in mind a little mission for you, that's the thing. I'm told you're on ah, friendly terms with Group Captain Towle."

"With Face? Yes sir."

"Never mind station procedure, Flight. You're familiar with his history? Medical history? Good." He looked at me for a moment. "That's the trouble, you see. All the games you chaps play, all this, ah, cat-and-mouse nonsense—you don't know when to stop. No wonder you lose your marbles. What d'you make of Towle? Is he a homo?"

"Sir?"

"Nothing in his records. Never know, chap with looks like that."

He studied me a little suspiciously, but seemed reassured by my gargoyle features.

"Fellow's got a bee in his bonnet about General Jessen. Comes in here and talks my head off, Jessen this and Jessen that. Jessen and his . . . his—" Potts forced it out, "his need for love. Has he, ah, talked like that to you?"

"No, sir." General Jessen was one of our most distinguished prisoners, so much so that he found our hospitality a little meagre, and his cry "I haff complaint!" had become a regular greeting among us. He was tight-lipped about military secrets, but voluble about our food, our bedding, and our failure to iron his trousers; and he demanded a batman. We gave him one: Franz, our best stoolie, a most willing collaborator and consummate actor. This produced quick but mixed results. The General took Franz into his confidence and, just as promptly, into his arms. "I haff complaint" acquired a new meaning in Sisdick circles. Our stoolie insisted on being delivered from the General's embraces, and an accident had to be contrived whereby Franz fell down the stairs—or pretended to—on the way to the latrines. "Ach du lieber Gott!" the General had cried, hearing the fall and the distant cries, "Ach du lieber Gott! Hilfe! Help! What has happened to my Franz?" Since then "Face," as far as I knew, had been questioning Jessen in vain; but when I last saw Denis he'd seemed in full possession of his marbles. "Has the General been, ah," Potts' hesitations were catching, "importuning Group Captain Towle?"

"Ask Towle. Right now he's upstairs on his bed. Been there three days."

I heard myself groan.

"It's all right, he's *compos mentis*, more or less. Best thing for him, I thought. I don't mind a chap taking a day off now and then if he's been overdoing it or, ah, got cause," and to my surprise the man was looking at me with a positively human expression on his face, "but we can't have senior men going round spreading rumours about poisoned coffee."

"Sir?"

"Towle thinks Jessen's putting something in his coffee, that's the latest thing. Trying to poison him. Switches their coffee cups when Towle's not looking."

I hesitated.

"What?" said Potts. "It's absolute balderdash."

Whatever else, Denis wasn't a fantasist. I was sure of that. "I don't think the Group Captain would invent a thing like that, sir—" but I got no chance to explain Towle Syndrome.

"He wanted me to send Jessen to the dentist," Potts broke in, exasperated, "says he's got false teeth full of cyanide. I asked him *why* General Jessen would want to poison him. Well, according to Towle, the General feels, ah, rejected by him. Can you believe it? Silliest thing I've ever heard. *Rejected* by him? Damn it, Towle's his interrogator, not his bum-boy! I told him so, and he's been sulking ever since."

"Sir—"

"I've read Towle's dossier. Did you know that before his crack-up he started accusing the other pilots of trying to shoot him down? His own Wing?"

This shut me up; I hadn't known.

"I can't think what to do with Towle. The fellow's a security risk, we don't want him running all over the countryside in his, ah, present state. Talking to God knows whom." Potts raised his eyebrows at me. "I've told him to go home for a week, but he says he won't. Very polite about it, says he'd rather not. I told him it was an order. He thought about it, said he wouldn't go home, thank you very much, but he *was* prepared to go to Dobwalls. Does that mean anything to you?"

"To where, sir?"

"Dobwalls. Aren't you a Cornishman?"

"Yes, sir."

"Well, you ought to know, then. I didn't. Had to get someone to look it up on a map. Dobwalls. It's near a place called Liskeard. Know where that is?"

I should have stopped Potts then and there. He wanted me to drive Denis to Cornwall, to "some place for the ah, religious, that's what Towle says it is, full of spies and conchies for all I know, so stay on the qui vive." I should have told him to find someone else and that I couldn't possibly leave Molly; told him I couldn't drive, something he seemed to have overlooked in planning this mission of mercy. But I didn't.

"Keep your eye on Towle. All the time. If he starts to shoot his mouth off, bring him back here toute suite. I don't want to straitjacket him, he's a good man. But I will if he goes off the deep end. Is that clear?"

And it wasn't just pity for Denis that made me say yes to the mission. At the very mention of it I realized how badly I wanted to get away from Molly for a while, from her distraught face, her pleas, her threats, her little legs pinioning me to her body as if she wanted to devour me, take all of me inside and regurgitate me as her child. I was already thinking up excuses for going off to Cornwall with Denis, as I bounded up the stairs to the officers' quarters. Excuses; guilty ones, hiding behind rancour. How dare she turn me from a lover into a failed inseminator?

"Denis?"

"Hello," he said, a tinge regretfully. He was lying on his bed, fully dressed, eyes closed and hands folded across his chest like the Egyptian figurines at the Slosh.

"Are you all right?"

He opened his eyes and looked at me in answer, expressionless.

"What's all this about Jessen?" I said. "He hasn't really been poisoning you?"

"I know my own cup, Richard. He swapped them round."

"Perhaps he was afraid you'd slipped something in his."

Denis thought about this solemnly. "I hadn't considered that."

"You put the wind up Pottsy, you know."

"He wanted to send me home. Did he tell you?" Denis glanced at me, unsmiling. "The poor old parents nearly died trying to hide their shame last time."

"Come off it, Face. You're perfectly all right."

He gave this some thought, without umbrage. "Potts won't let me go to Dobwalls unaccompanied. You will do it, won't you, Richard? There's . . . well, it's rather like a kettle just before it boils, there's a sort of pressure. It was like this before. A little hole in the skull would do the trick. Or some benzedrine. That's been known to help." He saw my expression. "I'll be all right when I get to Dobwalls, and if anything happens on the way, at least you'll be there. I'm really sorry, Richard. It's the only way out of it."

"Out of what?"

There were tears forming in his eyes. I should have guessed but I didn't. At that moment, in his featureless, overly tidy quarters, all I saw was a man on the verge of tears who said he felt like a kettle about to boil.

"Denis, why are we going to this Dobwalls place? Is it a monastery or what?"

"It's Hanbury's ark," said Denis. "You'll understand when you meet Hanbury."

Molly's reaction, when I told her I was taking Face to Cornwall, was worse than the row I'd pictured, as I armed myself with plenty of Dutch courage in the mess that evening. She went completely silent, as if she'd been expecting it all along. As if she'd known I would abandon her. She didn't say a word. I wanted to give in at once, to cancel the journey and comfort her. But her set, round face had assumed an impervious look. She was rapidly becoming a stranger, and much as that frightened me, it made it easier to leave. The only way Molly was ever going to make a clean break with her pills, her fears and her suspiciousness and her dependence, was by being deprived of her chief drug: me. That's what I told myself. Perhaps it was my own fear and dependence I was addressing, but I had no experts to advise or help me to keep open the lines of communication with Molly, they were all busy with "serious" cases; it was wartime and people were supposed to keep their beak above water, as Alec liked to say, or sink.

"You could go down to Hambledon for a few days."

Over breakfast I made myself say it, although it was what I was most afraid of. I could see myself trying to retrieve her and falling, but I felt she was less likely to do it if I suggested it myself. Less likely to leave; to bolt.

"Don't go with Denis," she said. "Please."

But I did, and it was one of the few things in my life that I did absolutely right.

Knowing I'd been detailed to do the driving, and knowing I couldn't drive, Denis had devised a Byzantine scheme to cover our departure from Latimer House. His own car, a Standard, was driven by his batman to a nearby hospital, in Rickmansworth. Denis then insisted on a blood test to prove his allegations against General Jessen, and had us both taken by ambulance to the hospital where his car was waiting and no-one would remark on the fact that when we set off Denis would be the driver and I the passenger. This ingenuity and forethought would have been reassuring if I'd thought the blood test was purely a ruse; but Denis insisted on waiting for the results from the laboratory. Not the slightest trace of cyanide was found in his system. Looking on the bright side, I hoped Denis would now accept that no-one was trying to kill him. As we climbed into the Standard I also prayed he wouldn't kill me.

"Is there any petrol in the back, Denis?"

"Petrol? Where?" He turned and sniffed, briefly.

"I mean in cans. Spare petrol cans."

"No."

He gave me a fishy stare. It would only alarm him, I decided, to explain about Auntie's warning.

Driving to Liskeard with a man at the wheel who might go into catatonic trance at any moment is an experience you don't forget. It was the same route I'd travelled so often with Alec, right to left, as it were, across the country, but sitting next to Denis made me see the road with new attention, mainly because I wasn't sure how much of it Denis was seeing. He appeared to look through it. Where Alec drove fast and joyfully, Denis drove steadily, distractedly, and not very straight. As we veered slowly towards the left-hand verge, I tried to cheer him on with what I took to be aeronautical terms, "Right aileron down a bit, I think, don't you?" Sometimes his gaze was so fixed and trance-like it made me wonder if he was going to turn the wheel at all, as we approached a bend.

"Denis, you're not suddenly going to . . . you know . . ."

He turned on me one of his startling, humourless smiles. It seemed to be something he'd learnt from watching other people do it, like the rest of us, but without grasping the animating intention.

"Angels one o'clock," I alerted him. "Crossroads approaching fast."

"I know, Richard."

"Newbury road. This is where we peel off."

"Sorry?"

There must be some reason why so few beautiful people have a sense of humour. By which I mean a sense of irony, not the capacity to laugh at a joke. Even Denis Towle must have laughed at a few jokes. I suppose that if you're trying too hard to be what you seem, to be what you see in the mirror, irony intrudes. More than intrudes; it's the shadow of death. Is it for the same reason that so few beautiful people have any erotic imagination to speak of? Irony and sexuality, both divorcing truth from seeming, meaning from ostensible reality? Both a mockery death, a dream-play, shadow-play death, certainly. But Denis—who had no sense of irony at all, and no sexuality that I could identify—was in worse case. Truth and seeming were not at loggerheads for him, they were complete strangers, he could no more lie than he could tell the truth; he was stuck somewhere in between. He had rejected his own beauty but found nothing to put in its place. It was truth and meaning, twin guardians of sanity, that were at odds in his life. He worried about everything you said to him, and even more about the things he said himself. You could see him mulling them over—in this he was the opposite of Alec, who could be seen mightily thinking, on occasion, but for whom controversy was over as soon as he spoke. Denis, who you thought hadn't heard what you said and wasn't going to answer, Denis who apparently wasn't thinking at all but was patiently waiting for thought, would suddenly speak, as if hearing his name called by the Almighty. This brought him no relief. Having spoken he looked like a man in peril of his soul, less troubled by whether he'd said what he meant than by the impossibility of meaning what he'd said. Since this applied to other people's utterances as well, it gave him the air of a sad paranoiac: "Oh dear, what did you mean?" his glance seemed to say, adding, "But then, what did *I* mean?" It was a blessing for the rest of us that Denis' melancholy took the wind out of his persecution mania.

"You'd better tell me about Hanbury," I said.

"Yes."

"Well, come on then."

"All right, yes. I met him at Alfriston. He got me through my crack-up."

"Hanbury was the squadron chaplain?"

Denis nodded, glancing at me. He was never sure what he'd said and hadn't said, and to whom. "Did I tell you that?"

"You didn't tell me his name."

I squeezed a few more details out of him about Hanbury. Nice chap. Very nice chap. Church of England. Believes in prayer. Good listener. They had kept in touch since Hanbury had chucked the R.A.F., apparently deciding that he wasn't cut out to be a service padre. "Not enough chaps like me around, I suppose," Denis explained without a flicker of a smile. "What he's done is gather the lame ducks together, some of them anyway, to ride out the storm."

"Potts told me to watch out for spies and conchies."

"Did he? Does he think I'm a spy?"

"No, he thinks you're queer."

Denis nodded seriously. I didn't push it any further, though I wondered if he wished he were queer; better than nothing. That morning Molly and I had got out of bed as we'd got into it, without touching. I pushed that thought from my mind too. My job was to keep Denis talking. "What have you been telling Pottsy?" But he didn't seem to hear. "Denis?"

"It's all right, Richard."

I forced myself to look away at the passing countryside, at an England largely unmarked by the war. Here and there an airfield had been attacked, a hangar gutted, its girders splayed and silhouetted against the sky, picked clean like the limbs of some metallic dinosaur. As we passed an imposing, unmolested country seat at Theale, Denis began to recite monotonously under his breath, like a man trying to keep himself awake. It sounded more like prayer than poetry, Hanbury's influence, I assumed, and left him to it until I began to hear words that didn't belong to any breviary.

"Speak up."

"Griffon rampant gules, bar sable dexter on a field argent," he went, in the same droning manner, but louder. I stopped him for long enough to establish that he was plodding through the coats of arms of the great houses along our route. I didn't think the Towles themselves sported griffons, and I knew that Denis, despite all appearances, was a product of state schooling; a childhood spent, as I now imagined it, dreamily trying to provide a local habitation for his looks. At any rate his knowledge of heraldry was prodigious—it made a curious litany but an appropriate one, all frozen profiles, and anatomy without perspective—and it kept Denis sane as we traversed the South of England from country house to country house, through a landscape of mythical beasts decked out in fleur de lys and ermine.

At Wincanton we stopped for petrol and an early tea. I was glad to hear no more of bars dexter or sinister, but the presence of other people, real other than armorial, made Denis begin to shake. I guided him out to the car. Bars saloon and whisky rampant were what I most needed, but this would have to wait. We were barely halfway there.

"Denis?" After a few miles he had begun to cry, soundlessly. "Don't give in to it, will you?"

We kept going, but there were periods when he was convulsed with weeping and couldn't seem to keep his foot steady on the throttle. We jolted down the A303, the car convulsing too, as if in sympathy.

"Call of nature," he said. It was the third or fourth time he'd said it. The tears had dried up at last.

"Well, pull over then."

"Yes, right."

I watched him stroll away, an unavailingly erect and dignified figure. He went into a spinney. I waited. After five minutes, and then another five, I began to fear the worst. Stuck on the Honiton bypass unable to drive and with Group Captain Towle catatonic, perhaps, in a crouching position under a nearby tree. I went to find him.

"Denis?"

"Come and look," came his voice. "But quietly if you can."

I tiptoed heavily towards the sound. He was standing gazing out of the foliage into the field beyond, a bone-dry, harrowed field. A bank ran up one side of it, and there, against the mounded, dusty soil, lay a dog-fox, basking, panting slightly in the afternoon sun.

Foxes; something weaselly about them, even serpentine. I shuddered, glancing at Denis.

Denis was watching the animal with rapture. Life had returned to his face, transforming it; with any luck we'd make it to Dobwalls. But I felt almost jealous of the fox. I'd seen this expression once or twice when Denis was playing with Matty at the cottage, utterly happy, released. He was more than beautiful then, his features were irrelevant, subordinated by love.

"Look at her sunning herself," he breathed. "We must be downwind of her."

I thought: she's not sunning herself, you fool, she's a he and it's autumn and he's putting off the evil hour of his return to an over-crowded earth, the cubs too big now, tormenting the vixen. And if he can smell two uniformed men watching him from a spinney, he doesn't give a damn.

"Isn't she beautiful?"

"Molly's sister wears one round her neck," I said, and Denis turned to me in shocked distaste. Then something else clouded his features. After a moment he turned and headed back towards the Standard.

"There's something I've got to tell you," he said.

We had been driving in silence for a while.

"I got Jessen to talk a bit about the bomb attempt on Hitler. I'm afraid he's rather proud of the Luftwaffe's record of loyalty. Only two traitors. That's the way he puts it." Denis hesitated. "The sad thing is . . . they'd have done better to keep their powder dry, really. I mean, the war's pretty much over bar the shouting, even Jessen knows that. These two Luftwaffe boys . . . they were on Stülpnagel's staff in Paris. Jessen says they've both been executed. Chap called Hofacker, and another called Lützow-Brüel. Is that your brother-in-law?" I couldn't speak. Denis sighed. "I was afraid so, Richard. Well . . . you can be proud of him, you know. Very proud. There are good chaps all over the place, but I often think a good German's the best of the bloody lot. Have you ever felt that too? I think of the people I met before the war, marvellous chaps. I asked Pottsy if he knew what I meant, but I don't think he did.''

That night I dreamt about Peter, as I still do from time to time. I wasn't able to take in his death; he wasn't really dead, in the same way that he wasn't really a German, as he'd put it himself. I was a pilot racing my shadow on the fields below, bone-dry, harrowed fields, and I knew that Peter was there too, airborne, and what I wanted to do was find him and show him that I wasn't trying to kill him: the war was over. In the dream I felt masked and tense—I think I was really still on the road with Denis, in my head—and as soon as I recognized the tension, once I'd framed the thought, the dream changed course to express it. There was fire somewhere in the fuselage, unseen but with nowhere to come except towards me. It was the second time I'd dreamt of fire without seeing any flames, and I was beginning to learn what this invisible fire was, something coming at you down a tunnel, down a corridor, it doesn't have to hurry because it devours everything anyway, chokes and sears and scorches and comes on. Fire is a thing that advances like an animal, that consumes a dream like a slow motion wave of light licking you to death, that eats up the past and catches up with you and backs you into an ever smaller space and makes you ashes too. In the dream I burst through cockpit glass and I can fly.

In Dobwalls the war might just as easily have been over long ago, or never taken place, and the time I spent there—longer than I'd intended—was as happy as any I can remember in my life; reading from Hanbury's extensive library, gardening, now and then attending prayers, listening to Denis recounting his childhood at unusual and mesmerizing length, and later on being driven round Cornwall by Hanbury himself. It was a dreadful time for Denis. But I wonder if he looked back on it that way, afterwards. It was the peace and routine, and the friendliness of Hanbury's crew who welcomed us as if we were savages redeemed, that frustrated his longing for a second crack-up; prevented it by the sheer obstinate bliss of life at Dobwalls.

After the day-long drive, we had crawled at last through the dull, dark town of Liskeard, and there, a few miles further on along the Bodmin road, we branched off into a valley where

Denis' instructions led us to Hanbury's "ark." It was a converted farmhouse, whitewashed inside and out, brightly lit that night and set against a wooded hill containing a small, ancient, and disused chapel which had served to house livestock for generations, with pasture in front of it and sloping vegetable gardens all around. Hanbury kept cows and bees, both of which provided a surplus, and revenue. It was a valley literally flowing with milk and honey, and we had arrived in time for the plundering of the hives, a regretful joy for their keeper. Instead of the gaunt old sage I was expecting, Hanbury was young and eager, with carrotty hair and an eaglet's face, thin beaky nose and no chin; he flapped about his domain in a black robe, baggy and stained and fastened at his waist with a black leather belt, a touching, hopeful figure, queer as a coot I assumed from his dancing gait, but under control. There were no spies or conscientious objectors aboard, as far as I could tell, in fact there was hardly anyone under fifty except for a wall-eyed local youth who didn't say a word, understandably since he turned out to be a mute. Many of Hanbury's "lame ducks" were kindly Christian cranks who laughed at each other's eccentricities and, though hopelessly fey, made the least abrasive group of people I've ever come across. God willing, Hanbury's ark is the spot where I intend to rest my bones. Wall-eyed Colin will dig my grave in consecrated ground beside the cowshed-chapel, and Miss Platten will sprinkle a few of her dried herbs on the coffin; Hanbury, if he outlives me and hasn't been hauled up before the Bishop and defrocked for giving in to his natural inclinations, will read the elegy.

These idyllic surroundings brought out a different Denis, even, it seemed, against his own will; a Denis talkative to the point of tedium—though my appetite for his life story was a match for his stamina—but suspicious of my motives for listening, hour upon hour. Was I making notes behind his back, for a full report to the C.O.? Far from it. In fact, in the first few days, when I reported back regularly to Potts, I dreaded the phone calls and couldn't think what I was going to say. How's Towle coming along, Flight? Well, sir, he's *trying* for a breakdown, sir, I think we're nearly there . . . that's it, one more good heave . . . I think it's coming, sir! Instead I assured Pottsy that Dobwalls was having a wonderfully calming effect on the Group Captain.

It was partly true. But in the process I could only watch Denis struggle. It was one thing to listen to his woes, another to live with them. I was fighting not to be drawn into the quicksands myself, I had a bad conscience about my wariness, and he knew it. Or rather, guiltily attributing to him the sixth sense of the drunk and the psychotic, I assumed he knew it. Why else was he watching me so guardedly, while he talked?

For a week or so he alternated confessors, spending part of the day with me, exploring the woods and country roads, and the rest with Hanbury in his study. The stories he told me were harmless tales of his childhood and parents who'd idolized him. He reproached them tenderly for their love, as if they had failed to notice the alien in their midst. I gathered that he'd been a model of obedience; perhaps, as a result, they'd expected too much of him. There was something darker beneath his reproaches. Last thing at night I joined Hanbury as he walked the perimeter and looked in on the animals, and from what he felt able to divulge of his sessions with Denis I learnt the missing elements of the story.

Behind the Towles' doting attention lay a grief, one they had hidden from Denis at first out of solicitude, later out of habit and long inhibition. I could believe they'd almost forgotten it—almost. He had been born one of twins; the other had died at birth. Denis had discovered it during a conversation with his mother, by chance, quite casually, he said, while he was convalescing at home after his breakdown. The subject had gone unmentioned for so long, it was only when a crack appeared in Denis that the family façade began to slip. That was how I imagined it; I had to reconstruct the story from Hanbury's daily report. Until now Denis had told no-one about it, and the information had begun to ferment in his mind. He was convinced that the stillborn twin had taken with him into limbo all the complementary attributes which would have redressed Denis' lop-sided existence—as if a single nature had been divided between them in the womb in such a way that one twin received all the blessings of form and the other all the blessings of substance. It struck me that even if there had been a small portion of truth in this, the disparity would have been crueller if the twin had survived; but Denis was grief-stricken. This was more than belated mourning. By a kind of osmosis, so he insisted, by a long intermingling of their lives, he would have traded some of his physical grace and composure against the secret of inner self-possession. I was hugely intrigued by this fantasy, no less than by the idea of a Denis twin. Denis now felt compelled to give him a name, perhaps, as Hanbury suggested, to heighten and try to overcome his sense of loss. But unfortunately he named the dead twin Derek, which had just the opposite effect on me—I'd regretted him more when he was a nameless unfortunate, and although Hanbury pointed out that it was just the kind of name the Towles would have chosen themselves, I couldn't say it with a straight face. As a result, Denis became evasive with me and spoke in riddles.

"D'you ever feel cold down the right side of your body, Richard?"

"Just on one side, you mean?"

"Yes, the right side."

"Only if I've been sleeping with the covers half off."

Denis studied me. "Does that mean you sleep on Molly's right?"

"No, I just said it for a joke." I thought about it. "But as a matter of fact I do sleep that side, on the right. What are you getting at?"

"When we were driving down here, did you feel cold down the right hand side of your body?"

"Not that I remember. Why?"

"I did. I felt cold down the *left* hand side of my body. I've often felt cold there. Don't you see what it means?"

"No. What *does* it mean?"

But he just gazed at me. "Think about it." And after a moment, "It's Derek. Don't you see? He was on my left, in the womb."

"Yes. Yes, I see. Of course."

I was completely at sea. Worse still, at other times I'd ask about Derek and Denis would pretend not to know what I was talking about. And the story seemed to be growing and changing—or so it seemed to Hanbury; later when I thought back to the left side/right side conversation I wondered if it hadn't been full-grown in all its variants, long before we came to Dobwalls.

One day Hanbury reported that Denis was fretting over whether he might himself have been responsible for the twin's death, strangling him with his umbilical cord as they struggled to emerge from the womb. Neither Hanbury nor I could substantiate the likelihood or otherwise of this, anatomically speaking, and a discreet enquiry among the other inmates of the ark revealed the curious fact that we were here one by one rather than two by two: none of us had experienced or witnessed childbirth (and if Colin had, he couldn't tell us about it).

The infant murder theory seemed lurid and unnecessary, but already by the following day geminicide had been forgotten.

Denis was now obsessed with the idea that the twin had not been stillborn at all, as his mother claimed, but was born deformed. This fitted the notion of the twins as polar opposites, but it led Denis to the conclusion that with the collusion of parents and doctors the disfigured child had been "put down like a dog." More than that, Denis now felt that the murdered twin, as he now saw Derek, had been a kind of sacrifice whose effect—this had the logic of a grisly fairy-tale—was to heighten the survivor's characteristics, gilding Denis' beauty but, in return for the blasphemous act, denying him a soul. Hanbury, to my surprise, seemed pleased by this development. We were getting to the point, he said. I hoped Hanbury knew what he was up to. On secular matters he often sounded foolish, with his nervous, fluting tones and squeaky laugh. He was well-read, but seemed embarrassed about it, putting on a funny voice to quote Virgil on bees. On matters of faith, though, he spoke with a soothing finality—it might have been disquieting in other circumstances, but I was glad of it now—as though his authority came not from the books he quoted but from within himself.

"Should goodness fail," he recited, the Adam's apple, wriggling beneath the chinless face, carrotty hair lifting insipidly in the breeze, "then weariness may toss him to my breast at last," and his quavering voice and eaglet eyes told me he knew something of this.

Meanwhile Denis was determined, it seemed, to take responsibility for the death of his alter ego. His beauty, the source of all his woes, was an accomplice in the murder: it had encouraged his parents to rid themselves of the monster who, unknown to them and against all the visible evidence, incorporated not only his own portion of the godhead but Denis' portion as well. But would a double portion of the godhead, if such a thing were imaginable, produce a monster? I had to remind myself that all of it, the whole rigmarole, was Denis' delirium, that there had been no evidence of deformity, let alone murder, in the story Mrs Towle had told her son. The demonic overtones belonged entirely to Denis. Or were they Hanbury's? I felt like a novice exorcist on his first house call.

And this was in effect what Denis wanted Hanbury to do: to exorcize the vengeful spirit of his twin, to absolve Denis from complicity in the murder and release him to wander like a penitent, newborn, free at last to receive God's sweet rain, the food of souls. I was no longer sure if this was Hanbury or Denis speaking, such was their *folie à deux*. But where Hanbury, thank goodness, was rather crisp when dealing with spiritual matters, Denis had begun to talk of them a shade hysterically. "Did your grandfather ever read you the Bible when you were little? What was your favourite parable? I bet it was the prodigal son! Everybody likes that one. I can just see God laughing at the chump who stayed at home, can't you? A great big thunderstorm, and God laughing? Boo-oom! And in walks the other chap. Boom!" It reached the point where I felt compelled to ask Denis if he'd ever thought of becoming a priest—"instead" I almost added, as though it were a plausible alternative to a nervous breakdown. "Yes, I've thought about that myself," said Denis. "I'd like to believe in God," he added, taking what seemed to be rather a large step back from his close acquaintanceship with Him. I took it that like most people flirting with conversion, he was waiting to see whether God believed in Denis.

One evening Hanbury came to me and advised me that I would do better to leave in the morning. Denis, he said, had begun to wonder whether the twin had really died after all, and this entailed some unforeseen developments. It was as though fantasy itself, with Denis in its grip, had achieved all it could with a stillborn twin, and now the only way to feed its raging appetite was to bring Derek back to life. "He says he thinks the child may have been given away." Hanbury looked embarrassed—at his failure to contain Denis' powers of invention, I took it. "I don't know if you can see what that means, Richard." I couldn't. "It means that somewhere in the world there is an ugly version of Denis, with all the inner self-possession he feels he lacks. So of course he . . . wants to find this person." I realized that Hanbury was looking at me meaningfully.

How was Denis going to do that? I asked.

"Richard . . . the problem isn't how Denis is going to set about finding him. The problem is that he wants to kill him."

I stared. "But surely . . . surely that was the thing, the dreadful crime that deprived Denis in the first place of—of whatever it is he lacks."

"Yes. But don't you see, if the twin's still alive, then the crime never took place. Instead there's someone, some living person, walking around with Denis' soul. And, of course, it could be anyone. It could even be someone he knows." Hanbury gazed at me in an anguish of politeness. "Someone, well, physically as unlike him as possible."

The penny dropped. And when I thought about it, Denis had been probing the oddities of my own childhood more than his own, during our recent talks. I'd been flattered. Now I saw his motives differently: I had a mental image, a Towle's eye view, of some benighted Watford vicar recoiling from the bundle on the church steps, a bundle with a pencilled note, "Derek," nappy-pinned to it, and Mr Punch, in miniature, peeping from the blankets. Ugh! Send him to Cornwall. It wasn't a compliment to be thought of as the missing Quasimodo. But on the other hand—as rich in soul, potentially, as Denis thought he was poor? Or merely demonic (a double portion of the divine) where he was wanly good? That evening I sought out Hanbury again in his study. Wouldn't it be a good moment, I asked, to send for Mrs Towle? If for no better reason, at least to remind Denis that the twin had been a perfectly ordinary baby, tragically stillborn? Hanbury pushed his chair back from his desk and peered at me over his half-rimmed glasses. "Oh dear: d'you really think there *was* a twin?" Then he saw I was taking this rather badly. "All right, suppose there was. D'you think anything Mrs Towle could say now would make a difference? Denis wouldn't believe her, he doesn't trust her any more. He doesn't trust any of us. And the Towles will only send him to a doctor. Don't you understand? That's why he's come to me, because doctors can only treat diseases of the soul as if they were in the mind. All the best doctor can do is try and help Denis to believe in himself, which thank God he doesn't, Richard, any more than he believes in me. He doesn't have to. A doctor and a patient can be as close as father and son. But there is no healing without the Name, not without the holy spirit to intercede between the healer and the sick. Have you ever thought about the Trinity, Richard? Do you know why there's no salvation without the Holy Ghost?"

I fled, on foot, to Liskeard. The trees gesticulated at me in the darkness, like anguished parents. Don't you know what priests are like? they cried. Give them an inch and they'll snaffle up your soul. Help him, help Denis, do something! The wind had dropped as I walked back again, full of Irish whiskey. Now I was the one who lurched, and they were perfectly still, the sullen trees, as if they'd given up on me. It was after midnight when I reached the farmhouse, and instead of going to our dormitory I chose a different room, planning to tell Denis I hadn't wanted to wake him by coming in late.

In the morning Denis was gone. His bed was empty but his belongings were still there, and we hoped he'd taken an early morning walk. We searched the gardens and, after lunch, the chapel and the woods, to no avail. I could see Hanbury was rattled now. We went out in his car and criss-crossed the Moor in vain, praying we'd find Denis waiting for us at home. He wasn't. We drove all the second day; on the third we went to the police, who took down the details, patiently. Wartime England, we discovered—emerging from our well-ordered cocoons, Hanbury and I—was teeming with absconded soldiers, dubious aliens, malingerers of every shape and size. Up to you, sir, we were told, if we wanted to search the haystacks. On we drove, questioning publicans and farmers, across a countryside shedding its leaves in glorious sunshine. But not a fugitive in sight.

It came to me that if Denis now thought I was the foundling Derek, he might have gone to find Mother and verify this. We drove to Padstow. Mother had seen no strangers either. Grudgingly she gave us lunch, and eyed me with Irish squintiness. Was I consorting with priests? Heaven help me. Married, was I! Saints be praised; I was past help. Why hadn't I told her, at least? I reminded Mother that I'd written to her, several times. "So you did," she said, "you're a good boy. Where's your brother now? Where? *Where?* What's he doing in *Burma*? Shouldn't he be fighting like the rest of you?"

At last the weather broke, and the following morning at breakfast time Denis walked in, drenched but sane. Our welcome seemed to puzzle him. He'd been on Bodmin Moor, he said. The old mineworkings were full of hidey-holes, comfortable enough while it was dry. Yes, he'd seen us drive by once or twice, but he'd been busy. Denis had a week's beard, his hair and clothes were filthy, and he had the haggard air of a Celtic prophet in a pageant, nourished on berries and visions. I'd never seen him looking better. Solemnly, he came and hugged me, and I knew without his saying so that he'd been busy burying Derek, hopefully for good, on Bodmin Moor. He had stories— almost gleeful stories—of standing dazed but happy among the Hurlers, a circle of megaliths on the edge of the Moor, trying to become one of them and ignoring the tourists until at last his legs gave out. He was brimming over; there was so much he had to tell us. But his explanations smacked of the old craziness, we led him to bed and let him sleep until lunchtime the next day.

"You go on home now." Denis studied me from the pillow, washed and shaved. I'd brought him lunch on a tray. And when I protested that I was under orders to stay with him, he said, "I'll square it with Pottsy, Flight. I'm still your superior officer. You go home to Molly. I'll only be a few days. You can see I'm all right, can't you?" He wasn't convinced by my nod. "Rich-

ard, don't ask me to explain it all. I can't. I don't suppose Hanbury'll understand it either, but I mustn't lose sight of it.'' He
hesitated. ''I know it sounds mad, but one of us had to die.''
Denis sat back and looked at me in silence, folding his arms.
''Have you ever been down a mine? No?'' He pulled the tray
towards him. ''Well don't,'' Denis chuckled. ''It's dark as hell,
you'd only bump your head.'' Then he put out a hand and touched
my forehead as if I were an old horse. ''Good luck, old chap. I
just need a few days on my own. I'll be back in harness by the
end of the week, don't worry.''

Under The Heavens was bare and bathed in a weak sun as I
tramped from the station. We had no phone at the cottage and
during my weeks at Dobwalls Molly and I had communicated
through a neighbour, Mrs Havelock. Over the telephone this
kindly, distracted soul either wouldn't or couldn't tell me how
Molly was doing in my absence. She spoke in platitudes, no
doubt reluctant to get involved. On one occasion she'd mentioned a visitor, ''I believe it's your brother,'' and I'd asked if
she would fetch him to the phone, hoping for impartial news of
Molly. But he'd already left—which didn't say much for Molly's
welcome. I walked slowly, expecting the worst; that she wouldn't
be there at all. The front gardens along the valley looked battered by the rains, the hollyhocks mown down like toy soldiers.
No humans to be seen. They were all indoors, hiding from the
ogre. No-one wanted to tell him the bad news.

There was no answer when I rang our doorbell. I walked
down the side of the house, and stopped, and I had all the time
in the world to let my panic subside. Molly was sitting on a
deckchair on the little lawn, wearing a polka-dot dress, one I'd
never seen before, with Matty at her feet. I realized: she'd been
out and bought a dress, out to the shops. It didn't flatter her
tubby figure. She was beginning to develop a striking resemblance to Nye Bevan. Nye Bevan, waiting for me in a deckchair, wearing small white spots on a blue background. A red,
white, and green deckchair. I blessed my absence, I blessed
Dobwalls, I blessed bloody Denis. Matty gave a start, shook
himself, began to bark, and Molly turned. She was sitting outdoors in the garden, reading a book. She wasn't even knitting.

On Fireworks Night that year Auntie was proved a true prophet
as Molly announced that she was pregnant; definitively pregnant. She was so proud of having kept it quiet, hanging onto her
hopes until she knew for certain.

I plunged straight in. "Well, at least this one can be called something other than Wilfred."

Molly glowered.

"Oh Molly—" I stopped myself saying it was bad luck. After all it wasn't like calling him Punch, after a dead child; not exactly, anyway. I told myself I hadn't really settled on a name, last time.

"I want my Wilfred."

"Don't you think that in the circumstances it would be a rather nice gesture to Denis, to . . ."

"Wilfred."

The Victory bunting was beginning to look tatty, it was the end of June and there was peace in Europe and electoral backbiting all over England, when Molly gave birth to a bouncing boy at Gerrards Cross. We called the little bundle Wilfred Denis Thurgo.

PICTURE A SPANISH ROAD, A MOUNTAIN ROAD: IT SEEMS TO have erupted, rather than been laid down, congealing on the dusty verges in rich tongues and burst bubbles of lava, trickling away over the rim into a dry ravine. And now the bend, the bend coming on, as the road dips. If this isn't the one, then why do I remember it so clearly? The road itself I see patched and peeling and blistered like skin, but the mountain roads were all like that, with vertiginous bends, a few wooden stakes along the outer edge, or nothing, just a precipice, and views that lured you to the edge. The view: for a moment there was something Carthaginian about this one, the word came to mind at once, without my knowing why. Palm trees and crags, strangely juxtaposed. Palm trees, crags, a herd of sheep, a house in the mist—then I knew what it recalled. It was a vista of Hannibal's soldiers climbing a mountainside, in Grandfather's study, the framed print with its Biblical colours, and something of a mirage about it, too, the palm trees, the robed figures, the animals, none of whom belonged, as if Hannibal's dream had brought Africa to Europe and hauled the desert up into the mountains, step by step. The view, and now the bend. The road dips, the bend comes on too fast, the parched ravine below opens its maw . . .

It was a death, now I come to think of it, that took me to Spain in the first place. The late Colonel Thurgo had left me some bonds, plus a few unspecified items—including, of all things, a lovingly annotated edition of *Mein Kampf* in Arabic— that were to "stay in the family." A week or so after his death I flew to Malaga, although from past experience I was wary of legacies. Neptune, lord of disappointment, in the house of inheritance, as Auntie pointed out; false hopes there, bonny lad.

I wasn't even all that keen to go to Spain, I imagined it a country of shallow, pomaded glamour, of poseurs. Rather subdued, as I pictured them now, licking their wounds. It was a place where people had stopped preening and torturing and blowing themselves up for long enough to sit out the real war, our war, in silence.

In the event Malaga reminded me of home in its drabness. Its cripples, patched and peeling, bared more skin than ours, and there was a one-legged man in a grey pullover who seemed to recur on every street, swinging a crutch and manoeuvring along like a pair of schoolboy compasses. In other respects Malaga town was not unlike Torquay, shuttered against a blustery March wind, it was a Sunday town, still in mourning. The countryside, however, was a revelation. What seized me by the throat, and later by the heart, was some attribute distinct from its features, though these were pleasant enough and often brought Cornwall to mind, and Ireland too, on occasion, where gorse and granite gave way to soft green pines, a tender green, so different from the melancholy obelisks of the Mecklenburg woods. I was reminded of Grandfather's lectures: Celt and Spaniard were of common stock, he told me proudly, remnants of a long coastal exploration. A prehistoric quest, perhaps, since now it struck me that they had sought out the same barren outcrops, the same stony places with their prickly, obstinate wildflowers. Grandfather hadn't mentioned this particular affinity; but then, preferring time travel, he'd never been to Spain. Welcoming as they were, it wasn't these homely aspects of the landscape that took hold of my imagination, nor its more exotic familiars, the burning rashes of bougainvillea, the magenta soil, the neatly trimmed heads of the olive trees, precise as pawns, filling a valley like the tents of a mediaeval army. It was something independent of its features, I couldn't place it yet, something as abstract as music and as exhilarating. As I stepped out of the aeroplane at Malaga, the squalid wasteland was like an orchestra playing full belt, serenading us. It had something tremendous to say—only it had forgotten what. In the distance a group of hillocks, softly humped like molehills, had an apologetic air; there were mangy palms and small, wilting cacti spattered along the roadside like dog-eared library books someone had flung away, but they too sang, parched and raucous. Houses closed in, we sank into the dusty town with its defeated faces, emerged from it, and there, at last, was a surprisingly, hearteningly angry sea.

"Richard, I've got some bad news for you." It had all started in Garnham's office, with the odd boy using pretty much the same formula as Alec on an earlier occasion. This was March of '48, and in the intervening years I'd been promoted from "Thurgo" to "Richard" as I passed my finals and joined the firm at last. The use of my Christian name only helped Pike-jaw to adumbrate his growing disappointment in me. I was for-ever under-charging the more poorly dressed clients, many of whom, as Garnham pointed out, were by no means as poor as they seemed. "We're not here to pass judgement, Richard," he spat at me on another occasion, when I'd foolishly told an un-appealing client that I thought he was guilty as charged. "What's the matter with you? You've got a good brain. Use it!" Until recently the firm had included an even more delinquent junior partner than myself, a balding youth called Brockway, dismissed at last for seducing the wife of a former Hungarian fencing champion whose property deals we were handling at the time. "I did not take possession of her body," Brockway had main-tained, "she surrendered it voluntarily." This last display of legal finesse didn't help him. With Brockway gone I was scape-goat elect, and Garnham must have seen the am-I-fired? expres-sion on my face because he added, "No, you haven't handed over money to another undischarged bankrupt. It's your uncle, I'm afraid the old boy's folded his tent." Died, I took it, and put on a suitable expression. "Heart. Keeled over in a café. On the seafront," Garnham said tartly, as though this was better than the Colonel had deserved. He advised me to proceed di-rectly to Spain before my clutch of shares and souvenirs van-ished. Instead I went to Alec who would doubtless be going out to Malaga to tidy up, and to collect the lion's share himself. He would see to my portion.

We met "at the office," by which he now meant the House of Commons, but "at the club" might have been more appro-priate as Alec led me from the vaulted lobby, past waving and yapping fellow-parliamentarians, to the bar. Everyone knew him. "Lecky!" they went (a few wartime intimates barked "Lucky!" with an unintentionally grudging effect), as firmly as if Alec's place in the ruling caste went back to the Conquest. I made a mental note to ask him for my Old Harrovian tie back; he clearly didn't need to fly borrowed colours any more. In his regimental cravat and double-breasted jacket he looked the part all right: Major Thurgo, M.C., M.P. for Cornwall East since the postwar election. Even the limp, acquired in Burma, suited him. He was in his middle forties now, a little ruddier, a little more lined and coarse-grained, but the face was still cherubic, and the golden hair and clear eyes kept his boyishness alive. It was hard to think of my brother as an elected representative of the people, much less a pillar of the establishment. But there were plenty of others there who looked just like him, brawny-faced men stalking the carpeted corridors with their hair still trimmed for parade, a cadre of Majors and Colonels and Naval Commanders who continued to carry their medals in their bearing but were now only a Tory rump, a proud, discarded crew.

I had to admit it, Alec fitted in. Grudgingly, (''Lucky!''), Molly had dubbed him Felix after the cat in the song: ''they blew him up with dynamite, but him they couldn't kill, miles up in the air he flew, he just murmured toodle-oo . . .''. Alec enjoyed the joke and would growl the song to young Wilf, as a bedtime lullaby—''landed down in Timbuctoo, and keeps on walking still . . .''. Alec had plenty of little songs and rhymes for Wilf, ones I'd never heard before. They derived from Father, I took it, and for the first time in my life I felt a genuine stab of envy for Alec's childhood.

> *Algy saw a bear,*
> *The bear saw Algy,*
> *The bear was bulgy,*
> *The ba-ba-ba-bulge was Algy . . .*

From time to time Alec fell into a stammer which, like the limp, he owed to the Burmese campaign. Uncle Alec had blown himself up, with his own dynamite, ''lobbed it at an ammo dump and caught the blast at silly mid-off.'' The limp remained but, unlike my friend F-F-F-Farquhar, he mastered his stammer and became a fluent if relentless public speaker, the scourge of the Labour benches.

It was a far cry from the future Molly and I had foreseen for him. We were quite sure that Alec was going to be a social misfit living on Scotch and anecdotes, bewildered by peace, but the war was barely over when fate and Freddie Launceston decreed otherwise. As chairman of the local Tory party, the Earl disposed of favours in a constituency once known as Liskeard-and-Launceston, now as Cornwall East, with an incumbent who had given many years of true-blue service. This sitting member had survived El Alamein, but the Victory Ball, Liskeard's VE-day celebration, proved too much for him. During the Grand Victory Dance he suffered a stroke, ''last casualty of the Western Front,'' as Alec termed it. We had no idea Alec had political ambitions. Neither had Alec, but the Earl knew better. Here was a Cornish war hero with a limp and a medal to show for it, a chap whose father had bought it on the Somme, or thereabouts, who'd worked for Vickers before the war—with the election looming there was little time for anyone to dig deeper into the candidate's past. As if to put Alec's Felix-like powers to the test, fate decreed a field day for Labour, and a catastrophe for the Tories; the Liberals ran Alec close, and elsewhere the county seemed, as always, unable to find its voice in party politics, demonstrating its bemusement by returning one M.P. from each of the parties; but rural Cornwall stayed loyal to their former, sitting member, and voted Tory in tribute to him. Alec's predecessor was now permanently sitting, confined to a wheelchair and still partially disabled. He watched expressionlessly, I remember, as Alec acknowledged the victory cheers.

I also remember being surprised to find that Molly had political views. I use the phrase in Alec's sense, as in "He'll vote Tory, he's got no political views." Was it to provoke Alec? I could well believe that Molly favoured Labour purely to spite him. She'd never mentioned any "views"; much less socialism. Secretly I was delighted to be married to a class traitor, I suppose because it reassured me that politics was only a kind of high-minded vindictiveness—Alec too, with his grammar-school background, was just as much a class traitor—and in no way superior to the low-minded vindictiveness I cherished. The class war, Us-and-Them: it was the great wartime preoccupation, but I never could find a role in it. I made a clumsy attempt to soothe Alec, who was fed up with Molly's tirades against the government, by pointing out that she was so used to hauling down her Churchills (for me, I meant, but it came out sounding otherwise) that it was only second nature for her to do it to their namesake. Unfortunately he repeated this to Molly, and she wasn't amused. To placate her I promised to vote Labour too. Now I had Alec on my back. "For God's sake, man," he sneered when I told him I'd pledged my vote to Molly, "have you forgotten Churchill's cry: 'Vote Tory, Sleep Labour!'?" It seemed to me that he was confusing Churchill with Mosley, but I did agree to go and help him campaign, or at least distribute leaflets; I would vote Labour but campaign Tory; I didn't care. No true Cornishman gave a toss for Parliament anyway.

A heavily pregnant Molly agreed to come along, to see the enemy at close quarters and provided, she warned, that she was allowed to heckle. I never imagined she meant it seriously, and when we joined Alec at the hustings we simply went our separate campaigning ways, meeting at night in our Liskeard hotel to exchange boastful stories. I hated every minute of it. The hotel was a pretentiously furnished little hole with a forbidding granite exterior and, inside, a scandalously expensive bar. The town, on closer inspection, seemed no less nasty than when Denis had driven me through it the year before, dingy and grey, like something that belonged in the rain, and drab even in summer, as drab as a stone plucked from the sea and left to dry. When I took Molly to Dobwalls one afternoon, to show her the Ark, she snubbed Hanbury and spoiled the visit for me. ''He's so bloody cheerful, isn't he,'' she complained. ''God's in his heaven and all's right with the world. How can anybody seriously believe that any more? Yes, I know he's a priest, it's no excuse. At least Daddy's decently mad.'' She was in a dangerous mood.

That evening Alec was to address the local Tory faithful at the Public Hall, alongside various worthies who'd arrived from London to try and lend some credence to the proceedings, as Molly put it. She'd made friends among the rowdier Labour supporters, and had probably urged them, it occurred to me later, to come along and barrack. They did, as soon as Alec's speech was under way. To my distress I saw Molly grinning enthusiastically beside me. Then she began to join in. As if this wasn't bad enough, coming from the candidate's sister-in-law, she started mimicking his stammer. That was when I kicked her, and thank goodness she was busy groaning softly and massaging her leg while her friends the rowdies were dragged out at the back of the hall.

I'd kicked my pregnant wife, a crime I would not be allowed to forget, she said, as long as I lived. Alec always maintained with relish that my kick had won him the election; it was the kick, as he liked to call it, that secured his seat. This was an exaggeration, but it was probably true that if Molly had been evicted along with the other hecklers, and a journalist had discovered who she was, the publicity would not have endeared Alec to the stuffier voters. Soon after the fracas Alec told me that, on higher orders, I was to remove my wife from the constituency. Since Molly and I were barely on speaking terms, this was easier said than done. Once more I attempted to conciliate, and we all met in a perfectly horrid room at the hotel, a sort of library with flock wallpaper of a faecal brown.

''Look, if Molly promises to stick to Labour gatherings, we

could go on as before, couldn't we? Would you agree to that, Molly? Molly?''

''It doesn't matter what she promises, I'm not putting the whole campaign at risk. If Freddie Launceston says she's got to go, she's got to go.''

''But surely, as an aspiring politician, you can see the virtue of a compromise?''

''Oh shut up, Richard.''

The more I played the peacemaker, the more it was me they rounded on, and in the end I retreated to bed and let them fight it out. We left Liskeard in the morning. Molly's face—I can see it now—was still puffy from the previous night's tears. I wouldn't discuss the politics of the affair, she wouldn't discuss the personal side of it, and we rode the train in silence.

Perhaps I was unfair, but I understood her socialism as a piece of Molly bull-headedness, another attempt to outdo Maggie, less flippantly but still with a finger raised at the vicarage world. According to Molly herself, it was her WAAF training at West Drayton that had opened her eyes. The working class recruits, the same girls who had taught her about nits, had also taught her about injustice. I saw no point in arguing with Molly; her newfound fascination with injustice only made my point that without it life would scarcely be worth living. And now that the war was over and with it, God willing, the most genteel period of my life—school, however genteel in dress, had been savage enough in manners—I was longing to get my Punch-nose back in the gutter, where injustice ruled. If in no other way I would do it through my criminal clients. As the old dreams revived I saw myself at their shoulders in the front page photos. ''Who's the ghoul in the pinstripe?'' ''Oh, that's the lawyer,'' ''The *lawyer*?'' ''Yes, that's Thurgo, he always acts for the syndicate.'' The ghoul in the pinstripe, the yokel dynamiter, the revenger, the thing from the bogs: I was still Grandfather's spy, waiting to be unleashed on the world. Wasn't I?

Within six months of the end of the war those of us whose studies had been interrupted by it were ''chaired through'' our finals, which meant that the examiners turned a blind eye to our rusty legal knowledge. Garnham didn't, though. The reference he gave me, when I set out to find a place in a practise specializing in criminal law, closed doors in my face. Slacker, dreamer, absentee: that was the message, although Garnham couched it in euphemisms. The yokel dynamiter had to tramp back cap in hand to Garnham and Coutts, solicitors to the distressed, the divorcing, the profitably bankrupt, and the dead. Not to mention foreigners—thanks to my German I got all the Jewish refugees with their naturalization papers and their tenancy disputes. They weren't exactly the syndicate I'd had in mind. But I had responsibilities now, the thing from the bogs had a family to keep in North London, where we lived cheek by jowl with the German Jews I represented, as if they, the disgruntled invaders of British West Hampstead, were my destiny.

There was no resisting it. For extra income we even acquired a bridge-playing Jewish lodger. I'd recently taken and lost his case to reduce the rent at his previous digs, on grounds of "persistent vermin," a term the judge clearly thought was better suited to Jews like my client. So much for my dreams: apart from our kosher dinners—Mr Mendelssohn liked to cook, which was a help since Molly didn't—life was just as it had been during the war, only a little bleaker. We even kept in touch with "Pitmarsh," another newly ardent socialist and back in Molly's favour. At least during the war I didn't have to listen to the Party line. Now I knew all about the higher austerity. Measly food to sustain a good conscience, and hiking for health—hiking! Germany might as well have won the war, I sometimes thought. Like most of the people we knew, Molly and I had developed a gruesome passion for making do and seeing who could cover a slice of toast with the smallest quantity of rationed butter. The taste of potted meat had wormed its way into our souls and become a taste *for* potted meat, filthying the English palate and even, for a time, the English appetite; the same thing seemed to have happened to the fucking, it had become bad form to revel in it—or perhaps I'd just been married too long. But no, everyone else seemed just as pinched. You could see it reflected in the children's faces. My clients' offspring always wanted to show me their stamp albums, they all collected these bright, spurious little tokens of elsewhere, glowing embers with names like Trinidad and Tobago, they'd open their albums for me as if releasing a flight of tropical birds. But for the children the best moment, you could see it in their costive little faces, was when they shut the albums (some had their own padlocks attached), shut the birds away for the night with a true collector's glee. Piggy-bank full; not a penny spent.

Days at the County Court wading through petty claims, nights playing bridge, Molly and I, with Pitmarsh and Mr Mendelssohn. That was what it came to, our Victory Dance. One afternoon a week I took tea with Ellie. Her "Hello, Punch" was

gently guarded; she wasn't going to let me come too close again.
The cat François, older than God, fifteen at least now and fat
and ridged and hard to the touch, like a mouldy loaf on legs,
eyed me cynically as I slid my attaché case out of sight, under
the armchair, and stretched out my hands to the broken white
pillars of the gas fire.

The cat was right, why try and hide the briefcase? I was what
I seemed, another bowler-hatted customer. Tea and a "cuddle."
In Leda Buildings all that remained of the past was a discount
for an old friend.

"No, there's nothing left in Spain for me," Alec drawled in
the Commons bar. "Didn't I tell you Tom and I had fallen out?
That's why he's made you his heir, I dare say. Not a dicky-bird
for muggins, I'm afraid: we dissolved the partnership years
ago." He sipped his drink as if to swill down the last traces of
this inappropriate liaison. "Mind you, it'd be worth your while
to go and rummage about a bit." Seeing my cautious expression, "I'll stake you, old bird, if you're short of the readies.
No? Well, good for you. One thing, though, I'd appreciate it. If
you find any private papers lying around, just burn them. Burn
the lot." He smiled a broad Alec smile; too broad. "And by
the way, give my love to Australia."

"I'm not going to Australia."

"I know. You're going to Spain. But you'll meet Australia."

He was right about that.

"Toor-go! Toor-go!" sang a dusty little man in black, in the
forecourt of Malaga airport. He announced himself as Luís,
seized my bag, and seemed anxious to bundle me into a car that
matched his size and appearance. I was still standing dazed by
my first glimpse of the country, by the powerful chords it seemed
to emit, and waiting for a melody to emerge, when I felt him
tugging at my sleeve. He was baring his teeth at me imploringly,
as if I was a large, recalcitrant mule. "Come, Toorgo. Come,
please," he hissed. My knees felt locked, I'd just spent long
hours with my legs uncomfortably folded, and I was in no hurry
to be packed into an even smaller space. "You see that man?"
Luís circled me quickly, rolling his eyes to direct my gaze. I
looked over his head, which only came up as far as my collar.
Another squat man, this one with cropped grey hair, was swaying towards us like a mechanical toy, arms motionless. His face
looked as if it had been held against a wall and kept there till it
set. "Is want to kill you." "Is *what*?" I stared. As the wall-
faced man approached, Luís pushed me off the curb and against

the open car door, then scuttled round the boot, jumped into the driver's seat and gunned the engine. I was still gazing at my supposed assassin when Luís yanked me down by my arm, I landed in the passenger seat, and we sped away across the tarmac.

"Is think you are strange man." Luís glanced at me as if to confirm this estimate. It seemed a poor excuse for murder, even in Spain. "You look like German," he added.

"I'm English," I said. I thought about it. "D'you mean he mistook me for someone else? Is that what you mean? For whom?"

"For German." Luís studied me some more. "You look like German."

"Well, I'm not a bloody German."

My head grazed the roof as Luís sliced across the traffic and onto a dirt road lined with slum buildings where everything but the washing was caked in orange mud. "Away to the races, hey Toorgo?" he exclaimed with sudden vivacity, as we bounced hard onto a paved road and turned back the way we'd come. "Is all right, I take you to la señora."

"Thank you."

For some reason, perhaps merely travel-weariness, I felt as if I was at a film in which the pictures and the sound were at cross-purposes, with the words arriving some time after the speaker had mouthed them. It seemed to me I ought to be riding a wave of exotic danger, a little comical but no less exciting; instead as we bumped along I felt bemused and sluggish, hoping the charade would end, or my emotions accelerate to catch up with it. I wanted to stop, get out and walk, take in lungfuls of Mediterranean air and scramble carefully along the scree with its prickly bushes, its yellow and purple blossom. But Luís was at, or perhaps in, a different movie altogether. It was all too familiar; I'd spent my life at the mercy of drivers.

Finca Thurgo lay nestled in olive groves, between the large mole-hump hillocks I'd spotted from the airfield. From the outside the house looked almost theatrically Moorish, with plenty of clumsy icing on the chimneys and external balustrades; it had fancy ironwork and overhanging galleries and what looked like dovecotes on the roof, heavily iced as well. This whiteness was offset by bougainvillea of a virulent red, a kind of crimson with a neon tint to it, like incandescent blood. The place seemed to be under siege. The gates were opened to us by armed police, and in front of the main building suspiciously clean cars were clustered round an aged palm. The cars belonged to lawyers, as it turned out. I was going to say fellow-lawyers, but these swarthy sharks, these swordfish—by their looks, la señora might have been interviewing unemployed bullfighters—were no kin to Garnham and Coutts. By comparison we were mere pikes, backwater pikes lurking in the pond-weed, snapping at small fry. And yet, curiously enough, old Garnham would have looked more at home in the Colonel's sitting room, his "sitting" as la señora called it, than these predatory creatures in their sleek suits and almost painfully white shirts. Entering Tom Thurgo's Moorish extravaganza was like walking from an oasis into a Harrogate hotel, or stepping into Valentino's tent to find it full of cheval glass and fumed oak. One moment I felt I was beginning to find my Spanish bearings, gazing at the lurid exterior, the next I was plunged into a gloom so British that even the local furniture looked Edwardian in it. I glimpsed hunting prints and brocaded wallpaper, I could feel pile carpeting under my feet. Luís led me like a blind man to the "sitting," and announced me. Dark panelling. Chintzes. A woman in a shawl held out a hand, from an immense sofa. Around her the toreadors rose suavely to their feet.

Before I left, Alec had warned me about Estrella—pronounced Estrelya, hence my confusion with Australia—or at least he'd told me to expect a fearsome person, the lioness who had shared Tom's life. La señora. She wasn't fearsome at all, I didn't think, though I did wish Alec had warned me about her hair, which was sparse and an implausible orange, and clashed so fiercely with everything in the house that it was hard to look at her steadily. She appeared to be about sixty, vacant-eyed and well-preserved in a doll-like sort of way. Doll-like . . . I have to hesitate, because the word doll conjures up Agnetha for me, and Agnetha was a marionette carved out of heavy wood, infinitely durable, while Estrella, beneath the powder and the rouge, was made of some thin substance that might puncture at any minute. Her puffed chest and stately port seemed distinctly fragile to me, and the small, hairless dog she carried everywhere under her arm gave a more enduring impression of life than she did. La señora seemed to be able to take in who I was, but not much more than that. I took it for an effect of grief, and once the pleasantries were over, thinking I might as well find out sooner than later whether my journey had indeed been "worth my while" as Alec put it, I enquired about the Colonel's papers. "Papers? Papers. . . ." Estrella turned, laughing, to the lawyers, to confirm the absurdity of this request. Everyone laughed along with her, as she spread her hands helplessly. Papers were all with the police. Estrella "knew nothing of papers," and smiled and shrugged to prove it. The police would explain. "Papers . . .". It was hilarious, apparently.

I decided to explore the premises a bit while my hostess was busy, as she made wanly clear she was. Or was I simply unwelcomed? There had been no invitation to stay, unless I was supposed to take this for granted. In the lobby I found that Luís had placed my suitcase beside an elephant's foot full of knobbly Lake District walking sticks, in a way that vaguely suggested arrival. Or, on the other hand, departure. The open front door, a massive item that looked as if it dated from the times of El Cid, revealed the ancient palm tree in front of the house. Another mediaeval relic, by the look of it. It was the tree equivalent of a toothless old man; fat and short of leaves on top, it sat there sulking in the drive like a gigantic pineapple, as a large dog appeared from behind one of the cars, sniffed at a tyre, glanced at the old palm tree, back at the tyre, and then, cocking its leg, decided to squirt the tree. Something about this depressed me. "Hector! Hector!" came a voice, and Luís materialized out of the darkness behind me, in a reek of tobacco. Perhaps I was imagining it, but the defiant way he belched the cigarette smoke into the lobby seemed to convey the pleasure of flouting his late employer's house rules. "Hector!" The dog, a German shepherd, padded towards him. "We go for a little walk, hokay?" After a moment I realized it was me he was addressing, not the dog. "La señora want to see you later," murmured Luís from the side of his mouth, as though the dog might overhear and pass it on. "Right," I said, and went out into the sunlight as Luís pulled the door shut behind me. I was fed up with being treated like a lackey. Was this a door El Cid would have allowed to be slammed in his face? No, he'd have kicked it down with one delicately-incised metal boot. "Take me to the police," I said.

"Hokay." Luís ground his cigarette underfoot, while the dog sniffed the trousers of my de-mob suit. I saw it in his eyes: My suit ran the old palm tree close. A few more years of conveyancing and petty claims and Hector would be pissing on me without a second glance.

The police claimed to know even less about Tom Thurgo's papers than Estrella did. They too smiled and shrugged a lot. They were polite but, in Luís' translation, "confuse." They would for many years have given much to see the papers of El Colonél. In fact they seemed eager to recruit me to obtain these for them, although their interest, they shrugged sincerely, was of course purely academic now that he was dead. How long was I staying? From their tone I understood that they wanted no Spanish succession in the Thurgo line. As we emerged I saw Luís wave at someone in a car parked across the road. It was Wall-face, our friend from the airport. Behind us our policeman smiled benevolently from the steps of the Guardia Civil. I felt "confuse" myself: who was with whom? Luís glanced at me.

"Is not kill now," he said cheerfully, "don' worry, Toorgo."

Once more we screeched away from the kerb. I gripped the seat. We were away to the races again.

It proved to be a long journey home. The best of it was that by the time we made it back to Finca Thurgo, Estrella seemed to have mellowed. In fact she greeted me as if we hadn't met before, pressing me to her ballooning chest until I was afraid I might asphyxiate the dog still clamped under her arm. The lawyers had gone; an armed guard remained, watching me suspiciously. It had been a puzzling afternoon and an uncomfortable one, but I was feeling no pain, having persuaded Luís that we could best shed any pursuers by stopping now and again at a side-street bar.

La señora now led me on a tour of the garden, using the dog-free arm to gesture at her favourite plants, naming them helpfully but slowly, as if addressing a child. Beside her orange hair, the bougainvillea became a waterfall of gore, and I kept my eyes on the plumbago blossom, shards of Spanish sky that seemed to have fallen and splintered on the hard ground. Afloat on *anis*, I followed Estrella through the Thurgo olive groves towards what she announced as my "living."

This was good news. Evening was coming on and the noise of the crickets was pulsing in my head like a record that had reached the end of its grooves: ssa—ssa—ssa—ssa . . . I needed to lie down and switch off the record.

After the grandeur of the Colonel's "sitting" I was anticipating a pleasant guest house, but the building I could see ahead of us, flanked by dismal eucalyptus trees, looked like an old barn. It was an old barn. As we entered I had to duck to avoid the low ceiling—and how the place stank! If this was my "living," it was the Prodigal Son story the wrong way round. But never mind, in my state even pig litter looked inviting.

"Upstairs," Estrella nodded at a dark corner of the barn, where I could dimly see some rickety steps. "Follow, please."

To my surprise, upstairs was clean and positively cosy. The floor was swept and there was a little bed with an oil lamp beside it, a comfortable-looking bed of a decent length. A hole had been made in the rough plaster walls to provide a window. By its light I could see a basin, a mirror, and behind me, as I turned, a small, ornate desk. Estrella was standing beside it, patting it. She smiled, seeing my expression, and nodded.

"Papers."

Later that night I took the oil lamp from the desk and set it beside the basin, to clean my teeth. My eyes were sore from trying to read by a flickering light, which now showed me a haggard face in the mirror. I rather liked the effect; it was a face that would only improve with age, and its gross features were beginning, I thought, to settle; I was coming into my face at last. But that was all I was coming into. The contents of the desk didn't seem to be worth a damn.

"I never know what is in your uncle's drawers," Estrella had said, straight-faced. "I am not permitted." Her sing-song voice made it clear she also didn't want to know. "Perhaps is some old rubbish. You take look, then we have dinner."

I had taken look, had dinner, and looked again. There was plenty of old rubbish in Tom's drawers. Old passports, assorted travel documents, some in what appeared to be false names, permission for a so-called Thomas Schäfer of Zurich to enter Germany and travel on business through various occupied zones; I could picture the old gun-runner appraising battlefields of rusting tanks. Beneath these papers I found some of the promised shares, Rumanian bonds at 15%, Bulgarian at 7%, a mass of useless pre-war stock only worth keeping for the calligraphy. Young Wilf might find them pretty, I decided. The second drawer contained books, and a sheaf of typescripts corrected in green ink. Military treatises, to judge by the names they cited. In the third and last drawer I discovered more shares—and these I recognized. I knew them well, the files were full of them at Garnham and Coutts; in fact Pike-jaw had probably recommended them to friends like Tom. The Russian Lena goldfields, the Buenos Aires-Pacific railway. Extinct ventures, wiped out and cancelled long ago. 1898 Chinese bearer bonds for something called the Tientsin-Pukow Line. My bet was that it never reached Pukow. But I had, this was my Pukow, the end of the line, the bottom of the drawer. No, there was something else, beneath the last Chinese bearer bond. It was a cheap-looking pistol, with a dozen rounds. Ha ha, it seemed to say. Perhaps the Colonel had had a sense of humour; I began to doubt this, though, as I looked through his books.

Some were in Arabic and *Mein Kampf* was the only one of these with its title reproduced in Western script. Inside, the printed text consisted of Arabic squiggles except where Tom had scrawled "quite right!" in the margin, in his distinctive green ink. I was glad the squiggles couldn't tell me which of Hitler's ravings had given my uncle particular pleasure. And yet they too—the squiggles—were oddly appropriate, I came to feel as I gazed at them, suggesting a long stream of grunts and cries which could only be expressed on the page in tortured hieroglyphs. Each marginal "quite right!" and "exactly!" now read like the soothing comments of a nurse in a mental ward.

I turned to the books in English: a handful of adventure stories by Henry Treece and a fragile copy of Byron's poems, Volume Four, pocket edition, one of a series printed, according to the fly-leaf, in 1837, in "Francfort." Its heavy, ribbed spine had broken free of the binding like a piece of pie-crust, and a strip had flaked away. What was left proclaimed "The Works of Lord Byro." Opening it I found a letter, or a rather a note, undated, presumably unsent; a draft, perhaps. *Dear Father,* it ran, *since receiving the Xmas bonus from Patrick, Greta minds the baby very capably, life is rosy in Foulsham Grange, and George's worries over Uncle Ned seem trivial. Grateful hugs, yours, Rupert.*

Foulsham Grange? Patrick, Greta, George . . . Uncle Ned and Rupert—none of these people were familiar to me; and that was all it said. But for a moment it seemed to offer me a glimpse of a world a long, long way from Finca Thurgo. As I replaced the letter in the battered Byron I saw that the fly-leaf had a few words scribbled on it in the same neat handwriting. A reference: "Don Juan, Canto XIII, verse 73." I looked it up, and found:

> *Firstly begin with the beginning (though*
> *That clause is hard); and secondly, proceed;*
> *Thirdly, commence not with the end—or, sinning*
> *In this sort, end at least with the beginning.*

No matter how I often I read it, this struck me as gibberish, more worthy of Lord Byro than Lord Byron. It reminded me of the clues made up by smart-alecks for treasure hunts; we'd had those at school, as a special treat, and I hated them. All that toil, and at the end of it an Easter egg or a ten bob note. As I put away the books, Auntie's words came back to mock. False hopes, for those who journey under Neptune. Useless shares and riddling souvenirs—was this all Tom had left me?

Not quite all. Looking in the mirror, I could see a legacy coming through. My O'Malley nose was a monument to the other side of the family, to Mother's side, but alas I lacked Grandfather's splendid, equine teeth, "all his own" as he liked to say, a boast which puzzled me terribly as a child; it seemed to imply that unless you were careful you could end up with other people's teeth—stolen, obviously, but how? From graves? Did dentists sell used teeth? It was a prophetic anxiety. My own teeth were crumbling, and my uneven lips seemed to be trying to hold them in. Now I knew who to thank: they were just like the Colonel's lips in the photographs Estrella showed me as we waited for Luís to bring dinner. Taut, uninviting lips, carelessly sliced at a bias, and perfect for Tom's lop-sided smile, which was half hidden by the moustache. A little, insolent goatee; a grinning face, under the Panama. A thief's eyes, gloating over his adventures, gloating as if he'd stolen mine. What he'd left me were his teeth, like bad debts, and to cover them, his crooked mouth.

Dinner, once the family album had been laid to rest, was largely silent. Or rather I did most of the talking, since Estrella was busy hand-feeding the dog from her plate. With its popping eyes and folds of hairless skin, it looked like a plucked terrier, all but ready for the pot itself. Coffee arrived at last, and with it another unwelcome discovery about my uncle. This one was gruesome. I was trying to interest Estrella in an account of life in London, mentioning my work with Jewish refugees, when she came to life and drew herself up on a loud, hissing intake of breath. "They kill Tomasito," she said, fully inflated and staring fixedly at me. Seeing my bewilderment she spoke slowly, in her talk-to-an-idiot voice: "The Jews, Richard. The Jews kill him." Since my first taste of life at Finca Thurgo, I think I'd known in my heart that the version Garnham had given me in London, with the Colonel simply "keeling over," was too peaceful by half. The seafront café had played a part, though, it was there "they" had "hired waiter for poison him," Estrella explained, picking up the sugar bowl to demonstrate. "He take three spoons. They put glass in his sugar, fine glass, every day little pieces until finally . . ." she put down the bowl.

Luís, by her side, pointed solemnly at his stomach. "Too many holes."

"I'm sorry," I said, trying in vain to imagine the likes of Mr Mendelssohn suborning a Spanish waiter. Glass in the sugar . . . what had Tom done to earn this macabre death? I began to search for a tactful way to enquire, but when I looked up I saw that Estrella had returned her attention to the dog, carefully wiping its mouth with her napkin. I was grateful to be ignored. After a while Luís began to clear away the dishes, and I studied him instead. Food-stained black clothes, unshaven jowls and that oh-so-unctuous expression; he had the knack of conveying devotion and resentment at the same time. I could picture him in a failing monastery. The abbot was dead, and lay brother Luís was piling up the dishes in a noisy, careless fashion. A touch of sacrilege, but too late.

It was all too late—the thought kept recurring as I stumbled back through the olive groves, towards the barn—too late for gruesomeness and bloodshed, years too late. It was as if the flight to Malaga had taken me back in time. Not into war; just a violent pantomime. All I wanted to do was take the first flight home.

But what had happened to the eighteen-year-old self who'd revelled in conspiracies, real and imaginary, at the Schloss? Here at last was the stuff of my dreams, dark deeds and revenges to nourish the old O'Malley spirit, car chases, death threats, even a treasure hunt, real or imaginary, for Spanish gold. Hints of green ink. "Firstly, begin with the beginning . . ." The barn beckoned, full of secrets, as dark and rich in stinks as Herta's treehouse, there, ahead of me, where the eucalyptus trees shivered like lost souls. And I felt no sense of anticipation, none at all. I stopped to take a quiet inoffensive piss, but no sooner had I begun than a distant whining noise came on the wind. It sounded as if it might be Hector, the dog who'd sniffed my trousers so contemptuously when I arrived. The Colonel's German shepherd, scenting me now—or perhaps he was just keening for his master. If so, he was the only one.

Standing listening under the trees I found myself thinking of Denis Towle. And couldn't for the life of me work out why. Denis tottering about beneath the stars, on Bodmin Moor? No. No, it had been Flight Lieutenant Thurgo tottering about in the Cornish darkness, with Denis on my mind, Denis my guilty burden as I walked to Liskeard for a drink, and weaved back full of Scotch. Forget Denis; a drink—wasn't that just what I needed now? Yet even that old compulsion was losing its charm. After a promising start, my prospects as an alcoholic were growing dimmer every year. I didn't drink to become intoxicated, or to forget. I drank, I saw it now, to remember what it was like to get drunk when it was fun to get drunk: when I was fifteen. And the memories were fading, the days of schoolboy drinking were almost out of reach, that was why I would go to bed clearheaded. In the barn; just a few strides away. All I had to do was step out of this enchanted circle, where the crickets trilled their broken record. Just a few more steps.

And here was the room again, and the lamp, and the stink, here was the face in the mirror with its great twisted nose and shifty mouth, welcoming the lines and wrinkles at last: hello, Punch. But there, too, were the solicitor's eyes staring back at me, awake, alert to all the unwanted echoes of the day. My words returned, my contempt for foreigners, for preening Spaniards . . . no wonder I felt remote, I'd become a canting Englishman, a jingoistic old fart. Like Alec. What had I said? "I'm no bloody German!" I'd even repeated it, in one of the Malaga bars we'd visited during the afternoon—it clearly wasn't the first time Luís had brought in friends of Tom's, "strange" men, and when the barman misinterpreted my silence and addressed me in bad German, offering to show me some cherished mementoes of the Condor Legion, a Mauser carbine among them, what had I done? I'd stormed out.

No bloody German? I who'd loved the German soul as if it were my own heritage, loved it from the first, and not only in its droll, ethereal form, its prancing von Lützows, but in its coarseness too; loved it in its very doubleness, vulgar and disembodied at the same time. I who'd delighted in its voice, the willful, pedantic syntax wallowing in saliva and phlegm: *selbstverständlich, Herr Graf!* I who'd loved the German soul for its sheer bloody absurdity—the bewildered sense of relish, the mechanical salute; who'd adopted it as my standard; taken it, without mockery, as the emblem of humanity. And hadn't the war confirmed it? Was there anything more absurd, more dizzyingly human than the expression on the faces of the concentration camp guards as they were herded into line for the newsreel cameras? No grief or shame, no fear, just bafflement, and on every face the same question: *Aber, meine Herren,* do you really think we enjoyed this?

Such blankness! God knows it was monstrous, but sublime too, almost endearing. These were men and women outside destiny, without past or future, they were anything you wanted them to be (and by Thursday they'd be better at it than you were): they were Germans. Twice now I'd been mistaken for one, and denied it twice, as blithely as if I were still wearing my prissy little wartime tunic.

"You'll never pass for a Jerry."

I could still see Wing Commander Potts cracking his knuckles at me. He'd been wrong, even then. I'd made him eat his words. But it was better not to think about the last few months of Sisdick, after I'd left Denis mad and bedridden in Dobwalls. They were too full of painful memories, they brought Denis with them again. Forget Denis.

The more I tried, the more promptly he returned. Denis, and General Jessen; and my short-lived incarnation as Gruppenführer Rautenberg. We were all a bit crazy then, by the spring of '45, and bored to death with the old cat-and-mouse. The prisoners made it too easy, they wanted to spill their guts now that the war was lost. The only fun had come with the arrival of American interrogators. Their casual approach, tie loosened and feet up on the desk, so offended the Germans that even the most lowly Feldwebel returned to ramrod stiffness and went silent for a while. But London didn't care about Feldwebels any more, London wanted to know about the higher echelons, and we only had one representative, one source: "I haff complaint."

General Jessen had been uncommunicative since Franz the stoolie fled his clutches. I saw my opportunity, now that Denis was no longer there to woo and comfort him. Where was "Face?" I didn't even know. Hanbury had written to me from Dobwalls. The Towles had come to fetch their poor demented boy, and he'd heard that Denis was now hospitalized, incarcerated was the bitter word Hanbury used, somewhere in Surrey. The letter waffled on about the Holy Ghost, its ubiquity, its inscrutability. It hadn't enabled Hanbury to cure Denis, that was the fact of the matter. Laziness prevented me from tracing his whereabouts, or more likely some twitch of guilt, some instinct that I hadn't heard and didn't want to hear the full story. I was on a different trail: Maggie's. It was from Jessen that Denis had learnt the news of Peter's death as a traitor. By all accounts the families of the conspirators had been persecuted too, and Jessen might have heard of Maggie's fate. If he had, would he tell me? Not across a table. These days the General was sulking, to Potts' frustration. I'd never been assigned to interrogate Jessen, and that was my trump card.

Potts fretted and snapped his knuckles, it just wasn't done, he said, for an interrogator to play stool pigeon. I'd never get away with it. But after little Franz's tales, none of our German stoolies were in any hurry to volunteer as Jessen's cellmate. "Just one day with him, sir," I pleaded. "One night." Potts had nothing to lose—and if he could impress the Ministry with information about German High Command, what price Air Commodore Pottsy? I too, though I didn't mention this, had less to lose than he knew; certainly not my homosexual virginity.

If I was unmasked, I'd simply leave. If Jessen got aggressive, well, I was bigger than he was. He had a white-washed hut all to himself, no other prisoners to recognize me . . . why shouldn't I bring it off?

When the moment came, and the General arrived back from interrogation to find me at the corner basin, morosely washing my socks, his expression nearly made me laugh out loud. He hesitated, as if he'd been brought to the wrong place; I'd anticipated this, it brought to mind the evening at the Schloss when I'd recoiled in the same way, finding Peter in the room. Though now I was Peter. Slowly, as Jessen realized that it was no mistake, his stony interrogation-face flooded with pleasure. It wasn't at all what I expected—I'd prepared all kinds of stories to allay his initial suspicions, how I'd demanded a cell of my own, how over-crowded the camp was and how badly organized. Instead it was the General who went out of his way to reassure me, remarking on my "Mecklenburger accent" before I even had to talk about my origins, welcoming me to "a little piece of the *Vaterland*." This was gratifying, though as time went by he said less and less, and studied me more.

At last it came to me that the man was just too lonely to care whether the companion he'd been given was a stoolie or not, and that the long, searching looks he was giving me were part of a valiant attempt to quicken his desire, rather than quell his doubts about me. I gazed back soulfully. To little avail; I could see the effect my face was having on him. It may have convinced him I was genuine. Would the English have been so stupid as to present him with someone so totally unappetizing? No, he'd been saddled with the ugliest fly-boy in the Luftwaffe. And the largest; I had to present myself as Gruppenführer Rautenberg, ground crew captured in France, a role for which my own interrogation victims had provided ample detail. Perhaps the hardest part of the impersonation had been finding clothes to fit me, in musty cupboards full of confiscated and unlaundered uniforms. But whether it was my face or the smell of my clothes, it was clear that I was not to the General's taste. By bedtime even his politeness had waned. If he knew any secrets, he didn't seem to be about to confide them. Should I take the initiative? The trouble was, the repulsion was mutual, and my loyalty to London and its need for information didn't extend to sodomy in the line of duty.

By nightfall I'd elicited no news of the Frau Gräfin von Lützow. It was rather hard to probe for facts about a traitor's wife while maintaining my claim to be a rabid Nazi. On the other hand the disappointment was outweighed by the fun I was having. God, was I enjoying myself: I keened for Germany, I rhapsodied the Führer, even Göring acquired a Wagnerian dignity in my speeches. If Jessen did suspect I was an impostor, and English, he must have concluded that Hitler had recruited the wrong allies. I went on to produce an unrehearsed stream of loathing for the English that even took Jessen aback, and little by little I persuaded him to join in—he was a bit of an old woman and I could tell he liked to gossip—by providing me with verbal sketches of his interrogators.

That was when the whole thing backfired on me.

Not that I let slip my true identity; I didn't. But when I loosened Jessen's tongue I began to hear camp tittle-tattle, from the other side of the fence. It was enough to make you wonder who were the information-gatherers at Sisdick, we or the Germans. Sordid domestic details, professional jealousies, pregnant barmaids—Jessen knew more about the place than I did. And who was his chief informant? "Der Schöne." The good-looking one; Denis Towle. It conjured up a bizarre scene, the prisoner doing the interrogating, the interrogator leaning forwards confidentially and dishing out the secrets. "As a matter of fact, old boy . . ." Perhaps it had been a relief to Denis. He hated games. Or was he taking some barmy revenge on us all? Perhaps something more confessional . . . it seemed he'd recounted a lot of smut about himself as well, to judge by what Jessen was telling me. Denis the philanderer, Denis and his scandalous passion for a fellow-officer's wife. The wife of a close friend. The wife, a pretty, willing—*Ja*, notoriously willing—former WAAF. I didn't even take it in at first, it sounded so implausible. Denis? Passion? Surely not. But so it seemed. Jessen didn't know the colleague's name, the one whose wife Denis was *vögeling* with—fucking, not to put too fine a point on it—only his nom-de-guerre: Rat.

I was sitting on my camp-bed; Jessen, lying on his bunk. He didn't look at me, thank God, and I had time to adjust my face.

It was nonsense, of course. I knew better than to believe it, and hopefully only the Germans knew about Denis' ravings. Then with a chill I remembered that the microphones were on in our cell, and every word Jessen was saying would be served up tomorrow in the *Scheisse*, translated, circulated in the typing pool and sent out to every office in Latimer House. What I'd anticipated as a permanent record of my triumph, my brilliant impersonation, was now going to be the laugh of the camp. Twenty years on, I could see it now, I would still be the butt of a celebrated saloon bar story. The man whose daring masquerade fooled a German General into spilling one of the best-kept secrets of the war: that his wife was cheating on him. I began to sweat. My need to get out was greater than Franz's had ever been.

But how? The first chance of a plausible escape would come in the morning, once I was led away to a supposed interrogation. If I made a bolt for it now on some half-baked excuse, Jessen would rumble me, clam up for ever, and Potts would be furious.

I lay back, rigid, humiliated, listening to Jessen rambling on about his childhood in Koblenz. Until at last he began to snore instead.

Only then did I allow myself to think about the other aspect of this Denis-and-Molly business: what if it was true? Please let it not be true.

When morning came I was at least able to forestall the distribution of the dreaded *Scheisse*. After being escorted from the cell—protesting strongly and demanding my rights—I hurried to the typing pool and offered to do the transcription myself. Lots of obscure Mecklenburger colloquialisms, I said, you might need a little help with those. Oh yes, sir? Thank you, sir. In place of Denis' slanders I attributed to Jessen some lively stories about Göring's entourage, which was infiltrated, I wrote, by Russian spies. I even named a few names. It would keep Potts happy—and it hardly mattered whether Jessen denied it all later, provided the Wing Commander never had recourse to the tapes themselves. I mutilated those, too, just in case.

To explain my hasty retreat from Jessen's hut, I hinted at disgusting German habits, and Potts was quick to let me go for fear of hearing more. Meanwhile the guards who removed Gruppenführer Rautenberg's bed and belongings were instructed to tell the General that his erstwhile cellmate was now undergoing corrective punishment for abusing the King; to wit, taking down the royal portrait and pissing on it. Jessen received this news with what was described to me as a rueful smile. At the time, I preferred to think of it as an admiring one.

By mid-afternoon my exploits were the talk of Sisdick and, although I wasn't in a mood to celebrate, it would have been churlish to deprive the officers' mess of a first-hand account— at least an account of the less embarrassing moments. So once more I was well and truly sloshed by the time I cycled home to Molly.

I can't say I was feeling no pain, I'd thought of nothing but Denis and Molly all day, imagining how I would react if Molly confirmed Jessen's story. And yet . . . it was strange: along with the pain, and a great deal of anger, I felt a distinct sense of relief. Relief, and something rather more distasteful. Excitement? Curiosity? Not quite. Of all peculiar things, a sense of power. As if by withdrawing—and this brought back old, puzzling feelings about Maggie and Peter—I regained control. Not of my emotions, but of theirs. As if by some kind of surrogation I participated more fully. I didn't want to watch, I don't think, it was more like wanting to be there in someone else's body. Both their bodies, as a matter of fact. I hardly liked to dwell on this; but the sense of relief still demanded attention. It had to do with Denis alone. I realized I'd felt responsible, all along, for his breakdown—not solely and fully responsible, but complicit in some way, as if I'd guided it from behind the scenes, prompted it, shaped its peculiar course. I never felt guilty of causing it. And yet there was something almost parasitic about the way I'd encouraged him to discuss his previous collapse, and about my fascination with his symptoms. Together we had mapped his soul, and while I'd done little more than fill in lines between the dots of Denis' recollections, wasn't the final portrait as much my work as his? I had idealized him, I knew it, as a kind of delicious freak, a man so offended by his own appearance, by his voice, his mannerisms, his whole personality as he experienced it, that he was driven to efface his own image in order to find peace; to start again, from chaos. Whose portrait was it, his or mind? That's to say, we had collaborated on it—

but which of us did it show? When Denis had transformed me into a lost twin, at Dobwalls, I felt he'd found me out: the alter ego who had sucked out his essence, refined, defined it, and described it to Denis himself, as if casting a spell. Or casting out my own demons.

No wonder I now felt relief. I hadn't engineered his breakdown. It wasn't my spell, it was Molly's. An affair with his best friend's wife would have been quite enough to unhinge Denis, in his fragile state.

So was it true, then? Of course it was. All the little clues came back to me, the clues I'd missed. Evenings we'd spent together, just the three of us. Molly saying Denis was the only one she could bear to see, after her miscarriage—because he *didn't* try and comfort her. The lying cow.

Denis himself trying to tell me, the day we left for Dobwalls. "It's the only way out of it." Denis gazing at me from his bed, willing me to understand. But how could I? For Denis—Denis who I believed was entirely asexual—to conceive a passion for a woman as fretful and uninviting as Molly seemed then, was unthinkable to me; Molly who was so jealous herself, jealous of me. And there was the dreadful logic of it. Only a capacity for similar transgression could make a person so suspicious of others. It was Kuno's breastplate all over again. To find our hidden vices, look in the mirror of our accusations. I was the accuser now, of course . . . but was there no such thing as righteous anger? I entered the cottage breathing fire, ready to brush aside any evasions, and, to my amazement, promptly burst into tears.

"Oh for God's sake, Flight," said Molly when I'd stopped crying long enough to stammer out my story. She'd taken to addressing me by my rank when she wanted to annoy, and now it had become a fixture. "Don't you see, you blithering idiot? Your Jerry must have recognized you right away. He knew exactly who you were. I bet he was laughing up his sleeve, inventing a lot of wicked nonsense and watching you squirm." And with contempt, "Oh, Richard, *really* . . . !"

I stared. She sat before me, wearing her mother's furiously composed expression, the knitting spread out on her pregnant lap.

"Don't you think it was rather stupid of you not to see through him? But I suppose you're too vain about your *fearfully* fluent German. It doesn't hide your face, Richard, everybody knows who *you* are, *look* at you, you stick out like a bear at a picnic. You're famous for it.''

"For what?''

"Your face, you fool. Of course Jessen knew who you were.''

I tried to interrupt, to explain to her that the General and I had never met. But Molly was barely getting into her stride.

"That's *one* thing,'' she barked, dropping the vicarage tones. "As for *believing* him . . . how *dare* you?''

During the invective that followed, I tried to think back to the night before. Was it possible that Jessen had made a total fool of me? If he did know who I was, what better revenge? He had me pinned. So long as I pretended to be a fellow-prisoner I'd have to listen to his insinuations about my wife. I'd come to deceive, and instead I rose to his bait, barb and all. The biter bit. But no—how had Jessen known so much about me, the very fact that I was close to Denis, that I was married, that Molly was a former WAAF? Denis had told him.

"Piffle,'' said Molly. "They all know stuff like that. They've got nothing else to do all day but suck up to the guards and swap stories.''

I wasn't entirely convinced. And as her anger passed its zenith and the subject swung back to Denis himself, a few cracks began to appear in Molly's defences.

Well, of course Denis had "mooned around her''—hadn't I noticed, for goodness' sake? He was always mooning around the girls. He was frightfully soppy.

Denis? Not the Denis I knew. This led to a bombshell. If I knew so much about Denis, did I know where he'd been during his famous disappearance from the Ark? I thought I did; on Bodmin Moor. Molly held my gaze. She must have realized, it occurred to me later, that she had to tell me about it, before Denis did. Yes, here, right here, he came to me, said Molly calmly. Hitched a ride to London, walked to Sarratt through the night. To her arms?

To my friendship, Molly blazed back, and to get away from you and that ass of a priest. That was why he came to me.

Yes, perhaps; and because he loved her; it was all too clear now. I recalled our neighbour Mrs Havelock telling me about a visitor. Alec, she'd thought, but no, it was Denis—I pictured his erect stride, Denis marching through the suburbs to reach Under The Heavens and Molly. But not to fall into her arms. Could I believe her? Molly as desperate in those days, as vulnerable, as Denis himself, Molly adored by this beautiful man, *der Schöne*, and married to a blithering idiot increasingly revolted by her jealousy, a husband unable, it seemed, to give her a baby. The baby she would do anything for.

Molly saw me gazing at her, calculating. Dates . . . she was three months pregnant, so she claimed, and it was nearly four months now since I'd left Denis at the Ark. Could she be four months pregnant? Her tubby frame wasn't telling. I saw Molly's hands tighten on her knitting needles as she waited, daring me to say something, and I thought better of it. Time—with any luck—would supply the answer.

It didn't, not conclusively at any rate. But what affirmed that the baby was mine, affirmed it as clearly as a sign from God, were its Thurgo features. The sunny side of the family, thank God, not the O'Malley gargoyle heritage but chubby, open-faced Thurgo looks with blue eyes and a jutting Thurgo chin. He was the image of my father; I prayed that his life would be longer and nothing like as feckless.

I'd known all along, I think, that Molly hadn't been lying to me, it wasn't in her character. She was a truth-teller even if it hurt. Even so I'd spent the remainder of her pregnancy in self-imposed torment, already convinced that the child wasn't going to live, lying awake beside Molly and placing my head against her belly, listening to our little Jack (or Jill)-in-the-box, or else finding relief by playing off one anxiety against the other—if it wasn't mine anyway, why be so anxious? Let it die. This was bitter medicine, and I made Molly pay.

Now it was I who hoarded suspicions, she who was pushed further and further away by jealousy, by daily questioning. In the end I drove her to the very thing I'd always feared: to leave. It was only for a weekend, supposedly, to see her parents, a long overdue visit but one that under the circumstances she wouldn't have made at all. And one that could turn into an indefinite stay.

We spoke by telephone on the Sunday, neither of us prepared to take the first, painful step towards each other, and each growing slowly angrier with the other for not doing so, until the inevitable row erupted. It was over the baby's intended names, Wilfred Denis. Innocent mooning or not, I wasn't going to have that man's name attached to my child, I declared. Molly was clearly expecting this. Oh, and how did I think Denis would feel, she said, Denis whom we'd actually asked to give the child his name? He'd think I preferred to believe what a Nazi told me. And if I did, why didn't we call the child Wilfred Jessen Thurgo?

I slammed the phone down; Molly stayed at the vicarage.

Could I really love a child named after a friend who'd carried on with Molly behind my back? I tried to see it differently. He'd loved her too. And I loved him. And wasn't it more likely that his breakdown had resulted from the conflict between disloyal yearnings and loyal restraint, than from unbridled passion? Argued that way (counsel in my head raised objections but was overruled), Denis had sacrificed his sanity for me, and deserved my love. The Saturday after the row, Molly and I arranged to meet in the restaurant at Gamages, her favourite London store. Neutral ground, well stocked with penitential offerings. I bought her lingerie; she bought me socks; and we went home together to Under The Heavens.

And what of Denis? I often wanted to see him again, but I never managed to take the necessary steps. Pitmarsh, who stayed in touch with everyone—a relic of his ecclesiastical upbringing, I sometimes thought—brought me a letter from Denis, a year or so before I came to Spain. There were no confessions in it, and I wasn't expecting any. Denis was a resident at somewhere called Horsham House, which conjured up gardens dotted with solitary loonies, but he sounded happy enough. He'd adjusted to his ''illness'' and enjoyed, he said, following the careers of his former colleagues, in the newspapers. Unless he subscribed to the *Hendon Gazette*, and studied the legal reports with unnatural patience, he wasn't following mine. Perhaps he meant Pitmarsh, now an aspiring captain of industry, or Potts who had risen to Air Commodore, despite my efforts; or even Alec. Denis expressed a wish to see me, though without sounding overly enthusiastic.

''There's a chap here I play chess with,'' he wrote, ''who doesn't seem to get any visitors and it rather upsets him when people drop in on me. Sundays are best. Do come if you feel so inclined. Trains to Horsham are quite frequent.''

Six weeks later Pitmarsh turned up for bridge with the news that Denis had committed suicide. I had no reason to connect it to my failure to visit him, but that didn't make me feel any better. Trains to Horsham were as frequent as ever and now it was too late to catch one.

Denis still returned to haunt me; as he did that evening in Spain, under the olive trees. It took more than a pillow and the late Colonel's stale sheets to put him out of my mind. Something to read . . . I couldn't face Lord Byron, so I tried Tom's type-written manuscripts, and fell asleep at last over a bizarre plan—when on earth had he concocted this?—to reassemble the Axis forces in North Africa. Once the Russians had swarmed all over us, as the author clearly believed they would, the forces of civilization would gather in the desert. Then they'd re-invade Europe under the swastika. With Berbers? Camels? Elephants? Hannibal had tried it. It didn't work.

I woke to a cold dawn, got dressed and shaved and headed for my uncle's Moorish folly in my overcoat. My British Warm! or Alec's, rather, he'd given it to me when his first Parliamentary winter loomed, and he'd bought himself a dark, fur-lined affair instead. This would be another day at the Commons for him. He was an early riser, perhaps on his way to Westminister already. Molly too would be up and about by now, feeding young Wilf. I could almost smell the musty corridors and the bacon-fat luring me to the kitchen, almost hear the grandfather clock, a belated wedding present from Wilfred senior and one which I always suspected of being church property, looted from some rectory and now ticking away at the bottom of the stairs at number 17, Parsifal Road. I pictured the shadowy entrance hall, the newspaper waiting on the mat. It was March the 25th, a date I hid from myself for years to come, though I've always known, in the back of my mind, when the anniversary was coming up. March the 25th, 1948: the date of my death, twenty years ago. Not the kind of date many people can celebrate in retrospect.

Nothing could have been further from my mind than dying, that morning. On more than one occasion, it's true, I'd thought that other people's driving would be the end of me, but—but I mustn't anticipate. As Byron says, firstly begin at the beginning.

I was swigging coffee in the kitchen at Finca Thurgo, that was when it began, while Luís bustled around me in a collarless shirt. It was British Army issue and presumably acquired from the Colonel. La señora sailed in at the door, complete with dog in armpit. If death can take unexpected forms, so, clearly, can his messengers. She was dressed in curly black fur—nothing second-hand about this outfit—and the dog too wore a neatly tailored coat. They looked more than ever like ventriloquist and dummy; but which was which? Swathed from head to tail in billiard-table baize, the dog didn't seem to belong to the natural world at all. In fact he had the smug air of a being from another planet who had brought Estrella with him as a form of inflatable transport. She and I exchanged good mornings.

"I see you are dressed for cold. When you are finish your coffee, I show you something very spiffing."

I finished off the bowl of coffee and followed her, saying that I had thoroughly explored Tom's drawers but found nothing to my advantage, and would be returning today to London. She seemed deaf to everything I said. We had emerged into the chilly sunshine and arrived at a garage.

"Can you open? Please." Inside sat the dusty black car I was already familiar with, and next to it, even less carefully looked after, a battered object: a jeep. "For you, Richard," Estrella smiled, and to my astonishment pointed at the jeep. For me?

"Why for me?"

"Is my wish," she insisted proudly. Of all things: the perfect present for a non-driver. I explained this to her. "Is easy," said Estrella, and climbed into the driver's seat to demonstrate. She was completely mad, I decided.

All along the walls of the garage stood plastic containers of Olio de Olivas Thurgo—perhaps I could take one of these home with me. If not "very spiffing," at least a more practical bequest. I was rather tickled by the idea of Thurgo olive oil, and it would make a change from the smell of lard in Parsifal Road.

"Here, try boots, Richard," came Estrella's voice from the jeep.

I leaned in. A large pair of old black boots sat on the passenger seat, military boots, the kind I never wanted to see again. But there was a pleading twist to la señora's smile. She wanted to give me something, apparently. With any luck the boots wouldn't fit. I sat beside her on the passenger seat and tried them on. They fitted. Along with his teeth I'd inherited the Colonel's feet—the better, Estrella seemed to think, to drive his car.

"Accelerador, brakes, is easy," she was saying, over a squeaking noise from the pedals as she pumped them.

The back of the jeep was piled high with useless items I now feared I might be given too: overalls and dirty workshirts, sagging suitcases, and beneath them more Olio de Olivas Thurgo, container after bulging container, as if loaded for market.

"Look, I wouldn't mind some olive oil if that's all right," I said, or started to say, because at that moment something whined under the bonnet and the engine cleared its throat with a ghastly roar.

"Accelerador! Brakes!" shouted Estrella as the garage filled with exhaust fumes.

To my relief, the thing juddered and I swung my legs into the jeep as we backed out into the sunlight.

Estrella turned the wheel towards the entrance gates, started forwards, and stopped again. "Clutch, neutral, is easy!" Patiently I explained once more that I didn't drive. If she was determined that I should have the wretched jeep, and if she really didn't need it herself, perhaps she could sell it, I suggested, and let me have the proceeds. She nodded as if at an intelligent pupil.

"Good, you sell. I tell you where to go. Plaza de Bailen *tres*. There you can sell, Richard."

There was a curious, intent look in her eyes.

"Plaza de Bailen," she repeated. "You want me to write down?"

"Couldn't we go together?" I said, but I'd lost her attention once more.

She was staring through the windscreen. I followed her gaze. Two men stood chatting by the gates, the guard with his machine gun dangling from one arm, and a squat, familiar figure. It was Wall-face. Estrella seemed to have frozen. A long, childish moan came from her lips. Then I realized it wasn't Estrella moaning, it was the dog making its first utterance. She was squeezing it half to death.

Now Wall-face was showing papers. The guard took them, studied them, and began to open the gates. A cry came from beside me, and this time it was Estrella making the sound.

Abruptly, she scrambled out of the driver's seat, yelling at the guard in Spanish, and hurrying towards the house. The two men at the gate watched her without moving, and Wall-face retrieved his documents, making a comment to the guard which seemed to make him laugh. I noticed the guard was returning something to his pocket too. And at that instant I noticed something else. The jeep was moving.

Alec once told me, after we'd had a close call with a lorry on the North Circular, that there was only one true test of a driver's mettle, namely how he reacted—she-drivers weren't even starters, in Alec's terms—to "a prospective prang." To the "born" driver, everything would appear to slow down, facilitating the correct manoeuvre; for the rest, for "non-drivers," it was all over before they could respond. I must have been a born driver who'd mislaid his vocation, because the events that followed were so slow that I had time to think back, or so it seemed, to every car I'd ever been in, while I wondered what to do. It didn't help; even the born driver needs a few lessons. Handbrake? There didn't seem to be one. How was I to know that the curious handle on the dashboard was, as I discovered later, what I was looking for? I stared at the pedals on the floor. Accelerador, brake . . . is easy! Si señor, but which was which?

We were gathering speed, I noticed when I looked up. The two figures in front of me didn't seem to have moved. If there was a "born pedestrian" category, they clearly belonged to those who froze before a prang. Either that or they assumed I was going to stop.

Brake? I slid across behind the wheel and lashed out with an army-booted foot. No: accelerador. I was thrown backwards, and from that moment nothing went slowly any more. The guard flung himself to his right, dragging the gate open and almost falling as he did so. Wall-face was standing open-mouthed as I bore down on him. I was too scared to enjoy his expression at the time, but remembering it gave me a good deal of pleasure afterwards. Is want to kill me, eh?

Not that I wanted to kill him, I just couldn't move my feet. Nor could he. Then just as I expected to see his already mashed-in face coming through the windscreen, he'd gone and I was plunging forwards on a bumpy track that led through olive trees to the main road.

The quickest way to learn how to drive, and I speak from experience, is by trial and error, or in my case terror: to find the brake there's nothing like having to save your skin. And having found the brake I had to start up again, unless I was going to abandon the jeep in the olive grove where we came to a halt, intact and with the motor still growling, to trudge back to a Finca Thurgo where Wall-face might greet me with more than advice about my driving. It would be better to steer clear of Wall-face for a while. Learning to turn the wheel was easy enough, as long as I went slowly, through the trees and onto the track. The gears were more of a problem, but they didn't seem to mind unduly whether I found the clutch pedal or not. Altogether it was a very tolerant sort of machine. And by God I was driving it! I was Ascari, I was Nuvolari—I was Alec—gripping the wheel, lurching round curves, slowly now, slow down, man, slowly, past mules and muleteers and long files of unattended goats, past men who waved cheerfully at me, recognizing the jeep if not the driver. There were few other cars, thank goodness, but rather too many animals, and once, as I passed a farm, I made an unsuccessful swerve to avoid a dog, heard a yelp and felt the bump and glanced back to see it scurry across the road into the bushes, where a fat, unappetizing-looking man staggered to his feet with an astonished expression. He shouted after me. I drove on cautiously; downhill, soon lulled again by the incessant, winding bends, as by a childhood swing.

Driving! I did it once, for one day of my life, and it was glorious. If I'd sprouted wings and flown it couldn't have been more exhilarating. Even today, when I see men hunched in their cars, in the grey Hamburg rain, I feel positively sorry for them. What do they know about driving? That March day in Spain I drove like the first man ever to sit behind a steering wheel (and at much the same speed): with wonderment. With anxiety too, of course. The airborne dream about Peter hovered all day on the edge of consciousness, waiting for its moment. I had the good sense not to try and negotiate streets full of traffic, and when I saw Malaga approaching I took a side-road back and up into the hills where I could creep along undisturbed. Plaza de Bailen would have to wait; I never wanted to stop driving.

Even the sights seemed more vivid than they had when I was a passenger, it was as if I was discovering them myself, the hilltop villages each clustered at the furthest end of a ridge and perching there like shining epaulettes, the valleys now more expansive, the earth a bloodier magenta, the olives prouder, as we left the scrubby seaboard behind. No more eucalyptus; how I hated the dismal things! By comparison the weeping willows along the Thames were as waggish as party hats. And no more fatuous hillocks. The mountains of Andalusia rose into misty peaks, challenging me to climb higher and higher until at last, as if reaching another, hidden country, the road dropped away to a great basin of farmland, and the clouds fell back as if they too respected the frontier. Rough pasture, fields of winter wheat, a few farmhouses, orderly groves and disorderly slopes leading to granite-shouldered hills: the sun shone on a majestic landscape, and I was at nobody's mercy any more, I was free to explore it as I pleased.

Dear God, the glory of that plain with its fleshy pastures and its arrogant, bony hills beyond, its low white farmhouses throwing back the light like fortresses against the glare; a landscape transformed by work, sculpted into fields and terraces, but without softening its pride. Instead the land had quickened the imported olives, burnishing them, harmonizing them, and made them an expression of its own spirit. Not even harmonizing: there was no interval between spirit and place, they sang in unison, expressing destiny itself—yes, and now I'd found the melody I was waiting for, the one obscured by the mindless rhumba of the seafront. It rang like plainsong and with the same sense of threnody, death and a limitlessness that absorbs all fear and dissolves it, a hymn of reconciliation. Now and again, when I hear a piece of Spanish music, it takes me back to that March day, the last day of my old life; and each piece I hear, single and complete and requiring no other, seems to capture the landscape as if it were the composer's dying testament to Spain. Singleness is the word it always brings to mind. Singleness is its meditation, the attribute of a landscape at one with its destiny and still inhabiting its transformations at our hands; and the strangeness, the singularity of our presence in the place around us, the place where we are. I hear it quite distinctly, this meditation on the ground of being; a world away, or so it seems to me, from the music of tortured emotions, so much of it Teutonic, the voice of vanity insisting: here I am, significant! I am the world! A music born of solipsism, consuming everything in its path, maddened by exile and beautifying its despair. What I hear instead—what I heard that day in Spain—is a voice exiled into knowledge, and in accepting the exile, receiving this: without sin there could be no redemption, without exile no reconciliation. Hanbury's promptings about the Holy Spirit had irked me, but I was ready to acknowledge it that day, in a form I could understand, a companion, more than a ghost perhaps, almost a witness to my existence: the place itself.

I passed a family decked up for an Easter rehearsal in gaudy clothes and headdresses, grinning at me from a horse-drawn cart; a dog sitting up watching its master, who was squatting in the roadside dust, eating his midday sandwich, bicycle propped against a milestone. The dog turned out, as I looked closer, not to be a dog at all but a goat sitting erect on its backside, with its forelegs perpendicular. And a little further on, two men lying on a sloping ploughed field, their heads together and their bodies stretched out at right angles to each other in a neat V, the V of a viewpoint inscribed on a plan, welcoming in the uprushing furrows of the field and, spread out like a tablecloth, the valley beneath. They lay there on their side, each with an elbow in the orange earth, and their heads together, talking. It was too scorched a setting for a rustic idyll, but these two weren't merely taking their ease, they lay on the planet as if it was their own, all of it, and waved at me to include me in their domain.

By lunchtime I was thoroughly lost. I didn't care. I didn't need to go home; I was home.

A pleasant illusion, while it lasted. I knew I didn't belong here. And that released a different longing, one that always crept up on the sly. One I hardly knew was there, I was going to say, but that isn't true, I knew it was there. Isn't there always somewhere we long to head for, drop everything, obey the hidden compass, and set out for? One person or one place that orients us even while we're unaware of them; one place we mustn't set out for—so I told myself whenever the longing surfaced. It isn't home or happiness the compass indicates, only which way to turn to find our own magnetic north. And what happens to a compass when you reach the pole? It goes haywire, presumably. That's what I'd told myself about Fold Farm; for years it was my secret haven, the one I was too canny to return to. I drifted, day-dreaming about it, and the more I idealized the place the less I wanted to measure it against reality. When it was gone I wasn't even sorry. I'd been spared a disappointment. And then, a few years later, under the billowing, Ellie-pregnant balloons, the barrage balloons that made the moon seem flat and silly that night, and thin as a wafer, I'd mistaken someone else for Maggie and felt myself wrenched adrift again. She had been shadowing me ever since, slipping up to tap me on the shoulder; Grand-mother's Footsteps in the snowbound vicarage garden.

Once, one rainy Sunday when we couldn't face our customary walk with Matty on the Heath, Molly and I had taken ourselves to the British Museum, and wandered round an exhibition of Anglo-Saxon jewellery, featuring strange twisted animals de-vouring each other, and more frequently themselves, in poses described by the catalogue as "ritual depredation." Whatever that meant, all I saw from one end of the gallery to the other was a fox stole on a moss-green dress, the fox biting its tail on Maggie's shoulder. Ritual depredation: it sounded like looting and pillaging, and that was appropriate too, I'd looted my mem-ories of Maggie, reconstructing them until each one mirrored a lost opportunity, an invitation I'd misread at Hambledon or at the Schloss. There had been so many occasions—I told myself luxuriously—when I could have mistaken her truculent manner for indifference; when what she was really signalling was im-patience at my absurd restraint. As with Fold Farm, these day-dreams were consigning Maggie to a fool's paradise. Was that what I wanted? Sitting in the jeep by the roadside, I took out my wallet, extracted Maggie's photograph, and studied it.

I'd owned two photographs of her, over the years, the first one sent by her from Germany in '38 and showing her in a short-sleeved pullover, long socks, and a pair of hiking shorts filleted by odd, unnecessary zippers. This photograph disappeared from Belgrave Road, stolen, I always assumed, by Ellie, and no doubt ripped to shreds in Leda Buildings. I'd begun by carrying it around with me, but after a time I thought I would see it more often if I stuck it up on the wall, or by the bed, though that would hardly please Ellie; or on the mantlepiece, somewhere visible. In the end I stood it in the kitchen, where I watched the trains pull in and out of Victoria Station. But somehow her image was less inspiring now that it was on show, it only brought home to me the anxious business of looking, whereas taking it out of a pocket to renew my sense of it, merely to see it, had brought Maggie alive. Back in my pocket it went. Then one day I saw a small oval frame, in a shop in the Strand, and was tempted to try again. To fit the frame I cut Maggie's figure from this photograph, only to find that what was left of the original, the square perimeter around an oval hole, had developed a life of its own. All it showed were bits of tree and sky, and blurred, muddy earth, but they'd acquired a hypnotic veracity, almost as though they were addressing me personally, while Maggie, in her oval, gazed not at me but at an invisible past. To let my puzzlement settle I put the various bits in a kitchen drawer, and by the time I disinterred them Ellie had pounced—it must have been her, no-one else used my kitchen—and made off with the bit that showed her rival.

The second photograph, the one now safely stowed away in my wallet, I'd stolen myself, from the vicarage. When Wilf was born I became personal grata there again; all I could find of Maggie in the Trimble family album was a school photograph, circa 1932. Molly knew I'd taken it. Her sister's fate was still a mystery, and the photograph came in handy. I was able to show it to refugees and homecoming members of the army of occupation, anyone returning from the Hamburg area—I'd even shown it to Auntie in the hope of a psychic breakthrough—though this excuse for carrying it around was growing thin, as time went by.

If she's still alive, Molly asked, why hasn't she been in touch? Why hasn't she got out?

We'd written to Schloss Brüel and gone through the official channels, both without success. Brüel had ended up outside Bizonia, as the newly merged American and British zones of occupied Germany were called—it was a name that rather foolishly evoked the operetta dukedoms of its past, it seemed to me; the Schloss was in the Russian sector, but the Soviet consulate in Rosary Gardens couldn't help us either. Three years now of fruitless enquiries; ten since we'd heard from Maggie, in '38. Why hadn't she written, if she'd survived? From what I heard, life in the Russian zone was no operetta. It was too soon to give up hope—and if anyone had trusted the inscrutability of fate, it was Maggie.

I looked down at the photograph, for confirmation. Maggie smirking, defying the camera, cocky in a way but only acting. That was her; but was it encouraging? I'm not getting anything, dear, I'm sorry, Auntie had said as she handed it back to me, under Percy walls. Another migraine day, no doubt.

I closed my eyes, as I'd seen Auntie do, and touched the surface of the photograph with my fingertips. The face it showed was too fresh in my mind, and that was all I got. Cockiness, innocence, but they seemed ominous now. A school photograph, evoking ranks of vanished girls. Of course I'm dead, Maggie smiled back, and broke my trance. I opened my eyes and read the smile again. Of course her schoolgirl self was dead; long gone. On the verge of crumpling it up, I put the photograph away.

I realized I was sweating, and no wonder, the breeze had kept me cool while we were going along, but now I was sitting in my overcoat inside a stationary jeep with the engine running and the afternoon sun in my eyes, roasting from head to foot. I'd come to a halt on the outskirts of a town, unsure whether to brave the traffic or turn back, and found the handbrake by a process of elimination, taking care, all the while, not to let the engine die on me. I thought I knew how to start it again, but I wasn't about to take the risk.

I took off my coat, replaced the Colonel's ghastly boots with my own familiar shoes, and looked around. Where was I? Antequera, said the sign, but that meant nothing without a map. I tried the glove compartment. Locked. After a fruitless search in the back of the jeep I was about to give up when I noticed the second key hanging inside the one in the ignition. With a little jiggling I got it off the key ring and tried it in the glove compartment lock.

Bingo: the little metal door opened, and inside sat a neatly folded map, a new one, as if waiting for me. Underneath it lay a diminutive leather bag with red and green canvas trim, zip-fastened, the kind of thing a person might buy in Jermyn Street, to hold his shaving soap and his cologne. I'd seen its like in Alec's bathroom. It too looked new. I lifted it out; it felt new, stiff and new, and surprisingly heavy. I opened the zip and found myself gazing at two brightly coloured wads, each as crisp and clean as the map, but thicker. And inscribed with zero after zero. Bingo indeed. Money, pots of it, or rather two tight bundles of it, in the largest bills I'd ever seen.

I couldn't take it in at first, and then my disbelief gave way to an obscure unease, an odd sense of accountability. Accountability? The very word brought to mind the cash I handled at the office, and Garnham at my shoulder: "Handing over money to another undischarged bankrupt, Richard?" Ridiculous, I wasn't at the office now, this was a dead man's money, unaccountable pesetas. This was Thurgo money, and for all I knew the Colonel had meant it for me. And yet that wasn't right either. It was Estrella who'd offered me the jeep. "Is my wish," she'd said. Knowing what was in the glove compartment? Perhaps not, perhaps it was Tom's final takings, for . . . for olive oil, or . . . no, there were tens of thousands of pesetas, and notes in other currencies too, I found, when I examined the second bundle. Hardly the proceeds of good old Olio de Olivas. But never mind its source—what if I was the only person who knew it was here? Suppose it was the Colonel's stash, a secret hoard kept handy for a getaway? Suppose nobody knew? To calm myself, I began to count it.

The figures blurred. I felt as if the sky, the hills, the olive trees with their unblinking stare, were watching me, even the jeep was watching, waiting for its share. I blanked them out, but I still couldn't concentrate, I lost count every time, my fingers trembled and my mind went racing off ahead. I'd barely found the stuff and I was spending it already. It was a bloody fortune, even without counting it I knew I had enough here for—for what? A new house? I didn't want a new house, I liked smelly old Parsifal Road. A new overcoat, certainly, no more hand-me-downs. New clothes for Molly; except that she wasn't really interested in clothes. A fancy education for Wilf, then. A flat for Ellie? A mistress in Holland Park, a son at Harrow. A partnership at Garnham and Coutts, or rather Garnham, Coutts, and Thurgo. Was that what I wanted? The years ahead yawned back at me, and comfort only made them less enticing. But money in the bank—that had charm.

I heard a whirring noise. A man came past on a bicycle, freewheeling down the slope into the town, eyeing the jeep. When he was gone I looked back at the money. The sense of unease had never left me, and it wasn't accountability, it was danger. With this windfall the convulsions at Finca Thurgo had become real, I was part of them now. Or would be if I wasn't careful. A quick escape was of the essence; make my way back, collect my things, my passport; safer to keep Estrella in the dark, tell her I was off to Plaza de Bailen to sell the jeep. Leave it at the airport. Take the first flight out. But not so fast: what if Wallface had taken over Finca Thurgo in my absence? Find a way of sneaking in round the back, through the olive trees, to the barn, and just pray Hector wasn't on the loose. Unfolding the map, I traced the road from Antequera, across the plain, back through the mountains to the coast. It seemed impossibly far, but lingering only heightened the unease. Handbrake off, turn the wheel, gently down on the accelerador.

It was the same road and the same jeep, but now they were both against me. No petrol gauge on the dashboard. I couldn't remember passing anything resembling a pump, along the way. The landscape was still watching too, trying to hold me back, defying me, drawing on my strength. I willed the jeep onwards, mile after mile, coaxing it home.

As we chugged up into the mists I worked myself gratefully into my British Warm again. It was a good coat really, perhaps I'd keep it and buy suits instead, plenty of suits. I'd think about that later, when I was clear, only bad luck to think about it now; but I couldn't resist the pleasure. A bloody fortune. Plenty to spare, I could even lend some to Alec. Short of readies, old man?

In my glee I felt like singing, and what the hell, why not? This was what I'd come for. My inheritance. Downhill at last; the sea, in the distance, and Malaga. She'll be coming round the mountain when she comes, when she comes, she'll be coming round the mountain when she comes! I found the main road and turned back towards the hillocks, cosy now, inviting. Somewhere Finca Thurgo nestled in them.

Yes, and this was how I'd remember it, the oleanders and the olives in the afternoon sun, the ploughed fields with their furrows in shadow now and the long files of mounded earth curving away like juicy purple coils squeezed from a tube of paint. The hillsides bristled with red and yellow blossom, cactus, bramble, thorns and barbed leaves, the oleanders spiky too, defending their outrageous blossom with a show of force. I was going to get to the airport with the little leather washbag, no matter what it took.

After a winding climb the road levelled out, a long stretch of road with a farm on the far-off bend, and where the curve began I saw a figure rise slowly out of the bushes to stand gazing down the road at me.

A fat, unkempt figure, vaguely familiar. Then I recognized him: the man who'd run out into the road, shouting at me after my encounter with the dog. He stepped out into the middle of the road, squarely, with his arms extended, palms up, signalling me to stop.

I wasn't going to stop now. If nothing else, I knew how to deal with foolhardy pedestrians. But by the look of him, this one wasn't planning to leap out of the way, as Wall-face and the guard had done. He wasn't built for leaping. On either side of the road, stout bushes sloped away down to the fields, the bushes into which the wretched dog had limped, and I didn't want to end up there. No need to panic, play it safe. I braked firmly, coming to a halt some fifteen yards in front of the fat man.

"Clutch! Neutral!" Estrella's voice reminded me, but too late. The engine shuddered and died. Damn the man; damn the dog. Its owner was walking towards me, nodding, as if to say: at last! As surreptitiously as possible, I reached across to open the glove compartment, pulled out the little bag and stuffed its money-rigid bulk into my overcoat pocket. With any luck one bill would more than compensate him for the dog.

A balding head, a white shirt streaked with sweat, shoes and trousers caked with roadside dirt. He'd been waiting for me all day, I could see it in his eyes.

"Buenos días," I called, but he just kept on coming, expressionless.

A round, fat, peasant face; a surly bastard, I decided. Perhaps I wouldn't give him my pesetas.

He reached the jeep and stood there gazing at me through the windshields, winding up his shirtsleeves to reveal huge, moist arms matted with black hair. Then again, what were a few pesetas? He put his head on one side and said something in Spanish, a guttural sound, heavily accented. I shrugged and raised my hands in apology, hoping to bring him round to one side of the jeep, out of my path. For a moment, as we waited each other out, I thought he was going to take hold of the bonnet and bend it into scrap metal, but eventually he stepped back and padded round to the passenger side.

"I'm afraid I don't speak Spanish," I said as he approached, sticking out his stomach. The dusty trousers were held up by an incongruously new belt. "But I'm sorry about the dog. Is it all right?"

He leant down, put his cannonball head through the open canvas flap of the door, and stared at me.

"Who are you?" he asked, in English. Guttural, accented English; and an accent I knew well. He wasn't Spanish at all. He was German.

"The dog," I said, faltering now. "Is it all right?"

"The dog, I don't know. Who are you, please?"

We gazed at each other, warily. Could he be one of the Colonel's "friends," living off the land? Despite his bulk he seemed less threatening, close to. More puzzled than angry. "Thurgo's the name," I said. "Can I help you? If it's something to do with what happened this morning," I began, but got no further.

"Thurgo?" His eyes had lit up; then the animation faded. "No . . ." he said, "Thurgo is an old man, I think."

"If you mean the Colonel, he's my uncle. Or was. He's dead." I watched his expression change again, as he withdrew further into himself. "What is it you want?" I said, but something in his face told me not to wait for explanations.

I glanced at the ignition. Turn it, that was all, turn it and punch the accelerator. The man was leaning in towards me, across the passenger seat. "Schäfer," he enunciated slowly. "I am Schäfer."

"I'm sorry, Mr Schäfer, but I'm in rather a hurry."

I turned the ignition key. Or tried to. Nothing happened, the key wouldn't move. "I've got a plane to catch," I heard myself say. The name Schäfer was echoing in my head, Schäfer in the Colonel's papers. *Schäfer, Thomas. Permission to travel in the Occupied Zones.* My hand was still on the ignition. Had I turned the key the wrong way? "You'd better stand back," I warned. But he ignored my bluff and leaned in further, looking round the interior of the jeep.

If the ignition key didn't start the engine, what the hell did? I stared at the bits of metal in front of me, the various knobs, the wiring held together with insulating tape.

"Good," Schäfer remarked, "I am looking for boots like this." Plucking the Colonel's pair from the floor in front of the passenger seat, he inspected the soles and new heels, heavy enough to crack open a coconut. Or a man's skull.

"I don't think they'd fit you."

"Oh yes, they fit me." One foot on the passenger seat, then switching to the other foot, he was removing his filthy shoes and trying on the boots, under my nose. His feet slid into them too easily, but he didn't seem to care. "You see? They fit me very well."

"Glad you like them."

Perhaps he was simply down on his luck; anything to be rid of him, let him have the boots. I watched him step back from the jeep and toss his shoes into the bushes.

"If you need some olive oil, perhaps we could come to an arrangement. I'm a little unfamiliar with this jeep, and . . ."

Turning and advancing on me alarmingly, he gripped the roof above the passenger seat. Thunderheads gathered on his sweaty brows. "You don't understand?" he said. "I am Schäfer."

"I understand perfectly, but I really must be going. As I say, I have a plane to catch."

"I come with you."

"No thank you. Really."

But he was climbing in. Grunting, he deposited his enormous backside, and stretched one foot across onto the floor beside mine. His leg jerked; the engine gave a roar, the jeep jolted forwards, and stalled. Schäfer adjusted the gear lever, and nodded at the floor. Beneath his foot I saw a worn metal button. "Vamos, muchachos," said Schäfer cheerfully, pressing down on the button, and the engine came to life once more.

At least he'd started the damn thing for me. From what I remembered, Finca Thurgo was barely a mile or so up the road, and if the worst came to the worst I could make a run for it when we got there. "I'm only going to my uncle's house. If that's any use to you."

Schäfer nodded. "Vamos," he said. And vamos, shakily, I went.

As I drove I could feel the bulk of him pressing against my overcoat pocket, money-bulge to bulge of fat. But the man was scanning the landscape attentively, oblivious.

"You are not an experienced driver, I think," he commented mildly. "But that was perfectly correct, what you did this morning. Always hit the dog. Better than to go off the road."

"I suppose so." I glanced at him.

"It is not my dog, you don't have to worry."

"What happened to it?"

"You don't have to worry," he repeated. "Not about the dog.

Worry about the road, please. You are driving a little fast.'' I adjusted our speed, and he nodded graciously. ''Thank you.''

''Do you live here, Mr Schäfer?'' I asked, hoping to preserve the affable tone.

''At the present, here in Malaga, yes, Mr Thurgo. I was sitting five days now waiting too long, I walk here to see him and then . . . then here you are this morning, with my jeep.''

''Your jeep?''

I assumed he was joking, and grinned at him. His eyes told me I'd got it all wrong.

''You don't know this?'' He studied my reaction. ''It is for me, yes. I thought you are coming to see me this morning, to bring it.''

His jeep? ''Really? Where do you live, in Malaga?'' But I knew the answer, even as he said it. Plaza de Bailen. His jeep; any moment he might look in the glove compartment, empty of money. ''Yes, as a matter of fact, I was told I could sell the jeep to someone at Plaza de Bailen.'' Keep talking, I told myself. I could see Finca Thurgo coming up at last. ''The, ah, the lady of the house told me, the Colonel's widow, you might say.''

''Yes?'' Schäfer nodded, gravely. ''And . . . how did he die, your uncle?''

The gates were right ahead of us.

''Oh,'' I said. ''Heart.''

''You go too slowly now.''

''I'll tell you what,'' I began.

''Drive a little, soon we find a place to talk.''

''Why don't you take the jeep? I'm on my way back to England, so the jeep's no use to me.''

''Mr Thurgo,'' said Schäfer, reaching into his pocket and bringing out a small revolver, a revolver dwarfed by his hairy hand. ''Drive a little further.''

A Spanish road, a mountain road, patched and peeling and blistered like skin, congealing on the dusty verges in rich tongues and burst bubbles of lava, trickling away over the rim into a dry ravine. Vertiginous bends, a few wooden stakes along the outer edge, or nothing, just a precipice, and views that lure you to the edge. Palm trees and crags, strangely juxtaposed; palm trees, crags, a herd of sheep, a house in the mist. Barely a house, a little whitewashed wall. The road dips, and the bend comes on. This is the one, I see it clearly every time, the bend comes on, the parched ravine opens its maw . . .

And then?

Nothing. Darkness, exploding in my head. The scalding, and the fire. And I have to begin again. Again I drive past a beckoning, deserted Finca Thurgo, on past other farms, fewer and fewer, away from soft hillocks and up into the mountains, knowing the fat ape is going to take the jeep and kill me, telling him again that he can let me out, I'll walk home, arguing with a Schäfer turned to stone.

The jeep stutters, drowning my words. Pines, friendly pines, then nothing but rock and scree and precipice, and the jeep juddering, sputtering, and Schäfer smiles. We have Benzin I think, he says.

The smile, again. The glance at the back seat.

And finally I realize: it isn't olive oil at all, it isn't Olio de Olivas Thurgo, the blackish stuff oozing so sluggishly in its plastic containers, behind us, stock-piled in the back, it's petrol. Petrol. And all at once the palm trees and the crags, the herd of sheep, the house in the mist. Carthaginian; yes, but no-one there, no Hannibal, no-one in sight as, once again, the road dips and the bend comes on, too fast. A voice, from nowhere.

Schäfer's voice.

"Here, go left."

Go left where?

And now I see it.

Yes: a track, pitching away at the far end of the bend, as if flung down the mountainside.

"Here!"

The gun pokes into me, I turn the wheel and we career down the slope, along a reddish, pitted trail no wider than the jeep. The sheep scatter, the house is straight ahead, empty, a useless, spavined thing, its rafters crumpled inwards. Schäfer telling me to slow down, slowly, man, slow down. The ruined house ahead, down in the dip. Bouncing towards it. Gathering speed now, but plenty of time to take it in, the blocks of fallen masonry where the door once stood, the broken timbers, and one wall still standing, held together by the plaster. The chimney like a monument over the rubble, with its long, grieving shadow stretching away downhill. At the bottom of the ravine, a dry bed sprouting oleanders, red and white, with spiky leaves, spear-headed and defiant.

Hurtling now, bouncing.

Schäfer's voice. The fat ape sounds alarmed.

"What are you doing?"

"Getting out," I say, with surprising calm; struggling to rise, my overcoat caught under Schäfer's fat behind.

One foot out, falling, trying to jump free.

And now it comes.

Darkness exploding in my head, shards tearing at my clothes, my skin. And still trying to jump, on and on, in the darkness.

Now I can let it come at last.

Fire, coming for me down the tunnel, scalding, goading me until I burst through cockpit glass and I can fly.

Have a jujube, came the voice, but I stayed where I was, face down against the hot, pebbly earth. I knew Grandfather was holding the boiled sweet down to me at arm's length as if I were an importunate retriever; it was his way of dealing with a wounded, squalling child. Kept loose among the strands of shag the jujubes tasted foul until you'd sucked off the tobacco taste, the taste of pocket. I wanted my apple, my digestive biscuit, and my milk. I didn't want a stinking jujube. I wanted to be picked up and carried to the kitchen where I could sob until my hands and knees stopped hurting.

The heady smell of rosemary told me I'd made it to within a few yards of the French windows before I'd stumbled in the herb garden, in the usual place, among the broken paving stones that lay in wait to trip me as I rushed in for elevenses. I could smell burning too, the place was burning. Some corner of my mind reassured me that it couldn't be Fold Farm because the house hadn't burned down yet, that was later, when I was older.

What was it that was burning? Looking up I saw that Grand-mother's dilapidated herb garden had been tipped dizzily down-hill as if by an earthquake, and turned to ash. A curious, blackened hillside met my gaze, devoid of colour, still smoking in places.

I waited patiently for it to stop pretending and resume the colours of the past; yet at the same time it made perfect sense, turned to ash. The hillside still belonged inside me, it was time announcing itself in this charred form, in dream-language, a black tide that had scorched its way up to within a few yards of me, consuming everything up and until a little circle of the living present at my feet, and bringing me up to date. This seemed perfectly natural—I felt no surprise that the blaze had stopped short and spared me. It was my tide, my time, all part of me as if my past had come disguised as fire and, reaching my feet, woken me with its message of finality. A kind of summons, too:

by moving I could detach myself from it. To see if this was true, I crawled a little way upwards through unharmed, crackling gorse, to the track. Pain in my legs and hands and head seemed to coat me in a fiery substance of my own, I picked myself up, aware of nothing else, only the clinging pain and someone inside it, shuffling down the hillside like a ghost. Cinders blew in my face, charred scraps, brush them away, spit them out. Bursting through cockpit glass; trying to jump, but the pieces clung to me, and now the house ahead, this was mine too, this carbonized thing. The rafters were still smouldering. The blackened stone seemed to have fused with a tableau of metal, bubbled metal stripped of paint, as uniform in colour as a sculpture in some dull, volcanic matter. Bits of it littered the ground like clinker. Shreds of metal had landed in the gorse, igniting it; it was as though a furnace had exploded inside the house, ripping the jeep apart.

The jeep—with the word came Schäfer, the fat ape and his gun; the fear, and a last thought as the bend came on. Petrol, don't drive with petrol in the back. Olio de Olivas, bouncing in the back. I could feel my mind faltering again, but attention kept the dizziness at bay. I let my eyes lead me. The jeep had dived straight in and somersaulted in the rubble, or else been blown onto its side, the tyres had melted and the glass was gone, but I could see a piece of the front seat hanging below the chassis, a great chunk of torn kapok, almost untouched. Above it, in the footwell, singed rags had settled on the Colonel's boots, as if Schäfer's last act had been to let his trousers down. The legs and what remained of the trunk lay among the springs, cremated; one arm hung down below the jeep, grey and swollen but intact, the shirt gone and the hair burned off. Looking closer at the chunk of kapok beside it, I saw that it wasn't kapok at all but a hairless, bulbous head with gashes where the skin had burst, seared by the flames and oozing what I had mistaken for seating material.

A few hardy flies—concentrating, I watched them settle—were beginning to brave the heat. I watched them hover, hesitate, and settle. And I was grateful to them; I was still having difficulty detaching things, distinguishing what was inside my head from what was outside it. The flies knew the difference.

In the dip, where the oleanders were, I found a trickle of water and brought it to my face. My hands came down red, there was a sticky, swollen place above one temple. Hair matted with blood. And when I glanced in the mirror, I saw the neat little hole in my overcoat. In the mirror? No; no, that was later. There in the ravine it was only the dirt and cinders I saw on my clothes, as I bent to the water to clean my hands of gorse needles and wipe off the blood. Bending, feeling the weight in my pocket as if I'd filled it with stones, and remembering now, remembering the money in my pocket. I was alive, and I had the money. But neither of those things seemed to matter, they had both been superseded. The money didn't seem to matter. It was dead weight. And that was when I knew, I think, that I wasn't going home.

There was a swollen place in my head, a bruise on the inside that I didn't want to touch. I waited, oh, a long time, long enough, for it to go away; for continuity; I waited, sitting on the hillside, up a little way above the fire line, and gazing at the jeep in the ruins, as night fell. Watching over Schäfer. Or was it Schäfer watching over me? Dead, or watching? It was like a little song, in my brain. Dead, or watching. Dead or watching. It went round and round, a perfect circle: perfect, surfect, surfeit, circuit, circle.

From time to time I broke off and tested the sensation, the swelling in my head, to see if it had gone. But it hadn't, it was dense and resilient, like drunkenness, releasing thoughts that bubbled up and burst too soon and were sucked back again into a warm, droning consistency. Beneath it everything converged. I knew perfectly well what I was thinking, what it was, the thought I mustn't voice. The droning in my head protected me from it, warning: quicksand. But it was there, all the same. I told myself a story, as a way to keep it strange. I had descended the hillside to see whether I was in the jeep or not, and I was, and I was dead. The flies had settled on my lifeless brains, and I was free to go, to Maggie's wedding. The words were there ahead of me, I knew I hadn't thought them up. I didn't need excuses. No, I was going to Maggie's wedding. Interesting. The man was obviously concussed. Confused, poor chap. He seems to have mislaid the last ten years. Yes, but if that was true, how did I know it myself? Concussed, or faking? It was the same question: dead or watching. Both perhaps, a perfect circle. The hillside was too dark to see now, but a sweet, pungent odour confirmed its original message. The past had come full circle—Spain, I thought, Spain, Grandfather! Like the dream that woke me, all evidence of my existence had been turned to ash and I was free to go.

Banging popping sounds came from the invisible jeep, as the

metal cooled, burps of uncontrolled glee. The gorse still hissed, subsiding, and now and again a car passed, way above us, throwing out splinters of light. No-one came. I could have stayed there happily, soothed by the hissing, belching night so full of promise, at one with my fate. The truth, it had seemed to me for so long, lay in things infolded. But it was too late now, the bomb had gone off and the minefield stretched ahead.

Walking back across the mountains was a fatuous, unsteady business, a lesson in pain, planning every step as if learning to walk again, tripping and sliding down the scree, jarring my hands and side and feeling the blood start to trickle afresh under my clothes, until in the end I savoured every jolt like a child picking at an unripe scab. Sweet, tingling pain forcing a track through clogged ways, as my brain cleared. There was a moon, a battered old moon, abandoned by its convoy of balloons, world-weary now, a fat disfigured face lighting my path. After a time the night air began to turn stale. There was a sour stench beckoning like a slum. A stench of wine; but I could see no lights. The smell rose rank and steamy. Had I pissed myself? It was everywhere, like an open sewer. I staggered, wading down a little slope and fell headlong into the stink, coming to rest against a bloated object, something with a head, black in the moonlight. A horse's head. Then I saw it had wheels on it, it was a little hobbyhorse, a child's toy. My croak of terror turned to laughter and I lay back, inhaling the fumes of a thousand empty bottles. I'd wandered into a rubbish dump. Welcome to the gutter. Once more I picked myself up and waded on down-hill, keeping the road in sight. I could smell the sea now, on the wind; I'd never loved the wind so much, it seemed oblivious to everything, even death and decay. Now barking dogs handed me on from farm to farm, the howling rose and fell, mapping out the darkness. And there it was below me, glistening Finca Thurgo, a blob of melting ice cream on the dark valley floor. Leaning into the wind, I lurched down the slope towards the trees, unseen. Through olives and brittle eucalyptus, tossing dark, streaming heads of hair like demented mourners. Beyond them, the barn.

I inspected myself in the mirror, by the light of the Colonel's oil lamp. The hole in my overcoat was around naval height, a neat round hole in my side. I'd been shot. I stood, hardly daring to open the coat. How on earth was I still going, shot? If this was some ghostly ordeal then the dead suffered too, life clung to them like a dream. But there I was, alive, reflected in the mirror, scratched and smeared with dirt, and standing at the basin. Under the coat my clothes were stuck together with dried blood. I loosened them with water. The bullet had passed on out again through the shirt, the jacket, and the coat. Darkness exploding in my head: the fat ape had got off a shot before I'd fallen clear. Searching, I swabbed at the aching, sullen flesh. There was no pleasure in this pain, only the fear of what I'd find, a sunken place, a blueish hole, starting to fester. But the bullet had only grazed me, scoring a groove along my hip. I fetched a vest, wrapped and knotted it round my middle, and slumped down on the bed, beside my suitcase.

Shaky now, examining my belongings to try and keep myself from stretching out to sleep. There would be time for that once I was safely on the train. I told myself the story once again: now other people were descending the narrow, rutted track towards the ruins, they were coming to the jeep, finding the corpse. Never learnt to drive—poor chap, he chose the wrong moment to try. Died with his boots on. They were going through his belongings in the barn, as I was doing now. The suitcase and its contents would be sitting here intact, because I was dead, in the jeep. Richard Anstruther Thurgo, tragically and suddenly, in a road accident, in Spain; no flowers. Mechanically I said farewell to shirts and socks. Plane ticket, passport. "We, Ernest Bevin, a member of His Britannic Majesty's Most Honourable Privy Council, a member of Parliament, etc., etc., etc." All three etceteras stared back at me. I felt a little giggly sitting there holding the thing, as if to console it. "Request and require," it blustered, "all those whom it may concern to allow the bearer to pass freely, without let or hindrance, and to afford him every assistance and protection of which he may stand in need." Kneeling at the desk, I sifted through the documents again. The Colonel's drawers were fair game, if no-one knew what they contained. Bugger Ernest Bevin—these were my belongings now, my start in life. And here it was. *Schäfer, Thomas, Permission to Travel in the Occupied Zones.* There might be more such papers where Schäfer lived, at Plaza de Bailen *très*. But my mind balked. No, it was Plaza de bale-out for me. A mistake: I felt the nausea revive. Who was the bolter now? The bloody man, he's done a bunk.

The room began to close on me, the trees outside were swaying and sighing, lashing the barn. Maelstrom; the word returned from something I'd read long ago, a vortex at the end of the world, a whirlpool miles across. And a ship sucked round and down into it, under black, howling skies. No: terra firma, hillside, rock and gorse. Still kneeling, I gripped the desk with both hands to steady myself. The foreground gradually returned. I reached down and began to stuff the travel documents into my jacket. Concentrate. Shares and bearer bonds could stay. Beneath them lay the gun, an unconvincing-looking weapon, plastic handle, stubby barrel with, when I turned it over, some lettering clumsily incised on one side. Isidro, it said. And in italics, *The Destroyer*. I put Isidro in my pocket, with the ammo.

Take me too, said the words of Lord Byro, Volume Four, pocket edition. Begin at the beginning; and secondly, proceed; that was my motto now. I took the little broken book.

We, Ernest Bevin. . . . Should I bring the passport? But it would lead verisimilitude, abandoned here. Leave it, I wanted no part of Richard Thurgo's life; I never had. Commence not with the end—or sinning in that sort, end at least with the beginning. Leave it. I had money, the universal passport. I returned to the bed and sat a moment longer, husbanding my strength. Concussed or not, I knew what I was doing; I was obeying the compass. Concussed; compulse; compass. Come-to-pass: behind me everything had turned to ash. The fire had made itself visible at last, and burnt itself out at my feet, it was the summons I'd been waiting for, all these years of wondering when my real life would begin.

TEN, MAYBE TWELVE METRES ABOVE THE WINDING HAMburg street the train veers wildly on its iron cradle, slowing down.

"Sankt Pauli. Reeperbahn."

Next stop St. Pauli and the Reeperbahn, comes the voice distorted by the S-Bahn speaker system. Once more: "Zanpowli . . ." Some remnant of English stirs in my head. Through the crackle "Zanpowli" rings like a plea: "Some*body*!"

No-one moves, then as the train stops and the doors slide open one or two commuters fold their half-read *Welts* and *Zeits* and *Morgenblatts* and join me jostling on the platform alongside other sober-suited avatars of the new Germany. Yes, even respectable people, some of them, commute to the notorious Reeperbahn (the Devil's birthplace, we tell our customers), to business offices in high-rise blocks, to publishers and shipping offices and God knows what all, not just to visit its porno theatres and bookshops, or its whores; respectable businessmen, *Wunderkinder*, model democrats, kindly, cultured, the salt of modern Europe. I look like one of them. (Well . . . perhaps not. At any rate I'm dressed like them.) Some nights on St. Pauli station there's a drunk who patrols the platform crying "Ein Volk! Ein Reich! Ein Führer!" but now, twenty years on, no-one pays him any mind. Gone are the days when Walters and I, even into the 'Fifties, could walk into a bar, murmur *Heil Hitler*, and watch a volley of hands rise in involuntary salute. Our favourite pastime then.

As we emerge this morning into the dull grey nullity of the Reeperbahn, far too bland to be the birthplace of even a very minor devil, how many of my companions still see it as it was? The rubble everywhere, people drifting like algae through the

256

wet streets? Furtive groups at the corner of Hamburger Berg, where the black marketeers huddled. Now it's the memories that are furtive, our yearning for the glory of the rubble.

Yes the glory; God knows the devastation was shocking even in '48, when I arrived from Spain, but I had never felt so conscious of human splendour—I don't mean splendour in defeat, or courage or resourcefulness though there was plenty of both. No, it belonged to the devastation itself: that was what revealed some old, immutable, long hidden ground for joy. A permanence. In the terrain as it gazed back at me it was as if a face emerged, more obstinately human than that other image of endurance, the drab figures straying in the wreckage; more human, yes. And as splendid as a savage seascape. You could say this was the splendour of it, but its features, this rubble, these ruins, came from inside that splendour and that permanence, disgorged like the womb on the floor of the stall at Schloss Brüel: what was there, always there, but not meant to be seen, now made available to touch and sight and smell, the innards of a city, and not the city of stone and glass but the place, Hamburg, where people gathered, the city as a body of men. I wandered its viscera like an explorer finding there what no slums could ever fully disclose, shapeless pulped and agglutinated things, shining, splendid in their fall, in their extrusion to the light. I had never felt so human, so invigorated. I wasn't glorying in destruction. On the contrary, in permanence, in the fullness of time made physical.

I wanted it to last forever, the stink and the spray of plaster dust that blew off the bombed houses, and the mulch underfoot. Disintegrating furniture, rags, sodden carpets and books: tilth, a gift from the hidden complement of life, from the death that gave it dimension, the dark side of the moon that turned the pale papery thing into a globe. To me it was a resurrection—it was not only my own resurrection, it was the final resurrection itself, the ruined buildings were like so many corpses raising their torsoes out of the great cemetery of the city, breathing into dull existence the sweet sickly life-giving breath of decay, reviving us, revealing what it is that preserves us, we humans, the threat of decay that quickens our sap. The prostitutes patrolling the streets knew it, their thronging clients knew it. They were all but fucking in the streets in their need to respond to it, yes to respond, not to react against the desolation; inspired, breathed into lust by the skeletal city, often going at it in the ruins themselves, in the flaming willowherb and the grass that grew out of the bombed sites like the timeless hair of the dead. Oh they were haggard, the whores, they were sick and desperate for money, but triumphant too. Day and night, cries came from bombed houses and backyards heaving with copulating couples, the scent of sex mingling with the faint, lingering, marzipan stench of the dead.

A ghoulish image, a *Walpurgisnacht*? Not at all, believe me. I felt more aroused than I ever had in my whole life, I had an erection swollen up as though I held the whole of Germany in my penis—and you must understand, this was not a demonic Germany, it was just a place, a city like any other, now made real and powerful and abundant by the presence of death, not by its aftermath but by its vital, ordinary presence, its loamy presence. Tilth. And more: a plant erupting with involuntary milk, saluting life. I walked those streets like Pan, like Punch, like a Bacchus spreading power and blessings, fructifying Hamburg by my watchful, withheld seed. A pandar, not a client; not yet, not once, those first few weeks. At first I thought this was because it was too pitifully easy—though I knew I didn't despise the girls for their availability; or the boys; men and women of all ages. Far from it; no, it was because I was them, I was one with them in the vitalizing power of my erotic magic, I contained every last squeezing German orifice in my arousal, and I needed to find my own client, I needed to impregnate poor sad defeated Hamburg (which was not, despite what we'd been told about the Germans, crowing in some demented Nazi *Götterdämmerung*'s delight; I was the only delighted person there), or at least, I felt, I must fertilize some representative of it; be a seedbed. I was the Great Whore, I had taken all of death into myself and sprouted branches from the grave, the whores were my leaves, my own, in all Hamburg they alone embraced the great energy of its ruination.

To repeat: there was no dark Nazi ecstasy here, no twilight of the gods, this was common humanity stripped of everything but the essential mystery and urgency of living. While as for the energy to rebound, to rebuild after being razed to the ground, the impulsion to build a new city . . . no, not yet, this was survival. It was in its fallen state that Germany was beautiful, not because it had earned it or somehow desired it, not as the mighty crash of impossible ambition, not because of the horror of the Reich, no, not because of any aspect of what had been: simply because of what it was, musky as earth beneath the plough. Forget the guilt, the sackcloth and ashes. There was liquor here. Here the husk of things had been torn off by the bombers as a bear rips open the honeycomb.

Besides, I think I was a little mad at this point.

When you're mad are you aware of it, do you direct your madness as in a dream, half at its mercy and half willing it in one direction or another? I was concussed, in shock, yet sufficiently aware of it to feel guiltily responsible for my actions, and to keep guilt at bay I fostered my bewildered state, or tried to. I had no sane reason to be exploring occupied Germany while my family and friends were coping with news of my death. But here I was. Mad or bad; dead or watching? Which part of myself was in charge?

No matter which, I had an interest in finding a higher significance in what I saw on my travels. Portents everywhere; and they all harked back to my awakening in the ravine outside Malaga as the brush fire reached me, waking to see the little ruined house with the burned out jeep which now seemed a herald, a true summons. I had felt summoned even then, and so it was: the fire, the gutted house, and Schäfer's corpse: each one pointing me towards this city of firebombed streets as far as the eye could see, and corpses by the thousand, still being disinterred. Time to rise from the dead, ran the summons, and Germany was the place for it. *Stunde Null* we called it then, hour zero, not midnight when the cycle repeats, but the intimate hour, a time shown on no clock. All bonds were broken, the streets were pure mischief, pure fellowship, the buildings nakedly human too, calling me home to Brüel and Maggie, to the permanent. To Maggie's wedding. No, I knew perfectly well that was a lie, a fiction to parade poor Richard-in-shock, though I clung to it during the long train journey to Hamburg, not only as an excuse but for the portion of truth it contained.

"Papiere!"

The train compartment door opening, and a German voice, but not always. British, American. Asking to see my documents, Thomas Schäfer's documents. Like a good German I had plenty of those. At one point a ticket inspector entered the compartment and, search as I might, I found I'd mislaid this one item, the only piece of paper I'd actually bought and had a right to. None of my washbag-currencies would do, it appeared, to buy another. I accepted this with a serenity that surprised me, and after some conversation the official said that in my condition I didn't need a ticket. It was some while before I realized that this whole encounter had taken place in my head.

The ravine kept coming back to me, on the train, either that or I was holding onto it as I had held onto the Colonel's desk in the barn that night when the little room began to toss and spin like a cabin in a high sea. Vertigo—that was still real, not faked. The hillside was still there below me, the ravine, that burnt grey thing which was my old, blasted existence, more real than I was, for the time being, as if I was its dream and not the other way around. Then, in recollection, came the flies, landing on the piece of kapok, the chunk of upholstery from the jeep which wasn't upholstery at all but a human head. This was a different moment, but the sequence wasn't clear. I had difficulty holding onto the present, that was the vertigo, it came from trying to hold onto the place, the space in which not only I would be, but other things would be there with me. What other things? There were times, in the train, when I thought I really would go mad. It was space that was the present, only I wasn't sure whether things were happening now, that's to say later than some things but earlier than others, or whether they'd all happened already and I was reviewing them.

I couldn't let go of the head because while in one sense it was merely horrible and I had survived a crash which burned a man to death and now there were flies on his melting skullcap, it was also sublime and what was sublime was a threshold, a pain where my senses met the world. And a foreground. There was space there. In it little atomies like the starfire seen behind closed eyelids; no they were flies, carrion flies, blue-green their abdomens gleaming like armour. I needed them. They made unpredictable movements, flitting around between me and what I also experienced as me, the head, they were the difference yet they seemed like agents of my mind, differentiating agencies. And when they settled, everything blurred again. I had an insight into things then, or rather an overwhelming sense of them as they took form outside me, yoking me to them at the very instant they disclosed themselves as separate: just as the head, Schäfer's head, became my likeness when I understood it wasn't mine; and I reclaimed this as my own death, as my dead self. My likeness, that is. Not me at all. It as not my head the flies were swarming on (like an echo I received this), and across the threshold which was pain itself joining me to what I saw, the flies gathered me into the world and made it familiar, mine. At that moment I loved the thing I was seeing—no matter that it was carrion, grotesque—and I loved it as I had loved nothing in my life before.

And I understood now why, waking in the ravine, I had felt as if transported to the moon. The charred, colourless look of the hillside was only a clue to it, hinting at a further secret: the curvature of what seemed flat, the moon's fat face. How did I know it was curved? It came to me slowly. Transported to the moon, my first thought was: what if I moved, becoming part of what I saw? Entering it, this dead landscape; now; calling me. Time was on the dark side, it said; it was death that gave dimension. Of course: of course it was death that gave us perspective, but more than that, death gave us time, and time had no dimension outside my head except as space, the place I was in. In time, then, everything was geometry. Sacred geometry. And by repeating this like an idiot, like an initiate, I became human (or so I felt) and, for the first time, lived.

''Papiere!''

Plenty of documents in my pockets. But what did they say? I was having difficulty focussing on print. Forged documents? Or real, perhaps? Who was the man I'd killed? Or rather who'd tried to kill me—but I took pleasure in thinking of fat Schäfer as my victim.

Schäfer, Thomas, Permission To Travel In The Occupied Zones. Studying this one, I finally noticed that it had expired. International Red Cross passport. Good, this seemed to be in working order. Thirty Day Business Permit. No dates on this at all that I could find, it didn't seem to have been stamped. And these last two seemed incompatible. Thomas Schäfer, businessman or angel of mercy? Hardly both.

There were other official-looking papers too, among them an interzonal pass, and an identity card from the International Refugee Organization, whatever that was. Valid or not, the fact is I bore no resemblance to the puffy face in the mug shots, other than unshavenness. I was altogether too thin, too gaunt. But looking round I saw no fat faces among my fellow passengers, we all looked emaciated. Did that help? With hindsight I dare say nobody looked quite themselves in the great weary migration that was Europe then, thirty million on the move, forty perhaps, sixty, the figures are all guesswork. We looked strange and smelt strange, and wellfed officialdom was happy to pass us on to the next control point. The working part of my brain decided, I think, that if fate wished me to be caught I would be, and that I might as well invite this as hide from it. It would be a relief in a way, to bring my little charade to an end, plead amnesia, and go home. And if instead I was allowed to continue, it would be God's will. Absolved, I reached into my pockets and thrust before me whatever papers came to hand.

I thought I was playing a grand game of dice with fate. What I didn't realize was how little control the Allies had—the Great Powers as we were learning to call them—over their newly-drawn borders. Travel regulations changed from month to month at Whitehall's behest, decisions were made in Washington or Paris but the officials on the spot barely knew what kind of permits they were looking for. Besides, they were more concerned with people trying to get out of Germany than with those trying to get in. A little luck, that's all it needed; even at the best of times the sharp-eyed frontier guard is a fiction sustained by a bad conscience. During the 'Sixties I employed and became friendly with an exotic dancer from Ipswich, Louise by name, who'd had her passport stolen by a jealous boyfriend in Amsterdam. Undeterred, she travelled extensively as a Norwegian on the strength of her one remaining document, a passbook from the Norwich Union Building Society. If challenged she would reply with double-Dutch in a singsong Scandinavian accent; but then Louise was fearless, hardly surprising since one of her specialities as a performer involved standing on her head stark naked while singing Rule Britannia—this appealed tremendously to the Germans—between pulls on a Churchillian cigar, and blowing out a series of candles with what appeared to be a puff of smoke from her vagina.

Lacking Louise's sangfroid I still feared German officialdom, and at last, as we pulled out of a city with people still hanging onto the train and squeezing into the compartments, I heard an authentic German voice, no foreign twang to it, proclaim inspection time. My bravado crumbled. Documents aside, would my German really pass muster? Perhaps I hadn't fooled General Jessen, that night in the Latimer barracks, perhaps he'd just toyed with me.

I forced my way down the corridor, away from the voice, and got off at the next station. Somewhere after Köln it must have been, in the American Zone. Köln with its cathedral in the distance—I know I glimpsed it from the train while I was still in my trance, and what I saw seemed delightful and extraordinary, a lace or latticework of snowy, silhouetted house fronts, the windows merely holes revealing more façades in the street beyond, tattered as if giant caterpillars had been munching on them. Actually what these chewed façades reminded me of were the chains of paper snowmen linked at arm and leg that Ellie made each Christmas, to give Auntie's consulting rooms a festive air, cut out of cheap, shiny lavatory paper; appropriate, now I think of it, to those dear stinking rooms in Poland Street. Here too, in Germany, it smelt sour; a smell of rotting rubbish and of corpses, even now, even in the snow; a foul sewer exhalation from dry taps. Disinfectant everywhere, too. Lysol and decay. And the people with their own distinctive smell of course. Starvation has a smell, a sickly sweetish smell as if the body is exuding a reserve of honeyed innocence, a last resort, held back to lure a careless predator. No shortage of these, as I soon discovered, in the Occupied Zones. In poor, crafty Bizonia.

Smells; did Spain have any, aside from the barn with its animal droppings, and the ravine of course, smoking, aromatic perhaps, but why can't I recall the smell? In post-war Germany everything stank. I remember being glad to be rid of the acrid breath of the locomotive. Distinctive, and suffocating. Then waking in a frozen field, the trees so black, the blackest I'd ever seen, and being unable to puzzle out how I'd got there. The diesel stench of the road still in my nostrils. No turds, there were few cattle left uneaten. A sugar beet lorry took me to the Ruhr, with its dead chimneys, dust everywhere. I remember other chimneys in the towns we went through, puffing smoke and indicating life beneath the rubble. Black crosses on a chimney meant the opposite, the driver told me: corpses not yet dug out. He seemed to navigate by chimneys, chimneys and churches, they were the only landmarks left. Hitler's Autobahns now ran from one heap of rubble to another, cars scuttling between them, black Volkswagens mostly, like ladybirds in mourning. Muddy trucks and troop carriers with their ribbed grey canvas humped like woodlice. I remember another dungheap looming up before us, I forget which one, another scarecrow city. This was how the world would look after an earthquake had shaken it to pieces, or a meteor collision. Or a war of the worlds fought with weapons beyond our imagining, using sound waves perhaps, because what was left resembled cities less than some kind of solidified noise, the mummified echo of a gigantic explosion from horizon to horizon, an echo in stone. Rubble, millions upon millions of tons of it, the silt left behind by a tidal wave of sound.

And no colour. No flowers, winter clung on that year. No

buds. I'd come from sunny Spain, festooned with bougainvillea. No blood, perhaps that was why the bougainvillea kept coming back to me. Its colour of course but also its imperviousness, those gaudy florets more leaf than petal, papery, different somehow from the effect of the whole bush though that too is brash and heartless, making you wonder how a creeper so mean in its parts and so vulgar as a mass, odourless, charmless, can pierce your heart. Odourless; it helped to think about bougainvillea in this place. It was disturbing, the feeling that it was my place, my grief, and that as yet I had no idea why.

Before the war I'd loved Peter, relished his homeland, relished the Branntwein and the language. But I hadn't felt at home here until now. Now, in this landscape? I kept finding myself humming *O God our help in ages past*, and at first I thought it was some kind of reflex piety, to ward off disgust, till I remembered that it was the background music, the theme tune as it were, of the newsreels I'd seen in London. "At Last The Reich Feels The Tread Of Conquering Armies," proclaimed my favourite. Week after week they were shown, by government decree, and I'd relished them like Branntwein. We watched German women in ragged smocks trading round-arm punches in the ruins, fighting over the rations being handed out by our boys, crates of liver sausage and other things dear, as the commentary put it, to the stomach of the Hun. Then, to ease any envy we might feel towards this largesse, we were shown how the so-called liver sausage was made entirely out of pine and beechwood shavings, no liver or meat in it at all, and in case we began to feel uneasy about the stomach of the Hun, the voice added sternly that it was costing us a lot of money to keep the Germans in food. To gloat over the defeated is not the British way, gloated the commentary as we watched child victims of malnutrition queueing up for treatment and families wandering the streets with their worldly belongings on their backs. Germany asked for it, the voice added, and Germany has got it. Pathé News won the gloating contest: "The Heil Hitlerites with obsequious smiles try to make friends," their announcer told us, over a close-up of grinning German rustics, "but Europe's backward race will have more lessons to learn before we take those smiles at face value." To Wagnerian music, the angle widened to show a pretty hamlet burning down in the background. "Lessons such as the people of Wallendorf learnt when the Americans set fire to the whole village because of persistent sniping after surrender," and finally, Pathé topping their loathing of the Hun with their contempt for the Yank, "but only a fool would repose trust in a German."

I lost count of how many times I returned to see those newsreels; I returned because of what came next. "Horror In Our Time" it was called. By way of introduction, Churchill's best growl: "What tragedies, what horrors, what crimes . . ." It was time for the stick insects of Belsen. Time too for something else, a moment of recognition that stopped my heart the first time around.

Death camp survivors in overcoats, in singlets, or still in prison uniform, wandered the compounds in a dream, among sleepers and heaps of clothes which proved to be more sleepers, and the dead, piled high, heaps and fields of the dead; while Allied observers looked on with handkerchiefs over their mouths. A few years later when I visited some of the camps I found to my amazement that a number of these survivors had never left, or had left only to return, unable to tolerate life outside the old compound, which now sported chintzy curtains and well tended windowboxes, and contained their former inmates, still in residence; bound by an experience which isolated them from the rest of humanity. Already in the newsreels I was struck by how similar they looked, the survivors, with their sunken cheeks and beaky noses, a separate tribe, looking at once exaggeratedly Jewish and identical to one other—conveniently for their exterminators, I thought. Then I was jolted out of this gruesome reflection. The screen now showed a line of death camp guards being led past at gunpoint, identifying themselves by name and rank. Some gruff, others defiant. Among them a scruffy blonde woman, plump, but unkempt. A slack-jawed, bullocky face. She stepped forward, spoke her name in a low mutter. "Herta Bote": that's how I heard it, perhaps already convinced I'd recognized her. She refused to say anything more, and was herded out of view. Herta, or had she said Hella? Or Helga, or Gerda? The voice was guttural and indistinct, the sound recording poor. Herta? Herta from the treehouse? I couldn't recall her surname or that of Ludolf her grandfather, and "Bote" rang no bells. Then again this creature, this criminal, might have been giving a false name. But her face . . . well, the truth was I could no longer picture Herta all that clearly, and with her heavy, bony looks and thatch of blonde hair she was one of a hundred thousand such farmgirls from the North, dull-witted Friesian stock, as Alec would have put it. No reason to think it was my Herta.

All the same I sat through the films again and again, listening to the mumbled name, studying the eyes for proof, in vain. It was no hardship. As I say, I was enthralled by those newsreels, I gloated with the best of them over the downfall of Europe's backward race, their suffering and their squalor. Germany was a place I never expected to visit again. Postwar England was quite squalid enough, thank you.

And now here I was: et in Bizonia ego, in the American sector, distributing sugar beet, wordlessly passing out rations like the soldiers in the newsreels, in that landscape familiar from a darkened cinema. The Americans got the scenery, so we'd been told, the French got the wine, and we got the ruins. Nobody said what the Russians had got; but they had Schloss Brüel, that was all that mattered to me. It was rumoured they shot strangers on sight, and the less Russian territory I had to cover the better, which meant crossing the British sector first. Then what? I'd walk. The Slosh was forty, fifty miles from Hamburg, due east, a walk in the woods. Travel by night. I could do it. The wound on my hip, where Schäfer's bullet had scorched me, was healing up pretty well. I had it dressed by a "Dr med. Roting" whose waiting room I remember for the stuffed owl that sat in a glass case wearing a stern consultant's expression and, more incongruously, an Iron Cross around its neck. No questions were asked about the wound or who I was. Don't tell me, said Dr med. Roting's eyes.

For ten years and more the Germans had been fed lies and they didn't want to hear any more. It took me a while to grasp this. Afraid that he'd penetrate my German disguise, I'd told my lorry driver I was an American journalist working an undercover story about everyday life in Occupied Germany. He made no comment, and I don't suppose he believed a word of it, or could have cared less. His mouth was set so firm it looked as if he was trying to punish it for ever having opened. All I could prise out of him was that he'd been in the merchant navy, he'd served as a stoker in a *Himmelfahrtkommando* ferrying arms across the Mediterranean to the Afrika Korps, from Naples. I thought he was going to tell me more, but then his lips clamped tight again over his bulging, swollen gums, and he resumed his impression of Beethoven's death mask. *Himmelfahrt:* literally heaven-journey but last journey is what it means, suicide mission. As I learnt later, the ships used in this particular exercise were little more than deathtraps, built in flimsy sections and sent overland to Italy, where the stokers were locked into the engine room for the duration of the journey, to prevent them jumping ship before it sailed. And once at sea, no escape if the ship was torpedoed.

I offered him money to smuggle me into the British Zone. He refused. I upped the offer to a thousand Reichsmarks. "Neh," he said, dismissive. He knew a *Himmelfahrt* when he saw one. Pulling up at a railway halt he opened the passenger door for me, wordlessly, and drove off without looking back.

The Hamburg train announced itself with two specks of light becoming larger, than the hissing of steam and a red glow from the driver's cab. Old German coaches clattered past, slowing, followed by Belgian cattle trucks and rain-soaked wagons with markings from France and Italy. Hurricane lamps waved us aboard.

As before, the inspecting officials were German; the further north, it seemed, the more administrative powers had been restored to them. I sat numbly, waiting my turn, clinging to Alec's dictum: if your papers say you're the Kaiser, you are the Kaiser, as far as Jerry's concerned. All you need in Germany is a lot of chits, well stamped.

Was it true? Clearly the Germans did have trouble identifying people by appearance rather than credentials, not only had they embraced *der kleine Adolf* in the name of a flaxen-haired Aryan ideal, little Adolf as they continued to call him, but they had embraced as their leaders a whole gang of dark-haired, utterly unprepossessing persons, Hitler and Himmler and Göbbels and Göring, who looked more like the woodland gnomes and greasy goblins of German folklore than the blond warrior types they themselves extolled; leaders who looked more like specimens of the races they were telling the Germans to exterminate. Had nobody noticed? But presumably their papers were in order and their chits well stamped. Germans couldn't *see* each other, was that it? Perhaps they couldn't smell each other either, they couldn't sniff out true from false, and like the titles and orders of old, documents served to ground German vertigo in the face of the world, the smelly, shifting, sentient world. Well then: no wonder the Germans were philosophers, no wonder they were musicians; no wonder they wanted to exterminate every smelly, shifting, sentient being who reminded them of their sensory inadequacy. At this very moment, and in the same spirit, as the inspector came nearer along the train, wasn't I too winding my reflections around me like a magic cloak, a spell to make me invisible, unsmellable?

Papiere! Abracadabra for a people without identity, only identity papers. I showed my interzonal pass. The inspector studied it painstakingly. Moments passed; my overweening faith in German obedience to print began to falter, and I held out my other documents to distract the man. He glanced at them, then at me. Finally he turned away without a word and went off with them along the stationary train. I saw him climb out and make his way into an office and I knew my goose was cooked.

Should I run? Where to? I'd already done a bunk and I was running now and there was nowhere else to go, except home.

The yellowish faces in my compartment were averted from me as if I had a contagious disease, though they were the ones looking ill, with their ominously sallow skin. I began to feel a pleasant lightness: it was over, I was going home to Britain and a decent bed and Molly's breakfast, and these disdainful wraiths beside me could have their nightmare to themselves.

The inspector had returned. He was beckoning to me.

I stood up, glancing round the compartment. *Adieu*, I said firmly, suppressing my giggles. *Auf Wiedersehen* seemed inappropriate, we wouldn't be seeing each other again. I was led down the platform, a prisoner of war, but nonchalant. In how many war films had I watched this scene? The heroic escapee recaptured (and secretly admired by the better sort of Boche). I was ushered into a dark and dirty office with cleaner spots on the walls where portraits had been removed. A uniformed man with a prematurely elderly face turned and came towards me, holding out my documents. Without thinking I took them from him as I heard the door close behind me. We were alone.

"Sturmbannführer Dieter Verg," said my interrogator, and he began to reel off a list of medals and wartime campaigns.

I wasn't having any of this. "How do you do," I said in English.

He smiled, indulgently it seemed. Then I noticed that there were tears in his eyes.

"Jetzt Reichsbahnbetriebsingenieur." This in a low, apologetic murmur, giving his current rank and role on the railways; an engineer, nothing to do with police or passes or border security, I realized, as he came to attention, gave the Hitler salute, stepped forward, reached up on tiptoe and kissed me on both cheeks.

We stared at each other as he took a hasty step back again.

Then he looked down, to try and stem the flow of tears, or else abashed, perhaps, by his own audacity. Either way, it was just as well that he couldn't see my own look of bewilderment. "My car is at your service," he said, adding "permit me to escort you to your destination," in what I recognized from Sisdick days to be a German officer's tone when addressing a superior.

For a moment I was still too flabbergasted to reply. "Nein, danke," I managed eventually, and then more sharply, "Nein."

Whoever he thought I was, it would be one charade too many, I wasn't ready for it. He bowed and I fancied I saw a conspiratorial look when his face came up. Yes, definitely sly.

Taking my cue I demanded to be allowed to return to the train. Another brisk salute and off we went, back to the platform and the hissing, waiting train. Before I could protest, a compartment was cleared for me; and there I sat, in baffled, solitary state, all the way to Hamburg.

As we lurched through the ghostly landscape I could still feel the Sturmbannführer's tearful kisses on my cheeks. It hadn't been Richard Thurgo he'd kissed, of course. It was old moonface Schäfer, Thomas Schäfer who by now, perhaps lay rotting in my grave. But who the hell was Thomas Schäfer when he was at home?

When the Buddha was young he left the palace and his wife and son, abandoning them one day to become a wanderer, and on his way he encountered the Four Great Sights: an old man covered in sores, a sick man, a corpse followed by mourners, and a yellow-robed recluse sitting in calm and meditation. Why these should be four great sights I can't imagine, they sound like the kind of thing you could hardly avoid in India, but if they were supposed to be the signs that a man was on the trail to enlightenment I was in good shape on my arrival in Hamburg, scoring three out of four. Sores and sickness everywhere you looked. I don't recall a funeral with mourners; yet oddly enough there was a yellow-robed man on the platform, hawking his spiritual wares in horn-rimmed glasses, yellow socks and sandals, and a yellow sweater over his saffron robe. This was the Bhikku from Rangoon, Bhikku Thunanda, a familiar sight and a striking one in the Hamburg of those days, and in time when I came to meet him regularly in the company of Wolfgang Zimt— known then as the King of Bizonia—*der Bhik* told me about the Four Great Sights and other Buddhist lore. *Der Bhik* was a bustling fellow, hardly sitting in calm and meditation like the figure in the Buddha's story, but anyone who could have achieved that in the frenzy of the Dammtor, our terminus that day, would have outshone the Buddha himself. We could hardly get off the train for people thronging us, pawing at us, searching our faces, calling out names in hope of an answer from a longlost son, husband, brother, lover. I saw few embraces to reward these pleading women, and from the faces of my fellow travellers I knew I wasn't the only one to feel unaccountably ashamed, as if we owed it to the women to console them, to cry out yes, it's me, I'm the one you've been waiting for with your hungry eyes and your placard spelling out the name of the beloved in case a stranger recognized it and had news of him—of him alone of all the soldiers still missing, of all the prisoners yet to be released, of the millions of evacuees who fled the city when the bombing started, the millions more of refugees dispersed as they fled west before the Russians, separated by exhaustion or by illness, by bureaucracy, by chance; among them thousands of young children lost to their parents, some for so long they had forgotten their own names. And now I knew why this was my place. Everyone seemed to be looking for someone, every family in Germany was searching, sifting through the human rubble, scanning the daily parade that plodded through the streets. Gypsy nations *auf der Walze*, on the *Treck*, the tramp. Now for the first time I was caught up in them, pushed against them, past and through them, first the women assaulting the train, then the shoals of young vagrants feeding off the crowds and then the cripples with their bowls, their blunted cloth-bound limbs, their improvised crutches and wheels, past them and out, I let myself be carried by the jostling, churning tide, out at last into the street, closer now, my heart was pounding and I could hardly wait: out into that glorious that triumphant rubblescape, that heart-assuaging desolation, the city naked and disassembled, opening herself to me.

Not the city I knew from the 'Thirties, you might think. Oh but it was.

There's a music hall ditty Ellie liked to sing, about being one of the ruins that Cromwell knocked about a bit, and while she sang I used to picture her old and knocked about. It was delicious; not because I was excited by wrinkles and sagging skin, not at all, it made no difference, if anything the person within only shone through more clearly, the pulpy, desirable essence. In that Hamburg street you could look round and in every direction see buildings crumpled into shapeless mounds, walls sagging, chimneys tottering. I didn't want to shore them up. I didn't want to cover up the fissures or drape the walls with fresh paint, it would be like blinding them, I wanted to push a few more over and get even closer to the Hamburg I had known, to dig my hands into it.

Bulldozers had pushed the rubble back out of the main thoroughfares, and there were cheerful teams of women in headscarves and aprons over their heavy skirts. Some wore goggles against the dust that flew as they passed down the ruined walls brick by brick, bricks to be shaken, cleaned, sorted, graded by size and fitness, stacked and counted with military precision. Defeat hadn't robbed the Germans of their passion for statistics, and the newspapers kept a tally: three million cubic metres of rubble cleared, only forty million to go, so many hundred million bricks extracted, so many doors and windows, every girder, every radiator, every heating pipe was listed. In one hour a person could remove, dust down, and stack fifty bricks; houses were being assembled out of serviceable pieces from all corners of Hamburg, Frankenstein houses with a window from Hamm, a door from Altona, roof tiles from a dozen shattered districts; a city shuffled like a deck of cards.

To put Humpty Dumpty together again would take at least another thirty years, according to the statisticians, thirty years to make good the work of two July nights in 1943. It was a time nobody talked about, and when I learnt the facts I understood why. On the Wednesday, as the bombs fell, the firestorm had reached a thousand degrees Centigrade in some parts of the city, melting the cars and shrinking the roasted people until what was found of them on the Thursday, in streets and backyards, were curious miniatures, doll-sized corpses littering the inner city. Three million sticks of explosive had been employed, though somehow the bombers still managed to miss their dockland targets, and the following year Hamburg produced more U-boats than ever before. The avowed aim of the bombing mission was to destroy the submarine industry, but the raid had a name, Operation Gomorrah, which suggests a grimmer purpose. Sixty thousand died, as many as in England during the entire war, in this, the so-called Battle of Hamburg, a one-sided battle. In the city only one house in five stood untouched. Worse than the rain of explosives was the hail of phosphorus bombs. Its victims ran through the streets with their clothes burnt off and their skin on fire, they flung themselves into the boiling canals, dying instantly, or clawed out pits in the public parks and covered themselves in earth. Only to find they'd dug their own graves. As soon as the buried tried to emerge, the touch of air ignited the phosphorus again, and they burst into flames.

Air, water, earth, and fire, all four at once conspiring to kill. It's said that for a week or more Hamburg was an infernal landscape of heads protruding from the ground, crying for food and drink, for comfort; that in the depleted city there was no cure for their self-igniting burns and that at last a volunteer force was assembled to go out, by darkness, armed with spades, and one by one silence the moaning. Can any city recover from such a night? It can of course, from that and worse, if worse exists; most cities have. I learnt all this later, and at the time, proof that the worst of times falls prey to time itself, along with the best, what I saw in the wreckage of the city was a toiling, haggard people who smiled at the least provocation, yes smiled, grateful to be alive.

I had planned to hole up in a small hotel for a night or two, some little place on the outskirts of town, both for anonymity's sake and to savour the rubble. There were no such hotels, and I felt rather foolish. What had I expected, a cosy inn miraculously spared and with a view of the ruins around it?

My first walk through the city brought me to the Alster, a lake ringed by elegant buildings, mostly hotels and restaurants, where a miracle did seem to have occurred. They were virtually undamaged, as were several other well-to-do neighbourhoods, spared, I suppose, by default as much as by design; the more densely populated districts had been the RAF's priority targets, so as to dismember the workforce; unless perhaps the kinship of the rich and powerful dies hard, and our military strategists just preferred to kill the poorer kind of civilian. I found myself facing the grand old Four Seasons hotel where I had stayed in '38, in my ten-guinea suit from Burtons. Here on the pavement I'd been greeted by a tipsy Peter and a giggling, hysterical Maggie in her belted camel-hair coat, the one that looked like a dressing-gown. Jokes about Hitler; shall I have the carpet wrapped for you, mein Führer, or will you eat it on the way home?

Their images, so vivid, Peter's long stride and flapping suit, Maggie's hair in her eyes, threatened me with tears, and worse, a sense of the absurdity of what I was doing standing here at all, and I shoved them away. I marched past the Four Seasons— it was a fateful decision—and on to the even more palatial Atlantic Hotel.

I was still unshaven, and horribly unkempt after nights in the lorry in fields, and in the train. My rumpled overcoat, my dirty hands and hair had helped me blend in with the crowds, but in the gilded lobby of the Atlantic I looked and felt like a beggar. Never mind, my money was good; I straightened my tie and approached the desk. Cheery-byes and cheery-ohs rang out around me as uniformed Britons filtered through the doors, top brass by the look of it, some with five inches of medals. "I'll get my titfer and be off," they cried. "Toute suite. Where's my kit?" What ho; I was starting to feel light-headed again, as I waited in line for the concierge's attention.

"You bloody old rogue," said a middle-aged officer in front of me, while he waited for his bill. "You're pulling my leg."

"I'm not," said his companion, dressed in a trilby and a pale overcoat, a British Warm in better condition than my hand-me-down one. "He's flogging it at fifteen Marks a gallon. Curaçao's even cheaper, if you can bear to drink the stuff."

"Dear God," muttered the officer, shaking his head, "what an orgy this has turned out to be." He bent and signed his name with what seemed to be a regretful flourish, and departed.

When I stepped forward the concierge eyed me in disbelief. "We are full," he said curtly, ignoring my documents.

"One of the gentlemen who just left," I began in my best German, "appeared to be checking out."

"The room is booked."

"I'd like to see the manager. I'm with the International Red Cross." I pushed Schäfer's Red Cross passport across the desk. The concierge's gaze reminded me that, far from resembling a Red Cross official, I looked like a refugee in need of their assistance. As he examined the passport I toyed with saying I'd spent a hard week in the field; but thought better of it.

Like the official on the Hamburg train before him, the man retreated with my documents, vanishing into an office. I turned to scan the lobby. British newspapers were rustling sweetly in well-scrubbed, soldierly hands, here and there elderly gents dozed in the armchairs. It was like Eastbourne on a bank holiday weekend. I waited, feeling positively jaunty. After the effect of my documents on Sturmbannführer Verg I was ready for anything. Perhaps other doors would open for me now as if charmed. Wasn't that what Auntie had said? "All doors will open for you, and you will fall on your feet." Though by the sound of it trapdoors were what she had in mind.

I heard footsteps behind me, and a disgruntled voice. "Herr

Schäfer.'' When I turned, the concierge was studying a guest roster and spoke without looking up. ''How long will you be staying?''

During the 'Sixties, '64 I fancy since that was the year my friend Zimt exiled himself to Capri, I visited the Baths of Caracalla, in Rome. Are they in Rome? Somewhere in Italy. And I was reminded of the Hotel Atlantic. The Baths of Caracalla! If I'm remembering rightly these sumptuous Roman bathhouses had walls thick enough to accommodate corridors for the slaves and bathhouse servants to go about their work unseen, while the rich lolled in the steaming, marbled halls; two worlds carrying on simultaneously, one inside the other as it were, and both invisible to each other. Yet only a membrane away. So it was at the Atlantic. When the evening meal was over and the guests had retired, a host of furtive Germans would materialize in service corridors and stairways. Shades of Schloss Brüel too—ten years on and I was still a midnight prowler, a seigneurial snoop in search of life backstairs among the leftovers. It was open house in the kitchens for pimps and spivs and anyone from the street whose livelihood depended on the hotel, the Kippensammler or butt-collectors whose haul was soon back on the streets as a pack of virgin cigarettes, the contraceptive merchants, the dealers in goods filched from the visitors, even a few schoolteachers who came to collect old British newspapers, not to read them but, since exercise books were in short supply, to hoard the margins and the blank spaces in the advertisements. The waiters and their clients were my first friends in post-war Hamburg. They were bewilderingly honest, and rarely tried to cheat or steal from me, which puzzled me at first. (According to Wolli Zimt, even in the Hitler years Nazi officials couldn't be bribed; the fools! as Wolli commented.) It was my forbidding appearance, I took it, that discouraged people from taking advantage. One of the chambermaids, Karin with the faint hare-lip that gave her a perpetual sneer, warned me not to leave my money in my hotel room, no matter how well hidden. She had found the Colonel's washbag, and its contents, with ease; it was a fortune to her and she could have taken it but she didn't, not a penny of it.

It was a fortune all right, when I got round to counting it. Almost a hundred thousand Reichsmarks, five thousand pounds' worth by the official rate of exchange. In another bundle fifteen hundred dollars, priceless in those days in any part of Europe—one black marketeer assured me a dollar fetched eleven thousand trillion pengoes in Budapest, he swore to the exact figure though he didn't say what you could buy with your pengoes. I also owned three million lira, a stack of British fivers, French francs and Spanish pesetas, plus a quantity of things called "bafs" which were issued to Occupying Forces personnel and which I now traded freely for Marks. How my uncle had got hold of these I neither knew nor cared, they were mine to spend, my inheritance, and with it in the Hamburg of those days I could have bought anything from cigarettes to platinum, from a racehorse to a looted Rembrandt.

Not that I wanted any of these things. I wanted to pierce the membrane that hid the real Hamburg, and for that I didn't need shillings and pence, let alone pengoes. "The veil is thin here," Mother used to say, no doubt quoting her own mother (I like to think so anyway, the words have a good Celtic ring to them), when describing a spot which for her had a particular magic. To tell the truth I never heard her say it, but Alec must have done, since he recites it mockingly when evoking our mother in one of her mantic states; and Auntie sometimes used the phrase in a disappointed voice, to announce a lapse in her visionary powers. Perhaps she'd picked it up from an Irish crony and misunderstood it, because what Mother surely meant was the something very different, that in certain places the true light shines through the veil of appearances. And if ever that veil was thin, it was thin in Hamburg. The streets were nameless, they were barely streets, more like animal tracks in the rubble, and on my first few excursions I got hopelessly lost. The parks were nameless too, little more than clearings, scavengers had picked them clean, stripped the wood from the benches and the last rowan berry from the trees. I liked the nakedness. I even liked getting lost. All the same there was something about the city that was beginning to irk me, something slack and passive. I could sniff it in the air. A birdless sky; no cats or dogs, all dead and mostly eaten, I assumed. I met a rat or two, some at close quarters, and in deserted places after dark I took pot shots at them with old Isidro the Destroyer, the Colonel's imitation Browning, out of sheer frustration. The veil was thin all right. But what was it that was shining through, exactly? Anything at all?

One sitting target I remember well, one motionless emaciated rat ten feet away when I took aim. Still no movement from him, perhaps he was dead. Something odd about him. Even with his ribs sticking out, starved as he was, he looked more like a stuffed rat than a live one. Stuffed? Wait a minute. One of Alec's war-time tricks had been to shower German dockland with stuffed ratskins, they were filled with plastic explosive in the hope that some benighted stoker would shovel the dead-seeming thing into the boiler and blow up the ship. Unlikely as it was that this was one of Alec's, I hesitated. What a way to go: brother Rat blown up by brother's rat. Now come on, get a grip, Thurgo. I took aim again. At that moment the rat showed signs of life, I saw a flash of teeth in his upper jaw as he raised himself, and a white patch of belly surrounded by reddish-brown fur. He sat back on his haunches, as if imploring me to shoot. His paws were trembling. His teeth actually chattering, from cold I thought, but no, it wasn't that. He was afraid, he was simply too frightened and too tired to run. Bloody German rat. I couldn't bring myself to shoot him as he cringed before me. Servility, that was the true light shining through, that was the light shining out of Hamburg's craven arse. Talk about stuffed. They'd all been stuffed. Honest spivs, and chambermaids who didn't steal. Now even the rats were surrendering.

I began to see how abject they all were, the people in the streets, behind their edgy smiles. Pitiful really, and hardly surprising; it made me angry all the same. Now and then I was tempted to pass out my hoard of banknotes like some mad philanthropist, but I could picture the fear and suspicion deepening in my victims' faces as they waited to hear what favours were expected in return, then scuttled away when I asked none. If they had the gumption to scuttle away. Once I saw a woman carrying a bouquet like a wedding posy, wrapped in newspaper, I watched her sit down on the counter of what had once been a shop, peel back the newspaper, and at the same moment that I realized the posy was grass, she brought it to her lips and began to eat it. I approached and by way of introduction handed her a cigarette, which she took and placed in her lap, putting down the posy. I saw to my relief that it wasn't simply grass she was eating, there were some chives mixed in with it. Then she inserted the cigarette in her bag with such heartrending care that I gave her the whole pack. Without a word, still cudding, she lifted her legs onto the counter slab, pulled up her coat and with it her dress, and lay back, legs apart. *Aber madame*, I remonstrated, and for the first time some real emotion, contempt, came into her eyes.

"Give it a year or two, half the kids round here will be little Anglo-Germans," said the Tommy beside me in a noisy little bar. "Perhaps that's the whole idea. Bit of English blood to sort you out."

"I think so, *ja*," I said. By my stained clothes and unkempt look he'd taken me for a native, and I was in no hurry to disabuse him.

"You reckon?" Slow country vowels dripped from his mouth; he was a sergeant, red-haired, with pallid skin that called to mind the waxwork faces at Madame Tussaud's. In the smoke-filled air between us nostalgic, familiar smells of beer and sour sweat mingled with an unfamiliar one, a pong like rotting cabbage. "They tell us not to fraternize. But what do they expect? Some of my lads have had the clap eight or nine times, it doesn't stop them. Doesn't stop the Frauleins either. No pride," he said, and I couldn't argue with him, "that's the trouble with you lot. Where's it all gone to?"

I shrugged as he studied me.

"Were you a Nazi?"

"Yes," I said.

"You *were*?"

"*Ja natürlich.* Of course."

"Blimey," he said, "that's a relief." He saw my puzzled expression, and grinned. "Three months and you're the first one I've met. First one to admit it, shall we say. You'd think Hitler had fought the war all on his own." He paused. "So you're a Nazi. Or you were."

"Sturmbannführer. Waffen SS. Odessa . . . Stalingrad . . ." What else had Sturmbannführer Verg mentioned in his list of campaigns? I'd have done better with the Luftwaffe, posing as ground crew. Waxwork looked me up and down, and finally nodded.

"So what do you think of Hitler now?"

"That mad dog." It was a phrase I'd heard in the Atlantic kitchens, but it came out without conviction. "He has ruined us," I added.

"All his fault then, was it?"

"*Bitte?*" I pretended not to understand.

Amid the din I saw rather than heard him mutter: "Typical."

"You should have fought with us against the Russians," I said raising my voice. Behind us Cockney songs rang out.

"What?"

He came closer, till I could smell the beer on his breath. "Together we would have won," I grinned, and repeated what I'd said, in German.

"You in business now?" The sergeant was fingering my battered British Warm. "Nice coat, isn't it, won't ask you where you got it."

He stood me another drink and, while we waited, showed me pictures of his kids. Big toothy smiles, young Vikings from the Essex marshes. Then he steered the conversation towards photography and asked where he could get a decent Leica, cheap.

It was my first brief go at masquerading as a Nazi, crude enough but I enjoyed it. If anyone had told me I would be doing it for the next twenty years I might have felt differently, of course. Perhaps not; if I'm honest, I've enjoyed it all along.

But why, I wonder. In a spirit of mockery? If so, whom was I mocking? One thing I know for sure, I didn't enjoy my adoptive role because I secretly approved of Nazi ideas and behaviour. Their cruelty continues to enrage me, and to fascinate me as it fascinates us all. No good pretending it disgusts me, though, it doesn't. What disgusts me is the way people wring their hands and talk about the death camps and the village massacres and the gruesome experiments on children, the whole familiar litany of horror, as the work of one race and one creed, one dreadful hour of history. Wringing their hands—and washing their hands of it at the same time. When people talk like this I want to shake the truth out of them, the admission that these were thoroughly human atrocities (good human atrocities I almost want to say; true to our barbaric nature) and unless we recognize them as our own we only hasten their return in a different uniform. Cro-Magnon man most probably devoured the Neanderthalers. Sargon, king of Akkad, flayed his enemies alive, the Romans crucified theirs, the Spanish Inquisition used the fire, the water, and the cord, the British and the French sold smallpox-ridden blankets to Indians who wouldn't give up their land; the Germans, nothing if not a thorough people, went at the job systematically, and I suppose you might argue that they've earned their role as scapegoats, earned it by their ghastly single-mindedness. But scapegoats, if they are of any value to us, should wear a crown of thorns. Was it this that made me feel so peculiarly and proudly human, adopting the name of Nazi less as a stigma than as stigmata, or was it something more mischievous—to stand up for Sturmbannführers, now, at this of all moments, when the fire had been doused, when the old incense stank and the satanic robes were looking fatuous, now when the uniform was at its least alluring? Perhaps I just wanted to be found out and get myself arrested.

Britons love to cheer the underdog, so people say. To side with the defeated is another matter altogether. And a different impulse, surely. Explaining myself under interrogation I would say I spoke as a Cornishman, Cornish and Irish, no Briton but a true Celt with a score or two to settle. Too late for underdogs now that the fight was over. No, to me this was the dog beneath the skin, thriving on abhorrence, never more potent than now when it was universally reviled. A German dog. A Nazi dog. "Europe's backward race" . . . who could resist that call? Have you ever tried giving a Nazi salute, I saw myself asking some po-faced Intelligence officer, giving it in earnest I mean, not as a joke? I defy you not to feel the thrill of it. Try it if you don't believe me. Go on, man. That's it, now put your back into it, feel the blood rush to your fingertips. See what I mean? Whoever devised that salute was a bloody genius.

I was looking in the wrong places, it wasn't till I located the whores that I felt the energy glowing from within, behind the veil of my rubble kingdom.

First thing every morning I walked to the town hall square, Rathausmarkt which had been Adolf-Hitler-Platz when I last breakfasted there, and stoked up on ersatz coffee, *Muckefuck* we called it. A descriptive name if ever there was one, but I rather liked the stuff, I preferred it to the chicory substitute we had at home. Sipping my *Muckefuck* I'd watch the trams wobble past with people clustered along the sides like swarming bees, then I'd set out across the city, past the demolition squads towards the mounds of icy earth and rubble, hard as iron underfoot, monotonous débris punctuated by an occasional stovepipe that reared up like a single-fingered gesture to the gods. Which it was, in a way. Each one was a periscope marking the spot where some obstinate soul had stayed on in the cellar, hoping against hope that Fritz, somehow alive, somehow released from Russia, would come looking for his family at the old address. Instead it was the wind that arrived daily from the Steppes, a vicious, teasing, Cossack wind, abating suddenly then pouncing at the corner of a ruined building, sabre-toothed.

Ice Age Relics Found, declared my Rhine Army News one morning, it was a mammoth I think they'd come across. In the frozen, devastated suburbs of Hamm and Horn I wouldn't have been surprised to meet a live one trudging blindly up the street. The stillness was unearthly, prehistoric, just the wind, the silence in the shelter of a wall, sometimes a bicycle clattering over distant cobbles with a sound like a collection of loose nuts and bolts being smacked along by a flapping mudguard. And then the voices, children's voices, luring me through this stony maze towards the few streets where a pavement had survived, creating a hidden domain. Here, in the oddest clothes, huge lederhosen, Daddy's braces and army cap, some with rabbitskin hat and mittens (or perhaps it wasn't rabbit fur, if you're going to eat cat and dog you might as well put their skins to use), the children gathered to play hopscotch, and here, too, sharing the precious pavement, huddled over a brazier or marching and stamping their feet against the cold, were the prostitutes. For them and for their clients this was sanctuary, far from prying eyes, from shopkeepers and policemen. It was their precinct, here in shattered Hamm; or shattered Horn perhaps; the names meant nothing in the rubble. Casual passers-by were rare, though now and again you might see a dazed traveller standing staring, a Fritz come home at last to find the street flattened, no stovepipe for him, a Ulysses returned to find Penelope vanished and his Ithaca a desert peopled by children and whores. Whores in their rage, the leaves of my beloved tree of death.

They looked just like ordinary citizens, which came as a surprise to me. Many of them wore no make-up and they all wore practical clothes, it was too cold for anything else; they could have been the wives and daughters of old Erfurt greeting Napoleon's conquering hussars, in Peter's story of the breastplate. Whereas their clients—these weren't the conquerors, who preferred less squalid meeting-places, but the conquered—were the ones in costume, by the look of it. Vegetable dyes had given their old uniforms a civilian lease of life, and now their owners had a circus air, mockery soldiers beetroot red or sorrel yellow, sometimes ivy green, according to the dye, and smelling of it. They all looked odd even if they weren't, they looked worn out, the younger ones stunted by malnutrition or, for the same reason, erratically long in arm or leg. Somehow the roles had been reversed: the whores like housewives out shopping, the men a cabaret of freaks, waiting to be chosen, pacing back and forth along the cobbled street. On either side of it the pavement-girls wooed softly, like spectators at a zoo. Come, come my little tiger, come. Come ape, come little bear.

It reminded you what a country of women Germany was now, like France after Napoleon had reaped its manhood. What women, though! Some, like Kriemhilde from Lübeck, who soon renamed herself Monika, remained in the business, and became a friend. Erika too, who in those days used to flaunt a cyanide capsule issued to her vanished father: she'd pop it in her mouth, swill it around, pretending to chew, and suddenly . . . *du lieber Gott*! I didn't mean to! . . . she'd go very still, mime a ghastly spasm and then spit the pill out intact, laughing. Oswalda—dear God, the names that Nazi piety dredged up from German history—and Wanda; Hannelore who smelt of leeks and lived underground in Billstedt, where I once came across a pair of British soldiers tossing a cricket ball from one end of a ravaged street to the other, the slap of leather in their hands instantly conjuring up summer schooldays, there in the frozen Hamburg slums. Blonde Alwine, pale and soulful as a mediaeval artist's Eve; Paula, nicknamed Rockefeller for her abject poverty rather than her riches, though she was generous with what little she had. She was a veteran of Rostock's Sperlingsgasse and its dockside bordelloes. "Tipptopp" was her name for me, picked up from a British customer. "Hallo Tipptopp! Alles tipptopp?" Sometimes I have to remind myself that my lifelong love affair with whores didn't begin here, it had started earlier, much earlier, with Ellie when I was sixteen, and before Ellie with Grandfather and his tales of Dublin tarts and the brothels of Aragon. But I'd been Ellie's "friend," not her client; her female friends and rivals were little more to me than painted faces glimpsed across a dance-hall floor. Now and in the years to come I discovered their callous vitality, the stridency of their fights and their despair, and that this was an ordinary unremarkable despair born of tedium, dependency, and a longing for money, as in other bourgeois professions. The work is too monotonous and too mechanical to interest bohemians, which in turn is why most whores grow to respectability, it's in the nature of the work from the beginning. In one respect they're anything but bourgeois, mercifully, rutting without sentiment or spurious mystery. Few hearts of gold among them, but no pretence of it; and no attempt to hide their attachment to their own, their sisters. Men, as I gradually came to learn, are always an intrusion on this primary, clannish passion of women for each other, a bloodthirsty passion, competitive but obstinately loyal. Ladies of the street don't bother to disguise it, and for that I bless them.

Contraceptives were in short supply. I bought them cheap in the kitchens of the Atlantic and sold them cheaper to the girls, under-cutting the black market price. It didn't buy their trust, but there in Horn (or Hamm; somewhere between the two perhaps) I wasn't looking for trust or intimacy, not even, as I think

I've mentioned, of the physical kind. I exulted in a positively Yogic self-denial, my power grew by re-absorbing my desire, drawing it upwards, homewards to my brain (this made sense at the time, my brain as a fountainhead of sperm), until I was one phosphorescent reservoir from scalp to scrotum; until, in fact, it wasn't self-denial at all, it was fulfilment, "tipptopp!" I was stroking the magic, buffing it like the shine on a military toecap. I didn't want anything from the girls, their appetite for life was all the nourishment I needed, with their laughter and their grim, competing tales of winter harder than this one, '46 and '47 when everyone from children to elderly professional men looted coal from goods vans along the railway lines, and a piece of your own floorboards to put on the fire was the most cherished gift of all, when trains pulled into the Dammtor with their passengers frozen to death, when thousands died of TB and pneumonia and just plain hunger, and cannibalism was more than a rumour. Survivors' tales; without self-pity, thank the Lord. No self-abasement from these girls. They were awed, their eyes grew innocent as they told their grisly stories. If customers were scarce we'd give up the pavement and withdraw into the nearest shell of a house, free accommodation, squalid it's true but there was no landlord or pimp to pay: one of the benefits of working the hidden domain. We sat around on piles of smashed débris, our rubble mattresses, and talked and hugged for warmth, while joyous singsong voices reached us through the blown-out windows; hopscotch cries.

Whores and smiling children—my father-in-law's pulpit dream come true. Only he'd got it all wrong, the poor old curate. Hope, not the devil, lay with them, yes with the whores above all, while they held on to that precinct. Imagination ruled there. All the money in the world could only buy a rubble mattress and a drab, unpainted lady, nature unadorned. They pleaded poverty, the girls, but the truth is they were still faithful to their upbringing and an ideal that old Trimble could have hymned, ironically enough, along with Hitler: no rouge, no nylons, no "decadent" frippery! They'd been raised on Adolf's vision of shorts and kneesocks and a clear complexion. A pederast's dream I suppose—or you could call it wholesomely Nordic. Either way the dream was fading fast as Germany woke to the sticky kiss of American fashions; Hollywood and jazz, the unsung winners of the war. The whores would soon succumb, replacing Nazi kitsch with Yankee kitsch. For now, though, in the lull between the two, imagination was a harder currency than marks or bafs or dollars. In the long run it's the only currency that counts, and the clearest memory I have of those days in the rubble is of stopping somewhere in my tracks to watch a little girl in a dark coat above long white socks and black shoes, skipping across an empty dusty space between the ruins, it was a bright sunny day and the way she skipped she could have been crossing a pasture full of dandelions, I can still see her with her arms a little extended and her white legs catching the light as if she floated in it, as if she made the light herself.

On my tours of inspection did I visit Innocentiaplatz and the area where I live now, leafy, elegant Harvestehude? I think I did, because I noticed one odd thing. Of the many surviving buildings here, some had no snow on their roofs, by contrast with their neighbours. It took hare-lipped Karin from the Atlantic to explain it to me. Around Parkallee and Innocentiaplatz, named after a vanished convent (and an ironic name these days, since the rape and murder of a young girl, quite recently, in the bushes of the square), the British had requisitioned the better mansions. They could afford to heat them, which in turn melted the snow on their roofs. Karin knew about such things, she was a chambermaid by night but a rubble-woman by day (a rubble-girl really, she was twenty, barely more), in gloves and goggles, trading gossip as she worked. God knows when she slept, week-ends perhaps. She was a quiet creature, sullen, with cropped black hair and greenish eyes, a soft-skinned face attractively spotted with moles but marred by the twist of her lips; less by the birth scar on her upper lip than by the way she chewed the bottom one, compulsively. Like Maggie.

That brought it home each time I saw her: what was I doing loitering here in Hamburg, day after day, instead of setting out for Schloss Brüel? I don't know how many times I told myself I'd be leaving tomorrow. Everyone in Hamburg was doing the same—we all had plans to leave tomorrow, we'd emigrate to America, to Canada, or we'd set out for home, when in truth we were all taking life one day at a time, as if shellshocked. I never wanted it to end, because I was already home here in this family of dreamers, I had a place, a role, I was Tipptopp the contraceptive man, slipping invisibly between worlds.

Not quite invisibly. Sometimes I had the oddest sense of being followed, or worse, that strangers were discussing me wherever I went, in the hotel, in bars, in streets, until I heard my name in every whispered conversation. Often in the Atlantic lobby there was a fat boy, one of the "Cheerybye!" crew, very British, fat as Schäfer, yes, but unlike Schäfer he was young and jolly. He seemed to stare at me. He couldn't take his eyes off me, and it gave me the eerie sensation that he really was Schäfer, Schäfer who remained a presence in my dreams, his face less and less clear and merging now with fat Cheerybye. Dream-Schäfer was turned away from me in the jeep, refusing to respond, and I felt so sad about this—which seemed absurd when I remembered it, awake—because I knew in the dream that it meant he was dead, and I grieved. Sometimes I felt I could smell him on me, in the rubble dust I washed from my growing beard and hair each night, with its marzipan smell. Which in turn was another reminder, it was the smell of the sweetmeats at Schloss Brüel.

I told myself I would leave for the Schloss as soon as I'd found someone to guide me across the *Grüne Grenze*, the thickly wooded "green frontier" that separated us. My earlier idea of a solo walk through the woods seemed less and less feasible as I heard about the border posts equipped with searchlights and machine guns, and the trained dogs that patrolled with the guards. Details of successful routes, so-called black crossings, were passed from mouth to mouth among the racketeers who travelled them for profit, and the refugees, some of whom made repeated journeys to ferry others or to fill suitcases with belongings previously left behind. Most of these *Grenzgänger* or frontier walkers eventually made one journey too many, and never returned; those who'd survived till now were to be found among the bunker people in the old air raid shelters, a warren underneath the Hamburg streets, where the old metal signs remained in Nazi red and black, telling us how to behave when the bombing began. The signs might have been left there as a memorial, or out of indifference, but knowing the Germans it was probably because they were waiting for someone with the proper authority to come and remove them.

There too, in the bunker-warren, I met the other face of Germany. One old man was risking his life, week in week out, to rescue his library from an apartment in Schwerin, in the Russian zone. A single suitcase full of books was as much as he could carry back on each trip, hurrying through snowbound forests and a deadly game of hide and seek with armed patrols. All for books. Print. For the sake of words, ideas: and no-one in the bunkers was at all surprised by this. Perhaps ideas bloom most fiercely, like desert flowers, in adversity, perhaps war fertilizes them, since there were surely more philosophers to the square mile in that underground city of air raid bunkers than in any university or monastery in the world. Here men reflected aloud, in the stinking darkness thickened by our breath, about human cunning and human folly, long rhetorical utterances punctuated only by the coughing, men coughing and railing at the intolerable burden of hope which would not leave them. Faced with so many bombs and bullets, with incarceration, with starvation, would a deer or a fox continue to hope? No, we agreed. Logical, sensible animal; curling up to die in peace instead of hoping against all reason, like man. My favourite bunker-dweller was a former chorister, Vlad was his name, an involuntary humourist I think (I've known him twenty years and I'm still not sure if it's deliberate), his voice resonating with the basso profondo of his first vocation. Devout as well as cynical in a peculiarly Russian way, peasant and nihilist at once, he had defected to the German side during the Eastern campaign, and lost an arm during a skirmish outside Odessa. The arm had been blown off in an orchard, and Vlad had crawled back through the grass while the fighting raged around him, to find it and retrieve his wedding ring. "Life is a string," he liked to announce when all but speechless with drink; and you have to imagine the Russian accent and Vlad's basso rumbling in the dark, "I pull it . . . and I cannot feel the end!"

Sometimes, in my dream, I saw Schäfer's featureless head hanging down from the chassis of the jeep, and I reached out to find his hand, with something held between my fingers, my own wedding ring. Even in the dream I shuddered at this mockery wedding to evil which would seal my presence as the dead man in the jeep, confirm that I was him, that I was dead; but when I looked I saw no hand, no arm, nowhere to attach the ring. As I bent then to place the ring in the ashes below the upturned jeep, the movement seemed to wake me, convinced that I had done this in reality, dropped my ring in the débris to ensure identification. But I hadn't. The ring was still on my finger.

There was a good deal of death, as well as talk of death, in the bunkers. We had a so-called rubble-murderer at work in the city, who ambushed his apparently random victims in the ruins. He used a noose of knotted string to strangle them. Sometimes he shot them. Or perhaps there were two rubble-murderers, or more. In my haunted state I felt all eyes on me, even in the darkness, when these murders were discussed; no doubt I was imagining this, but I also felt an unmistakable excitement in myself, a guilty thrill. Armed with old Isidro in my trance, in my timeless concussion . . . could I have done such things? To this day, so far as I know, the crimes remain unsolved. I wouldn't have liked to try and account for my movements at the time; but I could have accounted (to my own satisfaction at any rate) for my bullets, each one used to dispatch a rat; and there was no suspicious, unaccountable blood on my clothes. In the bunkers, as I say, there was plenty of death, from exhaustion and disease. Murder too: I witnessed one, of a man who had been exposed as a *Grüsseschwindler*, one of those who made a living by peddling news of missing relatives, fictitious news of course, and by begging money from the victims of his false reports. Harmless enough in those desperate times, you might think, but to the bunker people his callousness was worse than murder. One night he was pinned down and a bundle of old clothes were used to suffocate him—*würgen* is the gurgling, evocative German word, a sound like water going down a plug-hole. I took no part in it; but there, in the bunkers, I met the next man (counting Schäfer as my first victim) I was to kill. His name was Henry. Not Heinrich, though he was German, Hamburg-born and bred, but Henry, as the sons of this perversely anglophile city are still called Fred or Jonny, or Jonathan, as if we had never bombed them to hell and gone, or as if they only loved us the more for it. In the bunkers I had resumed my disguise as a journalist, British this time, looking for someone to guide me on a daring sortie into Russian territory. Henry was a black marketeer, or so he told me then; youngish, late twenties, with a quiff of dark hair and an arrogant, snub-nosed face. He volunteered to be my guide. I said I'd mull it over.

Most nights I left the bunkers around ten p.m. and made my way to the precinct in the rubble, with a bottle of black market Schnaps and a pocketful of contraceptives. Other shapes were dragging themselves in the same direction. It was *Krüppelstunde*, cripple-hour, when the girls entertained their deformed clients by firelight. They crowded round the braziers and the backyard fires like a nocturnal tribe; hordes of the limbless. I read not so long ago that there are still a hundred and thirty thousand one-legged men in the Bundesrepublik, ten thousand legless and God knows how many one-armed and armless men. Certainly the precinct filled with hundreds of them in that hour before the three blasts of the curfew horn, and what the Kriemhildes and Oswaldas dispensed was something more than motherliness, there was an eager appetite on both sides then, revealing how sexually potent is our fascination with the cripple and his hidden, stunted, penile limb.

Hundreds of them—it was an unforgettable scene, and one which I was later able to put to use by recreating it on the stage. A little glimpse of the divine in this, perhaps, as the threads of our life recur in the weave; and the overlapping veil of time seems thinner, for an instant. The air raid bunkers too have returned to haunt me. I acquired one of them in the 'Fifties and turned it into a night club, the "Grotto Azzurro"; later it became the Vegas-Girls, Hamburg's premier porno venue, and the voyeurs' cubicles and the film shows are downstairs where the beds once stood and people lay coughing and dying and spouting philosophy. (Happily Vlad the String survived to share these transformations with me, and I installed him as the Grotto's bouncer-in-chief; to this day his one arm is as feared as any in Hamburg.) As for the scene in the whores' precinct, I revived it a few yards down the Reeperbahn from the Vegas-Girls, with the help of my friend René who runs the Grand Théâtre Érotique. Now and again I made an unscheduled appearance there in some of the lewder acts, until at last he allowed me to choreograph a number we called *Trümmerbumsen*, "Rubblesex"— part, I like to think, of my enduring desire to raise to public consciousness an attribute we prefer to deny, our nostalgia for catastrophe. Rubble and rags: it was cheap on scenery, on props and costumes, and it ended of course in the compulsory fucking, or in most cases pretend-fucking, that drew our audience in the first place. But I was quite proud of the dance routine with which it began, a scampering and slithering of beggars, tarts, and cripples, as they sang a song of my own devising.

> *Oh the Bizonesian tribe are we,*
> *With a tralala and a tralalee*
> > *They say we're cannibals,*
> > *They say we're animals . . .*
> *We serve no fancy dishes,*
> *But you should taste our kisses!*
> > *They say we're cannibals,*
> > *They say we're animals . . .*

Who is it that giveth this woman to this man?—as they say, or words to that effect, in the wedding service, where the answer is presumably her father; or in my own case Denis Towle, since in view of Molly's pregnant state the Rev Mr Trimble didn't grace us with his presence. But my question is, what is it that attracts us to this woman, this man, as opposed to that one? Who or what, in a wider sense, giveth a woman to a man? Perhaps it's always her father. That's how it was between me and Karin the chambermaid: her father brought us together, regardless of the fact that he was ten years dead. He'd been arrested for expressing anti-Nazi sentiments in his pre-war newspaper column, and held in Fuhlsbüttel prison, a grim set of red brick cell-blocks on the northern fringes of the city, hidden among suburban streets. It's a place I've had cause to visit in its current guise as a house of correction for younger offenders; a shuddersome place, I would think, even if you knew nothing of its past. From the middle 'Thirties until the fall of the Third Reich, a steady trickle of men and women guilty of hostility to the régime, or suspected of it, entered the prison by its imitation mediaeval gateway, and few of these ever came out again. Some died under interrogation. Others, like August Posener, Karin's father, cheated the torturers and took their own life. At the time of her father's death in '38, the chief interrogator at Fuhlsbüttel was a man called Hermann Wackernagel, and Karin, who had also lost both her brothers to the war, emerged from it with a mission: to bring Wackernagel to justice. I got the impression even then that failing justice she would do the job herself; I mean kill him. There was nothing murderous about Karin—she seemed gentle through and through. But it was the kind of gentleness you can only achieve in despair, when you have given away your life; a gentleness more and less than human. Because who can be gentle through and through? Or anything through and through, for that matter—even Wackernagel must have known a tender moment, between interrogations. The man's curious, distinctive name had made it easier for Karin to trace his subsequent wartime career; it was just as well, she said, that he wasn't called Müller. But records of Wackernagel apparently petered out after the liberation of France, where he had taken part in more atrocities, so it was quite possible that now he was called Müller, and all the harder to trace. When I pointed this out, Karin merely shrugged, in silence. She was obsessed with Wackernagel; I was fascinated by her obsession. Saddened too, and impressed by it. But it wasn't I who made the first moves in our friendship, it was Karin, egged on by gossip she had picked up about me from her fellow-workers at the Atlantic; that's to say gossip about the Red Cross official registered under the name of Schäfer, Schäfer of the savage appearance and solitary ways. She had concocted a version of my true purpose in Hamburg, and it was better grounded than the gossip. But still off target, not surprisingly—she could hardly have guessed that I was in Hamburg for no sane reason at all. There were plenty of people here on secret missions of one sort or another, I can vouch for that, and mine, as Karin divined it, could have led her to men like Hermann Wackernagel. Even, perhaps, to Wackernagel himself; so she hoped. Had I realized this I could have disabused her, but she didn't tell me, not until our entanglement was such that its origins had become irrelevant. And in a way it was lucky she did keep her fantasies to herself, less because they kept her hopes alive than because they kept her silent about my disguise, skimpy as it was, and this in turn helped to prevent my early exposure as a thoroughgoing, or Thurgoing, fraud.

Come to that, wouldn't I rather believe she was drawn to me for personal reasons, and that these led her to invent a usefulness for me in her Wackernagel-world? Oh I would. But the images of Wackernagel and her father were her personal world, all of it. Is this hard to understand? It certainly was for me.

"Your German is good," she remarked one day, to let me know she had my number. Until then we had only exchanged pleasantries.

"Thank you."

I studied her as she folded back a corner of the bedsheets, for the night. They were frayed and painstakingly mended, like the curtains and the threadbare carpets, and the thin towels in the adjoining bathroom. Somehow this only drew more attention to the anachronistic grandeur of the suite, my Caracalla suite, designed like the rest of the hotel for an age as remote as Imperial Rome, each bedroom spacious enough to hold an archduke's retinue, and furnished as if for an impromptu conference; armchairs, desks, settees, on one of which I sat watching Karin at work, all keeping a respectful distance from a four-poster bed which wouldn't have disgraced a royal levée. My windows overlooked the hotel's own Winter Gardens; the lakeside view was reserved for even more expensive rooms. Karin finished fluffing up the pillows, and I waited for her to press home her advantage. How had I come by a German name? Why did I address everyone in German if, as her comment had implied, I clearly wasn't a native?

"Gute Nacht, Herr Schäfer," she said instead, smiling politely, and slowly made the long walk to the door. ''Schlafen Sie wohl.''

Sleep well; that's what she said to me then, in the days of our first acquaintance. It was the appropriate expression, yet what true Hamburgers say to one another is ''schlaf schön,'' sleep beautifully. Yes; schlaf schön.

The following evening, as she changed the sheets on that noble, enticing bed, Karin asked me if I had noticed any spiders in the room. Spiders? No. Was I sure? Quite sure, thank you. I was baffled. Spiders? Why? She held my stare and asked me what the English was for spider: how do *you* say it? I told her, and rather than let the opening pass again I asked her how she knew I was English.

It was the first time I'd seen her smile, her soft mole-spotted face wrinkling in amusement, positively boyish now, the harelip overshadowed as other dimpled planes surfaced around it like a hidden continent, deeply grooved. Ironically it took a smile to expose these lines of suffering, but the mounded flesh rising over her cheekbones seemed all the softer for it. Revising my first opinion I'd decided she was in her early twenties; but no, a little older still, perhaps.

There was no hiding my nationality: Karin's amusement made this clear. Was it my accent? She wavered, probably out of politeness. What, then? Everything, she said, suddenly voluble, everything from my choice of breakfast to the way I folded my clothes. The clothes themselves might be ''U.T.'' merchandise, acquired *unter der Theke*, under the counter; but—I wore a belt, and it was relatively new. A belt? Yes, such a thing could not be purchased here, even on the black market. She rested her case.

I shrugged, surrendering. Could I assume, I asked in my most formal German, that her curiosity was shared by her colleagues, and was it her conclusions?

After a moment Karin shook her head.

Awkward now under my gaze, or perhaps to forestall further questions, she turned back to wrestle with an enormous blanket, darned at the edges. Without thinking I stepped forward to help her; I took the other end of the blanket, about to ask why she had kept her conclusions to herself, when I saw her expression, and stopped. There were fully eight feet of sheeted bed between us but Karin looked as shocked as if I had laid hands on her rather than the bedclothes.

"Aber, Herr Schäfer." Her protest held one reassuring note. I was still Herr Schäfer, pending further revelations.

Karin gave me a mulish look: the blanket was hers to spread.

"Surely," I said as I pulled it taut across the sheets, "in a spirit of Anglo-German co-operation . . ."

The tautened blanket exposed what a counterpane usually hid, a central seam uniting what had evidently been two smaller blankets, now one huge one. The seam was rotten and a gap yawned between the unmended edges where they had been sewn together, leaving a long open slit like the sheet over a patient awaiting the surgeon's knife. It was too comical; I could have been our Bizonian overlord Sir Brian Robertson himself, rehearsing an address to the nation: good citizens of the new Germany, let us together wind the sheet of forgiveness (no, that would sound too much like a shroud), or rather, extend the blanket of solicitude (more like it!) over the tattered body of your country, putting our hands together to restore, no, to revive your ancient dignity . . . I wasn't so foolish as to say any of this, but the grin on my face had already added insult to injury. I had robbed Karin, or so I assumed, of that reproachful pride that servants take in unassisted toil; in fact, though I didn't know it then, it was a double indignity since she was far more educated than I was, and her ancestry gave her a better title to the bed itself, with its fluted mahogany columns and its canopy, than any Thurgo. For a long moment her face brimmed with humiliated rage. When she spoke it was almost in a whisper.

Anglo-German co-operation? She made it sound like a curse; and now proceeded to turn my aborted metaphor against me as pointedly as if I'd asked her to help me steal the four-poster and sell it back to the hotel. What co-operation, please? What choice did Germans have, but to co-operate? To whom could they complain? Co-operation! Did I mean, for example, the systematic dismantling of their industry, provoking strikes which only reduced the pitiful stock of goods available in the shops? I gaped at her as she recited the industries in question. Where had this demagogue come from? Or, she continued, did I mean the plundering of German valuables irrespective of their owner's record of resistance to the Nazis, witness the Duchess of Mecklenburg whose castle had been stripped of heirlooms, and who had been reduced to appealing for help to her relative the King of England? Had I heard of this? I hadn't? The King, I said, no longer consulted me. Karin frowned, in puzzlement I think; certainly unamused. Did I know about the looting of machinery and even of industrial secrets? Last week alone, she said earnestly, armed men had broken into the home of Germany's leading perfume manufacturer and only refrained from forcing his widow to reveal the secret of Eau de Cologne 4711 when the poor woman stuck the precious formula down the front of her dress. Seeing my stifled response to this, Karin changed tack. By co-operation did I mean the food rations we so kindly supplied? Had I seen them, the weekly rations? I shook my head, though the subject stirred a memory; I'd read about it in the London newspapers, I couldn't remember what; "Huns In Clover!" had been the headline. Karin waited me out. Very well—perhaps I meant the sharing of Hamburg's few remaining houses so as to leave the surviving natives stacked ten to a room? Gruesome figures tumbled from her as if they'd been dammed up all her life, awaiting me. A whole month's rations would fit, she claimed, on an Atlantic hotel teatray, four hundred calories a day, half—did I realize this?—yes half what Belsen inmates had been fed by their SS overseers. By the SS, who were surely the worst monsters in history: hadn't we said so ourselves?

This couldn't be what Herr Schäfer meant by the spirit of co-operation. No, I must mean the de-nazification programme, or re-nazification as she calmly called it, a policy which confirmed Nazi dignitaries in their old positions, while at the same time running the country down so thoroughly that not even in the days of Hitler's rise to power had a more fertile ground been created for fascism. And to what end? We exonerated the warmongers, generals and industrialists alike, all but a few scapegoats victimized to appease the public hunger for revenge; worse, we left in place the petty tyrants who maintained German obedience. Judges, policemen, bureaucrats . . . a low, sibilant roll call of Hamburg's hated names now echoed through the bedroom. Why were they still in place? It was obvious. We were preparing Germany to face the Russians so that those who hadn't died fighting against us could die fighting for us, or better still instead of us. Was that my idea of Anglo-German co-operation? She paused and then, as abruptly as she had begun, turned away and began to tuck in the blanket.

I let my side of it fall. Don't blame me, I wanted to answer, I'm just a poor benighted Celt on a romantic quest, a Tristan searching for his Isolde. Don't tar me with an English brush, I'm as Wagnerian as you are. Not that she was tempestuous; she never was. She said it all so sadly that it left me speechless.

More to the point, Karin's murmured tirade had completely

distracted me from the matter at hand, her reasons for keeping mum about my Englishness. I was too busy contemplating this new Karin, while she finished making the bed in silence. Then she headed for the door. No hint of an apology, though she could hardly have guessed how much better I liked her now that I'd discovered her grudge against the British, and her defiance too, her refusal to mince words or mollify me in any way. Before I could try to express this Karin cut me short.

"Herr Schäfer."

"Yes?"

"You will let me know, please," she had one hand on the doorknob, "if you come across a spider."

Ja freilich, I agreed, watching her hesitate, then issue her obligatory "sleep well," and leave. I still had no idea what she was on about.

Simple, really. If I'd been who Karin thought I was I'd have picked up the reference. And I might have chosen to play innocent, as Karin probably realized; so she was none the wiser. Neither was I. It wasn't till the likes of Walters and the wretched Philby (now *there* was a man after Karin's heart) came into my life that I learnt about *die Spinne*, the spider, a Nazi organization devoted to bringing together the dispersed threads of the Third Reich, devising and maintaining the routes which ferried loyal survivors out of Germany to havens abroad. And, more surprisingly, back into the Fatherland itself if occasion required. Big fish like Bormann, and Mengele too it appears, swam in and out through the security net, visiting relatives under our very noses. Hermann Wackernagel was a minnow by comparison but his exploits in France had made him a wanted man, and Karin was looking in plausible quarters for her prey. Someone—it was months before I discovered this source—had slipped Karin the word that I was implicated in the spider's web. She knew Herr Schäfer was no German, and now her own cunning misled her. Aside from Philby and Co there were several shady Britons in the neighbourhood, among them a chap who went by the name of Hirt, an undercover operative "trailing his coat" as the saying was then, hoping to flush out leading Nazis still in hiding by posing as a spider-emissary. Karin supposed me another Hirt, and in point of fact his was a job I'd have enjoyed. But I was busy trailing my coat in a quite different direction. Karin's outburst had earned her my full attention and from then on I couldn't get her out of my mind.

I thought about her as I drank my morning *Muckefuck* and

ploughed an increasingly familiar furrow through the rubble towards the whores' domain, loaded with contraceptives. I wanted to see her smile again, and enjoy the way it gave a worldly cast to her sweet, smooth features. But how could I achieve this, since I was one of the detested British? To my surprise she agreed to meet me outside hotel working hours, for a walk in the sole remaining park with any claim to the name, known to Hamburgers as Planten un Blomen (Plants and Flowers, the *un* a coy tribute to dialect, in place of *und*) and to the Occupying Forces as Knicker Valley. In retrospect it was hardly surprising that Karin accepted. To breach my disguises and win me to her cause she had to wheel up the big artillery: the story of her father's ordeal, a tale requiring longer than a change of bedsheets. All the same it wasn't only with pathos that she wooed me but, being Karin, with candour.

"At first my brothers and I were very much for the Nazis, which upset Father," *Vati* she called him, Daddy, though in German it's less of a nursery word, combining affection with respect, "and he tried hard to explain to us the shame he felt at the way Germans were treating other Germans. After all the Jews were Germans, loyal Germans, and so were others persecuted groups of course, though I don't remember Vati going out of his way to complain about the way the Communists were treated. In '34 he and my mother already knew about the camps, if you wanted to know about such things you only had to keep your ears open. But I was fifteen and didn't listen to anyone, because Vati had brought us up to be independent in our thinking. Also to be concerned for those worse off than we were, the workers, the majority. You see, we were comfortable, I wouldn't say rich but Mutti is a "von," von Hollenbeck, her family derives from the Margraves of Einsiedel; and we were cultured, Vati counted as an intellectual, he was a highly respected journalist and when we entertained . . ." she broke off, and finally shrugged. "We belonged to the intelligentsia, *voilà*. We had been taught to be afraid of Communism, as of all things Russian: it went with purges and terror, with oriental despotism masquerading as democracy. And the Nazis were clever, at their meetings they welcomed dissenting voices and put on a listening face—only at first, but I can vouch for this because I attended them, just as I also attended Communist gatherings. There all the talk was of putting the lampposts to good use," *alle Laternenpfähle vollbummeln*; hangings were what she meant, "when they came to power. The Nazis were careful not to say such things. And of course they too stood for work, for pride in ourselves, jobs for all, they were for the poor and against the rich, which is to say people like the Poseners and the Hollenbecks, and I was drawn to them precisely because of this. And not out of perversity, not at all, I was raised with a social conscience and being privileged by birth and upbringing I was twice as passionate as a socialist. And there you have it—I was being true to Vati. We might have gone with the Communists, Lothar and Georg and I, but we retained our liberal prejudices, and the Nazis appeared more interested in political dialogue than the Communists. Do you understand what I'm saying?''

I nodded; like the Nazis I put on a listening face, and it wasn't easy, because Karin was a revelation in her Sunday clothes. I loved the white blouse with a wide, sharply pointed collar peeping out from beneath her dark coat. Darkish but milky flesh showed below her neck; and—o joy—more moles.

We were granted a deceptively mild day, and everyone seemed to have paired off in response, as in a cartoon of a springtime park. No Hamburger wastes sunshine. Couples strolled past, by the look of them less interested in political dialogue than Karin was. Others lay and hugged or even, in the case of the fraternizing British Tommy, lay and fraternized in plain view, spotty buttocks showing above coiled woollen long johns and uniformed trousers; rising and falling with a girl somewhere beneath, a bit of frat, a jolly old frat sandwich. A distraction; but I really was listening to Karin. By her account it seemed she was fifteen in '34. Born in 1919—my God, that made her twenty-nine, only a year younger than me. Surely not; it wasn't just her schoolgirl looks she'd kept intact, but the solemn manner of a child in the presence of adults. How? Add to these her knowledge, her vocabulary—her wisdom—a wise child, that knows its own Vati; it was as if she had stopped growing, it occurred to me, when her father died ten years ago, or stopped aging as certain long-term patients in asylums seem to do; and entered some strange limbo in order one day to be reunited with him in her childhood guise. By an act of will? Everyone else in the city looked prematurely old, not younger. A pact with the Devil? No, come, she did seem older now, outside the Atlantic, so it must have been the girlish hotel uniform, I told myself, that had deceived me.

Karin was chewing her underlip again, as we walked along. Her tale was faltering. ''I know why I felt about it the way I did, but. . . ." She had reached the year of her father's arrest. "*Natürlich . . . doch*—of course that doesn't make it any easier to forgive myself. I knew he was a good man, and it made no difference to me, in fact it made it worse that he should be so reckless in his newspaper articles. Strange, isn't it? I should have admired him. But it was Vati himself who taught us to distrust heroism. By '38 I was completely disenchanted with the Nazis, but in my own way I was still just as selfish, I was angry with him, Vati had done this against us, his children, he'd deliberately put himself in danger to show us how a German should behave. As a reproach. And then to kill himself . . . it's true, I felt ashamed. But not of us. Of his. *His* selfishness. We needed him, we Poseners, more than we needed another German martyr. I hated him for abandoning us."

She glanced at me, and instead of looking away again she'd held my gaze, seeing something in my face. It was the moment for a comforting intimacy from my own life. But I drew back from it, knowing that once I began I was lost, if I let even the slenderest thread peep from the labyrinth my name would follow and I'd find myself spilling the whole damn yarn all the way to the faceless, devouring thing at the heart of the maze, and I didn't want to come face to face with it myself, not yet. Instead I let her tell me about her own blind journey, burdened by the inability to mourn her father; and how time itself enabled her to grieve and finally to rage on his behalf. Time, and August's resurgent ghost.

Among the little pile of his belongings retrieved from Fuhls-büttel prison was an unused packet of cigarette papers; unused, that is, for cigarettes. "God knows," Karin said, "what inspired me to take one out; years had passed and by now it was a conscious effort, a willed effort in the face of my own resistance, to come closer to him. To imagine what he'd suffered. Beneath the first thin white rectangle of rice paper I saw another, folded waiting. But it wasn't white. It was almost black with pencilled script. Vati had kept a diary."

It was this journal, with its minute, abbreviated entries fanning out like a wafer-thin papyrus—damp had glued the cigarette papers to one another—that once decoded had restored to Karin her father's courage, and his unceasing concern for his family; restored August himself, the father she could love and mourn all the more proudly—to be truly Wagnerian; but these were Karin's own words—for the freedom he reclaimed in death. And one thing more: punctuating the tiny, crowded script, under the magnifying glass, the letter *W* revealed to her his chief tormentor, and numbered Wackernagel's crimes.

"Beside each 'W' the date and time, and then another sign. Interrogation, midnight beating, execution, each one recorded in Vati's own shorthand. Sometimes longer sentences too. Elegies for those who've died." She left silences now, and I pictured her studying the journal through the lens, mouthing the words as she deciphered them. "He talks of Germany of course, and to Germany, as a man of his generation did. And he talks to me." Then: "As though he knew I'd be the one to open the packet of cigarette papers."

Karin reached into her bag. Out came a man's wallet, the leather expressively old and stale; no need to tell me it had been Vati's. She slid her thumb and middle finger into the wallet to extract its loosely enclosed contents—and in my mind I already saw the accordion of cigarette papers as she carefully offered me something folded, yellowish, black with writing. With print, rather; newsprint; as I unfolded it I saw it wasn't the journal at all but a newspaper clipping. More than one, with photographs in common. The same face, above a pre-war football jersey; Vati had been an athlete, then. A prematurely balding head, pale thoughtful eyes. Not a bad face, unremarkable really, a bit piggy in a German way. But handsome enough. Thank God I didn't say so, because a glance at one of the accompanying articles told me this wasn't Vati I was gazing at, it was Hermann Wackernagel. Feeling foolish I replaced piety with a harsher inspection. Local footballing hero and sadist in the making—the face in the photographs grew piggier by the minute, as I studied it again. Were these the lineaments of brutality? Try as I might to dismiss my first, mistaken attribution, the pale eyes remained as thoughtful as ever. I refolded the clippings with care. Despite a temptation to ask if I could keep one, I handed them back and we walked on in silence.

"If I've understood," I said at last, "you're telling me you need to find this Wackernagel as some kind of atonement, to show that . . ."—put it tactfully, Thurgo—"to show that you've changed, that the years of disloyalty are over. Not just to bring a man to justice. Am I right? To make it up to Vati?"

In short, still searching for a parent's love; dear God, I sounded just like Peter. I'd laughed at him, and the irony came full circle, for although I'd despaired of seeing Karin's smile today, now it flooded her face with its fine, caustic rivulets.

"Im Gegenteil," she said: on the contrary. "The person I've

become cannot hope to atone, least of all to my father. You see, I am a Communist.'' The smile held fast but it was rueful. "It would be so bitter for him to know this. Vati would never understand.''

A Communist; now I was courting a bloody Communist. Found a soulmate at last eh Ratty? How Alec would crow if he knew. Always a bit of a Bolshie, my lad. But I was no Bolshevik, not I.

They say the young Göbbels flipped a coin to decide whether he'd be a Nazi or a Red; which pretty much summed up both gangs as far as I was concerned. I taunted Karin with this apocryphal tidbit, but all she said was "Tscha'': well I never. Drily, unimpressed.

Something else occurred to me. "Do your employers at the Atlantic know that you're a Communist?''

"No, they don't know. But the Party is legal again, it's not a crime.' Karin glanced up, breaking off. "Why do you ask?''

She seemed genuinely puzzled. I was only looking for a counter-threat to match her hold over me as a closet Briton, a Briton pretending to be a Red Cross Kraut. Well, let it go. I shrugged, and studied Karin, once more trying to fathom her. She knew about the Russians, Stalin and the purges and the rest of it. How could she turn to Communism? Why? Why now?

"Because I am a practical person, unlike the rest of my family.'' Yes, including my father, said the gaze she turned on me. "Look at this country, and look at the Russian sector. There they give us back our dignity, they give us jobs. Work. And you, what do you give us?'' I knew the litany by now. No work; just promises. No food, or precious little. "No fat now since November. This is why so many are going back again, the ones who fled before the Russians.''

"Why not join them if it's such a paradise,'' I said, fed up. "What's stopping you?''

But I knew what was stopping her. She had to find Hermann Wackernagel. So then . . . what earthly purpose did this "practical'' political activity serve, in the meantime? Unless the comrades kept track of missing Nazis, and Karin never mentioned any such connection. Instead she was spouting the Party line at me.

"You don't think we need the voice of reason here too? Only the workers can prevent another war, by making a common cause. This is what matters now.'' Her eyes remained friendly, in fact she seemed unaware that the drill-sergeant tone of her bedroom tirade had returned. "We have to make our voices heard in every country. Starting now, before people forget. Especially here. In the kitchens of the Atlantic, if necessary."

I nodded. The flush of rhetoric, or perhaps it was the sunshine, waning now as evening came on, had added an interesting spray of freckles to her other, nubbier discolorations.

Dimly, and I didn't much want to explore this, I sensed in Karin's lurch towards the herd mentality something like an identification, surely unwitting, with Wackernagel himself. Dignity, jobs, food, the things Karin was saying the Russians could provide; weren't they the very things the Nazis had offered, in their time? Pushing the thought away I eyed her mottled flesh while we walked along. Karin could have been an Anabaptist or believed the earth was flat, she could have loved her father, hated him, or both at once, her emerging freckles and the moles on her neck and the soft swell of her upper bosom would have remained as cheerfully indifferent to it, praise God, as the stars beginning to come out above us. And just about as distant, for the time being: how I longed to touch them, these constellations of dark spots clustered on her milky skin like a negative of the heavens; like a scattering of brown and black seed. Her skin enthralled me, even its flaws. Best of all its flaws and faultlines, I wanted to trace the stitching of her hare-lip with my tongue, taste each mole separately, large and small, lighter or darker, hairy, some of them, I'd sniff the whole intricate map of her, pore over it like an antiquary in thrall to crumbling things, to parchment, incunabula, tattered papyri with their message intact but literally hanging by a thread—and—yes!—if only humans shed their skin like snakes—

Except that nothing could replace the living skin, skin with its cargo pressing back against the lightest touch. Looking at Karin my head swam at the thought, at what a bag of bones we are: feel them move under your hand, beneath the pulpy canteen (the pliant kind I mean, plenty of stuff sloshing around inside) of your lover's skin; hers so extravagantly featured with its bumps and tumps like troubles bodied forth, extruding Karin herself, yes now I understood, it wasn't skin and careless freckles, mere integument, it wasn't an indifferent sheath at all. Witness the way each smiling seam as it came and went threatened to exude her rage—the rage that was such a mystery to her—like a volcanic fissure. Or like the oubliettes I'd read about in books, the unsuspected trap-doors in the castle Dornford Yates had dreamt up for *Blind Corner*. And there was the rub . . . a real castle beckoned, eastwards. The Schloss. I'd leave next week, I was telling myself now. Or the Monday after. But with Karin it was as if, out of sheer fascination, I'd become assimilated to her skin; I couldn't tear myself away.

At weekends we visited the newly opened Café Keese where thanks to the shortage of men (two-legged ones anyway) it was the women who chose dancing partners, mimicking the whores in their rubble domain. Then on to the Dom, Hamburg's permanent fairground site, where we ate sausage in the shadow of the gun emplacements. I say sausage, though I suppose it was largely wood-shavings; you can get used to anything and at the Dom I did, to rat and squirrel, even jackdaw, rendered indistinguishable from each other by the oil they were cooked in. It was machine oil, and the thin, grimy pancakes on sale at the fairground stalls were about as inviting as fried gaskets.

What I relished about the Dom was its spookiness. Dom means cathedral, but Hamburg's cathedral is elsewhere and always was; in times gone by a yearly carnival was held in its precincts, until a stricter breed of clergy banished it to the Heiligengeistfeld in St. Pauli, at the edge of the city, secular land these days although its name continues to honour the Holy Ghost. A pair of titans dominate it now, monstrous spectres of *der kleine Adolf's* thousand-year Reich: the *Flaktürme*, twin "flak-towers" a hundred and fifty feet tall and two hundred wide, grey-black featureless islands of weatherstained concrete. Windows have been blasted in their sad slab faces, little holes with broken masonry around them like an old *Shockboxer's* eyes— but nothing can demolish the flak-towers. In some places the concrete is twenty feet thick and it can't be torn down, blown up, chipped away, moved, or anything at all except perhaps repainted—though this doesn't seem to have occurred to the Hamburgers—and reinhabited. The flak-towers, hideous as they are, spattered with bird-shit like two lonely, gigantic outcrops in the Hebridean seas, induce a kind of rapture in me. I like them best in winter when they dominate the empty spaces of the fairground and I can picture them outlasting not only Hamburg but the planet itself, sinking intact like evil Dioscuri into the melting core of frenzied atoms and turning almost gracefully into anti-*Flaktürme* in the black hole (the maelstrom! and the flak-towers spiralling down into it!) that devours our exploding sun.

During the war the towers served at once as gun emplacement, bunker, and Gestapo headquarters; in post-war days when I was courting Karin they hosted a variety of entertainments, the official radio station and the Scala Cinema where on special evenings the screen came down and the likes of Cary Grant gave way to portly Kalanag, Hamburg's favourite magician, in his horn-rimmed spectacles and paisley smoking jacket. The irony of this setting were never lost on Kalanag. No-one caught the phantasmal air, the jaunty insubstantial promise of our postwar years better than he did, whether turning water into Schnaps and back again or calmly partitioning his assistant, the lovely Gloria, with a rusty saw. The feet waggled as the saw chewed into her, and the head continued to smile. Kalanag glanced up. *"Weiter?"* Shall I go on? Our cheers came back at us—*weiter, weiter*!—off walls made to keep out the Allied bomb-blast and keep in the cries of the Gestapo's victims. Up sprang Gloria at last, intact. Now it was we who screamed, with glee, and bow-tied Kalanag who raised an innocent astonished face as if to say: why so surprised? If we can turn this torture-chamber into a pleasure dome, why not this wand—watch carefully—into a handkerchief, disclosing a bewildered rabbit? The old routines, but inside out and back to front: he swung the creature through the air, gave a black marketeer's quick shifty glance from side to side, then brought the rabbit down on his head as a top hat. Karin adored this (was there a Marxist joke in it? If so I missed it), clapping and bouncing up and down beside me like a child at a birthday treat.

Sometimes we visited the depleted Hamburg zoo with its humorous baboons, one of whom liked to wear a burst tennis ball on his nose and play a cheaty kind of blind man's buff with his females; in those days most of the other creatures seemed to be dead or, like the great sad Kodiak bears, hibernating, and the zoo's lifesize model of a diplodocus dinosaur was in some ways its most compelling and emblematic exhibit. But our favourite rendez-vous was still Planten un Blomen, where we met under an ancient plane tree. The tree was gaunt and uncomfortably reminiscent of London avenues, but its enormous height made it distinctive and identifiable as a meeting place. It had a bench under it, I was usually late and arrived to see Karin sitting over a book. She would rise, smoothing her skirt, putting the book— the place carefully preserved with a bookmark—into her bag. And we'd shake hands. I remained Herr Schäfer; listening solemnly, as we walked, to her discourses on proletarian rights and the future of Germany; both of us ignoring the greedy couples to our right and left—I never even took her arm—like Heloise and Abelard strolling through a brothel, arguing over the Nicaean Creed.

She had answers to everything, I complained. If I questioned them, I was splitting hairs.

"You don't understand Marx. History is process, it's one big question mark."

"Oh yes?"

"By answers you mean truth, don't you, a kind of eternal truth? This is bourgeois idealism speaking."

"Then surely Marxism is the last word in bourgeois idealism. Isn't the triumph of the proletariat the answer to everything?" It was the logical end and the purpose of history. The ultimate truth. Where was the question mark in that?

"You're talking about an ideal. Not at all the same thing as idealism, which is what happens when you turn a process into an idea. You don't understand the difference? Proletarian democracy is the ideal, yes, and the intended outcome, because it's the only rational way for human beings to live. But until then, history is process. Conflict, struggle. Not idea. Read Marx."

I tried, briefly. Somewhere in Marx, I never discovered where, Karin found the principle of uncertainty I cherished so, in those days. To plan is to die, I said. I agree, she said. No you don't, I said, you've got a Party meeting set for Saturday at seven. I was already jealous of the blasted Party and the time Karin gave to it.

"That's not planning," she said, "it's organization."

"All the difference in the world," I jeered.

"Yes. They are different. Example: since I warned you not to leave it lying around, you keep your washbag with the money in it hidden now, don't you, you hide it in the webbing underneath the red settee. Yes?"

"Oh," I said. "I do, do I?"

"Yes, and that is organization; it is not planning."

"And I bet you know what's in the washbag, every last *pfennig*."

"Bestimmt," she agreed: certainly.

"I see. Is that planning, or organization?"

She laughed, and I was so pleased I simply let it go at that. Didn't I wonder why she was so curious about me? No, I was flattered; flattered blind. Once, later, she said, "I'm a cheat and a liar,'' yes, she even said so to my face, but I preferred to think that she was lying when she said it; crediting her with consistency, if nothing else. I believed in her fundamental honesty, and I still do. She'd only pretended to care for me, that's what she meant (I assume with hindsight) when she said she was a liar. It's what she believed. But what if she was growing genuinely fond of me, even in those early days? Then she wasn't lying to me but to herself. At once lying and not lying: paradox resolved, Karin fashion.

If I'd made a pass at her, would she have given in? And if she had, what would her motives have been? Would she even have known what they were? I think my own uncharacteristic reticence had less to do with the fantasies of power through abstinence that took hold of me in the rubble domain, among the whores, than with the fear—perhaps Karin felt something of the same—of waking to myself; ending the trance. (In the trance I was saving myself for Maggie, whom I'd similarly never brought myself to touch—because, I always told myself, she was too close, too much resembled me. Instead I'd possess her chastely, more intimately in a way. Power through bloody abstinence again!) Also, I found Karin's sadness inhibiting, even though it was precisely her sadness, like a promise of truth, that had attracted me in the first place. Odd, that; in Molly it had been her vivacity, though I soon discovered the impenetrable solitude that underlay it, feeding and sustaining it. And Ellie? Ellie was penetrable, God knows, all short-lived sulks and smiles but when we reached the centre, when we fucked, Ellie wasn't there. She'd gone glassy, leaving behind a body perfectly contented, ticking over in her place. I never did discover what it consisted of, that glassy country. Wherever it was, she was happy there. In a different kind of solitude perhaps, a glad absence. Only Maggie, of the four of them, lacked sanctuary, some place of repose, or that's how I divined her, like myself a loner by consequence of this—certainly not by choice—and so in permanent search of company. When she found it her swirling moods only left her more vulnerable; they were all of her, making her continuously and discomfitingly present.

By contrast, Karin. Karin dense to bursting with the hidden stuff of herself, so prodigal her very skin couldn't contain it and spoke in eruptions. She was the queen of solitude, I was merely lonely (in effect the polar opposite) and I suppose . . . I suppose that drew me to her, no two ways about it, as to an alter ego.

I had begun to insinuate myself into Karin's life by bringing her black market items for her family. Nappies, I discovered, were especially prized, as were safety pins, both needed by her sister-in-law who had remarried since the death of Karin's brother Lothar. Sister-in-law Christa had spawned two more mouths to feed, regardless of poverty; in some way incited by it, perhaps. I gathered that this marriage was already rocky and that Christa's husband was away a good deal, but Karin didn't seem to want to tell me why. So whether it was sheer incompatibility or the difficulty so many couples had in adjusting to peacetime—the tally of divorces now matched that of the war dead—I couldn't tell. Clearly Karin was reluctant to involve me in her home life. I knew the Poseners' old house on the Alster was a burnt-out shell, that there were nine of the family living in cramped accommodation somewhere in Wandsbek, once a prosperous suburb. And the details gradually emerged: the nine consisted of various children, among them Karin's niece and nephew, Lothar's offspring, plus his widow Christa's new brood, and some unspecified members of Christa's family including her father, described by Karin as a good-for-nothing. He drank a bottle of wine a day, she said, a habit acquired while occupying France. Now he occupied the bath, sleeping in it with a bottle on the floor beside him. The doyenne of the household was Frau Posener, Karin's mother, whose von Hollenbeck origins seemed to avail them little in financial terms. There had been a von Hollenbeck aunt, maiden Aunt Elsa; she'd owned a house spared by the bombing, and the surviving Poseners had stayed with her before the move to Wandsbek, which was occasioned by Aunt Elsa's death and the requisitioning of the house by the British. There was little mention of this interim period before the hardships of the Wandsbek years, and even less mention of the maiden aunt herself. In time I discovered why, and although it left me with a lasting admiration for the old girl, I could understand why the others kept so quiet about her. After August's suicide they'd had their fill of Roman deaths, no matter how honourable. Aunt Elsa kept a tin beside her bed, containing her worldly worth in Reichsmarks. When the tin was empty, she said openly and apparently quite cheerfully, she would make an end of herself. And she did.

Surely Karin's father, however reckless an idealist, hadn't left his family destitute? Didn't Frau Posener receive a widow's pension, at least? Apparently not. Her daughter-in-law Christa had a pension, forfeited in part by her remarriage and spread thinner among them all than their margarine ration—they hadn't seen bùtter for years (I made a mental note: butter). No, the fact that August had been indicted as an enemy of the state deprived his widow of her right to a pension, despite the downfall of the Reich and its disgrace. And this, Karin pointed out bitterly, while the widows of Nazi officials, including those condemned for crimes against humanity, continued to be supported by the new Germany. The Vaterland forgave everything except disloyalty. Wasn't it an outrage? Karin was quick to compare the arrangements in the Russian zone, where the relatives of those who'd died resisting Nazi rule were being generously compensated. So she insisted, unaware of what this evoked in me. Hadn't Peter died resisting Nazi rule? I had a bizarre vision of Maggie living in Communist splendour, whatever that might be—Schloss Brüel translated into a People's Palace thronging with members of the proletarian classes lined up to vote on the day's menu . . . Gräfin Agnetha once more barricaded in her tower room against the *Pöbel*, while Ludolf the Kommissar still wore his majordomo's weeds, black tie and tails. A guilty vision; I realized I was telling myself there was perhaps no need to rescue Maggie from this Marxist paradise—if I believed Karin's glowing version of life *dort drüben*, over there.

Once Wackernagel was found and brought to trial, she explained, her father could be officially rehabilitated. Pension and compensation—both could be applied for. I was relieved to hear this, not only because of the restitution involved but because Karin's words began to lay to rest my image of her gunning down Wackernagel. This had persisted, though I couldn't tell whether it was in Karin I sensed murder or in myself, on her behalf. For some reason I saw it taking place out in the countryside, on a remote, tranquil farm, where a penitent but furtive Hermann shovelled muck, combining atonement and obscurity until one day: *krak!* Karin's slight figure at the corner of a barn, pistol in hand, and Wackernagel face down in the slurry. But a dead Wackernagel would butter no parsnips; old Mother Posener's well-being and that of her chickens depended on bringing him to trial, not assassinating the man. They were fully aware of this, I was sure. Karin too, for their sake if for no better motive. Yet her rare and breezy references to her family made her seem the odd one out, somehow, less of a Posener and at the same time more of one, prouder than the rest, and an outcast because of it. She was the heart of the family, their talisman, August's only surviving child. So why was it that when she talked about Wandsbek I perceived her as apart, displaced less by fecund Christa and the rest of her in-laws, or by her politics, than by her grief? After ten years her mourning must have appeared extravagant, reproachful even, now that everyone was putting tragedy behind them. She was still August's victim, it seemed to me; more than that she was still his daughter, the child of his recklessness. And she didn't seem to know it. I wanted to penetrate her family, to gather up its loose threads and forestall . . . what? Danger if not disintegration. Danger to Karin, that is; I was the last person to be preaching family togetherness for its own sake, at that precise moment or at any other time. All of which, I'm afraid, led to the evening of the butter fiasco.

The nappies, safety pins and the various goodies I had procured for the Poseners—women's underwear were in especially short supply, and found favour, though Karin maintained with ill-disguised loathing that Christa scorned such things; "always ready for action" was Karin's phrase—led at last to a dinner invitation. The way Karin issued it showed that she was rather less enthralled by the prospect than I was. She could very easily make my excuses, she said, no-one would be offended if I cried off, they'd have shown their thanks by inviting me but would be spared the embarrassment of revealing their impoverished circumstances and the meagreness of their hospitality. It was quite a little speech, and I fancied I heard her father in those Teutonic formalities; all they lacked was a final click of the heels. I also fancied it was an invitation Karin had already rejected once or twice on my behalf, until this gave our liaison an air of secretiveness—or worse, implied some shameful intimacy which was the very opposite of the truth. In the end she'd have to bring me home, and in doing so confirm me as a suitor. Hardly surprising that she was nervous about the whole thing, she'd probably had to endure a good deal of teasing about the mysterious Herr Schäfer. I sensed something else in Karin, however, a different fear: that my presence would somehow make her feel even more the outsider. Happily it didn't work out that way at all.

My first thought, once I'd over-ridden her attempts to spare us this ordeal, was to find some special contribution to the evening. But what? It was no help at all that I had almost unlimited funds at my disposal. The Duchess of Mecklenburg's stolen silverware, over a thousand pieces of it, was rumoured to be for sale to the highest bidder; but this would be de trop in Wandsbek (even for a von Hollenbeck) not to say a case of rubbing gentlefolk in their own distress. The same applied to the Rembrandt and the racehorses available via the kitchens of the Atlantic. Vlad the String offered to locate for me an ounce of pure deuterium stolen from an atomic fission laboratory, currently the most sought-after item on the black market and the object of many fruitless *Razzias* or raids by Hamburg's street crime squad. I didn't want to blow up Wandsbek, I explained, but simply to enliven an evening there, and show my appreciation. Vlad bent down and took the cuff of his jacket between his teeth like a dog, pulled the sleeve back to reveal an arm—his arm I should say since it was his only one—lined with wristwatches, and raised a heavy Russian eyebrow at me: one of these? I shook my head, no thanks; wondering by what contortion he'd attached them to the arm in the first place.

Then I remembered Karin mentioning the margarine rations, and that they hadn't seen butter for years. That was the answer, not just a square of butter but a slab, a tub, if possible a vat of it. Real butter; even the Atlantic only served margarine, and in tiny pats, one each per meal. Vlad looked grim when I told him what I had in mind. Butter! Now I wanted the moon, said his expression. We could ask Wolfgang Zimt. Zimt would find us anything. From Vlad himself I'd heard stories of this Zimt, a black-marketeer with a legendary temper and a way with a knife; like Zorro it amused him to leave his initial as a calling card, especially on a customer he felt had slighted him; Zimt as a last resort then, I said, but surely we could find some butter on our own initiative? Vlad muttered something under his breath. Repeated, it emerged as: first find cow. No cow, no butter. Where do we look, I asked? His shoulders heaved expressively. First cow we find in Vladivostok. Come on, you old misery-guts, I said, don't give me that, I bet people have got cows hidden all over the place. Farmers, I mean.

We took the train, across the Elbe and down to rural Lüneburg where, less than three years earlier, the Reich had formally surrendered. Vlad sniffed the air, grunted, and shook his head in dire prophecy. He was right. Searching the rapidly thawing countryside for cows, with a melancholic one-armed Russian lurching and swaying along in tow, proved to be a futile, time-consuming exercise; though exercise it certainly was, as we tramped through the mud from farm to farm. Their owners laughed in our faces. Cows? All eaten long ago. Even when creeping up on barns unannounced we drew a blank, not a moo to be heard, and by mid-afternoon Vlad's vocal impression of a lovesick bull was getting on my nerves. I was ready to give up the whole idea; though it was hard to accept that there was a part of the world where you could more easily butter your bread with pure deuterium than butter itself.

In the end it was a deer, not a cow, that led us to butter. Hirsch is German for deer (more precisely stag) and the Henry who'd offered to guide me across the "green frontier" was Henry Hirsch by name. He'd fetch us butter from the Russian zone, no trouble, and prove to me his competence as a frontier-walker while doing me a favour—for a price, of course. Plenty of butter *dort drüben*. Over there, the Holstein herds were still intact. A likely story, I thought; more propaganda. But lo and behold, after a two-day absence Henry showed up in our bunker with a pound of butter, swathed in cheesecloth, in his pocket. His odiously smooth young face shone with pride beneath the cowlick, the dark wing of hair which reminded me uneasily of Peter's. Only a pound of the stuff, he said sorrowfully, while charging me a fortune for it, eight hundred Marks. But real, Holstein butter, taste it! We did, passing the cheesecloth around in the twilit bunker, where the butter glowed like an ingot. *Bogu moyu,* my God, Vlad murmured at the sight of it; no mean tribute, since Russian soldiers had a strict swearing hierarchy and in ascending order of seriousness, as he'd once told me, this ran: shit, fuck, mother, Lenin, God. In turn we each shaved off a tiny wafer of the precious stuff before handing it on. Vlad put the cheesecloth in his lap and raised his butter-fragment high into the air like Kalanag about to perform a trick, dropped it into his mouth, and sighed. "Butter": it was all anyone could say, and the truth was that our palates were so coarsened by the likes of *Muckefuck* and machine oil that we had to draw on memory as much as on the clues provided by our startled taste-buds. But it was butter all right. Vlad lifted it back to Henry, who once more wrapped up the golden oblong. I passed him the money, he passed me the butter, and I all but ran back to the Atlantic, afraid at every corner that I'd see ahead of me the dull green Schakos of the police.

On the evening appointed I made my way to Wandsbek by tram with the butter still wrapped in its original cheesecloth. No point in tarting it up, its origins would remain unspoken but obviously illegal. And as with my earlier gifts, no less acceptable because of it; the Poseners lived in a world of stolen goods like everybody else, taking their chances. Enjoying it too. Even proud of it. Arrests for theft had reached three thousand a day, and the Hamburgers were proud of that, too. Crime was bring-

ing people together as no government edict could, and conferring a kind of nationhood, a community of resistance (though
nobody admitted this) to expiate the long years of compliance
with the Nazis. I wanted to enjoy this with them, but it wasn't
mine to share. All I had was the fear of being caught. Several
policemen climbed on the tram and descended again at different
points on the journey, and my bulging pocket cried out, I felt,
for their attention, as urgently as it had when it was full of money
and pressing against Schäfer in the jeep, on the winding Malaga
roads. We reached the Wandsbeker Chaussee at last, I got off
hastily and watched the tram slide away up the street till it swallowed by the darkness. Standing there I felt more alone than I
had since fleeing Spain, as though the anaesthetic were beginning to wear off. I gazed round, wishing I'd asked Karin to fetch
me or, failing that, brought Henry Hirsch as a native guide. But
in houseproud Wandsbek the street signs had been restored,
along with a few lamps, and where houses remained the numbers were legible.

Finding the house was the least of my problems. It stood in a
thoroughly respectable-looking street with little shops at one
end, though one or two of these were boarded up and gave off
a whiff of latrine. Further on, the doorsteps looked scrubbed,
the windows sported curtains, one step more and I'd be picturing family life behind them, modest, tidy, Parsifal Road and
Molly at the bay window—but here it was, thank God: number
65 in curly gothic figures. No bell; and as I shoved and the front
door swung open, Germany returned in a wave of sweat and
carbolic, *Sanitätskarbol* and tobacco and what Hamburgers insist on calling *Parföng*, cheap scent. And cabbage, immemorial
German cabbage. Karin had promised me time-controlled stair
lights, I found them and pressed the buttons in turn as I reached
successive landings, reading the names outside the doors. Not
so much names in the usual sense of one to each apartment,
these were lists, dozens of names stacked one under the other,
a surname or two followed by a roll-call of Christian names as
on a family tombstone. Whole dynasties seemed to be tucked
away behind each door and I missed the Poseners altogether,
probably because on their nameplate they were outnumbered by
the Danziger clan, Karin's in-laws. Finally, although the house
had looked intact from the outside, I found myself on a completely ruined top floor landing, open to the stars. Descending
again I pressed a few bells and the confusing instructions I received, on one occasion out of a catacomb-like darkness where

candlelight showed a coven of faces over a skimpy meal, led me to more wary tenants, suspicious of officialdom I suppose, before I found the right door by a process of elimination.

The Posener household had electric light, thank God. Or maybe they'd rented it for the evening; everything in the dingy apartment that night looked as if it had been specially imported for my benefit—Karin later admitted this—from the tablecloth, the napkins, and the paper doilies under each dish, to the armchair with its immaculate antimacassars, on which I was obliged to sit since no-one else would. Not even Frau Posener herself, despite my urging.

She was a doughty woman, smaller than Karin, sharp chin and dyed black hair, and between jaw and hairline a little withered nut of a face criss-crossed by tiny lines, showing how her daughter's would become in time, when Karin's teasing fissures became permanent. "Herr Schäfer," she greeted me with a fierce, steady smile, nose bending towards her chin, and her cheeks turning to crumpled graph paper. That smile! it went beyond courtesy, bespoke forgiveness. Her arms were extended but her body drawn well back in case I mistook her gesture to mean an invited embrace. We were still in Hamburg, and formal. It was an honour, she said, to meet their benefactor. Having all my life identified with Magwitch, the hoary old convict and Pip's secret patron in *Great Expectations*, I should have been delighted at the name of benefactor, but Frau Posener's tender dignity shamed me. Not so, thank heavens, the shifty Danzigers lined up behind her for inspection. Their nakedly greedy faces put me at ease as I shook their hands in turn, reaching Karin at the end of the queue, and turning back to distribute the smaller gifts I'd assembled. Leaving the butter till last.

It was Karin I watched when, in due course, I presented it. It was for her, really (and it was Russian butter after all!), for her and her mother, and bugger the Danzigers. Sister-in-law Christa was a brassy creature, blonde hair newly permed and out to get my attention, though clearly subdued by Frau Posener's presence. The Danziger father looked drunk and unaccustomed to the light, as did two louts Karin's age who turned out to be his sons; while the younger children were at least uniformly silent, boggling at me but managing with an effort not to paw the benefactor to make sure he was real—this trace of good manners due once more to Karin's mother, I decided. They all wore their Sunday best and as we surrounded the table, where I had placed

the still-shrouded butter, we attended it with a solemn and impersonal air, restrained, like ushers at a wake.

Pre-prandial conversation had been fitful, since everyone must
have been told not to ask me any searching questions. We discussed the welcome spring weather, the early vegetables, the
coming attractions at the Scala; no politics, nothing controver-
sial, it was a suburban dinner party out of time and all but
irrespective of place. The butter awaited. When I unveiled it
Karin's eyes told me I'd brought exactly the right thing, and I
gloried in her smile, amid the cries of Danziger approval and
Frau Posener's gentler wonderment. It was *kapital, famös, en-
orm,* even *tipptopp.* I was accepted; as at Schloss Brüel when I
recited ''The Shirt'' and won my spurs.

Soup came and went. No sign of bread. The butter sat, in
state. I could imagine it sitting there forever, a symbol not to be
spoiled by anything as vulgar as eating it, token of all that a
luxurious future might bring; or as if the imminence of butter
could never be matched by its taste. At last, after the soup, the
sausage, and the fish, between a stew and the cake that threatened us with a *nachtisch* as lavish as dessert at the Schloss,
Karin appeared with bread and cheese—the loaf quickly begged
from a neighbour—and Frau Posener invited me to do the honours.

''Bitte . . .''

''Überhaupt nicht,'' I demurred, handing her back the knife.

''Aber bitte . . .'' she insisted, returning it.

All eyes were on me as I buttered the first slice of bread, and
offered it to my hostess; once more Frau Posener shook her
head, so I passed it to one of her grandchildren, Karin's nephew,
a boy of five or thereabouts.

He took a bite. Munched solemnly.

''Na, Hans-Dietrich? Gut, was?''

Good? It was . . . it was like nothing he'd ever eaten before,
his nod and his round eyes declared.

The family applauded, and I began to pass out more buttered
bread, starting with the other children, until everybody had a
slice. Hans-Dietrich's loyal little face, as he continued chewing,
seemed to me to betray more puzzlement than delight; but I let
it pass. Soon they were all eating, exchanging murmurs and soft
cries of gratification.

''Tscha . . .''

''Ogottogott . . .''

''Ach du lieber . . .''

"Mnja . . ."

More, anymore? No, it would be a crying shame, said down-cast eyes, to eat it at all once.

I had refrained from taking any butter myself, and nobody, I noticed, was urging me to do so. Quite right too, I thought, it was their treat, they were the deprived round here, not I. But I was sick of playing Father Christmas—Magwitch would have joined in, surely—so I carved myself a small slice, stuck it on a wisp of bread, and popped it in my mouth.

I felt Karin's hand touch mine under the table, and give a warning squeeze. At pretty much the same instant a taste of mashed potato hit my palate. I chewed some more, in disbelief; appalled but trying not to show it. It tasted fatty. But definitely not buttery. No, it was mashed potato, mixed for consistency with some vile kind of animal fat, and coloured yellow. I stared at the eight-hundred-Mark object on the table before me. Impossible: it had been butter, good Communist butter, that we'd all tasted in the bunker. Butter, damn it, not this . . . this rancid impostor. Glancing discreetly round the table I saw fixed smiles, and understood the message of Karin's fingers. The family had pretended it was butter so as not to embarrass me. I was to pretend it was butter so as not to embarrass them. I squeezed back that I'd understood, and Karin's hand rested on mine for a moment, of her own accord.

When it was all over, and Schnaps had washed away the worst of it, we said goodnight at the front door, between the smell of cabbage and the urine smell of the street.

"I swear to you," I said, "it was butter when I bought it. I tried some."

"Macht nichts," doesn't matter, she said, and I saw from her expression that she was tickled by the whole affair. I'd tried to play the grand seigneur and instead had gained a taste of their life of deception and disappointment. "The children wouldn't know the difference anyway, it's been so long since they had butter. They enjoyed the treat. That's more important. Thank you."

"Bitte schön," not at all; my pleasure. I still felt galled.

Behind us the time-controlled switch clicked off, leaving us in shadow and suddenly awkward, as if the house had commanded us to kiss.

"Gute Nacht . . ." goodnight left hanging and then "ja—wie heissen Sie eigentlich?" What are you really called? The outline of her face, cheeks pouched, told me she was grinning up at me.

I hesitated. Then I had it—I wanted to say: Jonathan Mansel. Yates' *Blind Corner* sleuth. But at that moment Mansel's name escaped me. Once it had slipped my mind I couldn't bring it back, and Karin was still smiling, waiting for an answer. What shall I call you? "Richard," I heard myself say, and felt a curious sensation in my face as though I was blushing, and of the possible reasons I wasn't sure, I really wasn't, which one I was blushing for.

It began to snow in huge dull flakes, friendly, fuzzy things that melted on my coat, as I emerged from the Atlantic for the last time. So much for an early spring. That morning the heavens stormed down snow in communion-sized bites as if to absolve us of false hopes as fast as possible.

Time to go; and not only because I'd begun to reveal myself to Karin. "Hey, Pinkerton," one of the Atlantic bellboys hailed me, just a few days earlier. Luckily we were in the kitchens at the time. Everyone had grinned—I don't think they took me for an American agent, that was just the boy's way of saying "snoop," but it made me feel I'd pushed my luck far enough. All it would need was fat Cheerybye or some other Britisher taking a closer interest in me, to reveal that I was about as authentic as Henry Hirsch's butter. Who'd cover for me then?

Through Vlad the String I'd arranged to meet Henry in Rathausmarkt at noon, though I was pretty sure he wouldn't show up and risk my wrath over the butter. Wrong; I was always wrong about Henry. His features were so bloody insolent, tilted nose and smiling red lips, it made you want to slap him just for the pleasure of it. I had slower torture in mind, on this occasion. And there he was, lounging on the expanse of cobbles, not a care in the world. Unless it was a pose. The way he pushed his hair back when he saw me seemed less assured. Alec's voice came: give the blighter a boot in the stern.

As I approached, Henry's troubled gaze took me in from my bare head to the battered black shoes on my feet. I tried to ignore this inspection but I couldn't help remembering Tom Thurgo's army boots: where were they now that I needed them? They'd be no use to Schäfer in my coffin, perhaps they stood in Parsifal Road, in a closet somewhere or by the bed, or: stop. Concentrate on the journey ahead. We were setting out by tram, then foot. Twenty, thirty miles at most. Say twenty-five. But my mind kept sliding off, sliding back. Even in my hare-brained state this part of the journey seemed distinctly crazier, more dangerous than what I had done so far. Fifty-fifty, I'd been warned, the chances of getting safely across the border; one in five of staying there undetected. But it was too late to stop now. On a journey, I told myself, it's only the first step that counts. One path among many; all paths the same, our own only the hardest to find because it's nearest at hand, because we're already on it. Why else had I abandoned my passport in Spain, and there in the ravine the remains of a corpse that would be buried in my name?

Tram, then foot. Travelling light. I'd left my bulkier possessions with Karin, the eighteen-forty-odd pocket edition—what pockets they must have had then—of "Lord Byro," as well as the washbag with a sizeable chunk of Thurgo cash still in it. I was taking enough with me to bribe a Russian division, and I wasn't planning to stay long; if I was going to get caught I'd prefer to know I was enriching the Poseners with what I'd left behind, rather than the Red Army. Old Isidro came with me, The Destroyer of rats. Rats only, so far.

Henry was smiling at me, gleaming in fact; had the butter met with approval, Herr Schäfer?

Bare-faced nerve—or was he as innocent of the switch, what if it was someone at the Atlantic who'd replaced the butter with potato and pork fat or whatever the filthy-tasting coagulant had been? No, I'd kept it in my possession the whole time, from the bunker to the Wandsbeker Chaussee. The bunker: I saw Henry wrapping up the butter again, crouched in darkness over the cheesecloth. Easy enough to slip a substitute and palm the real thing . . . and play the innocent now in the hope that I hadn't been the consumer myself or, if it was a gift, that I wasn't present when it had been consumed. My silence did nothing to alter Henry's smile.

He came closer. "You have the money?" He meant his fee for the journey we were embarking on, costlier than the butter by a clear four hundred Marks. "Half now," he said, comradely. His expression changed as I shook my head. The cowlick crept back down his forehead. Together we played at ignoring the snowflakes landing on our faces, and I held his gaze, enjoying every moment of it. "In that case, Herr Schäfer . . ." He let his shoulders droop in a gesture of helpless regret. His services were no longer at my disposal.

Pity, I said, turned and headed for the tram stop. Bluff called. I heard his footsteps and then the murmured voice in my ear.

"But you do have the money with you? At least show it to me."

No. He wasn't getting a sniff of it, now or later—though I didn't tell him that. I'd already paid over the odds for worthless goods, and the extra four hundred Marks, a pair of *Blaue*, blue banknotes, would be the price I charged for the humiliation.

I had to endure a disgruntled Henry all the way to the tram terminus at the edge of the city. He'd been cheated before, he complained. *Schade:* alas, I said. Did I give my word, he asked, that I'd pay in full when we reached our destination? I did. He was still grumbling about promises as we struck out through dismal farms towards the open countryside and the woods beyond. It had turned colder still, too cold for snow to fall but at the same time preserving the layer that had fallen and freezing the mud beneath into hidden iron ridges. At school I'd exercised in harder weather than this, I had the edge, I felt, over thin, shivering Hirsch whose lips were turning blue despite his scarf and duffle coat and the woollen hat he now pulled down over his ears. Henry began grumbling again. "Halt's Maul, Henry," just shut up, I said, cradling Isidro in my overcoat pocket. Fellow's a broken reed. He could suffer in silence, damn it.

Was I too hard on him? If I'd known who Henry Hirsch was I'd have shot him then and there, in the first clearing we reached.

Now the only sounds were the munching noises of our steps and, in the woods, the sudden thump when a fir branch shed its waxy load, making Henry start in alarm. "Nearest Authorized Crossing Point," announced a sign in English and German, with an arrow pointing us southwards. Henry ignored it and walked on past. His route led us in a straight line regardless of woodland or open country, as if following some ancient trackway, the shortest, quickest way I assumed, surely best in this weather; leave deviousness to our nocturnal crossing of the *Grüne Grenze*, the green frontier. A "black" crossing—black and green were our colours, the colours of no flag I'd ever known. At the thought I realized I felt saner, clearer-headed than for weeks. I was venturing into Russian territory to rescue my missing sister-in-law. Yes, and about time too. Wasn't I responsible for Maggie's plight, at least in part? In the spring of '38 I'd failed to deliver Alec's message and aborted his own rescue mission, I'd lied and left Maggie to stew in Germany. A shaming confession, this, one I'd never fully made to myself, and even now the lawyer in me threw it out as false and posturing—just as Maggie and Alec's belated romantic alarums had surely been. She wasn't going to leave Peter standing at the church, it was Peter and the Schloss she'd wanted, Peter and the Schloss she got. But now Peter was dead. That was the simple fact of it.

And I could still picture this as a rescue mission, which helped me deal with another fact, less simple, the fact that except on rare occasions I hadn't been thinking romantically about Maggie. Not even prior to Karin; the risk of disappointment was too great, and there was comfort enough in thinking of Maggie as the only person I could tell my whole story to, she was home in that sense, my only home, and wasn't I hers, in all her fretfulness? Orphans of the storm: a Maggie posture if ever there was one, but I indulged it now, enjoyed it, especially when the afternoon brought another, more protracted flurry of snow, blowing straight at us and slowing Henry's progress as he led the way. At times we stumbled forward with heads averted, glancing sideways out of one blinking, snow-shuttered eye, or gazing downwards at our feet; we even walked backwards on occasion to give our cheeks a rest from the stinging flakes, and watched the snow blurring our tracks.

Hamburg had been an odd old time, I decided, a kind of airless trance, the city reflecting nothing back at me but myself, there was a glad kind of Saturnalia going on there, just what I was after, but it wasn't mine. Or mine too easily, the same thing somehow. I couldn't locate the grit, the obstinate and unassimilable; until now.

Perhaps there's always something wilful about travelling east, something eerie too, instead of following the sun you set off as if to outface him, brazenly, to joust with him, and as the day goes on you end up heading for the darkest part of the horizon, your own shadow steadily overtaking you, hurrying home, it seems, into the darkness, as the sun sets at your back. We were burrowing against the grain, Henry and I, the easterly wind said so, pelting us with snow: go back. The trickle of hurrying refugees said so, as evening drew on and they passed us coming the other way. Some ran off into the trees, suspicious, and we saw them only as scurrying figures weighed down by suitcases, crazed picnickers surprised by winter, dragging their children home; once we came across an abandoned suitcase, burst open, belongings heartrendingly exposed and wet with snow. Other groups, past caring or too tired to run away, plodded past with incredulous looks, like men who'd harrowed hell: were we mad? Did we know where we were headed?

Suddenly it occurred to me that unless she had received our postwar letters Maggie didn't even know I'd married her sister. How would she take the news? A hoot of laughter, that's how. Molly? You married *Molly*? Before I could put a halt to it the images came rushing in—Molly intent, spreading a tiny blot of marmite all around her toast, Molly squinting at her bridge hand, lips drawn back in a soft snarl. Her face set in pained determination on a Sunday hike. And I couldn't keep it at bay: Molly tearfully sorting through my things, no, she'd be dry-eyed, angry even, angrily but dutifully going through my papers, her late husband's briefs, as it were, going through his drawers, even rotten jokes were welcome. I'll be back shortly, I wanted to tell her, don't give up on me, I'm just on a hike; absurd—I must have known I wasn't going back, but even when the waxwork sergeant from Essex had shown me his family snaps I'd refused to let it affect me. I was on a walking tour. Molly's hiking grimace returned, its ugly rage; those awful bracing bustling hill-climbs . . . if I was trying to get away from all that I'd chosen a funny way to do it, walking backwards into Mecklenburg in my not-so-sensible shoes. The blizzard was letting up a little and I could face front, concentrate instead on what was coming up.

Henry seemed to be heading for a fat beech, gaunt above, at the edge of a field, where the last light reflected off the snow showed the figure *88* smudged on its bark in black paint. I took it for a frontier-walker's secret sign. So it seemed: Henry paused as if greeting a friend, went over to the tree and slowly settled on one of its drier roots, sheltered from the snow. Without looking at me he pulled a hunk of bread, damp at one end, from his duffle-coat pocket. Following suit I devoured the corned beef *Butterbrot* Karin had prepared for me with Atlantic margarine, though Hirsch-fat itself would have been a lip-smacking feast after our efforts.

Karin hadn't asked where I was going, so I didn't tell her. I hadn't mentioned Brüel to Henry either, it was none of his business. Once inside the Russian zone I'd make my own way to the Schloss, trusting to local guidance in the forests of the Friedrichswald. I'd no idea where Henry intended to make the crossing, I was in his hands, but the oncoming file of refugees was reassuring. Due east lay the Schaalsee, a long thin lake whose waters formed the border; hard to patrol, that much Henry had told me, when it was frozen. If it still was.

Not far now, surely? Henry merely nodded and we started up

again, shaking off stiffness and the clinging snow like a pair of sleepy hounds. In a distant lane I spotted a British scout car, parked and apparently unoccupied. Henry saw it too, and accelerated. We jogged deeper into the woods. An hour passed. No sign of border guards; no distantly barking dogs. It seemed too easy. What if a Russian stepped out from behind one of these trees, rifle at the ready? Bunker gossip said Ivan used dumdum bullets that could tear your leg off. Failing that there was the Bolshevik execution special, the *Genickschuss* fired into the spinal cord at the base of the kneeling victim's neck. Never kneel to a Russian. That was Vlad speaking. I wouldn't like to be in your shoes, he'd said, if they catch you with forged papers. Cheka men now at the border, GPU, NKVD, bad men.

If we said we'd come to help build true socialism, would we be fed and housed as Karin claimed, put to work on a collective farm? I'd have a hard time explaining what Isidro was doing in my pocket.

Would I use it to avoid capture? Doubtful, very. More Alec parlance, I couldn't seem to get my blasted brother out of my head. Beware the Russkies, he'd said, unlike the Krauts they mistrust everyone, with or without credentials. Rockefeller on the other hand—Paula from the whores' precinct—who'd left her native Rostock and escaped to Hamburg through the Russian lines, had made it equipped only with one protective phrase in Russian: "ya vas looblyoo." Lacking Paula's charms I wondered how Russian soldiers would react to the words "I love you" coming from a shaggy brute in a British overcoat. I'd never grown a beard before; it was jet black and curly, ringletted almost, some Mediterranean or even more exotic heritage—O'Malley blood enriched by Armada survivors if Grandfather's tales were to be believed. Give me a robe, a cross, and I could pass for Rasputin. Peace, little brothers, put down your weapons! Silliness did nothing to improve my nerves; I was jumping at the smallest sound now.

No refugees any more. I hoped Henry knew where he was going, I'd lost my sense of direction and began to suspect him of leading us in circles. Hadn't we passed that tree before? The number "88" was everywhere, as if to confuse us. We hadn't spoken for hours, and I wasn't sure if I could speak at all. I pointed to an *88*. Henry nodded and grunted several syllables which sounded like "Heil Hitler!" Heil Hitler? Later I learnt that was precisely what the inscription meant; we were surrounded by coded swastikas. At the time I thought Henry was losing his wits.

The snow had stopped falling again, I realized as we emerged once more from the beechwoods into a huge printless tract of farmland, empty in the moonlight, with a dark wall of firs facing us in the distance. I couldn't feel my feet, and even pressed against my crotch my fingers felt like useless, pounded meat.

Henry had stopped. It wasn't a field at all. It was the lake, the Schaalsee. Thank God. But looking closer, my heart sank and I groaned out loud.

"Is' was?" Henry managed. What's the matter?

I aimed a hand. The sparkle of moonlight on snow ended a hundred yards or so from the shore in a murky, darker expanse gradually declaring itself, as we stared at it, as floe and water.

We tramped wearily north, eyes trained on the lake in hope of an ice bridge. Spitefully, the wind veered with us, still lacerating our faces. Out on the lake the water grew wider. At last we gave up, turned and struggled back in our own footsteps, this time trying to avoid the hidden roots and ridges, southwards past the place where we'd encountered the lake, and on, hour after hour. Several times the level snowfield narrowed and a headland pointed our way to what seemed like an unbroken passage across the ice. On closer inspection it wasn't. Now another spit of land, reaching almost across the lake, the most promising so far. Light flickered, farther south. The end of the Schaalsee. This causeway—if it was one—was my last chance.

The ice appeared intact, right across to the opposite shore. No telling how thick it was, short of testing it. Steer clear of water. Hadn't Auntie said that? A stock warning, not very inventive. And this was ice, wasn't it, not water. Go on, try it, bonny lad.

Past the dead bracken at the shoreline, among reeds, the crust was thin and slushy. The ice was thin here; never mind the bloody veil. Further out it looked more solid and I tossed a stone which skittered confidently away into the darkness. For a moment or two we could still hear it squeaking and pattering on the bumpy ice, like a small animal. I gazed at Henry's rime-encrusted face; he at mine; both afraid to speak in case even our whispers carried to the Russian lights downwind of us. Looks would have to do. With a nod and a smile I tried to convey "I'll risk it." I couldn't read his face at all, but finally he brought out one trembling red hand, expressive enough: the money.

Na denn Tschüss, bye Henry, I wanted to say out loud and to

hell with the Russians, I made to speak but not a sound came
from my frozen jaws. Well, it's the thought that counts. I grasped
the proffered fingers in a quick, empty-handed farewell, took
half a step and then a huge stride through the reeds and slush
onto the ice, and set out hastily, before I knew it was holding or
not, to keep my weight moving across the surface. For a pace
or two the ice beneath me creaked exactly like a wooden floor,
but that was all. It held.

A furious hiss came from the shore, and then Henry found
his voice: come back, *du Schwein*! On the last word the voice
cracked like an adolescent's.

Schwein yourself, you little cheat.

After a moment, a different sound. Henry had jumped out
after me onto the lake, but I was running, I had twenty yards
on him now. The woods on the far shore would hide me if he
followed.

"I'll kill you," came his voice, and the change in tone made
me glance back, then stop, though it took me several tip-toeing
steps, arms out, to do so without falling.

He was ten feet out from the shore and perfectly steady, standing with some sort of pistol aimed at me. It looked natural there
in his hand, the pistol, and to my baffled brain it was my own
behaviour that seemed absurd. Why hadn't I anticipated this?
Was I going to be shot, now? Here of all places, in the middle
of nowhere? Not quite nowhere. The Russian lights, a mere
quarter of a mile away, seemed positively friendly. I was sideways on to Henry, legs spread for balance. Stalemate: surely he
wouldn't fire and risk drawing attention to us? Yes he would,
he was near enough to the trees to make a run for them. I was
the one exposed.

Well, why die for a pat of butter? For a couple of thousand
Marks that weren't mine anyway? "Okay, Henry." I reached
into my pocket and rummaged. A burning sensation: I couldn't
unstick my fingers from something hard, metallic, colder than
my own skin.

Henry's face, watching me, gloating. He was going to kill me
anyway and take whatever I had. His plan all along . . . no, that
made no sense, he'd had ample opportunity to do it earlier.

Nu mal los!—he was trying to make a beckoning gesture with
his free hand, the fingers didn't obey but the gesture said it:
everything you've got. Hand it over. Yes, and then he'd kill
me for sure. Could I fire through my pocket? I'd only miss.

Draw it then, *tu man*, said a voice in my head, a Hamburg voice, do it.

I watched Henry's face as I brought out Isidro. I was afraid but my body was completely calm as though my British Warm were armour plating. Lucky Lecky's magic overcoat.

Looking back it's easy to see the funny side of our showdown on the moonlit ice, a sort of Arctic Western, but even at the time it felt childish, as if we were kids playing. Go for your gun, pardner. Eat lead. I saw the flame at the end of Henry's gun, and continued to observe. Bullet, I'm dead, I thought, as I heard the report. A second shot, from behind me. No, an echo off the far shore. Ricochets of sound everywhere it seemed, we were both done for now. I stared at Henry, at his arm coming up to take aim again.

Given the rate at which news from my body was reaching my brain, I could be full of holes before I even realized it; full of little holes like Uncle Tom in the café, his guts sieved out by shards of glass. I saw that Henry's arm was shaking now as though it held a crippling weight. He fired again, and this time I heard the ping as the bullet scored a track along the ice, well wide. With a shuddering effort he sighted down the barrel for a third attempt. Why couldn't I move? Amid the echoes of the second shot, this one whirred above my head. Enough target practice for God's sake. I brought my hands together and lifted the Browning between them. Alec chuckled in my ear. Damn grenade was frozen, don't you know, I fell on it and the bloody thing never went off. Yes, what if Isidro was frozen solid?

A long death-rattle rasp of engines starting up, further down the lake, they sounded creaturely, I thought, whinnying with cold. We'd woken Ivan.

Henry too was making noise, gasping something, he was scrambling back across the ice, torso lunging forwards, arms outflung and his legs splaying out beneath him like a seabird on a take-off run. Seagull; great slow clumsy thing on Galway beach. I had all the time in the world, and after the rats I'd picked off with Isidro the shot was shamingly easy. I sighted, arms rigid to breaking point, wait any longer and they'd snap like icicles. No need to shoot him in the back, I thought, he's running away. Brain to body; come in, body. No need to shoot. Messages were subject to delay, and my extremities seemed impossibly distant, I could have been the diplodocus in Hamburg zoo for all the speed of my instructions to them. Don't shoot, ran the message, but my dinosaur finger had long since squeezed the trigger. The impact threw Henry forward, one leg going down in the watery gap where slush divided land from ice, and the rest of him following in a flutter of clothes as if he'd turned to dust inside them. No cry as he vanished from sight. The duffle-coat broke the surface, humped, like one of Grandfather's failed inflatables. But no head. Bye Henry.

Headlamp beams. The engines closer now and the first head-lamps sweeping the reeds where Henry lay, lighting the shore and cutting off my retreat. Engines stopping, releasing voices, shouting, yelps. Dogs!

Brain to body: run for the far shore, with any luck they'll assume it's where you came from and you've turned for home, come on run you idiot, don't think just run.

How long had it been? Hours or days, it no longer mattered how long. Same old pines and beechwoods, open spaces, snow-filled furrows, heath. Tangle of roots. Four or five times I'd fallen, more perhaps. Half asleep before I hit the ground . . . so why get up?

I must have got up, I'd been going all day and night now it seemed, the same night or another, no idea how long but I'd survived snowblindness, delirium, days without food, just drinking snow to keep alive, I was in a strange triumphant state, in tears and shouting fit to wake the dead—old Ludolf was emerging now, greeting me in disbelief—when at last I found myself there standing gazing at the Schloss, the sky had cleared and on the lawns pinpoints of light glittered like tiny shards of glass in sugar, under a moon reflected in one of the upper win-dows . . . I was gazing up dazed and triumphant, unaware that I'd contracted pleurisy, perhaps it was pneumonia, aware only that I'd made it, that I'd held on and made it, that I was on the verge of collapse and that . . .

That there was no Ludolf. And no Schloss. That I was gazing up at a great glistening snow-ruin of a wood, at the moon be-tween embracing branches, thin frosty trees huddled together against the cold, a scarecrow graveyard.

That I'd better keep going if I didn't want to end up like them, frozen in place.

That I'd just, that I'd.

My mental and physical condition must have begun to dete-riorate quite soon after the shootout and the border crossing (I was in the Russian zone as soon as I reached the eastern shore of the lake, slipping and sliding and expecting automatic gunfire at any moment, though none came) and afterwards the stages of this process remained clearer in my mind than the journey itself.

Even before the business on the lake my mind had been switching frequencies without warning, Alec's voice was there and Vlad the String's, and Grandfather and Galway Bay, seagulls and inflatables, I was perfectly aware of this, even to the point of thinking that freezing to death might follow the same route as a slow drowning on the surface, holding you afloat for a while on an icy wash of memories.

But at this stage I still rather enjoyed the conditions, I liked the way they stopped me thinking, and by calling my attention back to every painful step the effort of walking interrupted thoughts and reveries alike, and stopped me drifting off altogether; until it finally got so cold that my body issued no further bulletins, there was nothing left to do but think, and walking continued under prior instructions, like the bucket-wielding broom at the service of the sorcerer's apprentice. My face, first merely cold then raw as if a layer of skin had been flayed off by the wind, went numb, a papier-mâché mask of perished, immovable features behind which lurked eyes that could see, a nose that still breathed, a mouth that could exhale freezing breath but no words; a brain still functioning inside dead bandages of flesh. You don't want a report from feet and fingers, believe me, said the brain, you've probably lost some bits and pieces already. As for your nose . . .

My nose felt no more my own than if it had been the remains of a snowball flung between my eyes. My proud Punch hooter—what if I lost a piece of that? At its size you could well afford to. Let it go.

I did; and during the night, as the pain receded—a dangerous sign but I was too buoyant still to care—I entered a new phase. I began to glimpse the Schloss ahead of me, virtually at will.

More of a waking dream than a hallucination, if there's a difference. I wasn't delirious yet, I could still create and control the illusion, in fact that was it precisely: I was moulding what I saw. Which didn't alarm me in the least, it took me back to childhood, when I'd found it so unjust and so infuriating to have to wake up without the toys I owned in my dreams—toys solid enough to the touch the instant before I woke—that I'd worked and worked at it and finally succeeded, by sheer determination it seemed, in waking one morning with a gaudy, unfamiliar,

evidently brand new lead soldier in my hand. Done it! I thought.
I was clutching him so hard that for the rest of the morning my
palm retained the imprint of his metal limbs: he was a flag-
waving Swiss Guard, the nearest thing to a Spanish swordsman
that old O'Malley had been able to find me, and with a warlike
air achieved in time by filing the flag into a rapier. I'd told
Grandfather about my running battle with the dream world and
its unrelenting customs officials; something in this had moved
him to buy me a new toy and put it in my sleeping hands. He
ran the risk, of course, that I'd hope to repeat the trick indefi-
nitely. And when I rushed to show him what I'd salvaged—I did
it! I did it, Grandfather!—from the sea-bed of sleep, Grandfather
solemnly explained that everyone was allowed to do this once
in life. One pick from the dream-treasure chest. (Dear good
man, never granted this himself by the waters of the bay: how
much more loving of him to foster my dreams when his were
barren! And to do it secretly, claiming no thanks, tiptoeing into
my bedroom with the painted figurine and tenderly passing the
baton from his old hands to mine.) I had made my choice—a
good choice too, he added, pretending to examine the Swiss
Guard for the first time—and from now on I must respect my
dreams, learn from them, borrow but not steal: I must make a
life worth dreaming about, rather than dreams to be looted. But
I was seeing row upon row of Swiss Guards, armies of them.
Couldn't I have one more raid? Grandfather shook his head.
Only the once; I must be satisfied. I nodded, while secretly—
what child would have done otherwise?—resisting this, the painful part of his lesson. I had to put it to the test. I managed to
drag several more reluctant toys across the dream-threshold, but
my sense of triumph faded when I recognized the toy in question—and realized I'd sleepwalked to the toy cupboard and back
during the night.

Such crazed determination! Perhaps I should blame Grandfather for that. But eventually I admitted defeat, left dream-treasure
to dreams and never sleepwalked again, to my knowledge, until
my journey into Russian Mecklenburg; and now I needed all
my willpower not to give in to it completely, one step too far in
sleep and I'd belong to the dream world for good; now it was I,
stiff-limbed and leaden, held in the grip of an unyielding landscape, who might never wake.

Snow on my face, on my tongue. Snowing again. So dark I
couldn't see it but I could feel it on my cheeks. Footsteps in

crusty snow, my own. Steady now, skirt the woods and stick to open ground. Less likely to trip and fall.

Sooner or later I'd have to sleep. Scott and Byrd, heroes of my childhood reading . . . how did they keep going, the old polar explorers? How did Kuno von Brüel keep going, on the retreat from Moscow? I could remember everything else but that, remember Peter telling us how some of Kuno's companions ran off into the woods, where friendly-seeming peasant women took them in, fed them broth and murdered them in their beds; how other soldiers fell asleep around the regimental bivouac, in the snow, fell asleep and never woke again, and how the living then ate the dead . . . how Kuno took part; and Peter's voice . . . we have a good expression, *über seinen Schatten springen* . . . after such things, can a man jump over his own shadow? Spring over his *Schatten*? Jump his own shadow?

I didn't have one here, a shadow, not while it snowed. Left it in sunny Spain. Come to that, I could have slept on in Spain and saved myself all this trouble. Was it for this I'd been woken by the brush fire in the ravine, woken by the heat it must have been as the fire camp up the hill towards me? Only to land up in this hell of ice where sleep was fatal too, not so very different really, after a time even the snow falling felt like little cat-licks of fire, they helped keep me awake along with the thoughts that came with them, the fiery cat-licks, a teasing foretaste of hellfire, I'd killed a man outright this time.

Snow on my tongue, and Maggie's wedding in the little church at Tempzin . . . Tempzin of the box hedges and their sweet-urine smell, Maggie's wedding where—it was the candles!—out of nowhere I'd remembered going to Mass with Grandfather. And now the host as I stick out a thirsty tongue to receive the burning round of snow.

Embarrassment is a much underestimated force in human affairs. I'd be willing to bet that people have put an end to themselves because they were too embarrassed to pull back from doing it, once they'd committed themselves to the idea and invested everything in their despair. Better death than exposure as a self-pitying fraud. For the opposite reason (I'd invested all too little in despair) but just as effectively, embarrassment kept me alive—the sheer embarrassment of my unreadiness to die. I wasn't ready to review my life and I knew this would follow if I admitted to myself how near I was to dying of sheer exhaustion, of exposure to the elements. I'd find myself doing the accounts, happy memories and otherwise, the shameful ones too. I was determined to do nothing of the sort, it was more than death was worth.

And the hallucinations, when they came, weren't at all like life flashing before a drowning man's eyes, thank goodness. They were riddles carved out of ice and branch and shadow, fantastic script bared by the snow on glistening bark as dank and black as ink, woodland turned skeleton and casting up its meaning. Dead or watching? That was the question! At a distance I could glimpse gigantic figures frozen to death standing up and pointing the way to Brüel, sometimes animal shapes tall as the trees and once a frostbound gingerbread cottage which seemed curiously two-dimensional, as if incised in crystal, right down to the motionless wisp of cross-hatched smoke emerging from the chimney, and giving me a vivid and frightening sense of having stepped into my mother's world of glass. I saw clearly that the small wood or spinney I was skirting was in fact a bowl Mother had breathed into life with her usual patience, using a snow-tipped diamond point, the stippling so tiny it seemed like foggy breath, and I was in the bowl myself in a sense left unclear by the hallucination (I was afraid it might shatter at any moment, fragile as the plume of my own breath, and aspirate me out of existence). In fact that was the adventure, to find out whether I was in the bowl or outside it, or caught in the engraved crystal which formed it; that's to say in the engraving yet free to move— or not: this too was for me to discover.

But how? And what if I made a wrong move? I'd end up like the wisp of smoke, presumably, transfixed. Yet this was my own hallucination, I was setting the riddle, which meant I knew the answer. I was magus and pupil, both; much good this knowledge did me. How to proceed? The sensation was one I'd encountered in dreams, Alice-in-Wonderland dreams, the kind where everyone appears to know the rules, except you; and where, as in my hallucination, it has to be that way to maintain the pretence that the dream isn't your own creation but an adventure in which you find yourself taking part. Which is surely why so many dreams are like awkward social situations, or bouts of amnesia—you have to pretend to know who people are, what's going on, even who you are, until you can find out what everyone else seems to know already; what the dream itself seems to know. Or is it only to me, after twenty years in disguise, that dreams appear largely to consist of bluff? That and the fear of being found out, or worse, of being found to have forgotten everything? I doubt it; if dreams are a kind of improvisation then any dreamer capable of monitoring this (or rather any dreamer incapable of surrendering that watching-self) will suffer the terror of the improviser, the actor, the spy: that you'll become aware of a silence on stage—my God, how long has it lasted?—and everyone staring at you. You've forgotten your lines.

I had some help with my hallucination, mysteriously given, this too was like a dream, in the form of two pieces of information. Firstly that glass was a kind of solidified breath and remained glass only while time stood still (at first an unhelpful and alarming piece of information). Secondly that this was no ordinary bowl of Mother's, it was a punchbowl, and I was plainly conscious of the significance of this—it was profound and moving at the time and impenetrably silly when I remembered it later: the message of the bowl was that I was fated to the nickname long before Worthing Pier and Ellie at my side; I was Punchborn, in fact. And this useless announcement was what I was to bring back from the nether regions, from Mother's glassy woods.

I also knew that I was in the bowl in the sense that my life was in it, it spoke my life like a frieze—the wood, the spinney spoke it; the spinney that was crystal, and a bowl—and if I kept walking around the wood and keeping to the open field I could read my entire story until it curved round on itself and began again. But was I allowed to? If I walked widdershins, counter-clockwise—yes, making time stand still; that seemed to be the clue—could I walk round it (I'd be reading my life backwards, and that was right, my mind assured me: when I got to the beginning I'd begin again), or was I in it, waiting to live it? Take a step and see; and another; praise God I could, I could walk round it, and there was my entire life (if only I could read it, it was splendid and I appreciated it greatly although it made no sense at all) inscribed in its crystalline forms, in twigs and desiccated bracken, in forms and figures hidden among the leaves and in their own intricate cuneiform, in bird's foot scrawl along the snow-topped branches, in the filigree of frost-etched spider's webs, my story coiling around the wood until it came full circle on itself and, as I would, began again; beginning again: that was the meaning; if I kept walking round the wood, if I kept walking, if I could.

Whether this was a short interlude or a prolonged one I don't know, any more than I know how long the whole trek lasted.

Several days and nights, most likely. Could it have been more than two? How much longer can one survive out in the open, at those temperatures, on a bellyful of snow? (A lot longer, I later gathered from newspaper accounts of people lost in snow, though most of these dug a pit, saved their energy, and sat there waiting to be found.)

Thinking back I wonder if my vagueness about just how far it was to Brüel was entirely innocent. After all I had no mental image of my future with Maggie, none, and subconsciously at least I may have wanted to postpone the moment of arrival. In some respects I'd equipped myself well for the journey, warm coat, weapon, and sandwiches (courtesy of Alec, Uncle Tom, and Karin); plus a guide (expendable); in other respects poorly, footwear for instance, and no map. Perhaps as on the train to Hamburg I was simply giving hostages to fate: if I came through it all safely, despite some piece of deliberate negligence, that would mean the gods not only forgave me but approved, applauded. It looked a pretty-safe bet when I set out, I wasn't risking much more than wet feet and having to ask for directions. By the time the weather had tipped the scales I wound up paying dearly for divine approval, and the cost of the last stretch of the journey is still with me, the physical cost. From the Schaalsee to the Schloss: a mere thirty-odd miles on the map, fifty kilometres. But that's as the crow flies, not as the lost traveller stumbles, certainly not as he goes round in circles in the snow; round and round the same spinney under the fatuous impression of undoing a spell and escaping the threat of being frozen to the spot.

Fifty kilometres. The terrain is rolling farmland with hills and dales but no climbs to speak of, and in ordinary circumstances you'd hike it in a day. A good hard day, with lunch halfway, in Schwerin. I never knew where I was; I just toiled on, waiting to see which would crack first, my legs, my lungs, or my mind. I have no memory of Schwerin's twin lakes, which lay directly across my path, the lakes I used to visit with Peter, and where we buried the last of Alec's bombs. It doubles the distance again if I strayed far enough to north or south to miss the lakes altogether, and I can't believe I threaded my way between them along the ancient toll road causeway where Peter's ancestors used to fleece the travelling public; a road now seething with Russians, surely I'd have noticed that, or they'd have noticed me, a wild-eyed blue-nosed fellow with ice and frozen snot in his beard—hardly a respectable citizen going about his business. I'd been warned to keep clear of roads because of police block-ades, where identity papers would be demanded. And I avoided all signs of human traffic so successfully that later, when I was desperate for help, I couldn't even find a farm track whichever direction I took.

If they were frozen harder than the Schaalsee I may have walked clean across one of the Schwerin lakes of course, without realizing, under the impression that it was an immense flat field. Hard to tell when the horizon is bounded by fog, nothing but whiteness above, below, and all about. It would explain why I couldn't find a track, much less a farm.

What I feared most was the moment when I couldn't think any more. Thinking was becoming hard. Use your loaf, Thurgo; by all means, but where were the words? I felt as if speech itself was being erased from my mind. White everywhere you looked. White feet. White earth, white sky. It wasn't just the cold, it was the featurelessness that seemed to be finishing me off. In the next Ice Age would words survive? An universal whiteness buries all, page after blank page of snowfall effacing our prints. Save the word and stay alive.

Begin with A. Algid. Algid? Like a book falling on my head. Grandfather's shelves. Algid what? Algid saw a bear, the bear saw Algid, the bear was bulgid, the bulge was Algid.

Try again. Algy saw a bear, the bear saw Algy, the bear was bulgy, the bulge was Algy!

Repeat aloud. Try thinking now, at the same time.

Algy bears in Mecklenburg?

Must be.

Algy bulgy, argy bargy.

Algy balgy, Mecklenbargy.

Here comes something. Beginning with A. Aeroplane lying on its back in the snowfields. Not dreaming! Huge aluminum plane belly up, cockpit underneath it, tail fin buried in the snow. Don't touch, burn your skin off. Surprised look of it, as if still flying, frozen in mid-loop-the-loop. Bird lost in fog, emerging upside down, astonished. Would it fall out of the sky?

Grey falling. Not another night, please not another. Hurts so to breathe . . .

And now there were two sets of footsteps, I could hear them distinctly. A voice, *Buck up, Flight!* and Pottsy snapping his knuckles at me. Go away, I shouted, you killed Denis! And for the first time since his death I wept bitterly for Face, for his fine profiled nose, his pained mouth, his hunter's head. The footsteps were gaining and it was Peter overtaking me, skating along in his wind-walker's stride. *Weiter, Junge!* Keep going! Peter hectoring me, repeat after me The Shirt, the story of Count Archibald the Douglas as the Scottish call him, in German *Graf Doo-glas*, Count Archibald the pilgrim who comes to beg the king's forgiveness for his brother's treachery and to redeem his name. He struggles in his rusty suit of mail, say it with me now, *er sah in Wald und Feld hinein*, he saw into the woods and fields, he saw within and closed his eyes, *die Augen fielen ihm zu* . . .

No, mustn't close them, Peter. Long as I can think. Can think as long as I can see. German I spy, *mit mein* little eye . . . beginning with A. *Atem*, all I can see: my own breath. Ahtem, ahhtem, every breath ahhhtem. Hurts like glass ripping inside. Think! *Atem*, gender . . . masculine, *der Atem*. Or is it? *Der die das*. Ahhhhtem. Help me Peter, help me think. Can't breathe for pain.

Der Atem, Richard, masculine of course. It's no harder than Latin, *Junge*, didn't you learn your *hic haec hoc* in English public school? For a young man not so hard, I think. German is the more romantic language, Richard, you can think of this when you learn your *der die das*. For instance, time is feminine, *die Zeit. Die Stunde* too, the hour. But the girl, *das Mädchen*, is neuter. *Das Weib*, the woman, neuter. There is a logic here, you may not understand it but it understands *you. Die Frau*, the woman as a wife, is feminine. Like Maggie *das Mädchen* isn't yet a *Frau* so she is still a neuter, and *das Weib* too is not a wife but woman in the abstract. Now. The path, *der Pfad*, is masculine. Likewise *der Weg*, the way. So—*der, die, das*: the way, the hour, the woman. Are you with me? *Der Weg, die Zeit, das Weib*. Yes?

Final stage: three memories, the last three, they make most sense in the following order. The man with the jack, the bodies, the bear (myself).

First the man with the jack. I must have stumbled upon a road, and followed it—no recollection of this, just the stationary truck and the acetylene lamp, the man crouched, changing a wheel by its light. I was a pretty threatening sight I suppose, six and a half feet of frozen Rasputin silently tottering towards him out of the dark. He lifted the jack to drive me off. I don't recall any blows but I must have fallen over, I remember lying in the road amazed that I could still cry, that tears would come, unfrozen.

And some other part of me finding it comic. Going to stand for it, Thurgo, or take it lying down? Flat out in the middle of a frozen little German road, or Russian road, lying there dying in tears of self-pity. No memory of this either but I must have made it to my feet, I don't know what happened to the truck or the man. I'm in the piggery. I must have walked along the road. Perhaps it saved my life, the piggery and its shelter, but unless this too was a hallucination it had human bodies in it, a family long since frozen to death, pray God in their sleep because their faces were gnawed, unrecognizable, hands completely gone and parts of leg and arm and torso, but the job had been left unfinished. Plenty of wolves in Mecklenburg and they must have been starving now. Or dogs? Bears perhaps. The bulge was Algy. It wasn't me that ate their hands and faces, that much I know. Not that I was too finicky, I was quite hungry enough. I touched them, the bodies. They were ice.

I thought this too was funny, I remember. Frozen food. How did Kuno's comrades manage, though? First thaw your dead friend . . . hilarious, it was. Let *me* thaw him. No he's mine, I thaw him first.

Now I was standing in the street in the middle of the village and no-one wanted to come out of their house. I'm a bear, I wanted to explain, I've become a bear, I've come to confess that I've failed in the forest, I'm ready, I've come to take off my fur. Please someone take me in.

Ludmilla was her name, I was told afterwards. An old woman, very circumspect. (I can see her quite clearly, stooped, with grey hair in a bun, grey face, long ratty nose and dark moustache hairs at the corners of her mouth; and the inside of her house, I can see that too, dirty unpainted wood, cobwebby as a garden shed.) She had the courage to take in a fearsome stranger—I really was a thing from the bogs now—and the kindness of course, the simple human kindness, unremarkable you might think. But it took courage. From what she kept repeating there was an organization called People's Control or perhaps People-Control, which sent representatives round all the villages to account for food consumption. Everyone kept accounts, down to the last rationed ounce. (Pitiful rations too; worse than ours in Hamburg, despite what Karin had so piously believed.) If anyone was harbouring or feeding strangers, People's Control would soon find out, the old girl said; she didn't dare give me more than a slice of bread, but I could drink as much soup as I liked.

Slowly did it, a sip every few minutes. And then . . . then didn't I collapse and sleep for days? I longed to, but my will was clenched in spasm. My mind too, it wouldn't give up its ghost companions. As I thawed I read murder in the old woman's face. I knew I was among friends, I was a man being rescued, no longer a bear surrendering his kingdom. But the human part of me was locked in Peter's voice, I was Kuno von Brüel and all my comrades had been lured into farms where smiling Russians fed them *schchi*, the peasant broth, and stabbed them in their sleep. Broth I'd accept but not a bed. Not a chair either. No, I stood. Stood and kept watching her, I wasn't going to turn my back. When she came close I wanted to growl, but couldn't. When the bowl was empty I stepped back out into the algid hell, that Algy's hell where my bearhood awaited, a frozen death. Old Ludmilla was begging me to stay in the warm. Smile, you murderous bitch, I thought. Smile, you don't fool me. I'm safer out there.

And so I was. Too many people would have seen the old girl take me in, they were peeping from their icebound windows as she came out into the street and led the bear-Mensch indoors. They would have reported her, Ludolf assured me later, unless she'd informed the authorities at once, if not that very night then first thing in the morning, while I slept. I'd have woken to an official welcoming committee. So Kuno saved me, in a sense; or Peter rather, Peter's voice; like other kinds of madness perhaps all hallucinations come equipped with a key to survival in the everyday world, if you can find its hiding place, this key. It's there somewhere in the house of illusions, but of course if you stay too long it may be the last thing you see. By then you've forgotten the way out.

And I had another reason to step back into my arctic nightmare rather than do the sensible thing, and sleep. I knew where I was now, geographically. On this Kuno and I were one. Our Schloss was within reach, we knew it when we heard the name of the village from the old woman's lips: Weisser Krug, "White Jug"—the butt of jokes and etymological forays on the walks Peter and I had taken in the Friedrichswald woods. From here I knew my way, even in the snow. The road I must have been on since the piggery and before: the old post road—my inner compass was working!—that led through Weisser Krug led past the Schloss.

The stars were out and the sky really had cleared just as it had in my earlier, wish-fulfilling vision, when I'd pictured myself standing before Schloss Brüel, dazed but triumphant—yes, as I was now, standing there in reality and gazing up at the moon reflected in one of the snow-lined upper windows, a moon haloed as if it too were frosted over.

From the road the first thing I'd seen was the gatehouse, bless it . . . wonderful to come upon, looming out of the darkness like a ship at anchor, as it always did, with a lamp lit in the captain's cabin. I could have stopped there, turned aside and knocked at the door; but I felt as if I'd come halfway round the world, I wanted the Schloss itself. Face front, finish the race. Main entrance for me.

Past trees, past lawns sprinkled with shards of glass, just as I'd seen them in my delirium, snowfields full of winking facets. Harbour lights, waving me on.

And there it squatted, uncannily the same, the little old layer cake with its dark horizontal stripes of terracotta, and the pale turrets above, all of it sweetly, festively outlined in snow. Just as I'd conjured it, in my mind. I was home. I'd never felt that so much in my life, not even in boarding school dreams of Fold Farm.

I suppose I'd put so much into getting there that I couldn't afford to feel anything else, at that moment. I'd put more into it than I knew. I did have pleurisy, as I'd predicted (I should have settled for pneumonia), and one lung had collapsed, it was a useless flapping bladder in my chest. The other lung would have to be drained and my chest treated with decoctions of filthy-tasting leaves, then wrapped in stinking herbal salves. One remedy after another, until I wasn't sure who was fighting for possession of my body, the fever and I or the succession of head-scarved witches Ludolf summoned to my bedside. They quarrelled over me with their competing potions. In the end I was lucky—everyone agreed on this if on nothing else—to escape with my life.

Escape I did, though my lungs, as every winter reminds me, have never fully recovered. The re-inflated one is liable to collapse again, and various extremities exhibit partial atrophy, so-called. Sensation in them comes and goes. Also, by the time I reached the Schloss three of my toes were already beyond recall, two on my right foot and one of my left, lost to frostbite.

A steep price for a walk in the woods. And these days when I get trouble from lungs or feet or elsewhere I remember it all with bewilderment. Why did I do it? At times I've thought I understood why, then memories surge up (I'm crawling out of the Malaga ravine again, I'm walking over rutted snowfields) and I find that I'm still asking myself who or what it was that kept me plodding forwards through that long blind journey. Adored or not, Maggie seems a curiously insufficient answer.

What, then?

During the 'Fifties I came to know a Frau Professor Doktor Anna-Maria von Doderer, socially that is (she was a distant cousin of Karin's mother Frau Posener, and Karin herself was for a while one of the Dodderer's patients), socially rather than on a paying basis, despite her eagerness to have me as a patient. Unless they have outsize couches for outsize neurotics, I'd have had to lie folded in a foetal position, not an appealing thought. We took lunch regularly at the Four Seasons, and the Dodderer of course concluded, like Peter before her, that Mother, *die Mutter*, was the thread leading me through the Algy's labyrinth of my life; it was for her I'd made the journey and its sacrifices. In view of the fact that my mother gave me away when I was a speechless infant it was a conclusion readily to hand; also in view of the fact that I couldn't help flirting with the Dodderer, who was a very sexy eighty indeed, and almost exactly the same age as my mother. Faced with her insinuations I'd protest once again that as a form of personal grail my mother's nature was too coarse (more of a beer mug really, more Weisser Krug than silver chalice) and somehow too familiar to resonate for me with echoes of a lost paradise; I felt I knew exactly who and what my mother was, as if I'd spent my whole life with her. She was both devious and frank, brutal and mystical, I explained, as only a Catholic peasant can be—to be truthful I should have said she was a landed farmer's daughter, but a peasant at heart. She went to the quick of things, and since she never listened she couldn't be flattered or distracted. In that sense, I told the Dodderer, she cleared the decks, followed her own imperatives without a trace of guilt—it was all God's will—and left me intact. What was there about her I could possibly want to retrieve?

The Dodderer would merely shrug: if not this mother of yours then an ideal mother or simply mothering itself. That was my goal. I pointed out that I had never wanted to be mothered by my partners. Ah, precisely! Hungry as I was for mothering, I punished my lovers, sighed the Dodderer, by denying them the opportunity to mother me. Why? Because they weren't *die Mutter* herself, the unique original no matter how frightful, and to allow them a mother's role would end a search in which I, Reinhard the inconsolable, would accept no counterfeit. And so no comfort. Then she'd smile wickedly, showing teeth almost as bad as mine.

I could have added: my mother was in her forties when she had me and why else have I been attracted to older, crumbly skin, the frailness and the grain of it? Like the skin on the Dear Nose's rice pudding. Or it may have been her sago or her tapioca pudding, they've all faded into one.

Let it be mother, then; I never tried to say this to the Dodderer, who hated all mystical mumbo-jumbo, but let me try now—let it be mother, but in the widest possible sense. I dare say that like the Schloss all destinations have something motherly about them, serenely waiting for us, anticipating us. If the pilgrim in us all is simply looking for his earthly mother then this earth is a less mysterious place than I've understood it to be, less of a conjuring trick, and surely what drives us forward is the sense that somewhere behind the signs and illusions lurks a mother reality, waiting and watching—(not something you could sense, I would guess, in the Dod's consulting room, panelled as Karin described it, and smelling of old carpets and furniture-cleaning fluid, where I imagined myself bedding the Dodderer on her own couch, in a thoroughly Oedipal reunion). No; no, what drives us on is always out of doors, not at the mercy of the light switch with its mocking on and off but out there in the light that modulates incessantly, instant by instant, steadily modulating and reiterating time, time, sovereign time and time dissolved by sheer recurrence, the time that was there before us and whose indifference alone can release us from the time that cramps our lives, time which is surely what every traveller wants to locate. Every place that is sacred to us, every place worth a pilgrimage is really there waiting for us (as we imagine it to be) like the first place of all, the world we were disgorged into. The world already waiting when we were belched up into it. It's not the place itself that matters, nor the people lodged so vividly before it, too much so sometimes, in Peter's phrase too vividly to be entirely real. The place is neither here nor there. Wherever it is, our chosen place, it's simply time's face staring back at us—*die Zeit* as Peter would say, time feminine—that's whom we're hunting like our own personal source of the Nile, whom we see in every dream of home: old Mother Time.

Her features were what I'd fought all this way to see, and I must have fancied I saw them as I gazed up lovingly at the Schloss, proudly too, as though it was mine. Here I was, I'd caught time by the tail. Half crazy with the cold, I wanted to prolong the moment in all its elation. I gave a thought to Master Piloot the architect and the hundreds of years his work had lasted, old Dutch Piloot who must have stood here in the front pasture with a sketchbook in one hand and compasses in the other, planning it all, mapping out the site. J.B. Parr too, whoever he was, Englishman (younger, as I imagined him) adding sixteenth-century curlicues to this dear funny building. Parr Towers, Alec used to call it, I hadn't remembered that in years. I gazed up in the conviction that it was the Schloss I really loved, not Maggie or Peter but the Schloss as a glorified Fold Farm, part farm part fortress, smelling at once of dung and antiques. Dung and antiques! The smell awaiting me in those old corridors.

It was then, while I was gazing up at the moon reflected in one of the upper windows, that I realized it wasn't reflected in the window. It wasn't reflected at all. It was shining through the window. Through it? Then it wasn't a reflection; no; there was no glass in the window. No back wall beyond it. Nothing but sky.

I continued to stare, caught in the weightless confusion before you realize the landslide's under way and your life is changing forever in that instant; the moment you touch a loved one's face and realize they're too deeply still for sleep, they're gone.

Not a reflection but the moon itself shining through the window. The Schloss was a shell, a derelict façade. Gutted, empty. There was no Schloss, only a stone and terracotta mask, the moonlight profiling the snow on the tile and windowledge and lending the building substance like a draughtsman's cartoon; when in fact all that was left was a kind of hoarding, a hollow mockery Slosh, fronting a heap of snow-covered débris. My mind took pity, letting the tiredness hit me all at once as if someone had thrown a weighted cloak over my shoulders, dragging me down.

"Hal-lo?" came a voice, a familiar voice, old and querulous now. "Ja hal-lo?" It was all that saved me from blacking out.

* * *

I have no memory of when it was that Ludolf recognized me or how long it took before he told me about Maggie and the rest of the family. I couldn't speak to say who I was, let alone ask for news. He must have told me soon enough I suppose, but it's gone completely, unlike the earlier moment when I realized the Schloss was a ruin.

They were all dead. All of them, except old Ludolf, dead. But there, you see, not even saying it gives it finality, I don't think I believe I wasn't entirely surprised, I knew it was true and that I wasn't being lied to, and at the same time there was nothing in the world that could help me believe it, not even a body, because those you love can always be dead and cold and still fully alive elsewhere.

Peter dead; as I knew, though there was more to discover about the manner of his death, things I wish I'd never known. Old Agnetha dead, Peter's mother. Maggie and Peter's child, their only child, a little boy named Egon after Peter's soldier father, dead. Maggie dead. And the house derelict, nothing left, no staircase, no kitchens, no bedrooms with framed orange birds and fat wobbly eiderdowns, no Greek and Roman busts, no figurines, no flags no breastplate no portraits, no Rittersaal at all, no long refectory table. No Maggie.

They were buried at Tempzin where Maggie and Peter had been married. Or rather there was a family headstone at Tempzin and everyone's name was on it. I didn't see it until weeks later. Peter's parents were both inscribed on the grave in Gothic script, with Peter and Maggie's names below theirs, and then Egon their son. But only Peter and his father are buried there. Agnetha, Maggie, and the boy were ash, Ludolf explained, ash blown over an East Prussian field and (as I pictured it) soon leached into it, an unavailing human mulch dissolved by rain and snow.

Perhaps I could have pinpointed the field, with time and research. I could still do it, or I could try. But what for? All my enquiries have corroborated the story Ludolf told me in '48, which with regard to Maggie's death is substantially all anyone can be sure of.

Sippe is an ancient German word for family; put it together with *Haft*, the taking of a prisoner or hostage, and you have *Sippenhaft*, the name given to a law under which a traitor's family was arrested by the Gestapo, the children in many instances given away to other families under strictest secrecy and re-named to hide their shame forever; the traitors' sisters, wives, and mothers dispatched to concentration camps. Maggie had been allowed to take Egon with her for medical reasons, fraudulent ones, Ludolf said, but they enabled her to keep him, on condition that as soon as the boy was stronger he would be separated from his mother. This stratagem gave Maggie another year with her son—he wasn't yet three years old when the Gestapo came for them. A fatal stratagem, and Ludolf cried the first time he told me this; we both cried every time I made him describe it. It meant that Egon was still with Maggie and Agnetha early in '45 when they were evacuated before the advancing Russian armies, and sent by train to a camp further west.

They never reached it. The train was strafed by Allied planes, almost certainly British, though this too I haven't cared to try and confirm. They either knew or guessed that the train contained more than civilians. That is, I'd rather think they knew the Nazis were transferring ammunition and explosives under cover of civilian evacuation transport—because if the Allied pilots didn't know this then they're guilty of cold-blooded massacre. The train went up like a rolling ammo dump, which in effect it was.

Years later I saw a film in which a pair of Spitfires attacked a train. Or it may have been a pair of Messerschmitts, I don't remember anything at all about the story, just the incident with the train, which stops to let the passengers jump out and take cover. As they do, the planes continue to rake them with bullets. You see a woman crouched in the shadow of the train, and she turns to her husband and child—a little girl, in the film—to see that the husband is dead and the girl has only half a face, dead too. The woman rushes out onto the road that runs along the railway track and stands there alone as the aircraft wheel lazily and come back for another strafing run. Everyone else is hiding under the train now but she stands there in the empty road, right in the path of the aircraft, shouting, "Here! Here I am! Take *me*!"

The scene made such an impression on me that I became quite obsessed with it (at the time I remember I left the cinema and wandered the streets full of nausea and trying unsuccessfully to be sick), and it merged with the little I know of Maggie's death to the point where it became her death scene for me. Once I even told some strangers over a meal that this was how Maggie had died, before realizing with embarrassment that it was the film version I was telling; my shame wasn't for Maggie I'm afraid, it was for me, in case one of my listeners had seen the film and took me for a liar and a fantasist.

But that is how I see Maggie's death, even though the woman

in the film didn't die at all, and the force of the scene was that
the aircraft bullets spattered on either side of her, leaving her
cruelly alive; or perhaps it's because she didn't die—as a way of
making Maggie's death a lie—that I've given Maggie the death
the woman wanted but never got. At least it's a death of her
own, not just extinction, a choking expiry in a storm of heat and
terror, trying to save her son. . . . That was the image I couldn't
bear, my stomach churns, bile rises, I have to think of something
else.

My convalescence was a long one, I called it that in my mind
because that's what it was but it was also a kind of breakdown,
a breaking through of everything I'd been trying to keep at bay
by frenzied movement, ever since Spain. (Anything rather than
face reality, it seems: in order to immobilize myself at last I'd
had to sacrifice three toes and almost kill myself in the process.)
Recuperation, really; convalescence makes it sound like the kind
of thing you pay through the nose for, at a Swiss sanatorium. It
was rather different at the Hof.

This was the little low farmhouse where former Schloss Brüel
retainers spent their declining years, or had done when I'd visited it ten years earlier with Peter and Maggie. A chalet for
dwarves I thought it, then, never imagining I'd have to try and
fit my huge frame into one of their rooms. The few surviving
retainers were still there along with an assortment of the elderly
homeless, under Ludolf's care. What had happened to his own
family he wouldn't tell me. It was a closed subject, one of several. The refugees at the Hof were his new family, and his devotion to them was as untiring as his service had been at the
Schloss. They were hardly nobility, the Hof-dwellers, but Ludolf treated them like honoured guests. Two or three of them
were in worse case than I was; after months of wandering the
forests, when the war ended, they had no idea who they were at
all. They couldn't say where they came from or even their own
names. It could have happened to me—I'd been lucky that three
years after its virtual destruction Ludolf still couldn't bring himself to move away from the Schloss, that he insisted on living in
the gatehouse.

It was there I spent my first, comatose night. The next morning I was wrapped in blankets, hoisted still unconscious onto
four kindly shoulders like a corpse, and taken to the more se-
cluded Hof. Someone must have provided me with a huge
coarse-woven nightshirt, I had a mass of stale bedding on top
of me and a kind of pallet underneath me on the floor, up in the

attic. Presumably they'd given up trying to wedge me into one of their beds. No light, no window I don't think, it's the candlelight I remember; I was only sporadically conscious and what I can reconstruct of that time belongs largely to the spring and early summer when I was beginning to hobble around again. Until then, with the help of the aged inhabitants there and the doctoring crones from the village, Ludolf kept me hidden, secretly cared for, and fed, undetected by People's Control. Though such were his resources that I wouldn't have been surprised to discover that he was People's Control itself, the spider at the heart of the whole Mecklenburger web.

I could still remember him catching me stealing Branntwein at the Schloss, when I was eighteen; his expression as I'd translated "nightcap" directly into German. "Nachtmütze!" And the gleam in his eye as though he somehow approved, even wanted me to misbehave. He looked splendid as ever, silver-haired, gaunt of face, a little stooped; seventy now, and all the more aristocratic in his manner. The blessed Ludolf as we used to call him in his butler days—Ludolf was a saint's name, Peter had explained, a saint and a crusader. The blessed Ludolf: did he understand what I was doing here, my attachment to Maggie, that is? He knew me only as the younger brother of Peter and Maggie's friend Alec. Yet even before he knew any of the details of my life Ludolf had informed the others at the Hof that I was the late Countess' brother, from England. A good disguise, to elicit their help in hiding me and tending to me. More than that, an apt disguise; and not only because I was indeed Maggie's brother-in-law. Ludolf watched me crying as we talked about Maggie. He knew.

A knock on the door of my windowless room under the roof meant a visit from Ludolf, with or without a village potionmonger to inflict clammy herbal compresses. I must have smelt like something recently disinterred, with all the moss and leaves they strapped to my chest. Ludolf said a doctor might have felt obliged to inform the authorities about me. These village women, by contrast, were to be trusted. To this day I don't know if they saved me or merely prolonged my illness, which seemed to go on and on until I felt I was living in some echoing bronchial cavern that I was trying to cough to destruction, like Samson pulling down the temple. It gave Ludolf and me plenty of time together. He wanted something from me. I remember sensing this while I was still feverish. I'd wake to his voice telling me about the war years and the Russian nightmare that followed.

His eyes full of tears. His sighs, "Ach Gott, Herr Thurgo . . ."
The tales washed over me, but I found it comforting to be called
by my name again. I'd let myself be lulled to sleep and then
wake to his face examining me, silent now, the candle close to
my face, searching for what? Something more than a listener.

But I was certainly that, if he needed one. I didn't mind how
many times he described the day of Peter's arrest, or told me
with what dignity Maggie had spent the hours before her own
arrest; or conjured up for me the last days of the Schloss as the
British and Russian armies approached from either side and any
Mecklenburger who hadn't already fled lived by the wireless,
waiting to hear whose vassal he was going to be this time. Listening to one of Ludolf's stories I would drift off and the footsteps on the stairs outside would be Molly's, coming up the dark
stairs to my study in the attic of the little house in Parsifal Road,
where I sat among the piles of musty, beribboned papers, in the
old red armchair by the gas fire. Knock on the door. Elevenses:
a cup of tea, an apple and a biscuit. Tea at four. Knock on the
door. Supper at eight, don't be late. Or if I wasn't in my fever-
dream I might see that the knock on the door had brought soup
and sour bread with sugarbeet or the metallic rutabaga jam I
learnt to crave. The coffee too, not Muckefuck, some other
roasted root. Grandfather's frugal table, boarding school meals
and wartime rations: I was well prepared for strange food. Soup
and jam and Ludolf's voice out of the darkness . . . horrors he'd
seen, prams by the roadside with frozen children inside, bodies
abandoned in the road, pounded into the snow, dead horses
everywhere too; and Agnetha's herd roaring in the throes of
starvation, you could hear them for miles around. Mecklenburgers had had it easy during the war itself, he told me, no bombing, plenty of food, making the starvation and the brutality that
followed all the more shocking. With no idea of the atrocities
their own soldiers had committed in Russia, they'd welcomed
the invaders. In return their women were raped and killed, their
animals slaughtered and their bedrooms littered with the bloody
carcases, human and animal. Ach Gott ach Gott, Herr Thurgo.
Before Ludolf's eyes one old woman had thrown herself against
a file of Russian soldiers, pleading for death: "Please, soldier. . . ." Ludolf was clearly haunted by her and soon I was
too, pierced by the suspicion that this was Ludolf's wife, although his face forbade me to ask.

In my dreams I allowed myself a funeral at last, with mourners. Molly and Wilf, dry-eyed. I woke if not to Ludolf's voice

then to a withered crone with a compress. Coffee and a rutabaga sandwich. Once more I saw Molly going through my things, I saw little Wilf there too and let myself cry with them now, though my shame kept me from speaking, from saying, "Here! Here I am!" Candlelight. Ludolf was studying my features, as if to trace some sign of doom, or recovery. I slept.

". . . *zu dem stillen Landstädtchen Brüel, in ein breites von niederen sandigen Höhen umgebenes Wiesenthal eingebettet,"* so reads the reference in a little book Karin found for me, a 1930s gazetteer: thence to Brüel, it says, a quiet hamlet, population under two thousand, *"eingebettet"* which is to say bedded into, lying in the embrace of, a valley of broad and pleasant meadows. Light sandy soil. *"Umgeben,"* "given round" by low hills, low hills all around. *Paradiesisch*, adds the gazetteer, a paradisal place, where the fields and forests greet the eye much as they must have done in mediaeval times, the farms and the barns hidden away on the edge of remote clearings and kept profitable only by unceasing labour, by a devotion to the land which will not, the author remarks sternly, survive sharing the work with farm machinery. Backbreaking work, that was the price he didn't mention, but you could see the love in the way the fields were carved and turned and tidied. Cultivated, husbanded by the people of Brüel, not just farmed. And their reward was to belong.

No doubt spring is always *paradiesisch* in Brüel, but in '48 it was exceptional, the earth was returning to life from a winter that had seemed as if it would never end. So was I, emerging from my hibernation under the eaves of the Hof. I'd had to face the loss of the toes, amputated weeks earlier when gangrene set in. It was done while I was drugged for the purpose, Ludolf explained, and oblivious. No-one asked me, no-one told me—I hadn't even realized that the bandages on my feet hid lasting damage, and it was a shock. Walking had to be relearned in earnest, with a stick provided by Ludolf. It had been Peter's, and before Peter his father Egon's. This noble cane had survived the looting of the family valuables only because it hadn't been in the Schloss, but was having repairs done to the inlaid ebony handle, where some ivory had come loose. It was a princely stick. But something in me wanted nothing to do with it. A touching memento of Peter, daily to hand: why didn't I want it? I cut myself a length of ash in the Friedrichswald and used that instead. I have it still, though it looks no more than it is, a brittle dirty old piece of sapling.

I found I had a similar reaction to Schloss Brüel when I saw the place again after my weeks at the Hof. I wanted none of it. And when I think of all the love and longing I'd felt . . . but it was the same with Fold Farm too, I remember, after it had burned down—or been burned, by Alec and the unscrupulous lawyer. Once beyond recall I no longer mourned it. I couldn't, I needed something alive to long for. And as for keening, I didn't understand that at all.

All the same it was the last thing I expected, to be left indifferent by the Schloss. Upon emerging from the attic I'd made it the target of my daily hobble, coming closer each day, over a period of weeks—it was a little more than three kilometres from the Hof, and I used the forest to get there, so as to reduce the risk of being seen and challenged by officialdom. The woods were as gay and glorious that May and June as they'd been in '38 when they seemed to me the very woods of childhood. Or of fairyland. Which is just what they are, the sweet, airy, deciduous forests of folklore, of Nordic myth and children's stories (these tell of darker woods, too, but the Friedrichswald is the place of sunlit enchantment, not of imprisoning gloom). Towards the end of the war, people had taken refuge here. They'd become a tribe apart, and this had revived the old folk tales and superstitions of the region. At the Hof there was talk of *Petermännchen*, Peterkin, of woodland elves. Of leaving food out in the woods, for the *Petermännchen*. It made me think of the effigy I'd seen in Herta's treehouse, the gnome with the huge meerschaum pipe stretching along the ground in front of him like a Punch-sized penis.

I'd often thought of Herta, especially while Ludolf's old eyes inspected my face by the light of the candle-flame, and when, without his knowing it, I returned his gaze, pretending to be asleep. He looked somewhat like the ogre deciding whether or not to eat his guest, and he didn't especially resemble his granddaughter; but I thought of her nonetheless, and wondered how to tell Ludolf that I thought I'd glimpsed her on a British newsreel. Whether to tell him at all. When I asked him about Herta, he'd given a small, barely perceptible shake of the head. Dead? I asked. Another tiny, desolate movement of the head, again from side to side. Not dead, then. Gone.

I had to take it further, out of my own curiosity; but without provoking his. If it really was Herta I'd seen, she was probably in prison somewhere now. Perhaps Ludolf would rather know this and know she was still alive, whatever crimes she'd been a party to; or perhaps he wouldn't. And what if it wasn't her? Bote was the name the girl on the newsreel had given, as she lined up with the other guards to identify themselves. Before the war Peter had told me that Herta was illegitimate, that Ludolf's daughter had never married. So perhaps Herta carried Ludolf's surname, whatever that was. I found a way to ask him and in answer Ludolf made a sound I didn't fully grasp. I made him write it down: Pohl. Say it as I might, it wasn't Bote, there were two syllables in the name I'd listened to over and over in the darkened cinema.

So I said nothing to Ludolf. And though I still don't know how much he knew himself of his granddaughter's fate, I've no regrets on that score. Peace be with you, old saint Ludolf, wherever you are. Today I alone—thank God—know all of Herta's story, the true story, down to the last grisly detail.

Herta was a long way from my mind—so much so I even forgot to look for the treehouse—when I finally reached the Schloss on one of my slow, lame progresses through the Friedrichswald. I was wearing special shoes made for me by one of Ludolf's farmhouse elves, a round-faced man who looked like a mediaeval friar, and who never washed. He was one of the refugees whose memory had been cut adrift, a small man with creased jowls but completely youthful eyes of the palest blue. Martin he'd been named by the others, Martin as in Luther, in honour of his clerical looks. The one thing he hadn't forgotten was how to make shoes, and the pair he made for me were extraordinary, huge things the size of giant clogs but soft as moccasin, fitting sweetly and caressingly around my bandages. Where on earth had they found the leather? I asked. Ludolf looked shifty. When Gräfin Agnetha's herd had died and the last one had been skinned (we shared a pious glance: a mercy the old girl hadn't lived to see this sacrilege), the hides had been put to use making coats and jerkins, leggings and the like. All except certain parts, for which no better use had been found. Until now. What did he mean? Which parts, exactly? Ludolf smiled his butler's smile at me, enigmatic. Examining my Martin-shoes, I saw what he meant. The heels were cow's arseholes. The anus had been sewn up, and the tail slit open and artfully curved back to form the sides, the sole, and the toe of the shoe. As I made my slow way through the Friedrichswald I did wonder from time to time whether I wasn't treading, in a

manner of speaking, on Waltraut's end, or that of her son the
bullcalf Willibald whose birth had caused so much distress, all
those years ago; whose birth, in fact, had delayed our departure
and sealed our fate, Maggie's, Alec's, and mine.

Was this the Schloss? This decrepit thing? By day it didn't
look remotely intact, it was hard to see how I could possibly
have thought it was, even for a moment, moonlight or no moonlight.

There had been times in my convalescent reveries, inhaling
the strange, rank salves coating my chest, when I'd dreamed that
I was living rough in the leaf-strewn ruins of the Schloss. Unlike
the Hamburg rubble this débris held no charms for me, but I
was poking around in it for souvenirs, without success. Now
that I was here in the flesh I couldn't understand what had even
led me to dream of the Schloss; couldn't feel any of the attraction. It was a perfectly fatuous building. Architecturally absurd,
a silly confusion of styles. What were these ridiculous stripes
encircling it? Rococo frippery grafted onto a squat, stern country seat. What idiot (J. B. Parr, was it? Or Dutch Piloot?) had
decided to interrupt a perfectly good stone front with stripes of
terracotta, of all things? With its layered pinkish brown and
cream, it looked like an enormous public lavatory, tiled in alternating colours and designed by somebody who should have
been working in marzipan.

Inside it the remains were just as disappointing. Not a trace
of Count Egon's antiquities. All looted, or blown to smither-
eens. None of them saved, despite ample time to have removed
the busts and the figurines, the portraits and other heirlooms.
This had been Ludolf's responsibility, as he admitted to me. But
where to hide them? The guns of both approaching armies could
be heard from the gardens, he said, and as he described this I'd
pictured the Schloss caught between the pincers of East and
West, all that was left uneaten of Europe as the steel jaws closed
on the last unconquered portion of the Reich. At the heart of it
a house caught in a single file of sunlight: anticipating the outcome of Ludolf's story I saw the Schloss as the innocent, accidental place on the map where all the swooping arrows of
invasion met. Then, in sheer frustration that there was no more
of Germany to be devoured, both sides would sink their differ-
ences and instead of going at each other as they really wanted
to do, they'd vent their rage on the Schloss . . . but no, that
wasn't how it happened. The evacuation of the house's valuables

had begun and the lawns were littered with antique furniture as if for some outdoor theatrical performance, when the wireless declared that by High Command agreement Mecklenburg was to be occupied by the British. All would be well; the British were coming. Back went the portraits, the busts, the sofas and chairs—and next morning it was the Russians who arrived. To make things worse the depleted remnants of the German army, falling back before them, chose the Schloss as their last stand. Or perhaps this made no odds, and the looting would have been just as savage if the place had offered no resistance. Instead (and I suppose it would have comforted Peter's father to know it) for thirty-six heroic hours, until the Russian artillery caught up, the Schloss held out like a true castle, finally come of age—its first and last experience of warfare.

Armed with Ludolf's stories of the siege, I gazed at the façade. And couldn't feel a thing. Brüel's finest hour had emptied it of everything I loved and left it architecture. What did I, a large prowling mongrel with a mad look in its eye, have to do with this whimsical and tarty pedigree kennel, now fallen into disrepair? Give it a quick disdainful sniff, and back to the woods.

I really felt no desire to burrow into the rubble in search of souvenirs; but walking inside the building brought back memories I couldn't so easily disown. The lobby, then to the right the skeleton of the drawing room, where someone had daubed the figure *17* on the walls, over and over, like a tally of victims— painted in some places, in others burned or drilled by gunfire. Peter at the piano; straight backs and Bach-faces, where briars now sprouted from the floor-mulch and cracked walls. The Rittersaal was barely recognizable, but I could still picture Ludwig Beck, old butterknife-smile, at the head of the table. He too was dead, Ludolf had told me, in July of '44 he was to have been the interim Head of State and had killed himself when the assassination plot went awry. It was only later that I discovered the shambles behind the Roman veneer of the story; how Beck had indeed been allowed to take his own life, had fired his pistol at his head—and missed, or bungled the job. He was renowned as the greatest of Germany's military tacticians, but he'd never actually fought a battle, poor old butterknife-smile. Even killing himself proved too much, without help from the enemy. It had taken one of the arresting officers to finish him off.

Like Beck, Peter had been in Berlin on the day of the intended coup, waiting for news and phoning Maggie at intervals. The wireless reported Hitler dead in the blast; a small crowd gathered round Maggie and the telephone, a crowd dispersing slowly, Ludolf said, as each successive phone call brought worse news, and as the radio bulletins, once more in Nazi control, confirmed that Hitler had survived. The traitors were being rounded up. They would be chased to the ends of the earth, and suitable retribution found. Peter had played no active part, but his moral support for the conspiracy was evidenced by his presence at secret meetings, and he was named by other revolutionaries. He belonged to the overwhelmingly loyal Luftwaffe: this, and his known association with Beck, made him conspicuous. In the end Beck was more fortunate than Peter, who was allowed neither a Roman death nor even a brief firing squad in front of whom to cry "long live Germany" like Stauffenberg, the would-be assassin. No, an example was to be made of Peter and others of the aristocratic co-conspirators. In Hitler's terms this meant garrotting with piano wire. Hanging, but slowly, in effect slow strangulation, dangling at the end of a metal noose, and all recorded on film for the Führer's pleasure.

Somewhere this film exists, and on it there is gruesome footage of Peter and the rest twisting and dying. To think about anybody dying this death was bad enough, to imagine Peter undergoing it was almost past bearing. How it must have haunted Maggie; would have haunted her forever—and when Ludolf told me about it I couldn't help wondering, with little Egon in mind, how a son could have lived in the shadow of such things. It wasn't just the manner of the death that appalled me, all fathers have to die and some die cruelly and tragically, but the fact that the images of this Calvary still existed somewhere, keeping it, in a sense, alive, perpetually dangling, incomplete; that anyone who wished to so could see it, on request, over and over again if needs be. One's father's death: in any case the most metaphysical of all events, the event that symbolically endows us with the space in which to live. It has to happen, to be over at last. But how can it transcend the Tiberian mockery of a lingering, filmed death? What if it's never really over? Preserved on celluloid, rendered physical and at the same time eternal, ready to be run, over and over, available to be witnessed—even if you never do so yourself—once again: if this isn't an all-powerful curse, I don't know what is.

Or are we only haunted by the spectres we invite in and nourish, out of some perverse need? Can we say no, shoo devil, begone foul fiend?

In my dreams Herta's treehouse too dangles, twists in the

wind like a cage suspended from a branch. Of course in reality it doesn't, it's not a cage but a corrugated iron box wedged securely in the branches, above a crotch of the trunk. It sits there firmly, high up where the tree divides into two lesser stems. But the treehouse—the treehouse is where my association with Peter's death really begins; and my guardianship of its evil.

The treehouse was far out of mind, that spring and early summer in Brüel, or so I thought. Then it was in the forefront of my thoughts again and I think I know what recalled it, what it was that directed my footsteps that way. As I emerged again from the wreckage of the Schloss, descending the steps where I'd been so ingloriously sick on the night of the ball, I looked back at what was left of the front elevation. There, still intact, was the fresco of terracotta plates from the workshop—Peter's lilting voice returned—of the artist Statius von Düren. Huge painted disks like a giant's dinner plates, incorporating Christian and pagan scenes. A demon, half bird and half serpent, with a scaly face, a beak, and a snake's tongue, his shoulders flecked with small feathers or leaves; a cross sprouting larger trefoils, hung with fetishes and branched like an espaliered apple tree; reindeer, one ridden by a boyish Christ, straight-legged, ecstatic. And I realized once more—or was this the first time?—where Herta had drawn her inspiration for the woodland ritual we'd engaged in, after Maggie and Peter's wedding. The mockery marriage of forest demon (that snakeskin mask! I'd forgotten it entirely, but there it was on Von Düren's frescoes) to . . . what? Woodsprite? Herta had been more like a nubile heifer. We had wrestled—no; no, that was no part of the recollection. Was it? She had blown out the candles, in the treehouse reeking of animal blood, and . . .

Yes of course it was, because after that we'd wrestled in the clearing, no hanky-panky, just chasing and childish wrestling, that was all, I was too sozzled to go on and she'd run off into the trees.

So why did I feel such a welling up of dread at the thought of the treehouse and the clearing below it? What came back of that whole drunken afternoon after the ceremony in the church at Tempzin, apart from the raucous sense of absurdity, of lusting after the bride when I'd had the bridegroom instead . . . what came back just as clearly as the grisly face-painting with Herta was the spell cast by the woods beforehand—before ever seeing the treehouse, standing groggily watching the little shallow stream, so clear and pure only the twitch of minnows showed where sandy forest floor ended and streambed began . . . and the waterflies dancing, and the frogs eyeing them like sated potentates, and the whole intricate mechanism of the forest clock whispering aloud that life itself was there, that there was no mystery that could not be unravelled, right there, at that instant, just by looking. By looking.

That was the memory that led me aside to the treehouse as I limped home from the Schloss. It was that and not the vile and farcical ceremony with Herta.

But beautiful as it was when I found it, the glade with the stream and the frogs, their magic wasn't what possessed me now. They were still there, frogs, minnows, water-flies; waterflies more frantic, frogs more despotic than ever; but it meant nothing.

When I saw the rusty awful corrugated-iron sides of the treehouse high up in the beech tree, poised between its tender grey arms and the vast rustling effusive glory of its leaves, some emotion clutched at my throat, heat rose through my head, I couldn't name the fear . . . an overwhelming mix of terror and exhilaration as if the very fact of this treehouse, ugly patched metal thing hanging there between heaven and earth and violating this most gorgeous of scenes, were the spirit of transgression itself in all its childhood-heady power.

There were memories, and I didn't want to explore them. Feelings I knew I'd come here to explore, too large for me altogether, they'd shake me apart.

I had the uncanny sense, the conviction, that I was being watched.

To break the spell I stooped and found a pebble, threw it at the treehouse. After a couple of shots I rattled one metal side. Silence. I didn't want to climb up. I didn't want to go inside, it would be dark and smelly and awful, like burrowing into some wormy corpse, into a dead woman's womb.

I was going home. I'd go home and be an adult. This whole trip would simply become known as Daddy's crack-up and never be referred to again; or perhaps, more humorously, be known as Daddy's crack on the head—he was in a car crash, in Spain, for weeks he wandered round Europe in a daze . . . how extraordinary, Richard! And where did you go? Lord alone knows, all over the place I gather, ended up in Germany. . . . You didn't! Really?

I was perfectly aware that this glossed over far too many

things, Molly's pain and Wilf's and the fact that I'd killed a man, and the deliberate way I'd left my passport behind to convince everyone I was dead. It was the best I could come up with, to make the homewards journey bearable. By lingering in Brüel I was endangering Ludolf and the others. The longer I stayed the more chance there was of my being caught and asked for my non-existent papers by some uniformed person. And the whole Hof would suffer for having hidden me, Ludolf and the crones, little fat Martin too with his blank blue eyes and his hands working of their own accord, their finger-memory unimpaired. All the same, I dreaded leaving. The Hof was planning a thirtieth birthday celebration for me, I'd mentioned to Ludolf that it was coming up at the end of July, and the response was in keeping with the love I'd felt surrounding me there in the farmhouse. It wasn't that I was particularly loveable all of a sudden, simply that I'd been brought back to life by these people, at great cost to them in time and effort and at the risk of their own freedom, I owed them everything and they loved me for it.

They also knew I had to leave. The proposed birthday celebration was, we all knew it without saying so, a send-off party. In the morning I would be gone; as if the whole thing, my very presence in Mecklenburg, had been a dream, and they could safely deny ever having seen the tall black-bearded foreigner who walked like a drunk.

I could in fact walk a great deal better now and, with my ash cane for support in case I toppled, I threw myself into step after step at virtually normal pace. I was ready to go, I'd memorized the map of the whole area until I could have travelled it blindfold. I'd been told exactly where and how to cross the border. No conveniently frozen lakes this time, but there were routes as easy and surer than Henry's; so I'd been assured. And it was Henry, or his presence in my increasingly jumpy mind, who finally pushed me into leaving. Now that the reckless fatalism of Hamburg days had gone, I felt like a man waking up to find himself on a tightrope over Niagara, no idea how I got there, no idea how to get across or get back. I was Richard Thurgo again, London solicitor, no outlaw but an ordinary frightened person, minus a few toes, and with them I'd lost my nerve, the fine edge of madness which had lured me into Russian territory without documents. In Hamburg when I'd thought I was under surveillance it only invited me to greater daring, sometimes I'd complete a black market transaction in the middle of the street and under the nose of the police, imagining myself a matador of crime. Now I was so jittery I had to fight the urge to surrender to every stranger I saw, just to end the suspense. If I glimpsed a woodsman in the Friedrichswald a stray cowlick or a red cheek would convince me it was Henry himself come back from the dead to take revenge, stalking the woods axe in hand. Or asking my whereabouts of a pair of billow-skirted housewives pushing their bicycles up a sandy track through the forest . . . yes, there he was again, a fresh-faced peasant Henry, this time in a maroon-coloured smock and a rakish yachtsman's cap.

He'd replaced Schäfer as my accusing shadow—but what had it been about the man other than his maddening arrogance and his ridiculous English name? He'd cheated me, then tried to kill me, and got his just deserts. Somehow the retroussé nose had seemed to be flaunting its nostrils at me as if rearing up at a bad smell. Below them the slobbering redness of the lips, a bright orangy red like an internal organ without its protective covering, smiling and smiling; and the thick, lank, inexhaustible hair, that cowlick I could still see him flicking back with a toss of the head—a toss of the head! With something so infuriatingly German about it . . . and just the general pertness of him, as though no defeat could rob this particular Germany of its smug resourcefulness, the Prodigal Hun (my friend Walters' phrase, not mine) bagging the fatted calf every bloody time. One afternoon I returned to the Hof from my daily walk to see a dusty Mercedes parked on the rutted track outside, and thoroughly incongruous there. I waited in the woods, until Ludolf emerged with two uniformed figures. Russians, by their epaulettes. Then as one of them paused by the car to look back at the farmhouse, I glimpsed a Henry profile, with a reared-up pointy nose. Below it a red slash of a mouth, and although I was fifty yards away the reminder made my heart turn over. I watched the Russians drive off down the rutted track, before I came out and crossed to the little chalet doorway.

Yes, Ludolf nodded, fixing me with his rheumy eyes. "From the Central Administration for Popular Enlightenment. Looking for a man with a beard, very tall. It is a pity you are so tall, Herr Thurgo. By now everyone from here to Schwerin is wondering who you are."

Hardly, I thought, not in a region seething with a million and a half refugees. But it was clear Ludolf wanted me gone. We held my birthday party that night, even though my actual birthday was still four days off. Everyone crowded into the low-ceilinged kitchen, where I felt like a cuckoo in a nest of tits—

or, given the subterranean gloom, like something more larval, the butterfly whose survival as a grub, if I remember rightly, depends on being carried off by ants, dragged into the anthill and fed on their secretions till the spring. What the grub does to repay his hosts—for his part Ludolf wouldn't take a single Reichsmark for my food and keep—I don't recall. Perhaps it's a piece of insect altruism, but somehow I doubt it. Finally I persuaded Ludolf to accept my British Warm, a bit long in the arm, but the sleeves could be taken in again to where Alec had worn them. The old man seemed pleased, and I enjoyed the vision of him striding round Brüel in it like an elderly Brigadier in Hyde Park; in return he gave me a cape made from a horse-blanket, to keep me warm at night on the journey home.

In our Hof-cavern, we had a cake with candles, the old retainers sang Mecklenburger ditties, and I attempted to return the favour with ill-remembered school songs. Martin had made me a special present. It was a second pair of soft shoes with the same cow's arsehole heels, to replace the originals, which were showing signs of wear. The old crones had packed me a week's supply of rutabaga sandwiches in a hempen bag. And then Ludolf, from God knows where, produced the pièce de résistance. A bottle. As he poured us each a glass, my heart caught at the old, familiar, forgotten smell; the fumes of Branntwein. Ludolf pushed my glass across the table. I knew what he was going to say and my eyes filled with tears, I had to look down because the Schloss came back, and Maggie, and everything intact as it had been.

"Nachtmütze, mein Herr." The Hof-dwellers chinked their cups and glasses. They repeated Ludolf's words, like a solemn oath. A nightcap, sir!

Apart from the moccasins I set out on the return journey in the same old outfit. My suit had held up pretty well, considering. The trouser turn-ups and the knees, torn on the way to Brüel, were freshly mended. I had my cane. In my pocket, Isidro. I had food. I had my route rehearsed in every detail, farm by farm through to the green frontier. No hurry. Only one awkward decision to make: whether or not to bid a last farewell to the Schloss. It was more than a detour, it took me in the wrong direction altogether. At the same time I knew it wasn't really a farewell to the Schloss I was debating, in my head. I'd seen it, I didn't need to see it again. It was the treehouse, it was what was inside the treehouse that I hadn't seen.

The bottles of blood and entrails, the animal heads, they might be there—or they might not; just an ancient stink. Unappetizing either way. So why were my slow steps taking the path towards it, instead of west towards Schwerin?

For the best part of an hour it felt wrong, as if I was tempting fate, even walking into a trap. But of whose making except my own? I'd told no-one where I was headed. Finally my tension yielded a little to a dreamier state, and the memories I'd interrupted on my previous, abortive visit to the treehouse, when I was so sure I was being watched, began to intrude again. Herta, the afternoon of the wedding, bending low in the treehouse, bending to blow out the candles, and the smell, suddenly stronger in the dark, of blood congealing on my face . . . once more my mind baulked, slid away distracted by the brightness around me, the birdsong, and my painfully throbbing feet. Not much further now.

The rope was gone. No rope ladder. I hadn't even noticed, the time before. Now when I reached the clearing it struck me at once, and I felt immediately grateful: no way up. Or was there? Here and there in the beech tree's giant trunk there were stumpy footholds, hard to tell if they were natural or contrived. No helpfully low branches, to begin the climb. And higher up there were dangerous stretches too, where agility would be more use than size or strength. How badly did I really want to peer inside that foul little tin hutch? Such a curious structure—I couldn't imagine anyone wanting to build a treehouse without windows. It looked more like a wartime latrine or farmyard shed, whisked up into the air by a Wizard of Oz tornado. Tiny up there, caught in the treetops like a child's kite. My feet were crying out for relief and I sat down in a patch of light between the roots of the tree, where some grass had poked its way through the lead mould. Sweating heavily now in my cape, I eased it off and let my head back into shade to gaze up at the treehouse without having to squint; legs and chest soothed by the coolness beneath and the sunlight above. The vanished rope ladder had decided it for me. Whatever trace was left of Herta's amateur taxidermy, I wouldn't see it now. But glad as I was, there was something in me that refused to be let off the hook, something balled up inside. Not disappointment, it was more toxic than that, fiercer.

Darkness, a whiff or candlesmoke and the blood like paste sticking the snakeskin visor to my cheeks . . . what followed, or rather what I followed as the images came, seemed more like a reverie invented at some later date than a memory of a distant, wine-soaked afternoon; but once I gave in there was no stopping it. That darkness and the "what next?" I'd felt at the time had reproduced themselves in memory, interrupting it—yes, because what came next was a moment of fear as jolting as the brush of a bat's wing, in that little space. I'd fancied I knew exactly what Herta wanted, and I was sufficiently aroused by the day's proceedings to be ready for anything, ready to shag the hind legs off a goat if needs be. Then I heard the small metallic sound in the darkness. I'd seen the skinning knives there on the bench beside us, close to hand. Had I come all this way to be a sacrifice to some bizarre woodland cult—or simply to Herta's fascination with entrails? I must have taken a step back in panic because I felt something bang into the back of my head, it was another head, a furry one, and I was close to screaming but it was suddenly all right, light flooded in and Herta stood framed in the doorway. No knife in her hand. The sound I'd heard was the metal latch, opening. Herta beckoned me to follow.

Then I was out and breathing deeply to expel the stink. I felt clumsy in Herta's home-made cloak of fur and skins, but excited too, making my way down the rope ladder to the forest floor. Herta had gone. I couldn't see too well out of the snakeskin mask but enough to see I was alone in the clearing. Earlier on I'd felt like an intruder here—now even more so in this forest camouflage, this mockery pelt, but the smell of it and the mask were thick in my head, with the smell of the blood, and the alcohol in my veins. Disguised as I was, no-one could outface me, not the woodland gods themselves, and if I went along with her game perhaps I'd fine that mute little Herta had a gift to bestow which words could only violate: the right to belong here in these woods. I knew she was watching, waiting for me to show I understood. I paused a moment to catch my breath; my heart still pounding, I set off at a loping run into the undergrowth.

Remembering this, as secure in the memory as if I was in trance, I felt my body responding to it as I lay in the heat and the scented grass. The sunlight on my weary legs and all the accumulated energy of my long abstinence seemed to come together in my groin, teased along by memory until I had to free my insistent penis into the air where it belonged—after its hibernation this felt like adolescent arousal all over again—and let it guide me through the rest of the memories, certain of their innocence.

Yes their innocence, because as soon as I'd caught sight of Herta it all became silly and simple and childish again, nothing feral or satanic about hide-and-seek with a funny fat girl in a party dress. Both of us laughing too hard to be anything other than stumbling humans. I glimpsed her white-blonde hair, pretended not to, and the chase began. Joyous now, I flapped my arms, bursting through foliage like a blind brute as I circled back and trapped her and she shrieked in surprise. I caught her easily, pinning her plump wriggling body to the ground under the outspread wings of the rabbit-skin cloak.

Where had this happened—here in front of me in the clearing? No, somewhere further off, out of sight, but the sensation of it was so clear and so delicious to recapture that with a couple of strokes (was someone watching me now, further off, out there? Let them envy my Punch-cock its majesty!) all my blood seemed to rush to it and for a long instant my erection seemed the one fully alive thing about my lame, clumsy-footed body in its stale old clothes. I was as musty as the leaf mould I lay in but at the centre of it rose a startled, happy mushroom, now proudly flinging spores to the wind.

Herta and I, in memory: there we were as I delivered myself back to recollection. But the game was boyish wrestling, not coupling. The submission was all, I obtained it and as I relaxed Herta threw me off and onto my back, pulling off my cap and visor, grinning, pleased with herself. And yes, the whole thing was pleasantly childish, licking blood and smearing hands, fancy dress and a tumble in the leaves. After all she was little more than a child herself, fourteen, fifteen at most; I was nineteen and at a disadvantage here, trying to puzzle out what she expected of me. I sat up beside her, removing the cloak to examine it. Her work, I asked? Certainly—"Bestummt!" Her only word, *bestimmt* distorted by her accent; certainly, all of it, she smiled. The stuffed creatures in the treehouse, too? *Bestummt* they were. I began to ask her why, what were they for, but she interrupted me by jumping to her feet and offering to help me up, for another chase perhaps. I pleaded grogginess. When I tried to tug her down towards me, she pulled away and pranced back a few steps to safety. Seeing me still lying there grinning, she shrugged, swept the cloak and visor into a bundle in her arms, then she was up and marching back towards the tree-house, shaking herself, brushing off the leaves. . . .

That was it, that was what had happened. *Bestummt* it was.

So when had I burnt Alec's letter? Herta was present, but it had to have been the next day, before I left. I'd brought the treehouse an offering of my own. Herta had granted me admission to her mysteries; in exchange I burnt Alec's letter to Maggie, his pledge of love and rescue. Alec had burnt my past—I thought of Fold Farm as vengefully as I could, while I watched the flames—and I was burning his future, here in these regal woods. An Anglo-Saxon mystery to set before a Teutonic, woodland king. And Herta had knelt in the leaves and clapped her hands, and . . . and for years . . . for years it was Herta and that damned treehouse full of stuffed animals, that was what I remembered when I thought of Maggie's wedding—

No, that wasn't it at all. And as I lay there in the sunlight feeling acutely vulnerable, foolish now, sticky and detumescent, the sense of being spied on recurred abruptly—as if to distract me from something worse. I actually pictured the red epaulettes and Henry creeping up on me in Ivan-uniform to deliver the Russian coup de grâce, the shot through the back of the . . . the neck! but too late, even my self-induced shudder came too late to save me because at that moment, with my wilting, contented cock in my hand and despite the image of a gun being levelled at my head, I saw in memory something so troubling that both the imaginary gunman and Herta's applauding smile vanished simultaneously, along with the remains of my erection.

The images came so fast I didn't know what to make of them at first. Herta's blood, Herta squirming under me like an animal, my hand over her face and above my hand her eyes screaming at me. Blood on her chin and neck, and blood under our bodies, spreading out. The leaves were running with it.

That first rush of memory was so awful that I had to stop, I did it by sitting up quickly, making myself dizzy and then focussing on my surroundings, on the trees, the quiet clearing. I wanted the other to be a lurid daydream, some sordid and macabre fantasy intruding in my head. But no, it had its own unerring life, it knew where it was going.

And then I saw what it was that had drawn me back to Mecklenburg, up out of the Malaga ravine and on into the snow, all the way back to the clearing where I lay, right here on the soft coppery leaf-mould, under the arms of the beeches. Leaf-mould running with blood, at Maggie's wedding.

It wasn't till I'd ridden the memory all the way to the end, sitting up now, shaking but too terrified to cry, shaking and staring, that I knew I hadn't killed the girl. But it was almost as horrible, in some way even more so, because it wasn't the violence that was so shocking, it wasn't the savagery of what I'd done that had me bury it all these years. It was the joy.

Sitting up in the leaves over my shrinking, forgotten cock, sitting shaking and staring and unable to cry yet—I still couldn't quite believe in it as a memory, it was like something injected into me in my sleep, like a nightmare I was recalling, not something I'd actually done. But it was no longer confined to a few brutal images, the vista extended forwards and back, unfolding, all the details waiting there to tell me it wasn't a dream, it was a memory, it had happened.

Not the afternoon of the wedding; no, because after our rough-and-tumble mimicry of consummation in the leaves, Herta had run off, I could see her running with the bundled costumes, cradling them as if my scent in them was all she needed now. Nothing happened that afternoon. The wind was getting up, the branches flailing as I stumbled home on my own. It was the following morning, after some fitful sleep and half the night spent listening to the storm. I can't even claim drunkenness, I was hung over but in control of my actions, sober and angry after the long empty wedding night thinking of Peter and Maggie together . . . oh so cosy, wrapped around each other as the wind rattled the windowpanes. And yet wasn't this what I'd worked for all along? Conniving with Peter from the start, and now scuppering Alec's plans by failing to deliver his letter, buggering him as I'd already buggered Peter, I'd had everyone except Maggie and I wanted to burst in and have them both. My manoeuvring, my futile sense of power, my frustration—all knotted together and demanding release.

And no-one around as the morning hours advanced, they were sleeping in as if it was everyone's wedding night except mine.

A few servants stirring, the old faithfuls, but it was Herta I wanted. I could still feel her body against mine, tubby but firm, Herta with animal blood smeared on her face, ready for darker mysteries. If she hadn't yet solved the riddle of her body, then all too clearly she was asking me to do it for her. The treehouse itself cried out for blood, in a high wind like last night's there would be branches clattering against it, bottles falling inside, smashing. Blood leaking from the metal corners to form a perimeter of dark spoor on the leaves below, a sacred floor where . . .

Where I would burn Alec's letter to Maggie.

But I knew already when I found Herta that morning that this satanic rigmarole had nothing to do with her treehouse world. I was the one crashing around in a high wind. Shame at betraying Alec. Rage at having stymied myself. I'd got what I wanted and I didn't like it. Even my lust was fuelled by rage, and Herta must have sensed it too, she wouldn't come with me until she'd finished all her chores, the milking and the feeding and the cleaning up. When it was over at last I took her hands and danced her past the stables and then as we ran through the wet fields she began to get caught up in our adventure again, I could see it. She liked the burning of the letter, here in the clearing; a bright spurt of flame, the paper had gone up fast once it had lit. She clapped her hands and I gazed at her slabby face, roly poly features almost hidden in fat. I wanted to pierce her body, puncture it like a sausage too fat for its skin.

Roly poly, rumple tumble round the tree stump, that's how it began. All utterly deliberate on my part, and it was sickening to recall it now, that I'd tried to pretend this was a rekindling of the previous day's fires, no more than a last whiff of the erotic fumes we'd basked in after the wedding. It wasn't; Herta knew it when I forced her legs apart and pulled at her clothes. Her protests grew louder, I had to keep her quiet, and as soon as my hand went over her mouth she knew the games were over and she bit my palm, bit it hard until the blood ran down her chin and onto her neck.

More blood underneath us, slippery everywhere. I knew that virgins bled, but so much? Either she was menstruating or I'd torn her badly, both perhaps, the blood spreading and squelching as it had when Waltraut's womb came out on the straw of the stall. But this was Herta's blood, and her body squirming, fat white heifer under me. Nothing could match the joy of it, I loved the pain in my hand and the pain in my cock, more of it as she bit into the meat beneath my thumb, the mound of Venus, bonny lad, you've got a big one all right. Yes I was afraid I'd harmed her, ripped her, suffocating her now with my hand, and the eyes screamed but I wanted to do more, bite her head off in one animal crunch.

That wasn't what had scared the wits out of me, though, and made me shovel the whole thing, once it was over, down the deepest shaft that memory could find. Not the brutality. Not shame. It was the joy, the appetite exulting in me, I was reptile and rat, I was teeth snapping sinew in my devouring joy, my prowess. I fed. So blindly I was neither male nor female, I was blood and sinew replenishing itself on other blood, on weaker, snapping sinew, and there was a sense of coming home in this as if my fingers, clawing Herta's face, the other hand clawing the earth where my forearm pinned her shoulders to the ground, as if my fingers extended into the woodland roots. I had the whole forest in my blood and I was home as savourously as it was possible to be home, I knew this was the deepest joy anyone could know, and that I must never open the door to it again. I told myself I'd learnt what anyone could learn, any and all of us if the rank earth and the stench of blood mingled in our nostrils when the fit was on us, lust and rage at once. It was as if my scalp had opened to let in the forest, as if the rootways of a million years of memory could open up like veins to course with what humanity was, the killing that had got us here, that we had to forget.

But when it was over and she wasn't dead, just hurting and humiliated, eyes pressed tight shut now as if she never wanted to see again; when I could no longer summon up the feeling that she'd courted this, begged for it, that this was what she'd wanted and why she'd peopled the treehouse with blood and entrails, what she'd invited me in for; when I knew what I'd done, there was no primeval shout of triumph. I was sickened and frightened both for her and for me, I was a vicious nineteen-year-old bully who'd raped a German girl, a child almost, and who deserved to be strung up.

And didn't I deserve it? The tears came now as I sat there remembering, tears of self-pity God knows, but of shame too, and fear and disbelief at what a stranger I was to myself. How could I have forgotten it, buried it? And yet I hadn't succeeded; my mind had dragged me back here at last, made me face what I was. What I couldn't be, any more than any of us could. My whole body shook with the release of it, like a carapace falling off me, the stinking shell of ten years lying to myself, remembering drunken fun with Herta in the leaves, blow out the candles and . . .

Forget. But the part of me that couldn't forget had grown and swollen and pressed against my brain like a tumour until—and now I knew it as clearly as if I was seeing the newsreels all over again—until I'd been seeing Herta where Herta wasn't. The newsreel girl, the girl in the death camp line-up, I could see her now, she was nothing like Herta any more than her name was Herta's. My mind had simply been erupting with Herta and my lies and the forbidden images, just as I'd been seeing Henry at every turn of the forest path. And because I was too slow, too stupid, just too frightened to understand, it had finally taken me by the hand and said come along, you're going to Maggie's wedding, and I'd said, I see, thank you, it was ten years ago, that means I must be dotty, and the mind had said, you believe anything you like; just come with me.

And brought me here.

Tears were pouring down my face now and pooling in my moustache, but it wasn't just shame, damn it, be truthful: even now it wasn't just shame, it was loss too, the loss of that utter self-fulfillment, no matter what the cost.

At last I stuffed my long since wilted cock back in my pants, and lay back again, no longer trembling, recapturing my sense of safety, ten years had passed after all and we'd all changed, war had done its work and what was my puny atrocity compared to what had been endured by millions? I was safe. If Herta had told anyone, at the time, I'd never have been allowed to leave the Schloss unchallenged. And if Ludolf had learnt about it later he'd have killed me on sight, surely, no matter what the last ten years had brought; he wouldn't have rescued me and cared for me, much less set me free again.

Then why did I still feel I was being watched? Watched as if I were watching my self of ten years ago lying there in the leaves, shaking with fear at what I'd done, praying that Herta wouldn't tell, not knowing what to do, ready to swear it had never happened, swear it to anyone who asked, swear it first to myself. It never happened.

No-one was watching. Nothing stirred in the bushes, in the trees around me, no shape, no face. Until I looked up towards the treehouse. And there, among the leaves of a branch below it, met a child's eyes staring into mine.

The way he was just sitting there perfectly motionless above me, the first time I saw him, while I was still caught up in the events I'd been remembering; the way he appeared to belong to the treehouse, perched below it like an old man on his front steps; most of all perhaps the way the calm in his eyes told me he'd be watching for some time . . . all this made the child seem to belong to the memories, to spring right out of them as if— absurd as this was—he was the child of that morning's violence ten years before, condemned to live in the treehouse where it had all begun. The fact that he looked to be nearer five years old than ten, that he could have been any village child or farmer's child who'd adopted the treehouse in the meantime: I must have sensed these things however dimly, but given my state what could I think except that he was my child, mine and Herta's, conceived here and bequeathed to the forest.

A moment earlier I'd imagined my nineteen-year-old self shaking with guilt, somewhere in this clearing—and then to look up and see the child's unwavering eyes like the most still and innermost part of me gazing back . . . at that instant he seemed in every way a part of me. It was as if I'd conjured him into being, I'd brought out my cock and conjured him with my body as well as in the ghastly-joyous memories my mind had been restoring to me; summoned him, rehearsed the way he was conceived and here he was, he had to be my child. *Bestummt* he did. Herta's *bestummt*: I whispered it aloud, gazing up at the boy. Whispered it like a spell, an open sesame. Then louder, still gazing up. ''Bestummt!''

Wasn't there something in his face—the eyes widening, the slack mouth opening a little—that remembered? *Bestummt!* I whispered it again, loud, confidently, like a bond between us, willing him to understand. But he didn't move, he sat as if he was carved out of the tree itself.

Bestummt . . . it was the sound of a heavy-laden tree struck by the wind, it was an ogre's footfall on the leafy forest floor. Gazing up, I willed him to remember.

Legs and arms were thin, I could see some baggy shorts and a leather bib, no shirt, brown hair long and straight, falling over his face as he looked down, hair shoulder-length. Boy or girl? A feline child, but I think I knew it was a boy, or just assumed it by the brazen way he stared. I must have been unlike anyone or anything he'd ever seen—a large, masturbating cripple in a pair of bulbous clown-shoes, first playing with his cock and then crying; hardly an everyday woodland occurrence. He didn't seem in the least perturbed. It was so obviously his tree, his clearing—I wasn't the ogre sleeping at the foot of the beanstalk, trapping Jack above, no, I was an intruder again, gazing up at the castle and its master, a Jack in the sky who'd outlived all the ogres.

And still he didn't move. Did I dare try and climb up to join him? I couldn't, even if my feet had permitted it; the rope ladder was gone, no beanstalk. How did the boy get down? The same way he went up, of course, he'd found a way of shinning up and down, using whatever toeholds there were.

Picturing this, a part of me said: he's just a child from the village, playing in the woods. Nothing extraordinary in that. No reason—other than my embarrassment at having shown the child so much of myself—to make a fantastic association between him and Herta and the things that happened a lifetime ago, or so it seemed; I was beginning to come to.

And then he moved.

A village child? This was no village child, no farmer's child, no-one could move like that who merely frequented the woods to play. Before I could open my mouth to call him back, he was gone: jumping to his feet, scampering along the branch, back to the treetrunk, vanishing round it and appearing again higher up to dance soundlessly along an upper branch and into the treehouse. The latch went clang as he shut the door, the metal latch, the same sharp chilling Herta-clang I'd heard when she blew out the candles and I'd thought she was sharpening a knife. With the clang he was gone like a squirrel into its lair. And if he'd never been there on the branch, this thing of the woods, elf, *Petermännchen*, Peterkin.

I'd come to Mecklenburg with such a sense of purpose, and now, as I walked, I didn't know where I was going, or where my feet were taking me. I'd abandoned everything to come here; no matter how much I'd been mocking my life of bridge and baby and Petty Assizes, it was still my life, I'd thrown it all up to get here—and now what was I doing wandering the woods as if waiting for someone to appear and tell me where to go and what to do? As if the trees might part to show a distant castle with banners flying from its turrets, beckoning me on . . . when that was now over and done with, the lady dead, the Schloss in ruins, the truth exposed of brutal barnyard dealings, out the back door savaging the kitchengirl, all that was over, done with. I'd come through fire and ice to strip off the fairytale mask and find the animal lurking beneath, little red riding wolf licking his chops, I'd braved all kinds of terrors to get to the heart of the maze—and now why wasn't I free of it? After all that mad perseverance what was I doing wandering about as if I didn't know the way out again?

My mind did, though. I was going back to the Hof. It was the Hof-dwellers who put out food for the Peterkin, so they claimed.

I had to know about the child. Better not to have come, than to walk away without knowing.

I still couldn't separate him fully, in my head, from what I'd been remembering this morning about Maggie's wedding. And as I thought about it now, hobbling along, I saw how cunningly my mind had tricked me into coming back here. Maggie's wedding! Maggie had been the lure—and all along the trap, the truth, had been there right under my nose, in what I'd taken for a comic alibi: what would a man in shock do? Why, set off to attend a wedding from the past. I'd thought I was shamming amnesia, rather adroitly too. The joke was that I hadn't been shamming at all. Where Herta was concerned I'd had amnesia for ten years. And I really was going back to a wedding from the past; that had been the truth, and as I realized it I had a sudden image of myself as a child circling round a garden, stalking imaginary prey, but with no quarry there except myself. Like Maggie the Schloss had been a decoy—no wonder it disappointed me on close inspection. Meanwhile my mind was prodding and nudging me round, I was less the great hunter than the butt of blind man's buff being shoved on into the treehouse clearing, where the parlour games came to an end. I'd pinned the tail on the donkey and pulled off the blindfold and . . . and now—what was my prize, exactly? A good look at the donkey; at my happy bestial self. Then what? Forget it properly this time, forget the joy anyway, because it was too horrible to live with? Morally that made sense. But forgetting it was what had got me into trouble in the first place and brought me stumbling back here, forced to remember it again; and now forced to forget it again. It was like being slapped from side to side.

I know I should have felt ashamed of these thoughts, I'd taken vicious advantage of the girl and should be asking myself how best to atone and instead I was wondering what to do with the intoxication of the memory. To deny it would be the worst possible course, that's all I knew, it was mine and I had to incorporate it somehow. If only I could work it out. Perhaps atonement was the only way; but I didn't fancy grovelling at Ludolf's feet. The prospect of meeting him again was bad enough, with my mind full of what I'd done to his granddaughter.

As I came closer to the Hof I kept stopping to shuffle back and forth in one spot or another, in and out of the sunlight, debating, telling myself I didn't have to go back and face the music, whatever that music might be; knowing I had to, that I couldn't go home otherwise, that I was only putting off the evil hour. I made myself go on, wishing the earth would swallow me up. A voyage under Neptune leads . . . to a kick up the backside, wasn't that more or less what Auntie said before I left for Spain? Neptune was up to no good in the zodiac. Neptune in transit, that was it: beware of false enchantments. Stay at home. She was right, I'd wound up sitting with Luís in that dreary Fascist bar in Malaga, surrounded by Hitlerite mementoes—and lost my bearings. Even as I protested that I was British, my wartime contempt for all things German had begun to give way, like a local anaesthetic, to the old prickings of kindred feeling. The old enchantment—I'd lost touch with it for purely patriotic reasons, so I'd thought, but it was kinship with myself I felt returning as I blundered on to Hamburg, with myself and not, as I imagined for a time, with Nazi criminality. It resonated in me, certainly, but my demons weren't of the uniformed variety. My ties to Germany were obstinately personal, I saw that now, my Germany had a corner in it which, if not forever England, had my mark on it, my clawprints in the carpet of decaying leaves. Beneath them a trap-door gave into a world of nightmare belonging, the world of true belonging from which—was this too part of Neptune's plan?—I was barred. I'd made the voyage and I had nothing to show for it.

Until I saw the child. No matter if this was another false enchantment—at that moment the past had been closing behind me to be discarded like a dream, consigned to the dark like the phantom lead soldiers of my childhood. And now . . . look, Grandfather! Look what I found when I woke up. One hostage from the nightworld, one and one only, in a lifetime, could be salvaged; so he'd promised me. And the toy he'd placed in my sleeping hands that morning had been counterfeit. This was a living thing retrieved from Herta's world, Herta's and mine. I pictured her pregnant, her tubbiness disguising it, Herta bearing the child alone up there among the bottles of blood and the animal skins and heads and rotting things, suckling him, rearing him in the woods, in secret. The way he scampered up the tree only confirmed it. His world, he was heir to it now . . . seeing him there I'd felt the loss of it again, just for an instant, but what was that compared to what I'd gained? I'd sat and sat, waiting for the boy to come out of the treehouse. No matter either, that he hadn't; he'd broken the barren circle of my journey.

As I emerged from the Friedrichswald I could see the little Hof with its pagoda of roofs and tiny windows under each one, almost invisible behind the pink and orange blossom of the win-dowboxes; there it was, half a mile away across empty, sloping pasture. No cows, no turds. Buttercups and molehills, for the moles of Brüel it was business as usual, come German, come Russian, come Briton. I hesitated in the sharp breeze at the edge of the wood, knowing that once I set out across the meadow I'd be visible from the Hof, I couldn't turn back and I'd have to hear the story to the end.

I can see myself taking that decision, stepping out into the sunshine of that deserted pasture filled with light, and I can't help envying myself the moment. I was a wounded creature, I know, I with my clumsy feet, staggering a bit but surely still dangerous, still full of youth and its store of infinite, unex-pended, unexpendable energy, stepping out unaware of my shadow, into that warm bright buzzing field.

I must have been halfway there, my patent Martin-shoes sink-ing at each step into the turf, I was a little dazed by the sunlight but I had the Hof in my sights, when I saw all the faces at the little farmhouse windows, peeking through the geraniums. Faces at every window, on every floor, gazing at me. Was I so strange a sight? True, it must seem odd that I was coming back—we'd said tearful, definitive goodbyes the night before. But was my return after this false exit really so fascinating that it had drawn every inhabitant of the Hof to the windows, to stare at me in awe? As if I were a parade. Or—they weren't calling to me in greeting, or even waving, they seemed struck dumb—as though I was a spirit come to earth. It was only when I got closer, close enough to see their eyes, that I realized they weren't looking at me at all. They were looking past me, and I turned and saw a small figure some way behind but plodding resolutely after me. A boy in lederhosen with bare arms and legs and hair down to his shoulder-blades, mimicking my slow, gingerly-treading walk, like the African witches I'd read about in Grandfather's study when I was little older than the boy was now. As I stopped, he stopped.

"Ja . . . Egon!" It was Ludolf's voice that first pronounced his name for me, I heard it ring out from behind me in the most curious tone, wooing but mistrustful too, as if addressing a neighbour's growling dog. "Komm, kleiner," come! Come, little one; but the child made no response, merely turned aside and pretended to be interested in the turf. I looked round at the Hof. Ludolf had come out from the front door, and stood gazing at us across the rutted farm track. "Egon!" he called again.

This time the boy looked up, reluctantly acknowledging his name.

"Also, Herr Thurgo, da habt Ihr unser Gräfchen mitgebracht," Ludolf said quietly, and to the boy, "Schau mal, Graf Egon, das ist dein Onkel aus England." I stood staring at him, then at the boy, taking this in. Ludolf's words hung in my head as though I had forever to consider them. *You've brought Count Egon back with you, I see. Count Egon, meet your English uncle.* I replayed the words again; turned back to Ludolf. Count Egon? Ludolf didn't seem overly surprised to see him. Egon? Little Egon who he'd said was dead and gone, who was ash in an East Prussian field?

He'd followed me back to the Hof out of sheer curiosity, I think; later, when the boy took to playing his hands over my face, I saw in his eyes a kind of pleasure in me—a delight, even, in my uncouth features, more than anyone had ever shown; but that came slowly, with time. And if anything other than this secret physical affinity induced him to follow me further, away from the Hof and the Friedrichswald, it was the little coat Ludolf gave me for him. I saw how Egon watched it as Martin brought it out and handed it to Ludolf, who made a solemn show of handing it to me. He spoke to Egon but the boy wasn't listening, he was staring at me as I folded the jacket-length coat over my arm. It was Martin's work, a small but bulky thing of dirt-stained leather lined with wool, Egon-sized, patched where the child had torn it during successive winters. When the nights began to turn cold, Ludolf explained, they left it for him by the treehouse, and retrieved it again in the spring from wherever he'd discarded it.

Time and again they'd brought the boy home, by force, but he'd always escaped. When the woodland stream dried up in the summer, he might come sniffing round the Hof like a deer after water, but he wouldn't stay. A savage, Ludolf had said while I was still standing there stunned by his first words to the boy; a beast, *ein Tier;* and when I'd made a move in Egon's direction he'd called out to stop me.

I was still dazed. This was Egon, Maggie and Peter's Egon? How was that possible? How had he got here? And why on earth hadn't Ludolf told me earlier? At first my questions drove the old man back into himself, as if I were shaming him before the world. I didn't mean to reproach him, I said—but I wasn't getting through. Stepping from the spongy grass onto ridges of dried mud like brick rubble, I made to join him, but when I looked up Ludolf was already striding stiffly away from me along the track. I hurried after him as best I could.

Answers came slowly, and sometimes not at all, sometimes Ludolf just stopped and stared away into the distance, ignoring both me and the boy. I knew that proudly-grieving look; he was back in his old role at the Schloss. And while we talked I had the feeling it wasn't me he saw beside him, I wasn't the delinquent English boy he'd known ten years ago or even the traveller he'd rescued: I was all that was left of Maggie, an emblem for her, or rather for the responsibility he owed the dead. Words came more freely as we walked back down the track and past the Hof with its windows still peopled by elderly faces; then we'd turn and walk uphill once more. Egon too would turn and follow. He stayed level with us, moving idly up and down the pasture, picking at the grass. Now and then I saw him glance at me; keeping his distance like a stranger's pet, shy but intrigued.

Yes, this was Peter and Maggie's son; no, he hadn't died with Maggie and his grandmother; hadn't gone with them at all. And the names on the family gravestone, Egon among them? Ludolf shrugged. It was done in '44, to protect him, to fool the "hats." The "hats?" Gestapo, men in suits instead of uniform, with soft voices and soft hats. They'd come to fetch him, his mother, and his grandmother, and Egon had been hidden from the "hats." Hidden in the woods; nobody had dreamt it would lead to this, they'd done everything in their power . . . no doubt, I said, but why hide him from me? Why had he lied to me? Ludolf avoided my eyes, and we continued to pick our way up the track. "He is my punishment," he said indistinctly, gazing out past the boy towards the woods. I asked him what he meant, and after a while he stopped, looking directly at Egon now. "Tell me, Herr Thurgo . . . are you pleased to have such a nephew? Take him by the hand, you'll see. He spits at you. Hold onto him and he bites." Ludolf stretched out his elegant, emaciated hands, palms down, and gazed at them; if there were scars I saw none, but perhaps he did, scars visible only to him. "If you take him indoors he will take off his clothes and relieve himself everywhere. When you let him out he runs away." Ludolf fixed me with a glare. "I gave my word that I would always look after him. I loved this family, I think." The "I think" was assertive, proud. It hung there for a moment. "But not enough. You understand?" *Ihr versteht?* I shook my head. This was his punishment for not loving the Lützows enough? By the sound of it the child would exhaust anyone's love. Why did he hold himself responsible? "I gave my word. I was the one who said we could do it, I said we could hide him. My granddaughter would look after him, for a few days. A week or two, if necessary."

And the weeks turned into months. They'd fetched him back to the Schloss, Ludolf said, as soon as the "hats" had left. But Egon had run off when he found that his mother had gone, and no matter how many times they brought him back from the treehouse and explained that Maggie would return to him, that she would expect to find him at the Schloss, at home, not at the treehouse, he wouldn't listen. They'd lied to him, he couldn't trust them now; only Herta who never spoke, and the world they'd made for themselves. The treehouse world in which she fed him, played with him, comforted him. And at some point . . . simply abandoned him? When I asked what had happened to Herta I was met with silence. In my presence Ludolf wouldn't reproach her for the boy's estrangement, I took it. The stony lines of his face said it was no business of mine; he blamed himself, that was enough. He'd given the Frau Gräfin his word that together he and Herta would look after the boy. In my mind I saw Herta leading the way into the clearing, and Maggie following with the child. It's all right, *kleiner*, little one, stay here and play and I'll be back soon. Wait for me, I'll be back.

Didn't the "hats" come looking for Egon? Ludolf shook his head. Why not? I asked. He went stony on me again and we completed a full circuit, down one side of the rutted track and up the other. Egon was still following us, pausing with us when we paused, much as he must have done when he was stalking me through the woods on our way back from the treehouse. Stopping and starting; what had he made of my strange behaviour? The way he looked at me now, when the three of us came to a halt again, almost made me laugh. He cocked his head to one side as if exasperated—just like Peter, although Peter had done it to apologize for his height, and this child was small, so small for his face. Quite unlike Peter with his little narrow head and long neck. But no, the shape of the head was the same, when Egon's body grew it would be in proportion, a long, bony head like his father's. He looked oddly dwarfish now. An old tramp's face full of dirt-etched lines, stuck on a child's frame; it was a wiry little frame, he was light and airy and yet wizened at the same time, like Peter shrunk into a pint pot. And there were other resemblances: something risky and headlong about his strides, as though he came from a heavier planet and was taking advantage of the release from gravity. He was all Peter, at first, to look at, I couldn't see anything of Maggie in him; but it was there somewhere. I glanced at Ludolf. He was looking down at his feet, waiting for my attention.

"In '44," he began, "you have to understand . . . the Schloss was like an orphanage. They brought us children from the village when they could no longer feed them, sometimes the father was dead, sometimes both parents. The Frau Gräfin wanted us to take them all, but it wasn't possible. We fed them as often as we could, and some we took in, the orphaned ones. One in particular was her favourite . . ." he hesitated, "and mine too." I looked up at him, trying to keep my expression steady. Since I'd reached the Hof and Ludolf had called out to Egon, the image of a Herta-child had been driven out, along with the shame I was carrying. Now with this talk of orphans . . . Ludolf met my glance, but he seemed reassuringly oblivious, *Der Franzl, armes Vieh*, poor Franzl, he was weak here in the lungs," he said, tapping his chest, "trouble with asthma. Only the Frau Gräfin could calm him. And so . . . you see, the Frau Gräfin agreed, sometimes I think she too had thought about it, if we hid Graf Egon and she took little Franzl in his place, the 'hats' would never know," his eyes were pleading now as the words tumbled out, "and the Frau Gräfin thought so too, it was the best for everyone because the boy would go to a good family if they took him away from her, and Egon would be still here with us at the Schloss, no-one would know except for us." He stopped, willing me to understand. "We would all be together again, afterwards, when the war was over. That was what she said."

Ludolf fell silent, leaving me to draw my own conclusions. It was this "poor Franzl," then, poor bloody Franzl the asthmatic, who'd died with Maggie and Agnetha? The old man nodded solemnly. In the train, as he'd described to me?

The nod, repeated, was at odds with the pain in Ludolf's eyes. What was it he was pleading for? If it was forgiveness he could have it gladly, but it wasn't mine to give; rather the other way about, I should be begging his forgiveness for the way I'd treated Herta.

What did he want from me? And it was to keep up the pretence, I said, that they'd put Egon's name on the grave? To fool the "hats," yes. Yes, all well and good, but to treat me the same way, to have left me thinking he was dead—

Aber versteht Ihr doch nicht, Herr Thurgo? "Don't you understand, they *are* all dead, the Lützows. All of them. Our Egon too, the one . . . the Egon we loved.'' He faltered as a sudden movement distracted us. It was the boy tossing his head as he looked up impatiently, then away. *Klug war er,* came Ludolf's voice, ''A clever and affectionate child . . . that was the Egon the Frau Gräfin placed in my care. You think we haven't tried to keep that child alive? But we lost him, little by little we lost him.''

For a moment I stood there without thinking, aware only of the field and the child in it, and the Friedrichswald further off. ''He still knows his name,'' I said.

''Sometimes. But only as a dog knows it, Herr Thurgo.''

No, he was wrong—looking at the child I knew he was wrong, I wanted to prove it. And there was more. I wanted to submit myself, not to Ludolf's judgement but the boy's. No, that wasn't it, that wasn't all of it; then with a shock I knew.

''Even the women won't go near him now,'' Ludolf was saying, ''no-one can make him obey, not even Martin with all his patience.''

''I can,'' I said.

He paused, seeing that I was serious. ''You'll see, he bites.''

''I'll bite him back.''

The old man looked positively shocked, as though for all he'd said this beast, this *Tier*, was still a count and I was offering to bite a small defenceless aristocrat.

''He's my nephew,'' I said, ''and I'll bite him if I wish.''

We stared at each other. Ludolf must have known from my face what it was that I wanted, that I had to take the boy with me. Words came up—about England, how Molly and I would look after him as our own . . . I began to say them but they sounded false, they withered under Ludolf's gaze and I didn't believe in them myself, they weren't what I meant.

''No,'' he said at last, shaking his head.

I looked across at Egon. The boy seemed to be growing restive. Would he follow me, regardless of the old man's wishes? I felt Ludolf's eyes on me.

''This is his home,'' he said gently.

''I think my sister-in-law . . .'' I forced it out, ''if she knew how hard things were for all of you here . . .''

Wasn't that what he wanted me to say, what he'd wanted from me all along? But I'd lost him again, ''I have to think about it,'' he said, turning to Egon.

"No," I said. Any moment the boy might dart back towards the woods, as he'd done before, scurrying up into the treehouse.

Ludolf was still gazing at Egon; I wasn't sure if he'd heard me. "Please," I said, surprising myself with the word, and as I spoke I felt something give inside me. "I think this is why I came." A mile of rotten bandage giving way inside me; I was almost frightened to go on and, worse, it was so strange I felt I couldn't trust myself, but I said it anyway, "Let me take him, if he'll follow me."

If Ludolf had looked at me then I might have lost my nerve. But he didn't. After a time he turned from the boy to walk slowly back down the track towards the Hof, with the two of us trailing separately behind him. He went up to the doorway and I heard him call for Martin to bring the coat.

With my ash cane in one hand and the sackful of provisions in the other, the bulky coat was awkward to carry, so I wrapped it round the sack, tying the arms together. Egon refused to wear it, even at night—it was high summer and he was having none of this molly-coddling, and when I tried to put the coat on him he squirmed and fought until I gave up. He never bit me though, not once. At the time I thought this was because he liked me. He did like me, but he was no fool and I decided later that he'd been listening to my conversation with Ludolf outside the Hof and followed a good deal of it, especially my threat to bite him back.

It was hard to gauge how much he really understood and whether, when he ignored instructions, it was just because it didn't suit him to understand. I talked more and more to him, along the way. I talked about things he couldn't possibly have understood, about Maggie and Peter—about the good times, it became important to me to remember those now—just for the pleasure of telling him, and with a sense that perhaps no-one had ever talked to him at such length before. For that matter I couldn't remember when I'd last talked for so long, or so freely. Egon rarely spoke, and never in sentences. His sense of grammar had clearly vanished, it was like holding a conversation with someone who didn't speak your language but knew a few words of it and made up for the rest with signs. From time to time he would lead me insistently to a stream or a pool he'd found. *Wasser*, water, he would explain to me, making drinking gestures, as if I were an old spavined horse who'd mislaid his instincts.

A placid summer landscape dozing in the sunshine, a jumpy, unpredictable companion at my side, as jumpy as the landscape was serene . . . travelling with Egon sometimes reminded me of my journey through the West Country with poor mad Denis; the same fits and starts and general anxiety, imagining the shameful consequences if I lost him. He too had been my ward, in a manner of speaking. But where Denis had been tearful and distracted (and of course he was driving, which made it worse), Egon was joyous and distracted, every wood was a new game, a new house to explore like a frenzied terrier. Each time I had to wait till he exhausted himself. If I'd walked on regardless, keeping to my route, Egon would probably have caught me up however far ahead I got, he'd have sniffed me out. I could believe he had the tracking powers of an aborigine, but what if he didn't? Better not to risk it. So we dawdled in copses and along hedgerows, while Egon climbed trees, chased some unseen creature, or explored abandoned holes in the ground.

His toes and fingernails were ragged but not particularly long, I saw, abraded by digging and climbing. His teeth were far from white, but they were whiter than mine. He wasn't all that dirty either, although his skin was weathered in a way I'd seen on no child before. Or rather certain surfaces were weathered, hands, feet and elbows, forearms, neck; while the underside of his arms, from shoulder to elbow, was perfectly soft and babyish in texture, and not all the crawling in the world had managed to transform his knees into anything but a child's knees. The leather breeches, in effect short pants with a leather bib and straps over his shoulders, looked like more of Martin's work, purpose-made, sewn together with corded thread as tough as wire, and the leather itself hard as a saddle in places. The seat especially; this was baggy and hung down behind Egon like a great pad of rhinoceros hide. It was bull-hide I suppose, and it gave me pleasure to think that we were both wearing some remnant of his grandmother's herd. My new arsehole-shoes were still pale and virginal in colour, while by contrast the leather Egon was wearing was a dark brown, stained by forest life, greenish in places and close enough to the colour of Egon's tanned skin to make him look naked from a distance, a small brown thing of the woods but unmistakeably human—except when he was burrowing with his leatherbound backside in the air, hard and shiny as a shell, bringing to mind an illustration in my old childhood encyclopedia: the armadillo, with its long snout, loves to feast on ants.

What would I do with him in London? How would I manage? How would he manage? It was hard enough to picture him in a town, in a street—in Hamburg, if we ever got there. And how would his presence affect my own reception in London? To put it mildly the boy would be a source of trouble; long-term trouble. Also, with any luck, a source of reconciliation. That had been at the back of my mind from the moment I discovered who he was, but I hadn't yet steeled myself to think it through. Never mind what we could make of him, or he of us: he was Maggie's child after all, Molly's nephew, all that was left of her sister. And I'd rescued him at considerable personal cost. Was he, perhaps, my passport to Molly's forgiveness?

Passport, that was a thought: he didn't have one. Nor did I. Neither of us had any valid documents at all. But when we got to Hamburg, God willing, we'd throw ourselves on the mercy of the British authorities. Molly's mercy would be harder to earn. Either I was a poor mad wanderer or I was the fearless rescuer of Maggie's child and clearly sane enough to have informed my family that I was still alive; I couldn't have it both ways. Solve that later. First we had to get across the border.

My plan of campaign had been fairly simple, before I'd acquired Egon. At my own slow rate of progress, and allowing for the pauses I had to take to ease my lungs as well as my feet, I'd hoped to reach the frontier in two days and make the crossing at night. I hadn't counted on unscheduled stops while Egon darted off into the undergrowth to play, or hunt, hard to tell which. Darting was the word, he was the only human being I'd ever known to whom it could be properly applied. He always darted back again, but at this rate the journey might outlast our supplies. Ludolf had traded me some Stickermarks, the Reichsmark banknotes pasted with little stickers proclaiming them the currency of Soviet Germany, in case I needed to make purchases. Bearing in mind Egon's aversion to entering a house, I'd have to do this on my own and pray he'd wait for me. We had bread and sausage with us, plenty of it, but I soon found that Egon turned up his nose at the sausage. I wondered whether he was a vegetarian; for all his foraging Egon never returned with animal booty. Now and then I saw him chewing, he'd nibble beech mast like a pig, and once he returned with a horrible aged-looking slab of fungus off a tree, red as tomato inside. Either his dashes through the forest were just play, or he wasn't a very successful hunter. He'd always had the Hof-dwellers' food-care parcels to sustain him in the Friedrichswald; Ludolf told me they left him bread in the crook of the treehouse beech, and I'd imagined passers-by coming upon this mysterious offering in the woods, prompting more Peterkin tales. Bread, beech mast, mushrooms, berries probably . . . the stink of animal blood in the treehouse, it occurred to me, would be enough to put anyone off meat, for life.

The treehouse must have been horribly cold in winter. Perhaps he'd spent the nights in pits or burrows of his own making, old badger sets, fox earths perhaps, but what kind of child would do that when a warm bed awaited him at the Schloss, and later at the Hof? A deranged, retarded child? My mind kept returning to Ludolf's story. A clever and affectionate child, he'd said. A clever, affectionate child with an *idée fixe*—was that possible at three years old, to become obsessively attached to so harsh a life? A game at first, it was summer and the treehouse offered shelter, safety, food supplied in the crook of a tree, every boy's dream—for a day or two at most, you'd think. Not four years. Hard to imagine it, even though later on my friend the Dodderer told me that *Waldmenschen* or children of the woods weren't so unusual in Eastern Europe in the years immediately following the war. She'd known of several such creatures, and of several psychologists who'd have paid a small fortune to get their hands on one.

Was I prepared to abandon him if I had to, if as Ludolf had warned I couldn't make him obey? What if he chose the wrong moment to run off, under the eyes of the border guards? I tried not to think about this as I stood waiting patiently, yet again, leaning on my cane and peering into a thicket or a maze of pines where the ground bulged with roots. I couldn't chase him in there, for the first time in my life I had to look where I was going, every step of the way. Where was he, the little wretch? No use calling him. Then I'd look up to see him dangling above me, a Mowgli in lederhosen, dropping from the branch to land at my side. In other circumstances it would have been romantic and extraordinary. Right then I felt like someone planning an escape from Colditz with a playful half-wit in tow.

The only way he would consent to settle down was when I gave him a piggy-back ride or sat him on my shoulders, which seemed to awaken a memory. He'd perch there quite happily until a branch came along and he'd be off and gone again. At least—I felt this was promising—he consented to be touched. When I took his hand he didn't flinch or react at all, often he didn't even look up. But he didn't return the pressure of my fingers, either.

Maggie and Peter's son; and I was taking him home. Sometimes I felt quite dizzy with joy at the thought. I couldn't dwell on it, I didn't dare. Home was a word I wasn't yet ready to trust. From time to time I had a nasty glimpse of Molly dismissing us both, I could stay dead for all she cared and as for Egon she'd always detested Maggie . . . no, that was my guilty conscience speaking, surely.

I hadn't worked out where I was going to spend the first night, in the leaves somewhere perhaps, or in an abandoned shed if we were lucky enough to find one. As evening came on Egon seemed as much at a loss as I was. I watched him closely, but if I expected some preternatural familiarity with the woodland I was wasting my time, he looked as tired and disconsolate as any other child astray in a darkening countryside and I had to remind myself that he'd lived in a treehouse and been brought his food. He wasn't Romulus or Remus; hadn't been suckled by wolves. How would he manage without a familiar sleeping place? Perfectly happily, it turned out, cuddled against me inside my cape, at the base of a tree. I kept him firmly clasped, I had to be sure he'd be there in the morning, my gift from Grandfather's treasure chest. He slept soundly, which was more than I did. Shortly before nightfall we'd met out first real obstacle and had our first alarum, Egon and I; I was worried about the day to come, worried that if I fell asleep he'd slip away, and my dreams, when I dozed off at last, were worse than what I saw when I lay awake.

It was dark and cold and unpleasantly damp. My bandages felt clammy round my feet. Was I awake? I must be. I'd been dreaming about Henry and a murderous struggle at the edge of the lake, in the reeds. It came back steeped in dread, and for a time this dread was mixed in with the shock of waking in utterly strange surroundings, out of doors, no idea where I was or how I'd got there. During the first week or so at the Hof I'd had nightmares about lying down in the snow to die, I dreamt that people came to find me but it was too late, I was dying and couldn't tell them where I was—and this was similar except that the snow had gone and I'd survived, the snow had melted away to reveal me here at the foot of a tree, but where the hell was I? Then as I'd felt the child against me under my cape, remembering, remembering it all. First the dream that was still in possession of my soul. Then what had set it off, the day before. Egon and the lake.

We'd reached the lakes of Schwerin in the early evening after making better progress for some hours, with a worn-out Egon content to ride piggy-back, clinging to me sleepily. This hadn't made balancing any easier but once I'd adjusted we forged on steadily, covering ten kilometres this way by sundown. He was no weight at all, lighter than the knapsack Molly packed for our weekend hikes. I wrapped my arms under his legs, he knotted his arms around my neck and we were a contented unit, except when he began to ride down and would grab my beard to pull himself back up again.

I saw one of the lakes ahead of me, still an hour or two's walk away. It would be dark by the time we got there. Never mind, it was our halfway mark, another day-long slog tomorrow and we'd make it to the Schaalsee and the border. My feet were complaining bitterly, my lungs hurt too, but thanks to Egon's sleepiness and my own efforts I was back on schedule and determined to press on. Our intended route ran between the twin lakes, along the old toll road on its causeway. We'd cross it as late at night as possible, when the traffic had died down. Even so I was taking a risk. I'd be out there on a public road, no hope of running off, not on my bandaged plates of meat. If I was stopped for questioning it would be all over, *kaputt*. The alternative was a full day's detour round one of the lakes with my frisky friend. I just wanted to get him back across the border; rather go for the causeway and save time.

The plan fell apart the moment I saw the toll road, and I felt furious with Ludolf and the others who'd said it was unmanned at night, quiet as the grave. Unmanned? The road was patrolled at both ends. And lit up in between like a football stadium for an evening match. With hindsight I realize that at the Hof we might as well have been in the jungles of Borneo for all we knew about the political situation in the country, nobody there knew that the Berlin airlift had begun, that the Russians were moving troops westwards and mounting road blocks up and down the border. At the time I felt betrayed, and hysterically angry. I retreated up the northern shore until I was well out of sight of the patrols, and out of earshot. I wanted to kick something, to curse and shout. In my fury I'd almost forgotten Egon still asleep on my back and by now as much a part of my burdensome frame as a hunchback's hump, and when I bent down looking for a stone to hurl at the water he started to fall off; I caught him and he never made a sound, just fell asleep in my lap as I sat down on the pebbles, exhausted.

I didn't even feel him get up and move away. I jerked awake as my chin touched my chest, and saw Egon standing a few yards away gazing raptly at the lake. Just woken up, ready to go again, ready to play, I thought, and wearily watched him stroll towards the waterline. He didn't stop. As he waded in I had a vision of Henry's body bobbing darkly in the Schaalsee reeds and I heard Egon make a little noise somewhere between a gasp and a laugh as the water rose above his knees. By now I was on my feet and rushing. Trying to run I fell over at once, and scrambled the rest of the way, grabbing at his breeches.

He fought me like a wildcat, this time, trying to gouge my face, so I turned him upside down, held him up by his ankles and hauled him shivering and hissing back to shore. When I set him down the rage in his eyes told me I'd have to pay. There was no holding him, he skittered off across the pebbles and into the shelter of the trees, despite my imploring yells. After a while I sat down again, miserably, my shoes and trouser-bottoms waterlogged. The woods had gone silent, as if they'd swallowed him up: I pictured Egon deep in the pine forest, still running, and self-pity overwhelmed me. The day was a disaster, everything had gone wrong, if the border was as heavily patrolled as the causeway I'd do better to give myself up right away; and if I'd now managed to lose the boy, I didn't care what happened. If he didn't come back . . . I'd got my legs and feet wet, might as well finish the job—as time went by I actually thought about walking out into the water, letting myself sink. I thought about it calmly. Wouldn't you float, whether you wanted to or not? Perhaps it was a matter of filling your pockets with stones. Why not? As far as the world was concerned Richard Thurgo was already dead.

It was pitch dark when I heard the lightest of footfalls behind me, and turned. I had to resist the impulse to lunge for the child and hug him tight. I couldn't see his eyes, but whatever Egon understood by my reaction, as we waited each other out, it seemed to reassure him; when he approached I stood up and he let me hoist him onto my back without protesting. I tramped uphill into the woods, half a mile or so until the lake was out of sight, and by the time we were settled under the tree Egon was fast asleep again. Snoring gently, slack-mouthed. All innocence.

I was back at the Hof, in the dream I had that first night. I could hear my birthday party in full swing somewhere, knowing I should be at the heart of it, but instead I was hunched in one of the tiny corridors with Martin and he was begging me—with unlikely fluency—to take him with me to Hamburg, where he'd advertise in the newspapers and perhaps find someone who could identify him and connect him to a name, a past. I felt I owed him for the shoes, so I said yes, reluctantly. No sooner had I reached the party than Ludolf was taking me aside to tell me I must get up early and leave without Martin. From what he'd discovered about Martin's past it would be better, he said, if Martin never learnt about it. Ludolf's words puzzled and angered me. What right did he have, I wondered, to make this decision on Martin's behalf? But I felt relieved.

The next moment—and despite my conversation with Ludolf—I was being accompanied through fields by someone who looked just like Martin. I knew that this was all right because he was in fact Henry: I'd discovered the secret, which was that Martin and Henry were one. Egon was nowhere to be seen, he was an object of concern but in the dream I wasn't afraid of losing him. My fear was of something quite else. As we sat at the edge of a wood, overlooking a wheat field, a brilliant green with the wind doodling smoky letters in it, this Henry with Martin's dazed eyes offered to buy the child off me, and without his telling me I knew what he wanted to do with Egon. I pretended to be thinking about it and we were walking along beside the lake when I pounced on Henry from behind and forced him down into the water, between the reeds, holding his head under, and woke, woke myself really, to stop it. The dread clinging to me as I woke up had nothing to do with the murderousness of the dream. Henry in Martin-disguise had wanted to molest the child, I'd intuited it and now it clung to me as if it were my own secret desire.

It wasn't, though. As I felt Egon clasped against me I knew the excitement came from somewhere else; it was Herta pressing on my mind. Egon was sinewy under my cape, like a lizard, thin arms and pinching fingers and a scaly body, a scorpion almost. Anything less likely to arouse my lust I couldn't have imagined. He'd seen as much of my cock as he was going to see; more than enough, in fact. I only hoped he wasn't waiting for another exhibition.

As it grew light I discovered that we weren't out of sight of the lake as I'd supposed, I could see the dark mass of the farther, western shore quite clearly, and to my left, southwards, the far end of the causeway road. Patrolled, if the tiny, stationary figures I saw were soldiers. Away to the north there was a stretch of lake that looked familiar, with a long sandy spit of land, and I was confused by memories of the frozen Schaalsee and its promontories and sandbanks that failed to offer an ice bridge, when I realized the spit of land was familiar for a different reason. Walks with Peter. I remembered that we'd parked his car beside the causeway and walked north along the lake until we found a suitable spot, sandy earth with a fallen pine tree as a marker, opposite a spit of land. We'd dug a pit there, and buried the bomb with the silent, chemical-mechanical fuse.

Egon must have thought he'd finally taught me something: the joy of digging holes. Seeing me scrabbling away on my knees he joined in with delight. Both of us kneeling in the sand and digging, side by side . . . our first joint effort. Digging for victory, as the wartime slogan put it. When I stopped to begin a fresh hole he only dug faster and deeper to show me I lacked perseverance. My efforts to describe what we were looking for meant nothing to him, whether I used words or gestures. We were digging for pleasure as far as Egon was concerned. Now and again he paused to study me with a mentor's restrained approval—I'd come to my senses and discovered playfulness at last.

I couldn't remember if we'd buried the thing under the log or to one side or at the end of it, leaving it pointing at the place like an arrow. But I was pretty certain I'd found the right log. As we dug we were visible from the causeway. No reason for alarm, we were a man and a child digging in shoreline sand on a summer morning. Distant figures, digging for bait. The soldiers were busy anyway, there was a growing number of cars and cyclists and pedestrians for them to deal with. I saw with relief that not everyone was being stopped. But how many looked as outlandish, from close to, as Egon and myself? Without a diversion I didn't give much for our chances. I was still watching the causeway traffic when my fingertips scraped something smooth and solid.

I think Egon was more impressed by my finding the bomb than by anything else I've done since then, whether on his behalf or my own. My tireless efforts had shown him I was a good digger; this find showed I was a great digger. No fox or badger had ever come up with a glinting metallic box, its aluminum case untarnished, dazzling in the sunshine. Inside it everything seemed intact, the little phial of acid, the metal fusewire furred with rust but still in place; the plastic explosive was spotless; almost as if we'd buried the thing the day before. Little Egon was gazing at it with awe. I opened Ludolf's sack, cut us both some bread and gave myself a hunk of sausage, and as we sat chewing I addressed the child.

"Your father bought this from my brother," I said. "From your uncle's brother." I pointed at myself, trying to get Egon's attention. "Onkel Richard. Bruder Alec." But Egon was more interested in the box. "This funny-looking thing, this Alec-bomb . . ." I said, determined to make something of the moment, but I heard myself trailing away as I stared at the shiny metal. Sunlight bounced off it into Egon's delighted face; one dirty hand reached out to stroke the aluminum. If only his father had put it to its intended use . . . well, there was no point in speculating now; in case the boy started playing with it I leaned forwards and pulled the silver shoe-box across the sand towards me. Closing the lid I remembered how I'd felt when we were burying it here, Peter and I, as if it was a ritual farewell. We were laying to rest a different kind of explosive, our short-lived physical bond, So I'd thought then. But what bond? There in the Schloss, in the stink of Branntwein, fighting Peter in my under-clothes, Peter beneath me lying on his father's puke-stained dress suit . . . physical bond my foot. I hadn't asked his consent, I'd taken him by force, ravished him, and now it slowly dawned on me that in adopting Egon I'd managed to saddle myself—quite literally, I was his donkey-ride—not with the child of a girl I'd raped, as I'd supposed when I saw him beneath the treehouse, but with the child of a man I'd raped. The thought made me feel dizzy. It wasn't right though, "raped" didn't ring true. Ravished was a better term, if we'd both taken pleasure in it. The son of a man I'd ravished . . . that didn't sound much better. And to be playing uncle to the child; as punishment—even as atonement—it was eccentric, to say the least. My old law tutor's words returned: "Today we're going to take the three 'B's, Buggery, Burglary, and Bankruptcy." Until now I hadn't seen them as a sequence. Rape's progress. . . . Egon's hands were creeping back towards the box, he'd dropped his bread in the sand, and as his fingers worked the catch open I was jolted out of my trance. All we needed was for him to blow us both to kingdom come. I lifted the oblong metal case out of the boy's reach, holding it up like an offering to an emperor. "You'll see," I said. "A magic box." If it works, I added under my breath. Bang, I went, opening my eyes wide for Egon's benefit. "Bang!" This he liked. He made a throaty old man's noise which I decided was a rare laugh. Yes; today we were going to take the three "B" 's. Buggery, buffonery, and bombs.

There was nothing wrong with my plan. I simply never realized we'd been spotted from the causeway, or that the slightest interest was being taken in us. Perhaps one of the soldiers had binoculars trained on the shore. But if he saw us dig up a metal box, was there anything inherently suspicious about that? It could have been fishing tackle. Perhaps they weren't suspicious, only curious enough to send out a patrol in our direction. I've been over the sequence of events more than once in my mind, and I don't think I could have acted any differently. The fact is I never saw the patrol set out. We finished our meal quite unaware of it, packed our belongings and took the bomb back up into the trees, where I chose a spot close enough to the shore to make the explosion as noticeable as possible.

The fusewire had degraded, and I feared this might reduce the fuse time. To nothing, perhaps. No way of knowing until I broke the phial of acid. Then I'd know all right, one way or the other. Grandfather's exploding Spanish cannon, Alec and his grenades . . . the tremendous, sulphurous fart as the pasture erupted at Schloss Brüel when the bomb—when this thing's twin went off . . . holding the knife Ludolf had supplied with our bread and sausage, I stared at the little tube of glass. Do it, I told myself. Afraid to die? This new life I'd embarked on was like purgatory already, so far it was a guided tour of what I'd done wrong in the old one. The same life, without blinkers this time. I stabbed the phial. The glass refused to break. Stabbed it again; sawed at it. If only we had the silver sugar-tongs, the ones Peter used for our demonstration blast . . . as I looked round for another implement, so did Egon, imitating me. I could see he wanted to help but my worst fear was that he'd give me the runaround once I'd released the acid, and linger out of fascination with the box. I found two stones with broken edges, and returned with them. The boy was close, within arm's length. I crouched and reached into the casing.

As I brought the stones together I couldn't help shutting my eyes. The glass phial splintered and I turned to grab Egon, waiting for the world to erupt. I had his arm firmly in my grasp, he could scratch me half to death for all I cared, but no, he responded to my urgency, letting me drag him as we scrambled uphill. Above us, I couldn't see it yet, there was a path, the one

Peter and I used to follow. Further south it crossed the causeway road. Plenty of time, a quarter of an hour the fuse lasted—at room temperature, Peter had said. "Don't be afraid . . . you shouldn't be afraid, because this, old boy, is a British bomb." Fifteen minutes at room temperature.

We heard the soldiers coming before we'd even reached the little hillside path. Egon heard them too, he was staring intently. I crouched and pulled him down with me. Three of them; I saw their raw young schoolboy faces, their rifles held loosely at the ready as they left the path and trotted down towards the lake, through the trees. They were talking, unflustered, and it was German I heard, not Russian; just a bit of exercise for three lads sick of war, a woodland stroll to flush out a pair of odd-looking civilians.

I could have stood up then and cried, *"Ihr da, Freunde!"*— don't go down there, lads, there's a bomb about to go off! I'd have had to tell them how I knew, and got myself arrested for my pains. I could have stopped them going down there, but I didn't.

I don't know for certain whether any or all of them were injured, maimed, killed. They were certainly in the vicinity of the bomb when it went off, and given the size of the explosion I'm fairly sure I have those idly chatting, unsuspecting Germans on my conscience; in wartime it would have been a bonus, but it wasn't wartime and this wasn't what I planned, all I'd intended was a bang to bring them running, something to make them leave their posts. We were at the south-east end of the causeway when the blast came, tossing clods of earth and rocks and torn-off branches high into the air, a happy tissue-ball of smoke escaping like a sheeted ghost as the snapping and crashing sounds died down and the woods settled again. In the confusion that followed no-one paid us any mind, we were part of a crowd only too eager to get across the causeway and away from the noise and the danger.

The border crossing itself was a straightforward do-or-die effort, that night. Since June and the Berlin crisis the frontier had been shaved and turned into a treeless strip five hundred miles long. All we had to do was crawl across this strip, fifty yards or so, in darkness but thoroughly exposed if anyone was watching. Someone was out there all right, the distant tommy-gun bursts made sure we knew that. It was a terrifying sound no matter how distant. In time its steady, mocking recurrence made me wonder if this wasn't its main purpose, random firing into the dark woods to discourage new or faint-hearted frontier walkers. Frontier rats would have been a better term now that we had to slither across open ground. Egon thought it was a great game. So much so I was afraid he'd decide this was a perfect clearing to run dizzy circles in. I couldn't explain to him that he had to stay down, just pray that he'd imitate me. I was no great shakes at crawling. Egon was, thank God. He was an expert crawler and he knew it, and once he got the idea it was he who led the way across the shaved ground, showing his clumsy old companion what to do.

No doubt he thought I was unusually grateful for the lesson: when we reached the other side I hugged him tight in my glee. Still hugging him—I wasn't having the child go back for another demonstration crawl—I tucked my ash cane under my arm and hobbled into Anglo-German woods as fast as I could, ignoring the pain in my feet, easy now that every shuffling sliding step in the leaves cried safe, safe, safe.

It had seemed so much to ask of God, of destiny, to make it this far, that I'd barely thought about how to proceed when we got to Hamburg, other than to go to the authorities and, as I'd planned, throw myself on their mercy. Ask to be repatriated—along with a half-English, informally adopted child, my nephew by marriage. To all intents and purposes a German count. This was where problems could set in. I had plenty of time to think about it as we retraced my earlier footsteps, back towards where a tram would take us into the city.

There was quite an array of problems, I began to see that. Henry's body, fished out of the Schaalsee, might have led to investigations; or not—just another body perhaps. The border must have claimed enough of them. And would any investigations have led to me? Would they have pursued Henry's contacts zealously enough to come across a description of Herr Schäfer? It was all months ago; filed and forgotten surely, in the labyrinth of police paperwork.

So if I simply told the truth, omitting Henry, where would I stand? And where would Egon stand, administratively speaking? It wasn't as if he was a pet monkey I could simply keep on my person, hanging round my neck. How could I even prove who he was?

Getting Egon into the tram was a trial in itself. The rising number of houses, and cars, had already begun to unsettle him. But he'd seen some of each before, and he'd never seen anything like the tram, let alone found himself trapped inside a rattling yellow metal box, or confined in such a small space with other people. He was rigid with fear, now and again he shook convulsively. I could handle the rigidity and the shuddering by pressing him against me, but I was afraid this would increase his panic as it had in the water, any moment he'd turn into a crazed rodent trying to bite and claw his way out of my hold. Think of the treehouse, Egon, I murmured, uselessly, think of the treehouse in a high wind, in rain and hail, the corrugated metal sides flapping and shaking and the rain battering it, just think back to that and this old tram will seem like home. I sat him beside me, by the window, and stroked his back and shoulders. His eyes seemed to have gone dull, as though he was seeing nothing of the outskirts of Hamburg, too strange even to be reviewed. If he was looking inwards I hoped he was seeing something comforting.

Except for when he'd been asleep this was the first time he'd been so still and so close for a period of time, and I was able to see things in his face that I hadn't observed before. His eyes, which I'd first thought a greyish blue, then closer to hazel, I now saw to have greenish tints which in different lights had suggested both the blue, a cold blue, of his father's eyes, and the brown of Maggie's. On closer inspection the boy's eyes bore no similarity to either, their colour was by turns muddy and indeterminate in the way they deflected your attention to his other features; and then when the light found them through the tram windows they filled with luminous specks of green and brown and even a glint of gold, as colours will emerge from a canvas when a light plays on it, or from foliage when the sun comes out, where they'd looked dull and mealy a moment earlier. They were much his most expressive feature, at this age, the nose unformed, and the mouth undecided as to what shape it would take. Thin, sensitive, reddish lips, neither Peter's liplessness nor Maggie's moist and ill-defined ones; but with something of their mobility. Gazing blindly at the window, not following the sights with his eyes but simply staring ahead, the boy's mouth was drawn tight, his cheeks quivering as if in extreme concentration on the instant, and on containing his panic.

Without the slightest warning he was sick into my lap, and it seemed to surprise him as much as it did me; I remember his face quite clearly—he'd not been given any warning, his startled expression said, and he'd no idea what this fluid was or that it was possible to do this. I mopped up the worst of it with news-

paper. My clothes weren't exactly fit to meet the King in anyway.

Egon didn't. seem at all upset about having been sick, he
seemed more cheerful altogether. But how would he manage—
this was what was really beginning to prey on my mind—if these
nebulous authorities I kept invoking, I didn't even know whether
they should be military, civilian, or medical . . . if they took
Egon away while they tried to establish the truthfulness of my
story, a process that might take days, if not weeks . . .

Egon lost in a camp for DPs, displaced persons, unable to
cope with life there and with no familiar face to turn to: as I
pictured it I clutched the poor child tighter. Perhaps he'd adapt,
like a cat in strange streets. What if he didn't? I needed to know
who it was I'd be dealing with, in official quarters. I needed
advice.

From whom, though? The image of fat Cheerybye in the Atlantic lobby came to mind. He looked as if he'd know. He'd tell
me, wouldn't he, if I appealed to him for help?

But could I register once more at the Atlantic Hotel? Even
with the eccentric reputation I must have had there, which might
excuse the vomit on my trousers, surely not even Red Cross
credentials would be sufficient to explain my trying to check in
with my "nephew," a dirty, partly naked boy. It was hard
enough to imagine a hotel where that would be acceptable. The
Atlantic certainly wasn't it.

Of course! Why had my brain been so slow to clear? Karin—
it was Karin I needed. I felt released; even the tram seemed to
be sliding easier on its rails. Karin, to help me with the child
while I made my enquiries and prepared the next step.

We got off at Rathausmarkt, Egon and I. He stared at the
building facing us, a pseudo-Renaissance monstrosity from the
1800s, and I wondered what was passing through his mind. Did
he ever dream of the Schloss as it had been in his infancy?
"Town Hall," I explained solemnly, provoked by some of the
looks we were getting. I was beginning to enjoy outlandishness.

Egon stuck close to me as I made the telephone call to the
Atlantic and left word for Karin to meet me at our usual spot in
Planten un Blomen, under the old plane tree. The hotel em-
ployee who answered didn't seem to have heard of me, she was
new perhaps, but grudgingly she took Herr Schäfer's message.
I could hear the Mecklenburger accent in my voice, thickened
over recent months, and handsomely melodic. I lacked Molly's
gift for mimicry, but in my experience mimics are rarely lin-

guists; unlike her I could insinuate myself into a language, not just its song but its grunts and hesitations, they were more than a costume, they were a hiding place.

Egon continued to stay close to me as we made our slow way to the park, and I felt a little more confident. At least he wasn't tempted to run off any more. I hauled him up onto my back and took it slowly now, slowly in the sunshine, one step at a time and using the ash cane as if I were an old man. It was simply easier that way, but if I'd had a hat to extend to passers-by I could probably have bought us bed and board with the proceeds. They looked more prosperous somehow, the Hamburgers. The Jungfernstieg cafés were full of people sitting there pleasantly dazzled by the light. Out on the Alster a flotilla of launches stirred up the milky water and rocked gently in each other's wake, evoking something loved, familiar . . . an air of Maidenhead, that was it, lazy summer boating days with Alec and Peter, and Maggie with her parasol.

I felt their blessing, and now the sheer triumph of it all, of what I'd done, began to strike me. I'd given my toes—not intentionally of course, but I'd taken a risk, and had to accept the sacrifice—to bring home my nephew from a Russian forest, and by God I'd done it, I'd brought it off! Wouldn't this keep me in self-respect for the rest of my life, whatever my other transgressions?

Leaving the Alster behind us, we headed north past the Dammtor station. Egon tensed as new arrivals jostled us on the pavement, and I had to remove his anxiously tugging fingers from my beard. The Dammtor! Where I'd arrived in—what—March? Four heroic months. For all of us, it seemed: it wasn't just the Hamburg people who seemed better off and happier, the streets themselves were barely recognizable. In later years I learnt to greet this as the annual Hamburg miracle—one day you came out of your house and the gloomy damp was gone, the frog-city had turned into a prince. But there was more at work, this July, than the kiss of light. The rubble was gone from the inner city; at every corner there were neat rows of potatoes, turnips, beans. And goods in the shops! If I'd tried to buy any I'd have discovered that a new currency was in force and brand new Deutschmarks, replacing the old Reichsmarks, had been issued to every citizen. The shopkeepers were parading articles they'd kept hidden through the winter and spring, waiting for the spending spree to come. I saw shoes and suits and coats for sale, underwear, even bathing costumes. Irons, light bulbs, wireless sets. Fancy vegetables. Fruit! Streets lined with well-stocked stalls where there hadn't even been a street. I'd loved the dreary rubble and the scarcity, but this rejuvenated Hamburg suited my mood. The city's transformation seemed like magic to me, in my ignorance of the currency reform, or as if ten years had passed while I lay comatose at the Hof. Glimpsed in shop windows, my figure with its beard and horse-blanket and sapling cane had a touch of Rip van Winkle, and if I'd been the old sleepyhead himself I couldn't have been more amazed at the changes around me.

As we entered Planten un Blomen I glanced back at Egon to see if the grass and trees were a glad sight to him. But his eyes showed nothing, they were still glazed, and if he was seeing the greenery at all he may have registered it as a hallucination, a wish-fulfillment like my own vision of the Schloss on the way to Brüel. Seating planks had been restored to the park benches; I lowered myself onto one to let Egon down. But he didn't want to move. We still had bread and sausage left, and consumed it now like a strange two-headed beast, Egon clinging to me with his head on my shoulder and his jaws munching away next to mine.

I didn't know how long it would take for Karin to get my message and find the time to come to our rendez-vous, so I simply made my way there with Egon, prepared to wait as long as it took. As we came nearer to the plane tree I spotted plenty of fellow-Britons with their blue-and-white shoulder-flashes fringed with red, Control Commission people. The Continental Crackers Gang they liked to call themselves—they were all over, one here, one there, some with girls and some not. Clearly the warm weather was bringing them out.

I sat beneath the good old plane, quite the finest specimen I'd ever seen, and as I turned to make Egon comfortable I noticed that a plaque had now been installed beside the tree, naming the man who'd planted it here; a Dr. Lehmann, 127 years ago; and this touched me, absurdly. Millions had died but Dr. Lehmann's plane tree, like Hamburg itself, put out fresh leaves—whoever had put up the plaque surely meant me to understand this. Egon's head was lolling, it seemed the park was having a soothing effect after all, or perhaps it was the food, enabling him to doze after all the tension, the fear and nausea he'd been through.

We'd hardly sat down before I was conscious of people moving towards us from several directions as though we were a magnetic focus of attraction. Then I realized it was mostly men with shoulder-flashes who were approaching us with such unconvincing casualness. Were we breaking some law, Egon and I? Puzzled, I turned to see whether their target was behind us but what I saw were more grim faces coming closer, one had his hand poised at his hip, evidently armed. If it was me they were after—ridiculous—they didn't need gunmen: where could I run to? Egon's head still heavy on my shoulder, half asleep. I too couldn't, or wouldn't take in what was happening. It was like being an animal at the centre of a hunting party as the noose tightened, but when the puzzlement gave way my first, unexpected emotion was relief. Somehow it felt more honest than my previous high spirits.

The uniformed men had stopped some ten or fifteen yards away, at an invisible command, and now there was someone coming round the back of my bench to sit beside me, a man in a well-tailored suit. I'd never seen him before. No gun in his hand. Instead he reached into his pocket and produced an ancient, implausible pair of handcuffs, recently repainted and looking like a Christmas party joke. Someone had coloured in a tiny British lion on one of them, and on the other an imperial German eagle. I arrest you in the name of . . . whom? Of King and Kaiser?

"Richard Thurgo?" He was my age, nice chummy eyes, rather good-looking in a modestly dissipated, donnish sort of way. I stared at him, managed a nod. The cuffs were real enough, they felt cold on my wrists. I don't remember him saying "Come with us, sir," or anything of the like. Perhaps he didn't bother.

"Byron," said fat Cheerybye, his bow-tied, Bunterish figure perched on a corner of the desk, as he turned the pages of Uncle Tom's "Lord Byro." "Give me Shelley every time."

"Oh I don't know," said Philby judiciously from behind the desk. One chummy eye threw me a wink at Cheerybye's expense. He followed it with a conspiratorial, not-all-of-us-despise-Byron look, as if arresting me had made the two of us old friends.

They were waiting me out, and I couldn't quite make out why. Were they waiting for me to confess? But to confess about what? About Henry?

On the desk beside the battered Byron and the contents of my suit pockets, including the gun, sat the Colonel's washbag. Next to it, the money it had contained. And my stack of false documents. Everything I'd entrusted to Karin two months earlier, before leaving. I suppose I knew that she'd betrayed me as soon as I saw the CCG men closing in on me in Planten un Blomen, but I didn't realize the extent of her cooperation with them until I got to the interrogation room at Bad Neunburg and saw my possessions neatly laid out. Had she been in cahoots with these people from the beginning! Not wanting to dwell on it I decided I should be thankful she'd made herself so trustworthy in their eyes, because rather than holding Egon in some children's institution Philby and Walters (this was Cheerybye's name) agreed to put him in Karin's charge while I was being held for questioning. I'd begged them to do this, hoping that Karin felt some sense of obligation to me, after what she'd done. And at least until later when I started to hear about the hell Egon was putting her through, it helped to ease my mind; my body kept on remembering the two thin arms locked around my neck, remembering with a start as if I'd dropped him somewhere by mistake.

Of course they'd look after the boy, Philby insisted, I was among friends. Then why the arrest, why the handcuffs? Well, they just hadn't been sure how I'd react—I'd been armed, hadn't I?—to their invitation to talk things over.

Talk what over? Byron and Shelley? Perhaps they'd got the wrong man, I suggested.

"The curious thing," said Philby, ignoring this and easing back in his chair, "is that your uncle and my old father were such buddies, I'm only surprised we haven't met before now, you and I. They ran into each other in Damascus, back in '05 or thereabouts, and I first got to know him in the 'Twenties. Your Uncle Tom that is. What a rogue."

"He was a rogue," fat Walters echoed. Idly enough; though the weight he put on the first two syllables seemed to indicate a standard against which others (and certainly nephews) could measure themselves.

"Did you know," said Philby, "that he managed to sell arms to both sides in the Civil War and still dine out every day in the best restaurants in Barcelona, unharmed?"

"I want to know what I'm doing here," I said. "I'm a British citizen. Have I broken any laws?"

"Plenty," said Walters.

"Which ones?"

"All in good time."

His Cheerybye-manner of Atlantic days seemed to have vanished. He tossed aside the Byron in disgust and reached into the desk drawer, bringing out a slim file.

"Your uncle and my father fought a war once, in Mesopotamia," Philby was saying affably, "against each other, using rival Arab factions. One of them, Ibn Saud I think, was supported by the Foreign Office and my Dad. The other by the War Office and your uncle. Both armed by Tom of course, Lee Enfields all round. More of a thinker, my old man. Tom was a doer. Between them they founded modern Saudi Arabia, they used to say."

"Is that my file?" I asked. Walters was staring into it.

"Jawohl," he said heavily.

"Doesn't look as though you've got much on me."

"Cigarette?" said soft-voiced Philby.

"Look here," I said, "I was an interrogating officer, CSDIC, for five years."

"We're aware of that."

"Then spare me the double-act. What do you want? Why I am here?" I waved away the cigarette. "I don't smoke."

"Waiting for someone else to join us, actually," said Philby. "Just doodling around."

"Doesn't smoke," noted Walters, scribbling on my file. He wasn't dropping the mask or acknowledging in any way what I thought was my utter sangfroid. "We do know a fair bit about you," he said, turning a page, "but what we don't understand is why you killed Martin Bormann."

"Yes," said Philby, "we'd very much like to know that."

All I heard ringing in my head was "killed," and a strange name, not Henry's. "Who?"

"Reichsleiter Martin Bormann."

"Hitler's bosom pal."

"His bum-boy."

"So they say," Philby was smiling.

I grinned back and together we savoured the joke, until I saw their unwavering expression. They were amused all right, but there was something else. Now I could see it in their eyes: they weren't joking at all.

"Not me," I said.

But the ground had gone from under me. Martin. Martin? The little old amnesiac at the Hof with his true-blue eyes and his stunned face wreathed in middle-aged jowls? Martin Bormann . . . made my shoes? No, wait, he'd only been nicknamed Martin, after Martin Luther. And I hadn't killed him. Except in my dream where he was Henry. I'd killed Henry. Upturned nose, red cheeks and lips, insolent smile . . . far too young for God's sake. Not Martin Bormann, not conceivably.

"We found his body a couple of months ago," began Philby.

"You really have got the wrong chap," I interrupted, "I wouldn't know Martin Bormann if I saw him, but if nothing else I'm pretty damn sure I haven't killed him."

" . . . in Spain," Philby continued patiently when I stopped yapping.

I stared at them as the penny dropped.

A faceless, melting head. "Schäfer?"

They gazed back at me.

"Schäfer was Martin Bormann?"

"We think so," said Walters. "The evidence is all in here." And he tapped Lord Byro. "In your little book."

Evidence? My mind was whirling. "It's not *my* little book," I said. But things were coming back. *Begin at the beginning. And secondly, proceed.* . . . I looked from one to the other.

Philby was smiling again. "For a time we thought *you* were Bormann."

"What?"

"Well, you were travelling under his alias. Then we thought you were working for him."

"Or for Tom Thurgo," said Walters, adding as I turned to him, "Same thing."

"I *beg* your pardon?"

"We'd rather have had a word with Bormann first," said Philby soothingly, standing up and coming round the desk towards me, "but all the same . . . I'd like to shake the hand of the chap who killed him."

"Wait a minute," I said.

Philby pumped my hand anyway. I saw him flinch: I stank like a beast. He glanced at Walters but Walters refrained, without great difficulty I thought, from taking my hand. The phone rang and he moved to pick up the receiver instead.

"Ja, natürlich, sofort!" he cried into it, in an execrable accent, much more like the Cheerybye of old. "Warum warten Sie, you dolt?" He nodded at Philby as he put the phone down.

"In case you're wondering what Bormann was doing in Malaga in March," said Philby.

"Like hell he is," Walters said under his breath.

" . . . here's the man who can tell you."

Booted footsteps approached, the door opened, I turned, and for an instant I was back at Malaga airport. Quick, Toor-go little Luís was saying, tugging at me. Come, Toor-go, come!

"Well, Jakob?" said Philby to the man in the doorway, who was studying me and now gave an answering nod.

"That's him," said Wall-face.

Dimly, it seemed like years ago, I recalled nearly running down this man at Finca Thurgo, as the jeep rolled forwards, out of control. He probably remembered too. What on earth was he doing here?

"Jakob Mützel," said Philby, still amiable, doing the introductions. "Richard Thurgo." Neither of us responded. I broke Mützel's gaze to glance at Philby, who said, "Jakob is with the Mossad."

Walters saw me looking baffled. "Jewish Intelligence."

"Israeli," said Mützel pointedly, without deigning to look at Walters.

"Look what I've got for you, Jakob," Philby exclaimed, returned to the desk, where he opened the Byron and extracted a piece of paper marking the place. "La-Listen to this." In this enthusiasm a faint stammer, reminiscent of Alec's, had entered his voice. "It's Byron's Don Juan, canto 13, verse 73. . . ."

Wall-face Mützel was still staring at me and I was getting sick of it.

I stood up. As I did so both Walters and Philby stiffened, and I decided my appearance hadn't entirely lost its menace.

"Glass in the sugar," I said quietly. Mützel didn't react. Estrella's voice: the Jews, Richard. The Jews kill him. "Perhaps," I said, "you're the fellow who killed my uncle."

"I don't believe I had that pleasure," said Mützel, unmoved.

So much for my powers of intimidation. "You hired the waiter, then," I said, "to put glass in his sugar."

He looked at me a moment longer then burst into laughter. "Glass in the sugar? If I could have got that close to your uncle, to serve him sugar, I would have killed him much more simply. With a bullet."

"Don Juan, Canto 13," said Philby, clearing his throat like a schoolmaster trying to recapture the classroom's attention.

"Your uncle died of a heart attack," Wall-face said to me, "not glass in the sugar. Whoever sold you this idea . . ." he chuckled again, "has some imagination!"

"Don Juan, Canto 13," Philby repeated. "A b-book belonging to the late Colonel Thurgo, Jakob. With what appear to be several coded messages on the fly-leaf and a note referring us to four lines by Lord Byron." Philby picked up the book and declaimed:

" '. . . Firstly begin with the beginning (though
  That clause is hard); and secondly, proceed;
  Thirdly, commence not with the end—or, sinning
  In this sort, end at least with the beginning.' "

"Ye gods," Walters muttered.

"Now, the fly-leaf has several messages scribbled on it," said Philby, leaning forward to study it, "and the last one runs as follows." He sat back with the book and read aloud, carefully, " 'An elderly, muddled King may capitulate. . . . ' " Philby glanced up for effect, then went on, " 'but your city faces Greek brigandage unless Fate stands by Troy, Pa-Pa-Paris notwithstanding.' "

Was it a crossword clue? I did remember finding a message in the book. Had it been on the fly-leaf? Or on a piece of paper? *Life is rosy in Foulsham Grange* . . . nothing about Troy, that I could recall.

" 'Fat Menelaus,' " Philby continued with a sidelong glance at Cheerybye, " 'laughs, King Priam!' And that's it."

"So?" said Wall-face.

"I don't suppose you've ever heard of the Playfair code, Jakob?" said Philby. "Before your time perhaps. It's as old as the hills."

Wall-face grunted. Since his arrival the balance of power had shifted and I couldn't tell whether Philby was really the schoolmaster here, or who was being tested. He had produced a piece of paper from the desk and was scribbling on it industriously. "Watch this," he said to Wall-face. And, glancing at me, "You too, Richard, if you're not familiar with this stuff already."

Walters glared at Philby in disapproval. "You really think he isn't in on it?"

"In on what?" I asked.

"Look," said Philby, inviting us to bend over the page.

F	I	R	S	T
L	Y	B	E	G
N	W	H	O	U
A	C	D	P	M
K	Q	V	X	Z

" 'Firstly begin with the beginning'—and so on, you see?" Philby pointed to the little square of letters. "You make a five by five square of the letters of the alphabet in the order they appear in the text you've chosen. *I* counts as *J* by the way, so as to get the 26 letters into a nice neat five by five. Any letters that don't crop up you just add on to the end in alphabetical order." As he said this Philby added the bottom five letters, and sat back again. "Got it? Now. Know what a bigram is?"

Bye-gram, he pronounced it. A bye-gram? It was what I hadn't sent Molly.

"A bigram is a pair of letters," Philby was writing furiously again, showing us. "You add *X* if you've got an odd number, so "England" for instance would be *EN, GL, AN, DX*. Got that? Now, if you want to encipher the word *England* . . ."

He started to draw diagonals on the little square of letters, and then rectangles enclosing the diagonal lines. Cheerybye remained expressionless, but there was a look of faint distaste on Mützel's pug face, as though it were some decadent English vice that Philby was sketching for us.

"What you do . . ."—Philby scribbled madly—" . . . is *this* . . . or rather what you used to do in days of yore . . . as I say, the old Playfair went out with ca-ca-ca-ca . . ."

"Carrier pigeons," Walters supplied.

"Ca-ca-ca-loak and dagger, I was going to say," said Philby.

"I bet Jonathan Mansel used it," I murmured to see if anyone rose to the bait. The scene was quite as preposterous as any in a Dornford Yates book.

"Who?" said Philby, glancing up. Then a smile began, he couldn't keep it out of his eyes. "Yes, I bet he did."

"Who is Mansel?" asked Wall-face tautly.

"English agent," Philby said with a straight face, omitting to add that Mansel was no more real than Bulldog Drummond. It was a joke after my own heart; I loved him for it. He glanced from me to puzzled Wall-face. "Mansel was before your time, Jakob," he said, going back to work on his scribbles.

Without my knowing it the die was cast, the die of my life. All I was conscious of at the time was that alliances were emerging, Philby and myself on one side, Cheerybye and Wall-face on the other. Or was this the lure, I wondered, the illusion they were setting up for my benefit?

"Only your uncle would have used this rusty old method," said Philby, turning the piece of paper for me so that I could read it. "You take the first bigram, *EN*, see the diagonal they form on the square? Make a rectangle, and the other diagonal yields the cipher bigram: *LO. GP* for instance would come out as *EM*. Say your pair of letters don't form a diagonal; well, if they're on the same line as each other what you do is you encipher each letter with the letter to its right, starting again if you run out of letters, so *GL* for example, comes out as *LY*. Follow? And if your pair of letters are in a column, like *AN*, same routine but this time you replace each letter with the one beneath it. *AN* becomes *KA*. So: we've got *EN-GL-AN* coming out *LO-LY-KA*. What about the final bigram, *DX*?'' He looked up. "Richard?''

I studied the diagram. *"PV,"* I said.

"Well done. Like uncle, like nephew,'' Philby nodded. "You've got it. But all *I* had to go on was this,'' he pushed the book towards us, open at the fly-leaf; funny, I thought, that I'd never noticed the inscription. "I tried all kinds of codes on it,'' said Philby, "till I thought of the Playfair. Can you see how the message deciphers?'' We shook our heads. "Take the first letter of each word—ignoring *and* and *the*, by the way, they don't count—then simply decode them a pair at a time. Using the same premise as the encipherment process, only in reverse. Ready? 'An elderly, muddled King may capitulate . . .' starts you off with *AE*, *MK*, *MC*. Which comes out as *PL*, *AZ*, then *A* and *D*, it's an address you see, Plaza . . . de . . .'' A stammer hovered on his lips.

"Plaza de Bailen *très*,'' I blurted, remembering before I knew it. Estrella's words again: I tell you where to go. Plaza de Bailen *très*. There you sell jeep, Richard.

"Exactly, Plaza de Bailen *très*, Malaga,'' said Philby, writing out the rest of the decipherment. Walters and Mützel were staring at me.

"Plaza de Bailen *très*, echoed Wall-face. "How do *you* know it? We found Bormann's things there. But no Bormann.''

"It was where Schäfer said he was staying,'' I said, aware of Philby's eyes on me now, approving. Somehow I was doing it right. I didn't know what I was doing; only that I hadn't challenged the message he claimed to have found in Lord Byro. Perhaps it really had always been there and I'd never noticed it before, but now I knew that I was feeding the rising excitement in the room, and that it was what I was supposed to do, what Philby wanted from me. "Tom's ladyfriend Estrella told me to take the jeep there.'' I turned to Wall-face. "She must have thought you'd follow her if she went to deliver it herself.'' Wall-face nodded. "When I found the washbag with the money in it, I decided it was my lucky day,'' I went on, "I was on the way back to collect my things and get the hell out, then about a mile from Tom's place this chap stepped into the road . . .'' and I described the sequence of events leading to the ravine, the little downhill track, the ruined house at the foot of it, and the crash.

Wall-face took out a photograph and put it on the desk in front of me, without comment.

"That's Schäfer," I said, and was startled to feel a strong hand grip me by the forearm, twisting me away from the desk. For an instant I was reminded of Sturmbannführer Verg's embrace in the railway station office, as Wall-face reached up and planted a kiss on both my cheeks in turn. For his pains he got a whiff of the forest and let go of me quickly.

Philby and Cheerybye were bent over the photograph. "Taken where?" Philby was saying.

"Genoa, before Christmas," said Mützel, still grimacing.

I moved round the desk for another look at the photograph. It was too grainy to be a good likeness of anyone, all you could really see was a fat unshaven face under a narrow-brimmed hat. It looked like Schäfer, and half a million other people.

"We were so close," said Mützel. "One more day."

"That's him all right," I said, but no-one paid any attention. My story seemed to have put the identification beyond doubt.

"Why one more day?" asked Walters. "I thought you were there, in Genoa. Who took this, a tourist?"

"We took it. From a rooftop. You know what this is?" Mützel picked up the photo, one stubby finger pointing out the blur of shadows behind the face. "Cloisters. He was in the San Francisco monastery. One more day and we were ready to storm it."

"Flew the coop," said Philby. "One of our chaps in Spain intercepted this little signal," he tapped the Byron fly-leaf, "on the airwaves, so I alerted Jakob. Then old Tom died and all hell broke loose." He looked up at me. "No-one knew whether Bormann was still on his way to your uncle. Jakob was staking out the airport . . . and who should arrive?"

"You," said Wall-face, jabbing a finger at me. He seemed a bit more cheerful now. "My good friend . . . who tried to run me over."

"I wasn't trying to. I'd never driven before."

"What exactly were you doing there?" asked Walters.

"Tom's will," I said. My feet were playing up again and I sat down in the vacant chair, glancing at Philby. He knew about my amputated toes; I'd explained the problem as I hobbled out of Planten un Blomen with him. "I came to collect a legacy. That's what I was doing there."

"We've verified that," said Philby.

"Doesn't mean that's all he was doing." Cheerybye turned to me. "Why would he make you his heir if you're so bloody innocent?"

"I'm not his heir, Estrella is. I told you, there was supposed to be a bequest. A legacy. What I got was a lot of useless shares and a gun. Not a penny, until I came across the washbag. A piece of luck, I thought. I didn't know it was meant for Schäfer. I mean, having come all the way I thought I deserved something better than a few old bearer bonds. And possibly a free ride on the Imperial Chinese railway, if it still exists."

Walters looked puzzled. "Imperial Chinese . . ."

"Railway. The Tientsin-Pukow line. Tom had shares in it."

"You're saying that was all he left you?"

"That and a few books. *Mein Kampf* in Arabic. It didn't seem much of a legacy to me. Perhaps it was a joke."

"Or a game," smiled Philby. He was looking at the objects on the desk. "All you need are the dice." He was right; the crude wartime banknotes, divided into different currencies, looked like a starting share, and the little gun with its plastic handle was my token. Next to it the pile of identity cards. Walters smiled for the first time, lifted one of the cards, and pretended to read aloud. "Go directly to jail," he said ponderously, "do not pass Go, do not collect . . ." he gestured at the banknotes, "oh—about twenty thousand quid's worth, we reckon."

"Until I get out of jail, you mean."

Walters shook his head.

"If you get out," he said, leaning sideways across the desk to play with the piles of money, "if and when, I wouldn't take this stuff with you."

"Why not?" I said sharply. I didn't like him playing with my neatly stacked money.

"Because it's counterfeit."

"Come off it." I twisted aside to see past him, to Philby, but the chummy eyes were expressionless, for once. Cheerybye was still grinning. I began to smell a rat. "It's perfectly good money!"

"I'm afraid not," came Philby's voice, and Cheerybye moved away to give him the floor. "First-rate work, mind you. From the Arlberg factory. The Nazis were going to flood the market with it at the end of the war, just to cause trouble."

"Rubbish," I said, "I've bought things with it. I've had no trouble."

"Very possibly. First-rate work, as I say, but it wouldn't have passed muster where people had been alerted. Banks, say,'' and here I failed to decipher the all-too-guileless look on Philby's face, ''. . . or big hotels.''

"That's just my point," I said, "I paid my bill at the Atlantic with it.

Philby nodded, unimpressed. And then I realized why. Cheerybye's face confirmed it, as he set off on a little stroll around the back of my chair. They'd been toying with me all along, even at the Atlantic.

"We told the management we'd settle your account, or they'd have cried blue murder when you tried to pay with forgeries. You owe us quite a tidy sum, I'm afraid," said Philby. He gestured at the banknotes on the desk. "Can't accept this stuff in payment either. Got any real money?"

I hesitated, not sure how serious Philby's demand was. It seemed serious enough. But . . . what if he was lying, and they were out to steal the washbag money? "If that's counterfeit, why would Tom be giving Bormann a supply of it?"

"Pity we can't ask him, isn't it? Several possibilities, either they both thought they could pass the stuff off as real, which you've shown was possible, some of the time anyway. Or they simply didn't know it was fake. Or your uncle did, and he was throwing Bormann to the wolves. Any ideas, Jakob?" Mützel, squatting with his back against a wall, shook his head, and Philby turned to me again. "You might want to think about that, in case anything you saw or heard in Spain casts light on it. All of us here . . . we're just as much in the dark as you are.''

"Even more, perhaps," came Cheerybye's sarcastic tones, from behind me.

"You see, we heard on the grapevine that Bormann was back again, not for the first time by any means. Travelling under the name of Schäfer. Only it wasn't Bormann, it was you.'' Philby's face creased into a grin. "Bormann wouldn't have had the gall to stay at the Atlantic. All the same, the way you were behaving we were pretty sure you were here on spidery business, like your uncle. Carrying on his work. With luck you might have led us to some of the big boys.''

"On what business did you say?"

"*Spidery.* Spider business. You really don't know about *Die Spinne*?''

I really didn't; Karin's references to spiders had gone clean over my head. And now as I listened to Philby telling me about the Nazi escape network, I began to grasp why I'd been made so welcome by Karin. By others too.

"I came to try and rescue my sister-in-law," I said. "It was all perfectly innocent."

"Yes, I see. So that would fall under Compassionate Travel, eh?"

That's it exactly, I said. Compassionate travel.

Then where was my certification from the Military Permit Office, asked Walters. Or was I perhaps sponsored by the F.O.? I wasn't? Did I have a chit from the Home Office as a Visitor of Public Importance? Failing this, a chit from Martin Bormann, on behalf of the Fourth Reich?

"Look, I know what you're thinking, but I've never heard of *die Spinne* until today."

"You *were* meeting some rather odd people," said Philby.

Turning, I looked from one face to the other. Had they been following me round Hamburg? Everywhere I went?

"Perfectly innocently," I insisted, and ignored Cheerybye's guffaw. "I was trying to organize my trip into Soviet Germany."

"So then you headed east," Philby nodded, pausing. "And we lost you."

I wanted to keep the momentum going, but no words came, like Henry they fell into the gap between the land and the ice. If anyone was going to mention finding his body it was now. It occurred to me that I'd paid Henry in counterfeit notes for the counterfeit butter. No more than he deserved. But my God, if I'd known the scores were level when we set out for the border— that I was already even with him—

"Three months you've been there," Philby was saying, "in the Russian zone. You must be a resourceful chap."

"Or have contacts in the right places," said Cheerybye, seeing that Philby's meaning had passed me by.

"No, that was equally innocent," I began.

A grunting noise came from behind me.

"Gentlemen, if you no longer need me . . ." Wall-face Mützel stood up, impatient.

Philby threw up a hand to stop him, without lifting his gaze from my face. "Thank you for being so frank with us," he said. "We need to talk to Mr. Mützel now."

In sheer relief I couldn't stop, "I fell ill, you see, and then there was the child, he's my nephew . . ."

Philby nodded politely. "Tell us about it tomorrow."

* * *

What was I thinking, alone in my cell—hardly a cell; a room in a barracks, in a guarded compound—those days of my interrogation? That the boot was on the other foot? After all the Sisdick years of grilling prisoners, I was the victim now. Twisting and turning.

Did I have any glimpse of the future at all? All doors will open for you, Auntie had said, and you will fall on your feet. At that moment doors were banging shut, keys turning to lock me in. But I slept soundly, I remember that. Did I sense that I was home somehow, that I was backing into the espionage world? Just as I'd backed into Mecklenburg against the snow, watching my footsteps fill and blur. Twenty years it's taken me to tiptoe out again. God knows how many others there are like me, on the fringes of shady deeds, not sure if they're free to leave the scene.

There in the Bad Neunberg barracks my mind must have been seething with doubts and discoveries, retracing my steps in the light of what I'd learned, and what I could guess. Travelling as Schäfer-Bormann had earned me Gruppenführer Verg's kiss— one little tendril of the spider's web—and I'd been under observation in Hamburg too. By the British *and* the *Spinne*? Or only the British? Following me everywhere on my wanderings? Now every stranger I could summon up clearly enough, in my memories of Karin-afternoons, or romps in the whores' precinct, every figure at the edge of vision became an informant, stealing my privacy. Or was that all Cheerybye bluff? No-one tailing me at all.

Or Philby watching from the start, even in Spain? A phrase of Philby's nagged at me: "we've verified that," he'd reminded Cheerybye when I said I was in Malaga to collect an inheritance. "Verified" it—with whom? Old Garnham, Tom's executor? He was the one who'd sent me chasing castles in Spain. Or Alec? Who else knew? Molly. No, this was interrogation fever, with visions of everyone in league against me. Alec and Garnham, though . . . they'd let me walk into a hornet's nest. Alec had certainly known more than he let on. Burn any papers you come across, he'd said, as though he wanted nothing more than to be rid of an embarrassing association. Spidery business. I seemed to be the only Thurgo *not* involved in it.

Who else had been watching, in Spain, as I stumbled into Bormann's arms? Estrella, Wall-face, Alec too, most likely, at a distance. Philby's friends listening in on Tom. Others keeping tabs on me? Even my images of Spain were being corrupted now, like those of Hamburg. The two men watching me drive past in the jeep, that glorious afternoon, those two stretched on their sides at the crest of the ploughed hillside, each with an elbow in the warm red earth; heads together at the hinge of what for all the world looked like a pair of human compasses . . . how suspicious they became now, their divided bodies widening to plot the panorama at their feet. "Look," they'd appeared to say; behold! like emblematic figures on an antique map, on charts where angels puffed wind into expeditionary sails. They'd waved courage into me, lying there on the hill as if welcoming me to their tablecloth, to the feast of turned earth, root and worm and musky soil. Visualizing it again, I placed a walkie-talkie between their almost-touching heads, and it all became mockery.

In exchange I was being offered fame. Wasn't I? A place in the history books. Wasn't I the man who killed Martin Bormann? Trying to keep other thoughts at bay, I was already developing the story to give myself a less passive role. We were struggling in the bouncing jeep, Bormann and I, for control of the gun. Wounded, I flung myself out just as we hit the ruined house. I saw myself making headlines, giving interviews . . . yes, better still, before the crash I turned the gun against him, got off a shot, and . . .

One thing troubled me. I was seeing conspiracies everywhere, but I wasn't imagining Philby's sleight-of-hand with the coded message on the Byron fly-leaf. He'd written it in himself, I was almost sure of that. One of his "chaps" in Spain had intercepted the message from Tom, assuring Bormann of a safe house in Malaga: "An elderly muddled king . . ." decoding as Plaza de Bailen *tres*. And Wall-face said they'd found Bormann's things there. Estrella had given me the same address; confirmed by Schäfer, in the jeep. It all fitted together—so why would Philby want to forget an extra link in the chain, writing the address into Lord Byro? His stammer had become noticeable when Wall-face arrived. He was fluent enough when lecturing us on decipherment, and once Wall-face was convinced, the stammer faded.

Philby, Walters, Mützel . . . their machinations went on puzzling me for some time. All three of them, I think, fully believed Schäfer was Martin Bormann. It may be that they still believe it in Whitehall and that in some top secret document his death remains attributed to a civilian, one R. Thurgo. Only historians care now, I'd imagine; in those days, however, Bormann was regarded as the great prize and the most important of the Nazi bigwigs unaccounted for (unless you were one of those who thought Adolf was on the loose), Bormann the éminence grise of the Nazi Party, Lucifer's evil archangel as he'd been described, in his absence, at the Nuremberg trials. And a complete lunatic, to judge by what I've read of him since. The night before Hitler's suicide, an old General who'd been loyal to the last took Bormann by the lapels and risked a firing squad by telling the Reichsleiter what he thought of him, how Bormann had sacrificed the youth of Germany for his personal gain and glory; at the end of this stream of abuse, according to a surviving eyewitness, Bormann shook his head in mild reproof: *"Aber mein lieber Mensch,"* he said, "But my dear fellow . . . why must you take it all so *seriously*?" By this time, in '48, he'd already been reported dead, and then alive again, in several places and on several occasions. Yet when Philby shook my hand in congratulation I sensed that he did so sincerely. And did it with both his patriotic and his traitor's heart, so to speak; whatever else divided them, the Russian agent and the Briton in him both hated the "Nazzies."

In later years Walters evolved a different view of Philby's motives, but so did everybody once they realized he'd been a double agent. "Kim knew it wasn't Bormann," Walters then claimed, "what's more he didn't *want* him dead. Or captured. The more trouble-makers stirring the pot, the better. He just wanted the Hebrews off his back,"—apparently Wall-face and company were growing suspicious of Philby's lack of zeal where Nazi-hunting was concerned—"and this Bormann business made him look more helpful, thanks to you." But why did Philby want Nazis stirring the pot? Ah, post-war Germany! Walters crooned. That hall of mirrors! The perfect operational setting for a double agent . . . every move you made rebounded on itself and turned into its opposite, benefiting both sides. It was so easy . . . Cheerybye let the words hang, inviting me to wonder about his own loyalties in their light. Sheer vanity; he had unexpected virtues but he was too lazy, stupid, and corrupt to have survived as a counterspy, a profession requiring almost ascetic moral rigour; surely (I don't speak from experience) a lifetime of the most exacting discriminations. Or was it? In certain circumstances, if Walters was right, every shot in an undercover war would ricochet back and forth until no-one could tell whose cause it had advanced. In that kind of echo chamber even Walters could have been a double agent. According to him it worked like this: Philby's brief, conveniently enough, was to open the post-war intelligence offensive against the Russians. With regard to Hitler's former henchmen the British were divided, some wanted them prosecuted and the rest wanted them reinstated to fight Communism. So whether Philby was more or less zealous in pursuing war criminals, he could count on support from one or other Whitehall faction. The same went for his real masters the Russians, who were happy either way. If German captains of industry and military commanders were put on trial and jailed, it caused a scandal and undermined Germany; if they weren't, it undermined the Allies, caused a scandal, and put opposing factions at each other's throats. The latter was Philby's preferred course, since turning a blind eye to old Nazis earned him anti-Communist credentials. It suited the Russians best too, giving them lots to shout about. Everyone was dizzy with bluff and double bluff; only the Israelis, in their single-minded way, wondered about Philby's motives. "Then you turned up, trailing a corpse and dodgy documents. Ever see Kalanag at work?" asked Walters. I nodded, recalling evenings in the Flak-tower, Karin squealing as the lovely Gloria was sawn in half. "In the first place Kim didn't get Bormann's Malaga address from our own network. There *was* no intercepted message from your uncle. Kim got the address from the Israeli side, dressed it up in code and fed it back to Mützel, through you. You'd left a corpse in Spain, and now, hey presto, you had a code-book with Bormann's address in it. A little Lord Byron, a spot of crypto-graphic mumbo-jumbo . . . one dead Bormann, as required. Exit Hebrews looking happy."

All this of course with Cheerybye hindsight. Later still—Walters would have crowed, if only he'd lived to see it—road-works in Berlin unearthed a body near Hitler's old Chancellery, and it was identified as Bormann. If true it means that it was someone else who died wearing my uncle's boots, and is now buried in Highgate cemetery under my name. I hope so. Macabre irony aside, and tickled as I am by the idea of having killed a man like Bormann, I do have mixed feelings about housing a world-famous psychopath in my coffin. Especially with my son standing at the graveside, head bowed, as I sometimes picture him. Or laying flowers on the grave. I may not be virtue personified but I don't feel I deserve to be paired with Lucifer's archangel, even in death.

* * *

During the interrogations that followed I was able to piece together what had happened at home. Philby had been in touch with Alec—which was what I most feared, it was shaming, like being a schoolboy again and finding that the headmaster had been on the phone to your parents. He hadn't met "Lucky" Thurgo since Spanish Civil War days, Philby said, but after all they were colleagues, in a manner of speaking. What manner of speaking? Why, Alec's special responsibilities, as a Tory spokesman on German affairs. This was news to me. But he'd have informed Alec anyway, Philby said—good Lord, man, if an M.P.'s brother, supposed to be dead and buried, turns up on your doorstep under a false name, it wasn't something you'd keep to yourself without good reason, was it?

Dead and buried. This was the first time anyone had said it of me to my face. I *was* dead and buried then? Oh yes, so he understood. The remains found in the jeep had been buried in London under the impression that, indeed, they were my remains. My wife had identified them as mine, Philby added. Which was to say she had identified the feet as mine. The feet had been preserved by Tom's boots from the worst effects of the fire, sufficiently for an identification to be made. And everything else had been, well, shall we say charred? Yes, I said; I remembered.

Molly had identified my feet? Or rather no; she'd misidentified them. She'd identified Martin Bormann's feet as mine. What a wrong number, as our lodger Mr. Mendelssohn would say. He liked to recite a joke about a Jewish tailor who answered the phone to hear a voice say "Mr. Rothschild?" and who replied to this, "*Vot* a wrong number!" The way he said it always struck me as Mendelssohn's lament at ending up in our cheese-paring British household, and it annoyed me. But unlike the tailor Molly hadn't said "what a wrong number," no, she'd said it was the right number, she'd mistaken Bormann's feet for mine. Were they, perhaps, similar? (And what did that mean, if there were a science of feet, an art to reading feet, say, like palmistry . . . solistry, perhaps?) Or did it mean Molly simply had no idea what my feet looked like? An unsettling thought. On the other hand—or foot—could I have correctly identified hers? They were small and somehow crabbed, the toes turned down together in a bunch as if they were trying to hide. But so were lots of people's.

Nobody would ever mistake my feet again, three toes on one of them, like a sloth—wasn't there a three-toed sloth, or was it two-toed? And four toes on the other. Now that it didn't matter, I had identifiable feet.

"Interesting about the boots," Philby was saying. "Why did you give them to Bormann?"

I'm sorry? I was so distracted I made him repeat it.

Why, he wanted to know, had I given Tom Thurgo's boots to Martin Bormann?

I hadn't, I explained; I described how Estrella had given them to me with the jeep, useless but apparently specific bequests of Tom's to me, and how Schäfer had taken a liking to them on sight. I mean Bormann. Philby waited for me to finish, and then said, "Radio transmitter in the heel . . . did you know that?"

Radio transmitter? At that moment I was held by the rather ghostly pallor of Philby's face, and the way the grooves and shadows in it made it look like a face etched in coal dust, or a woodcut. Too much time spent in holes like this, I thought, talking to people like me. Radio transmitter, had he said?

Philby nodded. "This is only hearsay, but I gather they're standard issue now for people working with the *Spinne*. Without realizing, you simply delivered them to Bormann, like the jeep itself. And the cash. Any idea where he was headed?"

The jeep, the boots, and the money; and the Thurgo olive oil, I thought. The petrol, rather. Long journey somewhere. Radio transmitter . . . so much for Tom's precious boots! Not that I had to believe a word of what Philby was saying, but I remembered noticing how massive the heels were, and how heavy they were, the boots Estrella gave me. "I am looking for boots like this," Schäfer had said. Curious that while my own shoes, the ones I was wearing now, had an arsehole in the heel, Uncle Tom's had a radio transmitter. Was there anything to be understood from this? One had been made *by* a Martin, the others *for* a Martin.

"Pity you didn't hang onto the boots. I'd like to have studied the handiwork."

Still partly caught up in my trance, I pointed out that after the jeep had gone up the radio would most probably have melted. True, said Philby solemnly. Suddenly I began to feel nauseous. I was holding too much in, that was it . . . Molly and my feet, and above them—had they shown it to her?—that revolting corpse. Melted face, blackened arms and hands . . . the skeletal fingers that wouldn't hold my wedding ring, when I tried to fit in onto Schäfer's hand, and saw it fall into the ashes. No, that was in the dream. I looked down at my hand. There was no ring on it. I stared, trying to clear my head. It was only in the dream that I'd discarded the ring. It had been there when I set out for Mecklenburg. No-one had taken it from me, unless in my sleep at the Hof . . . but they hadn't touched my things. In the lake, struggling with Egon? I'd never seen my hands so thin, it could have slipped off any time. Philby was watching, and I tried to force my mind away.

What were we talking about? The desktop was empty, apart from my file. No washbag or money.

"I'd like to keep something of Tom's," I heard myself say. Absurdly, because that was the last thing I wanted. "Just one counterfeit banknote perhaps. If that's all right. You see . . . my grandfather's things were all sold over my head, I never got to keep anything of his."

I stopped myself right there. My voice sounded erratic, and Philby was sitting there all too calmly, gloating probably, any moment he'd start to purr. Careful, I told myself. When it was just the two of us, no Cheerybye, I was longing to spill more personal matters. I who thought I knew the tricks of the interrogation trade. It didn't seem to help. My eyes kept going back to my hand, as though any moment the ring would appear on it.

"To the best of your knowledge," I said, trying for an even tone, "does my wife know I'm still alive?"

"I assume so. Unless your brother hasn't told her." Philby paused. "But he'd tell her, wouldn't he?"

"Yes, I should think so." For some reason I didn't sound at all sure. Why not? Why on earth wouldn't Alec tell Molly? Again I was conscious of Philby studying me. I said, "And this was, what? Some months ago?"

"Oh yes. She'll have known for three months, probably."

He was watching me, but I wasn't going to think of Molly, I wasn't going to give him the satisfaction. Better not to think at all. Philby's gaze brought on the sensation I so often used to get when people tried to read my face, they'd see coarse features, small eyes and a huge nose, a broken mouth hiding bad teeth, a massive chin—now bearded but all the bigger. They'd try and square it with the impression of willingness I gave them. And they couldn't, quite. Inside this brute . . . what? At such moments I still longed to grow into my features.

I gazed steadily back; two could play at this. Philby clasped his hands together under his lower lip, and before they clasped I thought I detected a faint drinker's tremor. "Why did you do it?" he asked.

I took a long breath and expelled it, more noisily than I intended. "I'm not sure I've got an answer." Philby nodded patiently. "But I definitely went into the Russian zone to find my sister-in-law."

"Yes . . . what *have* you been doing there all this time?"

I told him. Or rather I gave him a version stripped of border incidents, of bombs and bullets. If he knew better, his listening face gave nothing away. Relieved to have a fresh subject, I told him at length about Peter and Maggie and the Schloss, about my convalescence at the Hof, and as I came to my birthday party and departure, I remembered that we'd celebrated four days early. A Henry Hirsch-face in Russian uniform, enquiring after me; and I'd left the following morning. I made a quick count. Stupidly, that did it. I looked down, but the tears came anyway, they'd been waiting for an excuse. It was my birthday and that wasn't why I was crying, bloody Philby didn't even seem surprised, he let me cry as if this was a familiar part of the interrogation process. Collapse of prisoner. At least he had the good taste not to offer me his pocket handkerchief.

"And now . . . you're thinking of going home?" he said, when I was done.

"Well, if there isn't anything stopping me."

There was a silence. After a while I rubbed my face, to be rid of the drying tears; when I looked up Philby was still studying me.

"Yesterday," I said, "what's-his-name . . . Bunter . . . said I'd broken the law."

Philby didn't smile. "You have, yes."

"Is that stopping me?"

"Depends how generous I'm feeling."

Before I could find anything to say, he closed my file and folded his hands on it.

"You've broken the law and incidentally run up something of a buh-buh . . . buh . . . of a bill. So what happens next is partly up to you. Think about it. When you're a bit less overwrought."

I had to face the fact that Cheerybye's absence wasn't going to make things easier. Not at all. In fact it enabled Philby to widen his repertoire. We'd had the gloved hand, now for the mailed fist.

"My colleague Walters," he said crisply, when we resumed our sparring, "is convinced you were thick as thieves with your late uncle. You can see his point. In the first place old Tom's been prowling round here since '45, supposedly buying up old war matériel while running errands for Bormann and his boys. Bormann's been in and out of Germany himself, with the help of people like Tom. They thought they were organizing a coup. Fooling themselves of course, but we don't want any more nonsense. Then up you pop with documents from Tom, travelling under a name that turns out to be a Bormann alias. The way Walters sees it, you and Tom disposed of Bormann for reasons of your own, perhaps he double-crossed you over money, or you'd double-crossed him with the phony stuff and he found out. You burn his body and hope nobody finds out. Then to keep Thurgo and Nephew looking innocent, you go about business as usual, organizing Nazi outings to South America and so forth.'' He saw my expression. ''Well, look at it from Walters' point of view. If you're so innocent it *is* funny you're carrying Tom's codebook with you, don't you think?''

It was time to get this out into the open. ''It's you who made it look like that,'' I said. ''It isn't a codebook at all, you made it seem that way by what you wrote on the fly-leaf.''

''Really?'' He was smiling. At that instant I was sure he'd done it simply to incriminate me. ''Between you and me, I don't think you were working for Tom. And I think I can handle Walters. But you do see his point of view?''

I said nothing.

''And there are still some awkward matters to clear up. Passing round false documents and forged banknotes, that's small beer really. But I don't think you've told me everything about your Russian trip, have you? Would you be surprised to hear that my Russian counterparts have been rather keen to find you? They've made that very clear. In fact we could be letting ourselves in for reprisals if I just let you slip through my hands. Too bad, you might say . . . all part of the game. But that's for us to decide, isn't it? Not you. Or do you think you can go rampaging around, leaving dead bodies all over the place, and walk off without a care in the world?''

I was back to cornered rat; it wasn't till a week or so later that I realized, thinking about it, how deftly he'd played on my anxiety, and never had to specify whom I'd killed and when. I was listening too hard for a hint of a deal, a way out, to hear the things Philby wasn't saying.

''I could let you go, I suppose. Clear up the mess myself.'' He paused. ''There'd have to be some sort of public accounting of course, a court appearance, that is, but you could hope to come off lightly in the end. Make an appeal for sympathy. Say you were a bit dotty at the time and didn't know what you were doing. Mind you . . . you do seem fairly *compos* now, that's the trouble." Another, longer pause. "On the other hand if we said you'd been working for us, that would change the whole complexion of it, I'm sure you can see that. Keep the police out of it. If we actually vouched for you." I watched him reel me in. "We'd expect something in return of course," he said, "call it a quid pro quo. And there'd be plenty for you to do here if you wanted to. For us, I mean. You could pay off what you owe us, for a start. Quite a few of you CSDIC people have been working for the Intelligence Division. You've learnt about interrogation, you know the Germans, you speak the lingo . . ."

"You're offering me a job as an interrogator?"

"I might be."

I said nothing, and after a bit he started drumming on the table with his fingers, like Wing Commander Potts. No; that wasn't a world I wanted to return to.

"Wouldn't that be rather a waste," said Philby, "given your aptitudes? Resourceful chap like you. Runs in the family . . . what with a brother in the SOE. I was thinking more of active duty. Incognito, obviously. The sort of thing I imagine you'd enjoy."

"Incognito? As a German?"

Philby nodded, adding quickly, "No need to sign up for life, you know. Just a few months, see what you think of it. We're rather short of people in the field. Immediately after the war there were lots of chaps who'd got into the swing of it and wanted to keep going. Or for one reason or another . . . didn't particularly want to go home."

He stretched out his hands, palms down, fingertips approaching the rim of the desk, and studied them. The tremor was still there. He touched the metal desktop, and we watched the blood draining and returning to his fingers as he bent them back and then released them again.

"They're mostly sick of it now," he said, "they all want to go home. But you don't, do you." He glanced up. "Not really."

I waited for him to say more, though we both knew he didn't have to. No cant about King and country or an ideal of service. He made me feel as if he'd recognized me and said, here's your ticket, Thurgo. Or perhaps that was precisely the kind of romantic twaddle he knew I'd be selling to myself, perhaps he simply saw a willing, feckless tool, a bit player, and snapped me up as effortlessly as a Friedrichswald frog picking off another water-fly.

"You'd get a passport," he said.

"What about Egon?"

"Who?"

"The boy. My nephew."

"A passport, you mean? We'd consider it."

He knew a hostage when he saw one. As I poised myself to insist on Egon's passport, Philby interrupted.

"Oh, before I forget. The other thing is . . . and I know this will sound a bit daft after what we've been discussing, but Brian Robertson's enormously keen on spa-spa-spa-sporting links with the Germans, so we've been doing our best for a couple of years now, and we've reached the stage where a representative match would give everyone a fillip. We've got it all fixed. Now, for the time being they're rather short of bowlers. The slow stuff would do fine, Richard, if you're not terribly mobile. And they haven't got a wicketkeeper."

Not a smile, not a flicker.

"How bad *are* the feet? You could always umpire, if the worst comes to the worst. What do you think? We're very hopeful about the future of German cricket."

Those of us who took part still refer to it as the first and only Test Match between England and Germany. It wasn't of course, it was just a knock-up game between two scratch sides, and you won't find it recorded in Wisden. But you'll find it in the *Neue Hamburger Zeitung* for August 15, 1948. No scorecard, more's the pity . . . Jones caught Schmidt bowled Sacher has a charm all its own. Just the result and the respective totals. We lost, of course.

We being Germany. Wolfgang Zimt's XI 111 all out—yes, we were all out for the dreaded figure known, though none of us could explain why, as "Nelson." "Nelson? *Was ist* Nelson?" rang round the home team dressing room. This total was in reply to the 170-odd for four amassed by the Control Commission XI. We put up a good fight, all things considered. Two years of practising had unearthed several local athletes with a good eye and they hit the ball hard, though it was true that bowlers were in short supply. Zimt, who according to Philby was a former SS clerical worker, gave me the new ball. I took two of the CCG wickets, the only Briton, as I like to think of myself, to have opened the bowling for the SS. In truth we were a multi-racial team—it was in the Displaced Persons camps that Sir Brian Robertson's decree had been most rigorously applied, and there were three or four very keen and energetic Latvians playing for German. The whole event was notably sporting, batsmen were applauded to and from the crease, and "Howzat?" came as a polite enquiry, from either fielding team. Ow*zet*? Only in Hamburg, I think, could the old game have been played in such truly British fashion.

"Örtlich bewölkt," said the weather forecast on the day of the match, cloudy in places, which was how I felt, myself. My trepidation wasn't about the cricket but about my "protector"— not a piece of cricket equipment but the man I was to meet at the game and who was to be my ally, my guardian in the months to come: the man Zimt.

Why had I agreed to any of this? I asked myself that daily. Poor old Walters used to say that most people who joined the espionage community did so for the same confusion of reasons and had to be wooed in the same way, with threats. They needed to believe they were being coerced into leading a double life; when in fact they were already, and had been all their lives. That went for most of them, Walters said; and then there were the romantics. Once Philby knew I was a Dornford Yates fan, he must have known my heart would miss a beat at the words like active duty and incognito. I'd sat out a war in offices, in interrogation rooms, I might as well have been a prisoner all through it, in a war that made a hero of plenty of others. My heart missed a beat all right.

It missed another when I learnt what my cover identity was going to be, initially at the cricket match. Subsequently too, if it passed muster. Team captain Zimt was in Philby's pay, so for the sake of convenience, as Philby put it, I would share his background. That way my "protector" Zimt could vouch for me. My name would be Reinhard Sacher, a purely invented name. Reinhard Sacher . . . it sounded innocuous enough. I felt I could probably get used to it. "Look, don't worry about all this," said Philby blandly, "I mean, if ever there was a pa-pa-perfect time and place to adopt a new identity without anyone noticing, it's Germany in 1948. Everyone here's doing it." Like Zimt I would be a former clerical worker who'd been attached, during the later stages of the war, to the SS. "Attached?" To the SS? Attached in what sense? Wolfgang Zimt would explain in due course, Philby said. No-one at a cricket match would probe into a team-mate's past. As it turned out, this was true;

but had I known how Wolfgang would later embellish his war record—and consequently mine—I'd have scotched the whole thing at birth.

And what was the purpose of this whole charade? I asked. To begin with I was to report on Zimt and his pals, even though they were "friendly" to us, which was to say rabidly anti-Communist. Zimt himself was a thoroughly reformed and remorseful ex-Nazi, Philby said, adding perfunctorily "if there is such a thing." Reformed Nazi or not, the man was now masquerading as an unreformed one, a neo-Nazi, on Philby's behalf. My job was to keep an eye open in case Zimt was more genuinely "neo" than he let on.

I knew of Zimt, everyone did. Back in the bunker-world Vlad the String had fed me tales of Zimt the famed black marketeer, the King of Bizonia, a shadowy but notorious figure whom nobody would dream of trusting. They were too scared of him. I now saw this as reassuring—if I was an intimate of his I'd be protected by the aura that surrounded him. And that Zimt could be the vice king of Hamburg and also working for the British came as no surprise. Everyone worked for the occupying forces when the situation called for it, they'd have been idiotic not to. How deep Zimt's devotion was to Britain, or to Philby, or to whatever money Philby paid him for information, was another matter. Or how reliable that made him, if my safety depended on his Anglophile tendencies.

But it doesn't, Philby said. Your safeguard is that he's been working for us and we can prove it. His neo-Nazi friends would have his guts for garters if they knew he'd been spying on them. If he shops you, we shop him. He knows that. You can rely on Wolfgang.

And what would good old Wolfgang do if he knew I was spying on *him*?"

Nothing, said Philby. He'll expect it.

Then what use was I?

Leave that to us, said Philby. Just get in there and stick to him like a limpet.

All very well, I said, but what about this "clerical worker" guise? Was that such a good idea?

It was ideal, I was sharply told. Over a period of time Zimt could train me in every detail of the life, as well as swearing to my presence as a comrade of his, in the camps.

In the where?

The camps, said Philby, ignoring my stare. Not concentration camps. Internment places, work and transit camps. No, of course I wasn't being asked to disguise myself as a concentration camp guard. Zimt hadn't been a guard, just a clerical worker. The word kept coming back, like a ghastly euphemism.

Sorry, I said. Absolutely not on. The chances of my making an obvious error were far too great, never mind the danger of being recognized, or rather *not* recognized. And weren't all the names of these "clerical workers" on record? Anyone in any doubt about my background could simply consult the records and I'd be exposed as a fraud. End up with an SS dagger in my back.

Philby shook his head sadly. Too much Dornford Yates; I didn't understand the sheer banality of undercover work, the lack of testing confrontations of the kind so dear to fiction. All over the world, he assured me, people lived out deceitful lives under the flimsiest of aliases. And in Germany no-one wanted to talk about the war; it was virtually taboo. Any evasiveness about the past was the opposite of suspicious, on the contrary it was suspicious to make any reference to it at all. The common history I would share with Zimt—not a man, Philby reminded me, whose word people challenged—was unlikely ever to be enquired about, and if it was, to draw a veil over it would be the most normal and appropriate reaction. Besides, he said, the records of SS clerical staff were by no means on file. Of the five thousand people who'd worked at Auschwitz, mainly office workers, only a few hundred were known by name. The SS themselves had destroyed the records, to protect people like Zimt. Even Philby only had it on Zimt's word, he said, that the man had worked in the camps. And yes, of course he believed it: who would want to claim that they'd worked in the camps, if it wasn't true? Didn't I see that this was the best part of it, my ace in the hole? Who'd be idiotic enough to *pretend* to a past like that?

I glimpsed myself as Philby described me, in the most exotic of looking-glass worlds. While former SS guards from Nome to Buenos Aires were insisting that they'd never been anywhere near the death camps, I'd be the only man on earth insisting that I had been, when I hadn't at all. There was no avoiding it: something in me stirred at that.

Had Philby mentioned at the time that from then on Walters would be my contact man, that he himself would disappear from my life and that in all likelihood we would never meet again, I might have hesitated. He didn't tell me. But Walters turned out to be an entirely different person from the moody, carping creature of the Bad Neunburg interrogation room. Different from the man I'd supposed him to be—and different from the man Philby and anyone else supposed him to be. A true friend to me, though. My Magwitch, in his way, my benefactor.

To reach the Displaced Persons camp in Halstenbeck, where the cricket match was to be played, took half an hour by tram from Altona Nord. When I was released from Bad Neunburg the Intelligence Division had found me a two-roomed apartment in Altona, recently vacated by a British sergeant and his wife. I was on edge from the moment I left the house. What if Herr Zimt already suspected that I was supposed to keep an eye on him and, despite what Philby said, didn't like it a bit? Vlad's bunker-voice rumbled in my mind, describing Zimt's reputed prowess with a knife.

I arrived at the DP camp and was directed to the pavilion. This was a white-painted wooden building on wheels, later moved to Blankenese where the Hamburg Cricket Club had its home until the middle 'Fifties. As I entered the little hut for the first of many times, that August morning, it was to the most curious mixture of smells and sounds: familiar smells of sweaty gloves and linseed oil, mingling with gossip in German. Cricketing terms surged up like reefs in German sentences, in the same bizarre way that English words punctuate a rugby harangue in Gaelic. I asked to have *der captain* pointed out to me.

All I could see of Wolfgang Zimt, until he turned and straightened up, was a smallish, slender young man in white trousers and an immaculate white shirt, bent over a pair of pads and attaching the bottom buckle to an ankle.

"Herr Zimt?"

He looked up. "Ah, Herr Sacher. Are you feet better? You will bowl a little? And where will you bat?"

He grinned at me, knowing perfectly well I was too overwhelmed, at that moment, to be able to answer. His smile was an insolent as ever, that red-lipped, red-cheeked smile, under the falling cowlick. I was staring at Henry Hirsch.

"You will see me make some good shots today," he said with a twinkle. "Better than the last time, I think!"

No matter what its citizens get up to, Hamburg always manages to keep its nose clean. ("Kept your nose clean, have you?" Alec used to say to me at the end of every school term.) Or to vary the metaphor to reflect my beloved, futile Reeperbahn, the "world's most sinful mile" and for twenty years my own corner of the city, Hamburg keeps itself in a state of perpetual douche. One of the prints hanging on my wall shows the story from the beginning. It's an ancient map of the region at the centre of which, painted pink, a small round cleft peeps out beneath a green and yellow patchwork skirt of fields: earliest Hamburg in its city walls, with a clitoral twist of Alster waters above it. Hamburg exposing itself with a bland nursery innocence, mocking God and the Devil. At a cinema long since gone from the Mönckebergstrasse I saw a film in which Satan, impeccably dressed, arrives at a rustic cottage. A girl opens the door to him. "Fräulein," he says (it was a French film but dubbed into German), "ich bin der Teufel." I am the Devil. "If you only knew," she answers, using the antique, painfully polite *wüsstet*, "how indifferent that leaves me. . .".

Hamburg in a nutshell.

It was Peter who told me that Christianity came late to Germany—a drive along the Autobahn had prompted this reflection from him, along with "*Pass auf*, there goes Wotan in his Mercedes!"—and I picture Hamburg taking reluctantly to the Cross. You want our souls? If you insist, Your Reverence. Are you sure you wouldn't prefer a good horse, and a saddle maybe?

In the Rathaus a curious fresco depicts the conversion of the pagan Hamburgers, though not in its original form. When first unveiled the painting showed a band of converts kneeling in the mud of the river Elbe, before the Bishop. Hamburgers kneeling?

Never! Protests forced the repainted citizens into a standing position, and today only the angle of the bishop's outstretched hands, pointing at his victims' crotches, betrays the heresy of the original design. Your flies are undone, gentlemen, he now appears to be saying. History books will tell you that in time the city rose to be the queen of the Hansa League, a powerful group of Nordic merchant ports; but this too is history repainted. Warlike Lübeck was the true Hanseatic powerhouse, while Hamburg quietly accumulated money in its shadow. Both cities prospered, but staying rich was easier in peace than war, and Hamburg usually found a way to buy or deal itself out of local quarrels. When they had to prove their loyalty, Hamburgers would march off to battle, slowly. Faster if their Lübeck allies were winning. Bismarck, on a later occasion, threatened to forcibly assimilate Hamburg into Prussia unless the city joined the war on Austria. Troops were sent, but they took so long to cover the distance that the fighting was over by the time they arrived.

The common thread in Hamburg's story is its distrust of autocrats. A wholesome, endearing trait, at first impression. It's certainly most un-German. The Bürgermeister is regarded as *primus inter pares*, and even the Senate, Hamburg's upper house of government, is elected to office. When Wilhelm was received at the Town Hall a reception room was appointed Kaisersaal in his honour; not the largest but the second largest room available, and the point wasn't lost on the Kaiser. The distrust has always been mutual. Like Bismarck before him, Hitler rarely visited the city, finding it too cool and independent for his taste, too English—the ultimate compliment here. But Hamburg isn't English at all, much as it loves to think so, and to ape English dress and what it supposes are English manners. Smug, self-sufficient, pedants of democracy, it's the sensible Swiss that Hamburgers resemble. British smugness is rooted in class distinctions, transcending money, but manifest everywhere. In Hamburg such distinctions are invisible. Along the Alster the rich matron in furs walking her Zwergdackel, the miniature dachshund scraping along behind her like a bloated insect, passes the tart in no less expensive furs, just as groomed, trailing a matching dog. The pets ignore each other as politely as their owners. A cool, impenetrable tolerance which only bankruptcy can shock: this is the key even to Hamburg's red light district, that misleadingly notorious place. Money changes hands, clients come and go, but depravity seems bogus here, a licensed sham designed for tourists and approved by the city fathers. Now and again a slot machine spills a jackpot like a luxurious, authentic orgasm. It's a good city for gamblers but a barren one for militant bohemians: the fact is, it's not much fun trying to scandalize a Hamburger.

A city of distances, courteous, remote, open to all yet closed to all. City of bridges, visible and invisible alike. A phantom city, drawn on glass: it has no smell, sniff as hard as you like. And yet the air is beautiful, the best city air in Germany, with the rank salt filtered out of it on the Elbe's long journey inland; what's left isn't sharp or especially bracing, just supremely, freshly alive, like some perfect and disinterested specimen of air. Good expensive air, fit for a shop window display. And the light—even in fine weather Hamburg light has a muted quality, forgiving, too discreet to pry. Or too arrogant, calmly reminding you that it pre-dates the city. Everything promotes the sense of space: the lack of skyscrapers, the new, wide streets, the vacantly unimaginative nature of the postwar buildings. These seem even further apart than they are, the avenues widening as if eager to reveal the sweet shaved pubis on my antique map, defenceless and unconquerable at once; Hamburg displaying herself with a stripper's indifference. And this remoteness, compounded by architecture and light and air, belongs to something more, to the personality of a city where distances are measured between people as much as places, where even lifelong friends still call each other by their surnames. Intimacy—so I was taught here—is the secret vice of autocracy: both are taboo in Hamburg. Its physical distances lack all grandeur, and are almost impossible to memorize. Hamburg has more bridges than any city in Europe, over two thousand, more bridges than Venice—and no man can remember one of them. Not one.

At first I thought I loved Hamburg because its past had been erased by fire, like mine. We shared a turning point, and now, it seemed, a common face, drawn mask upon mask. I learnt that fire was no stranger to Hamburg, city of dreamers and sea captains and merchants assembling paper fortunes. All of it combustible, ships and money no less than dreams. Here and there the old buildings survive, remodelled, dreadful—with that look of surgical approximation, almost-faces, like the RAF boys ravaged by their burns—but these are rare, thank God. Hamburg isn't the type of place where history stalks you at every turn. A city starting afresh, I thought, without false piety. A sea-port with a sea-port's raucous cynicism. I was quite wrong. Hamburg is beyond destruction, and incorruptible. Its past can be obscured but never totally erased, its true historic role that is—I'm speaking of the only past that counts in Hamburg, its heritage of light and fantasy; of theatre. The crowds who thronged its bridges to watch the great mediaeval conflagrations, one after the other—each of them accidental, Hamburg has no need of arsonists—gathered there once again to watch the firebombs raining down in filaments, through the searchlight beams. Bomber Command had come to strip the city naked. Its victims took this as their due, their destiny. But . . . it was their beloved English blowing them to phosphorescent hell—didn't they feel betrayed? No. In Hamburg anger is the only unforgivable sin. It wasn't a bombing raid. It was only Hamburg burning. Fireworks. And the English? Excellent people!

Child-city, refusing to grow up, stunned by loss and yet untouched. To understand this, you have to go back again to the paintings and the drawings, the engravings of a dark, canal-threaded emporium; to the bustling Hansa-port of quaint streets with its hurrying tradesmen and lingering crews. That warren of overhanging houses is gone forever—ethereal Hamburg in the perfect disguise, that of a dour North German port. But there's no mistaking the people. Here they are in the engravings, straying like souls released, people once stricken but who have forgotten why. Their pallor shows that they are dead, but their tender smiles show them to be patient, half oblivious, hoarding their nursery toys. By face, by size and shape, they're various as can be, the Hamburgers. All of them clearly city-dwellers if nothing else, a random selection, chosen only for their affinity with Hamburg. We're summoned here, they seem to say, by the purgatorial nature of our crimes; nothing can touch us now, we've nothing more to lose . . . we've even forgotten what they were, our crimes. This guileless, blameless fellowship—you can still see it in Hamburg faces. And you rarely see a lonely one. Everyone here is friends in a bemused fashion, like revenants. Hamburgers meet each other with surprise on the streets: *you* here? We hail each other joyfully, like former shipmates separated by oceans since our last encounter, as Hamburg's districts are by its strangely characterless, apologetic, almost unnoticeable canals—as if the Elbe had leaked across a city too polite to draw attention to it. (It's a scene that belongs to the Reeperbahn at night: an old sea dog, the Elbe, pisses in the gutter while top-hatted revellers look the other way.) Once the canals were waterways, busy barge-bound roads. Now they've come into their own and seep invisibly through the city, sullen as mercury, like thin streams of anaesthetic.

A city drawn on glass; perhaps the one my forest-haunted mother never would draw, even in the distance. But remember, Hamburg looks as solid as Gibraltar, that's its secret. Shock-proof, you might think, shatterproof. Until you hear the evening bells ring out, dissolving the city into melody. "Sticks and stones may break my bones . . ."—but that's only the descant, there's a darker undertow. These aren't angelic bells. The air is full of climax: streets and pavements, shoppers, buildings, all suspended in the last bars of a huge orchestral work. Listen and you can hear the city's violence—its adulthood—so long deferred, finding release in sound. All that pent-up, breathless time, disguised as stone. Waiting for nightfall. Poor stifled Hamburg—waiting—six o'clock . . . and as the evening bells decode her secret the maiden city takes wing, shedding her daylight inertia, perfectly preserved, ageless—like the vampires of legend. The violence she dreads so much is time itself, and in vampire-logic night doesn't count.

Someone drumming at the door. Who can it be? *Fräulein . . . ich bin der Teufel,* smiles the Devil. "If you only knew," the girl replies, smiling back, showing her fangs. Spreading her own cloak. . . .

Impossible to stay indoors at this hour, when the bells ring the city into life. They make you frantic, it's no good trying to sit still. A favourite walk takes me along the Isebek canal to the Christuskirche, and on, skirting the Reeperbahn, to sanctuary—into Altona, where with Karin's help I began to learn what Hamburg was.

Ten years I spent there, in Altona; they were the golden years, but it's as if I spent them in a foreign place, foreign to Hamburg, that is, and in a sense it's true. Before the suburbs claimed it Altona was a city in its own right, Hamburg's boyish, Nordic twin. A space between two city gates kept them apart. Now that strip of no man's land, that firebreak—is the Reeperbahn. The playground of my busy days and nights. Mornings belonged to Altona, and it was like waking on another continent. The difference is subtle yet unmistakable: Altona seems to have a history. There's a lightening of the palette, in tribute to its Swedish founders; even, in its greater simplicity of line, to Prussia. Look hard enough and Hamburg stone discloses a gingerbread house, childish and sinister at once, yielding in Altona to something more straightforward, dusty, gay, a kind of courtly peasant architecture, as I imagine old Stockholm or Trondheim. The Professor in Jules Verne's *Journey to the Centre of the Earth* lived here—although a more detached and inessential place you could not wish to find. Perhaps that's why Verne chose it. Altona leaves you parched for darker, subterranean things. Unlike their devious neighbours, the natives are openly innocent in the Scandinavian fashion, which usually suggests a maddening insufficiency of sin.

I didn't mind. It made a pleasant change after the barracks at Bad Neunburg, when I was first released. I liked the easy-going, village atmosphere, the streets with their little umbrella-shaded stalls. My apartment was anonymous and clean; the only drawback was that it still smelt of its previous, British occupants and their Naafi food. And they'd done the place up in the horrid Army issue fabric known as Married Families Chintz. Too many reminders of home. I promised myself I'd redecorate it, when I could afford to.

Home. Molly knew I was alive, assuming Alec had told her. But unless Philby was keeping them informed, she didn't know where I was. When I imagined phoning her and trying to explain the situation, the words seemed to add insult to injury. "Got to stay here and pay off a debt—I can't go into it now, it's government work . . .". Later, I thought; when I know where I stand, I'll write to her.

I knew exactly where I stood. My first walk through Altona told me. How on earth would I describe it to her? I felt as far from Richard Thurgo the solicitor as I did from Reinhard Sacher, friend of spies and gangsters—future friend, all being well. Where was I then? I was cold on open slice, as Walters liked to put it. Exposed front and rear. It should have been unsettling, to put it mildly. Instead I felt more exhilaration, more identity with my own existence than ever before. It wasn't the prospect of the espionage jungle that grounded me, or even the chance to sink my snout into the Hamburg milieu. Both seemed threatening to me now. That schoolboy visit to the law courts all those years ago, when I saw my own features mirrored in the faces in the dock, had launched me on a long trajectory: perhaps Hamburg was its target, but I wasn't yet convinced. My exhilaration came from somewhere else. Of all things, from the dead. I was in Maggie and Peter's world, the only one in which I'd felt comfortable. And I was drawing strength from it as though the dead were our true capital, giving us substance. The Lützow world . . . no, that was wrong; Mecklenburg and the Schloss were no longer its heartlands; Maggie and Peter's world—it was portable now, the legacy of their hopes and their confusion. Egon embodied it. At that moment, emerging from Bad Neunburg, the boy was all I had to hold on to. He was the whole logic of my life. But when I thought of him as Peter and Maggie's son, this diminished all of us. The Lützows weren't burdensome presences, telling me to raise their child properly—no—though I'd do that for my own sake . . . no: they'd released Egon. Germany was their bequest to me. I didn't know what to make of it, for the time being. That would come. It was the first gift I'd ever really felt was meant for me, was mine.

While I was still at the interrogation centre Philby had let slip that Karin was having "a bit of a rough time with the youngster." Egon had run off, the police had found him sleeping in the Jenisch park in Klein Flottbeck, at the other end of the city, and they'd retrieved him, Philby said, making it sound a routine affair. I could imagine the boy kicking and squirming, being overpowered. If I hadn't interfered in his life he'd be racing through the Friedrichswald, at liberty. I forced the thought aside. My own liberty was at stake then, and if I ended up in jail I'd have to sit it out, whereas no institution could restrain Egon against his will. Not for long. He'd find his way back to Brüel— I pictured his journey, and it comforted me.

On the day I was released I took the tram out to Wandsbek, where I'd visited Karin and her mother and the rest of the family, on the night of the butter fiasco. I still felt curiously serene about Egon. Less so about Karin; along the way I tried once more to puzzle out her motives, from the beginning of our liaison to her agreement to look after Egon. Was this purely out of remorse at having given me away? Surely not. No-one had forced her to take on the child. Why then?

I was finding it hard to concentrate; my companions on the tram were too engrossing. The smell of starvation had gone, I'd noticed that on my return with Egon, and the yellowish, cancerous hue had left their faces. Now both seemed to have been replaced by an aura of conspicuous consumption. I'd never seen people flaunt their clothes so much, their make-up, the cheap bangles they wore, their hair viciously permed and gleaming like a corrugated helmet. Even the purchases in their laps seemed to glow. Any moment now they'd unwrap them and do a rhumba down the aisle, waving toasters and gramophone records and mohair suits. This wasn't the Germany I'd come looking for. Would Karin be similarly primped and permed? I was even having difficulty picturing her face. I'd been so crazy when we met, I told myself, and so many strange things had happened since then, sleep and dreams and deaths that weren't dreams—my whole life had unravelled since those rubble-days. I knew I'd been fascinated by her blemishes as much as by her prettiness, I remembered her composure and her anguished skin. But I couldn't visualize her hare-lip any more, or place her moles. Four months ago I could have drawn a map of them, from memory. Walks in Planten un Blomen, among the randy couples . . . I recalled her Communist harangues, and her obsession with Herr Wackernagel, the hero (the villain rather!) of her father August's cigarette-paper prison journal; Wackernagel who'd bullied her father into suicide. Karin's photographs: the man's balding head returned clearly, pale eyes and piggy snout. And Karin quizzing me about spiders. That was where her Cheerybye connection came in: at Bad Neunburg I'd put two and two together and worked out that it was Walters who'd dropped her a few hints about "die Spinne"; that she must have hoped that whichever side this Herr Schäfer was on, my spidery connections would lead her to Wackernagel, or at least to people who'd know where he was.

I couldn't feel angry with Karin. Suppose she'd been in Cheerybye's pay all along . . . that hardly mattered now, and what came back most clearly from our walks and talks was my sense that she was genuinely fond of me. Perhaps it was true. Why else had she agreed to take charge of Egon? Even if Egon had been an angel of obedience her decision was bound to bring our paths together again—at the very least we'd have to meet, to hand Egon over. She'd have to look me in the face, knowing she'd played havoc with my life. "Wie heissen Sie eigentlich?" what's your real name? Her last words to me, and the first she'd said flirtatiously. Did she still want to know?

Before setting out for Wandsbek I'd made a quick inspection of the Altona apartment, showered and put on fresh socks and underpants and a new shirt, all bought with money from Walters; what he called an advance against salary. It was so modest I couldn't afford a new suit, but I told myself that for Egon's sake I ought to wear my old stinky one anyway, a comforting reminder of my smell and the forest's. Walking up the Wandsbeker Chaussee, away from the tram stop, it finally occurred to me how little I'd thought it through. Egon mightn't even be here, he might have vanished again for good, even the Poseners might no longer live in Wandsbek; they had no phone and there was no way to check beforehand. I had a sudden bird's eye vision of myself plodding stiffly along—I'd taken off the bandages but my feet still ached—like a pavement vendor's toy. Sticking out one clockwork leg after the other. I was proceeding in the same dim dreamy fashion that had served me well enough over the last few months. But this was no enchanted landscape, it was a bustling city street with people going about their business purposefully, rationally. To survive, I was going to have to wake up and become one of them, these new brassy Germans.

A bell had been installed outside the Poseners' door. It even worked. I heard it ring, inside. The names were still crudely inscribed beside the door frame, but the in-law Danzigers had been blacked out. Dead? More likely affluence had claimed them, and a new abode. As time went by I decided there was no-one at home. Then the door opened and Frau Posener stood there, raising her fierce crumpled eagle's face to inspect me. I'd forgotten how tiny Karin's mother was; her head barely came up to my breastbone. She too looked startled for a moment. It was my beard, I realized—and then she recognized me.

"Ach du lieber Gott," said Frau Posener softly, awestruck, staring at my filthy suit. There was a motherly tenderness in her voice that soothed and grated on me at the same time. Behind her on a sofa—a sofa! was my first thought—something stirred from sleep, uncoiling its limbs.

Until he moved I fully believed this was another child, not Egon, a boy in shirt and trousers, with cropped hair and a scrubbed face. He saw me and his mouth fell open as it had when I whispered "Bestummt" below the treehouse. Then he ran and flung himself against my body, and I knew it was me he'd been waiting for.

Try as I might to hold my feelings in—I summoned up shame as well as puzzlement; what had I done to merit this welcome?—it was no use. I cried. Frau Posener was watching us, but I couldn't even see her expression. *Tränenblind*, the word came back at me out of one of Peter's favourite poems; tearblind. A Morgenstern poem . . . what was it called? Come on, think—but nothing could stop the tears now. Although I'd carried Egon on my back it was the first time he'd embraced me face to face, arms around my neck, legs hugging my midriff, bringing intolerable memories of Wilf and the nursery at Parsifal Road. Egon's fingers were pinching me almost viciously, reproachful. "Schon gut," I heard myself repeating. *Schon gut*, Egon, that'll do.

Frau Posener was talking now, "Wolfskind," I heard her say,

wolf-child, as I tried to prise Egon's fingers from my flesh. He only held on tighter, and made a growling noise. "Er schimpft," he's scolding you for leaving him, she said. I carried Egon back to the sofa and we settled in a heap, his head buried in one of my lapels, while the old woman sat down at the table and, holding herself erect, impassive, like an Indian scout reporting on an arduous reconnaissance, began describing her days with Egon.

At first, she said, the Wolfskind must have been expecting me to come and fetch him. The next morning, when I didn't, he simply ran out of the door and down the stairs and was gone. Karin had made some phone calls—at the Atlantic she had come to know some influential people, Fran Posener said carefully, watching me, trying to gauge from my reaction, I felt, how much I knew of Karin's world. But my mind was elsewhere. Of course that's where Karin was now, at work, at the Atlantic; she wouldn't be here in Wandsbek during the day, and I felt stupid—realizing that I'd somehow imagined her giving up her job to look after Egon, or taking leave from the hotel—stupid, and sharply disappointed that she wasn't here.

Her mother was telling me how Egon had been found in the Jenisch park, and the struggle to retrieve him. Ludolf's warnings hadn't been exaggerated. Egon had bitten his police captors, he'd shat in the cells, shat again here in the little flat when he was brought back and locked in. I was grateful not to have had to take the brunt of this. The Danzigers had avoided it too—they had indeed moved on, to join Christa's Danziger husband in Bielefeld, leaving the apartment a cage for Egon and his trainers. Karin's name cropped up frequently in Frau Posener's account of the ordeal; her daughter had been in the thick of it, she said, but it was clearly the old woman who'd taken Egon in hand—the "mucky pup" as she called him: *Dreckspatz!* She told the story drily, without rancour, without disapproval even, and I liked her profoundly for it. This was a Wolfskind, so she'd been warned. Nothing surprised her. That was in her nature, it seemed to me, and the experience of the war had clearly added patience to her imperious Prussian soul. But she was still a disciplinarian. As she talked about her bloodier skirmishes with Egon, the battle of the haircut, the even fiercer battle of the bathtub, the prolonged campaign to dress him—he still wouldn't dress himself—I found myself thinking about my own mother. As always, this took me by surprise; I was pleased to find that it was a flattering comparison, to both parties. They shared a rigour and determination, and once devoted to their chosen task they needed nobody's approval. When my turn came to speak I told Frau Posener Egon's story as Ludolf had recounted it to me, but without elaborating my connection with his parents. I'd told Philby that Egon was my nephew, and assumed he'd passed this on to Karin. Frau Posener didn't probe. The boy was an orphaned Wolfskind, in my charge. I was the Poseners' benefactor; there was, she implied, an undischarged debt. That was all there was to it. That, and Hamburg reticence.

But there was far more to it, I could see as much when the old girl looked at Egon, still pressed against me and inhaling me as if I held the whole of the Friedrichswald in my suit.

"Sprich mal was, Egonchen." Say something, she ordered affectionately. I saw the anticipatory pride in her eyes. She'd been teaching him? Frau Posener nodded. "Komm, sprich!"

Egon ignored her.

"If you permit, I will teach him to read," she said. "In time he can go to school, but not yet. He needs special instruction."

To say the least, I thought; adding aloud, "I'll do my best."

Frau Posener laughed, and it was Karin's laugh, a brief peal of bells. "You? You'll never do it. He needs *me*." We studied each other. "I have time," she said. "And you can see him every day, we'll expect you for dinner."

She hadn't counted on Egon. He growled and wouldn't be parted from me, even at the voice of command. And to be truthful, I didn't want to leave him. "Pfui!" the old girl exclaimed when Egon lashed out at her, fed up with her blandishments. I felt the word was directed at both of us. "Du!" she threatened him, but her old face looked tired. At last, promising to bring Egon to see her regularly, I asked for his coat and breeches.

Frau Posener hesitated, and for an awful moment I thought she'd thrown them away, burnt them perhaps. Then she nodded, conceding. "Karin will bring them to you tonight," she said, "along with his other things. We've found him clothes, even a few toys."

"I can take them now," I said.

She shook her head. "You'll need both hands for Egon. Don't worry, I'll send Karin with his things. Also a list of instructions."

She was as good as her word. And by the time Karin arrived we were installed in our new home, Egon and I; Egon in a nest of faded, chintzy pillows he'd assembled in a corner of the room, while I fumbled happily in the kitchen with my newly bought provisions. The previous tenants had left all their poorer crockery and cutlery. It took me back to bachelor days in the flat overlooking Victoria Station. There were other reminders too. On the way back to Altona I'd lost my nerve about meeting Karin in my forest outfit, and bought a pair of slacks to go with my new shirt, throwing financial caution to the winds; on the same market stall I found some cheap Cologne, so crude it evoked Ellie's pre-war scent. I splashed it on as liberally as ever Ellie had. Looking in the mirror I felt a pang I hadn't known since Maggie-days, the fear that my brutal troll-face couldn't win a human heart. I thought of shaving off my beard. This might be too much of a shock for Egon, I decided, on top of my new aroma and fresh clothes. He seemed ominously subdued, clinging to me on the way home with an expression on his face I hadn't seen before. He'd been forced to accept the world of men, but compliance was only a subterfuge, to judge by his eyes. Suspicion lingered in them. If he no longer looked stunned it was because he'd withdrawn further and learnt a different kind of escape, into himself. When Karin knocked at the door, a soft tapping I recognized at once from her visits to my hotel room, I glanced at Egon and saw no response at all. I let her in and Karin's gaze slid quickly off me, all too quickly, looking for the boy. To my surprise I saw Egon cower back a little when she spotted him among the pillows, and I wondered what had passed between them.

I was hoping for a second glance from Karin, after all my efforts. No, she seemed mesmerized by Egon. Or was it simply to avoid looking at me? She was clearly uncomfortable. I took the suitcase from her hand, in silence. Seeing her I felt overwhelmed, and perhaps it had shown in my face when I opened the door. She looked so summery in her white blouse with its short puffed sleeves, a *dirndl* skirt, bare calves and sandalled feet. Make-up softened her features, the moles and freckles receded and the hare-lip was barely noticeable, as if I were seeing her through gauze. We exchanged courtesies, still painfully constrained. I offered a chair. No, she couldn't stay, she said. Why not? She gave a shrug. It was a gentler, shyer gesture than I remembered from her, but firm all the same, with a touch of Frau Posener in it. My breath was caught somewhere high in my chest. I couldn't think where to start, how to tell her I had no reproaches to make, that we were quits, more than quits after her help with Egon. She was still gazing at him. At least stay while I unpack his things, I said. You can help me read your mother's instructions.

I knew she was longing to get away, but I took as long as I could over the unpacking, examining each item and asking her about their provenance, hoping that talking would relax her. The "instructions"—I really did need Karin's help to decipher Frau Posener's gothic script—turned out to be a complete daily regimen, when to wake Egon and what to feed him, how to toilet-train the child, a list of words he'd spoken, under separate headings. The words included *bitte*, *fertig* ("finished!"), and *jawohl*. My God, I thought, they're turning him into a Prussian officer. Inside the suitcase there were clothes galore, assembled by Karin and her mother from stalls and shops and friends whose children had outgrown them. There was even a Matrosenanzug, a little sailor suit of the kind made popular all over Europe before the first war but hardly the rage any more. Karin insisted they were still to be seen. They were "schick," she said, chic. Then she admitted they hadn't tried to dress Egon in it. As we gazed from the sailor suit to the brooding little face in the corner of the room, her defences began to crack, and she had the good grace to smile at the absurdity of it.

The Matrosenanzug went back into the suitcase. Out came pyjamas, wash-things, toy cars, furry animals. Beneath them all, the coat and lederhosen, neatly pressed. I held them up for Egon to see. No reaction. Picking out one of the toy cars I ran it towards the boy, followed it on all fours and drove it round his feet, making appropriate noises. Egon didn't even watch the car, and eyed me in a lacklustre way. I had greater hope for the furry toys, until I saw the disgust on his face as Karin approached with one, a faded yellow bear with button eyes. It was so old, its chest worn smooth with love and cleaning, that it looked like the original teddy-bear on which all others had been patterned. I tried to fathom Egon's mistrust. Surely he'd had similar toys at the Schloss, before his treehouse days. Then I remembered Herta's gruesomely stuffed heads; perhaps what he saw advancing on him was a girl stroking a dead animal. Karin faltered, and glanced at me. I couldn't help grinning. We made such a comical threesome, Karin and I like supplicants before a boy-Emperor sulking on his pillows. Even with his scrubbed face he still looked wizened, as he had when I first saw him, and like no seven-year-old I'd ever known; like a much older child who'd never grown. I let the thought go by. He wasn't really sulking, he took interior time like a resting animal, without boredom or resentment—unless you disturbed him. As we knelt there bearing gifts, a red car and a yellow bear, Karin glanced from Egon's eyes to mine, and back . . . a scene that was to be repeated so many times, in different ways. All I wanted was to find out what elements of friendship or attraction underlay the ways that we'd been using each other, Karin and I. But Egon's presence was a shield between us and I think I already sensed it, that first evening.

"He's probably just hungry," I said. "I've got potatoes in the oven, and I bought some pork chops."

"He doesn't eat meat."

"I know. The chops are for us." To cover this, I hurried on. "I've got plenty of vegetables too."

Karin was on her feet. "Thank you, but I'm cooking for Mother tonight." For *Mutti*; the affectionate term sounded oddly defiant. "Mutti says to please bring him to Wandsbek tomorrow morning nine o'clock so that they can continue with his lessons." I felt a flash of resentment at having my life dictated in this fashion—foolishly, because I'd no idea how I was going to cope with the child without the Poseners' help. Then I realized that wasn't what I resented; it was Karin's impersonal tone, as though I were no part of it, merely a go-between. Karin had turned to Egon to say goodbye: "Tschüss, Egon."

It was time for a frontal assault.

"I want you to know how grateful I am," I said. "Not only for Egon. Everything's turned out for the best, it really has." I could see her starting to protest, and before she could stop me I blurted out my name, and as much of my story as I felt she could handle at that moment. "I'm working with Walters," I said. "I understand if you don't want to talk about it. None of that matters any more. I'm just happy to see you again."

She nodded, embarrassed, still clutching the teddy-bear. After a moment she leaned down and placed it on the edge of Egon's pillow-nest. The boy was watching me expectantly. He'd understood the references to food.

"Couldn't you stay a few minutes longer? There must be things you want to ask me."

Karin squatted, smoothing the *dirndl* skirt, gazing at Egon. "Tell me about him," she said.

I'd meant things she might want to ask about me, but at least I had her company for a little longer; and I retold Egon's story— as I was to do so many times over the coming years, until it became an empty litany. Everyone was fascinated by Egon, once they knew he was a woodland child. A real live Waldmensch! Like a universal ancestor standing before you. People gazed into his eyes as though they held the secret of humanity; our twin, licensed to growl and bite. When he wouldn't perform they lost interest. But Karin never did. Her fascination with the boy was compulsive, inexhaustible.

Over the next few months we fell into a routine, one that was to last several years. In the morning I'd feed Egon and walk him through Altona, crossing the Altstadt into St. Pauli and trying out new routes, so as to familiarize him with the city, or rather to convince him of its suppleness and variety; eastwards past the Alster, across St. Georg and finally up the Wandsbeker Chaussee to Mutti's house—as we all called it, Egon included. *Muttis-Haus.* In the evening Karin brought him back. After a while she began to stay longer, consenting to join us for supper but not, much as I longed for it, to wait till Egon fell asleep. Much less to stay the night. Walters had told her who I was, the things I hadn't said, that I was married, footloose, on the lam. The uncomfortable look returned to Karin's face when I tried to tell her about my past, as though I was asking her to share responsibility for it or to connive at what I'd done. I wasn't asking that. It was the present I wanted to share with her, not a fictitious present but myself as I was and had been; warts and all, as it were. If I loved her warts, her real, visible ones, why couldn't she at least address mine?

I wanted to talk about Molly; Maggie too; and Alec, and how I'd come to be Reinhard Sacher, so that at least there was one person who knew who I was, someone to come home to. Once or twice—twice to be exact—she called me Richard. Never Reinhard. And I remained "Sie," never "du." I could picture us in bed—and I'd still be "Sie," in true Hamburg fashion. Good morning . . . *wünschen Sie einen Kaffee?* At last a use for the phrasebook catechism Maggie and I had learnt at the vicarage. *Danke schön, gnädige Frau! Bitte holen Sie mir einen Schnaps!*

I soon discovered why Egon had cowered when he saw Karin at the door of our apartment. Their battles of will were fearsome to behold. If he refused to do something, Karin couldn't let it go at that. This normally quiet submissive creature flew into a temper without raising her voice. She locked eyes with him, trembling. They had to be in unison, or it made her desperate; unlike her mother she needed the boy's approval, and I suffered for them both. It's true I had an easier time with Egon. He treated me like a privileged being, and usually did as I asked. If not, I ignored him. I found his obtuseness rather calming. I had no desire to infiltrate it, in fact I wanted to preserve his Waldmensch spirit—within limits, anyway. At first he was barely housebroken, despite Mutti's boasts of toilet-training, and continued to shit anywhere but in the toilet bowl. I cured him of that by example. He liked to watch me in the bathroom, naked, something the Poseners naturally denied him; seeing me wash and dress myself persuaded him to follow suit.

At weekends I had him to myself. Egon treated this like a holiday after the Wandsbek regime, and the first time I went out without him brought swift retaliation. He wrecked the apartment. After that I took him everywhere. He'd play games with me in the street, pretending to disown me, disappearing, then I'd see him at a distance, tracking me more like a cat than a faithful hound. Hamburg was becoming his forest. When autumn came we went plum-picking, the three of us, on the south bank of the Elbe, along with other couples and their children. Egon scrambled up the trees, flinging plums in all directions and bombing Karin with them. For an afternoon we were the family I wanted us to be; that we could never be. Unless . . . it always came back to this, and though I dreaded it, I thought I knew what the proviso was: unless we found Wackernagel.

When she'd heard that Egon's father had been murdered by the Nazis, just as she felt hers had been, I think Karin took it as a sign from God. For years now finding Wackernagel had been her mission, a murderous one as I saw it, and here was Egon carrying—in ignorance—the same burden. He could be her healing mission. That was my hope. She talked less about Wackernagel; but Egon's rage seemed to threaten her with an image of her own submerged feelings. Give it time, I thought.

Sometimes I asked myself whether I really wanted to find Wackernagel, whether it wouldn't re-open the wound. Would revenge heal it? The man ought to be brought to justice, certainly, but . . . what I really dreaded was finding that this was all Karin had wanted from me, that it was still the reason for our friendship. We both knew that Reinhard Sacher, former comrade-in-arms of Wackernagel's, would be in a better position to trace him than "Herr Schäfer" had been.

It was on my mind from the beginning—from the day of the cricket match, Sacher's baptism day, his first outing. After walking Egon to Wandsbek I'd walked back again; the match didn't start until eleven, and it saved one tram fare. Cheerybye's meagre advance was barely keeping me going, with Egon to feed. I also wanted to repay Frau Posener, despite her protests, for the time she lavished on the boy. What I needed was a job on the side—the black market was still thriving, though in more expensive, esoteric items—working for the very man who could lead us to Wackernagel if he put his mind to it, and used his neo-Nazi contacts. In short a job with Wolfgang Zimt.

Alias Henry Hirsch.

The shock of finding him alive, standing there in whites and cricket pads, left me speechless. For a moment I forgot about Wolfgang Zimt and who and what this person was, in his ridiculous white outfit. It was Henry come back to haunt me. Then common sense asserted itself. It couldn't be Henry. Why was my mind doing this to me? I was going mad. Or perhaps Henry had a twin brother. Whoever he was I felt queasy at the sight of him. Tanned, smiling face. He was blooming. Confused anger was spreading through me. Somehow I'd been duped, and this . . . this creep was to be my protector? *This* was the fearsome knifeman Zimt? His words about "making good shots today, better than last time"—it was Henry all right. Reminding me that I was at his mercy. He watched the conflict in my face with satisfaction. *Brauchst Kleidung, was?* A glance took in my lack of cricketing equipment. Short of clothing? Smug, serious now— God how I loathed him—he nodded at a large communal cricket bag on the bench beside us, "Take what you need. We'll talk later."

It wasn't till mid-afternoon, when our side was batting, that we had a moment to ourselves. By then I'd had plenty of time to think about what happened on the Schaalsee ice. And earlier. I remembered Vlad the String suggesting that we go to Wolfgang Zimt for butter, and when I vetoed that, producing "Henry Hirsch" instead; devious Vlad. And later, in the Friedrichswald, I'd thought I was seeing Henry in a series of disguises. Impossible, because Henry was dead. Hallucinations.

But here he was sauntering along the boundary, intolerably cheerful. No, not rally cheerful, I could see that as he came closer. Smiling his red-lipped smile, that was all. Lips drawn back like a horse when the bit chafes. The pale, civilized, watery eyes looked as if they might roll up into his head at any moment. *Vollkommen verrückt,* I thought. Mad eyes. He's quite mad. *Ausgeflippt.* And I saw something else in them. He was afraid of me.

"Okay, *du Arschloch*," you arsehole, he said pleasantly, "you want to see the hole you made?'' He pretended to pull the back of his shirt out of his trousers. ''What kind of man shoots a friend in the back? *Du Arsch. Du Scheisskerl du.*''

''Let's have a look then,'' I said, and he glanced round before raising the shirt to show an angry indentation on his lower back, like a second, infected navel. He twisted his head to look at me, grimacing proudly. I stuck a forefinger into the pucker of the red-rimmed hole. Zimt gave a yell and rounded on me. Distant faces turned to us from the game. They turned back. It was all right, just a pair of *Arschloch* buddies horsing around. *Du alte, dicke Votze,* I said, calling him an old pussy—too late I realized this was an insult I'd picked up in the whore's domain—applied to women—what was I doing? I pressed on furiously, ''what kind of friend sells a man rancid fat and calls it butter?''

He stared, open-mouthed. ''Well?'' I demanded—(Keep going!)—*''Du Affenarsch!''* Monkey-bum! This fitted better. Fury was colouring his cheeks like a baboon's arse. I saw him hesitate, measuring me, and then settle for the offense to his professional pride.

''It was good butter!''

''It was fat and mashed potato.''

''What are you talking about?''

''And it cost me *vier Blaue*, four blue ones. Remember?'' As I said this I remembered something myself: they were counterfeit ''blue ones,'' if Philby and Walters had been telling the truth. Zimt hadn't discovered it, to judge by his expression. He looked genuinely puzzled.

''*Mensch*, I sold you good butter.''

''You sold me *Scheissbutter*. And then you shot at me.''

He laughed. ''You think I shot at you? I was trying to frighten you, to make you come back. Not to kill you.''

I faltered. Was it true? ''To frighten me?''

''Of course to frighten you. If I kill you, your British friends will scold me, *nicht?* I was supposed to stay with you. You idiot. Why did you run away? Because you didn't like my butter?''

My British friends. Philby had put him onto me! Through Vlad? No, I was an easy mark—I'd been asking everywhere, among the bunker people and in the rubble domain, for someone to take me across the border. ''How in hell did you survive?''

Zimt shrugged, tugging his cap back and pushing the rebellious cowlick under it. ''They pulled me out of the water. What do you think?''

"Are you saying the Russians rescued you . . . and gave you back?''

"What Russians? They were Germans. Our boys."

A motionlessness about his face. This time I was certain he was lying. I'd heard the cries in the Schaalsee reeds, as the dogs were released. Russian cries. And now I had a glimpse of him again outside the Hof that day, in Russian uniform, with another man. Pausing beside the Mercedes.

Applause jerked me back. A wicket had fallen.

"You are ready to bat?'' Zimt said promptly, pushing me forwards.

Ready wasn't quite the word. Three balls hissed past me like brimstone. Zimt in league with the Russians? Should I tell Philby? The fourth ball bowled me.

I went hotfoot to Bad Neunburg with my precious information. Philby wasn't there so I was stuck with Uncle Bumble, as the secretaries called him: plump Cheerybye, bow-tied and cleaning his nails as he listened. I told him how I'd first met Zimt as Henry Hirsch, making it clear I knew that he'd been sent along to tail me, and how Zimt had denied falling into Russian hands. And how I knew otherwise. My first day on the job and I'd made a discovery worth months of salary.

"It probably *was* Germans who rescued him,'' said Walters calmly. "Soviet Germans. The border guards aren't all Ivans, or hadn't you realized that? You say you heard them shouting. Shouting what?'' I racked my brains. "You speak Russian, do you?'' When I didn't answer, he looked up from his manicure, amused. "I don't see the mystery here. Russians or Germans, it makes no odds. When they found out who it was they'd fished out of the lake, you can be sure they gave him back pronto. They don't want Zimt over there. He spent last summer in Berlin, sniffing round the Stadtkontorbank, and a lot of industrial diamonds were missing from the vaults, not to mention ten grams of radium now circulating in the Russian sector. Left a few corpses in his wake—his way of making sure no-one could pin a thing on him. I'm not surprised they chucked old Wolfgang back at us, are you?''

"But I tell you I saw him several times in Mecklenburg!''

"In different outfits. Yes.'' I wished I hadn't told him, now. He studied me, patently speculating—or pretending to—about my state of mind at the Hof. "Saw him all over the place, eh?''

"You swear you didn't send him after me?''

"What, in a bloody Russian uniform? What makes you think

we could swing that?'' He leant back in his chair. ''For God's sake don't try and catch Zimt in any lies. Forget this watchdog nonsense. Never mind what Philby told you, just get in close and stay there. Do whatever you have to do, but don't ruffle his feathers. *Verstanden?*'' I nodded. ''You'll have your work cut out, I'd say. How did you get on with him?''

''All right, I think. Showed him I wasn't easily intimidated.'' I saw Cheerybye roll his eyes. I wasn't going to be intimidated by him either. ''Suppose I really did see Zimt in Russian uniform—''

Cheerybye tumbled his bulk forwards against the desk. ''Now look. The one thing spy novels always get wrong, old bird, is this idea that you've got a lot of clever-dicks playing different roles,'' he stressed ''clever-dicks'' to show what he thought of me and my theories, ''but that their heart's only in one of them. Believe me, half the buggers in this game don't even know which side they're on. Take Zimt. Born Düsseldorf in 1920. Joined the Party as a nipper, the Nazis that is, Hitler Youth. Claims they were going to drum him out for telling schoolboy jokes about the Führer, so he offered to join the Communist youth brigade as well, and spy on them. He's always played both sides against the middle. Zimt's not his real name by the way. It's Hickel. Wolfgang Hickel. Know what Zimt means?''

''Cinnamon.''

''It also means crap. Crap as in rubbish. Piffle, bunk. He was a byword for false information by the time he was fifteen. Wears it with pride. Do not make jokes about his name. The last smart-aleck who made fun of it had his privates sent to his mother in a cigar box.''

Wonderful, I thought, this was the man I'd just called an old pussy—while poking my finger into the bullet wound in his back. Come to think of it I'd called him a *fat* old pussy. It was just as well I'd inflicted the bullet-hole myself, if I was going to take liberties with it.

''During the war,'' Walters was saying, ''Herr Crap maintains he fought for a Totenkopf unit in North Africa and later on the Russian front. He didn't. He spent half the war in jail for forgery. Specialized in army requisition slips. They only let him out when the SS were drafting criminals to go and put the wind up the French, towards the end.''

I didn't like the sound of this. ''I thought Zimt was a clerical worker.''

''I'm coming to that. In France he was suspected of getting

up to his old thieving tricks again, so Himmler's boys gave him a desk job in a camp just up the road from here, at Neuengamme, where he could steal to his heart's content. Learnt his knife skills there too, I believe. Which reminds me. Get your armpit tattooed.''

''What?''

''Left armpit. Should have your blood group on it, that was standard SS procedure. Zimt'll probably tattoo it on you himself, if you ask him nicely.''

''No thanks.'' It was time to draw the line. ''No tattoos. I'm not playing charades with the SS.'' If it came to that, I'd much rather be in jail. ''I'll hang around as long as Zimt's word is my safe-conduct. But that's all.''

To my surprise, Walters didn't seem put out. ''Up to you,'' he said. ''It's your hide. As long as you understand that with chaps like Zimt it's easy come, easy go. And whether he's got Russian connections or not doesn't matter a damn, provided you don't tell him anything worth knowing. Don't trust him. And don't push him. I've got other plans for you.'' Cheerybye linked his hands behind his head. ''But they can wait. You're still a bit naive about the Krauts, aren't you.''

''In what respect?''

''Sounds to me as if you're afraid of them.'' And when all he got from me was an contemptuous stare, ''Well, *are* you?''

''No.''

Walters sighed, holding my gaze. ''All right. Now, I can see you're a logical sort of person. Like to think you're deep, don't you. A thinker. Don't say very much. Well, that's your first mistake round here. The German doesn't trust cold fish. Think of the Nuremberg rallies. They're an emotional people, Thurgo. I've had them crying in here, middle-aged men, officers—Prussians—crying! And d'you know what they're crying for? They're crying because they love me! Because I'm England and suddenly they love England, they've always loved England. Can you imagine *us* behaving like that if Adolf had won? They come here begging for their Persilchein, their Persil pass. Know what that is? Tells the world they're clean, no Nazi stains. Can't get a job without one. It's because I've got my foot on their necks, that's why they're crying. Someone's put them in their bloody place and they love him for it. But my God if it was the other way around! Eh?'' He reflected for a moment, as if struck by something new. ''Mind you, they'd still love us, if it was *their* foot on *our* necks. Brutality is a form of kindness, that's what they think. Get it over quickly. They'd expect us to be grateful, too. They can't understand why people didn't *want* to be conquered by Germany! D'you know what one chap said to me? Herr Oberst, he said—I'm not a ruddy colonel but it made him feel better to call me one—Herr Oberst, tell me truthfully, would you rather find yourself in one of Stalin's camps or one of Hitler's? I didn't give him the satisfaction of a reply. So being German he told me what the correct answer was. Hitler's of course. Why? Because you'd die quicker. More humanely. Humanely! You see how they think?''

Gazing at his expression I felt anger rising. You great smug bumblebee, I thought . . . I'll find a way to puncture you.

"Listen to me carefully," he said, "if you want to get along with this chap Zimt. There are two kinds of Kraut. The leaders and the led. Both equally dangerous. But you've got to make up your mind which you're going to be. If I was you I wouldn't try to lead Herr Zimt. Better make him think you're a bit of a fool. Impressed by him. Sitting there looking deep won't do it. It'll get you into trouble, pronto. He'll think, what's this fellow *really* thinking? Say something, butter him up. Like all Germans he admires you and he hates you, but they're all so bloody insecure they'll believe any little piece of flattery, doesn't matter if you mean it or not. They *want* to go along with us, now that we've won. You watch the next few years. They'll become a perfect little slave-nation, fawning on everyone. Work like beavers. Pots of money to be made here, Thurgo.''

He let it dangle, but it meant nothing to me at the time. I needed money now, pronto indeed, and not in some hypothetical German future. Hearing that Zimt was still in business as a thief had cheered me up. Industrial diamonds: a jewel thief? Precious metals worth untold sums, hundreds of millions of pounds, had been pilfered by the Nazis from all of Europe, so everyone said, and if Zimt knew where to lay his hands on it. . . . As Cheerybye prattled on, I looked round his dismal office. No, this wasn't the life for me. From corner to corner the place was piled high with tatty books, German books—but English authors, I noted. Jack London, George Orwell. Books on Indian Nationalism.

"Trying to educate the Krauts, I see," I said when he paused for breath.

"What?'' Cheerybye followed my gaze to the books. "No no no. We confiscated these, they're all from public libraries. Don't want any inflammatory stuff out there.'' I nodded as he glanced at me. "You haven't been listening, have you. Think you know it all." He sighed again, more gently. "You see now . . . that's just it. That's the difference. We're a lazy people, Thurgo. That's our secret. We're lazy because we can afford to be. Spiritually, I mean. Spiritually." He leaned forwards, relishing the word. "Hidden reserves! That's what we've got. Immense hidden reserves of self-belief!" Looking at his shiny face, I couldn't argue with him. "*We* don't need all this fanatical will, this work and sacrifice," he was saying. "Too much of a strain—just look at them, the Germans . . . no spontaneity, nothing but morbid introspection," he shook his head, "and what do they get for it? They're lonely as sin. All this arrogance and resentment and touchiness, it's insecurity, that's all. They're a young nation, compensating for it by arrogance. Got to remember they're the most mixed race in Europe, that's why this Herrenvolk rubbish appeals to them so much. Inferiority complex—love strong leaders. You see?" My lugubrious nod seemed to distract him. "Inferiority complex, superiority complex, guilt complex," he recapitulated for me, counting them off on his fingers, "and no wonder they've got a guilt complex, given what's in their hearts—"

"What's that?" I said.

Walters eyed me suspiciously. "Murder of course. Bloodshed. Rather drink blood than wine, any day—and they know it. Ever heard of the Teutoburger Wald?" His pronunciation was so bizarre that I hesitated, and shook my head. "It's where they massacred the Romans. Or the Romans massacred *them*. I forget which. But it doesn't matter—doesn't *matter*—that's the point! Hacked-off limbs littering some dark pine forest, that's what thrills them. Ever see the Hermannsdenkmal? Bloody great warrior in stone, hundreds of feet high. All this Kultur crap is just a lot of fancy dress, all these philosophers they hide behind. Try appealing to reason here! They don't give a damn about reason. Give them a legend to hang onto and they're happy as Larry."

In time I learnt Cheerybye's little lectures off by heart. The Modern Barbarians, Submissiveness and Domination, Extremist Tendencies. The Need For a Saviour. And so forth. Wartime cant. I don't suppose it would have angered me so much unless there was some truth in it, but coming from Walters I resented every word. At Bad Neunburg the story ran that when he first arrived from Nigeria, where he'd been a colonial administrator during the war, he asked for a list of his British and German staff to be drawn up under two headings: Europeans and non-Europeans. Who was he to mouth off about arrogance?

Listening to him I loved the Germans all the more. The Germans! . . . more intangible, more ample, more contradictory, more unknown, more incalculable, more surprising and more terrifying than other people are to themselves: so said Nietzsche. But it's far too grandiose a description. Typically German, in fact. "Surprising," "terrifying"—of the most predictable people on earth? Even "contradictory" misleads, suggesting murky depths. There are no German depths. Consider Hitler. To Walters a Lucifer—but take a look at the man's face; when Adolf wasn't trying to look stern there was a fatuous simpering sweetness to his expression, a helpless, feminine look which made people want to protect him; a contradiction, you might think, redolent of those cloying pieties about home and motherhood which lived cheek by jowl with Nazi sadism, filling German houses with pictures of chubby infants gathering flowers, under embroidered commonplaces—proverbs over the door and perverts behind it, as Cheerybye liked to say. There's no contradiction here. No depth. The truth is that in Germany nothing connects. Here the mask is the man. Who is he, the uniformed German who butchers a village before lunch and after lunch writes sentimental postcards home, describing the charms of the countryside? He's not Cheerybye's bloodsucking primitive, he's the most modern animal there is, a being who can be guaranteed to do what he's told, you feed it into him and it comes back at you like the chatter of a tickertape machine—soft words or automatic gunfire, according to orders. Yesterday chattering about racial superiority, today about democracy. Utterly biddable . . . the very image of the human creature rising to the light, absurd, ready for anything. I loved them viscerally. How can you *not* love the Germans? They are us.

But it was Wolfgang Zimt I had to deal with, and I never thought of Wolli (a name reserved for intimates) as particularly German. Neither did Wolli. In "Henry Hirsch" I'd seen an insolent German resilience. There was more to him than that. Zimt was a true fantasist, a rare thing in domestic German life (I don't speak of their poets, who have plenty of native literalness to react against), rare because Germans are such transparent liars. Innocents as Alec called them, rather than machiavels; the sadist and the sentimentalist aren't roles to be played, they're an authentic partnership, willed into being. But unlike most of his compatriots Wolli didn't invent himself, far from it, he was so deeply rooted in his being that he could afford a whole wardrobe of selves, each one meticulously acted out. By turns he was the thief, the victim, the cynic (a German cyniç! A *Tzü-niker*!), the tyrant, the Buddhist and follower of Bhikku U Thunanda, man of peace—though Wolli sometimes liked to hint that "der Bhik" was a celebrated Rangoon con-man amassing a private fortune from the faithful. (I always doubted this.) There was also the revolutionary Wolli who lectured us on politics, conjuring up the Free State of St. Pauli; the nearest Wolli came to it was the Freipuff or socialist bordello he founded, briefly and disastrously, since the girls couldn't get used to giving it away. Many customers also preferred to pay. One night loud screams of fear brought the whores running to an upstairs room, where Wolli held one of their number by the hair, both of them streaked with blood, the girl hysterical, Wolli brandishing a knife. Bloodspattered banknotes littered the floor. A warning! Betray the Freipuff, and incur the wrath of Wolli!

This too was a charade. He hadn't really knifed the girl, he'd cut his hand in the kitchen and used this as an opportunity to stage a scene. Threats failed to save the people's whorehouse, but Wolli told the story cheerfully against himself. He was a droll, another rare but not unknown German type. He savoured irony. A sly German. But in one important respect Cheerybye's cap fitted him: as the legendary Zimt he found it difficult to be my equal, or anyone's equal. Was I, Reinhard Sacher, his slave or his master? It troubled him, and I took great care to keep the question in suspense. Contrary to Cheerybye's advice, some instinct told me I was a dead man if Zimt ever pigeon-holed me. If I was his master, I must despise him—hadn't I seen him shivering in the snow, and turning in terror as I raised the gun? He couldn't allow that. (And it was true that when my nerve failed in his company I made myself think of him in the Schaalsee reeds, a frozen frightened squit pleading with me to come back.) If I was his slave, how dare I take such liberties with him, insulting him as no-one else in Hamburg dared? As we sat carousing at our Stammtisch, our regular table at café or restaurant, hardened thugs went very still when I called Wolli an *Arsch*. Only an old comrade could treat him like this—surely—which reinforced my cover story and made Wolli dependent on it for his dignity. In return, I could verify his more extravagant wartime adventures. I had to verify them. I was in them. Together we dodged bullets and quagmires in the deserts of Tripolitania, we were captured and dispatched to a prisoner-of-war camp in

Manchester, we escaped and rowed across the Channel. I was a boon to Zimt, a Reinhard Sacher sent by providence to corroborate his exploits. On the other hand, who better to expose them? In honour of our Manchester days we sometimes hailed each other in British accents: "Henry!" "Richard!" "My dear fellow!" like upper-crust explorers meeting in the Gobi. A teasing reminder of our earlier identities. A poisoned one, too, I could see it in his eyes. Wolli was trying to tell me that our shootout on the Schaalsee was only a rehearsal. He loved Westerns. The prospect of a final reckoning was shapely, and appealed to him.

Get in close, and stay there: those were Cheerybye's instructions. That first summer and autumn I did so without questioning his reasons. Philby had talked of monitoring Wolli's neo-Nazi contacts. But Philby was in Turkey. And Nazism, "neo" or simply nostalgic, never surfaced in Wolli's conversation.

Forget politics, said Cheerybye. The information he wanted from Zimt concerned the movement of black market goods. This suited me. It was what Alec would have called a sweet racket: in return for Cheerybye's protection, Zimt informed on his rivals, and undermined them in the process; I ferried news of various selected deals, then Walters intercepted them—and took the glory, I assumed. Whatever else he took was no concern of mine. I was learning discretion.

And I was on the inside now. Wolli sent me on errands, exchanging packages for envelopes; delivery-boy work, at first accompanied, later alone. One day optical instruments from the Czech mission, the next day penicillin from the Swedish Red Cross—no-one seemed averse to a bit of illegal traffic, not even the Jewish Relief people, whose stores were available at a price. Simple transactions. Profitable, since I took my cut. And safe. The gangs had yet to carve out their empires, it was a free-for-all and the milieu was in the hands of individuals. But somehow I felt disappointed. I remember sitting in Wolli Zimt's ostentatiously well-furnished apartment, drinking champagne, "shum-*pun*-yer," watching Wolli dance to the gramophone with dark-haired Sabine, his favourite then—*Das ist mein chère amie, Reinhard*—Sabine tiddly, Wolli flushed and singing along with the record. I Can't Give You Anything But Love, *bay-ay-bee*. . . . He was wearing a kind of ski-suit, a pale blue onepiece outfit like an overstretched romper, a cream shirt and a tie with a huge Windsor knot. I wanted adventures, not errands and a ringside seat watching Zimt do the fox-trot in his sitting room.

From somewhere he'd acquired a host of classical prints, chiefly Leonardos, which stared down at us from heavy gilt frames; later he mercifully took these out of the frames and used them to paper the walls and ceiling of his bedroom—I glimpsed them there on one occasion, and it was like peeping into an artist's grotto in hell.

There was no shortage of girls. The story was that I'd just been released from detention—as well as being true, it explained my sudden reappearance in Wolli's life—and must be ravenous for entertainment. This enabled Wolli to show off. And to show me off at the same time. He was proud of my size and ugliness. He began growing a beard, which I took as a tribute. It was as lank as the rest of his hair, but the sloppy moustache gave his red lips a certain animalistic quality, and he knew it. As for the rest of the Zimt entourage, the Catch-wrestlers and Shockboxers (fairground fighters, a vanished breed now) and other hangers-on, I was well aware that beneath the pretence of camaraderie they were watching me to see whether I fitted in. Taciturn silences were my best ally, I decided. Let my appearance do the work. For the first time in my life I felt I looked the part. But I was fooling myself to think I could pass close inspection as a German, no matter how well I parroted Hamburg grunts and casual insults. Wolli had anticipated this, making it known that I'd been raised in England by a German schoolteacher father and an English mother, before choosing the Vaterland in time to shoulder arms and learn the goose-step. All well and good; in this company I would still have to prove I was "ein fixer Kerl," reliable.

Our sorties to the Kiez, the cluster of St. Pauli streets around the Reeperbahn, made a pleasant change from Wolli's pretentious flat. The Kiez, the Reeperbahn, the milieu: I now learnt that they were different but interpenetrating worlds. Tourists spoke of the Reeperbahn, it was their haunt. The outlaw world, the milieu, was closed to them. The Kiez encompassed both, at once social and geographical—the turf, the Strip, the action. And the home of the paralytic. Even by day Kiez-dwellers lay sprawled on the pavement, out cold. Here the bars fed me their sour smells, welcome after Zimt's *Parföng*. I liked the ill-assorted faces; their desperation lulled me, even their boasts, their aborted fights and threats and shoving contests. We'd all troop back to Wolli's place, where now and then our host arranged an "all-the-way" striptease, the height of decadence in those innocent days, when strippers still had to leave pubic and nipples decorously masked. I was in close all right, to use Cheerybye's cricketing metaphor, I was at silly mid-off but in Wolli's company my mind was elsewhere, dreaming of Altona mornings, walking Egon through the city. Evenings with Karin, on my best behaviour. Sunday strolls along the Elbe, the three of us.

The three of us, and Wackernagel. Karin saw him every-where, it seemed to me. When we went out into Hamburg she was in enemy country. No-one was spared. Each passer-by of the right age was a killer—her eyes accused him, and accused everyone else of forgetting. And yet it wasn't true that everyone had forgotten; there were trials taking place in Hamburg and elsewhere, with former Nazis in the dock. If I pointed this out I received a tirade in return. Did I know why there were so *few* trials? Because the Generals we'd put in charge of the German armed forces—old Nazis, most of them, Karin insisted—had gone to the British and American military governments and ex-plained that their price for lining up with us against the Russians was the release and exemption from prosecution of the leading SS murderers. And we'd agreed. Even a Nazi butcher was "fam-ily," in Karin's phrase, and Germany merely the black sheep of the capitalist family, the blackshirt sheep—compared to the real threat: the Reds. The history of our century was a tortured love affair between Russian and German, full of pacts and violations and revenges; we in the West were merely a diversion with whom German and Russian dallied and fought from time to time to make the other jealous. A truly Germanic view of the world, though Karin wouldn't have thanked me for saying so. For the time being the Germans had "won" by losing, by isolating the Russians and turning the world against them. This was the only game that mattered, even to the "Great Powers" who'd fought against Germany; the fate of a few million undesirables was a mere bagatelle.

But for all Karin's cynicism the truth wasn't being suppressed in all quarters. Books on the death camps were appearing now in German, eyewitness accounts, and Karin brought them to me in batches. I found the experience of reading them repulsive, in the wrong way. After a while imagination gave out, over-whelmed; I couldn't go on reading, page after ghastly page, except as a covert fellow-sadist, not as a fellow-sufferer. There was too much suffering. It became a narrative punctuated by the joy of death, lovely tranquil death whose greatest charm wasn't the relief from pain and horror but from the shame of being human. I understood the stigma of survival. After such horrors extinction seemed not merely the final but the only solution: no wonder it was the death-bringers who commanded most attention, as I struggled to read on. Karin wouldn't let me off the hook. Read! She was educating me, as she put it. Meanwhile she followed the trials closely in the newspapers. If the reports were brief she was infuriated, if there was plenty of publicity this upset her too, it was an exercise in breast-beating, she said, the better to let the majority of offenders escape. Yes, but . . . what was to be done, then? Prosecute half the adult population? I was afraid to say this to her. It was both the official and the popular excuse, masking indifference, or worse, sympathy for the old regime. Karin often told me so. And there was no way round it: she was right.

I'd been racking my brains for a way to approach Wolli about finding Wackernagel.

"I need your help, Wolli . . ."

Simple enough. Except that nothing in the milieu was simple—and favours were the ultimate currency, a kind of gold standard that underwrote all other dealings. A weighty favour was a ball and chain; Wolli and I were nicely poised, so far, and I didn't want to change that. Such delicacy! But it was of the essence, in the touchy world of the Kiez. *Ganoven*—Kiez-rogues—might haggle over money for an hour or two, but they'd spend an evening arguing the moral balance of a favour and its obligations. You couldn't quantify what was at stake, or how precious it was to them. They were like mediaeval theologians proving the existence of the soul. The soul of the Kiez! Indebtedness was proof of virtue, negating every sordid detail of "the life"; even a Zimt might be trash in his own secret estimation, but if he kept his word he was a king and could look down on the lying, cheating, outwardly respectable bourgeois, the soulless man. At the same time favours were power, deadly leverage, and so were hoarded for as long as possible. A man's ranking on the ladder of debts was everything, it was the very rhythm in his step, the promise of a greeting—as precisely calibrated as a bank manager's smile—when he walked into his favourite bar. In some ways a beginner was safer on the bottom rungs of the ladder, I told myself; better to owe Zimt, letting him do me a good turn, than to have him owe me, and resent me for it. But the scale of the favour . . . what if his sympathies were with the Wackernagels of the world—what if he knew the man? I might be asking him to rat on one of his own. There was no way to prepare the ground, no opening in the daily gossip since the Reich was never mentioned, or only in bland, regretful terms. One morning in Wolli's flat someone read out a passage from a newspaper article, quoting an American professor who'd assessed the total cost of the war at three trillion dollars, enough, this smug *Arsch* told us, to have bought every family on earth a house, a car, a swimming pool. A swimming pool! A billion swimming pools . . . picture them and it made you thank God for the war. But of course Wolli and the rest nodded piously. *Mensch*, the madness of war! Subject dismissed. I'd have to tackle Wolli when we were alone.

"Wolli . . . what are your feelings now about the Nazis?"

After all the ways I'd thought of saying it I couldn't believe I'd chosen one as bald as this. Wolli didn't mind a bit.

"Tschahh . . ." he said equably.

We were sitting in the little pavilion in Blankenese. "Hamburg Cricket Club" had been inscribed in blue, our colours, over the door, and in winter it served as a meeting place for Wolli's lesser associates, the "Firma" (later this title grew more prestigious), also known as "das Cricket." That month the newspapers were full of the Neuengamme trials. Wolli knew the defendants well, they were his old colleagues; I prayed he hadn't been involved in some of their activities, the mildest of which was the extermination of children as the Allied armies approached. In court the guards said they'd been ordered to eliminate all potential witnesses, regardless of age, though this scarcely explained why they'd made the adult prisoners dig their own graves and then buried them alive—to me the worst of horrors—let alone why, at an earlier date, the children had been given infected toys and sweets in order to further research into tuberculosis. Wolli had the newspaper in his hand, he was reading about the trial and I'd taken it as my cue. After the "Tschahh"—which emerged with a puff of Novembernebel, Hamburg's wintry haze—he glanced at me, and looked back at the article. I cursed myself. He obviously thought I was probing about his time at Neuengamme. The guards' behaviour was a *Schweinerei*, he said at last. Filth. He'd had nothing to do with it. He read out the defendants' names. *Schweine*, every one.

"Have you been asked to give evidence?"

Wolli shook his head. *Schweine* they might be, but I couldn't imagine Wolli testifying against old comrades. Let alone hunting one down for me. I had to shift our talk away from Neuengamme. "Did you know any of the people at Fuhlsbüttel? The warders I mean?"

He shook his head once more, reading. "I knew some of the prisoners."

"You did?" I'd forgotten that Fuhlsbüttel held a motley crew, including petty criminals. "Did you know Dr. Posener?"

"Who?"

"August Posener."

I had his attention now, but he looked blank.

Jude? he asked, dispassionately. Hearing him say the word sent a shockwave through me.

"He wasn't a Jew. A newspaper columnist who'd written things about Hitler." I gazed at sloppy-bearded Wolli, trying to see in him the child Walters had described, the Wolli who'd got into trouble himself by repeating schoolboy jokes about the Führer. I couldn't imagine those pale demented eyes in a child's face. They looked at me from some inhuman distance, puzzled, speculating. Forever telling me I wasn't what I seemed. In his tales of the Russian front Malaparte describes a German officer walking along a line of deserters about to be shot, and suddenly pausing to single out a young man. "You bear a striking resemblance to my son," he remarks. "One of my eyes is made of glass, so skilfully fashioned that no-one ever notices. If you can tell which eye is glass, you may go free." "The left one," says the boy. The officer nods. "Yes indeed . . . how did you guess?" And the boy replies, "Because it's the more human of the two." When I read this I thought of Wolli.

"I have a friend," I said (should I, dare I call her a *chère amie*?), "Posener's daughter. He died there, in Fuhlsbüttel. And she blames a man, *einen Typ*, called Wackernagel."

Wolli waited. *"Und?"*

"That's all."

Watery eyes, studying me.

"The name means nothing to you?"

"Which name?"

"Wackernagel."

"No."

I had the feeling that he already knew what I was asking. But I had to say it. As I opened my mouth to speak Wolli looked back at the newspaper. In my mind's eyes I saw the *W* for Wackernagel inscribed, over and over, in August Posener's cigarette-paper diaries, which Karin had finally entrusted to me to read.

"Will you help me find him?" I said. There was no answer, and we sat in silence.

"Hitler made one mistake." Wolli turned to me. "Of course later when he was mad he made many mistakes. I mean at the beginning he made one mistake. You know what it was? He should have put the Jews in charge of the camps."

I stared at him. He seemed absolutely serious.

"Hitler should have put the Communists in the camps and let the Jews kill them. Then we would have won the war."

Wolli eyed me keenly, amused by my expression. Why was he saying this? To shock me, test me? Did he believe it . . . or could it be that Walters had told him about Karin, and they both knew she was a Communist? I was too appalled to ask.

One night I came home late to find Karin and Egon in terrible disarray. A Wolli-errand had delayed me. I was supposed to meet a man called Erik at a dockland rendez-vous and collect some patents stolen from a plastics factory; no Erik, though I waited for hours. Patents were one of Wolli's most profitable sidelines, and he wasn't pleased. A party must be thrown for our Norwegian friends, the gentlemen involved, and would I be so kind as to stay for the fun? A little more than a polite request. Until now Wolli and the Firma hadn't pressed me to join in their late-night revelling. They knew I had a child to look after. They understood; there were so many dislocated families. And the fact that I took my responsibilities so seriously . . . *na ja, der Reinhard* was *solid*, that's all, a bit straight. On this occasion I needed to show where I stood when push came to shove and the "party" erupted. It wasn't my first scuffle, but it was the biggest so far, a full-scale brawl. No weapons other than fists and knees and butting heads; a Norwegian jaw got broken and the Insel bar took a beating. Hurrying back to Altona I was walking on air, reliving the first punch I landed and the first one I received, the flurry of blows and the wrestling frenzy. Until that night I hadn't realized how bitterly alone I felt in Wolli's world. After the first few punches I was no longer alone. I'd been holding too much in, I thought—which at the time seemed to explain the feeling that unless somebody stopped me I'd lay out every-one in the house, and grind the tables to dust for an encore. But from then on it was always like that. Nerves beforehand, fear too, like a gathering of forces, then gorging myself as the scrap began. I'd found my *métier* and everybody knew it. Looking round at the Insel's bloodied mouths and noses I felt the same bewildered flush of shame as I had at school, promising myself

I'd be cannier in future—dodge the punches and hold my fire. Going for another boy's throat, his face, and I wouldn't stop until I'd left him a bloody mess; wondering afterwards what frightful demon had got into me. Big raw-boned chap like you (though I was only big and strong in the mirror, inside myself I was shapeless and I knew it wasn't by size and strength that I dominated the other boys, but by a berserker's will)—got to learn to control yourself, everyone warned me. Now for the first time in my life I didn't have to. On the Reeperbahn word soon got around and people wanted to test my strength, arm-wrestle, fight. I probably liked it too much; in the end I ran out of competition, except from the lunatics who wanted to be hurt—there were plenty of them here—and as soon as I saw that in their eyes all the fight went out of me.

At the Insel that night Wolli's cronies didn't seem greatly surprised by my feats (because of my size—or the rage they sensed inside me?); I wasn't surprised either, once I recognized my old berserker frenzy, and the only curious part was that at my most physical and ungoverned at last, flailing around with my great clumsy limbs, I felt I had the strength of something small, compact, invulnerable. Armour within armour, like a scorpion under a rock. The blows I took renewed my sense of it, they were futile percussive things. The pain came afterwards. Winning sweetened it; but best of all, pain gave me back my shape. As I strode home through Altona a giant popped out at me from successive shopfronts. My own familiar figure—newly familiar, as if bruising had made it real at last. I felt like the giant I saw, and I wanted to laugh with glee. Where had I been all these years? Cowering somewhere. I knew Karin would be worried by now, wondering where I was, chafing; Egon too, perhaps; but I felt capable of taming anyone and anything.

Up the stairs, keys in hand. I let myself in.

"Karin?"

The lights were on in the little sitting room. It was empty. My eyes went automatically to Egon's pillow-nest in the corner. No Egon. No pillows either, they'd vanished. I hurried to the bedroom door.

Karin was standing beside the bed, rigid, her face turned towards me. Glancing round I couldn't see Egon in the room. When I met Karin's gaze I saw such shock and rage in it—she was shaking, quite unable to speak—that my mind made a dreadful leap, one I'm still ashamed to recall. I saw Egon's body lying mangled in the filthy alley beneath the sitting room window, lying as he would be if Karin had hurled him from our third floor flat. Earlier that week she'd read me a passage about a prisoner at Bergen-Belsen, a girl who'd been employed in the SS compounds and who'd had a child by one of the guards; on her return to housekeeping duties for the child's father, she'd killed the baby and served it to him for dinner, naked and garnished on a platter. The look in Karin's eyes as she'd read this aloud! It was the same expression they held now as she faced me across the bed.

I was so possessed by the atrocious vision in my head that I didn't think to ask her what the matter was. "Where's Egon?"

Karin was still looking straight at me. She didn't seem to have heard, or to be capable of signalling anything at all. When she was in this state—I recognized it now—I couldn't expect answers. I crashed back into the sitting room, a part of me was still looking for Egon but I could see he wasn't there and I was heading for the front door anyway, down the stairs to shout Egon's name through the streets. No; that isn't what I was doing, I was rushing to the alley to see if my nightmare vision was true.

As I reached the far end of the sitting room I glanced into the little kitchen area. What I saw stopped me dead, one hand on the front doorknob. Egon was sitting there in his nest of pillows, perfectly happy, eating an onion. Scraps of peel littered the floor.

I could't speak, just stared at him wedged there contentedly between two cupboards. Then I saw something come into his face. A guilty flush, something I'd never seen there—and before I even wondered what had brought it on I felt a surge of anger; not at him, but at whoever had put it there. And at myself. This don't-punish-me face was Hamburg's doing. Looking closer at him—(looking closer! it turned harmless kapok, the jeep's upholstery, into a melting human skullcap, an innocent woodland clearing into a killing ground)—tears gathered in my eyes as if to ward off what I saw. It wasn't an onion Egon was eating. A wadded ball in one hand; curled, sticky little strips lying around him. Rice-paper. He was eating August Posener's prison journal.

It was all my fault; but now that I really had good reason to be angry at myself, I felt sick instead. For months I'd been asking Karin to let me read her father's secret diaries, and she'd refused. Nobody else had seen the diaries, except for her. Mutti didn't even know of their existence, Karin explained; she'd come across them some years after Vati's death, and it would have been cruel, surely, to submit her mother to the details of August's ordeal, and to renew the pain. I found this debatable, but I didn't argue. I began to wonder whether they really existed, these precious diaries. Perhaps my skepticism began to show, because finally Karin brought me the little cigarette tin, and placed it on the kitchen table. First World War army issue; inscribed with August's name. Out came the cigarette rolling device, then the crumbly, yellowing papers, glued together by age and damp. August's faint scrawls had faded almost to invisibility. Interrogations, beatings, fellow-prisoners' deaths—Karin knew the entries off by heart, just as Peter had memorized his ancestor Kuno's letters. But now she'd have to relive them in turn, once again, as we deciphered the minute, coded script. That was really why she'd hesitated to let me see them, I decided. Once she explained the code and I could follow the story myself, I wanted to spare her the agony of it, and I begged her to let me keep the journal for a day or two. To spare her? Hypocrite that I was, I didn't do it to spare Karin but to spare myself Karin's fixed, obsessional look, the one I thought of as her vampire face. I swore I'd look after the diary with my life. I'd been reading the wretched little papyrus at breakfast this morning, and what had I done? Left it sitting beside the stove.

I could picture it now: Egon arriving home with Karin and scanning the kitchen. He'd give anything a chew to see if it was edible.

I walked to the bedroom. Karin hadn't moved. I saw—I hadn't even noticed it before—a little accordion of cigarette papers hanging from her fist. She was clutching a chunk of the journal that she must have prised from Egon. Quite a large chunk, thank goodness. Seeing the compound of grief and intoxicated fury in her face I realized my own tears had dried up. All I wanted to do was hug her, something she'd never allowed. Hug her angrily as well as lovingly, pull her up short, shake her if needs be.

Karin saw it and backed away before I could move.

That tripped something in me. Damn her and her precious bloody diaries. I knew why she'd hidden them from everybody: it was written on her face. All that guff about her mother's feelings . . . Karin wanted Vati August to herself, yes, suffering and all! A vicious thought; and true or not, it was my bad conscience speaking. I'd promised to take care of the journal, and I hadn't. No apologies could suffice. Instead we stood there glaring at each other.

Of all things my unmade bed began to irk me, I wanted to

tidy it, at the risk of seeming callous. The dirty sheets embarrassed me. Here we were in my bedroom, for the first time; until tonight Karin had never even seen it. I always kept the door shut, precisely so that I could leave the bed unmade, and so as not to seem to be inviting her in.

Sod it, I thought, and made the bed while Karin watched me. I found myself remembering that it had once been Karin who not only made my bed, at the Atlantic, but stiffened in offense when I tried to help her.

When I was finished I sat on the counterpane, facing away from Karin, feeling deflated. God knows how long we spent like that, without a word. It was only the beginning of a long gruelling night. All the time I sat there on the bed I was afraid she'd leave. She was behind me and I expected to hear her move, she'd walk right past me, fling away my outstretched hand, march off into the sitting room, down the stairs and out of my life. Perhaps she was longing to do just that, but she didn't move, or couldn't.

At some point in that interminable bedroom silence, it came to me. I already knew what it was I needed to say to her; now I knew how. But this wasn't the place to do it. And Karin wasn't ready yet. I stood up and went to her, she was standing backed up against the wall and at that moment I also wanted to tell her how like Egon she looked there—the last thing she'd want to hear. Like a cornered vixen. Exhausted, using the wall to hold herself upright. She didn't try to stop me putting my arms round her and leading her to sit beside me on the bed. The fight was starting to go out of her; her slack mouth troubled me with its reminder of Maggie, and suddenly the hare-lip looked like a breach in her defences, as if her poor sad face were going to follow suit and break apart. As I held her by the shoulders, stroking, trying to soothe her, she began gasping for breath, taking long shuddering gulps of air and raggedly letting them out again. It was the nearest Karin got to crying, a good sign probably but it frightened me. On and on it went, until she was sitting perfectly still and limp against me. Hours had passed, and events that should have wiped the rest of the evening from my mind, but my body kept reminding me of the brawl at the Insel bar. My swollen face and hands sang with the pride of it. With all my being I wanted to make love to Karin then, lust and the release of tears and the softness of her body merging with the glorious feeling that I'd healed myself tonight, and at last I could heal others. And it was so easy to tell myself this was the only possible outcome to the evening, the logical one—for Karin precisely the right moment to turn from Vati and put on her womanhood, her own life. What else was there for us? Apologies on my part; more freshly sedimented grief on hers, as we pieced together the remains of the journal, the ark of the bloody covenant. No, either we fucked now or we parted.

But that was all in my head. At twenty I'd have gone along with it, I think, I'd have persuaded myself that I could save her soul by making love to her. Pitiful arrogance; but the saddest part of it is that looking back now I wonder if it wasn't exactly what I should have done. And what Karin wanted: it was she who'd taken refuge in my bedroom, for the first time. I was fresh from my Herta-journey, and I suspect what stopped me was less an idea of mature behaviour, of wisely loving restraint, than the memory of Herta and what had happened in the clearing. My own secret journal, that I didn't want to revisit.

So I held her instead, in what I decided was an adult fashion. I was so pleased with myself that night! I couldn't admit to myself that my self-control had anything to do with Herta; no, I told myself there was an old head on these Thurgo shoulders now. These Sacher shoulders, rather. A real man, ein fixer Kerl, beat the shit out of Norwegians and then went home and *didn't* rape his girlfriend. Mensch! the things you could learn in the milieu.

It was long gone midnight when I coaxed Karin onto her feet. I would walk her home, I said. She shook her head. I insisted, drawing her into the sitting room, towards the door. Egon was fast asleep, sprawled in his kitchen nest. "Stay with him," she said, at first so inaudibly I had to make her repeat it. Her face was a doughy mask, expressionless. I caressed it and she didn't stop me. Why do you stay with me? I wanted to say; why do you come here? I'm not helping you forget your pain. But I didn't say it. Her capacity for pain touched me too deeply, it was part of why I loved her, why I couldn't let her go. I fed on it. Bringing the cigarette tin I assembled all the surviving scraps of journal, placed them in the tin, fetched Karin's coat and put the tin into one pocket. The rest of the journal was still clutched in her fist, and I didn't try to prise it from her.

As we left I locked Egon into the flat. He knew he'd already done the wrong thing that evening—he knew all right, and I was haunted by his guilty look—so if he did wake up and find us gone, he might think twice before wrecking the apartment in reprisal. In a way I hoped he *would* smash it up, if that's what it took to restore the old shameless Egon.

It was a long walk, an hour and more, to Wandsbek. Every morning I walked it with Egon, but never through such perfectly deserted streets. That was part of my plan, the one I'd conceived earlier. I had a story to tell. Hamburg, sleeping like the dead, would be my sounding board; I needed Karin to feel how close they were, the dead, in the empty, kindly spaces of the nighttime city.

"Permit me to tell you . . ." Wasn't that how Peter had begun? "This is a story Egon's father told me," I said, "about a man he loved, though he only knew him through letters." Kuno von Brüel, Peter's forebear, who had saved Napoleon's life and followed him on his Russian adventure. I told Karin about the breastplate that had been in Peter's family since the Thirty Years War, and how Kuno eventually put on this piece of ancient, shining steel, to take the field against Napoleon, his former hero. Kuno's letters revealed a man scarred by the bitterest experiences, after the horrors of the Russian campaign. How to go on, to retrieve your own humanity, carrying everywhere the burden of intolerable memories? Trying to jump over your own shadow, in Peter's beloved phrase. It seemed to Kuno that this couldn't be achieved until he'd killed the tyrant. I described how Kuno went to Erfurt to do it, and returned to the theatre where Napoleon had so narrowly escaped assassination once before, thanks to Kuno's own intervention. And how he met Napoleon there in a ghastly dream. Napoleon standing beneath the fringe of artificial leaves, the dusty stage décor lit by a single, turbid oil-lamp in the auditorium ceiling; Napoleon helpless before Kuno's avenging pistol shot. In the dream. Dear God! I felt absurdly moved, telling the story as our footsteps echoed in the empty streets, telling it in the best German I could muster. Peter had told it in English for the benefit of the visiting contingent; hard luck on his mother, who didn't understood a word of English, though of course she knew the story. Agnetha's stern, distracted face came back to me so vividly that her presence conferred a blessing. I saw her at the far end of the table, in the Rittersaal, cudding as peacefully as the Lützow herd; no doubt she'd been thinking about her cattle while her son recounted family history. And here I was, retelling it in German—are you listening, Peter? I felt him so close—now that I'd mastered his language sufficiently to repay him in kind, in the original, the proper language of the story. And Kuno's words had meant so much to him! Kuno was Peter's conscience, his guide in slippery times; at the same time he was Peter's antagonist, the mentor whose fate he was struggling to avoid. Suppose, Peter had said, a part is thrust on you, unchosen: suppose the tyrant is placed in your hands, not in a dream, not in a theatre, but in reality. At your mercy. What then, if the play has already begun? There were times, he told us, when there were no honourable choices left—no pure-hearted ones, I believe he meant—but when not to act was more dishonourable still. He'd died, in a sense, for Kuno; and the image of Peter at the end of the piano-wire noose caught me in mid-story and I couldn't go on.

It was the only time Karin turned to look at me. She knew how Peter had died. I think she guessed what I was feeling, and I wanted to hug her and cry and shout my love for them both. But I was coming to the hardest part of what I had to tell, the nub of it, as cruel to the memory of Peter as it was to Karin's long-cherished dream. Kuno von Brüel had survived the retreat from Moscow with the remains of the Grande Armée, he'd come to Erfurt again, where Napoleon had assembled yet another army; come not to enlist but to kill him. *Sic pereunt tyranni!* Kuno shouted the words, levelling his pistol; but unable to fire. Waking instead, in terror—because now he knew it was a Liebesmord, a love-murder, that he was plotting. *Liebesmord*: I was ashamed to look at Karin as I said the word. Dare I attribute such feelings to her, where her father and Wackernagel were concerned? It was Karin who'd told me, as we walked through Planten un Blomen in the rubble-days, how bitterly she'd resented her father's suicide, his refusal to endure, if only for his family's sake. Kuno, I went on (let her make of it what she would, hate me too if needs be), was unable to distinguish hatred from despairing love. He enlisted in the forces of resistance to Napoleon, the Freikorps. At the battle of Lützen Kuno made himself a clumsy target, choosing to take the field not only in the breastplate but the full impedimenta of a mediaeval knight, and gave away his life. A deliberate, mockery death. He'd learnt—you never said this, Peter, and what gall to say it in your name—that revenge was itself a kind of suicide. Kill me first, the breastplate had read, so that I won't kill you. A lover's armour, not an assassin's. Armoured against love, for fear of loving too much, and losing.

It was three years before Wolli Zimt came through for me, and found Wackernagel. Three and a half years—I can put a date to it because I was sitting in the Onkel-Hugo-Grill, now the Olympia, watching the Coronation on Hugo's television. The place was crowded, from the way Hamburgers studied the proceedings you'd have thought we were the new Queen's most loyal colony. We knew who everybody was, archbishops, dukes, court officals. "Hier kommt der Duke of Norfolk, nicht?" "Aber wo, das ist der Duke of York!" "Aha!" It was all in the newspapers. For three hours Hamburg came to a halt, and we greeted the Coronation as if we too were entering a new dispensation.

In a way we were. That summer our two great post-war projects were completed: "Entnazifizierung," denazification, which had been in German hands for some while now, and "Enttrümmerung," clearing the city of rubble. Eight years of parallel toil. Clearing out the old Nazis, or making a show of doing so, had been the harder task. Everyone who wanted a job had to fill out a questionnaire regarding his political past; his answers were checked against the available facts. The whole process depended on its loopholes, since enough Hitlerite functionaries had to be let through to maintain some continuity in the civil service, the police and the judiciary, and enough of them had to be caught in the net to make it look as if political filtration were really taking place. Die-hard Nazis who didn't need a job, who had private means or Kameraden to support them, bypassed the net altogether and never even saw the questionnaire. They were still around. You just couldn't spot them. The old air-raid débris was another matter, you could see it was gone. So of course much was made of this. From Hamburg alone such a prodigious number of stones had been removed by hand—mostly by female hand, thanks to the army of rubble-women—and allotted to the rebuilding programmes, that statisticians were now having a field day summing it all up. Laid end to end the stones would have circled the earth one hundred times; would have reached halfway to the moon, or restored the entire Great Wall of China to its original glory. So the city fathers claimed. They were less keen to tell us the number of rubble-women laid end to end by British troops; let alone how far a line of denazified Hamburgers, "gecleared" as they were called, Persil-fast, whiter than white, would stretch. Probably barely round the Alster, never mind the world. No-one asked.

The human débris had been tipped onto the Reeperbahn, by the look of it. The Reeperbahn drew the tourists, and the tourists drew the legless and the armless. Also the impoverished, the

mad, the exhibitionistic. The daily parade—it's still what draws
us to the Kiez today, as it did then, on the day Vlad brought the
news about Wackernagel. A different parade, though, if I'm to
visualize it correctly. A 'Fifties parade. From my corner table
at the Onkel-Hugo my view of the street—as *der* Archbishop
von Canterbury intones out of the apparatus behind me—
includes an orderly file of disabled beggars squatting on the far
pavement, in between the girls, reminding me how far we've
come from the whores' domain in the rubble-city, with its Krüppelstunde, its happy-hour of the limbless. Perhaps I only imagined this, the cripple-hour, in my fevered state when I first arrived
in the city, but I would have sworn that all over Hamburg you
could see the disabled dragging themselves through the shattered streets, at dusk, towards the bonfires where the whores
clustered in their winter coats. Now that the war is well and
truly over—now that the very term "post-war" is going out of
use, seems irrelevant, apologetic, as in "post-war shortages"—
there are no more free fucks for cripples, at dusk or any other
time, not even a quick hand-job on account. These days they
can afford to pay, there's plenty to be made from begging now
that the tourists have returned, eager to help Germany back up
onto her feet. But they're almost all drunks, the kerbside cripples. Monika, who used to be Kriemhilde, steps right over them
to importune a potential customer, and they don't even look up
her skirt. A bottle's all they want. And they were so randy, after
the war!

Picture the Reeperbahn, my haunt, my theatre, beginning to
come into its own, in '52. Into its own again, I should say;
among travellers it was always a byword for nocturnal fun, a
Soho, a Tivoli, as Hamburg was once the Nordic sailor's Paris,
his haven of rest and entertainment, when the Reeperbahn was
the sail- and rope-makers' street its name records, a broad tree-
lined avenue flanked by pleasure gardens; when genteel amuse-
ments ruled by day, music, puppet-theatres, trials of strength;
and assignations by night. Duse, and later Richard Tauber, performed at the old operetta-house further up the street and thankfully out of view from my Stammtisch, the table Hugo reserves
for me. Thankfully because the developers have replaced its
charmingly colonnaded front with the usual eyesore in concrete
and glass. It's hard to make sense of this. It seems like yesterday
that the Reich foundered in ignominy, but Hitler's architects
have somehow conquered the world.

The street itself is just as wide as it was in Duse-days, though the double file of trees down the centre of it (a little Pall Mall once, where beaux strutted and ladies dropped handkerchiefs) is being replaced with ugly little cabins masquerading as shops. What you see (what I see from the Onkel-Hugo) is a rather ordinary, wide street, grey, dusty grey, a setting so drab it highlights the people in it, their variety and their every eccentricity of dress and eye, as surely as the dreariest pavement in a business quarter. It's not exactly staid, admittedly there are many garish touches, crude hand-painted signs and murals showing girls en deshabille, red plush curtains promising Arabian Nights (More! New!), plenty of bars, and street-walkers sporting fake leopard-skin and coloured boas. But it just isn't seamy, no matter how hard it tries, not even at night—in fact by night the Reeperbahn's most lurid feature is the police station with its purple neon sign and trimming. The New Germans have fallen in love with neon (and with espresso bars, and cha-cha-cha) and being Germans they have to have the biggest and brightest neon: pink, green, and yellow starbursts re-multiplied on the polished black curves of the parked cars, those belonging to the richer patrons, the ocelot-and-mink crowd. Vulgar, certainly. But squalid? Germans have no feeling for seaminess. This isn't because as a nation they're so orderly, so efficient and militaristic, but because they're so depressed. Squalor and depression are not the bedfellows orderly people like to suppose—no, true depression, as Karin Posener finally taught me, cleans its house, is tidy, leaves nothing lying around to remind it of life's natural devolution. So whatever genuine squalor has come to the Reeperbahn, with time, has been brought by foreigners, by the Greeks, the Italians, the Tunisians. Imported filth.

What we do have are native eccentrics, some of them specially dressed for today's Coronation in top hats, ersatz crowns, paper regalia. Squeeze the toothpaste tube of orderly-depressed existence and what squirts out of Germany at both ends—mad kings at one end and mad poets at the other—is wonderfully strange.

Here come Margitta and Heinz dressed as their favourite potentates, Soraya and the Shah of Persia—Soraya appears to have turned belly-dancer—who have hired Berber-Fred, when sober a repairer of antique musical instruments, to accompany their royal progress on the violin. And now as they dance *einen Slow* along the pavement, Heinz's pal Eddie distributes shredded newspaper among the whores and beggars, so they can shower the monarchs as they pass . . . or perhaps it really is their wedding day; pimps have been known to marry, and Heinz and Margitta have been together since they competed in the dance marathon at Café Keese two years ago. There goes Werner der Kellner, the waiter at the "Sorrento," a napkin over one arm and his tray held high above his head—no juggling today, he's carrying rollmops to a parked Rolls Royce. It was bought from the former military governor himself, it's said, by Münchner Manfred, a black-marketeer now fallen on hard times; such hard times he had to sell his private armoury, his racehorses and the Travemünde estate, and finally even his house in Blankenese, Hamburg's Hampstead-by-the-sea. But he wouldn't sell his Rolls. He lives in it: sleeps curled up in the back seat (a pigsty, says Wolli, who once travelled to Travemünde with Manfred), and receives clients in the front. Werner der Kellner threads his way through the crowd with Manfred's rollmops, past the girls and other regulars—I can see Ferdy, an old drunk with the head of a mangy lion, already three sheets to the wind and clinging to his favourite lamppost, straw boater askew. Ferdy and his lamppost dance! Soon he'll have slipped to the pavement, still hugging the cast-iron pillar. Visitors step carefully round him, foreigners, some of them, but now that Germans too dress in the latest American fashions it's growing harder to tell natives from tourists. Gone are the days when farmers from Lower Saxony arrived in their mud-spattered working clothes, pockets bulging, hoping to pay the girls in boxes of freshly-laid eggs. The new type of visitor pretends to ignore the girls while sizing them up; here's one now, working so hard at his conflicting missions that he bumps into a fellow-prowler, apologizes gruffly and crosses the street to shed his embarrassment, with Paula and Alwine closing in on him—he's vulnerable—as I watch, making me feel like a lazy-lidded cat studying life on the veldt—

Du, Reinhard!

It's Theo waving at me, paper bag in hand, as he makes his way towards my table through Hugo's clientèle. Theo with his bag of bananas; his stomach is shot to hell and gone from six years in concentration camps and he can't eat anything without tucking away a banana first. He's an old Romany, one of the elders of the Kiez, and a few years ago he wouldn't have so much as looked at me with his arse, as we say here. To him I was "ein Greenhorn," with or without Wolli Zimt's protection. Now he sues for my attention with an ingratiating smile.

Du, Reinhard!

Garçon! I call to Hugo, though I know how much this irritates him. Too bad. I point at my plate and then at the oncoming Theo. More—more Frikadellen and Gewürzgurken, rissoles and gherkins. God how I miss pickled onions sometimes—but there—

Theo is already sitting down, blurting out an important message. Has Vlad found me? No. Vlad is looking for me, says Theo. Should he go and look for Vlad, to tell him where I am? No hurry, Theo. I'm enjoying the ordeal of the British Queen. Have a banana. Eat your rissoles. Vlad knows where to find me.

Glancing back I see that out in the street Margitta-Soraya is dancing with Helmuth the police sergeant. On Coronation Day *tout est permis*. Like gypsy Theo sucking his banana at my side, Helmuth is one of the elders of the Kiez and worked here in the Zwanziger Jahre, in the 'Twenties, the good old days. Regularly transferred to other police stations on grounds of being too familiar, too lax with the "criminal classes" of the Kiez, Helmuth der Cop can't get along with his colleagues elsewhere, gets into trouble and ends up being posted back to the Reeperbahn, an old lag like the rest of us. He alone of the Hamburg police contingent knows how to separate an angry customer who's paid handsomely for his favourite perversion from an even angrier tart who couldn't be paid enough to do *that*; each girl has her limits beyond which she's as prudish and disgusted as any Hausfrau. Heinz and Eddie and the passers-by applaud the belly-dancer and the cop shimmying to Berber-Fred's musical impression of a night in old Baghdad, dimly audible above the crackly choral hymn from Westminster Abbey. The hymn: it's like a distant blessing on us pouring from this strange new miracle, a telephone with eyes connecting the Onkel-Hugo-Grill and its formica tabletops to Westminster Abbey, the dregs of Germany to the British crème de la crème in their ermine and their coronets; uniting victors and vanquished, so-called, though as we gaze proudly from the television screen to the show outside the window we all know where we'd rather be, here at the glorious water-hole of the Reeperbahn, watching the chase and the display on the mile of money (never mind the Mile of Sin). Everyone's here, except—so far—"der Bhik," the old Bhikku from Rangoon in his saffron robe, I don't see him working the street today. Perhaps he's watching television.

Suddenly shouts and laughter—"Free advertising!" cries one of the girls—draw our attention to a corner further down the street and an over-excited pair of dogs, dog and bitch rather, who seem to be showing Reeperbahn visitors what to do and how to do it. The animals are soon surrounded by well-wishers, and vanish from sight. They looked familiar, mongrels both of them, probably recently abandoned by tarts who thought they'd enjoy spending their love on them and then lost interest when they found they had to get up in the morning to take their pet for a walk. Glancing back I see that Margitta and Heinz are back together—someone has put a tiny black trilby on Margitta's bouffant hair—leading the procession past the police station towards the Herbertstrasse, and out of sight.

The Herbertstrasse! Herbert Street: was there ever so meek a name for a temple of debauchery? Long before the Reeperbahn began to share some of its fame (indeed eclipse it) the Herbertstrasse was Hamburg's established sexual headquarters. Even now it remains a jump ahead: so as not to be confused with the idle window-shoppery of the Reeperbahn, the little cobbled lane is closed off at both ends by a tall barricade, letting you know that you're entering a living museum, a House of Lords for ladies of the street, where advanced erotic artists crown a lifetime's practice. Down to business, says the barricade. At both ends of the street a sign warns female tourists to keep out. Ignore this, like so many males who bring along a girlfriend to ogle the tableaux vivants, the pouting divas posing behind plate glass in their satin and leather, luridly lit, like fallen angels in an airbrushed nightmare—ignore this law of the Kiez and you and your giggling girlfriend can end up pelted with water-filled contraceptives, or doused with a bucket of something less innocuous, from an upper window. Renowned for catering to the most exotic perversions, it's as well the street is closed off: not for innocent ears the cries of an elderly Hamburg Senator being whipped to pleasure, or the yapping of a captain of industry who likes to be led on a leash like a dog. If you know the right time to visit the Herbertstrasse you can even see him, in a muzzle that disguises his features, crawling the cobbles on his hands and knees, sniffing his way round the girls and cocking a leg on command. Inoffensive—if absurd—behaviour. The scatological German soul being what it is, obsessed with Arsch and Scheisse, the real speciality of the Herbertstrasse is a range of enemas, a secret menu including curried and vegetarian enemas-du-jour. A friend of Wolli's, as it happens a former Nazi bigwig, pays a thousand Marks on the Herbertstrasse, twice a year, for the privilege of wining and dining one of the girls—she has to eat fish, lots of it—before feeding the girl a huge dessert of laxative and retiring with her to his hotel. He brings with him his own king-sized rubber sheet to put over the bed, and there she releases the evening's intake onto his face.

Disgusting, but still harmless. Less so the fate of Herbertstrasse girls who try and hold back some of their exalted earnings. I've attended two funerals already in my three and a half years since joining Wolli's Firma. Heinz in the Coronation Day parade, who looked so amusing in his top hat and tails over a pair of baggy soccer shorts acquired from a local footballing hero—that smiling Heinz; that same Heinz stabbed a Herbertstrasse girl, one Gisela, to death. Plenty of people heard the screams, everyone knows who did it, some sent wreaths to the graveside, but no-one rats on Heinz. That too is the law of the Kiez.

If we're such bohemians here, such free spirits, why do we stand for it, this vicious, heartless code? We all liked chubby Gisela. Now we're stained with her blood. Why do we stay silent, obedient? Why do we stay at all? Some of us may claim we have nowhere better to go but most of us do, if we're honest. Why does Helmuth der Cop, respectable law-enforcing Helmuth, gravitate back here, of all places? And "der Bhik": why doesn't he recruit souls elsewhere? They're just as fallen everywhere you look. The romance of the gutter, if it exists, is soon extinguished by having to deal with Ferdy the lamppost-dancer in a belligerent mood and already soaked in his own vomit, or with drunk and hysterical petty criminals daring you to challenge their boasts at four in the morning; and a life of crime can be as stressful, as boring and as time-consuming as, say, practising the law. The company is a little more erratic, certainly more immediately pathetic, but more fantastical too, more fantasticating in their approach to life, their dreams, and if like me you need a license to be unpredictable, which is to say to be yourself, this is the place to find it. Nobody minds. By turns I can be vulgar, clumsy, brutal, tender—be myself without ever proclaiming it, without being obliged to *be* anything—and nobody minds. Erratic behaviour: it's expected, almost compulsory. So many times I've tried to put into words for myself why I feel so much at home in the milieu—I've pictured Alec sneering at me and I've tried to answer him and I can't; I can't—until I see Theo's face, or Berber-Fred's, or Hansi's twisted lips, his eyes gazing so eagerly, angrily almost, into mine. Nakedly into mine. What does he want? He doesn't know. It's written right there on his eyeballs, that he doesn't know. What the hell is going on? ask his eyes. And I love them for it. God knows it isn't the place that I love, amusing, shabby, sometimes sickening, always tolerable. It's the faces. Perhaps it isn't even I who feel at home here but simply the person whose features gladden Theo at this moment (probably because Hugo's finally bringing his rissoles, paid for by me), the person whose heart goes out so furiously, so possessively, to the pained, dangerous look of the Kiez-dwellers. Because they too see themselves in my eyes, their eyes in mine. You can see the look I mean in dogs' eyes (of all the parading natives it's the mongrels of the Reeperbahn, an endless supply, that I most identify with). A look of furious attention, but it isn't seeing you, it's saying: love me or I'll kill you. Here, to my joy, here on the Reeperbahn I've felt like a dog among dogs rather than a man among men, and it's been the best, the most wholesome and most loving sensation (erratic! yes—full of rage and inconsistency—that was the joy of it) I've known; not one I'm going to be ashamed of.

A dog among dogs. But of course I was having it both ways; I wasn't quite like the rest of the Reeperbahn zoo, I wasn't down among the dead men—the dead dogs—I was a man in disguise, a British spy on a daring mission in the German underworld, reporting to powerful men (one fat, bow-tied, powerful man) with a finger on the political pulse of Europe. So I was still telling myself. I wasn't ready to abandon myself to the Kiez yet. Walters was still my lifeline to Richard Thurgo, someone I was almost ready to forget, but not quite.

Now that Bad Neunburg had closed down and the British presence in Hamburg was moving—officially at least—towards a more traditional, consular basis, Walters and I would rendezvous at various locations on the fringes of the city. Many of these struck me as daringly public, but Cheerybye seemed undaunted. He would even arrange to meet at Carl Hagenbeck's Zoo—a regular, animal zoo, this, founded by a man whose first exotic specimens, brought to him by sailors, enlivened those old Reeperbahn pleasure gardens of bygone days—where Walters liked to visit Bobbi the once-famous parrot. Before the war this unfortunate bird had learnt to shriek "Heil Hitler!" and been amply rewarded in peanuts by visitors to the zoo. With the fall of the Reich embarrassed zoo officials felt obliged to withdraw the bird for political re-education. "Being Germany," as Walters commented, this had consisted of hitting Bobbi over the head with a rolled-up newspaper every time he demanded food in the name of the Führer. A silent, deeply confused parrot—Walters swore it was the very one—now sat in a far corner of the aviary, watching with a jaundiced eye as Walters cooed "Heil Hitler" at him. Peanuts, pieces of apple, it didn't matter what we brought him, Bobbi was not to be lured. They caught him young enough, said Walters approvingly. Apparently there was a forty-year-old parrot in an East German zoo who wouldn't stop calling for the Führer.

Sometimes Walters actually arrived in Altona to pick me up. He parked right outside the house in his Humber Super Snipe, the infallible herald of the British Secret Service. Every high-up in the Friends' employ had one, and all over Germany they must have stuck out like sore thumbs. I couldn't fathom this lack of secrecy. Spies (as, to be fair, Philby had warned me) never behaved like this in Dornford Yates. All very well for Cheerybye himself—but was he trying to get me caught, or what? When I suggested more devious arrangements I only got a withering look. Driving regally through Blankenese, on the way to his favourite restaurant on the Wedel road, we'd pass a house over-looking the estuary whose driveway was so full of black Super Snipes that it looked as much like a Surrey undertaker's as it did the local Field Security Section HQ.

It was this establishment that I'd telephoned one night, using the number Walters had given me for emergencies, when a group of undercover "Friends" flown in for a hush-hush trip into East Germany overdid it on the Reeperbahn, on the eve of their departure. Cheerybye himself was the duty officer that night. He sounded sleepy and distinctly ratty as I described the scene. The four Britons felt they'd been short-changed by the entertainment at the Sorrento, a night spot which must have promised everything they'd heard about Hamburg; one of them had been foolish enough to bring a gun, and by the time Walters arrived, this idiot had been disarmed by Stefan the club bouncer. Unlike Wolli and me, Stefan really had fought with the Afrika Korps in Tripolitania. Faced with a chance to re-stage El Alamein with a different ending, he was laying out Englishmen in every direction. It was no affair of mine; I watched impartially until I spotted Walters hurrying in through the red volour curtains of the Sorrento, cheeks and belly wobbling. What happened next made not only Stefan's jaw drop but mine too. Armed only with a little military swagger stick, Cheerbye stepped up to Stefan, who was throttling a sandy-haired young man with one hand while beating another, bloody-faced boy against the top of the bar. He poked Stefan with the stick until Stefan noticed him, dropped his victims, and turned, breathing fire. Plump, pale, unruffled Cheerybye then kneed Stefan in the balls with such calm ferocity that he had time to round up his team of delinquents and escort them from the club before Stefan had finished writhing and dry-puking on the floor.

The idea that Walters, this stupid, corrupt, fleshy person, was also as brave as a lion: it gave me pause. To me the British Empire had always been one of the great mysteries of the world—as it never was to Alec for instance, and I remember discovering this when we flew back from Germany together in '36 and I had my first airborne view of England (I was too scared to look on the outbound flight), that harmless-looking little quilt of fields which had somehow sired a race of tireless predators, generation after generation, conquerors and rulers of the greatest expanse of territory ever under one nation's thumb. The British Empire: why the British? What tribal characteristics had singled them out? How had they done it? Was there some clue to be found in the view from our Lockheed Electra, gliding in over Kentish fields and villages and steeples? I put all this to Alec, who looked up from his newspaper with a patient, lop-sided smile. Leaning over me to inspect the view, Alec nodded as if seeing his own explanation confirmed. "Pubs," he said, and sat back. Was that it? *Pubs?* "Pubs," he repeated, nodding at the little window. "You can see 'em. Not too far from the manor, not too far from the poorhouse either. We've always known how important it was to have a drink with the chaps. That's our secret. Know when to smile, when to threaten, when to order a drink." And when to deliver a kick in the balls, presumably, with a curious fearlessness, bred in—how?—where? My own courage wasn't fearless at all, it was born of rage and the sheer authority of my six and half feet of Galway brawn. But I wouldn't have tackled Stefan barehanded in the mood he was in, even if the fight had been my business. Without looking round Walters had marched out of the Sorrento with four subdued Jonathan Mansels in tow, and like Macaulay's ranks of Tuscany—forgetting for a moment that I was supposed to be German—I could scarce forbear to cheer.

Walters of course ignored me through the whole operation, quite properly protecting my cover. But neither did he mention it at our next meeting, not even to congratulate me on my prompt action in phoning him; I wasn't sure if he blamed me for letting the fracas happen in the first place, or for disturbing his sleep. I received no thanks, much less a promotion. It did make me wonder: what *was* my status in the British Secret Service, exactly? The Sorrento incident took place in the winter of '51, and I'd been working for them for three years. Shouldn't I at least sign the Official Secrets Act, at some point?

"If you like," said Cheerybye. It seemed an odd sort of answer.

"No hurry, then?"

He shook his head.

"Had a raid last night," he remarked in the car one day—this was shortly after I'd asked about signing the Act—"persons unknown broke in and stole a couple of files."

"Oh?"

"One of them was yours."

Walters looked out of the window while I tried to work out what, if anything, he was trying to tell me. When he turned back he was grinning.

"Want to see it?"

From beneath his coat he produced a file and handed it to me.

"Well, don't you want to look at it?"

I recognized it from my sessions under interrogation with Philby and Walters, when they'd first pulled me in. At first glance there was nothing of any great interest in it, and the only mystery was its classification: "DN."

"Damned Nuisance," explained Walters, and when I offered him the file back, "keep it, why don't you?"

So was I working for His—now (as of today) Her—Majesty, or was I just a Cheerybye informant, worth an occasional peanut? I didn't ask; I was better off with my dreams.

Its funereal evergreens always gave Blankenese a peculiarly English air, reminding me of driving West with Alec through the firs, the holly and rhododendrons of Virginia Water. Cheerybye clearly felt much more at home here than at the old interrogation centre, where he'd become increasingly irritable company, especially over lunch, complaining at the contrast between burgeoning German living standards and our Officers' Club fare, the thin soup, dried egg and mushroom omelette, followed by ice cream. Now, in Wedel, we'd been gorging ourselves along with the Hamburg "Schicker-*ee*-ya," the nobs, on what we'd got used to calling "pre-war" delicacies, fatty pork steaks swimming in butter, cream pastries heaped with chocolate sauce . . .

"Well, Dicky," Cheerybye would say at last. Since we became Schickeria dining partners he'd conferred this name on me; I hated it, and craved it too, it meant I was one of the gang. "How's our Herr Crap these days?"

With the passing years I had less and less of an answer for him. The tips about black market deals began to dry up as Wolli Zimt moved out of "Im und Ex," import-export, his polite phrase for what Cheerybye still called "ye olde Schwarze" or "the black," and into "invisibles." What Wolli meant by this, I found to my surprise, was property. Thoroughly visible, you would have thought, but to Wolli it was an abstraction when compared to cash in envelopes and stolen silverware in a hold-all. The profit—the gradual appreciation of invested capital—was "invisible," and Wolli was warming to it. "Thieving is for wartime when you have to carry everything on your back. In peace you can put it down, make it grow. Otherwise," he liked to say, "you end up in the back seat with Münchner Manfred, among the dirty clothes and the leftover food, trying to make one more deal. You have the big car, but at every corner history overtakes you and shows you its *Arsch*." I was afraid that with my waning supply of tips about "deals" my own usefulness to Cheerybye would also begin to dry up. Would he still treat me to lunch and slip me an envelope full of Deutschmarks when I no longer had "Pier 17, the *Arcturus* from Malmö, docking Thursday, Petty Officer Gonzalez has the patents" to murmur into his ear? It wasn't the loss of earnings I regretted—I made plenty on the Reeperbahn now, thanks to Wolli—but the loss of self-esteem. The loss of direction. My role as Cheerybye's informant separated me, in my mind, from the true, the desperate Kiez-dweller, the dregs. Even the danger of being unmasked lent a certain dignity; I was almost disappointed at how easy it was to get away with a double life. Without my Walters connection, my life on the Reeperbahn would be—in Vlad's words—like a string: you pull it . . . and you cannot feel the end!

Queen Elizabeth above me (looking, poor girl, as if the weight of the crown, the robes, and sheer concentration, have together wiped all human expression from her face, leaving in its wake a look I've seen before—yes, on Maggie's face the day of her wedding; the look that promised total erasure of the proceedings as soon as they were over, no matter how hard she would try to remember them) and gypsy Theo slobbering at my side: a tipp-topp combination, if only I could preserve it.

Wolli was distancing himself from Cheerybye, I decided, from all the old relationships forged by necessity. In a way, from me, too. Three months ago he'd put me in sole charge of a pet project of his, a plan to turn the former bunker complex beneath the Reeperbahn into a labyrinthine night-club. This was flattering, and remunerative too. Out of the budget Wolli had allotted I paid myself a good salary. I had power to hire and fire, to find designers, oversee the work, recruit staff. But it was also "sink-or-swim," an English term Wolli savoured. Whenever I asked him for advice, for suggestions, he clammed up. Show me when you've finished—that was Wolli's attitude, and it felt like a lot of rope with which to hang myself. What if he didn't like the finished product? He had already given the place a name: Der Grotto Azzurro. The rest was up to me. I wasn't going to paper it with Leonardos, like Wolli's bedroom; if that was his idea of a *schick* erotic ambience, it wasn't mine.

When I proudly told Cheerybye about this development he nodded, the last time we'd dined at Wedel; nodded a little too casually. The Reeperbahn bush telegraph had been at work. You knew? I said. "Of course I knew," he smiled, carefully wiping Eisbein drippings off his chin, adding, "it was my idea." And before I had time to recover from this, he said: "Who do you think owns the bunker, anyway?"

I stared. Who *owns* it?

"Poppa," said Cheerybye, tapping his chest. "Bought it dirt cheap in '47. Officially it belongs to a company full of dummy names, apart from Zimt's. And yours, of course."

"Mine? *My* name?" He'd said '47; I'd only got to Hamburg in '48—

"Not Dicky Thurgo, you ass. Reinhard Sacher. I invented him long before you arrived. Thought you'd fit the bill rather well, so I had Zimt suggest the name for your cover, and Kim bought it. I told you I had plans for you, don't you remember?" He watched me digest this. "But don't forget, will you, Dicky. The bunker's mine. Der Grotto Azzurro," he pronounced with relish. "Good name, don't you think? With all those tunnels down there, we could have plenty of 'blue' activities going on, eh? Think about it."

It had staggered me. It still made my mind swim. Walters a property-owner on the Reeperbahn? ("Ever been to the Tirol Hotel in Badestrasse?" asked Walters when he saw my amazement. "Douggie Collins from Signals bought it in '46, under an alias of course. Owns six of them now, three in Hannover, two in Berlin. Mind you, he had capital to start with. Father's in the restaurant game. I'm just a small investor.") Wolli confirmed it. But instead of reassuring me that I was sitting pretty at the centre of an Anglo-German web, it made me feel more exposed, somehow. I wanted to be able to come and go. This was getting sticky. And why were Wolli and Cheerybye investing in *me*? What am I to them, I kept wondering, other than a Damned Nuisance, a chap who now knows altogether too much?

A sharp dig in the ribs brings me back to the reality of the Onkel-Hugo-Grill. It's Theo, mouth full of gherkin, drawing my attention to the window. Pointing. A quartet from the Heilsarmee, God bless it, the Sally Army with its gleaming tubas and saxhorns, are setting up their music stands on the pavement. But that isn't what Theo means, I realize, as a figure appears in a billowy Cossack shirt, barrelling through them—which alerts me; as a rule pious Vlad never mocks the Salvationists—and entering the Onkel-Hugo to a panicky volley from the ting-a-ling bell over the door. Vlad sees me, and though his expression doesn't change, relief shows in his change of pace as he moves more slowly between the tables.

Theo, thanking me, makes himself scarce as Vlad arrives. This too must be deciphered (and thought about later): Vlad's business is too weighty for Theo, yet Theo already knows that this is so. His seat opposite me is barely cold as Vlad's huge bum descends on it. I'm holding court here, I realize with satisfaction. All I need is a chamberlain to cry "Next! Who's next for König Reinhard?" Vlad greets me gruffly, avoiding my eyes as he always does—as though too much affection binds us, too much to be able to show it in moderation. No preamble: from his pocket he brings out a folded scrap of paper, passes it to me across the Fromica. Am I to look at it now? Vlad's hyperactive eyebrows tell me at once that I am. That's to say, when I put the note unopened beside my plate, the eyebrows start to leap around like hares startled in a brake. Very well. I open it. It says: "H.W.," and beneath this an address in Karlsruhe. I look back at Vlad, who reads my puzzlement at once; don't ask *me*, his eyes reply.

I look back at the note. Who do I know in Karlsruhe? A city down south somewhere, I couldn't even place it on the map. The handwriting on the little note, familiar from other assignments: it's Wolli's. "H.W.?" Then it hits me, and I can feel myself flush (am I the only blushing desperado on the Kiez? Sometimes I wonder if people joke about it behind my back): Hermann Wackernagel.

No time to let it sink in, there are delicate matters here, nothing to do with Wackernagel or Karlsruhe. I have to think fast, with Vlad watching me. All innocence: just a messenger boy, his expression insists. A heavily moustachioed messenger boy in a Cossack hat, which he wears winter and summer, even, absurdly, in the wrestling ring. It's his trademark. Cossack Vlad the one-armed wonder, the cripples' champion.

"You know about this?"

Vlad shakes his head. "Something for you." Then a shrug. "And for me."

"A job for both of us?" But Wolli has left me to do the explaining—why? "Like searching for a milch-cow on Lüne-burg Heath?"

Vlad shrugs again. Too quickly. And starts in hungrily on Theo's half-finished plate of Frikadellen. It's the first time in years that I've referred to our futile search for butter to repay the Poseners' hospitality; yet it was on Vlad's mind, to judge by his response.

That little shrug changed everything. The butter—a pound of it, so meaningless now, so easily available—no longer mattered to me, it was eight hundred counterfeit Reichsmarks down the drain, and an evening's embarrassment, long ago. But it still mattered to Wolli. Yes, I thought, I should have realized that. I'd shot him for cheating me. The butter had nearly cost him his life. And since then it seemed we'd had the same thought: that the only other person in the old Reeperbahn bunker who knew that "Henry Hirsch" was bringing the butter there on that par-ticular evening, who touched it, tasted it, who could have switched it for lard-and-potato in the darkness, was Vlad. And now, with no word spoken directly to me, just an address on a piece of paper, Wolli had sent me Vlad as a partner in a far trickier business. A wartime Kamerad, "H.W.," was being betrayed. Which Vlad hadn't been told, though he was to be a part of it. In other words, the messenger boy was expendable, if I needed a scapegoat. It was Kiez-language, and Wolli knew how I would read it: Vlad stole the butter, he's yours now, you deal with him. But this interpretation, right or wrong, would be entirely my responsibility. Wolli was keeping his distance and wouldn't admit to anything.

No, not to anything, past or present; he never did. So what if it was Wolli who'd cheated me on the butter after all and, rather than admit it, was fingering Vlad to fool me? To test me. Vlad, ignorant of this, wolfing rissoles across the table from me . . . I pictured him again in the shadowy bunker (in the bunker at this very moment being painted midnight blue, being transformed into the Grotto Azzurro), raising the little tasting-slice of butter high above his lips, cleverly distracting us, perhaps— yes, it could have happened then, the switch—only . . . how exactly did one-armed Vlad perform the substitution? With his knees? Ridiculous. All I had to go on was one hurried, guilty shrug, just now. Devious Wolli—yes, it was coming clear—he knew that suspicious or not I bore Vlad no grudge, but he was throwing us together in the ring. Whatever the truth about the butter, it was a move in *our* game, the longstanding one between Wolli and myself. I had plenty of time to respond. There was always time, on the Kiez; where revenge, like Theo's rissoles, was a dish best eaten cold.

The Karlsruhe address called for prompter action. But in the three-and-a-half years since Egon had chomped away on August Posener's diaries (destroying a good deal, though by no means all, of the evidence against Wackernagel) enough had changed in my relationship to Karin, and in hers to August's death, to make me hesitate. It wasn't that my story-telling about Kuno von Brüel and Peter, or my subsequent efforts to moderate Karin's obsession, had made any in-roads. No, I'd put her on her guard, and she spoke less—on all subjects that might provoke an argument. She'd even given up trying to sell me the Party line, and I missed it, I missed the pedantic bickering of our strolls through Planten un Blomen. The educated talk that had flowed so strangely from her child-face was gone, censored now as if it too were a relic of her pride in being German. Her chambermaid voice had returned, childish, submissive; and it frightened me.

The question was whether an unsuccessful attempt to bring Wackernagel before the courts—I saw him laughing in our faces—would be more damaging to Karin than no attempt at all. And as for trying to bully a confession out of him, if that was what Wolli Zimt had in mind by offering me Vlad's services, it would probably be us and not Wackernagel who landed in jail.

Of course we could simply kill him. But was I prepared to do that? And Vlad? I doubted if Vlad wanted to get into the ven-detta business. As a Russian he had no love for former SS men, but no particular scores to settle. He was now a popular and successful wrestler, in a small way a celebrity. He wouldn't want to put all that at risk—not even if he did owe Wolli and me for the butter trick. I could perhaps hire an assassin. I didn't know any personally; the only Kiez-dwellers I knew with blood on their hands were pimps, and eliminating Wackernagel was a far cry from stabbing a frightened girl. Besides, something in me shuddered at the thought of having Wackernagel killed. It wasn't moral squeamishness, the bastard could roast on a spit and I'd be glad to watch. Bringing Karin his head, metaphorically speaking: that was was what troubled me. Whatever the role I wanted in the Poseners' lives, I knew it wasn't as their pet avenger. In time the blood would only drive us apart. And I loved Karin. I was in love with her. That was the problem.

All right then. Inform the Karlsruhe police. Provide them with such evidence against Wackernagel as we could muster. Then what? August's death was still officially recorded as a suicide. And perhaps that was the truth—according to his journal the Fuhlsbüttel guards had urged August that the best way to avoid further beatings would be to hang himself. If he had, it made little difference morally to Wackernagel's guilt. But legally? All Karin's attempts to have him charged with the crime, even *in absentia*, had founded on this and other technicalities. It wasn't a war crime: August had died in '37. His maltreatment was criminal, no-one disputed that, and someone was indeed responsible—*Selbstverständlich*! But equally self-understandable, *mein Herr*, was that while mass murderers were still at large, the authorities could hardly give priority to hunting down lesser monsters. The Jews had their own energetic pressure groups, and hunters. But the Poseners weren't Jewish. Also—and this was more frustrating still—I found Karin oddly reluctant to get together with other relatives of Fuhlsbüttel victims, in order to mount a broader case against Wackernagel. I had to do this myself; and I'd assembled a sizeable dossier. Over the years this process became disheartening. Each family I met not only had gruesome stories to tell of torture and killing—by now I could have walked through Fuhlsbüttel prison blindfold, I knew every cellblock and every corridor as if I'd been a guard there myself—but also stories of how the guilty were being protected by the state, ignored, or even (they claimed) found and warned to flee by one Ministry when another was searching for them. I couldn't judge how much of this was true, but there was something about the bereaved that began to revolt me. They were connoisseurs of injustice. Some were even competitive about their grief. "Your Fräulein Posener had it easy," one widow told me, "my husband endured Fuhlsbüttel for six years. Six!" And wasn't "my Fräulein Posener's a Communist? Fomenting more trouble? I didn't tell Karin about these conversations.

"She doesn't sleep, you know," said Frau Posener one day when we were talking about Karin. We were always talking about her, like parents fussing over a delinquent child; once it was Egon we clucked over, but he'd become a model of obedience, such a good learner; now it was Karin. She didn't sleep. This piece of information came as no surprise, in fact when we'd first met and Karin was working as a chambermaid by night and a rubble-woman by day, I'd wondered how she got any rest at all. "Sometimes I hear her going out."

"At night?"

Mutti nodded her eagle face.

"Where to?"

"*Ja . . .*" Who knows? she shrugged.

Wandsbek was a safe enough district to walk around in, even at night. But my suspicious mind was already picturing assignations.

Karin and I weren't lovers, in the strict sense: that was one of the more bewildering things about our years together. It didn't seem to puzzle Mutti, but I wasn't sure whether that was because she knew her daughter or because to a woman of her generation (she once mentioned the five years of her engagement to August, chaste years I assumed) this was just as it should be. We were courting. That's to say I saw Karin virtually every day, took her to the cinema, to dinner, bought her (and Mutti) flowers; used my contacts whenever I could to cut through Hamburg red tape for them—to have their telephone installed quickly, or a new bathroom suite, cheap. I bought them a television. I bought them a piano, when I heard they'd owned one before the war, and that Karin had been an accomplished pianist. And artist too, Mutti said proudly. At once I bought her paints and a palette, planning to give her an easel for her birthday. But when I saw how these gifts embarrassed her I decided against it. She didn't use the paints. Or the piano. (Mutti did, though, her tiny frame bent over the keyboard and her face almost touching it, her hands flying up between chords in old-fashioned flourishes, as if the keys were red hot.) Clearly this wasn't the way to Karin's heart. At this rate we'd be courting into all eternity. Mother and daughter both knew I was married, though evidently separated, and until I was divorced there could be no talk of engagement, of marriage, however distant. The idea of divorce never entered my mind, after all I was dead and buried, and dead men didn't sue (or get sued) for divorce. Molly might have married again for all I knew; I never did write to her. What was bewildering was that this chaste romance with Karin didn't fit my idea or my experience of myself, from Ellie onwards. And now of all unlikely times, now that at last I was an accepted member of the milieu, a lord of the Kiez—a night-club owner for God's sake—I'd have been laughed off the Reeperbahn if anyone had known the timid kisses I exchanged with Karin.

She didn't have to fight me off; it was enough that I sensed her reserve. Or perhaps she sensed a quality in me that bred caution. I couldn't tell which. Once the tearful evening in my bedroom had gone by, the evening of the mutilated diaries, I was afraid to force myself on her and measured my caresses by her encouragement alone. Soon after my release from Bad Neunburg I'd broken my celibate fast, in Wolli's company. And I went on having sporadic afternoon encounters, sometimes paid for, sometimes not. Absurd situation—sometimes I told myself that it was only now that I had the Herbertstrasse as my playground and could indulge to the full both the animal and the humanly degenerate, now at last the tender soul could peep out and enjoy a delayed adolescence. Begin again, with courting. At other times it seemed to me that I was locked into some compulsive, inexplicable and ghastly Totentanz, a dance of death (given her Wackernagel obsession, increasingly becoming mine too) with a neurotic thirty-three-year-old virgin. And if anyone had said that it was my feelings for Karin that were keeping me in Hamburg, I'd have laughed in their face. I was King Reinhard, holding court at the Onkel-Hugo-Grill, having the very kind of fun in the very kind of place I'd always dreamed of. The Reeperbahn was my passion; of *course*—I'd have said—I was staying put in Hamburg.

From Wandsbek to Fuhlsbüttel prison was an hour's walk. Once Mutti had told me about Karin's midnight excursions, I had a vision of Karin making a solitary pilgrimage through the streets of Barmbek Nord, up the Habichtstrasse, past the vast Ohlsdorf cemetery where Vati lay, to Fuhlsbüttel, and slowly back again. I even spent half a night in a shoeshop doorway in the Wandsbeker Chaussee, waiting to follow her if she came out of the house—not knowing what I'd do; just to follow her. But she stayed home that night. Or perhaps, I thought, Mutti was exaggerating about her night-time habits. The idea of the Fuhlsbüttel pilgrimage had come to mind because of our Sunday excursions, Karin and Egon and I; after putting fresh flowers on August's grave we went to Fuhlsbüttel airport to watch the flights come and go—Egon's choice of entertainment. As our tram passed the turning that led to the prison I could always feel Karin's reaction, she was fighting not to look, as if against a magnetic force. Once past the turning everything was all right. The aerodrome restaurant was full of sightseers, and Egon was in his element. He knew the aircraft so well that he could identify each tiny silhouette as it appeared in the distance, naming the model, the manufacturer, and the specifications, before anyone else had even spotted a plane.

He'd become a distressingly ordinary twelve-year-old. I couldn't understand how this was possible, after his start in life. It was a source of wonderment to everyone. He spoke slowly but clearly and well. After three years of Mutti's devoted work he'd been accepted at the Wandsbeker Gymnasium, in a class of his own age group. He was eager, solemn, considerate, and to tell the truth he bored the daylights out of me. There had been a certain priggishness to Peter; it was as if Frau Posener had tapped a supply of it in Egon. *"Nein, danke, Onkel Reinhard*, I prefer my potatoes without gravy, if you don't mind!'' "No thanks" would have sufficed. He was modestly shy in public—except when he wanted something badly enough, and then he was a terror. What Egon wanted was a flight in an aeroplane, any old aeroplane.

At Fuhlsbüttel he'd disappear off into the crowds for short spells, and we didn't worry until we discovered that he'd been hanging round the pilots, pestering them. Or rather charming them; because we only found out what he'd been up to when one of them offered to take us all up for a spin. His son Gerhard, he said, was in Egon's class. We were led to a little pre-war six-seater with an overhead wing seemingly held on by wires. At the sight of it Karin cried off, leaving me to stuff myself into the fuselage while Egon wriggled past me to peer over the pilot's shoulder. The noise and the discomfort were overwhelming but it was worth every minute. The rapture on Egon's face as he looked down at Hamburg, his jungle floor, broke my reserve. It was so long since I'd hugged him—and I might have done, I might have cried too, I think, if the rattling metal box hadn't scared the wits out of me. Not Egon. It was a treehouse with wings. I hadn't seen such glee in him since we left the Friedrichswald.

But perhaps I hadn't been looking. It was Karin I watched, unceasingly. Her face had acquired an extraordinary beauty, I thought; I had no idea whether others saw her that way or would be amazed if I spoke of her as beautiful. I no longer saw the hare-lip or the moles that had once fascinated me, and when I realized this I told myself I was seeing her face at last and not just her features. I still noticed the seams that crumpled her face when she smiled, and loved them the more they came to stay. Her face was acquiring much-needed character. Such a dear smooth round face, small, small-featured, with a deceptively soft submissive chin; dark eyes, dark hair—no, it wasn't quite true that I'd lost sight of her features, I'd become mesmerized by her eyebrows, an aspect of her face I'd barely noticed (or that I'd censored, rather, as unappealing and inconsistent with what I found attractive in her looks) when we first met. They were powerful, thick and dark, quite masculine—modest in size by Vlad's standards, and obedient by comparison, but with a virility almost obscene on her delicate face, evoking armpit and pubic hair. There was no such eyebrows in the photographs of her father, and her mother's looked to be entirely pencil. Where had Karin got them? She herself had no idea. I longed to know who he was, this hirsute ancestor; he was the survivor in Karin, surely. He was my hope.

"Where do you go at night? Mutti tells me you go out."

She nodded.

"Where?"

"Just walking."

I had my arm around her shoulders, on the sofa, the same old sofa from my first Altona flat, with its Married Families Chintz. I'd grown fond of it, and took it with me when I moved to a larger place a little nearer the Reeperbahn and one where Egon could have his own room. He slept in a bed now, with model aeroplanes dangling above it.

"You don't go anywhere special?"

Karin shook her head. "I'm used to working at night, that's all."

"Do you miss the Atlantic?"

"No."

But it had taken months of argument, pressure from Mutti and from me, to get her to give up working there. It was one thing, we insisted, in the barren post-war years, all hands to the pump . . . we refrained from mentioning her hopes of tracing Wackernagel through the hotel and its Control Commission guests. Now that jobs were available, teachers needed—surely—someone of her intelligence and education . . . on and on we went till she gave in at last.

"I like the city best at night," I said.

She nodded agreement, and squeezed my hand. No, I thought, it's the night she likes, the darkness.

Of all things she'd taken a job as an artist's model, by answering an ad in the *Morgenblatt*. The idea of Karin undressed, under so many eyes—she mainly sat for life classes rather than for one artist alone—offended and startled me. (Mutti, I think, took it as the first sign that her daughter was not quite right in the head.) Nocturnal walks I could understand. This was the very opposite of protective darkness, though. Karin naked, Karin who was so guarded with her body where I was concerned, so prudish; now offering it for endless view. For money. Why this, of all jobs?

"I enjoy it, that's all," she'd said. "I didn't know if I'd like it or not, until I tried. When I used to draw I always wondered how the models felt, why they did it. Now I know. You soon lose the embarrassment and start to think of something else. You're being paid for doing nothing at all, just sitting still and dreaming. And in the end it's nice to be looked at. Nicer than to be ignored. It isn't sexual," she added, seeing my expression. "Models are never sexual."

Never? And anyway, wasn't there something doubly provocative about stripping naked while declaring "this isn't sexual?"

"It's not a striptease. They don't see me strip."

"All the same . . . there you stand. Or sit. Defying them to find you sexual."

She laughed. "Im Gegenteil." Just the opposite. She loved to turn me on my head; *im Gegenteil*. "It's like being a child again, unselfconscious."

"Unselfconscious? Under all those ruthless eyes?"

"Precisely, under all those ruthless eyes. Looking at form, colour, texture, not at you."

It sounded plausible. Why couldn't I believe that was all there was to it? When she first took the job, I felt mocked; here I am, take me, was the message of her nakedness, her life class; rape me, my man can't do it. But she was always perfectly matter-of-fact when she spoke about the work, and with time I came to my senses and tried to understand it differently. It wasn't about me, I decided. If only it was. She was baring herself to prove she couldn't be hurt, as if to say, look, you've taken it all, there's nothing sacred left about me; you can't take anything from me any more. I longed to tell her it wasn't so, but her talk of childish pleasure made this impossible. By exposing ourselves to humiliation once more, I wanted to say, we think we're mastering the pain, but we aren't. I said it to her in other ways often enough, and bluntly too: "It was your father's death, no more, no less. It happened fifteen years ago. You're thirty-three, for God's sake." *Um Gottes willen!* Yes, you're right, she'd nod; it's my life, I know that.

I lived in fear that there was some darker secret to come out, that her father had, perhaps, molested her—I didn't want it to be true, but it would have explained an awful lot. Karin was evidently and innocently startled when I probed about this, I had to pursue it through increasingly perilous hints because she simply didn't see what I was driving at. All right, perhaps it wasn't that. What, then? Having discarded both parents myself I couldn't grasp—even allowing for the brutal circumstances, and much as I wanted to understand—that it could be so devastating, this loss, and so lingeringly, lastingly hurtful. Clearly it was more than her father Karin was mourning, it was Germany; but this too was alien to me, it was like grieving for a flag. Or a passport.

I didn't tell Karin about the Wackernagel address. Not for weeks. The delay seemed so much less important, at the time, than what was at stake, Karin's well-being. And there was an additional reason. Mutti had come to the conclusion that her daughter was ill; I didn't know whether I found it a brave conclusion or a foolish one, but she faced it bravely, where other parents might have gone on looking the other way. At her insistence Karin had recently begun seeing the Dod, Anna-Maria von Doderer, Mutti's psycho-analyst friend and distant cousin. (A friend, I suspected, only because she was a relative. The two women had little in common, though Frau Posener was proud of the Dod's eminence in her field. And their family connection meant that she could keep a closer eye on her daughter's progress.) It was a delicate juncture. I too wanted to consult an expert before I blundered in with momentous news.

Karin had taken her mother's injunction in silence, as she always did, and brought her protests to me.

"Do *you* think I should go and see Anna-Maria? That mad old woman?"

"Only if you want to." I sensed a secret acquiescence in her, welcoming the self-surrender. It was a relief, I could imagine, almost an erotic pleasure, to give your suffering official status at last. She *was* wounded, warped by grief. Why not acknowledge the cost?

Mainly she talked about how her Marxist friends would disapprove if they knew. Treatment of the mind was bourgeois solace, apparently; Freud and Marx were heads or tails, you couldn't pick both.

But her Communism was in abeyance, to my relief. If you were as intelligent as Karin you could hardly fail to see that Russian behaviour in East Germany resembled Nazi repression more than it did the withering away of the State, and that the boost this gave to anti-Communism in her own Germany made life there a lot easier for old Nazis, however ironic this might be. The comrades admitted no such conflict, of course, and maintained that only the Russians pursued war criminals with the proper zeal. I went to several of their social gatherings with Karin, and met none of the fanatics I expected, instead a lot of nice, depressed, quietly dogged people. As I saw it they had plenty to be quiet about. Recruitment had fallen off badly. What their fellow-Germans wanted were hula hoops, chewing gum, espresso bars. Under cover of this the government moved steadily towards banning the Party altogether; a law had already been passed banning Communists from government posts. No wonder they were depressed.

By contrast Anna-Maria von Doderer was exuberance itself—and it was this, it seemed to me, more than psycho-analysis, that promised well for Karin. In search of information about Karin's psyche, I began to court the Dod. Her roomy old face looked as if it had accommodated all the woes she'd ever listened to, stored them, and turned them into merry, benevolent tumours, into pouches, bulges, chins and wattles, and when she laughed, in a splendid bass, they shook like old adventures made flesh. We liked each other on sight and soon fell into the habit of a weekly lunch. (I paid the bill, which sometimes made me feel as if I too were a patient, paying handsomely for an hourly session but enabled to pretend I wasn't.) Our lunches took place on her turf, the well-heeled lakeside world of the Jungfernstieg, not on the Reeperbahn where she felt people would stare at her, "an old lady . . . looking for what? A gigolo with a Mercedes?" "But you'd love to have a gigolo with a Mercedes." "Hah—hah—hah," she went, delighted, in her stilted *basso* laugh. The Four Seasons Hotel restaurant, full of rich couples, was our usual rendez-vous, and it wasn't only the Dod's laugh that rang out with an embarrassing boom. She was a little deaf, and spoke loudly as if to hear herself better. As a result the entire dining room heard scandalous confidences, something I slowly grew

to enjoy, watching our prim Hamburg neighbours. But I kept
my own voice down.

Thinking this was the kind of thing that would intrigue an
analyst I told the Dod about my Herta-amnesia and how I'd
finally remembered the unpleasantness in question. (Actually
the Dod was much more interested in the richer obscenities of
the Herbertstrasse, and cackled gleefully over erotic enemas
and the like.)

"And so you don't fuck Karin," she bellowed for all to hear
when I finished my tale, leaving me wishing I'd never embarked
on it. I pictured Karin in the Dod's consulting room, and the
Dod exclaiming, "You don't do it? What's the matter with you
both?" I was also taken aback by how quickly she'd made the
connection between Karin and the after-effects of my Mecklenburg discovery; and how ruthlessly she associated them.

"Well, it's more complicated than that. Isn't it?"

The Dod always reduced me to painfully British noises, baffled protests in the main, even when we were sparring in her
native language.

She gave me a long-suffering look. "You went to Mecklenburg to expose your memory of this exciting rape *because* you'd
fallen in love with Karin. Don't you see?"

"Anna-Maria, I was already on my way to Mecklenburg when
I met Karin."

Ach! she shrugged, dismissive.

Clearly chronology was of no great importance to an analyst.
Or to women in general perhaps. They had a very odd sense of
time, it suddenly jumped up and slapped them in the face and
they were outraged, as if they hadn't noticed the smaller incre-
ments, as if time as a sequence had no reality for them. And no
claims on them. At thirty-three Karin already greeted her morning image in the mirror as though no sign of aging had been
visible the night before, she'd been sandbagged by time and she
was furious. I knew this because we had in fact slept together.
I hadn't mentioned it to the Dod out of embarrassment—I'd done
no more than cuddle Karin on these occasions, at her request—
and because if I told her the truth I thought I'd be in for a funny
look, or worse, a mocking cackle. Anna-Maria flirted with me
continuously, and while I took this as no more than harmless
fun, I didn't want to be seen as unmanly, let alone impotent.

Besides lubricious stories of the Reeperbahn, what the Dod
most wanted from me was a chance to get her hands on Egon.
She never actually said she disapproved of Mutti and her Prus-

sian code of behaviour, but it was evident that she loved delinquency in all its forms. ''The little beast!'' she glittered when I described Egon's destructive acts of old. *Viehchen! Untier!* Little monster! She promised to revive the primitive in him. Two afternoons a week. At reduced rates. Whatever I could afford.

I was already helping Mutti with Karin's fee; but it wasn't the money that made me hesitate. The Dod gave off such an aura of unbridled geriatric lust that I feared for Egon's soul—his soul, mind you, if it had been only his body at risk I wouldn't have given a toss, it's never too early to start. But hooked as I was myself on aging skin, I wanted to give the boy a fair chance to avoid this curious attachment. I mourned the primitive in him, it's true (no, it's not—that's a downright lie; I was angry with him, and with myself, and I didn't mourn the old Egon because I never really believed it had gone for good); but it wasn't some kind of ravenous sexual behaviour I wanted for him. It was his indiscriminate childish sexuality, so lavish, that I missed. I could picture the Dod giving this a focus again, and at twelve I fancied it could be decisive. (Had I lusted after the Dear Nose? The thought shocked me; if so, I'd forgotten it, and couldn't begin to imagine it now.) ''Too late, Anna-Maria, I'm afraid,'' I said. The Dod scowled and pouted; she thought I meant it was too late to revive the beast in Egon, and that I was being pig-headed and stupid and trying to keep the boy to myself. But it was too late in another sense. I wished I'd brought Egon to her when I first got back to Hamburg with him.

For professional reasons the Dod wouldn't talk about Karin directly, although she could be astonishingly indiscreet, in passing, about her other clients. Naming no names, of course. Like the Herbertstrasse whores she seemed to have a high proportion of coprophiliacs on her books, ''trying to eat,'' as she put it, ''the accumulated shit of Germany, bless them!'' An uphill task, we agreed, and when I named it for her, calling it the Sisyphus (or Scheissyfus) Complex, she promised me a footnote in a future monograph and—so I fancied—a place in psycho-analytic history: Sacher's Disease. I never told her my real name, and although I was disappointed that she didn't press me on the subject, I was also surprised at how little I minded, really: I could foresee a time soon when I wouldn't care who I'd been, either. As Karin's friend, I explained, I needed to know how it would affect her if Wackernagel were to be found, but couldn't be prosecuted. Should Karin know?

"Know?" the Dodderer erupted. "She should confront him, immediately. Do you know where he is, this man?"

Hold on now, wait, *think* about it, Dod, I thought. How can you be so certain? But she was.

"Suppose," I said, "I did discover where he was. I'd rather tell Karin about it in my own time."

"Never mind 'suppose.' Tell her *now*, you fool." *Dummkopf.*

"But what if we found the man and he laughs at her?"

"He *should* laugh at her. She is laughable."

No no, I thought. I can't trust *you*—you're crazier than I am. Whatever Karin is, her grief isn't laughable.

"Was her father's death laughable, Anna-Maria?"

"No!" Again the word exploded out of her, as if I were an idiot pupil. She returned to her food, and I watched her—I couldn't help it, I was used to the Poseners, small dainty women with precise movements (I was used to Kiez-girls too but I never sat down to formal meals with them) and it was always a pleasant surprise to see the Dod, a genuine aristo after all, a "von" Doderer, pitching her shapeless body over the soup and slurping it from her spoon as messily as any peasant.

I let her finish the soup. "Well then?"

Das bisschen Leben, she sighed: this little life. "Reinhard, you want her to go on and on eating her father's shit?" *Vatis Scheisse* resounded across the room as she pushed her soup plate aside. "Let her confront this Wackernagel. Let her see what he is, a brute who likes to gouge people, to spear them. Or that's what he *was*—now he's probably a respectable businessman and good to his family. During the *Nazizeit* he learnt to be a warthog who enjoyed the smell of blood. If she confronts the business-man . . ." the Dod shrugged, letting her Hapsburg lower lip droop, "he will deny everything. Wouldn't *you*? She must confront the other one, the warthog." The epithet fitted; Karin must have shown the Dod her Wackernagel-photos, I decided. "And what use is that?" she roared. "Can you accuse a warthog? Lecture a warthog? You don't think this is ridiculous—be truthful—. . . a grown woman trying to get a confession from a warthog?"

"But you're saying she should do it."

"Of course she should do it! Let her discover what he is. And what he isn't—then she can start work on herself, *nicht*?"

And still I dithered. Perhaps not for altruistic reasons; there was always my old fear that when I'd served my purpose in locating Wackernagel, Karin would ditch me. I hadn't actually admitted to the Dod that I knew where Wackernagel was. But the old woman kept at me about it. She wasn't fooled. I told myself I had to know more about Karin's condition, for my own peace of mind. I'd have to beard the Dod, and to hell with professional discretion.

"Help me, Anna-Maria," I lowered my voice, hoping to bring her usual volume down in sympathy and make her feel more able to betray confidences, "why *is* she so obsessed with her father's death?"

The Dod shrugged her enormous shrug, raising bison shoulders disguised under a lace shawl. She stared me out, and I saw her decide to speak.

"In the first place," she said heavily, almost as though she were telling me this to keep me satisfied and not because she truly believed it, "she didn't love him as she felt a good daughter should, a good Prussian daughter, a good Posener. He slighted her, without meaning to, probably. Ignored her. I had such a father and every day when I finish brushing my teeth I say 'Frau Professor Doktor von Doderer has brushed her teeth, Vati!' This is how I do it—still today. But Karin lost her father before she could show him she was equal to a son, or better perhaps. She hated him," said the Dod lightly, "perhaps even wished him dead at one time or another. Then it happened and he died and in her mind *she* did it. She is Wackernagel. Have you read Racine?" I shook my head, thinking how Peter should be here to cry "Natürlich!" and quote *Mithridate* at her. "King Pyrrhus falls in love with widowed Andromache," said the Dod, "you haven't read the play? *Ach!*" "Sorry." "And Hermione loves Pyrrhus," she went on witheringly, "and another fellow loves Hermione. What's the matter?" "Nothing." I was disturbed by the memory that I, Richard-I, had married somebody called Hermione, Molly for short; though the Dod couldn't possibly know that. "So Hermione tells this poor fellow to go and kill Pyrrhus. And he does!" she grinned in what seemed to me a slightly demented way. "Now! The poor fellow comes back and says 'I did it!' '*What* did you do?' 'I killed Pyrrhus! Precisely as instructed!' And Hermione says, with anger: 'Who told you to do it?!' *Ja?*" I nodded. No doubt it sounded better in French. "You see?" "No, I'm afraid I don't." "Wackernagel is the poor fellow. Karin is Hermione. He did the thing she dreamed about and it's killing her." Yes; yes, I did see. It was close enough to what I'd been imagining myself, but took my suspicions further, into crazy territory. Did people really behave this way, for these reasons? It made me feel drably sane by comparison; though from the way the Dod was looking at me she probably had me figured in a Racine play, and I didn't want to hear about it.

Six, seven weeks passed. It was late August, a rainy Hamburg August, before I broke the news to Karin. I came home late, to be sure she'd already have put Egon to bed. When I told her she stared at me, alert but otherwise expressionless. Somehow I felt immediately relieved; I don't know what I'd expected.

"How did you find out?"

"On the Kiez," I said. "I put the word about." I didn't want to have to tell her that Wolli Zimt, my friend and sponsor, was a former SS colleague of Wackernagel's.

"How? How did they know?"

"You can find out anything on the Kiez if you're patient, and people owe you favours."

She didn't normally ask about my Reeperbahn life. What I told of it she accepted without comment, as though I too were serving some kind of sentence and bringing her exercise-yard gossip.

"That's the way it goes, on the Kiez," I said, uncomfortable under Karin's gaze. "I give someone a job, they pay me in their own way."

"When did you hear about it? Today?"

"This morning." To distract her I brought Wolli's note out of my wallet; crumpled, but it was crumpled to begin with. Why did she sense at once that I'd been holding the information back? Or rather how was it that after years of duplicitous Kiez-life I was still as transparent as ever?

Karin was studying the note. Her lips moved as she read the address, but when she looked up at me I had the feeling she hadn't taken in a word of it. "What do we do?"

At least it was still "we." And as I watched her all I saw in her small face was growing animation. Bewilderment, excitement. Nothing tortured or perverse. No Racine heroine, just a person with consummation in her reach. "We inform the Bavarian prosecutor's office. There's the possibility they'll do nothing. More than likely they'll do nothing, you know that. Worse still they might warn him off and we'd lose him altogether. He could move, change his name."

She nodded, looked at the note again, turned it over, found no more handwriting. Turned it back again. "30, Albrecht-strasse, Karlsruhe."

We gazed at each other.

Would *she* say it? Should I? *Dummkopf.* The Dod was so bloody certain—all right then—"Or we could go and talk to him. Before he flies the coop." I couldn't read an answer in her face. "Would you want to do that?"

"I don't know."

But it seemed to me she was lying, pretending to be dazed because this was more decent; it *was* what she wanted to do.

"It's possible, I suppose," I said, "that he's the kind of man who *wants* to own up and . . . face the music. Who just needs a little push." I didn't believe a word of this; I was giving her an alibi almost before I knew what I was doing. "There don't seem to be too many of that sort around. But there must be *some*."

"Yes. There must be some."

"Think about it. Let's see what Mutti has to say."

But with that I'd lost her. She didn't want to think about Mutti. That night we went to see a film at one of the cinemas along the Steintor. I remember what it was because of the title: "Ich Suche Dich," I'm Searching For You. I chose it shamelessly, hoping it might be about a quest like Karin's. Instead, and much to Karin's contempt, it told the story of an atheistic doctor (magnificently played, I thought, by an unshaven O.W. Fischer) whose girlfriend brings him to the love of God, the "Ich" of the title.

The Karlsruhe train left from the sad-eyed jostle of the Hauptbahnhof, not my beloved Dammtor with its blaze of windowpanes. None of us drove, that's to say neither Karin nor I did and although Vlad volunteered I wasn't about to entrust our lives to a one-armed driver—not on the Autobahn, Wotan's racetrack; so it was the train for us.

To explain Karin's presence to Vlad I'd had to tell him what our mission was, or at least pretend that I knew. It sounded so implausible when I described it to him: we were going to face a killer with his victim's child, to shame him into . . . what? Surrender? A breakdown of some kind? Some word or gesture of atonement? I hastily explained that it was being done for Karin's benefit, even if, in the end, justice was mocked. "You really don't have to come," I said, though I longed to have someone there who wasn't caught up in the folly and the fascination of it, "I can handle this." Pah, he sneered. To Karin I said that Vlad was an old anti-Nazi—I hoped his evident Russianness would endear him to her, though he was no Marxist—

and a personal ally whose very appearance would enhance our bargaining power, face to face. A bodyguard on either side of her, as I pictured it.

I fully expected Karin to be offended, shocked even, that I'd involved this stranger in her affairs. She took it without a murmur. Let 'em all come, why not? That seemed to be her attitude; I don't care who watches. Accompanied, unaccompanied, she would accuse Wackernagel before the world. Everyone else was a stranger, as in life class. I watched her closely, but Karin seemed perfectly sane to me, she was her own small tidy self, wearing a suit, almost a travelling suit in the old style, like Maggie's moss green outfit, but this one was a grey tweed with tartan lapels. She wore a tartan-lined cloak and carried a pale pink travelling case, formerly Mutti's. It was Vlad and I who drew stares as we accompanied her, a pair of ogres who'd kidnapped Sleeping Beauty. Now that he was famous (in Hamburg at any rate) Vlad carried himself with a swagger; his walk had seemingly never adjusted to the loss of an arm, and he suffered from, or had begun to affect, an exaggerated sailor's gait, rolling along like a man in a hurry with a heavy suitcase in one hand. Crowds were an affront to him and he parted them ruthlessly with his bulk. At the Hauptbahnhof disgruntled travellers turned to Vlad, protesting, as we followed in his wake like royalty. Karin didn't seem to notice.

I made a mental note to search her pink travelling case before we closed with Wackernagel, and by whatever means—forceful caresses if needs be—make sure there were no weapons on her person. Vlad would be harder to search, and I was struck with my newfound fear that he'd known about Wackernagel all along and had been briefed by Wolli (I couldn't think why) to gun Wackernagel down on sight. For that matter the Russian could as easily kill him with a stranglehold, if he was going to, so I'd gain nothing by disarming Vlad before the meeting.

We'd left Egon at Wandsbek, in Mutti's care. She disapproved of our journey, intensely so. But the Dod had been severe with her. ''A crisis is imperative!'' she had roared down the phone. I heard this version from the Dod herself. A crisis? The word alarmed me, and had clearly alarmed Frau Posener too, who must have thought a crisis was what we were trying to avoid. She had already told Karin she was not to seek out Wackernagel—*Punkt!*—*Schluss!*—end of conversation! *Quatsch!* was the Dod's response to this. To Mutti she said, ''You must not ask your daughter to obey you.'' Karin's habit of obedience was in her opinion a sign of contempt for Mutti: this statement, also delivered on the phone, had been reported to Karin by Mutti herself (the Dod never mentioned it to me) and it had distressed both Poseners terribly. I wondered if Anna-Maria knew what she was doing with some of these sweeping remarks. Karin herself called the Dod *bekloppt*, mad, much as she had before their sessions began. She regarded the decision to go to Karlsruhe as hers alone. "After this," meaning the coming confrontation, "I won't need Anna-Maria," Karin said, adding, "she says so herself."

True, the Dod had said to me that Karin might be able to start working on her feelings once she'd discovered who and what Wackernagel was. But did that mean working on her own? Puzzling over these inconsistencies, I felt that no-one was entirely telling me the truth.

It was a day-long journey to Karlsruhe, with two changes of train and hours of silent travel in between, staring at magazines or the view from the compartment window. Whenever possible I sat beside Karin, with Vlad opposite, eyebrow to eyebrow, as it were. He was studying her too, now, and I looked forward to asking him what he saw.

Apart from trips to Travemünde where Wolli liked to frequent the brand new casino, and a holiday in Lower Saxony with Egon and the Poseners (we couldn't go abroad; we had no passports, Egon and I), I hadn't seen much of Germany. I'd seen nothing of central or southern Germany, of Bavaria, not since my crazed journey by sugar-beet lorry and later by train, through that dungheap of a countryside with its black trees and wrecked machinery, its shattered cities with people crawling on the rubble-mounds. In five years those busy insects had worked an unnerving transformation. I'd seen it happen gradually in Hamburg, street by street, almost stone by stone as a new face emerged. The old scars were everywhere, in memory. Here there were no scars to be seen any more, and the German landscape being what it is—"being Germany," as Cheerybye would say—you could no longer imagine them and began to wonder whether the fighting and the bombing hadn't spared the fields and villages in front of you, it had all taken place somewhere else, nearby perhaps, out of sight, but not here in this seemingly ageless, fresh-faced Germany. These days travel has brought everything nearer—Heidegger himself says this, or something like it—but without making any of it more present to us. It takes a German to understand this fully. The view from the train was unsettling at first, but slowly it restored to me the Germany I'd visited before the war, that portable landscape, sculptural, precast (in someone's head), proverbial. The Germany I'd always thought it was so easy to carry with you. Creepy but endearing.

In Karlsruhe itself there was still evidence of the war, the city had been an industrial powerhouse, you could see that, and also that it was still struggling to catch up with its old self; there were dozens of empty, burned-out warehouses in the outlying districts along the railway track. The centre of town came as a shock as we emerged from the station. It was like Hamburg. Of course it was, I realized: another new faceless city, when I'd imagined Hamburg as the only one, without knowing I was doing so. And this—this was how it might be to meet a twin after you've known her sister for years, with a curious sense of familiar features thinned or thickened, surgically amended; it might be like this, I thought, to go mad, everything would look slightly different but you couldn't put your finger on it.

As it was each new street brought quick, faint nausea and distrust, like the signs of a suspected unfaithfulness in a face you love. Karlsruhe was too much like Hamburg at first, even the people seemed like duplicates and I kept expecting to see friends among the passers-by. Vlad had wrestled here—I was so conscious of omens that day that I never asked him whether he'd won or lost—and led us to the small hotel where he'd stayed on that occasion.

I had a passion for hotels, though in jumping from pre-war British bed-and-breakfast jobs to the grandeur of the Atlantic and the Four Seasons I'd missed out on the common or garden variety. This was also my first experience of a "modern" hotel. Zum Alten Bock was what Alec would have called cheap but cheerful, but I found it so cheerless I thought even one night among its plastic ornaments might undo our resolve. If this was the new Germany I didn't want to confront it in Wackernagel; I saw his wife—in imagination I'd given him a wife, following the Dod's lead—ushering us into a sitting room with similar fuzzy yellow carpeting and imitation leather sofas. But Vlad liked it and Karin seemed so indifferent to her surroundings that I refrained from dragging them through the streets in search of somewhere more congenial—if there was such a thing in Karlsruhe.

"I haven't imagined it further than saying, my name is Karin Posener, my father was August Posener." She stared back at me defiantly. "I'm not planning to make conversation with him."

She said this now, as we sat on the bed in our hotel room; it was what she'd said before we left, when I asked her how she intended to approach Wackernagel. In much the same words—perhaps exactly the same words. This time I had to press her further.

"All right. Then what? Does he recognize the name, as you imagine it?"

"I don't know."

"Suppose he doesn't."

"I tell him who my father was."

"And suppose he slams the door in our faces."

"I wait."

"You wait till he comes out?"

"As long as it takes."

"And if he calls the police?"

She thought about it. "I'll still have looked into his face. I wanted him to see me—and—"

When she hesitated I couldn't help prompting her, "And for him to remember it." To see her. As I was seeing her now, the small intense face, pretty despite itself, the pretty features, small fine nose, dark eyes and eyebrows like mink, oriental eyebrows so black against the strange smooth bubbling skin with its moles and its tiny skin-covered bumps like more, nascent moles: seeing her like this? Or would she look different, faced with Wackernagel, savage, an avenger, the small mouth spread tensely, baring the hare-lip? Despite myself I was caught up in the trance of her imagining, I was finishing her sentences. Instead of shedding light on her groping, unclear images of the meeting to come, I was carried along by them as though they were my own. "Is that the idea? You want him to remember you?"

"I want him to know that I'll remember, and that as long as I'm alive I might be there around a corner, waiting for him."

The way she said it—I was wrong, I thought, she wasn't groping; she knew exactly what she wanted. "And that's enough?"

"Don't ask me that." We sat in silence. "It's what I want now."

"All right. We could go now, if you like."

"It's late."

"All the more likely he'll be home. If he works here in Karlsruhe he'll be out most of tomorrow. Unless you want to go there early, before he leaves home."

She gave a convulsive shiver. "Let's find the house tomorrow. And wait till he comes back."

"If that's what you want."

I thought I saw tears building, sometimes I saw them in her face before she knew they were on the way. But they didn't come.

"Mutti says . . ."

"What does Mutti say?" I asked when she let it hang. Karin wouldn't meet my eyes. "I love you," I said at last, knowing how ill at ease this made her feel, but unable to help myself. For once she squeezed my hands in answer. She looked tired. Frightened, too. I hugged her and she spoke over my shoulder, to the room, the walls.

"Mutti isn't even curious about him. Sometimes I feel I'm not either, any more." I held her, not knowing what to say. "But I want to go through with it."

What would the Dod say if she was here? Something caustic, that was for sure. I could hear myself sounding like a gentler, neutered Dod, a good Dod, but just as wise and all-knowing. Karin, why don't you tell me I'm a fraud, I wanted to say. Can't you see it? Can't you tell? The keener, more inflamed part of my mind wasn't here, it was with Wackernagel the reformed warthog, sitting stretched out in his imitation leather armchair, reading the newspaper. Mouthing the sports results. Unaware that his life was about to be invaded by a vengeful harpy. Why didn't she rebuke me for my oh-so-tender manner? At least Mutti was angry, and honest about it. But if I said it straight: no, I don't understand, Karin would say "Yes you do, when you think of Peter and the way he died." And that wasn't true either. I was appalled that anyone should have to suffer like that, as August had too, as millions had—but the men who killed them, what were they? Men intimately, exhaustively acquainted with death, enviably so, and lacking civilized restraint, unclean men who'd taken on the curse of human curiosity. *Mutti isn't even curious about him.* What was our murderousness except unbearable curiosity about death? These were men who'd braved taboo, the killers, or they were nothing. Nothing of interest, just warthogs.

"Would you rather we didn't come to the door with you, tomorrow?" When she didn't answer, I added quickly, "I'd like to see him too." Karin nodded, and I didn't pursue it, I didn't want to hear that it made no odds to her whether I'd be there beside her at the door or not.

Vlad was in his room, lying on the bed in a singlet and pyjama bottoms, the black lamb's wool hat still jammed on his head (habit—or vanity? Was he going bald perhaps?), puffing on a cigar. The singlet left his shoulders bare. I'd never seen his stump naked before—Vlad's wrestling outfit both hid and accentuated the loss of the arm by means of gaudy, gold-tasselled epaulettes, a supposedly Cossack effect, attached to his fighting vest. The stump was white, atrophied, in shape and colour like an uncooked chicken wing with the small yellowish end sticking out and the fleshy bulb lodged in Vlad's armpit socket. It took me back to the Dear Nose's kitchen at Fold Farm, where as a child I'd fingered the plucked, fatty flesh of the birds waiting for the pot—delicious sensation—when she wasn't looking. This Vlad-wing twitched, seemingly of its own accord. No, perhaps Vlad was working it himself. I wanted to touch it all the more.

"So," said Vlad, indifferent to my stare. "We have to do what to this man?"

"I've told you, we don't have to do anything," I told him again, while he gazed at me in open contempt.

"We do nothing to him? We shake his hand?"

Butter-stealing bastard, I thought, if you had two arms . . . though I knew his one arm was as strong as both of mine. When he saw me getting too cocky on the Kiez, Vlad would offer to arm-wrestle me, smiling tenderly as he pressed my fist to the table.

"What do you think of her?" I said. "How do you find her?"

"A terrible thing," Vlad shook his tight lamb's wool curls, ignoring my question. "How old she was? Six, seven?"

"She was eighteen, Vlad."

He stared, removed the cigar from his lips. "She was eighteen *then*?"

"In '37. Yes."

Amazed, "She's thirty now?"

I nodded. "Thirty-three."

"Then I find her very interesting."

"In what way?"

"Very unusual."

"Her looks, you mean?"

"Her looks, yes, what else?"

"You don't find her peculiar in any other way?" He studied me. "I mean, she seems normal to you?"

"For eighteen, normal. For thirty-three is something else."

"Yes. I suppose you're right."

"She's your girlfriend?"

"Yes."

Vlad raised his eyebrows, and I awaited his judgement, their judgement, poised to spring. "Interesting," he said at last, heavily. "You like them skinny." He returned to his cigar. "I like them fat like ox."

Albrechtstrasse was a tree-lined avenue, long and straight in the manner of the Wandsbeker Chaussee, and the Wackernagel end of it consisted of attractive two and three storey houses built at the turn of the century, with modest hints at Jugendstil in the curved lintels of the windows and the flaring gable ends. Some of these family residences, once stylish, had gone to seed—a poor reward for having survived the bombing—and needed painting. It was difficult to tell whether the owners were hard up or merely slovenly. Number 30, the Wackernagel home, was in good order, blue in colour, a smoky blue a little muddier than Wedgwood, with white trim. It looked gemütlich all right, teutonically cosy. But my images of leatherette and vulgar carpeting receded as soon as we came close enough to see inside. Chunky Biedermeier furniture was dimly visible, dark gloomy wood no doubt sprinkled with lace and knick-knacks. In one front window a cactus and a fleshy marine plant disputed the sill with a china cat. The cat sported a sea captain's hat—the only visible touch of Hamburg, Wackernagel's home town.

We'd found our way to the house in mid-morning and made ourselves conspicuous since then by loitering on the opposite side of the street; no convenient café, no car to hide in. "I don't care," said Karin. "Let them stare and wonder what we're doing here. If anyone asks, I shall tell them." Provided it isn't the police we end up telling, I thought, as neighbours came and went from overlooking windows. I suggested we take it in shifts to watch the house, since the three of us looked so grotesque as a group, but Karin wouldn't budge. "You go," she said with her mother's asperity.

A dumpy person—at first I took her for a cleaning woman—was occasionally visible inside number 30. We couldn't tell her age, but she wasn't young. In the early afternoon she emerged from the little, vinecovered front door alcove, and turned back to bring out a wheeled contraption, less elaborate than a pram, with a child in it of indeterminate sex. Its hair was tucked under a cap, the body hidden by a shiny blue romper suit. Red-cheeked, red-lipped, the child; a miniature Wolli Zimt. In the sunlight the woman looked more like the child's grandmother than its

mother. I'd allowed for a child, in my fantasies, a wife too—
(open-mouthed as we challenged her husband; how we'd shock
her!)—but not a Wackernagel mother. This seemed more gruesome, somehow.

Seen closer to, she was a small woman with iron-grey hair, a
snub nose and a dark shabby suit over heavy shoes. Obviously
she'd seen us studying her house, but after a brief glance the
same guardedness that was preventing her neighbours from ac-
costing us got the better of her, and she went her way down the
avenue, pushing the infant. Minding your own business, even
when the world encroached on your doorstep, was now a national obsession and it benefited us that day.

My whole body was aching. I don't think I'd ever stood in
one place for so long, and little walks up and down the street
didn't help much. A grumbling Vlad went off "to buy provision"
and came back two hours later stinking of beer, with bread and
sausage in a bag. By this time I was sitting on the curb. Karin
was still erect as a sentry, gazing at the house as if to memorize
it item by item. Looking at her I realized I hadn't searched her
for concealed weapons. Too late now, she wouldn't welcome an
embrace. I'd stay close to her when the moment came, ready to
intercept any surprise movement. But it was hard to imagine
anything concealed on her small slim frame. (Skinny? Did I
really like them skinny? I thought back hastily; no, Molly was
plump, and Ellie frankly fat like ox.) I turned to number 30
again, tried to see it through Karin's eyes. Wasn't there something fascistic, now that I looked more closely, about the languid
curves, the narcissism of its Art Nouveau touches; the connection had never occurred to me before, and it was probably just
my mood; but where the heavy Victorian furnishings we could
glimpse inside the house seemed to resemble the sentimental
ballast of the bourgeois period, wasn't there something faintly
hysterical about the architectural fancies that followed, the dramatic gestures, swooping lines? Perhaps I was getting slightly
hysterical myself. So was Karin, I could tell. During Vlad's
absence the woman had returned with the stunned-looking child,
and once again ignored us. Seeing us reduced to two, she may
have hoped that we were gradually abandoning our mysterious
vigil, whatever it was. Was the look on Karin's face, as she followed
the pair with her eyes, indicated a different theory at work: the
old girl *knew* we'd come along, that someone would come, one
day.

Evening came and a steady trickle of working men came home

to neighbouring houses, by foot and by car. Lights came on along the street. No-one returned to number 30. By now we were all sitting on the kerb with our feet in the gutter.

Wackernagel wasn't here, he was away, on business or on holiday: no doubt we'd all had the same thoughts. Unless he was in the house and had been there all along. If so he knew about us by now and wouldn't come to the door.

"Soon I go home," said Vlad.

"I think we all will." I looked at Karin, but she shook her head. "Karin, they won't go on ignoring us forever. The neighbours certainly won't, not all night." She wouldn't look at me. "Do you want to get arrested? What would that accomplish?"

I got no answer. It was time to break the impasse. I stood up and crossed the street on shaky legs, opened a low ornamental fence gate and went to the vine-circled door of number 30 to ring the bell. Footsteps at my back; Vlad and Karin hurrying after me once they realized what was I doing. I didn't want to hear Karin's protests. I couldn't find the bell among the vines so I beat on the door. Now there was no going back.

Um Gottes willen! came a woman's voice almost at once. She must have been watching from the window. *Was wollen Sie denn?* What do you want, for God's sake?

"We're looking for Herr Wackernagel," I called. "It's important."

Was? came the muffled voice.

I repeated myself, with variations. At last the door opened, as far as a heavy chain would allow. A cagey lot, the citizens of Albrechtstrasse; I almost expected a gun barrel to appear next. Instead the old woman's face came into view, belligerent, her snub nose flushed.

"Frau Wackernagel?"

"Who?"

"Excuse me, but does Hermann Wackernagel live here?" She looked completely blank. "Hermann Wackernagel."

"Who?"

Total bafflement is a hard thing to simulate; it comes from the inside. When you see it, it's unmistakable. If she'd closed the door I might have suspected that she was holding out on us. But angry as she was, she didn't shut us out.

This *was* 30, Albrechtstrasse? It was, and yes, it was the only Albrechtstrasse in Karlsruhe.

Feeling stupid, I brought out Wolli's note to see if I'd got the address wrong. I hadn't.

"Wackernagel, Hermann. You've never heard of him?"

She shook her head, studying us now.

I stared back at the note. Someone was playing games with us.

As we traipsed back to the hotel Vlad was looking increasingly disgusted, and Karin shellshocked. To cover our embarrassment I'd told the old woman at number 30 the truth. I couldn't think of anything else to say. And to my surprise it turned her anger into a touching welcome. Inge Scholtz she said her name was; she too had been devastated by the Hitler years—*unsere Schande*, she called them, our shame—and had lost a husband and a son; she invited us in, plied us with Schnaps, showed us photographs, the husband killed on leave in the bombing, the son a deserter on the Russian front who was recaptured and shot. His face in the photograph could have been the face of the boy who braved the officer with the glass eye, in Malaparte's story. Suddenly we were all crying, what with the drink and our pent-up emotion, Vlad crying for Mother Russia, Karin and Inge for their lost loved ones and I for the sheer pleasure of it, or else for what and whom I didn't dare think. Three years Inge had owned the place, she said, she'd bought in from a young couple called Börne. There was no Wackernagel in the house, she said once more—all of us laughing now like idiots—but we were welcome to search. She was so unaffectedly friendly and we, I suppose, were so relieved, that the sense of failure didn't set in till we were out of the house and halfway to Zum Alten Bock.

I put Karin to bed. She didn't want to talk, she looked dazed—and I wondered what the Dod would say. The Dod had wanted us to come to Karlsruhe, and perhaps that was all that mattered: the coming here, the concentrated anticipation of the day, with Karin meeting Wackernagel in her mind, over and over, during the hours of waiting—then the let-down, the release of tension, and none of the messier consequences of finding the man. Was it enough?

Perversely it was Vlad and I who now couldn't leave well alone. With our sense of disappointment restored, we felt foolish and humiliated, sitting at the hotel bar over more Schnaps. Regarding the Albrechtstrasse address I knew, as Vlad did, that Wolli wouldn't tolerate a phone conversation on the subject. I was probably supposed to have destroyed his note at once and with it Wolli's part in the affair. But why would he have sent us on an out-and-out wild goose chase? It made no sense. Somewhere in Karlsruhe there was a clue, a trail. To come all this way and then just traipse home . . . surely we could at least try the phone book. How many Wackernagels could there be in Karlsruhe? As we leafed through the pages I remembered Karin saying "lucky his name isn't Müller" when she'd first told me the story.

There were plenty of Müllers in Karlsruhe, but no Wackernagels. "Never mind. He's here," said Vlad, giving me the kind of look Auntie had reserved for cosmic messages. Come to that, hadn't she warned me once against "strange companions?" Did this apply to Vlad? He said again, putting his hand on my arm: "He's here, I feel it." I felt it too. Or rather I was hooked. I wanted to find Wackernagel—for my own sake, and to hell with the consequences.

The days that followed made a curiously precise impression on me, establishing themselves in memory hour by hour like a ship's log in a storm, in strict sequence, that is, with none of memory's circuitousness. It was the door-to-door life of campaigning politicians, salesmen, or true detectives, girding yourself for each encounter and the chance of a door, or a dog, in your face. I could remember each house I visited, in their correct order.

On the first day of the routine, a Wednesday, Karin woke in a fever. As usual she'd hardly slept, she said, but hadn't wanted to disturb me. She'd slept well enough the night of our arrival in Karlsruhe (I hadn't, myself, so I watched her sleep, glad of it, and hadn't pointed out this not-so-usual event, surely a good omen); but after the previous day's ordeal I wasn't surprised at the sleeplessness, or even at the fever. I could feel it on her forehead, and ordered her to stay in bed. After breakfast I found her in an alarming, speechless state, her face flushed even more. Clearly running a high temperature now. Her expression was fixed in a furious frown I recognized from somewhere. It was her piano-playing frown, I realized, I'd seen it once when we were visiting old friends of Mutti's and they implored her to play until she couldn't refuse any more; it was *that* frown, yes, a desperate offended look as though the Devil were after her, propositioning her through the music, and she had to play faster to keep ahead of him. She looked dreadful there in the hotel bed; but perhaps she was playing Schubert in her mind. When I touched her blazing forehead (even now I couldn't help stroking one eyebrow with my little finger) Karin barely responded. She closed her eyes, concentrating. Demons at work in there, I thought. Delayed shock. Must phone Mutti, I thought. And didn't.

By afternoon the fever had gone and she was asleep at last. I didn't wake her, much as I wanted to. We had glorious news. Taking along Karin's newspaper-clipping photographs of Wackernagel, we'd gone back, Vlad and I, to the Albrechtstrasse and begun questioning the neighbours. This time we'd concocted a story about Hermann our missing relative. (In the course of the day I noticed several glances directed over at Vlad and back up to me, as if wondering what possible consanguinity could link a bearded bean-pole to a one-armed bear; and both to a third party whose photograph showed a trim, smooth-chopped, balding person with pale, almost bleached-out German eyes.) Most of the Albrechtstrasse residents were recent arrivals and knew no more than Inge Scholtz did. Alas they too had missing relatives, other Hermanns and Gustavs and Stefans, and insisted on commiserating with us over coffee, cake, and photographs of their own. Vlad, a voracious eater, seemed to enjoy this more than I did. At number 41 a man came to the door: Herr Stockenreiter, emaciated, in his early sixties as it turned out, but older-looking. He'd lost a leg in the First World War, and when I heard this my heart sank, foreseeing Vlad and Stockenreiter exchanging tales of limblessness for yet another wasted hour. But not at all. He knew Wackernagel, recognized the name and the face from photographs, too: a lodger for several years with the Börnes at number 30, the people who'd sold the house to Inge Scholtz. Three or four years back, this was, said Stockenreiter. Could he be more exact? Three and a bit; he'd left in the spring of 1950, when the Börnes put the house on the market. They'd got on well, he and Wackernagel (I could see Vlad stiffening at this). Hermann was an insurance salesman here in Karlsruhe, he'd bought his own house in the Weststadt somewhere, Mühlburg perhaps, but Stockenreiter couldn't recall the address. Or the name of the insurance company. No. *Entschuldigung, meine Herren:* so sorry. Was he lying? Had he seen Vlad's frown as he began to praise our "relative?" A decent, hard-working man, Stockenreiter had said, perhaps assuming a family fondness on our part. And then Stockenreiter's memory had begun to go fuzzy. We weren't going to get any more out of him now, and though I could see Vlad straining at the leash, fist clenched, I motioned towards the doorway. I didn't want to watch a bout between the One-Armed Wonder and the One-Legged Pensioner.

If Wackernagel still worked in Karlsruhe, we debated on the way back to the hotel, why wasn't he in the phone book? Perhaps he didn't have a phone. Unlikely, for a salesman. Perhaps he'd changed his name. The first thing to do was to try the insurance companies. Before starting on that I phoned Mutti. Now that Karin's fever had passed I simply said she was sleeping, exhausted, which was true, and explained that we hadn't found Wackernagel—knowing that the relief of this, for her, would help to balance qualms about Karin's state. "Let her sleep," and wake in a Wackernagel-free world; although she didn't say it I could hear that this was Mutti's hope, "and then take her on a little holiday." Good, I said. Yes. As soon as she's ready. Besides, Karlsruhe itself is pleasant at this time of year. I didn't tell her Vlad and I were scouring it for Wackernagel like a pair of contract killers.

Karlsruhe *was* pleasant, and when my first queasiness wore off, the double vision of the city as Hamburg restored to me in a disquietingly alien form, I began to appreciate its southern flavour, its sunny places. Sly, shifty lot, the Bavarians, Walters liked to say, with a touch of the Eytye—the Italians; "up here in Hamburg the north wind keeps them honest, blows away the Bierkeller stink." It was true that you could smell beer everywhere, as if Karlsruhe bellies kept its air perfumed with lager belches. But the summer sunshine came back at us gladly off the grey cobblestones, where Hamburg always seemed too thirsty and absorbed the little sun it got. We had plenty of opportunity to savour it; after a Wednesday afternoon spent largely on the telephone to insurance companies who knew no Wackernagel and had employed none, we spent Thursday visiting them in person, each with a photograph, to see of they knew him by another name.

What if old Stockenreiter had deceived us and Wackernagel never sold insurance? Or what if he'd deceived Stockenreiter? Both thoughts accompanied us on our separate journeys across the city, Vlad taking the south and centre, I the north, east and west. One or other deceit seemed increasingly possible as the day went by and no employer claimed our man. By evening Vlad was discouraged—no more cosmic messages coming his way—and fretful too, he was booked to wrestle in Hamburg on Saturday and hadn't had a chance to train all week. On Friday morning I walked him to the station, thanked him, and waved him goodbye. It was a hopeless cause anyway, I thought as I returned to Zum Alten Bock. Why not take Karin on holiday?

Each morning the feverishness was there on her face, evidence of another sleepless night, and more, surely, the working up and out of demons. If not exorcized, certainly flushed out of their recesses. And perhaps Karin's sleep during the day was exorcizing them.

To offset reports of our failed search I brought her magazines, holiday brochures. "This *is* a holiday," she said once, smiling weakly from the pillows, after a good sleep. She still seemed dazed, but as the morning fever lessened, day by day, I hoped this had been the crisis the Dod demanded. A gentle one, but it seemed to reach deep. In the evenings she talked about Vati August, not about Wackernagel. Some of her conversation was strange, long rambling stories I'd never heard, including the entire plots of several historical novels August had apparently intended to write, or drafted perhaps and then thrown away, and which he'd described to Karin when she was little. She remembered them scene for scene. Once, she said, she'd embarked on one of them herself, writing it out as he'd told it to her and adding incident and dialogue; this was later, when she was sixteen. She gave it to him to read. By then he must have abandoned his own literary dreams, or rather consigned his ambition to dreams. For weeks he failed to read her efforts; when he got round to it at last the vexation behind the compliments he paid her stopped Karin dead in her tracks, and neither of them became historical novelists. Thinking of my quondam mother-in-law Laura Trimble, and her sagas—*At the Gates of Vienna* and so forth—*The Enchanted Flagon of Ostend*, that was another one!—I breathed a silent thank-you; though I could see how painful the episode must have been for Karin.

When these memories stirred and twisted her lips, I knew a bad night was coming. I could have phoned the Dod—I wish I had!—but I dare say I was jealous of her, of her power. I admired the Dod's brutal strictures, mostly free of jargon, her plain speaking, "horse sense" as she called it. "Speak horse sense, Reinhard! *Ach*, you complicate everything, always 'but,' 'although,' 'on the other hand.' " Unfortunately this encouraged me to believe I too could be a psychiatrist if I chose to be, if horse sense was worth more than textbook patter. "Goodbye, old horse!" Denis Towle's last words to me, on the pillow there, at Hanbury's Ark. (Don't think about that; tears thick in my throat already.) All right. I had the horse. Where was the bloody sense?

Walking back from the station, where Vlad too, in his parting words, had urged me to take Karin away, I found one incident from the previous day still nagging at me. At the Westphalian Insurance Company in Mühlburg, where Wackernagel had supposedly bought a house (but was not—I'd checked—on any available electoral roll under that name), a secretary had recognized his photograph without a second glance. Of course: Herr Fleischmann, she smiled. I'd mentioned no names. My heart began to pound, until I met the director, a grey-haired smoothie called Meise, who shook his head ruefully over the photograph. "Where's the scar?" he said. What scar? Why, Herr Fleischmann had a duelling scar from student days; the secretary agreed, a noticeable scar, quite so, but otherwise the features in the blurred photographs were similar, were they not? Herr Direktor Meise agreed. Similar. Perhaps the photograph hadn't picked up the scar. What was my interest in Herr Fleischmann? I knew that Wackernagel had no scar from student days; and the more I described Hermann to them, the less he tallied with Fleischmann. But I wasn't quite ready to let it go at that. Had there been a warning look (my imagination was full of them), one I'd missed, between smooth Meise and the secretary, alerting her to follow his lead about the scar? In the phone book there were two Fleischmanns with Mühlburg addresses. I'd tried them both, repeatedly. No answer from either. Was it worth going back to stake out the two addresses, in turn? Another couple of days almost certainly wasted, with Karin ready for a holiday, needing to be taken away from the Wackernagel-world now. Urgently perhaps. Forget Fleischmann.

As I entered the hotel lobby I was startled to see a fully dressed Karin pacing at the desk. Then she was rushing towards me. "It's Egon! Egon!" was all she could say.

For a moment I thought—I was certain—the boy was dead. An accident. I wanted her to say it. I couldn't speak to get the word out of her.

"A plane . . . he took an aeroplane!"

I'd seen nothing about an air disaster in the morning newspaper. Karin saw the horror in my face and shook her head frantically.

"He's all right. He stole a plane. He didn't fly it. It went into the mud."

He stole a plane? Egon?

"At Fuhlsbüttel. Mutti phoned—it happened this morning— he isn't hurt or anything, it's all right."

It was better than all right. I started to laugh in relief, and in pure joy too. I knew he had it in him. At last the little bugger had done something genuinely outrageous.

It's not funny, Karin was saying, bewildered at first but getting angry now. "He's with the police."

On the train back to Hamburg there was plenty of time for amusement to evaporate and be replaced by a guilty conscience. I realized I'd barely asked Mutti how Egon was, when we'd spoken on the phone, just a routine enquiry in passing; I hadn't asked to speak to him. I'd sent love. But not felt it, not even really thought of him. I didn't, these days. I believed I'd lost him, and I'd lost too many children to want to feel the loss again. Lost them all but one, of course—and that one I'd abandoned. To my surprise it was Wilf, not Egon, that I found myself thinking about on the train, once I'd extracted from Karin all she'd heard from a panicky Mutti about Egon's adventure.

We talked it through, over and over, speculating, puzzling over it. Had Egon been trying to fly to Karlsruhe, feeling deserted by us? (Feeling jealous of Karin, who had all my attention now? I didn't suggest this aloud.) It was the first time we'd been away from him at all, never meaning it to be for the whole week; but confident that he was busy with his schoolfriends, and felt safe with Mutti . . . yes, perhaps our absence had played no part at all. Perhaps if he'd got airborne he'd have headed east to the Friedrichswald. Except that he seemed to have forgotten Mecklenburg, and never talked about it. Once or twice I'd heard him disclaim all memory of the woods—he hated the Waldmensch tag, he didn't wanted to be questioned, pointed out, stared at as a freak. No, he just wanted to fly: that must have been how he understood it. It wasn't anger at our desertion. Egon had planned it carefully, weeks ago, that came clear as I sifted Mutti's information. He'd persuaded Gerhard, the schoolfriend son of the pilot who'd taken us up in the plane—a Focke-Wulf, apparently—to steal his father's keys to the cockpit door, and make duplicates before returning them. These he passed to Egon. (At a price? The thought made me ashamed, it was my Kiez-spirit speaking, and I hoped I hadn't passed the ethic on to Egon; no, it could have been friendship, an act of love, of shared conspiracy.) He'd gone to school as usual, but secretly carrying a forged sick-note from Mutti. I could picture him forming the antique Gothic letters, his mouth working like Maggie's as he drew them; a note which his fellow-conspirator delivered while Egon scampered away, I saw him running, running, all the way to Fuhlsbüttel with the keys jangling in a pocket of his short grey trousers. He was a familiar figure in the airport hangars, known to the mechanics from his solo tours of inspection at the weekend, ogling the planes. Slipping now unseen into the Focke-Wulf. How he'd studied the pilot, peering over his shoulder, as we'd taxied down the runway that Sunday afternoon! Watched the man flicking switches, adjusting flaps, testing the joystick—yes, it had been in his mind already then. But to do it! To actually *do* it! At twelve years old. (And mercifully not to take off but, as Mutti described it, skid into the cabbages at the muddy end of the Fuhlsbüttel runway; thank God.) But what resourcefulness, what nerve! Or had he never fully understood how lethal machinery could be, cars (we didn't have one and to my knowledge he'd never been in one), or trams like the one we rode to the airport from the cemetery every Sunday, so safe on its rails? Aeroplanes, seemingly secure to him in their sky-tenure, secure as birds? All the same he knew he'd get into dreadful trouble . . . yes, that was the joy and the mystery of it, after he'd been so priggishly obedient for years now. And that was the reproach too, besides the one to Mutti as mentor and disciplinarian-in-chief: the reproach to me for having abandoned him to the Poseners. And I *had* abandoned him, the real Egon, years ago. I was missing the point, with my vicarious glee. Even if he'd got off the ground and flown the thing, known the joy and somehow landed safe (he must have believed he could land the plane; I don't believe there was any desperation in what he did, or a full awareness of the danger), what came next was the police, and he knew it. The police—who'd picked him up in the Jenisch-park the night after our arrival in Hamburg, when I'd been carted off to jail and left him in Karin's hands. Can we go back to the beginning, please, he was saying; can you please get it right this time?

Had I known then, on the train, of the Dod's part in the escapade, I'd have been spared some of my shame. But it was good for me, I'd earned it. The Dod! Ruthless as I knew she was in pursuit of the truth, her truth, it never occurred to me that she was egotistical enough to disregard everything I'd said and delve right into Egon's life, seize on our absence as a chance to invade Wandsbek and take Egon off for evening instruction— for tea. For tea, Hamburg's eternal bloody British tea. But that's what she did. I learnt it later; Mutti never mentioned anything on the phone to Karlsruhe, during the week—she must have been ashamed of her capitulation to the Dod. I couldn't blame her. No-one could resist the Dod in full Blitzkrieg. Planting ideas in the boy's head, over tea and cake: do it. My sweet little delinquent, do it.

The presence of other travellers in our compartment limited what we could say to each other, Karin and I, though we stood in an isolated part of the corridor for several hours, watching Germany go by again and saying less and less about Egon. Her frown was back, only now it wasn't the piano frown but something less furious, the gentle frown of someone trying to recall an obstinately vanished word.

For my part Egon's wonderful piece of madness (and it was wonderful, no matter what the danger to him or the reproach to me) somehow broke my long refusal to think about Wilf. I'd come close to losing Egon forever, and was having to face how much I'd pushed him away, towards the brink. I'd pushed Wilf away too, long before Spain, and even though he was an infant, blameless . . . *blameless!*—as if anyone could achieve blamelessness on his own: blaming was what others did to you. He was my son, I knew that, but he was born in the shadow of Molly's affair with Denis. It left the feeling that I'd sired the child Molly wanted from Denis. And I could never say that, she'd have denied it fiercely. My feeling, then; perhaps not hers at all. And it seemed so poor an excuse for not having loved one's own child. He *was* mine, and Molly had stayed with me, not with mad Denis. But that was just it: what if Denis hadn't gone round the bend again? Had his affair with Molly been the cause of his relapse, and I the beneficiary? Old, discarded griefs that had once gnawed away at me daily. It was puzzling to find them still alive, these rat-memories, deep under the floorboards. And overwhelmingly sad to come upon them now, when it was Egon who needed me, when Wilf (God willing) thought I was dead. He'd have turned eight this summer. Last week of June. Almost to my relief I found I couldn't remember the exact date.

Karin too seemed shaken and preoccupied as if—this was an ignoble thought but I couldn't get round it—Egon had broken into her Karlsruhe reveries with the very act of defiance that had been denied her. He'd beaten her to the draw again. But one way or another we'd all ended up in the mud. This became palpable, like a slap in the face almost, as we got off the train at the Hauptbahnhof and saw the late edition headlines on the news stalls.

Das Fliegende Wolfskind! chortled one—The Flying Wolfcub! *Gräfchen Tarzan* . . . little Count Tarzan swinging through the air. There was a front-page sketch of him in the Friedrichswald, jumping from one branch to another with pretty blond locks aflutter and a Focke-Wulf hovering in the sky above. "Twelve-year-old Count Egon von Lützow-Brüel," the story began—how they loved his title!—"couldn't wait till his eighteenth birthday to take flying lessons and recapture the freedom of his extraordinary childhood. . . ."

We too were celebrities, it seemed, though we didn't rate sketches, and they'd turned up no photographs. "Reinhard Sacher, the Count's mysterious guardian . . ." I read on, quailing. Would Dornford Yates have stooped to this? It was pure Dumas. Mysterious guardian! And even the demonic Ellis, my beloved Yates villain, had redeeming features compared to Sacher, "a well-known figure on the Reeperbahn . . . 'very much attached to the child,' "—some drunken Kiez-parasite had volunteered this, making me sound even more like a notorious pervert—"the origins of whose relationship to Count Egon," yes, here it came, "no-one seems to know, or dares to say." A brief interview followed with a purported Lützow relative in Saarbrücken who declared himself willing and eager to save the child from the Reeperbahn and restore him to the bosom of the aristocracy. Where in time, no doubt, he could fly his very own plane. The Poseners were given a passing mention, but also as frustrated saviour-types, hanging around and rescuing Egon from the gutter whenever I passed out and left him there.

I even found reporters at my door in Altona though they parted to let me through, seeing the look on my face. At the Haupt-bahnhof I'd put Karin in a taxi to Wandsbek with strict instructions to stay there. A change of clothes and a telephone to find out where Egon was: they were what I needed. Among the letters I waded through inside the door, a week's mail, I saw a telegram with my name on it. I stared down at it for a moment, puzzled.

Then I realized what was odd about it. My name. Richard Thurgo, 11 Wolperstrasse, Altona, Hamburg.

I picked it up, tore gently at it, but my fingers wouldn't obey. Finally I got it open. It was in English, a language I wasn't used to reading, and for a moment not a word of it made sense.

"Mother dying wants to see you Alec."

Sitting on a British train again, I felt as if I were in some intense but unidentifiable danger. I was about to be exposed. It was absurd. Exposed as a German? Hardly as a Briton, there was nothing to expose, I had a British passport thanks to

Cheerybye; in a false name but perfectly valid. Saunders was my travelling name, Denis Saunders. Walters had chosen it without telling me. I enjoyed the irony of being a Denis, and on my way to Cornwall again. Perhaps it was Egon's presence, sitting opposite me and studying the pictures in a book on British aircraft, that was making me skittish. But he too had a British passport, in his own name. We both had a right to be here on this train, the train to Padstow that I knew so well that I could turn the pages of the journey before I reached them, anticipating each new vista.

This is how ghosts feel, I thought, they know the place, it's theirs and they can pass through walls, go where they like unless somebody comes and frightens them back into limbo. Molly could come walking down this train. But she wouldn't. (Or rather, I wasn't really afraid she would—I doubted if she'd recognize me beneath my springy black beard; it rose high on my cheeks, covered my mouth and chin, almost hiding my lips and their freight of bad teeth altogether. She'd walk right past me, gazing down the compartment, and be gone. The reproachful eyes I kept seeing in my mind were quite different: they were old Ludolf's. I entrusted the boy to you, they said. What are you doing with him?) No, Molly wouldn't be on this train unless today was the day of the funeral, and Alec had invited her. Even for Alec that would be in excessively bad taste, given the chance that I'd show up too. Mother and Molly had scarcely had a word to say to each other. For that matter, neither had Mother and I. I didn't want to think about that now. She might be still alive, fully recovered and furious at suggestions that she'd been anywhere near death. Come to think of it she might not have been dying at all, or even ill; "Mother dying"—Alec's idea of a joke, perhaps, a way to lure me back to Britain. How on earth did he know my Altona address? Cheerybye was my bet, even though he denied it.

The telegram, all seven words of it, was my only source of information. Mother had no phone, she'd had it disconnected when the war began, as a kind of protest; I'd tried to contact Alec at the House of Commons, but he was "away," I was told. Because of his mother's illness? "I've no idea, sir. Try the constituency Party down in Cornwall." The girl I spoke to there didn't know either. Was it possible for a Tory M.P. to vanish without trace? I could have phoned Molly, I suppose. I almost did, several times.

Cheerybye wanted me out of the country, fast. He couldn't

have cared less about Egon. But I insisted: two passports or none. Philby had promised these, I lied. My sense of urgency on Egon's behalf had nothing to do with the police or Egon's theft of the aeroplane—Gräfchen Tarzan was now the country's darling, and even a hint of official punishment would have brought a public outcry. No harm had been done, the Focke Wulf was intact, a few cabbages were squashed but that was the total damage. A newspaper had opened a fund to pay for flying lessons as soon as Egon was of age, and money was pouring in. No, the problem was the Lützow relatives. Not just the one found and interviewed by the *Morgenblatt* on the day of the incident, but previously unheard-of Lützows and Brüels (others too, a whole tribe of rich and related Blankenburgs) who popped up to claim Egon from all parts of Germany. They were baying for blood, competing to adopt the boy; whoever got him, the public would be on their side. After all, what was Reinhard Sacher but a sleazy figure who'd stolen him from East Germany? Much as, it was suggested, the Arabs were believed to spirit away Germany maidens to their harems. The fact that as Richard Thurgo I was legitimately the boy's uncle, but couldn't say so— this infuriated me. Should I abandon up the role I'd cultivated so carefully, these past years, risk my future on the Kiez, in order to keep Egon? It had never occurred to me that one day I'd have to choose between them. How would I live with myself if I sacrificed him—yet more of myself, of my past, another living child—to preserve my incognito? Would there be enough of me left that was worth preserving, under *any* name? Thankfully Cheerybye took the choice firmly out of my hands. His anxiety to smuggle me out of the country was flattering, at first. Thinking about it, I realized he wasn't anxious because I was so important to him, or because a minor informant unmasking himself would cause a scandal. It wouldn't. I was small fry. But what I knew about Cheerybye's business activities: that was the juicy stuff. That was my real capital. What wouldn't the newspapers pay to hear about a British Secret Serviceman investing in the Reeperbahn? Cheerybye could guess as well as I could, and he wasn't going to risk his career, be disgraced and drummed out—all as a consequence of a twelve-year-old's lunatic prank.

I was in the box seat after all. When he saw that I was serious about not leaving without Egon, Walters got together with his German counterparts, pointing out that although technically Egon's status was a German matter the boy's mother was British, and that there were at least as many British relatives—true if you counted up the Trimbles—with a claim to him. God knows what he had to trade, or threaten to reveal, to get his way, but in a day or two it was announced that the British had won the informal custody battle, and Walters even managed to leak the name of an imaginary Lord Trimble to impress those Germans still in thrall to the Coronation. There were plenty of them, thankfully; and the squabbling Lützow relatives were beginning to make an ungracious effect on newspaper readers. It made this British victory a little less galling. We left Hamburg early one morning on a military transport plane, much to Egon's delight, and without publicity—with any luck the press would soon find a new topic to replace us.

Mother dying wants to see you. She knew I was alive, then. Or did it mean she'd never noticed my death, hadn't been to my funeral? True, she hadn't bothered to show up for my wedding, but surely she could have made it to see me put to rest. Perhaps she had, and Alec had explained things to her since then. Wants to see you. She'd never wanted that before. It rang false.

I tried to interest myself in the English countryside as it passed in review before us. Had it changed? Did it feel home? Neither question seemed to have any meaning, I couldn't address them. Not even when a familiar landmark, like the white horse carved on a distant hillside, brought back earlier journeys. The hills and fields were obstinately different from their German equivalent, that much I could tell. Obstinate was the word; the Germans lived in a raised and contoured map (it might as well have Hügel inscribed on each hill, like the horse, and Wiese across each meadow) which corresponded gladly to their language. And what Englishman could be fool enough to think that of his countryside? The hills would laugh behind his back. Here and there I saw haystacks, a field already harvested, but the stubble looked murderous to me, and the countryside anything but compliant: the land itself, that is, not some conception behind it, not nature but the land, callous and prodigal and green. Impervious to thought; as Germany—that waxwork—begs for it . . . or as Ireland, for instance—as Ireland belongs to the sea, with Grandfather, who knew as much and threw away the plough to work the waves instead. As Hamburg is glass on muddy glass. It was no good, my mind kept on slipping back to where Karin might be at this moment. At the piano in Wandsbek (did she play secretly sometimes, when Mutti went out?), in the studio naked and abstracted among the apprentice painters (did they appreciate her moles? Her bumps and tumps? Struggle to reproduce them exactly?). Or lying on her bed staring blindly up—no, I didn't want to see that. Perhaps she was visiting my apartment as she'd promised to do; watering the plants. Or walking to Altona, down the Reeperbahn, wondering about me and my life there. It was the Onkel-Hugo-Grill I should be in now, right now, receiving petitioners, the cousin of a man who could sell me velvet plush, cheap, for the Grotto Azzurro, a recently disgraced waiter seeking a job there when it opened, with a recommendation from . . . it pained me to think of the workmen in the Grotto, unsupervised, drinking beer and exploring the bunker's tunnels when they should be painting, drilling. I saw them drilling by mistake through the wrong brick wall, into the cavern of the underground U-Bahn line—you could hear it down there, it was one of the objections to having a jazz cellar in the tunnels . . . but now, how wonderful it would be—yes—to have a window on the U-Bahn, curtained, draw the curtains back and you'd see the passing train, the startled faces reconciled to darkness and then suddenly seeing revellers, bar-girls, strippers in exotic outfits under fancy lights, through a window, right there beside them for an instant! What an attraction—U-Bahn revenues would soar! *Ja*, I saw a nipple today, I swear it, on the St. Pauli line . . .

After Exeter the London and South Western Railway nosed more hesitantly into Cornwall, up across the county to the northern coast, and the holy port of Padstow. I could have let in images of Denis running wild on Bodmin Moor, in his madness, but I didn't want Denis with me (now that I was my own Denis, Saunders Denis as German officialdom would have it) and I looked away. A surly taxi-driver drove us inland from the station, in a new black Rover. I couldn't restrain myself from asking, "How *is* Mrs. Thurgo . . . d'you know?"

"Who?" In all his years he'd never taken anyone to this address. I had to guide him through the lanes.

Preparing myself, I tried to picture mother's face on the pillow, wispy grey hairs, a lipless grizzled mouth, her stone jaw grown fatty and slack. Last words. "I'm a night-club owner in Germany, mother." And her response? I couldn't find it. "Which one are you? Alec, or the other one?"

No cars outside the cottage. I paid, watched the Rover turn laboriously and leave, then took our suitcases and led Egon to the door.

It was open. I called, but the little house was empty, the beds made, mother's bedroom tidy, spartan, everything in its place. Mother's clothes in the cupboard. Returning down the narrow stairs, I went to the kitchen. There was food in the pantry. Eggs, butter, the milk fresh. Fresh bread on the sideboard, and a pot of Gentleman's Relish. No other sign of habitation. It was as neat as a museum, but that was mother's way. Or had been mother's way. Even allowing for her monastic regimen there was a finality about the house, most of all in the sitting room where I found Egon studying the pictures. The hearth was cold and clean, and mother's glassware on the polished mahogany dresser looked like the skeletons of some exotic deep-sea creature, marine blowfish perhaps, the bowls more eerily translucent than ever, as if to say, "The breath has gone out of me."

I found nothing discomfiting about the empty house. I wanted to sleep, to doze here on the lumpy horsehair sofa. Penitentially lumpy, as if daring you to stay on it, but for once I didn't care. I felt at peace, soothed. No-one would come. Egon and I would stay a few days, I'd cook our meals and we'd walk out onto the broad plain of fields that gave no indication of the cliffs further off, the sharp drop to the sea. To be so close to the ocean and not to see it, only smell it—Mother could have found a cottage with a view of the Atlantic, but no, plumbing the waves had been her father's folly. The pictures on her sitting room walls supplied all the views she wanted, conventional prints of the Mountains of Mourne and other Irish beauty spots. Egon reviewed them in turn, like a critic at a gallery. He was happy too—we were travelling again, he and I, exploring, and we spoke as little as we had on our long walk back from Mecklenburg.

We'd been there a short while, perhaps no more than an hour or so, when a car drew up outside and we both went to the window to look. Alec emerged from a sumptuous machine whose make I didn't recognize, and glanced up calmly—same old Alec—as if we were just what he expected to see staring out at him, a bearded monstrosity and a boy with his unformed nose pressed against the windowpane. "Mein Bruder Alec," I murmured to him, as Alec entered and came to the sitting room doorway, resplendent in a tailored dark-blue suit, a natty club tie. "Onkel Richards Bruder."

"Where've you been, Ratty?"

"Is she dead?"

"In the ground three days. Where've you been? I wired you Tuesday of last week."

I nodded. The telegram had sat there in the hallway while I was in Karlsruhe on a wild goose chase.

Alec's gaze had moved on. "This is Egon," he said, feigning polite curiosity and no more. But I knew him too well, the sentimental English soul under the brusqueness.

"Maggie's son."

Alec extended a hand. "Pleased to meet you." Egon came forward, took the hand in silence and then, to Alec's alarm, gave a small stiff bow as instructed by Mutti. "Does he speak any English?"

"Not a word."

"Good. Then we can talk."

"Yes," I said, unaccountably upset. I couldn't tell whether this was because of missing mother's death, or her funeral—both perhaps, we'd have had nothing to say to each other but at least I'd have had that to mourn, and an occasion to mourn it—or because of Alec's words. We had to talk, of course. Yes, that was what I dreaded.

"Hungry?" said Alec, and patted his stomach in enquiring sign language, for Egon's benefit. It was tea-time, but we'd bought sandwiches and ginger beer at Waterloo, and fed along the way. Alec glanced at me. "Look as though you're going to cry, Ratty. If you'd rather not to do it before the boy . . . want to take a walk? I wouldn't mind stretching my legs."

"Yes all right. *Wir gehen spazieren, Egonchen*," I explained, *"willst mit?"*

He gave a faint shrug at the offer to join us. I knew fields and lanes held little attraction for him now, he'd become an indoor boy with a vengeance—taking his revenge on the woods (this was how I understood it) by ignoring them. Or his revenge on me. I told him we'd be back soon and he nodded calmly enough. What if he ran away? Absurd, I hadn't had that fear in years; put it aside, I thought, along with all this guilty stuff about the boy's revenge. I reminded myself that I had to learn to let go of him. Might as well start now.

"Trying to look like a tramp, are you?" Alec glanced at me as we walked away from the cottage, onto the road. I glanced down. My clothes didn't seem too bad—my one dark suit, admittedly shabby compared to his. He grinned, jutting his lower jaw at me. "No-one told me about the beard."

"Who gave you my address?"

Alec stroked his chin for a moment, without answering.

"How did you find out where I was?"

"Never lost you, old boy."

"How d'you mean?"

"Plenty of time to talk about that. How's tricks on the Reeperbahn?"

"Fine. How are the Commons?" Two could play at this game; why did Alec always drive me into the same old corner? I looked at him as we walked between the hedges, still high but with a gathering September leanness, brittleness. Alec looked ruddier, as if cut from a darker wood than I remembered, and his neck had surely thickened. Drink, I thought, and then, my God he's nearly fifty. Fifty next year. He knew I was studying him.

"London's not what it was. That's why I like coming down here. I remember when I first moved up there, I was living in Camden Town—Regent's Park I used to say," he chuckled, "living in Regent's Park, and there were days when I could walk to my tailor's and back without seeing a car. That's a thought, isn't it." Then after a moment, "Mother died pretty peacefully. If you're interested. She phoned me from the Dog one night, said she was on the way out."

"Phoned you from where?"

"The Dog and Admiral. The pub—don't you remember? No, I suppose you never did spend much time down here. Yes, she phoned me up, it was quite late, must have been closing time but she sounded stone cold sober. Said she was on the way out— those were her words. I knew what she meant. Didn't ask me to come, but I did. She'd already put herself to bed, wouldn't eat. I sat with her but she didn't want to talk much, just played with her rosary beads."

"Praying?"

"I suppose you'd call it praying. Saying the words. Is that all you have to do?"

I was trying to picture it, the two of them in the silent cottage.

"She didn't put much feeling into it. Just taking out insurance, I suppose. Strange old bird, our mother," Alec said, and paused. "D'you know who she left the house to?"

"No."

"Guess."

"I hadn't thought about it," I said truthfully.

"Some fucking Irishman," said Alec. "Some stupid Mick I've never even heard of, no-one knows who the hell he is. Back in the ould country," he mimicked crudely, continuing to insult his own Irish blood, "some rural idiot she loved once, probably."

"Why d'you say that?"

"I mean, he could be *anybody*. Joseph Michael Donovan, that's all it says—'from Kerry.' Perhaps," at last he cracked a smile, "that's why she always said, 'Joseph Michael and all the saints . . .' when she was out of patience. There must be forty Joseph Michael Donovans in Kerry, if he's still there. What are you laughing at?"

Alec on a wild goose chase of his own, in the West of Ireland . . . it made me feel better about Karlsruhe.

"I'm not going there," he said firmly. "The lawyers can do it. Put up advertisements all over Ireland, in the newspapers and so on, and thin out the impostors. Then I'll interview the final candidates. Can you believe it? Damn it, I was hoping for half shares at least. Bloody nice holiday cottage."

"I'm sorry, Alec."

He brooded for a bit, and walked on.

"But she did want to see me," I said after a time, "when she was dying?"

"What?"

"Your telegram. Mother dying wants to see you."

"Oh yes," he said vaguely. "She was a bit loopy towards the end but she knew there was supposed to be two of us."

It was an opening. I could take it now—or put it off a while longer—God how I loved walking along a country lane with my irascible brother, a packed, solid being the colour of cured ham. My cigar-store Red Indian. He still walked with military pride and bearing, even more so, in a way, since he'd learnt to disguise the limp almost completely; the "Burma limp" he'd called it proudly once, after its combat origins. Major Lecky Thurgo. Did they still call themselves by rank, the old warriors, or had the civilian years made that a joke? There were more important things to ask, and I was letting myself off the hook. Ask now; it's got to come out sometime.

"Didn't mother think I was already dead?"

"Nope."

"But when I disappeared, and . . ." I took a deep breath. "A chap called Philby told me there was a burial."

"There was, yes. You were buried," said Alec levelly.

"Philby told me he'd been in touch with you. But this was months later. When did you tell Mother I was alive?"

"Never told her you were dead, no need to. I knew you were alive from the beginning."

"How?"

"It's a long story, Ratty. But I suppose you may as well hear it now." He studied his gleaming toe-caps as we walked; they were acquiring specks of mud. "Look—you know old Tom Thurgo and I were in business before the war . . ."

"Yes."

"Well, we were still in touch in '48, right up to his death. I know I said we weren't, told you we'd fallen out, but I had to keep all that stuff dark. In my position."

"What stuff d'you mean?"

"Well . . . arms to North Africa. Gingering up the Bedouin. Wouldn't have looked good for an M.P. to be tied in with an old villain like Tom."

"Wasn't he far enough to the Right for you, then?" It was a stupid crack—if she were here, I thought, it was what Molly would have said; and I got comprehensively ignored for it. "Tied in with what, exactly?" I asked. "Never mind the Bedouin. You mean you were helping him smuggle Nazis out of Germany?"

"Are you mad?" Alec glared at me now. "Anyway, he was doing that for love, the old fool, not money. No, he was buying up war matériel like nobody's business. Let's say I hadn't completely severed my connection there."

"So?"

"Well, I also knew what he was up to on the Nazi front. I was in daily contact with Estrella."

"You knew about Bormann?"

Alec smiled. "Kim says you killed him. Took against the fellow, did you? Or was it panic?"

"Panic," I said.

Alec nodded, satisfied; only one war hero in this family. "I knew about the jeep, you see. I guessed you'd done a bunk with the money."

"The counterfeit money."

He seemed genuinely puzzled at this.

"Counterfeit? I'd written it off as your stake."

"How d'you mean my stake?"

"In the business. Tom should've cut you in, he really should."

"Well, it was counterfeit, all of it."

"Dear oh dear. Are you sure?"

"According to your friend Kim."

"The hell you say. I'd better check my deposit box then, hadn't I. I hope Tom wasn't unloading the fake stuff on everyone." Alec glanced at me, inspecting my smile. "Then again . . ." he walked on, "I wonder why Kim didn't tell me. He confiscated it from you, he said."

"To pay my hotel bill."

"Hmm," said Alec. "Well, everyone's entitled to his racket."

"Is that why you didn't tell on me?"

"How d'you mean?"

"You thought this was my racket, running off with the money?"

He gave me a queer look.

"I suppose so."

"Did you tell Molly?"

"What, that you were alive?" He hesitated. "Should I have?"

"No, that was down to me."

"That's what *I* thought. And somehow I couldn't bring myself to tell Mother you were dead, when you weren't. I don't know why."

"Because you loved her," I said.

Alec shrugged. "Thought I was going to inherit the bloody house in those days, didn't I."

"Come on, that's not it. With me supposedly out of the way you'd have stood a better chance. You loved her, Alec."

But he wouldn't admit it.

"What I mean is," he said, "she didn't pay attention to you when you were alive, so I don't know why I thought she'd be upset. Anyway—I thought, what the hell, if she talks to Molly and refers to you among the living, asks where you are and so forth . . . I mean, Molly knew she was bats anyway. She'd write it off as senility." A quick glance, then, "Know how old she was?"

"Eighty?"

"That would make her forty-five when she had you, wouldn't it? That's more or less what I thought too. She was eighty-four, Ratty. I found her birth certificate. Eighty-four. Means she was forty-*nine* when she had you, old bird. Same age I am now. You don't look much surprised . . . what I'm trying to say is, it makes a difference. Forty-nine—I mean, you can see why she wouldn't want to raise a kid at that age."

I nodded.

"Hell of a business, after all. Think what a handful I'd been. She wasn't to know you'd be the dreamy type."

I could see he was disappointed that I wasn't taking more comfort from his words; I appreciated the effort, but if he expected me to be touched by Mother's plight . . . well, that was just too bad. "What you said earlier, about Mother and Molly talking. Did that happen? Did they talk much?"

Alec shook his head. "Never, to my knowledge."

"You're in touch with Molly, then?"

"Well, that's the thing, Ratty, I'm not, I'm afraid. Haven't done much for the boy. Young Wilf. Molly won't let me." His face had gone a darker shade of ham. "In some idiotic way I think she blames me for your disappearance."

"You mean my death."

"Of course. Your death."

"She does think I'm dead?"

"Absolutely. But she knew Tom was up to no good, and when she found out there wasn't much of a legacy waiting in Spain, she blamed me somehow for sending you out there into a tight spot of some kind. She doesn't know what sort of spot, of course. All the same, why take it out on me? It was *you* Tom named in his will."

"Only because you already had the business, if I understood you right, just now," I said. When Alec said nothing, I continued, "And you did send me out there into a tight spot." (Damn you, Mansel!)—I must stop using Alec's language, I thought; five years speaking and thinking in German and I seem to have forgotten how to be myself in English. "You knew about it, and you even paid for my journey, remember?"

"So I did. Going to pay me back?" he grinned. "Tell you what, let's call it quits. I did send you out there—because *I* couldn't go. But I didn't think you'd start killing people right and left. That came as a surprise, Ratty. And I've covered for you since then. Seems to me you've got a pretty good deal out of it all." Alec studied me for a while. "Must be enjoying life among the Krauts, or you'd have come back, what?" When I said nothing he returned to the earlier topic of Molly and Wilf. It still seemed to be weighing on him. "Anyway, I send him birthday presents, Christmas presents, that sort of thing. Never so much as a thank-you-kindly."

"He's only eight, Alec."

"Molly could write, couldn't she? Bloody uncivil, your wife."

"She hasn't married again?"

Alec snorted.

"Is that so ridiculous?"

"You haven't seen her lately."

"How d'you mean? I thought you hadn't either."

"Not for a year or two, no. But unless she's lost weight. . . ."

She was never slim, but God she's a tub of lard now. Take a gorilla to get his arms round her.''

I'd heard enough of this. I didn't want to hear myself springing guiltily to Molly's defence.

"You knew about Egon, too," I said.

"Oh God yes. Maggie's dead, is she?''

I nodded.

He began to walk faster and I lengthened stride to keep up with him; then he slowed and finally stopped. "Think I've had enough of this,'' he said, and for a moment I saw him wrestling with the stammer that had come with the "Burma limp,'' and which he seemed to have mastered completely. He had; it came out cleanly when it came: "Bloody boring stretch of country-side. Why the hell d'you bring the boy anyway?'' When I hesitated Alec gave me a canny look. "Getting too much for you, is he? Cramping your style?''

We set out on the return journey. Was this the moment? I wasn't ready. I said, "Hadn't you heard? He made a name for himself last week.'' And I told Alec about Egon's recent adventure. To my relief, he was impressed.

"Wants to fly, does he?'' Alec mused. "Wasn't old *Pay*-ter in the Luftwaffe? Without ever getting airborne?''

"I don't think Egon knows that. Or how his father died.''

"You haven't told him?''

"Not the details. Just . . .'' my English foundered for a moment, "a hero's death.''

"Some bloody hero. That lot couldn't have killed Hitler if they'd had a Maxim trained on him at ten paces.''

I held my tongue. "You mean Egon's exploits didn't get into the papers here? He made headlines in Germany.''

"Did he? Well, that's Germany for you.''

I was glad it hadn't reached a British public, and that Molly wouldn't have read about it. Time to take the plunge, Reinhard. "I had to bring him here. Peter's relatives were clamouring to adopt him.''

"Well, good Lord—best thing for him, isn't it? Count yourself lucky. You don't want him cluttering your life.'' Alec saw my expression. "Thought that's what you were trying to get away from when you gave Molly the heave-ho.''

"Not exactly.''

"What, then? What *were* you up to?''

It was the wrong moment to tell him I'd been searching for Maggie. I said nothing, and at that moment the little house came back into view, half a mile further on. Lights on, downstairs. I realized it was getting dark.

"Michael Joseph bloody Donovan," he muttered, gazing at the distant cottage. "D'you think Mother was carrying on with somebody behind our back all these years?"

A steady wisp of smoke rose from the cottage chimney. Mutti, I recalled, had taught Egon how to light a fire, and at that moment I felt absurdly touched that he hadn't been too shy to take possession of the house and hearth in this way, Mother's cold, clean house and hearth. Alec saw it too, the column of smoke.

"Are we on fire?" he said, unalarmed.

"No, he knows what he's doing," I said.

"What the hell is the matter with you? Now you *are* bloody crying."

I managed a chuckle, which came out more like a croak. "The boy stood on the burning deck," I said, and paused, trying to think. "I can't remember the rest." Alec was staring at me in earnest now. "Alec," I said. "He *is* Maggie's son."

It must have been in my voice—or perhaps Alec had suspected what I'd come for all along and he'd hoped to make me back down . . . all that stuff about raising a kid at forty-nine—*his* age—he wasn't trying to comfort me at all, he was trying to tell me there was no way he'd take on a child; but he gave a groan as if he suddenly understood what I was getting at.

"Oh Christ," Alec said.

"I've got a life in Hamburg. If he comes back with me, we'll lose him."

"*We?* I've never seen the bloody child before." He'd stopped. "Ratty, for Christ's sake!"

We stared at each other; it was becoming hard to read a face, in this light.

"Let the Krauts have him," he said, more quietly now. "They obviously want him, from what you're telling me."

I had a sudden thought: "You're party spokesman for German affairs, aren't you?"

"Sort of," Alec nodded. "When Winston's not breathing down my neck. How d'you know that? Still take the *Times*, do you, over there?"

"Philby told me. What I mean is—wouldn't it look rather good, if you adopted a German orphan . . . I mean—English mother, hero father, murdered by Hitler . . ."

If Alec was taking any of this in, his answering tone didn't show it. "If I did *what*?" And in disbelief, "You're suggesting I *adopt* the bugger?"

"I'm saying it wouldn't do you any harm, would it, as a public figure—"

"What are you *talking* about, Ratty? You're telling me you've brought me over a German kid to advance my career? You must be mad. I couldn't look after him, even if I wanted to. Where would I find the time?"

"He's old enough to go to boarding school," I pleaded. "He's bright, he'll learn English in a matter of weeks—"

"And what about the bloody holidays?"

"You send him to me. The fuss about the stolen plane will have died down, no-one need know."

Alec studied me, mouth open in mock bewilderment. "You come back here, you say, hello, I'm having a ripping time, just hold this twelve-year-old, d'you mind? While I go back and whoop it up—"

"That's not the reason—"

"You think you can saddle me with some Kraut kid—"

"Alec . . ."

"No. No. You must be bonkers. Just because Mother did it to *you*. I'm not old O'Malley, with a housekeeper and acres of ground—an old codger with nothing to do all day but dream. You and your bloody daydreams, both of you! I'm a busy man with a flat in Whitehall the size of a broom cupboard."

"Buy somewhere bigger."

"No."

But a crack had opened in Alec's defences, I thought. Didn't we both sense it—that in mentioning Fold Farm he'd made a tactical mistake? What was the right move now . . . to go for the jugular? After all these years!

"You owe me, Alec. For Fold."

"Balls."

"Alec, I've never complained, you know that."

"Balls."

"You mean I *have* complained?"

"Every time you look at me you're forgiving me for what you think I did. Complained? I wish you bloody had! You could have asked for your share at the time, you ass."

"At the time you said there wasn't anything to share. Nothing. All gone up in flames."

"What about the insurance, then?"

I stared at him. Did he really not remember? "You said there *was* no insurance!"

"Did I? Perhaps there wasn't." He looked genuinely uneasy, and confused. Then a smile began to tug at him. "*I* don't know . . . was that really what I said? And you swallowed it? Bloody fool."

"I didn't swallow it. I loved you."

"Don't start that, Ratty." The smile had gone. "I'm not taking the bloody child and that's final."

"Maggie's child."

"You keep saying that." He was fierce now. I'd infuriated him with my talk of love; yes, that was the real tactical error here, I saw it too late. "You still think I worshipped that pretentious cunt."

I was more startled by his language than anything else, but perhaps he mistook my expression for hurt. It seemed to incite him.

"*You* loved her," he bellowed in the empty, darkening lane. "*You* worshipped her. Raise her fucking German fuck-fruit if you want to. Don't tell me what I owe you and what I don't."

We marched back to the cottage in silence—I had to march, to keep up with him.

That night, after a subdued and frugal meal in Mother's own tradition, I climbed the stairs with a heavy heart, thinking of times when Alec had told raucous stories in the little sitting room, scandalizing Mother; when, earlier, he'd sung us bawdy songs to the guitar, and we'd both clattered drunkenly up these stairs. This place was Alec to me, I realized, not Mother, who had refused to give herself to it, to infuse it with her smell or even her imagination. She'd kept that for God and her glassware. While I'd stayed here I lived for Alec's visits.

Before we headed for bed I'd cornered him in the kitchen.

"Alec, I'm not staying here with Egon. I don't want to live in England."

"That's up to you."

"If I take him back, he'll end up in Saarbrücken or some godforsaken place. D'you think that's what Maggie would have wanted?"

"Why not? You seem to forget she married a Kraut." He held my gaze for a while. "I thought you liked the Krauts. Ratty, I've told you my position. Germany's the best place for him. I mean, he looks German to me. Doesn't he to you?"

Egon was asleep on the horsehair sofa in the sitting room. I lifted him up—he was still small, light for his age—and carried him to the back bedroom, not really a bedroom but the lean-to, with a small bed in it, that had served as Mother's studio. There was no unfinished, half-engraved glass on the workbench. Not even Death could disrupt Mother's schedules, she knew him well and saw him coming, knew how long to allow for him and left everything tidy, finished. I did want something of hers, I decided, a goblet, something with one of her landscapes incised on it (I could see no punchbowls, alas, here or on the dresser).

I tucked Egon into the bed. Yes, he did look German, Alec was right, it was there in the strong sandy lashes perhaps, almost spiky, closed now over the indeterminate-coloured eyes. They bulged a little in sleep. Formless nose, slippery Maggie-mouth, lank hair. I kissed his head, feeling it damp and slightly sweaty against my lips, with a sickly smell.

That night I wanted so much to dream about Mother, I wanted to inhabit the house as hers, her house, more fully in sleep than I'd been able to during the day. Instead I dreamt about Germany, a lurid dream in which I felt besieged by Lützow relatives out to kidnap Egon (though neither they nor Egon made an appearance in the dream), I'd left the boy on the Reeperbahn in good hands but now I couldn't remember with whom and I was rushing from bar to bar in an agony of shame and anxiety, trying to find him. In the Onkel-Hugo-Grill old Ludolf rose to greet me from my usual table, and after an instant of fear—had he come to accuse me? Could I lie, say I knew where Egon was?—I knew he'd come to save me. "You don't have to worry any more." I'm not sure that he spoke the words but his presence conveyed it like a complete sentence in my head. "You can keep Egon, Herr Thurgo. He's counterfeit. He isn't Count von Lützow-Brüel, he's my heir, that's all. Mine." Ludolf's heir . . . in the dream his meaning was unmistakable: Egon was my son by Herta—I felt elated, terrified too, and woke with precisely the exposed feeling I'd had in the train to Padstow the previous day.

Descending the stairs to the kitchen in a dressing-gown bought for me by Karin on the Mönckebergstrasse, I found Alec fully dressed, fresh shirt, tie knotted, sipping coffee. His cheeks were flushed, the skin beneath his eyes so dark it had almost an olive colour.

"Sit down," he said, headmasterly. "You don't look as though you slept any better than I did."

I sat.

"Tell me if I misunderstood you yesterday," he said. "You said you'd take the boy during the holidays, is that right?"

"Reeperbahn . . . Sankt Pauli." Zan-*pow*li. . . .
More and more these days I find myself still sitting on the train after my station has gone past. I hear the voice announce "Zanpowli," "Some-*body*," and I don't move. Travelling on the S-Bahn puts me in a trance. Partly it's the soothing way the train sways on its elevated cradle, the rocking-horse ride, partly the pleasure of looking down at the streets like a sea-bird drifting in from the Elbe, amused by landlubbers.

The train creaks to a halt, the doors open but I stay in my seat as though dozing through the rattle of an alarm clock, savouring its last convulsive stutters—willing it to die. Pretending this isn't where I get off makes me feel I'm hiding a delicious secret from my fellow-travellers: playing truant and nobody knows. The doors close again, we slide forwards, and my stomach tightens as I look out of the window. We're over water. The roller-coaster dive is coming up. Below us the green water of the Fleet, a jolt of brakes shudders along the train from one compartment to the next and then we're hurtling down towards the water at the foot of the Town Hall. At the last moment a hole appears beneath its Western façade and the carriages plunge into it like a troupe of frantic rats, nose to tail. At the crowded Hauptbahnhof the ride comes to an end. *Endstation.* I resent this. In Germany everything is where and how it is for a good German reason, but I've always wondered about Hamburg's overground railway, with its profusion of overlapping arms like a Hindu deity embracing itself. The arms emanate from the central torso of the Hauptbahnhof, the city's main terminus. This is logical enough. But what's missing, among all these intertwining limbs, is a loop line: simple, practical, efficient. German. Then it came to me—a loop line would enable people like me to travel round for the sheer hell of it, without having to pay for the distance they covered. A good practical Hamburg reason for not having a loop line. Of course you can still prolong your journey at no extra cost, by going back and forth along the same line, or by switching lines in a random way. But what German would do this?

Twenty years a German and I end up complaining that they aren't Irish enough! Still—what did I expect? That every German would be a Peter von Lützow? That Mutti wouldn't turn Egon into a good little Prussian and take him away from me, yes, long before the Focke-Wulf rebellion that finally brought all the contradictions to light and put the Channel between us? Or that sheer persistence would make a German of me?

Life here without Egon wasn't as strange, in the end, as I'd feared. I ceased to view Hamburg through his eyes, but that had been tailing off since he started school and we no longer had our morning walks to Wandsbek, exploring back street jungle paths, crossing the greasy green water of the canals. Karin and Mutti took it harder than I did. It didn't help that for a while they received crank calls at the apartment, distressingly polite phone calls from women who thought the Poseners were hiding Egon, and who wanted to adopt him or simply take him out to tea. On one occasion Mutti had been reduced to tears, Karin said. But they both knew we'd have lost Egon to the Lützows if he'd stayed, and now they could at least look forward to the promised holidays. Mutti consoled herself that her years of concentrated instruction would leave Prussian metal in his soul, rust-free deposits to withstand foreign ways. She'd have been happier to consign him to a British education, I think, if it wasn't for the nearest example of its effect: me. Fond as she was of me, I displayed a sloppy, anarchic quality (at least where parental and domestic discipline were concerned) that she'd never thought possible in a Briton. If there were more like me at home, Egon's manners would soon need a refresher course.

As for Karin, I—as I'd hoped—was her consolation. We began living together shortly after my return to Hamburg. Mutti had mixed feeling about this. "Living together" was all the rage now, she understood that. Its scandalous overtones were gone. But it still violated her code. On the other hand she knew I was devoted to Karin, I'd proved it over five years. She knew, too, that Karin badly needed to leave home. Even, if necessary, against her will. The Dod agreed (though now this was no recommendation in Mutti's eyes, which had been opened to the Dod's excesses in sponsoring delinquency). Karin never did leave home, in her heart, always referring to Wandsbek as *zu Hause*; and I invariably felt I was taking her home when we were heading east up the Wandsbeker Chaussee, not west into Altona. Still, it was a necessary stage, I told myself.

The Dod took Egon's departure hardest of all. She admitted no responsibility for it, hadn't encouraged him to steal the plane and take to the air, "only in his mind, Reinhard! In his mind!"— although from what I'd gathered when I questioned Egon, she'd failed to make the distinction as clear as she claimed. Unless he'd been using the Dod as an excuse; he was a knowing child.

The Dod had only known Egon briefly but she couldn't stop talking about him. Our lunches became Egon-lunches, we slurped him with the soup and ate him with the plat-du-jour, as if we hadn't devoured his fate already, between the two of us. But other subjects were more painful still. It was hard to talk about Karin. I'd taken consignment of her, in a sense, and I both resented the Dod's advice—I've heard this all before, was my high-handed attitude—and felt ashamed of taking it behind Karin's back. Was it right to preserve this sense of Karin as my ward at the very moment when we were becoming partners in life, equals? I still longed for guidance, that was the trouble—because it made me feel we were the Dod's puppets dancing in her experimental theatre of the soul, and I wanted living together to be our experiment, not hers.

So did the Dod, to be fair. "You don't challenge her enough! You are polite, you suffocate her! Be brave with her. Neurotics are strong, they stretch and bend like *Gummi*, and rarely snap." (That "rarely" didn't slip past unnoticed; was the Dod taking out a little insurance these days, like Mother with her rosary beads?) "She is stronger than you or I, Reinhard!" If this meant I was excused from the category of neurotics, it was flattering, so I didn't interrupt. "If she is silent and you feel like shouting, shout! If she is rigid, shake her. What is she, glass? She isn't glass."

I wasn't so sure about that. Alec had allowed me to take one of Mother's goblets—he was in an expansive mood once he'd broken through his resistance to Egon, "take the bloody lot, I hate 'em, take 'em all," he'd said, but I only wanted one—and Karin took it from its shelf almost every night to wonder at it and admire it. Drawn to it by some affinity; or was it by an attraction of opposites, if, as the Dod suggested, Karin were the *Gummi*-rubber thing that couldn't break? She turned it slowly (I'd done the same as a child), treating it like an unfolding landscape. Which it was, composed of bushes with birds in them so small they might be no more than the light falling on a minuscule facet in a certain way, and tiny stippled leaves on trees so tall there were no hills visible beyond them, no horizon.

Karin did seem happier in some respects, now she'd moved in with me. We'd crossed the sexual Rubicon at last. It was a landmark for me as much as for her, since taking her virginity confronted me directly with my Herta-memories for the first time since I'd returned from Mecklenburg. And I realized I'd been putting it off at least as fervently as Karin had. It wasn't the blood itself I was afraid of; without the smells of earth and leaf-mold and sweat born of fear, the blood was nothing, leaking decorously onto the towel placed on my bed for the purpose. What was it, then? Karin's gasps as I entered her alarmed and excited me. If I surrender to the full excitement, I thought, I shall do more damage than the Dod ever dreamed of—yes, that was the fear—but Karin was an eager lover, and soon I knew I had no need to restrain myself. On later occasions her gasps were the same, as though she too were recreating the moment of violation. Her touchstone as well as mine. She was happy to make love, and happy in it; it raised no terrors in her, much to my surprise, and seemed a privileged area in which the demons, far from rising like startled wasps, were appeased, or simply absent (how could this be? The Dod would know!). But was she happy for me, or for herself, when we made love? Her pleasure, continuous, reached no climax, though she insisted she couldn't imagine greater pleasure and didn't miss what she'd never known. Oh, there was so much to ask the Dod! With Karin I was in new territory again, so different from Ellie's efficient but abstracted exercise and Molly's jovial repertoire.

"Make love to me": it wasn't a Prussian order, no, more a dignified child's request. But what followed was orderly in a sense, reliable, uniform, as much for me in the renewed delight— ravishment was always a part of it—as for Karin, it seemed to me, in the safe protected plane she reached so soon and where she remained steadily, neither passive nor thrashing towards orgasm (as Molly had, threatening to tear me out at the root) but simply glorying in it.

"Why not?" exclaimed the Dod. "What do you want from her? Screams? Not everybody screams. I prefer silence myself. But I am *not*," she added thunderously—there were now, I was convinced of it, Tuesday regulars in the Four Seasons who booked the best seats just to hear the Dod—"unresponsive, my dear! *Ich schwelge!* I luxuriate!"

"I'm sure," I said hastily, trying to bring the cabaret under control. "But that isn't really what I was asking. I don't want her to scream, particularly. I'm very happy with our sex life. I'm just puzzled by the fact that hers is so . . ."

"So . . . what?"

I hesitated. "So undramatic," I said. "If sex is supposed to be so deeply significant—"

Ach! An airy wave of one enormous hand.

"Well isn't it? I thought that's what Freud said. He said it was important, didn't he?"

"Who said it wasn't important? Of course it is."

"Not just important—what I mean is . . ." lowering my voice as far as I dared, "how is it possible for a deeply disturbed person to have such an untroubled sex life?"

She looked at me tenderly. "Because the *child* was not disturbed, Reinhardchen. Vati August was pleased with his little girl. Later the bigger girl bored and disappointed him, then the trouble began. Now do you understand? You, your mother gave you away. *That* I call trouble. You shouldn't be surprised that your sexual life is thoroughly disturbed, violent, vengeful even. *Ja?*"

Was it vengeful? It was only the Herta business that had opened my eyes—belatedly—to my own violence. Now it had contaminated me, that was true. I was complaining that Karin was too happy. And I was still seeking occasional companionship—companionship! it was the impersonal in these encounters that I relished—on the Kiez, behind Karin's back, and the Dod's. Normal behaviour by Kiez standards, of course; and by other standards too, judging from the Reeperbahn's thriving afternoon trade. I even wondered whether the Dod might call it perfectly normal appetite, the physical equivalent of "horse sense," and chuckle, "Give me details!" as she did where other people's casual encounters were concerned. Or would she say, "No wonder Karin denies herself a climax! You hide from her, she hides from you. If you want to hurt her, Reinhard, hurt her to her face." That was the Dod I feared.

Our aborted, interrupted pursuit of Wackernagel had certainly left scars. The Dod likened it to an incomplete analysis, in miniature. Karin was now sleeping better, but since she took pills to do so it was hard to gauge the positive signs in this, if indeed there were any. The medication was the Dod's idea. "Let her sleep, poor girl," she said, echoing Mutti, and adding in her own vein, "by the way, what kind of lover are you, that she needs pills afterwards?" Wackernagel was unmentionable now, as though we had actually found him in Karlsruhe, or found he was dead. But he wasn't, he was just around a corner, waiting, just as Karin had once hoped to haunt the man herself. He'd not quite vanished; a half-buried corpse. (Corpses were on my mind during the months following Mother's death—"in the ground" three days . . . why did Alec have to use that phrase? I'd found myself morbidly picturing her decomposition, stage by stage.)

On my return I'd taken up the Fleischmann lead, tenuous as it was, and without telling Karin. I'd never told her about my interview at the Westphalian Insurance Company. I phoned the two Fleischmanns who lived in Mühlburg. One was a young married man; that left the other, and his phone rang and rang without answer. The breakthrough came when I phoned the insurance company again, gambling that the secretary wouldn't recognize my voice, and asked for Herr Fleischmann. They employed no Fleischmann, she replied. He'd left, then? No, they'd never had a Fleischmann on their books. A Fürstmann, yes; no Fleischmann. I still couldn't be certain, but this barefaced contradiction, taken with the way the girl had identified the Wackernagel photograph as Fleischmann until Herr Direktor Meise got in on the act, argued that the two were one and the same. But also that if his employers were now denying Fleischmann, he'd been warned and was long since gone, covering his tracks once more. Now the mystery was why he bothered to do so, if all he had to hide was the kind of bygone thuggery less liable to prosecution, these days, than persistent littering. Perhaps he just wanted a quiet life.

No point in telling Karin, I thought. It was no advance on our Karlsruhe journey, and would only aggravate its effects.

And I had my hands full on the Kiez. I'd left Vlad in charge of work on the Grotto Azzurro as a kind of thank-you for his loyal efforts in Karlsruhe, and a hint of further responsibilities to come, if he wanted them. (This didn't mean I'd lost sight of Wolli's message, as I understood it to relate to Vlad—"he's your creature now, punish him as and when you will"—far from it, there was time, as Wolli intended, to consider, judge, fondle the Damocles sword.) The place would need more than one bouncer, a squad perhaps, all built like ox. Vlad could be their overseer, hire and fire them, lounge at the bar or come and go as he pleased.

Approaching the Hamburger Berg entrance to the Grotto that autumn, I already saw it in my mind's eye as it would be, one day soon: over the wide, curved, stone doorway a series of semicircular zigzags in pale blue neon, each one a little darker than the one beneath, as if reflecting jagged wave-light off the dance floor below, in the Grotto. Around and among the zigzags, leaping silver neon dolphins. Did dolphins leap in grottoes? No matter, the customers would be our dolphins. Der Grotto Azzurro (it was grott-*a*, one of our Italian workmen explained patiently, but I wasn't going to be the one to correct Wolli) in blue—or gold?—over it all, in curvy neon handwriting. That would be enough (and quite expensive enough) to draw them in, the gullible, greedy dolphins. Foreign tourists were returning to Germany now. We'd give them everything—not only the Berliner-style decadence they'd heard about but a glimpse of the justly-punished Germany they'd hungered for: see the bunkers where your victims cowered as the bombs fell! Dance on their bones (by implication; it wouldn't do to say so)! I was determined, against all advice, to keep the old metal air-raid warning signs, and outline them in flashing red neon. Achtung! Bombing raid! No need to evoke the noises (though I'd toyed with the idea) on a soundtrack loop—the passing U-Bahn trains would simulate distant, muffled sounds of destruction. On the day of my return there were similar and gratifying sounds of builders at work, walls crumbling. I came down the steps, ducking to avoid the low white-tiled ceiling over the stairway. Below, there was ample headroom. Vlad was around, I was told, somewhere in the tunnels.

I stood, inhaling the place. Not even the demolition and paint-work smells could quite obliterate the musty bunker smells of old; bringing images of the sick and dying, so talkative in the darkness, bunker-philosophers to a man. Even during the years to come it was still there in the mornings when the Grotto was empty, that faint stink of fear, beneath the stale perfume and the fumes of drink, tobacco, and sweat, clinging to the draperies. I set off in search of Vlad, through the tunnels and the former dormitories. I had a plan for each of these, I saw it as a gradual development as revenues increased. First the Tanzkeller, with a bar, a dance-floor, room for a cabaret; adjoining this the offices and a little warren of private rooms (later dubbed *séparées*) where customers could entertain undisturbed. I'd nicknamed this area the Kasbah and had a Turk working on appropriate designs. Elsewhere I planned a proper grotto with a heated pool for favoured guests. Stalactites above, and underwater lighting. There was room for a recreation hall (Sportsaal), showers, a sauna, even, I speculated, an underground squash court—if the Germans could learn cricket, why not squash? To the north, at the furthest end from the rumbling U-Bahn, the Jazzkeller. Jazz fans would have to walk several hundred metres underneath the Reeperbahn to reach it, but as long as we brought in foreign bands they wouldn't complain, it was only German products the Germans disparaged. The Jazzkeller would pay. All we needed were enough bouncers to keep the tunnels free of tramps and lovers. Finally, at the south end of the old shelter-complex, where I was now headed, a cinema with late-night porno shorts (innocent thought! I'd no idea then how twenty-four-hour porno features would become our staple source of income). I found Vlad sitting on a heap of masonry, reading a newspaper—an old discarded wartime rag he'd found there—by a working light. Seeing me, he tossed it aside onto a pile of old clothes that seemed to date from the same period.

"One day we find body here," he said grimly, after we'd embraced.

"You don't like it in the tunnels?"

He raised his eyes to the curved ceiling. "I like best up there. Where I come from, you see rider coming so far away you have his dinner ready when he gets off horse." He'd often told me about the Steppes, its great sky and its tumbleweeds hurtling before the wind. It sounded dismal to me, but I envied the heartache in his voice—at least until the day I discovered that although he might have visited the Steppes he'd been raised in the back streets of Odessa, a long way from riders and tumbleweeds. Vlad began to report on building work in progress. He didn't ask me where I'd been or how it went. You didn't, on the Kiez, you waited to be told.

Once he'd completed his report, and we began a tour of inspection, Vlad added: "Women come looking for you." This I didn't mind. One of them was "blonde, big, ugly," he said approvingly. I nodded, it sounded like Marianne, a recent afternoon-encounter. To be discouraged, if she was growing attached. No more Marianne.

My real worry was a different kind of unscheduled, pestering visit. The Kölner-Jungs, the Bimbos and the Georgi-Boys, rival gangs on the Kiez, sent scouts to watch our progress with the Grotto, hinting that Wolli and I were getting too ambitious. "The longer the neck," we found chalked on a tunnel wall one morning, "the easier to chop off the head." *Kopp abzuhaun.* Deliberate misspelling—or maybe plain illiteracy. But clear enough. There was enough room down here below the Reeperbahn for everyone, was the message: share out the underground chambers, rent them even, so as to preserve the balance of power above ground, on the Kiez. From time to time I found figures scrawled on the old dormitory walls, bids for a monthly rent. Our rivals saw the bunker-world as a second, parallel empire, a basement milieu. So did we. It tickled me to think how many bars and strip joints we were walking under, Vlad and I, as we beat the Grotto bounds. It would be no more than a night's work to tunnel up into rival property. They wouldn't dare leave cash there overnight, not any more.

We were making them all nervous. Soon the Kölner-Jungs or Bimbos would infiltrate our workforce (if they hadn't already—the warning in chalk covered ten metres of wall, someone had taken time over it), and sabotage would begin in earnest.

It marked the start of the gang wars that made our nights so lively for the next five years, my happiest on the Reeperbahn. Everyone's happiest, I think. When people talk about the good old days, and the Kiez as if it were a vanished Eden, it's this brief period they mean. And not because of the violence. We called them the gang wars, but nobody got killed; unless you count the Georgi-boys who overturned on the Autobahn, hurrying home drunk from Berlin one night and killing three of the five in the car. There were plenty of fist-fights, plenty of threats and nasty pranks, fires were set (famously so in the Grotto's case), and misdeeds leaked to the police, but it was only in the 'Sixties when the Tunisians took their clasp-knives into battle that people got injured, myself included. I'm not saying it was all sweetness and light until the "Tunis" tried to take over. Protection rackets, once detested on the Kiez, had grown alarmingly by then, as our rivals struggled to keep pace with Wolli's Firma, "das Cricket." Our title had long since become detached from the little pavilion where our forces once met, and where cricket itself was no longer played, but the word remained, now as mysterious and terrifying in the Hamburg of the 'Fifties as the Tongs or Cosa Nostra; it opened doors, got you the best restaurant tables in a hurry, even in restaurants that weren't "fire-proofed," as we call it, by us. Fireproofing was Wolli's invention, a scheme by which he sold fire extinguishers at a hair-raising ten thousand Marks a throw: "you never know when you might need one" was his sales pitch. But even the rivalry for this protection empire was largely a battle of wills, of bravado, almost Latin in its emphasis on threats and insults rather than physical violence. If you lost face you backed away muttering *Scheisser* (or if you belonged to the Bimbo gang, some dark Italian word for contraceptive, their rudest epithet). You didn't draw a knife. And over money people were prepared to recognize an honourable draw—the sign of civilization if ever there was one: *wir machen fifty-fifty, ja?* A Tunisian would rather end up in Ohlsdorf cemetery than accept "fifty-fifty."

True, it was the time when fighting sometimes spilled onto

the Dom and frightened the kids who'd come out for a good time among the carnival stalls. Breathing Schnaps-fire I once chased a member of the Wiener Gang who'd given me the finger, and when I caught up with him behind a food tent I pushed him clean through the canvas, spraying Zuckerwaren and sizzling, half-cooked waffles at the waiting customers. Women screaming; I was in some Hitchcock movie in my head; thinking too that I had a perfect right to do this, *my* Kiez, *my* empire, so what if bystanders got sprayed with burning grease? They'd come for a bit of excitement. I was providing it. But it was also the time of harmless stunts, when Boxer-Max would walk trouserless from one end of the Reeperbahn to the other for 50 D-Mark of anyone's money. These days the tourists would have hysterics—they're here for films and porno-treasure, secret smut not public outrage—and get Max arrested before he'd covered fifty metres.

It wasn't a street in those days, the Reeperbahn, it was (as anyone will tell you) an addiction, *eine Sucht*. I had to be the first there in the mornings, my blood began to pound as I glimpsed the empty pavements with no-one around except Robby at the Sorrento doorway brushing beer-stained sawdust and dirty water into the gutter—bald, partly deaf Robby who'd never fully recovered from wartime shellshock. Like the Karin of Atlantic days, he went entirely without sleep, and with no harmful effects, he insisted, other than boredom. Now that Karin's drugged nights left her feeling sluggish in the mornings, I would be up—earlier and earlier, pacing each half-finished room of the Grotto Azzurro in my mind, fretting over details—up and into the kitchen to make coffee, I'd prepare Karin's breakfast and leave it waiting for her, then rush off along the Königstrasse, running sometimes, to the Reeperbahn. It was a hangover in stone, stale smells, shuttered windows, a stunned look to the wide pale street under the spreading trickles of Robby's slop-water. I wanted to rattle the doors—*nu mal los*, let's go, wake up (Brutus awake! Thou sleepst, etcetera! A fever of impatience—I hadn't felt this way since childhood, frantic when Grandfather's afternoon nap went on too long and we were going fishing). I had the keys to the Grotto, and for company I woke any *Penner* I found curled up on the Grotto steps. There were usually a few, and I dragged them grumbling into the tunnels to help me with a spot of painting. Those stinking *Penner*! "Sleepers"—a mockingly polite word for the legion of drunken tramps. Tattoo-Dieter, Mintchev the Bulgarian, Alfons with his removable leg.

Each one had a jealously guarded trademark, "Little Karstadt" with his Bauchladen, an usherette's tray sparsely equipped with shoelaces, Opa Gerd in his top hat, Benno and his accordion, Sahara Charley (another Afrika Korps veteran) with his precious Moritz, a white mouse that lived among crumbs in the lining of his raincoat and emerged now and then to skitter round his filthy collar; every one of them with a bottle in his pocket. They knew they could earn a few Marks, enough to finance the next litre, by helping me in the mornings. Paintbrushes in hand, my grunting, stinking Penner-army, slapping on the midnight blue! Once the workmen arrived and I'd given them detailed instructions, the tramps and I were free to return to street level and take part in the day's Kiez-business, each in our way.

Wolli needed me again, if only to help intimidate our rivals. And I too, as befitted my rank in "das Cricket," acquired a "right-hand-man" (we used the English term), a lieutenant. Not Vlad, whom I regarded as an ally but who had his own circle among the wrestlers; I wanted to trust Vlad, but aside from the butter-business I couldn't quite forget what he'd once told me about his military education. Russian soldier, he said, is not permitted to have friends. Bad for morale when they are killed next day. No, what I had in Oxfart, my new *right-hent-men*, was a devoted acolyte.

His real name was Hansi Meynert, Austrian, queer ("a homo!" as Wing Commander Potts used to splutter), with close-cropped hair, eyes of an almost ochre colour and a thin, battered-looking mouth that seemed to promise as much cruelty to himself as to others. A criminal's face if ever I saw one. But he was trained, he swore, as an artist in Vienna—porcelain work, under *der grosse* Rosenthal, a genius, apparently—and had worked as a waiter only when times were hard. What Hansi called "hotel contacts" had brought him via Düsseldorf to the Four Seasons in Hamburg. I could believe it; he looked as if he'd been buggered by every head-waiter along the way. He'd been too young to fight in the war but still had dreams of naval uniform, cut his hair brutally short and affected a clipped manner of speech. *Zu Befehl, Chef!* At your orders. *Alles in Ordnung!* All Hansi lacked, until he came to Hamburg, was a true *Chef*, a *Boss* for all seasons.

While he was being buggered in Düsseldorf, Wolfgang Zimt's home town, someone there had given him an introduction to Wolli. Hansi moved on to Hamburg. With Wolli's help he soon found he could make more as a Reeperbahn waiter than he could at the Four Seasons. And the clientèle! "Transis," transvestites and trans-sexuals of every possible combination were flocking to the Reeperbahn now from all over the world. You could frolic with a former Guatemalan soccer star with breasts and no penis, with Tanya who had beasts *and* a penis and Tasha her twin who had neither, or with sylphs who had yet to make up their minds let alone their bodies. When Wolli bought out Hugo and re-named the Grill "Die Olympia" he gave Hansi a job there. The first time he brought me my Frikadellen, Hansi's search was over: one look at my face and it was permanent devotion. His doggy faithfulness made even Egon's seem inadequate; I don't think Hansi wanted me as a lover, he had enough of those, but as a father I fitted the bill "to the T" as he liked to say. Hamburg had everything he wanted. Here too, in the Colonnaden arcade, he found the gaudy, striped scarf that furnished his nickname.

Oxforduniversitätsschal! he snapped proudly when asked about it, pronouncing Oxford *Oxfart* with careful emphasis, as though he alone knew the true, the British way to say it.

"Are you quite sure, Hansi? Purple and green . . . I don't think that *is* an Oxford University scarf," I ventured.

"What would you know?" said Oxfart.

Unless you insulted his scarf he was a model of obedience, and our days then were enjoyably spent showing Hansi the ropes, introducing him to Kiez corners and customs. Which finger said "up yours" and which said "er ist in Ordnung," he's okay, "ein Glatter," smooth. Which finger met the thumb to make a circle meaning you were broke, "mause," and which one made a circle meaning "you can fuck her, she's anybody's." How to address a Casmus, a butch lesbian, so that she wouldn't kick you in the Eier. (Wolli's favourite, and over-used, line was "I'm a lesbian too, I only sleep with women"—it cracked him up every time—but being a Kiez-lord he could get away with it, and it wasn't a claim Oxfart could make, even in jest.) How to tell a Schmock, a would-be, failed pimp, from a true Loddel. Which bars to go into and which not. The battle lines were being drawn more strictly than before, and neutral territories like Hugo's place were having to commit themselves to one side or another. In the evenings Hansi went home to Mutti, to his own Mutti, that is, an aged mother brought from Vienna and installed in a Barmbek apartment. So he told us—no-one ever met or saw her. No-one asked to. Hansi's evenings were his own business.

I no longer had to hurry home to Egon, but there was still Karin to consider. Now and then she'd join me at the Sorrento or the Olympia for a meal, on selected peaceful occasions. She was as ill at ease there as I was among her Party friends, a glum assortment, exhausted young teachers with small children of their own, a few middle-aged eccentrics pretending to be dour and working-class. As slovenly as Kiez-folk in their domestic habits, many of them; all the squalor without any of the fun. Three nights a week Karin went home to Wandsbek, and sometimes we got dressed up and took Mutti out to a good restaurant or a film at one of the plusher cinemas. I wasn't the only person in the milieu living a double life of this sort—not by any means. There was Willi Bungert with his picture-perfect bungalow in Schenefeld and a wife who had no idea what he did for a living and never asked. He'd married her at eighteen and promptly joined the merchant marine. Willi was a Mischling, a half-Jew. His father's mother had been Jewish, and Willi's father Joachim had left home in '36 to spare his family from persecution; Willi once described his mother breaking down in the street when they passed Joachim and he made no sign of recognition, just walked on by. A few months later Joachim had disappeared to Neuengamme, never to return. Willi never forgave the Nazis, but some of his stories were a corrective to the indiscriminate loathing I'd learnt from Karin. Travelling by train to Norway to rejoin his ship, and full of rage at the suffering his family had endured, Willi unburdened himself to a fellow passenger in Zivil, civilian clothes. "Look me up when you get to Oslo," said the stranger, passing Willi a card, "I'm the new Gestapo chief there." As Willi's mouth went dry the man continued, "I'll help you any way I can—just show that card if your mouth gets you into trouble. You'll see, when the war is over the Führer will kick out Himmler and these SS *Schweine* . . .".

Willi survived the war and returned to the Reeperbahn and Renate. At home he made intricate model sailing ships, kept fit on exercise machines, grew roses and played with his children. I spent many pleasant afternoons there with him and Arno Schiller, Willi's *Chef*, over a game of Skat. (Beloved *Skat*! to my knowledge the only three-cornered card game in the world, a bully's dream—always two against one.) Arno later became my nemesis; but I always liked squat pug-faced Willi in his yachting blazer and silk scarf at the neck—comical now, but unremarkable on the Kiez in those days; any self-respecting pimp wore a suit to work. When his wife brought us sandwiches and enquired of Willi what he wanted to drink, she said *Und für Sie?* as though he were one of the guests, a perfect stranger. When we left his house together, there was no peck on the cheek for the wife. They shook hands, the two of them, in parting—Willi and Renate, Hamburg spouses.

One winter morning, a bitter February following my return from Padstow, I was taking measurements in what was to be my Grotto Azzurro office when I heard the familiar noise of Vlad's approaching footsteps, a momentary pause and a ka-*thump* each time he came down on his armless side. And another sound, further off but amplified, reverberating in the tunnel: an ice-pick clack of high heels.

Vlad peered in. "Someone to see you," he said, grinning so hard the ends of his huge moustache were turned up like a bandmaster's. His eyebrows were going a mile a minute. "Ugly blond woman," he explained and, as the high heels came closer, drew a generous outline in the air.

"Tell her to go away."

"Same one, from before!"

I went back to studying the office ground-plan. "Tell her I'm not here."

"I have said you are here."

"Good. Now tell her I'm not here." Downright rudeness: that should do it.

"She comes from Berlin to see you."

Now he had my attention. Marianne, my former afternoon-encounter, the one I'd thought was pestering me—Marianne was a stay-at-home Hamburg girl, born and bred here. "From Berlin?"

Vlad stepped aside. There was a woman behind him.

Even after fifteen years there was no mistaking her. Not all the make-up in the world could disguise that bullcalf jaw. Or her wispy white-blond Friesian hair, never meant to be lacquered up into a beehive. The hairdo made her face seem even longer and larger than I'd remembered it. I don't know how long we stood there staring at each other, Herta and I, long enough for Vlad—never quick on the uptake—to grasp that he wasn't wanted, and leave us together.

My beard fooled her for a moment. Then her hand flew to her mouth in a gesture that seemed pure cinema. It stayed there, the same big slab of a hand I remembered, flat against her lips like a calculated indiscretion it was too late to withdraw. But the tears in her eyes were genuine enough. Herta was even more astonished to see me than I was to see her, and at first I couldn't understand why. She was the one who'd come looking for me.

She'd gone pasty-faced, white with shock, and only removed her hand from her mouth at last to extract a handkerchief from her bag. She wrestled with the clasp for a moment; the bag looked brand new. Out came the hanky and she dabbed at her eyes.

The *Herr Graf*, she said—she'd read about Egon in the newspapers. She'd barely got the words out before her big cheeks were streaming with tears again. There was nowhere for her to sit in the old dormitory except rubble and she was wearing what looked like a new coat, too, of some smooth, brushed material, a dull blue. Seeing how wobbly she was I turned her round, pointed her back at the tunnel, and led her out through the serpentine of passageways onto the Hamburger Berg, where it looked ready to snow.

I walked her towards the docks, trying to think of a nice quiet place nearby where no-one knew me. You live in Berlin now? I said. She nodded yes. The handkerchief was still clamped against her mouth. And last autumn, I asked, remembering Vlad's comment, "same one, like before": had she come here to look for me in September, when the newspapers were full of Egon's story? Herta nodded again, more faintly. I wondered if she'd come more than twice. I'd been in England, I explained. Taking Egon to my brother Alec. As I said this I remembered something else, the series of crank calls Mutti had received—a woman asking for Egon over and over until even Mutti's defences had buckled. Herta had seen the newspapers; the Poseners had been mentioned there too, and they were in the phone book. Then again, the calls could have been from anyone, but it made me suddenly wary of the woman at my side. Was she a little ausgeflippt, perhaps? A little cracked? Her stunned, weepy state as I guided her across the Kiez began to make me uneasy.

It surprised me how collected I was, walking with Herta down the Hamburger Berg. Once the initial astonishment wore off, I'd felt nothing but disappointment at the sight of her. This lumpy person before me—was this really the source of my most potent erotic memories? She wouldn't be more than thirty, I thought, but she looked older than I did. There was no trace left of the teasing, chubby Herta, and I felt embarrassed—rather than guilty—at my youthful appetite: couldn't it have found a more attractive object? Or at least one that aged more gracefully? I had to take her arm as we crossed the Reeperbahn, or she'd have got herself run over.

I wondered how I looked to her. Then—idiot!—*Dummkopf!*

Idiot! the Dod would have said—I realized why Herta seemed so unprepared, so stunned to see me. Unless she'd been in touch with Ludolf there was no earthly reason she could have known that *I* was Reinhard Sacher, the notorious Reeperbahn figure (to be approached, in any case, with trepidation!) referred to in the newspapers as Count Egon's guardian. It was enough to knock anyone for six . . . having plucked up the courage to beard a Hamburg gangland boss and pervert, you found yourself face to face with the English boy—a solicitor's clerk straight out of school, a clumsy, raw-boned kid—who'd raped you when you were fifteen. No wonder she was in shock, and stumbled several times as we picked our way through early customers and brave tarts, red-nosed with cold, huddled together against the walls in their imitation furs. (They glanced at us, smiling at me—who was this weepy thing *der olle Reinhard* was steering down the pavement?) Herta in her modish coat and high heels looked like a shopgirl with pretensions and no taste; or—and I couldn't help the thought, by now it was an automatic recognition—a tart on her day off. To make conversation I asked her how Ludolf was, but got no answer.

It took several meetings, over a period of years, before I was able to piece together Herta's story. Just when I thought I'd heard it all, a new fragment would emerge, a new horror. "But I told you that already! I didn't? Are you sure?" she'd say, and sigh. She had supp'd full with horrors, and was entitled to forget a few. What I heard that freezing February day—my first instalment—will always belong, for me, to the port of Hamburg with its cranes like empty gallow-trees bending over the sluggish water; I only have to glimpse it from the S-Bahn's elevated railway windows and it brings back Herta's monotone, her solemn Mecklenburger growl untouched by Berliner cajolery.

She didn't want coffee or food, she insisted with firm shakes of the head. Cold as it was, we'd settled in one of the open shelters overlooking the Elbe, along the Landungsbrücke where the ferries come and go. A wooden bench, cement walls on three sides and a cement roof. We were protected if the snow began to fall. And no prying eyes or ears.

Herta was still crying, unable to speak. Now that we were off the Kiez I was happy to give her all the time she needed.

Straight in front of us, across the dreary slipway, rose Blöhm und Voss, the shipwrights who'd once kept turning out U-boats despite British bombs, who'd survived British indecision about their postwar fate—"those arses in Whitehall," as Cheerybye had put it, ''who can't decide whether to build the Germans up or rob 'em blind,''—and were now turning out tankers at a rate to match the Japanese. The distant noise of it floated across at us, thousands of hammers, drills, riveting guns at work on half a dozen huge ship's carcases.

It all reminded me why I steered clear of the port. I hated the stink of the sea, that human-hating rankness; worse still was the rancid ship-stink of machine oil spiked with seawater. By comparison Herta's smell beside me, panic-sweat turning her cheap perfume sour, was an elixir. It was the smell of the Kiez, a breath and body stew—sacred to me.

At last Herta put the handkerchief away, in silence. She'd put on a headscarf as we emerged from the Grotto Azzurro, and her jowls, protruding from the scarf, gave her face a pear shape, slack, putty-coloured. Not a pretty sight but at least it wasn't the face of the tight-lipped, taut-faced bitch I'd seen in the Belsen newsreels and translated into Herta. They shared a Christian name, blonde hair, a peasant jaw. The rest (as I'd hoped when enlightenment broke through, in the treehouse clearing) had been my mind punning grimly on my own sadistic past, still censored at the time, buried but not quite dead.

Egon was well, I said. My brother Alec—did she perhaps remember the elder Herr Thurgo? She did, Herta nodded—had written to me to say that in England he was regarded as an excellent pupil. We were all proud of him.

She nodded again, a servant's nod. It was no more than my platitudes deserved.

I began to tell her how I'd gone to Mecklenburg, how it was at about this time of year, in the snow, and how I'd been rescued by her grandfather; how Ludolf had entrusted Egon to me. That I'd tried to look after the boy . . . I couldn't tell whether the gaps in my account were troubling Herta or not. I said nothing about having married a sister of Maggie's or about why I wasn't back in England now myself. None of her business, I thought. It was quite dangerous enough that she knew who I was.

She didn't probe. Perhaps she thought it wasn't her place to do so. But Herta had never shown much curiosity about me—or else she was too baffled to know where to begin. I recalled her blank reaction in the kitchen of the Schloss when I carved the slice of sugarbeet into a swastika and ate it. I was a creature from another planet. Here she sat beside me, silent, waiting for what—to be prompted? To be released? If she was sorry to have met me again and simply wanted to get away, I could understand that. But there were things I had to know first.

Ever since the lurid dream I'd had in Padstow, the one in which Ludolf told me that Egon was "counterfeit," I hadn't been able to let go of the idea. Only a dream, I told myself, but Auntie was always there to shake her head. Everyone's psychic, dear. I saw Egon again as I'd first glimpsed him below the treehouse, as Herta's child. Ludolf's heir!—Ludolf whose bearing had spawned Maggie and Alec's jokes at his expense, in which he was Peter's dim-witted elder brother, the real Count, merely playing at the role of butler because he preferred it; Ludolf whose glances at me, proud and beseeching at the same time, had puzzled me so while I was convalescing at the Hof . . . was he wondering if he should palm off on me his own dim-witted relative, his Waldmensch great-grandson, as Graf von Lützow-Brüel? If he'd done so—then Egon would be three years older than we thought, if he was Herta's child and mine. Mine: that was the part I didn't want to think about any more. Having lost him I needed Egon to be Peter and Maggie's; gone for good, to Maggie's England. But after the dream I couldn't leave the itching scab alone. He'd be fifteen. Physically a stunted fifteen, but why not, after the treehouse years? A fifteen-year-old with the nerve to steal a plane made more sense, too, than a twelve-year-old. I'd reached the point where any day I expected a letter from Alec, saying, "Funny thing, old bird, are you sure he's only twelve? School doctor phoned me up, says there's an outbreak of mumps, says he's been checking the boys and our young German chappie's got the biggest pair of testicles he's ever seen on a twelve-year-old. And he's one that *hasn't* got mumps. Bit puzzled by this, the doctor. Asked me if the Germans have all got big balls. Do you know the answer to this?" No such letter arrived. Alec did write, but to ask me if he could keep Egon for Christmas. "Thought I might take him down to the cottage," he said—no sign of Joseph Michael Donovan as yet—"I like the place but it's dashed lonely on your own." He'd send Egon for Easter. Or the summer hols. I found I wasn't sorry. I wanted everything to stay the way it was.

"It must have been terrible," I said, trying a different tack, "when the Russians arrived in Mecklenburg. For women especially. Anyone who stayed around, as I understand it . . ."

Herta looked at me then. "You think I left Graf Egon? I'd have died first."

She said it without anger. Disarmingly, as simple fact. I nodded.

Her eyes were dull, the same dull blue as her coat, reflecting it perhaps, or the coat chosen to match her eyes. Then I realized why the colour preoccupied me—it was RAF blue. Molly blue.

"He *is* the *Graf*," I asked, trying for Herta's own disarming tone, "he *is* Peter and Maggie's son?"

She scanned my face as if trying to understand the question.

"Oh yes," she said.

It was the only time that day that I heard bitterness in her voice. I had no idea why it was there, but it gave her answer the ring of truth. She was the most guileless person I'd met in years—perhaps the only guileless person I'd met in years. It took a while to get used to it.

"Did *Opa*," she asked, using the German word for "grandpa," "say I left Graf Egon?"

"No, not at all," I said. "He didn't tell me anything."

Herta carefully put away her handkerchief and sat in silence for a time. "When the Russians came we went to the woods," she said at last, emotionlessly now, "all of us, except for Opa Ludolf. What else could we do? Everyone went there, thinking it would be safer. Why would they come to the woods to look, the soldiers? But there was no food left in the villages, we took what we could carry when we heard from the refugees what the Russians were doing. Hoping they would go on somewhere else to look for food, and let us be. We should have left them something. Or perhaps if the Schloss . . . if it hadn't been defended, perhaps they would have gone.

"For days we could hear the shooting, we didn't know what to do, where to go. Then they came looking for food, the Russians. To save bullets they used bayonets. When they found us, ten, twelve of us, the women and the children from the Schloss, we were too frightened to move—Mutti was the bravest of us, when she wouldn't stop cursing them one of them stabbed her in the stomach. That was when Egon ran, he was too quick for them. I ran too but he was quicker than me and when they caught me I thought they would kill me too. Later I could have done it myself, many times, but I didn't have the courage.

"Opa Ludolf stayed and fought at the Schloss, and when our soldiers left he wouldn't go with them, not while we were still in the forest. So he was captured, and because he was old they didn't kill him, they made a joke of him instead. They brought out all the old things from the Schloss and played at fighting with the swords, and they dressed Opa in armour and beat him if he didn't serve them properly, hitting him with the swords, sometimes with pieces of wood from the house, so that he fell over in the armour, and then they made him get up again.

"*Otryad 17*, that was their unit. They wrote it on the walls. And on us too, when they brought us back to the Schloss. It was their camp, in what was left of the place. And they did everything in front of Opa, taking turns with us and forcing more drink into us. They made Opa bring the drink. They did it with the children, doing the same things to them. But not Graf Egon. I didn't see him again, *Gott sei Dank*. Most of the women they left behind at the Schloss, but they had a truck and I made sure they took me with them, the Russians. I didn't want to be with anyone I knew any more.

"I went to the truck myself and I climbed into the back. Opa Ludolf saw me do it, but he didn't say anything to me. My clothes were filthy and they took them off and put a Russian uniform on me, and later when I took it off, in Berlin, in the hospital, I saw they had written their unit number in cigarette burns on my chest. And I had no memory of when they did it— only my face, in the truck, the punches to my face. They had cut my hair to look like a boy. Many of them preferred boys, I saw that at the Schloss. They gave me a helmet and a uniform, and a gun. A machine pistol. That was the worst, when I thought about it afterwards. I could have killed all of them. Many of them, before they killed me. Instead I went out with them into Berlin and shot at Germans with them. Gerda was my name, and Gerda was a good Russian soldier, and at a night a good Russian bitch. If one of them had been nice to me, then I think I would have killed him. I was sick, bleeding, and I didn't want to notice it. I could smell myself, that there was something wrong, but I didn't care. You know how gangrene smells? I wanted to kill Germans like a good little Russian bitch. At last the stink was too much even for my Russians and they threw me out. *Ins Lazarett*. To the hospital, with the wounded. I should have died there. But here I am, you see. It's easy to die when you don't want to, I saw that often enough in Berlin. And sometimes when you want to . . . well, you need courage and I didn't have it.

"Afterward I came to the West, I didn't want to be a Russian any more. I made a friend who works in a shop on the Ku-damm, and when I was better she found me work there. Everyone in Berlin. . . ." She faltered. "In Berlin life goes on, some days it's still hard for me, but my friend understands."

Her hands had begun to shake.

"When I read about Egon. . . ." She glanced at me. "Does he remember the woods?"

"Bestummt," I said.

She looked at me again, steadily now. It was still the stupefied shopgirl's face I'd seen in the Grotto, but I saw it quite differently. It was the punches on the face I was seeing, a face purpled with bruises.

A smile came, for the first time, when my bestummt registered—and for an instant the naughty child was there in front of me, the smiling Herta streaking animal blood on her cheeks and restoring everything I'd been keeping at bay, the treehouse, everything. Then it was gone.

"Na ja, bestummt," she said.

To obliterate the shock of that smile I told her some more about Egon, all I could think of. And about her grandfather, until the tears came again. I gave her Alec's address, in case she decided to write to Egon. Then I took Herta to the zoo. It was an absurd thing to do, but I was completely at a loss, I couldn't wait to be rid of her but at the same time I couldn't make the first move towards it, and she didn't seem to want to leave either. At the zoo it finally began to snow and all the animals retreated from sight—except the Abyssinian baboons, who thought it was the best fun they'd had in years and pounced and swatted at the flakes as if at slow, stupid flies. From Hagenbeck's Zoo I took Herta to the train, and felt enormous relief, nothing but relief now, to see the back of her.

She'd been too discreet to ask about my life, so I hadn't been called on to go secretive on her and give away, perhaps, how precarious my life was here in Hamburg; and how much she had me in her power. One whisper on the Kiez and within a few hours everyone would know my name and origin—the girls would soon pass it along the pavement, in and out of the bars and back onto the street; but that was relatively harmless, it would be amusing gossip, nothing more—now that I was established on the Reeperbahn I could have turned out to be Stalin's longlost brother and no-one would have turned a hair. Except Walters. His problem would be with the authorities, his "German colleagues" as he now called them. Because of what I knew about him Walters had gone to great lengths to cover for me during the Egon episode, telling them he'd personally cleared

Reinhard Sacher as an authentic and reformed ex-Nazi. If I now emerged as a Brit there'd be questions to answer.

I waited until Herta's train pulled out of the station, in case she wanted to seal our parting with a wave—give it finality—but she didn't. No, this was more final still, I decided. No backward look. You've got off lightly, Ratty, I thought, hearing Alec in my head.

Two weeks later the first letter came.

Ich wollte Ihnen alles erzählen, Herta wrote, *schaffte es aber nicht*. I wanted to tell you everything, but I couldn't.

"I never expected to see you again. Now I wish I hadn't. I only wanted to know where Egon was, perhaps to see him again or only to write to him, and I was expecting to meet a man called Reinhard Sacher, not the father of my child." I stared at the words, in the big clumsy writing. "Yes, the father of my child. I thought surely you knew, Herr Thurgo. I thought, he must have guessed. Then when you asked about Graf Egon and whether he was the son of the Graf and Gräfin, I saw that you didn't know. I didn't tell you the truth when I said I always loved Egon. I hated him too when I heard that Franzl was dead with the Frau Gräfin. Franzl who went away with the Gräfin was our son. The Frau Gräfin did not know this. When she took Franzl she said it was for the best and he would soon be given to a family to be looked after . . ." No; no, I thought; I knew at once it was a lie. Something in the way she set it out—too guileless altogether—I was reading but I was barely taking it in any more, "I never said anything. Opa Ludolf would have killed me, he would have thrown me out. When I couldn't look after him after he was born I took him to Frau Körner in the village, she was always kind to me, and she looked after him as her own until he was too much for her with his bad chest and she brought him to the Schloss where Opa Ludolf and the Frau Gräfin were looking after them all, the orphaned and abandoned ones."

There I sat in the Grotto reading it, and as soon as I saw the words on the paper I knew they were a lie, a cunning lie. She wanted something from me. That was it. And she did, damn it, she wanted money.

"Have pity on me, you know some of the things that happened to me, but not all. I am still not recovered from the first year in Berlin and have to go to the doctors often. The medicine is expensive and they say another operation may be necessary. It's difficult to work, I think I told you that I work in a shop but that isn't true, I haven't worked for many months. Life is expensive here and I have no-one to help me.''

Habe Mitleid. I wanted to feel pity. I felt nothing but rage; I was being conned. Operation! Reparation more like—it wasn't up to me to pay war debts, to make up for Russian atrocities. I crumpled up the letter without reading it again. No more children!—that was what kept running through my mind—no more bloody children, by love or rape. When I was calmer I uncrumpled it, but still couldn't bring myself to read it over. Or throw it away. I knew perfectly well what it said. I tried to be calm, to be fair, to. . . . The letter contained no recriminations, no reproaches. What's done is done, it seemed to say—and after what she'd been through with Unit 17 my brutal treatment paled into insignificance. Yes, she was just a suffering soul, who . . .

I wrote back acknowledging her letter, but I couldn't bring myself to make any reference to Franzl. I enclosed 500 DM, praying that would be the end of it.

Three months later another letter came. That operation she'd mentioned? The doctors—always these anonymous, plural doctors—said it had to be performed. She didn't have the money. Eight hundred Deutschmark, plus the hospital expenses. I sent a thousand, and received by return of post a gracious, brief but fulsome note—along with, to my horror, a photograph of little Franzl on his fourth birthday. Sitting among other children in the kitchen of the Schloss, happy little refugees (no Graf Egon to be seen, these were the underprivileged), was a sickly-looking blond creature. Bulging lips held in a cough, over his birthday cake. He had a bulbous forehead and heavy brows but otherwise not the slightest resemblance to Herta—he looked spindly, overheated, sallow—let alone to me. None to me. There was something distinctly loopy, as Alec would say, about his beady, close-set eyes and flushed face. Whoever he was I hoped he'd been an idiot, too good and too stupid to live.

The operation was a qualified success, I gathered from a letter six weeks later. She was weak, Herta said, unable to work. The doctors said that what she needed was a holiday. But where could she go, without money?

I debated with myself. Should I submit to this? When would it end? At the back of my mind was the fact that she knew who I was. She'd never mentioned this. She didn't need to, knowing I knew. Or perhaps she didn't realize the power this gave her over me. Perhaps she simply needed a holiday, as she said. In the end I sent Herta a smaller sum, hoping to indicate that our relationship was winding down.

Then for a time I didn't hear a word from her.

The grand opening of the Grotto Azzurro, Hamburg's most luxurious night spot, was due to take place at the end of that year, but didn't happen until a little over twelve months later, on Silvesterabend, New Year's Eve 1954, for reasons that have become part of Kiez-lore.

Everybody has their own theory as to which of our rivals set the fire that consumed the original Grotto décor and postponed the gala. But the truth is that the Georgi-boys were in disarray and undergoing a leadership crisis in the wake of their Autobahn disaster, the Bimbos didn't have the nerve (they had the best repertoire of insults but nothing to back it up), and it was only the Kölner-Jungs, who controlled three nightclubs, a *maison de passe* on the Herbertstrasse, and a high proportion of the Reeperbahn girls, who were still in contention with us for lordship of the Kiez. The arsonist left no clues. Anyone with purloined keys could have got in and done it. During the remodelling of the old bunkers our struggle with Hamburg's fire regulations (sharpened by experience to the point of paranoia) was by far the trickiest and most protracted of our legal problems, and Wolli handled it himself; by the time we'd satisfied the fire officers we had five separate exits to the street, and fire doors in every tunnel to contain the flames, in an emergency. Whoever got in that night made no attempt to make the fire look like an accident, preferring to make sure of the maximum destruction, and simply laid a trail of petrol from the Tanzkeller through the offices into the "Kasbah," soaking carpets and draperies along the way, opened all the fire doors, lit the petrol, and fled.

At three in the morning, as the flames took hold, a phone call from the overlooking Prinz-Eugen Hotel got me out of bed and brought me sprinting through the deserted streets towards the distant, revolving flare of the fire-engine lights. A crowd was gathering, dressed in whatever clothes had come to hand. With the tunnels alight and roaring at each of the five exits, it might as well have been a fire in an oil well for all the firemen could do. I'd no idea a great fire, when it was contained like this one, had such a range of voices—howling as a gust of wind rushed down and through the passageways from one exit to emerge at another in a whirlwind of carbonized dust and fading embers of wallpaper, paint and wood, gasping, grunting, snarling as the larger beams gave way. It had been raining earlier, and now the streets began to steam as the temperature rose through the tarmac from the inferno underneath. I could feel the heat through my shoes, it was a terrifying sensation, like standing on Etna—except that the volcano was invisible and I felt it might erupt anywhere, bursting up through the street in a pillar of flame. Sounds continued to pour from the exits, some great Ourobouros, or Fafnir the giant worm of legend, seemed to be groaning in fury as if the Reeperbahn's guts were ablaze, snorting greasy black dragon-plumes of smoke that floated across the Kiez from five fiery nostrils, and left soot up and down the house-fronts.

At first I was devastated and it was weeks before I steeled myself to go down into the bunker and face the mockery of my labours, my dreams. I'd had plenty of gruesome first-hand reports—the place in its charred state was almost as big an attraction as I'd hoped the club would be—so the blackened caverns with their twisted remains of glass and metal came as no surprise. Several wags had urged me to open the place exactly as it was. I could see their point. It was a true grotto now. The chandeliers were fused into exotic moonrock stalactites. The fixed metal barstools, styled like a pre-war American diner, had become obsidian mushrooms from hell. And the long steel-and-mahogany saloon bar, my pride and joy, was like a drunkard's nightmare, a buckled, weaving shape with a surface like a roller coaster. It would be the first night club designed to show the inside of a customer's head.

Privately, Wolli hinted that the fire was Vlad's work, doubtless suborned by the Kölner-Jungs: Vlad did have a set of keys, didn't he? Wolli had never asked about the outcome of the Wackernagel hunt, but he'd certainly noted that far from punishing the Russian for butter-crimes past, I'd promoted Vlad to overseer at the Grotto. He was still trying to make trouble between Vlad and me, I thought. I had my own theory, one I never discussed with anybody, that Wolli had instigated the fire himself; not only to collect on the insurance but to swing Reeperbahn sympathy against the Kölner-Jungs as the likeliest authors—the destruction was a little on the excessive side, everyone agreed—and begin the Putsch which left him, within a year, sole master of the Kiez.

Wolli didn't need the cash, though after a long, tedious investigation our insurers coughed up more than we'd actually spent on the club up to that time. And the money simply came back to me as the new budget for a revamped Grotto. Using his *Schore*, the accumulated proceeds of his black-market days,

Wolli had speculated cleverly; the radium stolen from the Stadt-kontorbank now glowed in neon over Wolli's bars and restaurants, the Santa Fe, the Alter Kai, Fischerheim, Olympia. Wolli had also become the proud owner of a country mansion in Sieg Holstein (the Hamburg flat was now "mein pied-à-terre"), with extensive grounds, where he'd assembled a menagerie to rival Hagenbeck's zoo. Tropical birds, Sittiche—some kind of parakeet—and brilliantly coloured lories, as well as a horde of flamingoes, were his latest craze. He spoke to them for hours on end, cooing and clucking like a latter-day St. Francis. "The day I get too fond of them," he said, "you know what I shall do?" "What?" I said, fearing the worst, a slap-up meal with parakeet hors d'oeuvre and roast flamingo as the centrepiece. "Release them," he said. "Over Hamburg. Reinhard, imagine my flamingoes settling on the Alster, and the parks full of little coloured birds!" Full of dead little coloured birds, I thought, if I knew Hamburg starlings.

Mercifully Wolli never went ahead and did it. But the richer he got, the more he talked about giving things away. Attachment, he said, was the curse of life—*Anhänglichkeit, Reinhard, unsere verfluchte Anhänglichkeit! Nicht?* The Sieg Holstein aviary period coincided with his new obsession: Buddhism. He'd tried to lure "der Bhik," Hamburg's own initiate of the saffron robe, into living with him as a resident spiritual guide and unpaid zoo attendant, but the old Bhikku was too canny for that. "Ick bin Mendikant, Herr Zimt," he said with a polite bow, though alas mendicant wasn't a word in German and I had to translate it for Wolli: Bettelmönch. Bhikku (the word means monk or some similar title) U Thunanda had been educated at an English school in Rangoon and it infuriated Wolli that I who was perfectly indifferent to Buddhism could chat with the master any time I liked. What's more I was needed as translator when Wolli wanted to debate higher matters with U—or "U-Bahn" as Wolli nicknamed him, since it was U's only mode of travel, apart from sandalled foot.

To be fair to Wolli, he never completely abandoned Buddhism, even after the Bhikku returned to the Far East (to get away from Wolli, I always suspected, though U said only "My work is done"). U had promised his order that he would make thirty German converts, and though it took him eleven years to do this he left where he'd fulfilled his numerical vow. I never asked him if he counted Wolli. In time it was Wolli's ideals of an inoffensive, unattached existence that led him to found the

Freipuff, his socialist bordello—a gesture I admired; but along the way his Buddhism caused bitter arguments between us. Our trips in Wolli's new "sled," as we called them on the Kiez, his huge Mercedes, often ended in a screaming match. As soon as the doors crunched shut like a discreet encounter of tectonic plates, I could feel the tension rising. The very smell of well-greased leather seemed to incubate our mutual distrust. In any case I was a rotten passenger—all my life; no matter what the car or who was driving—and Wolli knew it. "Learn to drive at last for God's sake! What's the matter with you?" I've never known what the matter was between myself and cars, I simply knew I'd got this far without one and I liked it that way. I was a big baby, that was Wolli's explanation, I wanted to be ferried everywhere. But I didn't. And I hated Wolli's car. I refrained from pointing out the contradiction between a large Mercedes and the Buddhist faith. I only lost my temper when Wolli insisted on screeching to a halt, to avoid running over even the smallest of God's creatures.

He liked me to accompany him to Travemünde, to play baccarat (or rather watch while *he* played) at the casino, and this longer, rural drive brought out the worst in him. Especially on the way back, if he'd lost at the tables. A dozen times or more he might jump on the brakes and send me hurtling at the Mercedes dashboard. The Travemünde road was amply papered with two-dimensional frogs, lizards, hedgehogs, and the like, but if so much as a beetle ventured into Wolli's headlamp beams we had to stop for it. Sometimes I offered to get out and personally guide the bug across the road. You should do so, Wolli would say, unsmiling. It might be your grandmother. If my grandmother (whom I remembered clearly, shapeless smock and all, in the hallway photograph at Fold Farm) had made such a poor fist of her human incarnation that she'd been relegated to the insect kingdom, perhaps she deserved to be run over, I argued. Wolli was not amused. We waited for Grandmother to cross the road. Even as atonement for the human beings Wolli had carved up during his life, this was going too far, surely, and I wondered if Wolli bothered with it when he was driving on his own. Or was it just to bait me, see how far I could be pushed? I called him a hypocrite, he called me a cynic, and once or twice—*zack klatsch klatsch* as we said on the Kiez—we threw punches at each other. But I was far too big for him and as soon as I landed a good one Wolli would pretend it was all in fun and give me a caressing slap on the face, approvingly, as if to say he'd just been testing my reflexes.

The Zimt appearance had changed once more. His wispy beard had gone, and now Wolli was cultivating what he thought of as his resemblance—faint except for the fruity lips—to Elvis Presley. Clean-shaven, fresh-faced but with an artificial tan and a razor-cut *Elvisquiff* in place of the cowlick, he looked younger than ever. The gaudy clothes were gone too; these were the days before a sequined Elvis gave in to showbiz glitter. Black shirts and black drainpipe trousers gave Wolli the blend of street chic and asceticism that a Buddhist Elvis might adopt. He mocked my baggy salt-and-pepper suits, but secretly I think he liked the way I dressed. It showed him off.

Oddly enough our worst row, which ended with us wrestling in the front seat of the Merc while a driver behind us hooted furiously on his horn, came not because of an animal in our path, but a red light. There were no cars behind us when the row began. It was the middle of the night, we were in a deserted part of Hamburg and in a hurry. Oxfart had phoned from a club in Barmbek, where the manager was refusing to part with Wolli's share of the monthly receipts and had assembled a group of bully boys to back up his resistance. Go on, for goodness sake, I said, keep going, as the lights turned amber and Wolli slowed down. "There's no-one around," I grumbled. Wolli said nothing. We stopped, engine throbbing in silence. Empty streets to right and left. The red light glared at us interminably. "Hansi said it was an emergency. He doesn't exaggerate." *Quatsch*, said Wolli. "And if you're wrong?" I said. "Come on, what does it matter, one red light? Everyone does it, at night." "*Ist mir scheissegal*. Because everyone does it *I* should do it?" The light was still red. Was he slighting me because it was Oxfart, my lieutenant, in trouble? "When we get to Barmbek," I said, "you'll threaten somebody's life if you have to, but you won't run a red light to get there in time to save Hansi's skin?" It was madness; I was trapped in a car with the vice king of Hamburg, we were going to battle and he'd stopped to be faithful to the highway code. "If Hansi gets hurt because we're late," I began.

"If Hansi gets hurt," Wolli mocked. "What is he to you, your bumboy?"

That was when I lunged at him. *Zack klatsch klatsch*, and once we'd got going the light must have turned green and red again and green before the car arrived behind us and Wolli pushed me away to turn and make sure it wasn't the police.

For the opening of the refurbished Grotto Azzurro—to satisfy the authorities I'd had to close off the tunnels altogether and restrict the club to dance floor, bar, and offices—Wolli graced us in all his finery, a blue mohair *Smoking*, ruffle shirt and blue satin bow-tie, a new gold Rolex (a surprise, this; it was normally a pimp's trademark, but it turned out to be a gift from Arno Schiller, prince of pimps) and gold rings. Oxfart was there too, having survived the Barmbek ordeal; he'd fled into the night, pursued by the bully-boys, by the time we got there, and the manager, now closing up on his own, was most co-operative. Vlad and his Catch-Wrestling friends, Willi Bungert, the cadaverous Arno Schiller, Loddel-Heinz and Loddel-Eddie the pimping twins, Werner der Kellner, Paula and Alwine, old chums from the days of the whores' rubble-district, Helmuth der cop: *le tout Hamburg*, as I liked to think of it, was there. It wasn't just the Kiez that was well represented. So was respectable Hamburg—well-to-do nightclub patrons from the business community, the slumming sons of old Hamburg money, a Senator or two; mixing easily (though I doubt if they knew it) with visiting underworld figures from other cities, some of whom might easily have passed for Hamburg "Schickeria." Their escorts were certainly polished enough to pass for Senators' mistresses. Entry was by invitation only, and having pruned the gathering of any drunks or troublemakers I felt able to invite Karin and Mutti, without a blush. The Dod too; I knew she wouldn't be embarrassed. This was my hour of glory, why not let them share it?

I even invited Walters, as a joke almost. But to my surprise he came.

It was his club of course, insofar as he and Wolli and I were co-owners, though the recent capital investment had been Wolli's and Wolli would expect the lion's share of the proceeds. I was the executive arm, at once functionary and dogsbody. Walters was the sleeping partner. I knew he'd be curious to see what I'd conjured up for the Grotto; but ever since our brush with the German authorities over Egon, Cheerybye had kept his distance from me. Aside from Kiez-gossip the last substantial piece of information I'd been able to offer him was during the Korean war, when Wolli told me that contacts close to Otto "Scarface" Skorzeny, once Hitler's leading daredevil, were letting it be known that Otto had three crack SS divisions ready to put at the disposal of the U.S. High Command. Things weren't going too well in Southeast Asia. Skorzeny had a Blitzkrieg all worked out. The Kameraden were trained and fit and assembled in Otto's Spanish hideaway, waiting for the word. They could be in Pyongyang in 36 hours. Would Walters care to act as go-between and speak to the "Amis," the Americans? In the event Walters all but choked on his fish when I told him this, over lunch at Wedel, and promptly changed the subject. His response was one of utter disbelief, I thought then; he'd never believed in Wolli's neo-Nazi contacts anyway.

Then something happened which should have made me revise my thinking altogether, if I'd had my wits about me. I needed Wolli to sign some cheques to pay for decorative touches above and beyond the Grotto budget; given a second shot at the design I now couldn't resist gilding the lily and I'd developed a siren motif which adorned the supporting pillars and the dance floor itself. I was having portraits of some of our more shapely Kiez-sirens incised (with a splendid vulgarity of line that would have appalled my mother) into the great glass mirror behind the bar. I dreaded facing Wolli with this extra cost, I didn't want to tell him on the phone and I'd left it so late that there was nothing for it but to go out to Sieg Holstein at the weekend, when the tropical birds had most of his attention. He was giving a party, as it turned out, an even more promising distraction. But why hadn't I been told? I thought resentfully, seeing the assembled limousines in the drive. Too posh for dogsbody Sacher? Groups of idling chauffeurs watched me march into the house in my creased suit. I found Wolli beside the flamingo pool, surrounded by admiring guests. Even with many of them in civvies you could tell this was a military gathering. And there were enough uniforms and beribboned chests there, elderly but erect, to have furnished a NATO conference, or at least a worthy sub-committee, sipping champagne among the flamingoes and discussing the merits of the old 98K carbine when hunting rhino. Or so I thought until I began to catch references to "the West Algerian war zone" and arms "arsenal-fresh." "The Tunisian Chief of Rural Police wants a thousand pistols—nine millimetre—from Finland of course. . . ." That didn't sound like NATO business. Or safari gossip. Clasping the pen and cheque-book I pursued Wolli through the seemingly sedated flamingoes, while trying not to nudge Hitler's former generals into the pool, or fall in myself. "Excuse me—*Entschuldigung, Herr General—Danke schön—Bitte schön*. . . ." Part of my problem was that Wolli wouldn't stop holding forth on the subject of his one-legged birds as he walked among them, offering them small fish from a silver bowl.

I followed, bewildered by fragments of conversation drifting across Wolli's lecture, ". . . they live until eighty, some of them . . . did you say *eighty*? . . . of *course* they can live on corned beef, *Mensch*, we're talking about half-starved guerrillas on the edge of the Sahara . . . I've clipped their wings so they can't fly . . . yes, United States surplus boots . . . 37 millimetre pompoms, one and a half million rounds, and 40 tons of TNT . . . port of Monrovia . . . the guerrillas insist on German bullets, they all have nine point seven centimetres . . . they're really quite easy to feed, are they? . . ." (The birds? The guerrillas? Or were the birds the guerrillas, in code?) ". . . yes, quite easy, but if one of them breaks a leg you have to say goodbye . . . no they don't mind using Czech carbines, it's the corned beef they can't stand . . ." When I got the pen into his hand Wolli signed the cheques with a quick indifferent flourish, and I escaped before it occurred to him to ask what they were for.

My head was still spinning as I paused beside the aviary on my way out, to wish the parakeets "Guten Tag." I was ready for a little conversation. But they wouldn't come anywhere near me.

"Here," came a voice, "you need some peanuts, Dicky, that's all."

Walters tossed me a small blue and white bag of them, as he approached.

"What are *you* doing here?" I hissed.

"Hello, birdies. . . ." He made tweeting sounds.

"Were you invited?"

"Natch."

"Well, have you seen who's here? The place is seething with old SS types."

"Hardly surprising," he said. "Being Germany. It's their country now, remember?"

"But they're making arms deals all over the shop, by the sound of it."

"Are they by gum."

"What *are* you doing here?"

"What do you think?"

"Keeping an eye on them?"

"*Jawohl.* Exactly that," said Walters, and waddled off towards the party.

Now as he waddled into the Grotto Azzurro in a huge wine-red cummerbund he looked like the cat who'd swallowed the cream, if not the canary too. "Spiffy!" he grinned. "Just what Hamburg needed. But don't get too fancy now, Dicky, we're here to make money, after all. Germans like smut. You've got to give it to them neat." I introduced him to Paula and Alwine, who could perhaps teach him a thing or two about what Germans liked; but as they escorted him to a table, I wondered about Cheerybye, beaming, sweating, being steered like a beach ball against the tide—I couldn't see him giving it to Paula or Alwine, neat or any other way.

The club really was looking spiffy that night. It was alive for the first time now that it was full of living sirens and sleek dolphins, or rather killer whales in the black and white of their tuxedos and stiff-fronted shirts. I'd known the Tanzkeller empty, under construction, for so long; even in the later stages when the electricians were done and I could simulate the final effect for myself, the soft lighting always seemed murky and threatening in the deserted club, as if everyone had backed into the shadows in horror at some invisible crime on the spotlit dance floor. Now, beneath my scallop-shaped wall brackets of misted glass, the gauzy, golden light had faces to soften, and my faceted chandeliers had jewellery to reflect. The company seemed positively awestruck by the vaseline flattery of soft lighting combined with shards of glitter, and couldn't keep their eyes off their own reflections in the incised mirror that ran the length of the bar. Thanks to the cheques Wolli had signed so blithely, what our guests saw there were their images dancing with ghostly cut-glass bathing beauties, as well as with their own more modestly endowed partners in real life. Behind the bar they saw the whole world of the Grotto in which they shone so splendidly; they ogled it as if it offered better confirmation than the flesh and blood beside them, and I felt like Captain Nemo displaying the submarine world to his visitors aboard the Nautilus—except that here the undersea splendours were on both sides of the glass, and accessible.

Wolli approved, I could see it by the way his brilliantined head was bobbing in time with the music of "das Combo," our resident band. The Mambo Neapolitano I'd renamed them; Die Drei Gauchos wouldn't do. When they played "Zambesi"—as a mambo—it even brought Wolli to his feet, to dance with his partner Andrée, a rare tribute since he hated being the smallest person in a crowd.

At the edge of the dance floor he extended a hand to Andrée—

making sure we all saw his new Rolex—and the dancers parted for them as if for royalty. One or two people even applauded. We were officially launched.

Karin danced with me, while Mutti and the Dod looked on like cautiously satisfied duennas at Don Juan's wedding. Mutti was wearing an exquisite black dress trimmed with jet which hadn't seen action, I suspected, since the 'Twenties; it gave me a glimpse of a darting, sinewy young Mutti, sexy in her vitality—yes, that was where Karin had learnt the sensual *schwelgen*ing beneath what seemed like an atrophied, unresponsive way with people. And Karin danced like a silkie, half land half sea creature, a wonderful, modestly sinuous movement of her whole body, tip to toe, that made me want to have her on the spot. Like Mutti she was dressed in black, a matt-finish satiny number with a high Japanese neck. She was delicious. The Dod, however, had gone mad. What inspired her to dress in pink I shall never know. I was used to her daily wear, the baggy cardigans and knitted shawls; though I could see that what she wore beneath them, the flowery silk blouses faded from years of wear, had been as expensive in their day as the brooches and cameos she alternated at her neck, or the antique diamond stud that wobbled among the greying folds of flesh on either hairy, pendulous ear like a very small maharajah clinging to an elephant. She wasn't poor. She probably had suitable evening outfits. But I'd assumed that what the well-dressed psycho-analyst wore to a nightclub was the same, in the name of truth, as what she wore to work, old cardigan and all; that she'd see herself as an observer (and consequently invisible) in hell, and would forget to dress for it. Instead The Dod was almost perfectly dressed for hell. She was a shiny pink satin all over, but bulging, rigid, stretched to the limit, about to come to the boil and explode her carapace and take to the dance floor like a great shelled prawn, white but segmented with red rings where the dress had cut into her flesh—it was so tight it hurt just to look at her. I had to conclude she'd hired the thing; surely no-one actually had such an item in their wardrobe. Taffeta from head to foot, stiff as armour, with wave-line flamenco flounces at the cuff and hip and a froth of them at the calf, the kind of dress a cruel stage designer might have dreamt up for a 250-pound opera singer in the role of Carmen. If "Zambesi" brought her to the dance floor it would be the end of my carefully choreographed Nautilus-ballet, replacing it with something more like the dance of the pink hippopotami in Disney's "Fantasia." The Dod stayed put.

I knew she was waiting for me to ask her to dance, but she was out of luck. In view of Vlad's taste for big women I could have asked him to put the Dod out of her misery and give her a twirl, but between them they would have cleared the dance floor, and then no-one who was there that night would be able to remember anything except the walrus and the heffalump dancing the mambo. I had a big treat in store for the assembled guests, one I did want them to remember, and I wasn't going to spoil it, even to please my beloved Dod.

The treat was Freddy Quinn, Hamburg's elfin charmer, as starved as a young Sinatra (how we all loved that! This was the real North Atlantic alliance—the child of our austere, war-chastened, meagre loins—but spunky! Look how we've skimped and saved, and how vital the hollow-eyed results!). His guitar seemed larger than he was. Freddy was our emblem in those days, he'd risen to be a national recording star from dates in St. Pauli bars and clubs, he was living proof of everything we wanted to believe about the Kiez—cradle of talent! Heart of Bohemia! Proof that by rights we could all have conquered Germany the way Freddy had, if we weren't so lazy—no, if we weren't so proud of our own fief, our place on the Reeperbahn. After such glory, what price the rest of Germany? We sent Freddy out into it as a favour, as our roving ambassador, a sample of St. Pauli nights.

I was picking my way around the edge of the dance floor on my way to the offices and the artistes' dressing rooms, to make sure Freddy was being properly attended to—he was on in ten minutes—when the evening slipped its moorings.

A Valkyrie with fat legs crossed and wrapped in lurid green *Twisthosen*, cut tight to the knee, was staring at me, following me with her eyes.

The way she did it stirred a memory. Someone else staring at me with the same hunger—years ago—yes, in the kitchen of the Schloss—I returned the Valkyrie's gaze, she grinned at me a little drunkenly, and to my horror I realized it was Herta. For an instant or two I thought it might only be a resemblance. Please let it be a trick of the light. It wasn't. With heavy make-up and her hair down she looked less matronly, but the sweet goofy smile gave away the peasant, sure as Scheisse.

Herta here in the club tonight—with everybody—Walters—Karin, Mutti—I could feel myself break out into a sweat. She couldn't be here. I hadn't invited her. She was still smiling at me, all teeth. The Combo were playing "La Paloma," I remember, our Kiez-anthem in those days, as a man in a *Smoking* returned to Herta's table with two fancy cocktails. I understood then; and in the same moment I knew that it was true, as I'd suspected all along—you get a nose for it, there's a knowing reserve, a fake demureness about an off-duty tart—that Herta was on the game. The man with her was Otokar Weiss, a Berlin pimp on Wolli's personal invitation list.

Swarthy Otokar was beckoning me towards his table. "Reinhard! I'd like you to meet someone. By a special arrangement with my good friend Wolfgang Zimt, Marlinda here," he waved a small fat hand at Herta, "who dreams of the Reeperbahn, is coming to work for Arno Schiller, here in Hamburg."

Marlinda? "Coming to work in Hamburg?" I repeated as it sank in. What was this, an exchange programme for whores? Realizing how rude I was being, I bowed.

"Enchanté," I said, "Marlinda."

"Herr Sacher." Still smiling fixedly, Herta offered her hand to be kissed.

And that was all—it was as much as I could take; drunk as she was, Herta behaved herself that night, thank God.

All the same I spent the rest of it on tenterhooks. Freddy Quinn was a triumph, the club was a triumph, and to judge by the tipsy compliments I received Reinhard Sacher was the master spirit of the age, the herald of a new flowering of European night life—but for me the bloom had already been taken off it by Herta's arrival.

Worse was to come. The very next morning she set up shop on the Reeperbahn, despite freezing rain. As her pitch she chose the pavement opposite the Olympia, which meant that from my Stammtisch I could see her hail the customers and come and go with them. To my surprise Herta was immediately in demand. Apparently a soggy Valkyrie was just what every middle-aged Hamburger had been waiting for. "Marlinda," I could hear Otokar's rasping voice, "who dreams of the Reeperbahn . . ." I'd had plenty of time, the night before, to work out the relationships involved. Herta was clearly Otokar's, she'd gone to him and asked to be allowed to move to Hamburg; if Otokar was to keep a share of Herta's earnings here, he'd have to ask permission from his friend Wolli, overlord of the Kiez; Wolli, who ran no girls, would ask Arno to deputize; Arno, who would now take a cut himself—without having to break in a new girl— gave Wolli the Rolex by way of thanks, making Wolli an honorary pimp. Kiez-politik. Everyone benefited.

But it wasn't the Reeperbahn Herta-Marlinda had been dreaming of, that much was clear. Not this grim rainy New Year's Day Reeperbahn, bleak as any Berlin street would be today. Selling herself under my nose: that's what she had in mind. If I wouldn't send her money, she'd procure it on my turf—was that the message? Of course, I could move to another bar. With Herta following, wherever I went. Between them Arno and Wolli, as she knew, could enforce pavement rights anywhere on the Kiez. Outside the police station, if they cared to. No; I might as well confront her. I sent gypsy Theo out to invite Marlinda to a plate of rissoles and gherkins with König Reinhard—a king besieged in his own palace.

The last thing I wanted was a public row, in full audience, as it were. But if I was the one who decamped, and arranged a meeting with Herta elsewhere, I'd lose face when the news got around. I wasn't going to surrender the Olympia to a faded girl from below stairs; even if I had raped her in a previous incarnation. And if Herta was going to blow the gaff on my identity she could do it anytime and anywhere. I had nothing to lose.

Theo opened the café door to her, led Herta to my table, pulled out the chair. She knew the routine; sat graciously, waiting for attention to subside a little.

"The operation went all right, did it?" I said.

I heard a faint snigger from a neighbouring table. Regardless of Herta's real (or imaginary) operation, the one she'd mentioned in the letters, this line was a standard opening gambit in Kiez conversation; on the Reeperbahn "the operation" meant a sex change and it was the usual, idle way of calling someone's behaviour into question. A woman's assertiveness. Or a man's lack of it.

"Till the next time."

"Oh?"

"The doctors say I'll never be completely right."

I was sorry I'd raised the subject now; Herta's hackneyed but unashamedly direct way with words was throwing me off course.

"So you're raising the money for the next time."

She nodded. "Don't pretend it's a surprise. When we first met here I could see you knew what I did for a living, Herr Sacher."

"Reinhard," I said.

Her expression didn't change.

"Tell me one thing, then," I said, "without beating around the bush. Why come here to do it?"

"I wanted to be near you."

She was keeping her voice down; but I didn't like to glance round in case that drew even more attention.

"Arno won't like that," I said. "You'd do better to stay away from me."

"If you're thinking I'll tell people who you are—"

"Tell anyone you like."

"Don't be afraid. I'm not here to make difficulties for you."

"Why, then?"

"I want you to give me a baby."

I stared at her, praying that any keen-eared eavesdropper was thinking *ausgeflippte Nutte*, another tart with a screw loose.

They couldn't see Herta's eyes, as I could. Calm, and clear. And absolutely reasonable.

Karin and I had begun to explore Europe together. For me it was a chance to broaden my own horizons at last and gradually to emancipate Karin from Hamburg and from Mutti. For Karin it was a matter of getting away from Germany. But so long as that remained the overriding purpose, as I often tried to explain to her, she wasn't getting away from Germany at all. Abroad, she often denied being German. She was Dutch, she said, implausibly; if challenged, Austrian. (This struck me as even more absurd, given the longstanding Austrian contribution to bigotry in general and to Nazi bigotry in particular.) She was becoming one of those modern Germans who derive pride from the denial of their homeland. National shame, I said, to her fury, was also nationalism, but *umgekehrt*. Reverse nationalism. If there was a defence against the kind of fever that had overtaken Germany in the 'Thirties, and other nations in their time, it began—I argued—with the recognition that the Reich was a source of human shame, not merely German shame. Karin was never more German than in her own self-hatred. But she wouldn't see it.

Until I got my passport we'd had to holiday in Germany or not at all. That meant not at all, after our first attempt—a week in Lübeck. We went *zu viert*, the four of us, Karin, Mutti, Egon and I, and stayed in the hotel where Mutti had spent her honeymoon with August in 1913. That was a mistake for a start. It was Mutti's idea, but several times we found her wiping away tears in her hotel room. Egon wanted a room of his own, and when he was forced to sleep with Mutti he complained about her snoring. In the end he slept with me, and Karin slept with her mother. We toured the flat lands of Lower Saxony by coach, but even its unbroken, sunny fields of grain seemed to fill Karin with dark thoughts. As always I found her mood infectious. When the twin towers of Ratzeburg's guild churches hove into view I saw them less as fingers raising our eyes to God than as sinister lances, ready to be lowered, and attack the infidel. We ended up, I remember, sitting glumly on the beach at Travemünde, each of us in an ancient wicker wraparound chair which offered some protection from the wind. Schoolkids patrolled the beach, renting binoculars. The object of inspection was a stretch of coast across the border, in the Ostzone. There was nothing to be seen on it. But it was still *dort drüben*; over there, and therefore fascinating. I rented a pair and found something better to study on our own coastline—a group of young Mormons from America, bathing fully clothed and defending their virginity with a determination worthy of Karin. At least I assume that's what they were doing. The effect of wind-lashed, well-soaked blouses stuck to healthy Mormon chests was as erotic as anything I'd seen on the Reeperbahn in years.

Our holidays were very different now. Karin was eager to make love in glamorous surroundings (in glamorous hotels, that is; the great outdoors never aroused her); we were alone, and we had money.

Maps became our Kabbala. We travelled to "innocent" countries, to Denmark, Sweden, to the Low Countries, to France. As the Grotto Azzurro established itself as a leading attraction of the Kiez, Wolli and I were able to persuade the fire officers to let us open up more of the bunker, little by little, first the Jazzkeller, then the cinema. Profits increased, and between them Vlad and Oxfart learnt to hold the fort while I went on trips, often by myself, "gathering ideas" as I called it. A well-earned rest, was what I told Karin. Both were lies. What I was really doing was getting away from Herta.

Right from the beginning I told her that if there was one thing she could be sure of, it was that I wasn't bringing any more babies into the world. She could find someone else to give her one. (Though as I said it I could hear Alec's voice in the hospital after Molly's miscarriage: "Give her another one, Ratty!") I think Herta knew as well as I did that there would be no more babies out of her poor battered womb. All the same I was haunted by the sight of her on the Reeperbahn, arm in arm with a new client; and she knew that too. She promised to go back to Berlin if I made love to her. She was a truthful person, and like an idiot I believed her. I wanted to believe her. "Just once," she said. "We can pretend we're making a baby." Then she'd return to Berlin and leave me alone.

There was a place on the road to Bad Oldesloe, a converted mansion, now a fancy hotel on a Landschutzgebiet, protected parkland. We arrived separately by taxi, had lunch, and retired to a room overlooking the lake.

Rather than tarting herself up, Herta had removed her Reeperbahn make-up for the occasion, and I was touched by this, although it left her looking less Wagnerian and more Neanderthal. Without mascara, rouge, or lipstick, the bulbous brow and heavy jaw dwarfed the rest of her face. Over lunch I couldn't help picturing her arms and thighs, no longer as packed sausage-meat but sagging on her heavy bones. To offset this I called to mind some of Herta's satisfied customers; I could remember them all too easily, the ones who came back for seconds. The leather-coated chap with the shaving cuts who looked like a Schmiermichel, an off-duty cop. The grinning one with the bowtie and fedora, full of himself. The one I called Einstein—he'd just visited the city, the real Einstein, that is, though the Reeperbahn wasn't on the great man's schedule—because of his droopy eyes and matching moustache. Was Herta showing each of them the Unit 17 tattoo on her chest? Explaining it? Was it exciting them, to go where so many Russians had boldly been?

As we climbed the broad, carpeted steps towards our room we still hadn't so much as held hands. Hers were as plump as ever, I'd noted that too during lunch, and now I tried to bring back memories of tugging Herta excitedly across the wet Schloss Brüel pastures, the morning after the storm; and couldn't. Not with the full-grown woman beside me hefting her big hips up the hotel stairs.

Wie schön, she said, admiring the view from our room. "Were you here with others, before?"

"Never," I said. Not in this particular room.

She sat down in one of the armchairs beside the bow window. "Who did you come with? Tell me. Some of the girls from the Kiez?"

Unlike my own private roll-call of Herta's afternoon-encounters, her interest didn't seem prurient, just curious.

"I haven't been here with any of them," I said.

"With whom then? They know you, here." Grinning, "D'you think I couldn't see that?"

"Business lunches," I said, grinning now too.

Herta giggled and I settled on the window-seat. The canopied bed seemed an endless walk away.

We sat in silence. A moment earlier, protesting my innocence, I'd almost called her Karin, something I'd never done with Marianne or any of the others. I racked my brains for safe subjects for conversations. Perhaps unsafe ones would be better, we might find we'd really come here to talk, not fuck. I glanced at her.

"Yes?" she said.

There was a small smile on her face as though she were a patiently reproving nanny, but I realized that wasn't the intended effect at all. She was trying to look dignified, to match the setting. Her hands clasped in her lap gave away how nervous she was.

"So, talk to me," she said.

"What about?"

"Your life on the Kiez."

And how I got there; no; "I want to talk about the Schloss," I heard myself say, to avoid the Thurgo-story, I thought. And yet that wasn't why.

"About Schloss Brüel?" Herta didn't take her eyes off me. I felt them looking harder, without humour now, but without reproach either, and I had to look away at the trees and the water below us.

The whole thing had been sculpted to look like British parkland, I saw that now, sloping lawns and tall oaks in isolated groups like stately, chatting elders watching a game of croquet.

"You said it was destroyed."

"Yes."

I saw the figure *17* the Russians had burnt into its walls as they'd burnt it into Herta. Crows cawing in the silence—no, that was in winter, when I'd first visited the Schloss; and the crows were here now, outside the hotel bedroom window. Ludolf with a candle in his hand, catching me stealing Branntwein.

"I married Maggie's sister," I said, gazing down at the oaks. "The Frau Gräfin had several sisters, and I married one of them."

When Herta said nothing I looked up.

"Because you couldn't marry the Frau Gräfin," Herta prompted gently. She was infuriatingly calm. Fat hands in her lap. Sitting there like—like Ellie almost, with the expression that had always maddened me, the worldly-wise look of the abused.

"Yes. Because I couldn't marry the Frau Gräfin."

No, damn it, Molly was her own erratic, battling self, I'd loved her for it and she wasn't to be confused with that . . . pretentious cunt, as Alec had called Maggie. I could see Herta fighting back a wider smile.

"Everybody knew, did they? How I felt about Maggie? Even in the kitchens?"

"You looked at her like a big dog, Richard."

Rishard she said it, making me feel faintly queasy, also that I was in the presence of a total stranger. Had she been calling me Rishard in her mind all these years?

"Like a good dog waiting for an order," she explained, and studied my response. "I can call you Rishard?"

"Richard," I said, thinking, she's going back to Berlin tomorrow. If I can get it up today.

"Rishard," she nodded.

I hesitated, then her nanny-face gave me the impetus. "Did you also know that I buggered the *Herr Graf*?" I said. "Without waiting for an order."

She shook her head. "That's not funny." And after a moment, "I don't believe you."

"It's true, I did."

Nein!

Doch.

Now I'd got to her. The servant in her. You didn't bugger the *Herr Graf*, certainly not without being asked.

"And I raped you," I said. So much for Thurgo the good dog, the lapdog.

"Raped?" she said. Puzzled, then amused. *Aber Rishard . . .*

For a moment I couldn't work out what was happening. What did she mean, *But Rishard . . . ?*

Smiling at me now.

What? I couldn't speak to get the word out.

Smiling at me. Genuinely surprised.

Vergewaltigt? she repeated the word, sweetly mocking. "Raped? I thought you'd *never* do it, you were so shy."

I found my voice. "You fought me!"

Herta shook her head.

"You bit my hand—you bit right through it!"

"Why were you so rough?" she said. "There was no need to be so rough."

I stared at her, as she leant forwards to me. Then she took one of my hands and began to stroke it with extraordinary tenderness, as if it weren't the lardy peasant hand I'd always kept out of sight whenever possible, but something finer and more sensitive altogether. And how they fitted, our pudgy hands, gloved paws with something beneath the mattocky tissue that cried out at its own clumsiness, made it angrier. My fingertips began to tingle the way they had as a child when I held something lightly and the nerve ends became drunk with touch, distorting the scale and feel of the object, a marble perhaps, so that it felt gigantic, airy, like a huge balloon, even though I could see the thing was there, contained, between my fingers. I began to cry but couldn't move towards Herta for comfort and she had the wit not to do more than stroke my hand as if I were a grieving animal.

When she led me to the bed I was shaking with lust.

"Rishard," she said.

"Richard."

She couldn't get it. But it didn't matter.

I'd misunderstood my life, that was simple enough to grasp, but it was another thing again to understand it correctly. What I'd been expiating all these years—angrily, defiantly—wasn't a crime, just my own stupidity, I decided. My sheer stupidity. I'd misread Herta's fifteen-year-old signals. Or rather I'd read them correctly, and then mishandled it. (And after Maggie and Peter's wedding I had blood in my eyes, I was blinded by it.) Yes, I should feel better about myself; just a clod, Your Honour, no malice at all in the fellow.

But I was still in trouble. Worse than ever in fact, and clod-hood was no more use in sorting it out than malice was. Every day trains for Berlin left without Herta.

We both knew why. It was no good pretending our meeting at the hotel had been just another afternoon-encounter. Which was why it wouldn't, mustn't happen again. I didn't really want it to happen again, I convinced myself. It was like sleeping with nanny—with the Dear Nose, indeed, who thought she'd been small and wiry had possessed a heavy, wattled face like Herta's. I dwelt on Herta's grossness, her unappealing flesh (even the "17" tattoo had been a disappointment, illegible and blotchy like peeling spots of sunburn). It was a matter of persuading Herta that it couldn't go on.

I begged her to honour our agreement, and return to Berlin. At this she began to cry and tell me stories of Otokar Weiss and how he treated his girls. If you complained to the police, Herta said, you could count yourself a *Lampenbraut*—a lamppost-bride: dead. She insisted that if she returned to Berlin there would be no escaping Otokar, and I believed her. Why hadn't she told me this before? That she couldn't go back to Berlin? Because you wouldn't have made love to me, she said with exasperating logic.

"But it's all right, Rishard. We don't have to make love." We could talk, just talk.

She wanted to talk about Egon and Ludolf and her shame at having gone with the Russians. She wanted to tell me about little Franzl, and when I tried to stop her and said I didn't want to hear about any of it, the tears came again. Opa Ludolf had known that Franzl was hers—though she'd never said who the father was, Herta kept repeating, as if I owed her for this—and it was Opa Ludolf who'd suggested to the Frau Gräfin that Franzl should go in Egon's place. This had been done without Herta's knowing; she would never forgive Opa Ludolf.

(Even as I blocked my ears to this, I saw her climbing into the back of the Russian truck, under Ludolf's eyes, giving herself deliberately to the savages who'd humiliated him—humiliated them both. Sweet vengefulness: "Look what you've made of me, all of you!" Yes, she carried as much rage as I did.)

Now it was all down to me, that was what I understood from her story. Was I going to be like all the rest and treat her as a slave, as the kitchen girl, illegitimate, disposable, a piece of meat to be thrown to the dogs?

It was she who was making herself into a slave. She would clean the Grotto Azzurro, cook and wash for me, do anything, she said. I could have other girls, she didn't care. She'd heard I had a *Fixe* at home, a "straight" girl. That was all right too. Just let me stay in Hamburg, she pleaded. Until the baby comes, I feared she would say, but she didn't. Herta wasn't crazy. Just addicted.

She began to follow me, at first trying not to be noticed. Since she was about as inconspicuous as Vlad in a blond wig, this didn't work very well. I didn't know what to do about it. What could I do? Buy a ticket to Berlin and put it in her hand? Call Arno Schiller and ask him to send her back to Otokar? Arno wouldn't be pleased—neither would Wolli—to know I'd been messing with one of his girls. Every night Herta was there at the Grotto, dancing with the customers as if she was part of the service. Vlad took a fancy to her himself, but she ignored his attentions. He offered to throw her out, if she was becoming a pest to me, as he put it, but I couldn't bring myself to do that. Not yet.

I'd find a way to make her understand; or perhaps time and a cold shoulder would do the trick. She was still plying her trade outside the Olympia, and if I went to the Colibri or the Sorrento to do business, Herta would arrive, order a drink, and sit watching me from the bar. Once I saw her in the compartment behind me on the U-Bahn and changed trains several times until I lost her.

Then one day she was missing from the Reeperbahn. That night I expected her to arrive at any moment in her apple-green *Twisthosen*, heading for her usual barstool. Kaspar behind the bar would have the crème de menthe ready almost before she got there. But she never showed.

Not the next day, or the day after. I was breathing sweet relief when Willi Bungert bobbed through the door of the Olympia. *Hé, Gartenzwerg!* I called, knowing I was the only man on the Kiez who could call little Willi, once a mettlesome amateur boxer, a garden dwarf. For once Willi didn't crack a smile. His *Chef* Arno Schiller wanted to see me. *Sofort, Reinhard*. Right away.

Arno held court at the Prinz Eugen Hotel, opposite the Grotto's Hamburger Berg entrance. I detested his style, which included a strings-and-piano trio in the lobby, playing popular classics. He was the only Kiez-baron who went in for corny gangster-poses. The armchairs seemed to have been chosen so that everyone except Arno in his corner chair sank into bottomless fabric. It was hard to maintain your dignity while being eaten alive by brocade. We exchanged the pleasantries Arno favoured; I admired his tie, he admired my shoes, which were indeed new—since Martin's arsehole-shoes I've searched in vain for comfortable footgear—and were all Arno could find about me to admire. After a boisterous version of "La Paloma," in my honour, the piano trio returned to Strauss waltzes.

Ja . . . die Marlinda. Arno adopted a finicky expression, grimacing at me. "Where is she, Reinhard?"

I feigned surprise. "Have you lost her?"

Arno disliked *Humor*. Willi was already flashing me warning glances.

"Is she not in Berlin?" I asked.

"Would I be asking you, Reinhard, if she was?"

''You've spoken to Otokar?'' Arno didn't bother to answer. ''Why *are* you asking me, Arno?''

Mensch, said Arno patiently, ''d'you think we're blind, on the Kiez? Every so often *eine Nutte* gets a notion about a man, and it ends badly. We all understand that.''

I glanced hurriedly at Willi. He was expressionless.

They thought I'd killed her.

''But now Otokar is out of pocket, *nicht*?'' Arno was saying. ''And I'm out of pocket too.'' He smiled. ''We're civilized people here. I decided I would speak to you before I spoke to Wolli.'' Arno smiled his catty smile. ''He's so busy.''

''We're all busy, Arno,'' I said, struggling to my feet out of the fly-trap armchair, ''it's only evil-minded ponces like you who can afford to sit around all day listening to cheap music. Let me know when you get a decent orchestra. Or a better tune.''

Arno had been moulding himself on ''Krimi'' novels for years and this gumshoe patter—it sounded twice as derivative in German—was the only kind he recognized.

Then one evening that week Karin came into the apartment wet and shaking herself like a frenzied otter, and ran past me, to the window. When I asked her what on earth was the matter, she said, ''Someone's been following me. A woman.''

I tried to muster incredulity, but I felt sick with fear. Arno was right; it would end badly.

''A woman? What does she look like?''

''Big. Dark hair. I think she's a mad person.'' Karin backed away from the curtains and turned to me, her teeth clamped tight over infolded lips to hold them still. ''You look, please. I think she's gone.''

Dark hair? Herta in a wig? Now I was really baffled. I looked, but there was no-one in the street below.

The woman had followed Karin home from the Atelier, the artists' studio, in the rain; she couldn't help noticing her—such a strange big woman, at first glance like a man—but she'd thought nothing of it. Just someone who lived in Altona too, perhaps, going home at the same hour. Then the woman had been there outside the house when Karin went out with Cäsar, and followed them into the park.

Cäsar was Karin's birthday present from me, that December: a Schnauzer puppy who'd won her heart at once. Now in July he was no longer an endearing black woolly bundle but a quivering monster with blazing dark eyes who looked as if he'd just been goosed by the city's main electrical supply and would short out, emitting smoke, unless earthed at once or given something to do with the accumulated energy. Karin named him after a childhood pet; I'd wanted to call him Wolli, or failing that Adolf, on the grounds that striding through Hamburg at night while calling "Adolf! Adolf! *Komm!*" might be as good a way of flushing out neo-Nazis as Philby had ever devised, and that to bellow "Wolli! Sit!" would give me personal satisfaction at the end of the day. Neither would have won me friends on the Kiez. But Cäsar was to be Karin's dog, and I didn't anticipate taking him to work. Poor Cäsar! in time he became the most famous of all Reeperbahn dogs. But in those days he was passionately attached to Karin, and although he tolerated me it was her he yearned for. As if embarrassed by our common gender, Cäsar would save up all his Scheisse for his walks with Karin. If I took him round the park he wouldn't so much as cock his leg at a bush. The truth is, she was more patient with him than I was, and took him for longer walks; it was probably Cäsar's way of showing his appreciation.

The dark-haired mystery woman put in no appearance the following day. Perhaps it hadn't been Herta after all; I only hoped Karin wasn't developing fantasies of being followed— thanks to Herta's behavior I now had a clear idea myself of what this felt like.

That night I heard Karin climbing the echoing stone stairs, after taking Cäsar on his final outing. Then came a knock on the apartment door. Assuming she'd left her keys behind, I went and opened it.

Herta stood there. A Herta in close-cropped black hair, dyed and cut to match Karin's, successfully enough that for an instant—I was so confidently expecting Karin in the doorway—I thought it *was* Karin, bloated by some ghastly accident to the face.

Gefällt es dir? murmured the grotesque apparition in front of me. Do you like it?

There was a smile on Herta's face, and the tone of her words was clearly intended to be coyly charming. But she was so evidently frightened that they came out already defeated, harsh; and the smile became a rictus as she saw my expression.

I stood there helplessly, unable to answer, thinking only that Karin might return with the dog at any moment and find us here . . . that I had to tell Herta to go—then realizing that it wouldn't do any good, she'd only be back, return and do something worse perhaps, and that I had to use this moment to bring Herta to her senses.

It was too late for reasoning. Herta reached out to me and all I could do was pray that I'd wake up and find that none of this was true. She took my hand and gently brought it to her cropped black head, rubbing it through the silky artificial curls, utterly unlike Karin's wiry little whorls of hair. As she did so I saw her left wrist, the underside of it, and I knew at once where Herta had been during her disappearance from the Kiez.

I let the waves close over me; it was no good trying to fight against it any more, trying to keep the worlds apart.

"Come in," I said.

She'd seen my eyes go to the fresh, livid scars below her fat palm, the cross-hatched stitching like a ghastly nest of spiders infesting the flesh, and now, too late, she hid her hand.

Come in, I repeated, took the hand and drew her into our narrow hallway.

Herta glanced round anxiously, strangely skittish. In profile the black cap of hair looked even more ridiculous and toupée-like, bobbing on her fleshy head. Somehow I'd assumed Herta had picked this moment knowing Karin was out, that she'd been watching the house, waiting to see Karin leave, but she hadn't.

Wo ist sie? Herta whispered. Where is she?

Sit down, I said we've got to talk; not knowing what on earth I'd say, but leading blindly—the kitchen was right ahead of us and some half-baked instinct, perhaps that Herta in the kitchen would strike Karin as less of a violation than Herta in the sitting room, led me towards it.

At once all I could see were knives, knives on the wall, Karin's lovingly honed set, an unwashed knife on a plate by the sink, another on the kitchen table where I'd used it to prise open a package. Did failed suicides try again so soon? I didn't know but I scooped up the knife from the table before Herta reached it.

Too obvious a gesture. I regretted it immediately. A moan came from behind me and I turned in terror, thinking I'd now put the idea into Herta's head, with so many other knives within reach—perhaps that was what she'd come here to do, in front of us—

Her blue eyes were staring as if she too had woken into a nightmare. Then in the next instant I realized she'd simply heard the sound of the key in the front lock, and in the instant after that, as I was still registering the opening swish of the door, an excited hellhound with tales to tell came springing into the kitchen, ears and frisky poodle-tail erect.

I've never been so relieved to see anyone or anything in my life. From the first Cäsar had been a rotten guard dog, treating every stranger as an invitation to play, and he stood there in the doorway looking from Herta to me and back again in furious glee, as if someone had told him there was a rabbit in the room, disguised, and he had just five seconds to decide which one of us was it. You could kill yourself in front of your lover, I thought, gazing gratefully at him, you could kill yourself in front of your rival, or your lover *and* your rival, or in front of the whole world on television, but there was no way on this earth that you could kill yourself in front of a wildly enthusiastic dog.

It was only a suspended sentence, a brief moment of grace. Karin was in the kitchen doorway now too, she'd gone puce, with anger I thought at first, then it seemed more like lack of breath, eyes bulging, standing there open-mouthed and staring at Herta as if a hideous twin had stepped out of a carnival distorting mirror and taken her place.

Wackernagel's arrest came out of the blue, in the summer of 1957. We read about it in the newspapers, without warning. Karin seemed glad and also somehow resentful, understandably so, as if this too had been stolen from her. But I found it harder than ever to gauge her reaction. Since Herta's irruption into our lives Karin withheld as much from me as she had when we first met—more perhaps; or else I just felt it more keenly now that we lived together.

We were still living together, after a fashion. I'd had to tell her what Herta was to me, there was no other way to explain her presence in our kitchen. Once I'd begun I had to tell her everything, right back to Schloss Brüel and the wedding—I didn't know how to tell the rape any more but I described what it had meant to me—and up to date, with the exception of my hotel afternoon with Herta. I should have included that, for honesty's sake, but even with hindsight I can't see how it would have helped. It seemed at the time as if I could explain Herta's fixation simply in terms of the past and what I'd done to her then, and didn't need to hurt Karin into the bargain. Especially since Herta was soon gone from Hamburg and from both our lives.

They had stared at each other that night, Karin and Herta, on and on as if Cäsar and I didn't exist. Gradually the high blood in Karin's face, which had given it a colour I'd never seen there before, began to drain, and I was afraid she might faint. Herta was the first to move, advancing on Karin, I couldn't see her expression, and before I could react Cäsar began to growl. The growl rose abruptly to a great snapping protective bark, barring Herta from the doorway and from Karin. It made us all jump. *Ruhe*, Cäsar! I managed, *Platz!* The dog ignored me. Herta had backed off towards the table. "I'll take him to the sitting room," I said, but I didn't like the look on Cäsar's face, and hesitated. When I glanced at Karin, hoping she'd call off the dog, I saw that her eyes were still fixed on Herta.

"It's all right," I said, as much to Cäsar as to Karin, "this is Herta, Herta Pohl."

But Cäsar had begun to stalk her, growling, twisting round me as I tried to block him with my legs. "For God's sake," I said, and Karin came to life at last and spoke. "Cäsar!" He obeyed and went to her, and as soon as Karin turned to push the dog down the corridor Herta bolted past me into the hallway, out of the open door and down the stairs.

A week or so later I heard that she was back with Otokar in Berlin, which got Arno Schiller off my back, though our games of Skat at Willi's bungalow never resumed after I'd called him an evil-minded ponce.

How clever I still thought I was then, keeping my distance from the worst of Reeperbahn behavior! I didn't see how thoroughly I'd become its creature, that even the gifts with which I now showered Karin were Reeperbahn gifts, jewellery and frocks, things that showed off the giver, the kind of gifts an Arno Schiller gave his favourite tart. It was so hard, I thought, to know what to give someone with Karin's frugal tastes. Giving anything at all amounted to a confession of guilt, I knew it but I couldn't stop myself. When I'd said I never had a fling with Herta, Karin seemed to accept this. But our sex life went rapidly downhill and when I asked why she was less and less keen, demanding a certain *Stimmung*, the right occasion, the correct atmosphere, Karin pretended to be surprised to hear that we were doing it less often. I hoped she was pretending. If not it called into question just how vivid our passion had been for her, in earlier days. Even in the throes of it she only said she loved me under duress, when I coaxed it out of her; she'd said that she was happy—no small thing, I told myself—and once or twice that she was happier than she'd ever been before. One day when she fended me off because the *Stimmung* wasn't right, and I started to complain, she surprised me by snapping, "No-one makes love in Hamburg.'' ''Oh, you mean they only fuck?'' I said angrily. She shook her head. ''No-one fucks in Hamburg either,'' she said.

For a second I took this as a barely veiled reference to the fact that the hotel where I'd met Herta wasn't *in* Hamburg, it was a mile or two outside. Then I remembered that there was no way Karin could know that. Perhaps she was simply mocking my claim that I hadn't done anything at all with Herta: as unlikely—was this what she meant?—as claiming that no-one in Hamburg did anything at all. But there was a calm about the way she made the remark that seemed to convey something very different, a conclusion long since drawn about the city. It was one that made precious little sense to me. We'd finally added the ''Kasbah'' to the Grotto's amenities, and underneath Hamburg if not in it there were customers fucking as if it was their last night on leave.

Our trips abroad had also slowed to a trickle. We couldn't go on leaving Cäsar in kennels while we were away, because he pined for her, Karin said; and after a few trial runs we discovered that he was too much for Mutti to look after, and knocked her down in his exuberance. I had a solution for this, however. It was precisely a trip abroad, a big one, that Karin and I needed, I was certain, to clear the Herta business; that and a change of apartment, to lay the kitchen ghosts.

We would go to Italy as soon as Wackernagel's trial was over. We'd go with Cäsar. And Mutti too. By car. Oxfart was an excellent driver—and I'd already discussed the whole thing with him. We'd hire a limousine, he could have a chauffeur's livery if he wanted it, I promised, yes, leather boots too; no doubt we both saw the same picture, Oxfart lounging elegantly in the piazzas, sizing up the talent. We'd even discussed the route. Karin had always wanted to retrace Goethe's own *Italienreise*. Oxfart himself was startlingly knowledgeable on the subject.

On our return, as I envisaged it, we would drive through Hamburg, past Altona (Mutti smiling, Karin puzzled and intrigued) along the Elbe to Bauernstrasse in Blankenese, stopping outside a little chalet in a row of charming, eccentric houses. Blankenese was Hamburg's equivalent of Hampstead, a community of artists and rich people with quaint tastes, a Transylvanian Polperro overlooking the severe, bird-haunted estuary. ''Home,'' I would say. I'd bought the house several months ago and begun to decorate it—tastefully, this was no Grotto—with Karin in mind. I'd shown it to Mutti and she approved. Cäsar certainly approved, since the place had a garden. Karin was the only one who knew nothing about it yet.

If that failed to cheer her up I'd marry her. In for a penny, in for a pound, and on the Kiez I'd discovered how many more bigamists there were in the world than I'd ever suspected. At a certain level of Hamburg society (not one that Mutti would have recognized, admittedly) it was almost chic, and no home was complete without its double.

When I look back I see now that my reckless period had already begun. I was no longer getting up early to rush to the Reeperbahn, where the faded stink of the morning Grotto was little incentive after a late night and closing up the club at four a.m. I was so busy with the Blankenese house I sometimes didn't go in at all. I was even making excuses to avoid my Tuesday lunches with the Dod. I hadn't cleared the Blankenese house with her, and didn't want to discuss what had happened with Herta, or any of the reasons for our prospective move; though it was also true, as I told myself, that the Dod as a taffeta lobster was an image hard to erase, discouraging somehow when it came to baring your soul.

Karin still faithfully attended her sessions with the old girl, and often returned with eye red from crying. I wanted to take this as a sign of progress, but when I asked what she and the Dod had been talking about, she said: "You." She was still taking sleeping pills and, I discovered, other kinds of pill explained to me as "mood-swing agents," and occasionally an obscenely large oblong green horse-pill, a gelatinous object that went by the name of Oblivon; all of which made Karin groggier than ever in the mornings. I still woke early out of habit and lay studying Karin, whose sleeping face disclosed a surprising range of moods from peaceful through vexed to combative, sometimes tight-lipped as if her dreams tasted like bitter coffee, sometimes strangely composed as if the night had aged her and given her the puffy, benign face of someone who'd reached a farther shore.

As the lines and wrinkles, still just as dear to me, came to stay on her face like dream-residues that persisted, they seemed to me to make more and more of a coherent face for her, a finished painting as it were, with all the dots joined up. The bumps and tumps were no longer isolated farmhouses on the map of a deserted region, there were lines criss-crossing the area as if civilization had overrun it at last, and I sent the moles along them on imaginary journeys down her cheeks, taking this or that intersection to go shopping at her mouth or follow the faint, downy, jawline hairs, to curve up before reaching her chin, up under the corners of her lips where the shadows gathered. The harelip was always a little pink in the mornings, as if blood had gathered on either side of the rift, looking for a place to cross. The small nose was at rest—when Karin laughed hard enough her nostrils would dilate and collapse in again, faster and faster like a rabbit-nose, enchanting, though I'd made the mistake of telling her about it and now she covered her nose with her hand when she laughed. Asleep, she gave herself away as guilelessly as Cäsar with his muttered hunting cries and jerking paws. I knew when Karin was dreaming by the twitch of her eyebrows; they were like something the Song of Solomon might have celebrated (and Cäsar too), a thicket alive with young roe deer. The rest of her face was quite still when she dreamed. At nine I'd wake her with coffee. Firmly; there was no other way to do it if I was to rouse her at all.

When she got up Karin would immediately make the bed, before heading for the bathroom; making me feel uncomfortably as if she were trying to erase all trace of our presence together in the sheets. It reminded me of the way her face seemed to be trying to renege on her words as soon as she'd said she loved me; when she did. "I'm a cheat and a liar," she said once, out of the blue, and I hastened to deny it before she could elaborate, afraid that what she meant was that she'd never really loved me. Just as worrying were the days when she wouldn't leave the apartment, even to go shopping. "When I think it's German air I'm breathing," she said on one of the rare occasions when I coaxed her into talking about it, "I feel as if I'm suffocating." "You're Karin Posener," I said, "why must you take responsibility for all things German?" "Because no-one else will," she said curtly. About this time there was a remarkable case of stigmata in Hamburg, affecting one Arthur Otto Moock, a middle-aged wood salesman with no religious leanings of any kind, who shared with St. Theresa the unsolicited eruption of Christ's wounds seven years after an accident of some sort: in St. Theresa's case a fire, in Moock's a car crash. When the story broke in *Der Spiegel* I had an immediate vision of Karin developing similar symptoms, and as I made frantic attempts to prevent her from seeing the newspapers I experienced once more the vertigo that affected me where she was concerned: was it my own morbidity I was struggling with, or hers?

As it turned out when we read *Die Zeit*—which had the fullest of the rather cursory newspaper reports that summer—

Wackernagel had been arrested in Baden Baden, where he was selling insurance for an unnamed company; arrested not for his pre-war Fuhlsbüttel crimes but for horrors committed at a later date. He had already been caught by the Americans in '45, we discovered, and extradited to faces charges in France, where he'd served with the Waffen SS. After two years he was released without trial, apparently for lack of evidence, and had gone to ground. *Die Zeit* didn't say where. There was nothing in the article to confirm or disconfirm our Karlsruhe lead. But, looking back, we'd hardly known what we were doing; we didn't even know the full extent of Wackernagel's wartime exploits. Following his French tour of duty it seemed that Hermann had returned to take charge of the SS contingent at Fuhlsbüttel on the occasion of its promotion from *Polizeigefängnis* to *Konzentrationslager* and outstation for its larger, sister concentration camp, Neuengamme. A British bombing raid had put the main runway out of action at the neighbouring Fuhlsbüttel airport, Egon's airport as Karin and I thought of it, then a vital Luftwaffe base. Faced with a huge hole in the tarmac, someone with a sense of urgency and the mind of an engineer from hell had calculated how many corpses it would take to fill the hole, this being the quickest way he could think of to fill it. It was not asserted in Die Zeit that this someone was Wackernagel; nor was this ever proved. What *was* asserted by the Hamburg Procurator was that Wackernagel had supplied the corpses, seventy-three of them. With two exceptions, both German citizens, the dead were Russian women being held in Fuhlsbüttel C block, in Wackernagel's charge. They were there for the crime of having gone on strike against conditions at the nearby factory, where they were employed as prisoner-of-war slave labour. An SS unit led by Wackernagel had allegedly herded the women into a truck, driven them up the road onto a patch of wasteland scrub called the Ohmoor, now a golf course, shot them and delivered them still warm to the airport for use as hardcore.

There were other charges relating to that period and to German prisoners at KoLaFu as Fuhlsbüttel was known for short, crimes similar to the torture and slow murder of August Posener; but they had the familiar ring of inconsistent, unsubstantiated accounts. The main work in bringing Wackernagel to trial had been done by relatives of the dead Russian women, themselves Russian-born but now German citizens with rights they had pursued in a more organized way than Karin or I. And with a better case, it seemed. The Beast of Kolafu—this was not *Die*

Zeit speaking but the sensation-loving *Morgenblatt*—would receive his just deserts. The newspaper itself claimed to have tracked down eyewitness testimony to the Ohmoor massacre, in case the prosecution case was below strength.

Now was the time, I suggested, to add our evidence to the rising swell of indictments against Wackernagel. "Would Vati want that?" said Karin. "Isn't 73 enough?" I was surprised by this, but I nodded, thinking that perhaps the Dod had been doing good work on mitigating Karin's old obsession. But "Isn't 73 enough?" lingered uncomfortably in my mind.

Puzzling over Karin's remark that no-one fucked in Hamburg, I'd begun to remind myself of some of the small, bizarre things she'd said over the years, infrequently but more regularly now. Unless I was just noticing them more. The odder comments she made contrasted so sharply with her customary restraint that I'd often decided the lapse was mine, not hers, that it was I who for some reason couldn't see how straightforward her words were. "I always fall in," she said once when I suggested we try a newly opened quayside restaurant close enough to the water to hail passing ships—so its advertisements boasted; and I laughed because she'd never fallen into the water when we'd visited the port, or anywhere else that I could think of, or that she or Mutti had ever mentioned. And when I teased her about on a later occasion, by Wolli's pool at Sieg Holstein, saying, "Careful, you'll fall in," she didn't respond and it was my joke that fell flat.

Another day she said, ". . . like the time you hid from me with Cäsar in the Jenisch-Park, remember?" When was that? I asked, and she described it to me in detail, a game of hide and seek in snow already so trampled that it gave no clue where Cäsar and I were hiding. But we'd never taken him to the Jenisch-Park together, it was far too long a walk, and I'd never hidden from her, there or anywhere else, and she agreed it must have happened in her dreams.

I didn't know whether it was a good idea for Karin to attend the trial or not. Perhaps she might not want to, in view of her reluctance to contribute evidence. Finally I phoned the Dod. "If she wants to go, take her." The Dod was very curt with me on the phone. I'd earned it, I knew, by cutting her out of my life. But I'd never imagined she could be so imperiously cold. I couldn't bring myself to tell her about the planned trip to Italy, or the new house in Blankenese.

A dear little house; the redecoration now almost complete, though I'd become superstitiously afraid of adding the finishing touches to it. There was plenty of time to find bedspreads, cushions, and the like, too much time as the months went by and we waited in vain for proceedings to begin against Wackernagel. He was in custody, though not in Fuhlsbüttel, I was sorry to discover. The old prison was an empty, abandoned hulk; all the more appropriate, surely, to have re-opened it for Wackernagel and held him there on his own like Hess in Spandau, in a *Gestapogefängnis* full of echoes, but no, the Germans were wary of theatrical gestures. The state was assembling its case, we were told—waiting, I took it, until the initial publicity had died down and Wackernagel was all but forgotten. This was ominous, but despite my fears that he'd be released again, as in France, a courtroom date was finally set, in March of '58.

The day before the trial opened I paid what I hoped would be a farewell visit to Fuhlsbüttel, on my own, and to refresh my memory. Gazing at the stunted, imitation-Gothic gateway with its toy turrets, I wondered about the sculptor responsible for the stone-carved head over the entrance. How could anyone have foreseen, in the 1870s, what was to come? Yet as an emblem for a mere *Zuchthaus*, a house of correction, the face—part leering man, part lion—was too demonic altogether, its mouth agape in a rapacious grin, eyes popping. Too knowing a face to belong to a hungering beast, but with its great animal tongue extended in gargoyle insult, no longer purely human. Don't be fooled, said the grime-blackened lion face, don't be taken in by the homely red brick cellblocks and their air of boarding school privation. We devour people here.

The court buildings on the Sievekingplatz I found to be almost as bleak, a series of matching palaces of an ochre colour. These *Justizgebäude* seemed to be paying off a debt to the Romans and their architecture, but in instalments, as half-heartedly as the Fuhlsbüttel gateway was to the Goths. The pediments still awaited figures, and the columns capitals. They looked much as one might imagine Louis XIV's stable block, here and there a curlicue but why waste more invention on horses? Just enough pomp to remind servants and stable boys who their owner was; and niggardly enough to remind them of their place. The same principle, applied to criminals, ruled the cavernous interior, where touches of marble and mosaic hinted at the civilities available to the fully reformed villain. Down the broad staircase a

coiled marble balustrade—purple, a most unpleasant touch—
writhed like an umbilicus to Mother Crime.

On the first, crowded day we were all there bright and early,
Karin, Mutti, and the Dod too, stiffly acknowledging me. Cäsar
had been left with Oxfart for the day; Oxfart was frightened of
the dog and Cäsar knew it, but if we were all to travel to Italy
together it would be good if they came to an arrangement to
tolerate each other.

Wackernagel was led in, wearing a neat grey suit and a blue
and silver tie which we were to see again on the final day; in
between, the suit remained the same but the tie varied, discreetly implying a businessman's wardrobe. He was quite bald
on top now, with sleek greying wings of hair flat at his temples.
Heavy lines ran from nose to chin and enclosed a firm, raw
mouth. It was a careworn face, but from responsibilities, it
seemed to say, from tedious duties, from filling in too many
forms; the face of a senior clerk. There were co-defendants in
the matter of the Ohmoor killings, and they filed in behind him,
less trimly dressed, as if to show continued deference to their
old boss. They all sat staring into space, giving the impression,
as the various counts were read aloud, that whoever was on trial
here it wasn't them.

There was little to make anyone feel a trial was taking place
at all. I never thought I'd yearn again for the formality of British
courts, wigs and gowns and a robed judge in the gods, beneath
a gilded coat of arms. Something about the civilian air of the
panel of judges seated at the same level as the prisoners threatened no more than a slap on the wrist, a taste of reform school.

When the witnesses were called, beginning with Fuhlsbüttel
survivors, my spirits rose. Instead, the effect was worse. It took
me completely by surprise. Faced with the grey courtroom walls
and the shellacked benches like a school examination hall, I
longed for some vile, tearful description to transform the place
into a theatre, despite its lack of ceremony; I wanted cries,
shaking fingers extended in accusation. They came all right. But
in a mere fifteen years the events recounted in testimony had
somehow acquired a coat of varnish as impenetrable as the grey
shellac all around and beneath us. No matter how vivid the
picture, it belonged to a bygone era. Sobs and dramatic gestures
only enhanced this sense of borrowing. We were all helpless
before it. Even the details seemed to have been studied at the
cinema, right down to the organ music reportedly played in the
KoLaFu prison church adjoining C Block, during the evening

hours of torture, to drown the victims' screams. It was real, it had happened, we kept telling ourselves; this thing of darkness I acknowledge mine—yes, only we weren't on a desert island contemplating the past, like Prospero, in a shipwrecked, penitential state. We were freshly rigged and sailing under another flag, when this forgotten thing, this Wackernagel-monster, surged up from the bilges. The Hamburg public knew it, even if we didn't. Apart from ourselves and the mostly Russian relatives of the victims, the public seats were empty. Three reporters attended the first day. Soon only one was left, though the other two returned for the verdict and sentencing.

For three days the Folterungen, the beatings and other punishments undergone at KoLaFu between '43 and '45, were enumerated before us. Old men had been made to stand all day and night revived with kicks and bucketfuls of water when they fainted, and made to stand once more; men and women humiliated, starved, flogged; one young man had refused to name resistance colleagues and his fingers had been chopped off in turn. The dead acoustics of Gerichtssaal 5 seemed to absorb it all, making the voices sound flat, rehearsed. Thinking this was perhaps a professional response, the lawyer in me used to more tensely resonant surroundings, I kept an eye on Karin, Mutti, and the Dod, but they too looked stifled and depressed. It was more frightening than the testimony itself: history and the choking indifference it brought was manifest in that courtroom as though it emanated from us, the observers, like sleeping gas. There was no statute of limitations on the crimes we were hearing about, not yet. But there didn't need to be, if emotion itself was perishable. Even the witnesses seemed to recognize this, and let themselves be cowed by Wackernagel's relentlessly sarcastic counsel, Herr Mühlendorf from Munich. It was easy for him, he had the room, the air, the very walls on his side. Is this all? the jaded courtroom atmosphere seemed to demand. We've heard better torture-tales than this! Come on! Where are the thumbscrews, the electrodes applied to testicles, the red hot wires inserted into the penis, the buggering with bullwhips?

At the end of the first day we walked blindly through Planten un Blomen, away from the court buildings, and separated at the Dammtor, unable to face each other. A good start to the trial, we said. It was indeed; certainly it was. Even the Dod was silenced. She and Mutti headed east in one taxi, Karin and I west to Altona in another.

We were the monsters, spoiled gluttons fed for years on the

most delicate cruelties that print and picture and selected anecdote could offer. The sense of anti-climax was too shaming to put into words. There was hope: this was only the beginning, and the Ohmoor shootings had yet to be anatomized in court. But that couldn't be said either. It would be too close to admitting our own hunger for the gruesome.

Karin seemed far away, going through the motions of preparing dinner. Silence, usually so comfortable for both of us, hung heavy that night, and we made desultory conversation over the meal until Karin asked me to tell her, of all things, about Herta.

Liebchen, I said, I've told you all I know about her.

Karin looked dazed for a moment, then suspicious.

"You've told me about her?" she said dubiously.

"Everything."

Then I saw it wasn't me she was suspicious of, but herself. It puzzled her that she couldn't remember.

"Tell me again," she said.

It was an unsettling echo of Herr Mühlendorf's favourite phrase. We'd heard it over and over in Gerichtssaal 5. "Tell me again," he would patiently demand of a prosecution witness who'd just described events in Fuhlsbüttel to the Hamburg Assistant Procurator; and as the witnesses found themselves unable, after so many years and so many re-tellings, to use any but the same words, Mühlendorf would let the appearance of contrived rehearsal speak for itself, along with the tedium of sheer repetition.

I hadn't told Karin more than a broad outline of Herta's experiences after she and Egon were parted and the Russians had dragged her back to the Schloss. This was just what Karin wanted to hear about, to judge by her rapt expression. I felt idiotic, as if I was the final witness of the day.

Had Herta actually killed Germans, Karin wanted to know, when she'd become Gerda and put on Russian uniform? It wasn't Herta herself but *Otryad 17* who'd put the uniform on her, to be precise about it, I said, though joining the Russians in the truck had certainly been Herta's decision. I could only remember Herta saying she'd shot at Germans; not whether she'd hit any. But Gerda was a good little Russian soldier, I recalled her saying, and by night a good little Russian bitch. She'd even repeated this to me in the soldiers' Russian. Who knows, perhaps she had killed Germans.

Something in Karin's expression seemed to say "Don't you understand, then?" But understand what? When I asked what she was after, Karin only shook her head. Go on, she said, tenderly, as though I were a pitiably innocent witness for the other side who was walking into her trap, incriminating himself word by word. But we weren't talking about Herta and me; just about Herta. Why were we discussing Herta at all?

"I've told you most of this before, *Liebchen*."

"I don't remember."

She clearly didn't. But at last Karin allowed herself to be hugged and taken to bed.

Her words anticipated Wackernagel's. Now it was he, the accused, who didn't remember. Again and again he said it, when he took the stand. "No, I don't remember. It's so long ago . . . *mag sein*, it could be . . . but I don't remember."

Was this an adequate defence? Mühlendorf seemed content to collect his client's forgetfulnesses like so many butterflies to show the court. Even the other defendants grew uneasy at these point-blank denials. "Come on, Hermann," one of them grumbled aloud, to my amazement. That's it, I thought, even his own men are turning against him. Now he'll break.

But Hermann remained steadfast. And gradually his protests of amnesia, uttered in the sane dull monotone, became oddly convincing. Perhaps he really didn't remember. Then, as the day went on, the words "I don't remember" took on a different colour again—as neither an evasion, nor a challenge to the evidenciary weight of the prosecution case, nor as an honest statement of the truth, but as an obstinate reminder of what the entire trial was conspiring to forget. *We* were the ones who didn't remember, who wouldn't bring ourselves to remember who and what we were now: a Germany without memory. He alone proclaimed the true spirit of the courtroom, as if he were the bravest of us and not the cowardly thug we knew him to be.

Every so often the past broke through, restoring a different, precarious kind of sanity. Survivors recalled him pushing and shoving the Russian women into SS transports in the Fuhlsbüttel courtyard. He was already waving a pistol, they said. These gentlemen—they were all *Herren*, in this case—couldn't have seen me, said Wackernagel. And Mühlendorf proved it, taking an afternoon to elicit from each witness where their cell had been and using a hugely enlarged map of the prison to show that none of them had a clear enough view of the courtyard to have made the identification.

The parade of witnesses touted by the *Morgenblatt* the previous summer, who'd actually seen the executions on the

Ohmoor, turned out to be one woman who'd heard shots from her house, and seen no more than distant figures. No-one denied that there were bodies under the Fuhlsbüttel runway, or that they were the bodies of Russian women from KoLaFu C Block. Herr Mühlendorf graciously conceded this and was thanked by the court. Heartfelt thanks; his concession prevented the appalling cost of having the entire length of the runway dug up to find and identify the corpses, interrupting civilian air traffic worth millions of Deutschmarks. Long, heavy compliments were made by Hamburg, in the shape of the President of the court, to her sister city Munich, in the shape of Herr Mühlendorf, for not taking advantage in the battle for tourist revenues.

Finally, the commanding officer of the Luftwaffe wing occupying Fuhlsbüttel airport at the time could not be called to give evidence about the unusual method used to repair his airfield, because he was dead, killed in France six months later; and his former underlings now claimed ignorance of the affair.

Yet *someone* had taken the women from C Block in the early morning of the 10th of August 1944, while it was still dark, driven them to Ohmoor, shot them by the light of the headlamp beams, loaded them up again and dumped them directly into the bomb crater at the airfield. There was no-one at KoLaFu, Konzentrationslager Fuhlsbüttel, with the authority to do this except Gruppenführer Wackernagel, the State Procurator pointed out in his summing-up. No-one else could have done it without the Gruppenführer's consent and cooperation. And why would some mysterious, unrecorded SS visitors have done it, as his esteemed colleague Herr Mühlendorf had suggested, when Wackernagel himself had the manpower available, in the shape of his former SS colleagues and present co-defendants? And the motive—that too was available. Letters entered into evidence had shown that the Gruppenführer was under a good deal of pressure from the Sicherheitsdienst to take in more prisoners at Fuhlsbüttel; that his appeals for correspondingly more SS personnel had been turned down. In some of these letters Wackernagel complained bitterly of being left short-handed, even that there was some danger of a break-out by the prisoners. By clearing C Block of the mutinous Russians and replacing them with more docile and exhausted internees on their way to Neuengamme from other labour camps, he could fulfil what was being demanded of him without risking his control of the prison. Now whether or not Wackernagel had been seen clearly enough, that murky morning, to be identified—said the Procurator—was not a question to be judged by every-day standards. Prisoners who had learnt to identify their tormentors by their footsteps, let alone voice or appearance, would not have mistaken Wackernagel's voice in the courtyard, shouting at the women as they were loaded into the trucks. The Gruppenführer's sadistic ways had been amply documented by witnesses; it could not be said that he was too tender-hearted a man to have committed the greater crime of mass murder. Only the harshest penalty must be exacted from such a man, one who showed no sign of remorse and could not be supposed to have suffered years of secret shame and expiation. Hamburg dared not hold its head high while this *bestialische Mörder*, this brutal killer, was alive and at liberty.

It was a pretty firm speech, though to me the "alive and at liberty" bit seemed at once to ask for the death penalty and to modify the demand. In reply Mühlendorf dwelt, as expected, on the circumstantial nature of the evidence, on war crime precedent, on technicalities of identification. Lawyerly arguments, and they sounded hollow after the Procurator's eloquence. Mühlendorf also used the word *Russen* a great deal more than was necessary, in referring to the victims, as though hinting strongly to the judges that to make reparation to the *Russen*, the Russians, would strike an unpopular note at a time when so much of Germany was still under the heel of this hated race. The judges looked unimpressed. You've got it wrong, Mühlendorf old son, I thought. You Bavarian oaf. Hamburg *loves* to be out of step. You've just signed your client's death warrant.

I could have got him off, I thought; and in doing so realized how far I'd moved during the trial towards seeing it purely from the viewpoint of a legal eagle, in Alec's phrase.

The night before the sentencing was the longest of my life, not because I was on tenterhooks about the outcome—I wasn't—but because I was afraid for Karin. She couldn't sleep, and wouldn't take her pills. She didn't want to be groggy the next morning, she insisted. And she would be, she said, if she took enough to get her to sleep that night.

So we stayed up. We walked Cäsar through Hamburg, round and round. He loved every minute of it. We even went out to visit Vati August's grave, though I warned Karin that the cemetery would be closed, and it was. But the walk to Ohlsdorf and back helped the small hours to pass. "They'll convict him, won't they!" she kept saying. It was as if she was appealing to me to argue with her. I didn't want to play devil's advocate, and in the process perhaps shake my own confidence in the judges. My refusal to substantiate her fears seemed to make her frantic—again I was bewildered, I couldn't follow what she wanted from me—and once she strode away from me when I shouted, ''Yes! Yes—they *will* convict him!'' as we crossed the expanse of the Dom, in the dark. The featureless concrete cliffs of the Flak-towers dwarfed her as she hurried across the empty square; in the distance I could see a silhouetted Bismarck on his monumental throne, sword in hand and brooding like a judge with Wackernagel on his mind. Cäsar bounded after Karin, and when I set out after them Karin broke into a run.

Was there anything else I could have done that night? I've asked myself that a thousand times and all I can see is the three of us running dementedly through the empty Hamburg streets as if the devil were after us, Cäsar yelping with delight, myself calling after Karin to stop, and chasing, chasing until I catch her, both of us exhausted now and leaning against the freezing wall of some apartment building as I hold her tight and the dog puts his paws up against my back, trying to get in on the hug.

After our restless vigil we should have been as groffy as if we'd taken sleeping draughts in the first place. But we weren't, we were both still frantic as we walked up the Reeperbahn to-wards the Wallringpark and the court buildings. The Kiez knew of my connection to the Wackernagel trial and along the way several people, including old sleepless Robby at the Sorrento doorway, wished us luck and a suitably merciless outcome. Ox-fart emerged from the Olympia to take charge of Cäsar, and gave Karin a good-luck kiss on the cheek. Then and there, see-ing this moment of tenderness from Oxfart, the first he'd ever shown her, I ached to tell Karin about our coming *Italienreise*, all of us together in the limousine as we'd glimpse the Mediter-ranean for the first time; about the house in Blankenese and everything I'd planned for her. But it wasn't the moment. She was hearing and seeing nothing in her excitement, and I doubt if she even knew it was Oxfart who'd kissed her and wished her well.

Since the first day of the trial, Mutti and the Dod had declared themselves unable to face any more of it; even today they wouldn't come, despite my pleas. No, we were to phone them at once with news of the verdict. ''If he's acquitted I don't want to be there in any case,'' said Mutti bluntly. But I wondered if that was the reason. It was conviction, not acquittal, that I feared at that moment, the futility of a revenge that—as Mühlendorf

had reminded us more than once during his summing-up—
wouldn't bring the victims back to life. Exemplary revenge belonged to the law, to the state; it would crumble in our hands if
we tried to squeeze private satisfaction out of it. Mutti understood that, I thought. But did Karin?

To warn her against the disappointment, not of failure to convict but of retribution itself, seemed almost impossible while
she was so anxious about the verdict alone. But I tried. I thought
she'd gone completely deaf and then, abruptly, when she understood what I was struggling to say, she threw me an extraordinary glance—as if I was at last saying what she needed to hear,
showing that I'd finally understood. I felt an idiot for not having
talked about it earlier, not a word on the subject since the night
of the prison diaries; but now (happy to get in my own summing-
up) as I elaborated my theme, the old legal theme of the role of
the state in relieving the individual of the intolerable burden of
punishment—of its perpetual inadequacy as well as of the need
to punish—I saw I'd lost her again. Reinhard, I thought: shut
up. Once it was over, that was when it would really hit her, the
emptiness. Which was why the trip to Italy was so important,
even if went by in a trance, or in despair; and the new house,
the fresh start.

The defendants were brought in, Wackernagel as impassive
as ever, the blue and silver tie seeming to deny the days since
he first wore it, at the opening session. Nothing had happened
in between, his expression said so as clearly as his choice of
clothes, the whole trial had been an illusion, already forgotten.

Then came the judges. I'd studied each of them at length
during the trial until I was certain I had their number. First the
woman President whose face told of some grief of her own and
who'd make Wackernagel pay for it; then the plump time-serving
ex-lawyer with his notes and questions, I knew his British equivalent—he'd recognize a fellow-spirit in Hermann Wackernagel
but would go either way on the verdict, content to follow Madam
President's lead; finally the ascetic, bespectacled one who'd sat
like a statue through the trial, not a flicker of an expression. I
had him pegged for an ex-Nazi, thère were more than fifty of
Hitler's appointees still serving on the Hamburg bench, Karin
had told me. He'd be for acquittal but the other two would out-
vote him.

The charges were read out once more, and a verdict announced at the end of each count. Wackernagel's indictments
were taken first. He was acquitted on every one. As the voices

droned on, dismissing the lesser charges against his co-defendants, I barely heard the verdicts. *Freigesprochen.* Acquitted. Freed—the word came over and over again, as we watched Wackernagel shake hands with Mühlendorf, snappily, in the unsmiling German fashion, as if sealing an insurance deal. Showing us and the world that there was no need to make a fuss, and hadn't the outcome been obvious all along?

Karin hadn't moved or reacted in any way that I could see on her face. I had her hand clasped between mine, but it was still cold, I remember, from our walk to the court through icy March winds.

The Russian relatives were on their feet, shouting and weeping and battling with the court ushers as Wackernagel slipped out with Mühlendorf. That's it, I remember thinking. That's all.

Karin stood up, pulling her hand from mine, and moved quickly through the crowds, sliding between people, towards the door.

She had her bag clutched in her left hand instead of her right, she was protecting it in the crook of her arm like a rugby ball. I noticed it as I got up to follow her, and in that instant I knew what was coming. I plunged through the Russian women, ignoring their cries and when I reached the door Karin was almost at the head of the stairs with the gun raised in her right hand and the bag swinging open from her left, spilling articles of make-up. For a moment their tinkling clatter was the only sound on the balustraded landing. Everyone had stopped moving.

I ran for Karin as she steadied the pistol, first high in the air, then pointing down the steps, and I grabbed her arm, pulling her off balance. Shouts came from behind us, shrieks, and in the pandemonium Mühlendorf was pushing Wackernagel down the stairs and away from us as I held Karin to the stone floor and took the gun from her. There were people tumbling over us, on top of us, court officers and would-be heroes, and I was shouting now too, punching, trying to push them off, with Karin being crushed beneath us. She wasn't fighting. She was heaving in the old, dreadful way, no tears, just long, shuddering rasps of breath.

The Hamburg police were surprisingly understanding. After the court verdict I felt I'd deceived myself about the city, underestimated its sheer malignity—or at the very least its cowardice. I expected the worst. But no, the authorities could now afford to be generous with Karin. If they could turn a blind eye to a Wackernagel's crimes, I thought bitterly, of course they could do the same to our abortive attempt at one. It was indeed ours, not jut Karin's: the gun was Isidro, my old Spanish Browning inherited—well, stolen—from the Colonel. It came as no surprise that Karin had known where I kept Isidro hidden. From the beginning she'd been shameless about going through my things—she'd found the washbag full of Tom's money even when I'd hidden it in the upholstery of the Atlantic armchair; my "Caracalla" suite, and her warning to hide my money better . . . that was how we'd met. Isidro The Destroyer: as much a misnomer in Karin's hands as in mine. Even Wolli had survived its best shot.

I was content to be regarded as Karin's accomplice, and refused to say she'd taken the gun without my knowledge. It wasn't just a matter of loyalty; as in Karlsruhe I'd omitted to follow through on my fears, I'd forgotten to search Karin and I couldn't put that down to carelessness. No, there was more to it than that. Thinking back to the moment of the verdict I realized I'd felt strangely glad, as though my own vengefulness had been given a new lease of life. And when I'd rushed to grab Karin's arm, it wasn't to save Wackernagel. She'd raised the gun—to aim it at herself, I thought. To kill herself in Wackernagel's presence. I lunged for her, but even then, as she lowered the gun, she could have fired at him. I was looking at her and not at Wackernagel, but I wonder if she wasn't waiting for him to see her; waiting an instant too long.

We left the court buildings in police custody. Much of that dreadful day is still a blur, with only Karin's stunned and silent face to show for it, in memory. *Ein Schnupfen hockt auf der Terrasse . . . bis dass er sich ein Opfer fasse:* one of Peter's favourite Morgenstern verses, and the wretched thing kept going round and round in my head. "Waiting on the terrace for a sacrificial victim, a head cold lurks . . . until he's picked him." We were released on our own recognizance, without bail, also without Isidro, for which I had no permit. Charges would have to be brought against Karin, both of us perhaps, we were warned. Eberts, the policeman in charge, was kind, I remember that (I remember, too, that he was a true Hamburger: he had absolutely no smell). He tried to tell us what we'd be up against in the days to come. The reporters at the court were no doubt filing eyewitness accounts, at this very moment, of the attempted murder of an innocent citizen—Eberts spoke the words with heavy disgust. Pity the bastard didn't fall down the stairs and break his

neck, he said; and ushered us out the back of the police station
so that we could avoid the crowd of newspapermen at the front.

They caught up with us again in Altona. If only we'd gone to
a hotel instead, as Eberts suggested! But I thought familiar surroundings would be better. Thoughtless, thoughtless fool. Once
I'd phoned Mutti and the Dod I left the receiver off the hook,
and when they arrived I left Karin in their charge, went downstairs to our neighbours and persuaded them to lock the front
door to the street and tell any reporters that we'd gone away.
Even so, voices could be heard at intervals, calling up at us from
the pavement.

Gradually, through that afternoon and evening, Karin came
round, but painfully, like a person thawing out from sub-zero
exposure, weeping and hugging Mutti, myself, and the Dod in
turn. I had Eberts' word that he would do all he could to keep
Karin from coming to trial; there were enough good men in the
Hamburg judiciary, he said, who would be shocked and ashamed
at Wackernagel's acquittal—and who'd know that to inflict more
suffering on one of his outraged victims would only drag Hamburg's name even deeper into the mud. That wasn't going to
happen, he said grimly. But while charges were still pending we
couldn't go to Italy either. Best not to tell Karin yet, I decided.

Instead I repeated Eberts' assurances, and we consoled ourselves as best we could. *Freigesprochen* . . . the acquittal still
bewildered me, but looking round I could see I was the only
one who was surprised by it. Mutti and the Dod spoke of Hamburg in the old days; of August and family outings before the
war. I rocked Karin on the sofa and let the talk flow over us. In
the early evening she fell asleep, without chemical assistance.
It was pitch dark when the Dod and Mutti finally left. I'd had to
endure stiff Prussian lectures about my casualness where Karin
was concerned. My mode of life. My behaviour in general. I
was feeling tired, sad, and sorry for myself when I joined Karin
in bed.

She was still asleep when I woke and brought her morning
coffee. When I couldn't wake her with gentle touches I let her
go on sleeping. In mid-morning I went to the bathroom for a
warm, wet flannel compress I'd sometimes used to wake her
from the soundest sleep, and it was then that I saw all the empty
pill-bottles in the waste bin under the sink. Each of them with
their top screwed carefully back on. A dozen of them at least. I
rummaged. More. They hadn't been there the night before, I
couldn't think where they came from unless Karin had kept

empty pill-bottles, years of them, and decided to throw them all away in the middle of the night.

Next I saw the empty vodka bottle on the shelf over the towels; that hadn't been there either. I went on refusing to believe what eyes and mind were telling me, finding other explanations—she'd got up in the middle of the night, without waking me, unable to sleep, had a drink or two and then, while looking for a pill to take, she'd cleared out her pill-cabinet, that was all. Of course; that was the only explanation. But for a long time I couldn't bring myself to go back into the bedroom to make sure, and discover instead what it was like to sit beside someone who wasn't sleeping any more, to know that the landslide was under way and that your life was changing forever in that instant; the moment you touched a loved one's face and realize they're too deeply still for sleep, they're gone.

WHAT DOES A MAN DO ON HIS FIFTIETH BIRTHDAY (A MAN! A one-eyed, seven-toed thing with a shock of white hair, with false teeth and a curious tattoo on his penis)? Smoke a cigarette, lying in bed, waiting for a thin-lipped, beady-eyed German queer to fetch me—*Morgen, Chef! Alles okay?*—with the car, to go and kill a man.

I don't know who he is, my blackmailer, the one spreading stories about me. I don't know what he wants. (Is he outside the house now, watching?) Perhaps he just wants to destroy me. Oxfart doesn't know who the fellow is either, only where we're supposed to meet him, to discuss terms. There's nothing to discuss; I've already been discredited by his lies. Only last week a boy spat in my path, on the Hamburger Berg—I keep seeing it over and over again—as I passed the entrance to the Grotto Azzurro, now *das Peepshowhalle*, "Voyeur-Paradies" they call it; I had no idea who he was, the kid who spat at me. Never seen him before. But he knew me. "Linker!" he said, and pouted up phlegm beneath his little blond moustache before depositing his spittle at my feet. *Linker!* "Lefty": meaning traitor, scab. Stoolie we called it during the war. I trod on his spittle, pretending I hadn't heard.

A short journey with Oxfart, to the Roman Gardens in Blankenese, our rendez-vous with Herr Blackmailer. I've pictured him with so many faces. Wolli's, Vlad's, even the blond boy with the moustache.

"Some*body*," crackles the St. Pauli announcement on the U-Bahn, yes, somebody, but who?

My secret benefactor in his way, and surely without knowing it. Pushing me along the path I've been avoiding for ten years. Not even Oxfart knows that I'm leaving Hamburg for good, he

586

thinks I'm slipping out of town for a holiday and to let things die down a bit after the deed is done. He doesn't know I won't be coming back.

Long before I understood that I had to leave Hamburg I saw it written all around me. My mind kept me abreast by humming songs whose lyrics were trying to tell me about it, by misreading newspaper headlines, even shop signs. Trauringe, engagement rings, written above a jeweller's shop, with the word Uhren, watches, next to it, I'd read as *traurige Uhren*, sad clocks. Or as I knew my mind was trying to say, hours of mourning. The district of Hoheneichen, Tall-Oaks, announced itself as Hohenleichen, tall corpses. Einrichtungshaus, furniture store, became "Ernichtungshaus." This was an interesting one. Richtung I'd made into "nichtung" or nihilation, as in Vernichtungslager, extermination camp. But where the prefix *ver-* assigns finality, *er-* is a more elusive qualifier, perhaps the most German and metaphysical of all; translucent as holy water, it brings out the colour of the verb and re-baptizes it; *er-* has the connotation of "becoming." "Ernichtungshaus": there's no such term, but if there were it would have to mean "the place of fulfilment through nihilation." Dissolution. All lose: whole find. My Hamburg in a nutshell.

Er-, ver-, zer-, how I shall miss these little shims and washers with which the German language engineers the finer tolerances of meaning; and the great spanner set of its prepositions. Truth prepositional. There is (German will tell you) no truth in nouns or verbs, only *ab und zu*, on and off, from time to time. Above, below, behind, before: truth is the grace of angles. And that sacred geometry I thought I'd glimpsed in the Malaga ravine, as the carrion flies restored me to time by way of perspective, found an echo in the dance of German suffixes.

Staring at the melting head that wasn't mine, and was mine. Inside, outside. The flies knew the difference.

Other deaths come to mind this July morning. Peter's, at the end of a wire rope, Maggie's in a burning train, Denis Towle's in the Horsham asylum. Life fills up with dead people as you grow older, it doesn't empty; they come and stay, getting nearer until you're bumping into ghosts all the time. Death—this morning perhaps, in the Roman Gardens—will be like being lifted up bodily by them (as I was from the gatehouse of the Schloss, carried unconscious to the Hof by those men—or were they women?) and taken to join them.

After Karin died I went overboard for a time, and did a lot of stupid things. I plunged into the life of the Reeperbahn as I hadn't done before. Many of my antics were ludicrous, shameful as well as stupid, and some of them I've mercifully forgotten. I took a trip to Morocco with René Durand *der Sex-Pabst*, the Pope of sex, and I was so spastic on a mixture of Preludin and hashish that I don't recall a thing about it except for René crying, "On fait la fête! On fait la fête!" wherever we went . . . yes, and standing shakily in the backyard of a farm in the Atlas foot-hills—where the air alone, perfumed by the marijuana crop, was enough to keep a man permanently high—while crooning Eric Burdon in a German accent, "Vee got to get out of zis place," to the scrawny chickens at my feet. That was Morocco. Along with the "Haschi" I became a cigarette smoker for the first time, at the age of forty. And when I met Louise, the exotic dancer from Ipswich who sang Rule Britannia standing on her head and puffing on a cigar with (on occasion) her vagina, I moved on to Havanas for a while. (She stood on her head in a cake stand; we spent hours in Mönckebergstrasse department stores trying to find one the right size.) I gambled, not at the Casino, that was too slow, but behind closed doors—locked doors, with a man on guard watching for the Schmiere—where Kiez-barons wagered thousands on one throw of the dice, merely because it was illegal. Squealing like girls when they lost. More then once I staked my share in the Grotto Azzurro, hoping to lose, but fate wasn't ready to let me off the hook.

One demented night at the height of it, we were drinking in the Sorrento when Wolli returned from the toilets with a hunted look and the news that a man had followed him in, apparently to get a look at his Schwanz from a neighbouring stall. The man had been shadowing him for several days with this inspection in mind, Wolli said. Inspection? We'd teach the peeping nancy-boy a lesson, I suggested, rising to my feet. Where was he? Wolli grabbed my arm. Sit down, *du Arsch*; didn't I understand? The man was from the Bund, the association. The Bund? What Bund? Keep your voice down, Wolli said. That's it, I thought, he's finally flipped. The Bund in question, Wolli was whispering now, was a tight-knit group of former Totenkopf SS men. *Queer* Totenkopf SS men? Nein du stupid fucking Scheisser, he hissed. Didn't I get it? I listened in growing dismay. Wolli himself had claimed to be a member of the Bund, and someone was putting his claim to the test: during the war all brethren of the Bund had swastikas tattooed on their penises as part of the initiation cer-emony. At the urinal Wolli had held his hand over his member, but we couldn't go on hiding from the Bund. They'd catch us sooner or later, with or without our pants down. *Us?* I said. *Aber natürlich.* In accordance with our old arrangement—we were former comrades in arms, weren't we?—he'd put it about that we both belonged to the Bund. Remembering the faces among the flamingoes at Wolli's party, I hesitated. Might he be telling the truth? And if so . . . . Wolli watched me as the penny dropped.

He nodded grimly. No, I said—not Trulla die Zigeunerin, I begged, not gypsy Trulla. *Um Gottes willen*, Wolli.

We were almost drunk enough, but not quite. A back room in the Grotto's Kasbah and a mixture of Haschi and *Rote* got us most of the way there. Reds, no Preludin for this one. Alwine's lascivious striptease did the rest, since we had to maintain erections while Trulla executed the tattoo. Even through the drugs it was almost unbelievably painful, like having your groin devoured by piranha while you watch, and I remember ranting, I'll kill you, I'll kill you, if you're lying about this Wolli I'll kill you, as a way of getting through the jabs of Trulla's ink-impregnated needle. Wolli was laughing and crying at once, and held my hand in a death-grip as Trulla started on him.

She made a lousy job of it too, on both of us, though the spidery ink-scrawl might have satisfied a drunken Bund-inspector glancing at a detumescent penis in a pissoir. Assuming Wolli was telling the truth, that is. Sometimes I think he invented it all as a crazy dare to see how far I'd go with him. Erect, the zig-zag scribble did look a bit like a swastika—with the help of an assurance that it wasn't a little-known form of North African dick-rot. And it became a considerable attraction on the Kiez. Jerking off the swastika gave the girls a good laugh. I thanked God Karin wasn't alive to see it, though, let alone be shafted by it.

I knew perfectly well that by all this craziness I was trying not to think about her. About her death and my part in it. About the loss of her. (And, as I thought of it in my guilty rage, about what I'd wasted, the years, the plans, what I'd put into our life, hers and mine!) As I say, I went overboard. Certainly, I was distraught. Equally certainly, I reacted badly. I took Karin's death as an accusation. My crime, I announced to any drinking companion prepared to listen, was that I'd loved her; though I knew this was the least of my crimes. One night in the Colibri I delivered myself of a loud speech on the subject. It's self-disgust that makes the world go round, I said, our precious self-disgust, and

God help anyone who tries to rid a person of it—by loving them! What everyone wants is someone who can take them or leave them. It's what we want of God, it's what we want of other people. We do not want to be loved. I repeated it, until people stared and then looked away, embarrassed: we do not want to be loved.

I even resented the dog Cäsar for mourning Karin. He was so disconsolate he wouldn't stay with Oxfart, and I had to take him with me on my Kiez-rounds. This culminated in the shameful evening at René's Grand Théâtre Érotique when Cäsar made his name. Overstimulated by the sight and smell of the squelching activities onstage, he leapt up from where he was sitting on the aisle beside me, bounded onto the stage, and ran madly among the exposed posteriors, jumping everyone and everything in sight—to René's delight, though not, in every case, his victim's. I made sure it never happened again, but that one night ensured Cäsar's fame on the Reeperbahn.

I wasn't entirely sorry. Every little helped—even turning Karin's pet into a porno star—to obliterate our old life. Our life! That was the joke. It hadn't been ours at all, or so her death told me. And now I had the task of going back over it day by day, tracing the signs—as we all do in the end, I told my listeners—and learning how much of our beloved's life was lived on the dark side of the moon. (Convenient words, letting me off the hook: even if I'd looked closer, I was protesting, could I have seen more? No-one can see the dark side of the moon. But *is* there something to see in a human being, some controlling plan, if you attend, look closer, think, apply wisdom? What—suppose—if Karin had no idea she would really go through with it until that night, when she woke and, in one of the countless ways I've pictured it, went to the bathroom for a single sleeping pill? Tired, miserable, facing trial by newspaper if not in court. And her pill-cabinet itself proposing a solution. . . .)

That's too easy, of course. No good pretending it was a sudden, arbitrary decision on Karin's part. She'd been saving up the pills, for years perhaps. Why stockpile them, unless with suicide in mind?

But suicide in mind, I told myself, is still some way from suicide in practice. So let me try once more: the act has such an aura of grim, serene certainty about it—but is that always the case? Even as they're jumping, slashing, swallowing . . . perhaps the suicide thinks, am I doing this? Do I want to do this? Even: I'm not sure I can face myself if I *don't* do this, after all the secret vows I've made; and—too late perhaps—I wish I knew whether I really wanted to do this!

All wishful thinking on my part, I dare say, anything to avoid the image of Karin rushing gladly into it, as into a lover's arms. The image of a Karin absolute for death; and my ignorance of this, my contribution to it.

Was it my fault for having stopped Karin on the steps, for pulling the gun away from her? Should I have let her do it? No, because . . . if she'd succeeded, her life was forfeit anyway. Killing an innocent citizen. She'd decided to kill him if he was acquitted. Which meant she was a dead woman, in her own eyes, from the moment the verdict was spoken. No matter what I did next; I'd only delayed the outcome. And the way she'd said, "They'll convict him, won't they . . .'', the night before: as if she was afraid they *would*—now it made sense!—and that she'd lose her chance to nail him.

To nail herself. Was Wackernagel really worth so much to her? If so the last few years, with Karin mentioning him less and less, had all been make-believe. That didn't ring true. What, then? What did ring true? I kept coming back to the sense that it was done against *me*, that it was me she was trying to kill. I even wondered, crazily, whether she hadn't found that she was pregnant by me and—for whatever reason—preferred to die; absurd, and I had no evidence for it, only a sense of how much Karin must have loathed me, to take the pills and then come back and lie down beside me. That was the hardest thought to bear.

Why *did* she do it? The Dod would have the answers. But I didn't want anything more to do with the Dod. The expert! Her answers had led Karin—how else could I see it?—to an overdose of the pills the Dod had been prescribing, and I hated her for it.

That too was Karin's legacy, the hatred. She'd left us each a little hand grenade engraved with our initials, or rather a ticking bomb with no instructions for defusing the thing. I kept remembering the look that passed between Karin and Herta in the kitchen, loaded with enough rage to kill half Altona—Karin's at being supplanted by this nightmare frump, and Herta's, faced with the privileged little survivor I'd shacked up with and preferred to her. (And Cäsar growling; a kitchenful of rage!) In memory the little mat of dyed black hair on Herta's head became the judge's cap, and death the sentence I'd demanded. For all my bluster I was haunted by the fear that in dallying with Herta I'd set it all in train, the final lurch of Karin's life; and, through

Herta, finally said the thing no-one had dared say to Karin: that she was a phony, that she hadn't been raped by the Russians or tattooed with burns, that she didn't know what it was like to stink of gangrene, and shoot at your own countrymen. Yet Herta . . . Herta was the one playing make-believe with me—let's pretend we're having a baby . . . playing it openly, that was the difference, while Karin and I kept it all under wraps, took make-believe trips and cradled her make-believe vendetta.

Real now; she'd died for it. Real all along, if pain is all it takes to purchase reality. But is it? Is it? How I've hated her! Pored over every martyred, self-denying trait—making my own case as a martyr!

Karin wanted to prove that she was the only one who remembered, who cared. (And it's true—Herta *had* forgotten. It wasn't for the Russians that she cut her wrist) Now I would be forced to remember. The suicide's dying curse, and I was stuck with it all right.

The Reeperbahn wasn't oblivion enough, I didn't think it would be but I rode it while I could. In the end I walked into the Dod. Our paths had to cross somewhere, I suppose, but I was scrupulous in avoiding Ohlsdorf cemetery at the weekends when I knew she visited the graves with Mutti. Karin's and Vati's, side by side. Mutti I couldn't face at all; after the funeral and its meaningless embraces it was five years before we spoke at any length. I was in a different part of Ohlsdorf, not the Posener part, when I ran into old Anna-Maria. I'd already been to Karin's grave to water the *Hortensien* I'd planted beside it (why did I do these things? Instead of kicking down the headstone as I dreamed of doing! Instead I plant hydrangeas! Why? To water my rage? *Dummkopf! Idiot!*) It was another of my graves that I was visiting—Cheerybye's, my old partner in crime and business. Import-Export, Im-und-Ex. Now he was Ex, he was the soundest-sleeping partner a businessman could wish. After the Grotto had opened he'd gone back to buying me lunch, at intervals, to hear what the returns were, monthly; and I've gone on telling him, even now that he's dead. It tickles me to think that passers-by suppose I'm murmuring a prayer, when (as befits Hamburg) it's the ledger I'm reciting, over the grave. He's listening, too, I'm sure of that. Whatever he may have said about Germany and the Germans, he never could manage to leave. The last time I saw Walters alive was in the smaller Pornokeller at the Vegas-Girls, where he was reading the *Daily Telegraph* by the light of the flickering antics on the screen; he'd obviously watched the film several times around because as I walked down the aisle towards his portly form I saw him glance up from the sports pages, which were all he ever read, just in time to catch the orgasm on the screen before returning to the cricket scores. He liked it here.

Along the Nordring, one of Ohlsdorf's main arteries, I saw the Dod's heavy, stooping figure approaching me. Too late to take another path. She'd seen me; she looked pleased. Close now, we stopped and studied each other in silence. One of the blessings of a cemetery is that empty *politesse* sticks in your throat.

"Come," she said, and I followed her down a side path between the graves.

I thought I knew where we were headed. Long ago Mutti had told me that Dod had lost a husband and a daughter, before the war; the Dod had never mentioned them. And here they were, two names and dates inscribed on one tombstone. The daughter dead—and this shocked me, somehow it wasn't what I'd expected—at six months old.

We said nothing. The Dod gazed at the headstone and the flowers, anemones, still fresh. To my alarm her eyes were full of tears, and I felt dizzy, seeing them.

"You know why I couldn't keep her?" said the Dod at last, very low, a growl almost. She turned to me. "*Now* I know," she said.

"Why?"

"Because I loved Christ too much."

Her eyes held mine, dared me to look away or to betray my astonishment. This caustic, gravel-voiced old person, this old analyst, invoking Christ? Without knowing what she meant I could see the force it had for her, now, not in some frivolous past when she might have had a religious phase, before finding the truth in Freud. That wasn't it at all. She meant it now. I couldn't take this in, all I could see and feel was the brimming pain in her face, pain nearly forty years old and as fresh as the *Anemonen* by the headstone. Pain addressing me directly, as though I had some gift to give her back, merely by being here to witness it. I who'd called Karin a phony for clinging to her pain. Looking at the Dod that day the first chink opened in my soul—in my heart I was going to say, and yes, that too—which couldn't fully open yet. Not for a few years yet. And you, her eyes said, what is it you don't remember, won't remember?

* * *

Bells. The beautiful St. Nikolai bells, waking me; I must have dozed off, waiting. For an instant the sound brings back a long buried image, something glimpsed from the train as I rode through Bizonia in '48, a riverside quay lined with church bells. Teeming with them, bronze bells of every size clustered on each other's backs like snails; thousands of bells from shattered churches all over the Reich, churches with their tongues ripped out. Those mouldering, weather-stained bells, heaped up like old cars! God's voice not only silenced but thoroughly mocked. After the Belson films I couldn't imagine ever wanting to enter another church.

Gone six-thirty, if the bells have started. But there's plenty of time. Our appointment at the Roman gardens: seven thirty on a Sunday morning, no more than ten minutes by car at that hour. When it's over I'll be going on a short holiday. That's what Oxfart thinks. He won't be surprised to see my bags packed and ready.

For months now—longer perhaps—I've noticed that waking arrives with the sense of a noise I've just missed, the one that woke me, still just audible—an echo (like some Haschi-born truth evaporating even as you think it)—somewhere behind the wainscoting, as though my mind had a hidden passage, a crawl space inhabited by urgent messages that aren't getting delivered. In the moment after waking you can hear them rattling around like mice. Not that my current apartment has wainscoting! Fold Farm had wainscoting. And field mice scurrying behind it. Wainscoting . . . this smooth rubbery-modern little place! Unlike my head this building I live in makes no noise at all, rather as if its walls had been injected with some solidifying foam, given a silicone job like the girls at the Vegas, and had every possible cranny stopped and fillered. No echoes here.

After Karin's death I sold the house I'd bought for her in Blankenese. I never spent a night in it. She never even saw it; but it was full of her all the same, full of the ways I'd imagined her in it. I needed to get out of Altona too, and bought this cramped ground-floor apartment as a temporary bolt-hole, in leafy, respectable Harvestehude. Everything I disliked about it encouraged me, in the end, to stay; its soothing hotel-room blandness, asking nothing, risking nothing, easy to leave.

My bags have been packed for a week, ever since Oxfart received the invitation to this meeting of ours, today. It was delivered by hand to the V-girls, by a boy Oxfart said he'd seen before, once or twice, in the kitchens of the Four Seasons hotel.

A clue to our Herr Blackmailer? Could Wolli have dared to return from exile, from his palace on Capri? The message ran: *Zahl voll du Linker du Leimi du Laberheini*, I was a squealer and a Brit, it said, *Drecktier zahl voll, zahl voll due Ratte*, pay up you rat; and gave the rendez-vous.

Half an hour to get dressed, put on my camel-hair coat and go out to meet the vampire at last. It was Wolli who gave me the coat, in the days before his empire fell apart. He'd enjoy riddling it with bullets. Or stabbing through it. If it's he who's waiting in the Roman Gardens.

The rumours about me began circulating last winter. They were more specific than the insults in the note delivered to the Vegas-Girls, but along the same lines, arguing a common source. The word ran that I was a squealer, I'd betrayed Wolli to the police. I was a "Leimi," indeed a Limey Jew, a Nazi-hunter who'd killed not only Bormann but other missing desperadoes.

Bormann's name had to have come from Walters, in the first instance. Wolli was the only one he would have told. But had Wolli told anyone, in the past? If so, I reasoned when the whispering began, then they and Wolli were the only plausible suspects. The rumour-mongers said I was still hunting Nazis—Wackernagel was a minor case in point, I gathered, but a corroborating one—long after the rest of the world had called a halt. I'd been working with the Leimi spy Walters who'd died in the car-bomb incident in Blankenese. Whether Wolli Zimt was behind the murder or not—many said he was—I'd ratted on Wolli to the Schmiere, forcing him to run for it. My motive? Greed. I wanted Wolli's share of the Kiez. I was a thief. Hence the "zahl voll" in the note: pay up.

It was all nonsense. Almost all.

If I'd been quicker off the mark I could have guessed twenty years ago what was going on between Wolli and fat Cheerybye. Easily said, now that I know the whole sordid story—in '48 I had no reason to doubt Philby when he told me that Zimt was his informer among the neo-Nazis. At the time I quailed when he asked me to report on Zimt's political activities; I wanted as little as possible to do with them, and when Cheerybye relieved me of any such duties I was only too pleased. Philby moved on, and I forgot about him. I feel sure now that he knew how thoroughly corrupt Walters was. It must have tickled him to bequeath Cheerybye to Britain's "postwar intelligence offensive." Hindsight again: when I saw Cheerybye joining Wolli and his former Wehrmacht guests among the flamingoes at Sieg Holstein—Sieg Heilstein as Walters used to call it, an idle joke I thought then—I should have made the obvious deduction. But I wanted to believe he was there to keep an eye on them, as he said himself. I was daydreaming. I ignored it all until it finally blew up—in my face, I was going to say, but it didn't blow up in mine. Daydreaming, as Alec loves to point out, costs lives, usually other people's.

Wolli may have been Philby's informant on the old Nazi network, but he was Cheerybye's contact to it. Or as I assume, and if I'm right it wasn't ideology that brought them together. It was the scent of money—Walters once told me that the Nazis had smuggled five hundred million dollars out of Germany, first to South Africa, then the Far East, dispersing it, investing it. The biggest, quickest killings (as Tom Thurgo knew) were to be made in armaments, then as now. Mausers were needed by the rebels in Algeria. The German army knew where to procure them "arsenal-fresh," with a little illegal help. Someone to steal the carbines from their own armouries. Wolli was in over his head—it was a world where sales talk began in millions, whether dollars or rounds of ammunition—but he wanted the cash. He wanted his Mediterranean hideaway, his palace on Capri. It was his dream, and he got it, for life.

Walters was in over his head, too.

"Fancy another trip to Morocco, Dicky?" He knew about my jaunts with René. "All expenses paid, this time."

"Oh yes? By whom?"

"Some Arab friends."

"What do they want?"

"Oh, all kinds of things. Cheap cigarettes. Corned beef."

"Corned beef?"

"Dicky," he sighed. "If you're unloading crates on a quiet beach east of El Djeb, how badly do you need to know what's in them?"

"Not all that badly, now you come to mention it."

"Attaboy," said Walters.

It was the height of my reckless period and I was game for anything. Besides, Herta had resurfaced in my life. Morocco sounded fine.

News travels from milieu to milieu, and I'd heard with relief that Herta had forsaken the streets and married "einen Fixer," not a fixer but a man from the straight or "*solid*" world, an accountant. Good news, and I decided it was no surprise, there was a ballast of sturdy good sense in the woman. I didn't expect to hear from her again. But news of Karin's death must have reached her somehow—it certainly reached the Berlin streets, since I received consolatory notes and there were wreaths at Karin's funeral from some of the most disreputable men in Germany. Lavish wreaths, too. Mercifully, Mutti was too distraught to ask who they were from. A year had passed before Herta wrote to me (a typed letter, one of her new skills, she explained). It wouldn't have been *schicklich*—"proper," very much a Ludolf word—to have contacted me earlier, "under the circumstances." I was touched by this. No other reference was made to the events of a few years back. She had followed the Wackernagel trial, she said. She'd been shocked by the outcome, and by its consequences. "The war still isn't over," she wrote, and that one sentence, unadorned, so startling from a German, took me by the throat and started me crying, knowing how much it would have moved Karin to read it.

Herta also informed me that she'd written to Egon, care of Alec, and received a reply in what she called "very good German," although Egon had apologized for it, explaining that he hadn't spoken or written it for years. He didn't remember Herta, but had been told who she was. With his letter he sent her a school photograph—which she would have enclosed, Herta said, except that she didn't want to trust her only copy to the mail: perhaps we could meet one day and she would show it to me.

Perhaps. I had mixed feelings about this, on several scores. I'd written to Egon, now seventeen and a boarder at a fancy school in Somerset, to tell him of Karin's death, but since then I hadn't been able to bring myself to write. Communication was strained between us anyway. Almost as soon as Egon had settled into boarding school life, Alec made it clear that he'd rethought the question of Egon's holiday visits to Hamburg. "One foot on the Reeperbahn and one on the rugger field is no way to grow up," he wrote, and to tell the truth I was glad, glad that Alec had taken Egon's upbringing to heart and glad not to have a censorious schoolboy breathing down my neck. His infrequent letters told of runs amassed for the second eleven, or tries for the third fifteen. They began "Dear Herr Sacher," and were signed—always in full—"Yours sincerely, Egon von Lützow-Brüel."

I was in no hurry to see a school photograph if it meant seeing Herta with it, and my reply must have conveyed this. All was quiet, for a time, on my eastern front. Then in '61, the year of Cheerybye's North African adventure, Herta's Fixer husband was jailed for five years on counts of embezzlement and fraud. Sturdy she may have been, but Herta had a gift for choosing the wrong man. He left behind a grim tally of debts. Loyally, Herta was trying to pay them off, and turned up on my doorstep asking for a job. An honest job this time, she pleaded, not as a bar-girl or a *Nutte*. She'd learnt book-keeping from her husband—not much of a recommendation, given his record, though on the Kiez there was always a place for a book-keeper who knew about bending the rules. Was that why she'd come to me, or was she here to see whether there was a place for her in my life? A husband in jail was an expendable thing. The only way to show her it was over between us, I thought, once and for all, was to give her the job and work beside her in total indifference for a month or two. That would do it.

I misread everything in those days. The one thing I couldn't grasp was that Herta really wanted to be my friend; and I saw every kindness as a bribe. She kept her distance, shook my hand and called me Herr Sacher in public, didn't follow me home from work. But she was always there, in the Grotto. She brought flowers to cheer up my office; one way or another she was in the club every day, checking the previous night's take, offering to type letters, run errands, making a pest of herself. Her hair had grown out and it was blonde again, thank God, in a mannish, page-boy cut. She was full of unwanted advice on how to make everything more efficient; she smiled all the time, Doris Day with a Hapsburg jaw. Hardest of all to take was Herta's concern over my wild Reeperbahn nights, especially my gambling. "Why must you throw it away, Rishard? Would Karin have wanted this? What will you do, if you lose everything?" Marriage had turned her into a bourgeois scold, and it infuriated me. She had all the self-righteousness of the convert. I'd liked the soggy Valkyrie better. Rishard this, Rishard that—I pitied her husband if this was the sort of stuff he'd had to put up with; perhaps he'd gone to jail to get away from her nagging, I finally suggested. Herta went silent for a time, wounded, and I thought I'd won the day.

"Gather you dropped quite a pile at the Tabu," said Cheerybye the day he offered me the Moroccan job. Softening me up, or trying to.

"I can spare a few *Blaue*."

"The hell you can. I heard their colour was red and there were ten of them."

He was right. Ten thousand, on the nose. "Who told you that?"

"That nice girl. Blonde. The one who works for you. Big Bertha with the bazooms."

It was the last straw. How dare she go behind my back? I thought. That's it, she's fired.

"Don't look like that," Cheerybye was saying. "She came to me knowing you were in a spot, to see if I could help. And knowing you're a fellow Brit, it seems. But she wouldn't dream of using that the wrong way, you know. She's very fond of you. Worse luck."

I saw an odd expression on his grinning moon-face. Distinctly boyish. Furtive.

"I could take a shine to her," he said.

So that was it! Herta thought she could make me jealous by flirting with Cheerybye! Ridiculous. And when Herta came to me herself to ask for a couple of weeks off, hinting heavily that romance was in the air, I gave her my blessing. I'd fire her when she got back. Jealous? Me?

Where were they going?

"Sunny Spain," said Walters blandly.

I knew it wasn't an innocent trip. He'd mentioned "Gib" in connection with the Moroccan venture. I said nothing to Herta. None of my business.

It wasn't innocent. On their return, as they climbed into Cheerybye's Humber Super Snipe in the Fuhlsbüttel airport car park, it blew up and incinerated both of them.

Everything I know about their death derives from Reeperbahn gossip, and from Wolli, an even less reliable guide. When I went to the British spy hideout in Blankenese to see if I could ferret out some facts, they said they'd never heard of me and showed me the door. This wasn't altogether a shock; ever since Cheerybye had offered me my file back, coded DN for Damned Nuisance, I realized Her Majesty wasn't going to reward me, in due time, for services to the crown.

These days the rumours—fresh growth on a long dead tree—have it that Walters and I were about to expose Wolfgang Zimt's connections to the Kameradschaft of old Nazis, and that Wolli retaliated. (Wolfgang Zimt! A name spoken in awe now—only six years later, my God! Now he's the king across the water, the exiled gladiator, the Spartacus who ruled over a noble-warrior Kiez, once upon a time. What Scheisse!) There was no such rumours at the time—and no wonder, since everyone knew that

Walters was as deeply tied to the Kameradschaft as Wolli. He was their diplomatic contact to the Wilaya people, the Algerians; the Arab cause was their new passion. Cheerybye's passion being money, he'd arranged the shipment, via Gibraltar, for a price. Wolli was to steal the Mauser carbines from German army barracks—or so the story went; Wolli never admitted as much to me. So who blew up Cheerybye and his "girlfriend"? It was all the mention Herta ever got. On the Kiez it was said that the guerillas' representatives had already taken a look at the stolen carbines, and noticed that they weren't German army issue at all, but Czech imitations, with bolts that erupted in your face. (Shades of the Spanish Armada in Grandfather's account, with their useless, exploding cannon.) Walters' death was the Arab revenge for this ballistic double-cross, ran the Kiez-tale. As to who swapped the real Mausers for Czech fakes, no suggestions were made; not while Wolli was still on the Kiez. Soon after his departure people said openly that he'd made the substitution himself and blamed it on the Leimi Walters. Same old Wolli, I thought; for butter read guns.

Wolli always denied it, of course. But in time I came to believe him. There was a little strutting Frenchman on the Reeperbahn in those early 'Sixties days, he came and went, a few months at a time, always boasting about the girls, always inquisitive. Vlad the String warned us he was up to no good. After the car-bomb little Napoleon vanished abruptly; a few years later a reporter called Engelmann described him "to the T," as Oxfart would say, in a piece on gun-running. He was connected to a rogue French espionage unit at odds with the Algerian rebels, and pretty free, apparently, with the explosives. *La Main Rouge* they were called, and it was their *plastique* that erupted under the Super Snipe—I'd be prepared to bet on it.

The Reeperbahn was in a frenzy for a time. Drugs and gang fights and protection rackets were small beer compared to international arms smuggling and Nazi gold, with Wolli *in excelsis*, spanning both worlds. Everyone wanted to be seen with him. But no-one knew where he was, not even the police, who wanted him most.

I knew where he was. On Capri.

We spoke every day, an appalling phone connection to what I gathered was a nearby village post office. He was building his dream *palazzo*, he told me proudly, overlooking the *real* Grotta Azzurra. He was getting a tan. He was never going to come back. But he was starving for news, for every drop of sordid

Kiez-gossip I could bawl down the line to his island paradise. He was desperate to return, it was obvious; just a matter of waiting for him to admit it.

When he did, I went to Inspector Eberts, the man who'd been so helpful after Karin's affray, and asked him on what terms Wolli might return. On no terms and under no circumstances, said Eberts. They were glad to be rid of him, after all these years. They had witnesses (he claimed; bluffing, I thought) who could tie Wolli to a raid on the armoury at Wiesbaden in April. The guns and the ammunition were still missing. And the Kameradschaft connection stank to high heaven in the public prints. If it wasn't for that particular association. . . . But there it was, Eberts shrugged. No deals. Wolli was out.

Bluff or not, the message was clear. If Wolli was to accept it, it would have to be delivered to him in person, I'd only get rage over the phone. And worse. Threats, commands. Hysterics. It would be like reporting to Hitler in his bunker.

And this was how, at last, I got my *Italienreise*, my trip to Italy by limousine, with Oxfart at the wheel. Alone of course, no Karin and no Mutti. Cäsar I left with Vlad, the only man in Hamburg with an arm strong enough to hold him. I had the back seat to myself and sat in state, puffing on my cigar, as German light slowly modulated to Mediterranean.

(Vlad too, it occurs to me now, bears me a grudge—not over the dog; no—a recent, heartfelt grudge. What if it's Vlad waiting in the Roman Gardens? Could I kill Vlad? For all my boasts, the fact is I've never killed anyone. Not face to face.)

After a spot of sightseeing we left the limo in Naples and crossed by stinking, turbulent ferry to Capri. Wolli stood waiting for us on the dock in white ducks and a natty sports shirt. The car journey had been glorious. Now came the part I was dreading. You can't come back, Wolli. You're out for good. It's over.

He knew. Surely, I thought, he'd heard it in my voice when I told him I was on my way to visit him. And now, seeing him standing there in his espadrilles and holiday trousers and his gaudy Neopolitan shirt—why did I feel such fondness for this slim, hungering German figure? In that Latin crowd Wolli was nothing more than a small anxious tourist with a febrile look, his lank hair streaked blond by the sun and held back in a pony-tail. That pony-tail! It suited him so well, somehow he looked even more German now with his tanned face, red lips and vulpine features, and the pony-tail proclaiming who and what he was. A chancer, a survivor, and a loser too—the next tantrum was always just around the corner. Lords of the Kiez! We'd come a long way from the Schaalsee ice, two frozen idiots shooting at each other, trying to keep their balance. All around us now men shouting, vendors clambering onto the boat with pleading hands and voices, and others leaping to the quay with ropes; and the rotting smells of garbage and gruesome sun-baked shreds of sea-food on the dock, flyblown sea urchin and squid. And Wolli waving, so absurdly glad to see us. I couldn't get over how tenderly I felt towards him in this setting, and towards my life. For an instant its strangest ties seemed just, and mine. Of all that crowd with its curious mix of knowing, innocent, and travel-weary faces, visitors aching and ready for the journey back to their Naples hotel, I'd still have picked out Wolli as my guide, a skinny rogue with pale demented eyes, pitiful some-how, quivering like an addict, grinning, moody, full of schemes. Probably a leech, I'd have thought, a crazy stranded foreigner. The anger was still there in Wolli's sinewy arms, the bony shoulders that made me want to hug him like a child.

For an hour we followed him in single file up narrow, dank, shaded paths, the stones steps worn smooth, the high walls be-side us jagged, sprouting wallflowers and blackberry shoots, and alive with lizards; stumbling and striding uphill between houses and walled gardens, reeling with the stink of dogshit and crushed figs beneath our feet.

At the crest of the hill we stopped to drink in the breeze, Oxfart and I, while it quartered our bodies along lines of freez-ing sweat, and we stared at the sea. Oxfart draped one thin, weary arm around my shoulders. *Schön, was, Chef?* Wolli, fit-ter than us, was marching on, calling us forwards and pointing towards an olive grove. Beyond it we caught a glimpse of white walls and green shutters.

The villa was more modest than I'd expected, though still under construction, Wolli was quick to explain. A smiling el-derly couple greeted us at the door, lined up as for review. Cook and gardener, we were told. Over veal and home-grown zuc-chini Wolli talked about the island and its history. Not a word of Hamburg. After supper he took us on a moonlit tour of in-spection, describing further bedrooms, patios and terraced gar-dens, a guest house. A woman's touch was evident in the completed sitting room, expensively chintzy. Anita, Wolli's lat-est flame, had come with him from Hamburg; I thought perhaps he'd lost her along the way, but no, she was on a shopping expedition to Rome. Dispatched to leave us to our business.

Wolli retired for a moment to put on a silk scarf, loosely tied, and a red sweater, and returned to sit beside me, cradling a Campari, studying what seemed to be a careful match between its colour and his evening outfit.

"Your little talk with Eberts . . . no-one knows about it, I hope. Not even Hansi."

I shook my head. Oxfart had unpacked his scarf and descended to the port for a tour of inspection of his own.

I knew I had to speak, but the wine and food lay heavy on me, and the exhaustion of the journey, and instead I sat there in a trance, lulled by the sound of the crickets. They restored Spain to me. Further off, waves hissing on the rocks a hundred metres below us. When in a sombre mood, the emperor Tiberius had pushed visitors off a cliff on the far side of the island, Wolli had told us over dinner, casually. The point was not lost. Bringers of bad news met a sticky end on Capri.

There were lights on the hill opposite, and above it somewhere in the dark were the remains of the imperial palace, its banqueting halls and vomitoria, the little cubicles where, according to Wolli, guests went to empty their stomachs between courses. Or perhaps they went there to be sick out of sheer terror. In the cypress groves beneath the palace there was apparently a small villa where a counsellor called Nerva made the mistake of distancing himself from Tiberius' policies as well as his palace, and starved himself to death as a kind of penance. I decided I'd prefer the quick shove off a cliff. I plunged in and gave Wolli the Eberts news, straight.

Wolli sat perfectly silent for a time, then abruptly and plaintively, "Remember the butter, Reinhard?"

For a moment I thought he was asking if I'd remembered to bring him some German butter. I'd brought him some Schnaps, but—

Schlauer Fuchs, you sly old fox, Wolli said, mistaking my confusion for bluff. "You *do* remember. In the bunker. When I gave you potato for butter. It was a mean trick."

I was too wary, at this moment, to be pleased that he'd finally confessed; given Wolli's silence about Eberts I took it as a prelude to something else, and watched him cautiously. But he was waiting for a response.

"How did you do it?" I asked. "The substitution, I mean."

"I didn't." This came out in the same plaintive tone, Wolli-

victim. "I put a *Stückchen* of butter on it, for you to taste. Just a little, on the end."

"And Vlad? He tasted it too."

"He knew. I paid him *einen Zehner* to say nothing."

Vlad dropping the sliver of potato and rancid fat into his mouth, swallowing and sighing, "Butter!" I laughed.

Wolli shook his head. It was the wrong response. He discarded his Campari and reached for my hand. His palms were unpleasantly moist. "You've always hated me for the butter. Now you won't let me come home."

"You know that's not true." I squeezed back, hoping to end the hand-clasp, but Wolli held on tighter. "Give it a year or two," I said, but I didn't sound remotely convincing. "They'll all have forgotten. And as long as I'm there you're still *der Boss.*"

He wiped his eyes and I pretended not to notice.

"*Du . . . Reinhard . . .* we'll live six months here, and six months on the Kiez, *ja*?" My own eyes were prickling now and I resented it, I'd never been a sniveller until I came to Germany; there was always someone crying on the Kiez. "They like us here," Wolli was saying, "we can do business in Naples. But I need *you* here, Reinhardchen." He made a fist of my hand, demonstrating, then gripped my wrist. I said nothing. He was mad; I could just see us muscling in on the Mafia. "Anita likes you, you know," Wolli added softly, opening even more disturbing vistas. Tiberian orgies by all means, but troilism with Wolli wasn't on my card at all.

"Italian girls, they like this," he jabbed my forearm upwards, suggestively, "with the fist." And he closed his fingers over mine again.

As I feared there was no lock on my bedroom door. I'd have been grateful for one, the way Wolli was talking before he finally let me go to bed. I sat up fully clothed, braced for a knock on the door. No-one came. But lamps stayed on in Wolli's bedroom, below mine. I could see the light reflected in the olive trees outside our respective windows.

After a while I slipped out of the house on tiptoe and took a long slow walk. It was too hot to sleep anyway, and the hills were as richly perfumed as they'd been during the day, when I was hurrying too hard after Wolli to enjoy them. The crickets' song seemed louder now, at night, and when it stopped—if I came too close to one of the hidden insects—it was like a ticking bomb falling silent just before the bang. My journey with Oxfart was the first time I'd been in a car since Cheerybye and Herta's bomb-deaths; it was all I could do to stop myself looking underneath it every time we climbed in. We were all still in shock, trying not to think about the explosion in case it gave us the shakes. Now at last I felt myself giving way to the place I was in, for the first time in months, and I lay down in the spiky grass and herbs and let the wild oniony smells wash over me. There were insect noises, close, and the wind in the grass, and further off the wind in the trees. I slept.

Walking back damp and stiff I saw the light on in my bedroom and a figure in the window, waiting for me. Wolli. I stayed in the olive grove till dawn came and he was gone.

"I have business to attend to, today," said Wolli at breakfast. Oxfart had returned, looking smug and rumpled. "Which boat will you be leaving on?"

Oxfart was humming a Neopolitan aria as we motored back up the Italian coastline with a certain guilty glee—it was like escaping with Alec after a Padstow Christmas. I'd delivered the message to Wolli—whether he took Eberts' advice was up to him—and got away. Our come-uppance came promptly as the black Mercedes began to stutter on the way through Ostia. *Scheisswagen!* Overheating, Oxfart muttered. At first I thought he was inventing excuses to force us to stop, so that he could prowl the beaches we were passing, and I ordered him to drive on. Oxfart was too loyal to remind me how little I knew about cars. When the radiator finally boiled over, I decided it was Wolli's anger catching up with us. Whatever it was, we were stuck on a lonely stretch of road. A turquoise sea to our left, and fields of yellow stubble to our right. In the middle a broken-down black furnace of a car.

Oxfart stripped off and ran for the sea, I didn't have the heart to stop him. The breakdown was my fault. I'd go and look for help myself.

I began to feel happily sunstruck as I tramped along that empty road, picturing myself a legionary on the march and feeling like an artist's wooden model of a man, all jointed bone, dem dry bones. All the slush gone out of me. At last a straggle of houses came into view, but they looked deserted. Not a shop, much less a garage. A bucket of water would be a start, if only I could find someone at home. I knocked on doors in vain, and even tried a chapel some way back from the road and dwarfed by umbrella pines, the only shade I'd found for an hour.

The chapel door was open and I descended some steps into

the subsoil coolness of a crypt. It was empty. I wouldn't find a bucket of water here, never mind a mechanic, but after my walk the air and the dim light were like balm, and I sat panting on one of the chairs.

My breath was as loud as a bellows in the silence. Panting— panting like a hart . . . where did that come from? Was it biblical? I was trying to remember, when I saw the fresco.

Now that my eyes had adjusted, the light was no longer dim; the narrow windows were chequered with yellow panes, giving the harsh afternoon sun a confusing morning tint that glowed on sandy stone with the fading remains of whitewash on it, like pastry with a dusting of powdered sugar. The chapel was small, no bigger than the one where Molly and I were married, in the grounds of Latimer House, that little knobby church with its pseudo-Byzantine boils outside and low curves within. This was the genuine article, so full of glowering undecorated arches that I couldn't see the altar without crouching forwards in my seat. That too—the altar—was plain, an oblong of stone more like a bier or catafalque. No altarpiece anywhere to be seen. Instead a shallow dwarfish ring of arches curling round behind the stone oblong. The dwarf-sized arches too reminded me of my wedding and Molly's coifed head bobbing under me, beside my Flight Officer's stripes; but that had been St. Mary Magdalene's, it occurred to me—"an admirable choice of saint," as Pitmarsh had remarked, out of Molly's earshot—and this one seemed to be dedicated to a different Mary, more piously pregnant than Molly and a good deal less amused by it. The Virgin's image, and the one patch of colour in the place, was on the side wall nearest to my chair. The paint appeared to hang precariously on a thin drift of plaster with ragged edges, evidently rediscovered in the course of laying bare the walls, and luminous with its original pinks and blues. The sunlight caught it perfectly, as if pointing it out to me, imitating the shafts of light in the painting itself, and I sat before it as its first beholders must have done, just as rapt.

I had no conscious sense of what the fresco showed—I didn't think of it then as the Annunciation, though I must have known that was what it was. I saw a conversation piece between two people, the woman barely listening, ignoring the speaker with his hand raised in admonitory fashion. He was threatening her. Or else pleading, since he was on one knee. His diaphanous wings had faded to an outline, like the once-gilded haloes; but for them it could have been a scene of domestic quarrelling, jealousy perhaps. The most startling thing in the painting, though, the one that held my gaze as if it carried a message for me alone, was a fire-breathing dove between the two figures, its small beak open to emit a long trail of flame spiralling down in ever tighter coils into the Virgin's lap.

It sizzled as it spiralled, emitting tiny puffs of flame and smoke. This fiery umbilical to God transfixed me, I could feel the pain in my own gut, although Mary seemed blissfully unaffected by it; and from nowhere, as if I were the one being violated, the idea of a sacred child burned into life in this way, into flesh, made tears start into my eyes. I wanted to get out at once, sickened by the sentimental power of the image. And this absurd mockery union! The woman's eyes were modestly lowered, she was reading a book—completely unaware, as far as I could see, that she was being impregnated. God's scorching fire-borne orgasm seemed to leave her indifferent; or rather she was somehow already with child, by the look of her swelling blue dress, as if the act were only happening for us the onlookers, only beginning for us, and for her was part of history already, quite forgotten. For her the event had no particular occasion. Only for us. I needed to understand why it upset me so; and couldn't leave. The afternoon sunlight shifted gradually off the Virgin and towards the angel kneeling opposite her. He too looked puzzled and frustrated, almost toppling over to get her attention. Listen to me! he was saying. This is direct from God, important! One hand urgently raised. The other clasping a slim green wand crowned with lilies like an unstoppable ejaculation. Mary went on reading. Orgasms all over the place, divine, angelic, it made no difference to her. Between her and the angel, and beneath the dove with its flaming tongue, lay a dizzying chasm. Once more this looked domestic: above, a darkening, receding set of arches, one within the other, led the eye towards a tiny, distant door; below, the runway of the patterned marble floor drew a perspective along narrowing, converging lines: an interminable corridor, as if the whole of time now lay behind the two figures—or before them—or both. Above, below, behind, before; and at the end of it, beyond the black-framed doorway, and so small that I had to stand and walk up to the fresco to confirm it, a glimpse of a sculpted garden, a topiary ball of leaves on a slender stem. A leafy head. Blue sky around it.

If I'd understood the fresco better, or rather acknowledged what was mine about it, there for me to grasp, I might have saved myself a good deal of suffering. Not to mention an eye.

But as soon as we got back to Hamburg (Oxfart having made certain mechanical connections on the Tuscan beach) I put Italy out of my mind. There was plenty to do. Word of Wolli's exile soon got out, and the Kiez-vultures gathered. I did my best to protect his empire—this included keeping the flamingoes fed and, later, finding them and the parakeets a home at Hagenbeck's Zoo where the Vogelhaus is now Wolli's one true memorial in Hamburg. A suitable one, too, since Vogel means bird, but the verb vögeln commonly means to fuck. (As do so many German verbs; in the Onkel-Hugo-Grill we tried to count them once, and gave up only when we'd found a different one for every day of the year.) I received offers for the Grotto from half a dozen sources including the wretched Arno Schiller, offers so insultingly low they constituted a veiled threat. Sell or else. It was a form of negotiation, all the same, and the Tunisians had no such scruples. They were the new kids on the block, out to make a quick impact. The Messerschmidts I called them: literally, knife-makers. They made their own, with olive-wood clasps. Notched—like the dive-bombers—with the tally of their victims.

The Tabu club was now Tunisian headquarters; in turn they started fights at the Fischerheim and Wolli's other, lesser properties, scaring off the customers, challenging me to retaliate, and I did. Oxfart urged me not to lead the raid on the Tabu in person. *Bitte nicht, Chef!* It was a matter of roughing up the place as unpleasantly as possible, and I think he was trying to tell me that at forty-six I was getting too old for *mano a mano*.

This was nonsense. And in the event, when someone pushed the huge old Tabu coffee machine over onto me, I'd have been slow to get out from underneath it no matter how young and fit I was. Then I saw the dull flicker of a home-forged blade, and after the knife plunged into my face I remember none of it, not even the pain and the roaring screams which I gather alarmed the Messerschmidts as much as my own boys.

There's no denying that it was a turning point, both for me and for the Kiez. That night my downfall seemed—briefly—to have heroic overtones. It had something of the death of Gustavus Adolphus, the Lion of the North, as Peter described it—at least in one respect: after I fell my men fought all the harder, and Oxfart managed to rip down the Tunisian flag and pass it on it before the ambulance and the police arrived.

But the Tunis had made their point. I was out of action, and it was they who, in Kiez-terms, had arrived. I lay in my hospital bed, helmeted in bandages like a half-exposed mummy, gazing upwards with my one good eye and, when faces entered my field of vision, adjusting to the world as one eye sees it, somewhat flattened. The other eye was gone, my Messerschmidt eye. It was out, removed, but for weeks I could feel the blade-thrust, as if the metal had broken off in my head. I felt cut in half and I raged over it. In the end it wasn't as brutal a loss as I feared; now I can't even recall how two eyes see. The eyepatch suits my Bluebeard face and I've come to enjoy the effect it has on other people. (The threat of the empty socket behind the patch is even more potent than the unsettling effect of the glass eye I had made a few years later. I hardly ever wear this. It's a pretty lifelike eye and not uncomfortable once it warms up, but nowhere near as convincing as the officer's in Malaparte's story; even at my most glazed I doubt if anyone would call it my more human eye. In fact it gives me a look of Mr. Carstairs the stuffed and moth-eaten bear in my school science lab, another reason not to wear the horrid marble in my head.) Best of all my empty eye socket excited my friend Louise, upside-down-in-a-cakestand Louise. She liked to sit on the scarred, unfeeling thing and grind herself against it until she shuddered with release. A lesbian orgasm I suppose, two sockets without a plug, but most of all the act reminded me of the whores and their amputee clients in the rubble precinct—a fascination with any flesh that was less than fully flesh. A child's itch, this seemed to me, a need to probe the horror of the created universe, that abyss between ecstatic receptivity and its frail, material vessel; intact one instant and vibrating with messages from the ether, a crushed beetle the next. Danger, absurdity, the maddened psyche quickening the flesh to self-awareness: what could be more voluptuous? That was Louise's secret. In orgasm she had the look—I'm speaking now of times when we made love in less extravagant positions, and I could see her—of a ten-year-old on a whirling fairground wheel, rigid, eyes wide, swooning with holy terror. Straight-legged in ecstasy like the boy-Christ on a reindeer, at the Schloss! I savoured this. At other times I felt abused, excluded, as if by rubbing against my useless eye with her vagina (that prehensile, cigar-smoking orifice) she were mocking my dead wound with her live one; as if hers were all eye, inside, all darkness crying to be seen, and punishing my blindness.

Lying in hospital after the stabbing, I told myself I wasn't half blind, not a bit; one eye was busy thinking (I could almost feel it doing so). Seeing required a little more imagination than before—that was all. Distances were a little harder to judge, but I'd always been clumsy. I was used to bumping into things. The doctors warned me that reading would be exhausting at first, and might give me headaches. So when I came out of hospital I withdrew to my little apartment in Harvestehude, and listened to music. Bach was my comfort: close my eyes (I was still working them in concert, reflexively) and I was in the church at Tempzin listening to Peter play, or at the Schloss, beside the Bösendorfer. I stayed away from the Kiez, and received only Oxfart, for business reports.

As the months went by this became a soothing routine. To preserve it, and to spite the Tunisians, I sold out Wolli's empire to Arno Schiller for a pittance. All I kept for myself was the old Tanz-keller in the Grotto, re-naming it the Vegas-Girls in accordance with changing fashions. Wolli ranted down the telephone that I'd bankrupted and betrayed him, but I didn't care. It was hard to feel sorry for Wolli. (And he didn't seem too upset about my eye, lost in defence of his territorial rights.) I did feel sorry for Vlad, since despite all his loyal service it was Oxfart I put in charge of the Vegas-Girls. Vlad loved nightclubs, but those days were over on the Reeperbahn, and the Vegas just wasn't his sort of place, it was a porno-palace jammed with film booths and magazines. Soon, as with so many of my old friends and lieutenants, I didn't see Vlad any more.

My days were easily filled. I took Cäsar for walks, and visited my assorted dead in Ohlsdorf cemetery. Karin beside Vati August; my Dornröschen, little thorn rose as the Germans call Sleeping Beauty. Walters next to Herta. *Schlaf schön*, I told them each in turn, sleep beautifully. After the car-bomb—filled with steel pellets as well as enough explosive to have destroyed several cars on either side of Cheerybye's—there had been little of him to bury, or of Herta. Less than the feet, long since rotted, in my own grave. I wrote to Ludolf, but received no answer, which left me in ignorance as to whether he was dead or still bitterly impervious to Herta's fate. I could have taken her ashes to Mecklenburg. I didn't want to go back there, that was the truth of it.

As for Cheerybye, he would be shipped home to Walters relatives in England, I assumed, care of Her Majesty's Government. But no, it seemed his family wanted none of him, alive or dead. Keep the scoundrel, they said. We did, and soon I was haunting Ohlsdorf like a cemetery gardener. I came to know the gravediggers, and the other regular mourners. I even watered their flowers for them when they went on holiday, as well as my own Hortensien, the hydrangeas I planted at Karin's graveside. Their blossoms are a deep reflective blue, and thrive.

I visited the zoo, fed Wolli's parakeets. Came home to Bach. *Ich will Jesum selbst begraben!* (But did this mean "I want to bury Christ himself"—or bury Him "myself"? With Peter gone I had nobody to ask.) Sometimes I put on Händel instead, in memory of Peter's other musical love, but it burdened me somehow, as though Händel were my former Kiez-self, expansive and delighted, the voice of the infinitely possible. Bach and Händel were arguing about God and the Kiez, while I tried to picture myself heading for the Reeperbahn again. It was just a short walk down the Grindelallee to the Dammtor, then a kilometre or so of botanical garden-stroll through Planten un Blomen; passing the old plane tree rendez-vous of Karin days; or worse, making a detour to avoid it. Or I could go by U-bahn to St. Pauli station and walk down from the Millerntor. Or even to the Reeperbahn station itself, its stairs to the street emerging opposite the Grosse Freiheit like a trap-door, centre stage, hidden and garlanded by newsvendors' stalls, where I saw myself appearing once more (*"Reinhard! Der olle Reinhard!"*) like a demon king in my old horse-blanket cape, my eyepatch and the cane I carried when my feet played up. Grandfather of the Kiez! But months passed and I didn't go. Like Tiberius, who Wolli said never returned to Rome once he'd exiled himself to his island fastness, I couldn't take the first step.

Gossip, Oxfart told me, held that I'd lost my nerve after the stabbing. Whatever the reason, my long slow walks with Cäsar took me in a different direction, away from the Kiez. Along the deserted canals, spying on the city. Beneath Hamburg's Händelface, they reminded me, lies the unforgiven, unforgiveable Bachsoul. Unshriven Hamburg. The architecture dissolves once more, mere frontage, and the people remain—each in isolation, as I first saw them—passengers and crew working out their destiny afresh, each as they must. Must is Bach's word. All you see around you is inside you, murmurs Bach. *Ach!* answers Händel pityingly (turning into the Dod in my mind, the Dod in a powdered wig); *ach!* solipsistic Bach! Yes, but God translates so imperfectly, Bach answers, listen hard and you can catch his syllables. That which is not solipsism: that is God. Which is to say, the silence after music. Then Händel, who hears God in the notes themselves, is silent, is rebuked but unrepentant.

I did my shopping close by, at the little outdoor Isemarkt. I discovered the public library, ten minutes' walk from the market; and when my eye (the outward-facing one; the other inward, as I'd grown to think of it) learnt stamina I revived childhood afternoons in Grandfather's study, pulling dusty books down off the shelves. What memories: pulling out a book and falling to the floor with it like a lover, unable to wait, devouring it at once on the sunlit carpet. The bay outside, Atlantic horizon greeting me with the smile of the illimitable. Now in Harvestehude when I looked in the mirror it was Grandfather's face I saw, distorted by the scars around one hollow eye-socket, twisted and tired as his had been—except that I didn't apply the boot-polish dye to my hair. It was greying fast, with a long, alarming streak of white above my dead eye, perfectly aligned with the scar. And one white eyebrow. (The other is still jet black, even now, so that unless I cover the white one with the largest of my eye-patches it gives me the piebald, grizzled look of an old Welsh collie.)

Apart from Oxfart, the only person I saw was dear Louise. And even with her there were barriers to break down—it wasn't all erotic eye-sockets from the word go. It took time, and a strange kind of courtship, to win her trust. This word held a special meaning for us. Under Oxfart's direction the V-girls also made short porno films, and the stills from these were incorporated into magazines with multilingual (the word was never more appropriate) texts whose wording brought me much quiet pleasure: her hands began rubbing my balls and kneeing the inside of my pride, declared one, until I pulled my clothes off and fell on top of her, defiling her lounges with one culving trust. Louise and I read my beloved Oxfart English aloud to each other until we wept with laughter; but enjoyed no culving trusts, let alone curving thrusts (into that trusted culvert! Poetic Oxfart!). She held out on me for six months, pleading a boyfriend in Paris, until I followed the time-honoured principle of giving a plain girl a hat and a pretty girl a book: carrying this to extremes I gave her Heidegger's *Being and Time*, which I'd been wrestling with in the library. It and my persistent ruminations seemed to amuse her, like a needlessly awkward jigsaw puzzle, all sky. We pondered the book together in English, spoke pidgin German in the street, and became fast friends.

Around this time I had the first of several dreams—they've recurred since then—in which I found myself in the Friedrichs-wald again. I kept my eyes down for fear of seeing a treehouse, but I knew I wouldn't see one because this was the Black Forest, not the Friedrichswald, and I was searching for a gamekeeper's hut, convinced I'd find Heidegger there. Louise was with me. We found the hut at last, but Heidegger had given up philosophy: a mug's game, he said, dismissively. *"Wurscht!"* He'd taken up wood-carving. He showed us an owl he'd made, which seemed rather crude, and I wanted to tell him he was a better philosopher than wood-carver, but didn't dare.

Sometimes in the dream we go for a walk in the moonlight, Louise and Heidegger and I, and I am feeling tearfully moved by this and can't understand why, and Louise begins calling him Martin and asking questions about his philosophy, which breaks the mood and embarrasses me tremendously, since although they are the very questions I have wanted to ask him I now know that he regards everything he has written as "Wurscht." At last Heidegger stops, exasperated, gazing up at the full yellow hunter's moon between the trees, and utters the sentence with which I awake as if clutching yet another lead soldier, another talisman. Convinced in my sleepy, half-awake state that the words I am muttering to myself are the ultimate revelation—I'm too sleepy to be able to tell whether they even form a sentence or not—I stagger to the table and write them down feverishly: *Moon, the dark side of being.* And that's it. Moon, the dark side of being. I could only decipher the words by turning them around. Being: the dark side of the moon. Which was to say the permanently invisible, the world inside the Caracalla walls; being, whose other face, living, was the one poor clue we had to the existence of its all-but-imaginary twin.

I refused to think of myself as having undergone a religious conversion, although my talk, when it wasn't full of Heidegger, was full of God. Louise didn't seem to mind.

But there were things I couldn't say to her, that I couldn't say to anyone. Time and the Christ are one. How could I say that to a girl who made a living singing Rule Britannia standing on her head? Without time—I longed to say to her—there was no sin. Without sin no need for Christ. But in a timebound life (one life, one only) there would always be sin, and only the Christ in us could meet this and redeem it. Not only my story but all stories, it seemed to me, Louise's, Herta's, Karin's, were Christian: because they *were* stories, and without redemption there was nothing to tell. Time: that was what was there to be redeemed, in the telling. Time and the Christ were one.

I did find myself going into churches, for the peace and the pleasant gloom, I told myself; I wasn't a churchgoer. I wasn't even religious, I felt, for all my talk. And in fact I couldn't find a church I liked. Impressive on the outside, many of them, but unconvincing within, as though no serious prayer had taken place there. Calvin had failed in Hamburg, and I could see why—there was no fear of God or Satan here, only of ill-advised investment. As for my nearest Catholic church, hidden apologetically in the leaves of the Eberstrasse, it looked like a rather well fortified bank.

(Besides, how bitterly angry I was in those days!) Yes, still furious, though I pretended not to be. Angry with Karin, in my mind as stiff, unyielding, deaf a figure as the Madonna in the Italian fresco, indifferent to my pleas. And angry with Germany. To forgive Karin was to forgive the Germans what she herself could never forgive: their rush to oblivion. But how else—yes, how else could they have endured their separate shame and become Germany again? Ten years it took me to make my peace with this, and clear the way . . . Dod, dear Dod, I know *you* understand this . . . to begin my own pilgrimage.)

It was my dentist who finally put me onto St. Lukas in Fuhls-büttel, an ugly new building that was his own place of worship. I'd gone to him because my teeth, crumbling since my early thirties—I'd seen it coming in the Colonel's mirror, in Spain—were finally unbearable. *Herr Zahnarzt* Fischer didn't seem surprised when I asked to have them all out. Cosmetic dentistry is a fine art in Hamburg (in the whole of Germany perhaps; if nothing else they know how to put a good front on things) and he equipped me with a splendid artificial set. Better than this, he bequeathed me the St. Lukaskirche, brickbuilt in the 1930s on older foundations and, like my teeth, newly remodelled. The inside walls heavily plasters, white, perfectly stark and soulless. In its nasty, cosy, modern way, and without trying to compete, the gently curving Norman arches reminded me of the little chapel in the Maremma with the Annunciation fresco. Or allowed me to dream of it, undisturbed by Gothic cobwebs. I returned to the figures in turn, the Virgin with her innocence and ignorance, the maddened, pleading angel, and that endless corridor extending back between the profiled pair, that tunnel (one I could no longer enter by the eye, I with my telescopic view) drawing the eyes towards a vanishing point. Time began here, it said; begins here, now at this moment of generation. The vista spread through all dimensions, re-inventing distance: Christ's matter, awaiting His redemption, and ours.

And then there was the bird, flame-breathing messenger. In

the library I found the tale of Raniero Ranieri, a crusader who abandoned his wife and family, using the crusade—so I understood it—as an excuse to get away, and found his way home again only by means of an extraordinary act of atonement: carrying a lighted candle from the Holy Land all the way back to his native village, replacing one candle with another but never letting the flame go out. At last as he reached home after months without sleep, and mounted the steps of the church, he stumbled, dropped the candle—and a bird flew down from the eaves, plucked the falling stub from the air and carried it, still flaming, to the altar.

It was that miraculous helping hand—or beak—that failed me when I went to church. I couldn't find forgiveness in Fuhlsbüttel at the St. Lukaskirche. (Half a kilometre from the prison; as far again from the airport.) Only Wilf, as I understood it, could forgive me, and in my mind Raniero Ranieri blended into the old Doo-glass of "The Shirt," in the rhyme Peter taught me, kneeling in his rusty "harness" before young King James.

It was one thing imagining it; I dreaded going back to England and doing it. I needed so badly to confess, and couldn't, walking around like a bag of tears unable to burst.

"London! *Mensch*, the most beautiful of cities," sighed an old man I met beside the Isebek canal. "You've never been?" he smiled, mistaking my expression. "Pity!" London . . . London should have been Molly to me, the smells of the house in Parsifal Road, but it wasn't, it was Ellie, Ellie and her pebble-glasses caught up in her feather boa, bringing me Turkish Delight so we could guzzle it together in the little flat overlooking Victoria Station. It was the smell of the kerosene that kept the ants out of my kitchen. Law books, and the hiss of brakes from the incoming trains; Salmon on Tort, and Underwood on Branntwein, and nights with Ellie in a world I knew.

Though when I imagine telling somebody about this, it's Wilf I'm telling, Wilf golden-haired like a young Alec; telling him how I got here, from the brisk wind in the bay and Grandfather's cries, "Inflate the balloon!"; Grandmother's snowy Footsteps at the Hambledon vicarage, and Peter at the Schloss, playing fugues. Can you hear them, Wilf?

Gradually everything else slipped away. Cäsar grew old and died. I told no-one. Although I'd shaken off my terror of the Reeperbahn I went there so rarely that none of my old friends noticed Cäsar's passing. There was no-one left to mourn him. Oxfart wasn't really sorry—the old dog had grown more cantankerous with age, and tended to snap at him. And Louise had long since continued on her travels. Thanks to my contacts at the cemetery, where I often took morning coffee with the Keeper of Graves, the dog was buried in Ohlsdorf in a child-sized coffin. Quite against the law of course, and for propriety's sake I had Cäsar Sacher, with his dates, fully inscribed on the headstone as though he were a son taken from me, like Egon, at the age of twelve. The gravediggers and the pastor of St. Lukas were in on the secret. They knew I'd loved the dog, and the funeral was achieved with dignity.

By then the vicious rumours about me had begun—*du Ratte!*— and the spitting in my path, for the absurd, unlikely crime of having fingered Wolli as Cheerybye's murderer, for having brought the golden Zimt-years to an end; and I was no longer welcome on the Reeperbahn. I didn't miss it. Arno Schiller had cut a deal of his own with the politicians who wanted to clean the Kiez. Get the whores off the streets! That was the cry, and Arno complied, in exchange for controlling rights in the new brothels, the Palais d'Amour, the Eros-Centre, where the girls were monitored by cameras and fined if they sat down on the bed to take an illicit pause between customers, or perched on the radiators, reading a newspaper. No wonder everybody hated it—and needed a scapegoat.

Herr Blackmailer (could it really be Vlad? Did he hate me so much for the Vegas-Girls, for passing him over and falling into stride with the degraded Kiez?) came like a saviour, jolting me out of my trance. Whoever he was, I was grateful to him. I'd kill him, then I'd have to leave. Shave off my beard, dye my one white eyebrow black, put in my glass eye, polish up my false teeth and head for England. That was the plan.

The bells have stopped, it's seven a.m..

Oxfart is in the doorway, coming through the door.

I seem to have got dressed, I'm sitting on the bed. We go out to the car.

We're driving through Altona, Flottbek, Blankanese.

In the Roman Gardens there's a figure waiting by the formal hedge, the topiary with cockerels and cannonballs of box leaf.

A figure in a suit. My brother Alec.

Hands in pockets; feet splayed wide. Alec. Of course! In the note, "pay up you *rat*. . . ."

Before he speaks, I understand what he's doing here. It was his money, Thurgo money—the Colonel's money—in the arms

deal, poured through Walters. North African arms, to ginger up
the Bedouin. Thurgo money. Alec thinks I killed Walters for it.

Now I shall kill Alec.

Once, twice. The gun Isidro makes a sound like a doorbell
ringing.

It *is* the doorbell ringing, and I wake.

Oxfart's arrived.

IN AUNTIE'S WAITING ROOM THERE WERE THREE CUSTOMERS sitting lined up for Madame Rita's services. A girl weeping silently into a handkerchief, and two clean-shaven young men with university accents—recalling for me the young swans from Ox and Cam who used to queue for Ellie's favours, in the high old days of Leda Buildings.

Madame Rita, Palmist and Clairvoyant: Auntie's sign was still in the corridor below, unretouched. The old Poland Street stink on the stairs. The same dirty cream-coloured door. The clients seemed incongruously young; but no younger than I was when I first visited Auntie.

Here we are again, I thought, as I took the fourth chair. I wasn't sure, in the state I was in, if I'd said the words aloud. I'd done precisely that when I was thirteen years old and six foot one and returning from a visit to the headmaster to answer for "repeated impudence" (my punishment was to write out a hundred times, in fine italic script, the sentence *Attar of roses is a fine perfume*); I'd stood there in the doorway with the whole class gazing at me and just blurted it out, "here we are again," as though it was they who were saying it through me, and indeed we all burst into helpless laughter, myself included. Laughing, but hating them all for it, plotting revenge. Grandfather's Irish spy! The ways I'd kill them, slowly. And in the end I had killed someone, face to face, after so many false starts. Yesterday. A little less than 36 hours ago.

I'd killed Herr Blackmailer with my own hands, in the car park of the Roman Gardens. The real blackmailer, that is. Not Alec. And not in a dream.

As we sat together in the black Mercedes, waiting for the mystery man to emerge from the shrubbery, Oxfart was trembling about the face and hands. Unlike him, I thought, to get the jitters.

Relax, I said at last. What's the matter with you?

Oxfart didn't seem able to speak. He was staring through the windscreen. I leaned over to look, to try and see what he was seeing, but there wasn't a soul in sight. Without warning, Oxfart started the engine.

Now what are you doing? I asked.

When he didn't put the car in gear but simply revved the engine, making noise, I should have understood what he was doing. But it never entered my mind. I checked my watch. *Wart mal*, hold on, it's only seven thirty-five, I said. He hasn't arrived yet, that's all.

Doch, said Oxfart quietly. Yes he has.

Where? I looked all around.

Oxfart turned to me and held my gaze.

Then I understood.

Oxfart; my Hansi; and he was running the engine to cover the noise of the shot. I wanted to smash his face in then and there. But that would have to wait.

"It isn't the money, *Chef*."

"*What* money?"

"There's a price on your head. But I wouldn't do it for the money." He could see I still didn't know what he was talking about. "*Der Boss,*" he explained. "In Capri he told me I was to kill you if you let him down."

"*Aber Hansi—*"

"I know. You fought the *Tunis*. But since then, *Chef*, you've let everything go. I tried to warn you." His lips were trembling worse than ever. "I refused many times to do this. I hoped some rumours would drive you away, back to England."

Back to England; clearly Wolli *der Boss* had told him everything. No, it was more than that, I saw now that he'd always been Wolli's creature, from the moment he arrived in Hamburg; even when I'd thought he was mine, Oxfart was spying on me. And now Wolli was calling in his markers. Poor Oxfart, trying to drive me back to England, to avoid this. I *am* going back, I wanted to say. I am going back. But not at gunpoint. Oxfart saw me about to lunge for his jacket pocket, and reached into it quickly. If he'd got off a shot through the lining it might have done some damage. He was shaking too hard to find the trigger, and once I'd got him pinioned I was far too strong for him, I wrestled the gun away and pushed him down into the seat until

I was kneeling on his upper arms. Then I examined the gun. It was a heavy thing, much too heavy for this job, a Scandinavian pistol as big as a Magnum. Oxfart gazed at me in terror.

"A Lahti?" I said, turning it on him. *"Bist du verrückt?"* Are you mad? "They'd hear it all over Hamburg."

As I wound the window down above his head, Oxfart made another grab for the gun, but I flung it out into the bushes, and took hold of his scarf instead, pulling it tight around his neck, ignoring his frantically clawing fingers. My knees were on his shoulders, my buttocks on his chest. His lips were pursed in agony as if begging for a Judas kiss. Too late for that. I'd found him, Kiez-reared him, promoted and protected him; it should have been like throttling my own son, but I couldn't forgive him this betrayal. And he'd have wept as he killed me. That disgusted me most of all.

I left the body in the car and walked until I found a taxi. It was all too easy, and at the apartment I went through my intended routine in a fever of haste, expecting the police at any moment, chopping at my beard with scissors, cutting myself as I shaved for the first time in twenty years. The black hair dye stung on my eyebrow. In went the glass eye, after I'd warmed it in my hands. Studying the effect in the mirror I added black dye to the white streak in my hair. I looked ten years younger but completely crazed, with my transfixed eye and my jaw bloody with cuts. I hadn't seen my beardless face since . . . since I'd stared at myself in the mirror in Spain, upstairs in Tom Thurgo's barn. Knowing I'd been shot and wondering whether I was a ghost. And suddenly it struck me that I'd left a body in a jeep in Spain, and now a body in a car in Germany. Bags packed, as they were then, to go home. But I still couldn't go as Richard Thurgo. The passport Cheerybye had fixed for me when I took Egon back to England was in the name of Denis Saunders. Richard Thurgo—I was giggling now—was the chap I thought I'd left in Spain. But now I was leaving him in Germany.

Looking round the apartment I was satisfied that there was nothing more I wanted to take with me. I'd left a letter for the Dod, and a note for Vlad with legal documents transferring the Vegas-Girls into his name. Perhaps he'd turn it back into a night spot. I'd given away everything else, mementoes and the like; Cäsar had mauled the Friedrichswald cane beyond redemption, and he'd chewed up my arsehole-shoes when he was a puppy. Mother's goblet was long gone too, I'd given it to Mutti when we made up at last, as something of mine that Karin had cherished. Mutti had been touched, and I was glad to be rid of it. Nothing to carry me with but clothes. No talismans. I grabbed my bags and took a taxi to the airport.

Loudly blowing her nose, the girl weeping into the handkerchief went in to see Auntie, as an elderly female client emerged. Young Ox and Cam both moved up a chair each, chortling with anticipation. I stayed where I was. And thought about people searching my apartment in Hamburg; about the Dod opening my letter.

Dear Anna-Maria, Of all the wise and provoking things you've said to me over the years, the one that sticks in my mind is—as I'm sure you know—what you told me in Ohlsdorf cemetery, that death took your daughter from you because you loved Christ too much. To be exact, what you said was that this was why you hadn't been allowed to keep your daughter; I never fully understood it—did you mean you were too wedded to the truth to be allowed an ordinary worldly life as well? But has it occurred to you that perhaps your sin, the one you had to expiate by losing your child, was that you didn't love Christ enough?

Recalling it now I felt ashamed of having written such crazy argumentative stuff, instead of simply telling the old girl I loved her, and saying goodbye. Perhaps I might write to her again, when I had a moment.

On arrival in England I'd headed for Parsifal Road, but no-one at number 17 had ever heard of her. Hardly surprising. It could be twenty years and more since she'd lived there. How to find her? All I wanted to do—I'd rehearsed the speech a hundred times—was ask if I could see Wilf, just once, or at least ask him if he'd be prepared to meet with me; he was twenty-three and should have the chance to make up his own mind. I didn't want to disturb her life any further, I would explain. Just see the boy.

But where were they? I drew a blank in the telephone directory.

Each time I rang Alec at the Commons he was busy, it seemed, unavailable, off in the Chamber, voting. Just as well, I decided; if Interpol were already on my trail, as I imagined they might be, no doubt Alec would rather be able to tell them with a clean conscience that he hadn't heard from me. Then I remembered something Alec had said in Padstow, after Mother's death. My quondam father-in-law, he told me, old Trimble, had had some sort of a stroke and was living in Alec's constituency; in Liskeard. While on his way to an ecclesiastical convention, he'd gone a bit dotty, and taken up residence in the hotel overlooking the main square. All this by hearsay—Alec hadn't seen him and couldn't fill in the holes in the story. If Trimble wasn't too dotty, he might know where his eldest surviving daughter lived.

Once more I took a train to the West Country. But when I reached dull grey Liskeard and tramped uphill to the hotel, an unkempt old man at the desk shook his head sadly. Dead these ten years, he said. A nice man, the deceased. A painter. This didn't sound like Trimble, but apparently it was; name and appearance both fitted. If I liked I was welcome to see one of his paintings. Even to buy one. I declined, and caught the next train back to London, where I holed up in a bed and breakfast place in Paddington, trying to decide what to do next.

Trimble dead too. Mad Trimble, who'd warned me that Molly was a bolter, and who'd sermonized the Unknown Father, dead. Time is the horizon of being, Heidegger had written, and though this statement seemed to vex the commentators, it struck me as simple enough. Time *was* the horizon, and in time we all toppled over it like the ships in a flat-earther's nightmare. My charts were getting less populous by the day, and Molly's bark was nowhere to be seen. Purely out of nostalgic humour I headed for Gamages, where she and I had met and made up, in the cafeteria, after our row over Wilf's name. We often ate there at Molly's behest, for the prices, rather than the food. A shilling for the Special Lunch, a Cornish pasty, mashed potato and spring greens. It brought back the London I'd loathed. And when I joined the lunchtime queue and turned to see Molly sitting there, now, only ten yards away, over her tray, my instinct was to back out and run before she saw me too. Calm down, I thought, no need to panic, she won't recognize me without my beard, and then remembered that I hadn't been bearded when we were married. When we were together, that is; we were still married, but it was unthinkable that this fat person—Alec was right, she was barrel-shaped—was still my wife. On the other hand, fat had preserved her, I decided as the queue brought me slowly closer to her. She looked younger than her years.

Molly had a spoonful of apple crumble in her mouth when she looked up and saw me, and it stayed there while she stared at me like a chipmunk caught thieving. I abandoned the food queue and walked towards her. She looked petrified. It's me, I said, reaching her table. "Mind if I sit down?" I nearly said *"Darf ich?"* and at that moment realized that I'd rehearsed my entire Molly-speech in German.

She gave a faint nod, eyes still on me, food unswallowed.

I sat down opposite her, trying to avoid meeting her knees with mine. How to begin?

"You still eat here, then."

She said nothing.

"I do wish you'd swallow that mouthful," I said. "You look as if you're going to be sick."

She swallowed obediently. There was a glass of wine by her plate, and I waited while she took a sip.

"I'm sorry. I should have warned you. I didn't know where to write any more." Absurd excuse for a man who'd vanished for twenty years; I corrected myself quickly. "Besides, I didn't know I'd be coming to London until yesterday."

Her face was still frozen.

"I've been in Germany," I said.

"I know. I knew that." She sounded hoarse, but I couldn't tell from her face whether it was emotion or the apple crumble in her throat. She pushed the bowl away.

"Did Alec tell you?"

"I don't see Alec."

The old, withering tone; I beat the memories down. "So he told me."

"I knew all along. Even when I buried you." Then, without looking at me, "I just prayed you'd never come back."

"I'm not. I mean, I'm not trying to come back. I'm on the run, actually." I was appalled to hear myself saying this, the one thing I'd sworn to myself not to mention. And suddenly I couldn't stop. "I killed a man in Hamburg."

She studied me as if I were a mad, importunate stranger she'd never seen before, who'd settled at her table.

"Well, don't come to me. I won't hide you."

"I'm not trying to hide. I had to leave, that's all."

Suddenly she was chuckling, that lovely boozy chuckle that accompanied our sexiest moments. The girl, the Molly who'd glutted herself on erotica in Trimble's library, was in there somewhere. Now it had all turned to fat, wobbling as she laughed. "You could have hired yourself for the defence, Richard. Just what you always wanted. Do they have capital punishment, over there?"

This wasn't at all the way the meeting was supposed to go.

"Well *do* they?"

"No-one saw it," I said. And I strangled him with the scarf. And my fingerprints would be all over the Mercedes anyway, as a matter of course; and it was none of Molly's business. But she was enjoying herself now.

"Then you shouldn't have run off, should you. Now they'll know it's you."

I tried ignoring her. They *would* know it was me, of course. Reinhard Sacher, alias Richard Thurgo, Her Majesty's Damned Nuisance—only there was no file on me at Section HQ in Blankenese; alias Denis Saunders, an identity contrived for me in secret by a dead man. Dear dead Cheerybye. I wasn't going to be easy to find.

"What's happened to your eye?" said Molly.

"A spot of trouble a few years ago."

She raised her eyebrows, and let it go. "You look terrible," she said.

"Thank you. You could afford to lose a few pounds yourself."

We grinned at each other, but the affability was forced.

"So you're in a pickle," said Molly, sounding more like her old brisk self. "If it's money you want, you've come to the wrong place. I haven't got any. Even if I had, I wouldn't give it to you, Richard. I don't want anything to do with you."

"I understand that. But I'd like to see Wilf. That's why I came."

She studied me without comment.

"He thinks you're dead," Molly said at last. "I should say he's better off that way, wouldn't you? Or do you think it would cheer him up to find that his Daddy's a murderer who ran out on him when he was three?"

As she looked away again I thought: she doesn't want to tell him she's been lying to him all these years.

I was afraid to stop, to think, to do anything to break my headlong momentum.

"Then let me see him," I said, "just see him, without explaining who I am, across a room, a street, I don't mind. I'd like to see what he looks like."

But I knew, I was sure, what he looked like, with his blue eyes and darkly golden Thurgo hair, thick as an adult's even in the crib. I wanted more than to see him, but perhaps to see him happy would be forgiveness enough; as much as I could ask.

"Give me an address," said Molly archly, "and I'll send you a photo."

It occurred to me that I had some bargaining power here. I could track the boy down if I put my mind to it, and Molly couldn't stop me telling him who I was. What could she do? She could shop me to the police—if she believed my murder-tale—yes, but if it all ended up in the newspapers Wilf would be sure to find out about me. So she wouldn't do that. I had the edge, it seemed to me, and Molly knew it, by the look on her face.

"See him by all means," she said. "It's up to you. But you'd better know one thing. He's not your child. He's Alec's."

He's Alec's. The syllables made no sense.

Molly could see I hadn't taken it in. "I wouldn't lie to you, Richard, because I don't care about you either way."

"He's Alec's?" I said. "What do you mean, he's Alec's?"

"I don't even hate you any more," she was saying. "I was in Sarratt on my own and bloody miserable, you'd gone off with your potty friend Denis and left me to rot in that nasty little house. And who should arrive to comfort me? Good old Alec. I didn't know what a bastard he was then. I shouldn't have done it, and I suppose I did owe you your freedom, in a way, because I couldn't bring myself to admit what I'd done." Molly stared at me defiantly. "But I don't know. The two of you . . . does it matter which bastard Thurgo sired the boy? It's all the same blood. And he doesn't know. I've kept him out of Alec's way, and he's turned out quite well, though I say it myself." She took a swig from the glass in front of her, and emptied it. "Calls himself Jack, by the way. Always hated the name Wilf."

But *you* insisted on Wilf, I thought, still quite unable to take in the full force of what she was telling me. Here in this restaurant you insisted on it.

"Are you going to eat?" she said, climbing to her feet with an effort. "I'm done. You can have my tray." And she wriggled out inelegantly past my chair and headed for the door, leaving me sitting staring after her.

After a while I went out and down the stairs into the streets and wandered in a daze. She was lying, of course, I thought; a good way to get back at me—and keep me away from the boy. But the truth stared me in the face. What I'd always called Wilf's golden Thurgo looks were simply Alec's looks. Not a trace of my O'Malley gargoyle in him. And Alec had indeed visited Molly while I was in Dobwalls with poor mad Denis. The old, malign voice in my head said, "See? There *is* a God. It's just what you deserve." He's Alec's. And Molly—their mutual hostility returned to mock me, and I walked faster, uselessly, as if by hurrying I could keep the memories at bay. Alec visiting us at Parsifal Road. Alec sitting at Wilf's bedside, reciting.

Algy saw a bear, the bear saw Algy, the bear was bulgy, the bulge was Algy.

The night we spent at the hotel in Liskeard, Alec and Molly and I, Molly pregnant and hell-bent on disrupting Alec's electioneering: they'd sent me off to bed, and in the morning Molly hadn't slept, she was red-eyed and silent, and I should have known it had nothing to do with politics. She'd told him the baby was his. I'd be prepared to bet on it—that all these years Alec had known about Wilf. I almost wanted to laugh. Because now I understood the curious act of penitence that had led him to take Egon into his care. I saw the Dod's eyes gazing at me. *Das bisschen Leben;* this little life; I'd burned Alec's letter to Maggie and played havoc—or tried to—with his life, and now . . . but none of it was proof of God, God put a Karin or a Herta through living hell and acquitted a Wackernagel, and he wasn't going to balance the books all of a sudden, starting with me.

I should have felt a terrible grief, perhaps. I had no son. No Punch, no Franzl, no Wilf. Not one, living. No Wilf to grant me absolution—assuming that were possible. No, he was Alec's. I didn't owe him a life. Now that I'd seen Molly there was no-one left to accuse me or absolve me, I was free to seek my own salvation, damn them all.

I felt a craving for a cup of tea, and realized where my feet were taking me. Down the Tottenham Court Road towards Upper Shaftesbury Avenue. To Leda Buildings, where my steps had led me so many times for a teatime cuddle. From the age of sixteen until—when? My last visits, at thirty, a furtive married man glancing round as he slipped into Ellie's apartment block, making sure no-one who knew him happened to be passing in the street. Now I owed nobody. I was Denis Saunders, a one-eyed man of fifty, free and with enough money in my pocket to keep me in style for a month or two.

"Hello, Punch," Ellie would say. She'd recognize me all right. "Where the hell have *you* been?"

In the Hamburg library I'd been finding myself drawn to the English language shelves, curious to sample written English again after all this time. The subject didn't matter; I got quite caught up in a book called *Progressive Fishbreeding*. Next to it was a tome entitled *Pulcinella: The Curious History of Mr. Punch*, whom I was intrigued to find had been born twice at the same time in different quarters of the same town, and to different fathers. In due course he became a magistrate, a poet, a master, and finally a valet. A valet! I put aside dreams of a progressive trout farm (though it would have delighted Grandfather) and began to see myself as a gentleman's gentleman, well paid, comfortable and obscure.

As I came nearer to Leda Buildings my longing to see Ellie seemed to acquire something more than its first sexual urgency. My feet had begun to lead me towards her before I'd even thought about that. They were leading me home. "Hello, Punch." Perhaps it was another pipe dream, but Ellie was still my first, I told myself, and longest-lasting love. Then it occurred to me, doing the sums again, that she'd be within a year or two of sixty now, and that cooled my ardour a bit.

The sight of Leda Buildings cooled it even more. The old place had been quit respectable in the 'Thirties—or if respectable wasn't the word exactly, then at least tidy. What I found there now was a slum defacing the centre of London, stinking of piss and dogshit, with vomit at the foot of graffiti-spattered walls. It was no surprise to find Ellie gone, and that no-one knew her name. She wouldn't have stayed in a tenement like this; she was a tart, but not a slut. Woe betide any customer who spilled Ellie's "Russian" on the carpet!

And so I tramped on down to Poland Street, scarcely expecting Auntie to still be there in her old consulting rooms. She'd know where Ellie was. Or would she? The last thing Ellie had said to me, on that nightmare journey to the underwater city, wartime London, when she'd told me about little Punch and his fatal "disptheria," was how she wanted nothing more to do with the stars—and all that bollocks, as she called it. Auntie had told her Punch would look after her in his old age.

Tea, tea from Ellie's samovar . . . I could imagine—following through my serving-quarters fantasy—happily spending my declining years as a valet-and-housemaid couple with Ellie, in a grand country house somewhere. Or as a butler even, a British Ludolf. In Conan Doyle, another of Grandfather's favourites, I'd recently come across an inspiring specimen of the breed, learned, lecherous, and formidable: "The butler of Hurlstone, sir," declares his employer, "is a thing no visitor ever forgets!" A thing! I could picture myself terrorizing guests and kitchen staff alike (threatening to take out my glass eye!); with Ellie as my consort. A setting in which to do more ruminative work, in my spare time. For years now I'd been writing—in my mind—a book of imaginary interviews with Heidegger on the subject of the German soul (did it exist?). The finished work would be dedicated to the memory of Walters, the person who

I felt would most have benefited from it, and was to be named after one of Cheerybye's favourite expressions, *Being Germany*. . . .

Dreaming of this—I saw myself writing in the pantry, late at night, adding the sub-title Philosophical Essays of A Butler (A Well-Travelled Butler?), and felt English again for the first time—I found myself in Poland Street. And there to my amazement, in the open doorway, sat Auntie's sign. Madame Rita, Palmist And Clairvoyant. Internationally Known. Business and Matrimonial. And the old Poland Street stink greeted me in the corridor, as I climbed the stairs and opened the same dirty cream-coloured outer door, to take a seat among the customers.

Now the second and last of the undergraduates emerged to join his fellow, their voices ringing joyously as they cantered down the stairs. They were taunting each other. From what I gathered Auntie had promised them all the success in the world, but had spoiled it by promising it to both of them in exactly the same words.

As I went through the inner door, another old smell hit me. Piss and carbolic! Carbolic soap, remorseless and germicidal, no false fragrance, no attar of roses, just the rough cheek as if shaved that Auntie always raised for me to kiss, and its dear pungent stink of cleanliness.

"Won't be a minute," came her scratchy voice from behind the curtain. "Take a seat, dear."

Same old routine. I could hear the rattle of kettle and teacup as her shaky hand poured the tea. I glanced round the little room. Nothing had changed. Same Alnwick Castle on the walls. Percy Walls. Curtains, carpet, even the chairs looked the same, but the dark satiny tablecloth looked new.

The small crystal was on the table.

"I'll have the big crystal today, Auntie," I said. I could picture it under its russet cloth in the kitchen alcove. "It's been a long time."

For a moment there was silence behind the curtain and I wondered if she'd heard me. Growing deaf perhaps. Eighty now, eighty if she was a day.

In front of me the small crystal, fist-sized.

It looked black as basalt, unreflecting. As I stepped up to it, I gave a start. There was something small and round and pale in it moving towards me like a drowned face surfacing from the depths. A child's face. Wilf's. Then I realized: it wasn't in the crystal, it was on it—my face, unrecognizable that first instant without the beard, distorted, all nose and gasping lipless mouth, ruddy as a baby's. My own face turned babyish by the curve of the glass. My heart was still pounding, slow to receive the message that it wasn't a Wilf-child, but my own child. Myself.

Algy saw a bear . . .

The curtain swished as a heavy body pushed past it. I looked up but I was still in the grip of the shock I'd got from the crystal as Wilf's face had swum up at me—surrendering to me, it seemed—not forgiving or waiting to be forgiven but coming to me, coming with me, mine again and crying out in pain, that lipless open-mouthed face, my own, making me want to take the crystal in my palms to warm and soothe it. I didn't want to be disturbed, but Auntie's pale eyes were blazing at me, shocked too—same old Auntie, barely a year older—I registered this dimly; unchanged, the same headscarf, the rings, the shaven-looking jowls.

Almost. What was it that was different?

"Hello, Punch," she said, with an almighty effort, and something in her voice stopped all reflection. It was Ellie.

Acknowledgements:

The author is indebted to all those who harboured and encouraged him during the writing of this book: to Heite, Hermann, and Joachim Jessen, to Horst Hesslein and to my other Hamburg friends and acquaintances who shared their memories of the Nachkriegsjahre, the postwar years; to the authors who educated me about the Germany of the period, from Stephen Spender to Douglas Botting, J. A. Cole, Jan Molitor, Erik Verg, Günter Zint, Wolfgang Köhler, Bernt Englemann, and many others; and to the memory of Wolfgang Borchert, prince of Hamburg writers; also to the late Peter Young and to those who, as he did, furnished me with stories, notably Alan Williams, Patsy Meehan, Pamela Blaxland, and Elfrieda Watson; to Charles and Betty Corman, to Bob Shearer, Carol Philpot, Reynalds Haas and my friends in Florida; to those in Sri Lanka; and in California to Billy and Shobhana O'Brien, Lawrence Waddy, Paolo Dau, Sabine McQuarrie, Jim Carmody and Laurie Edson, Susan Kirkpatrick and Darwin Berg; in New Haven to Emily Jayne; in England to Valerie Harrison, Jonathan Kebbe and Christine Simpson, Jeremy Paul, John Stevenson, and Steve Wilson; and Dr. J. F. Read of the Forensic Science Society. To Julian Duffus. To Maggie Noach, tirelessly sustaining; to David Godwin, and to Helen Fraser; once more to William Arctander O'Brien, fraternal reader; most of all to Catherine Lowe, whose love and whose poetic gifts nourished author and book.

About the Author

A playwright whose work has been described in *The Listener* as "intricate webs of fantasy, erudition, and comedy," Carey Harrison—born in 1944 to actor parents Sir Rex Harrison and Lilli Palmer—has over ninety performed works to his credit, including a dozen stage plays, numerous radio plays, and more than sixty television scripts. *Richard's Feet* is his first novel, and it is also the first book in his tetralogy, *To Liskeard*. He lives in Greater London.